## COUNT LEO (LEV) NIKOLAYEVICH TOLSTOY

displayed an extraordinary duality of character in a life filled with deep contradictions. He was born to an aristo-cratic Russian family on September 9, 1828. His parents died when he was young, and he was raised by several female relatives. In 1844, he entered the University of Kazan, remaining there only three years. At the age of 23, Tolstoy joined the Russian Army and fought in the Crimean War. While still in the service, his first published story appeared, a largely autobiographical work, called *Childhood* (1852). Tolstoy returned to his estate in 1861 and established a school for peasant children there. In 1862, he married Sofia Behrs and gradually abandoned his involvement with the school. The next fifteen years he devoted to managing the estate, raising his and Sofia's large family, and writing his two major works, *War and Peace* (1865–67) and *Anna Karenina* (1875–77).

During the latter part of this fifteen year period, Tolstoy found himself growing increasingly disenchanted with the teachings of the Russian Orthodox Church. In the ensuing years, Tolstoy formulated for himself a new Christian ideal, the central creed of which involved nonresistance to evil; he also preached against the corrupt evil of the Russian state, of the need for ending all violence, and of the moral perfectibility of man. In practice, his asceticism required that he repudiate all vices, even forsaking physical contact with his own wife. In spite of these changes, he continued to write voluminously, primarily nonfiction, but also other works, such as the play *The Power of Darkness* (1886), the novella *The Death of Ivan Ilyich* (1886), and the novels *The Kreutzer Sonata* (1891) and *Resurrection* (1899).

In 1910, still unable to reconcile the differences in the lives led by the aristocracy and the simpler existence he craved, Tolstoy left the estate. He soon fell ill and was found dead on a cot in a remote railway station. He was buried on his estate at Yasnaya Pulyana.

Bantam Classics
Ask your bookseller for these other world classics

# Anna Karenina
# by Leo Tolstoy

The modern American translation
by Joel Carmichael

With an introduction by
Malcolm Cowley

BANTAM BOOKS

TORONTO · NEW YORK · LONDON · SYDNEY · AUCKLAND

ANNA KARENINA
*A Bantam Book / published July 1960*

*PRINTING HISTORY*
**Anna Karenina** *was first published in 1876.*
*First Bantam edition / July 1960.*
*Bantam Classic edition / March 1981*
*2nd printing .. November 1981*

*Cover painting, "The Fur Jacket" by James Abbott McNeill Whistler.*
*Courtesy of the Worcester Art Museum, Worcester, Massachusetts.*

*Library of Congress Catalog Card Number: 60-6052*

ISBN  0-553-21034-3

*Published simultaneously in the United States and Canada*

*Bantam Books are published by Bantam Books, Inc. Its trademark, consisting*
*of the words "Bantam Books" and the portrayal of a rooster, is Registered*
*in U.S. Patent and Trademark Office and in other countries. Marca Registrada.*
*Bantam Books, Inc., 666 Fifth Avenue, New York, New York 10103.*

PRINTED IN THE UNITED STATES OF AMERICA

11  10  9  8  7  6  5

# INTRODUCTION

by Malcolm Cowley

AFTER finishing *War and Peace* in 1869, Tolstoy plunged to a series of violently unrelated activities. First he studied the German philosophers and rejected all but one, the most pessimistic; he announced that his summer had been "an endless ecstasy over Schopenhauer." But the ecstasy was soon forgotten, and he spent the winter of 1870 "busy with drama" —that is, busy reading the collected plays of Shakespeare, Molière, Goethe, Pushkin, and Gogol while dreaming about a comedy of his own. He also vaguely thought of starting a novel, which would be concerned—so he told Sonya his wife —with a married woman in high society who betrayed her husband. The author's problem, he said, "was to represent this woman as not guilty but merely pitiful."

In April he set out to gather material for a different sort of novel, a panorama of Russian life under Peter the Great. The project was laid aside in November, and he began to study Greek with daylong application. Reading Homer in the original, he became so excited that he decided "never again to write any such wordy trash as *War and Peace*." Then his health broke down from overwork or brooding—he was always subject to fits of depression—and he spent the summer of 1871 on the steppes of Samara Province, drinking kumys with the Tartar herdsmen. On his return to Yasnaya Polyana —"Clear Glade," the family estate—his interest turned to pedagogy and, with infinite pains, he wrote his *ABC Book*, designed as a complete curriculum for the sons of Russian peasants. He said in a letter to his older friend, Countess Alexandra Tolstoy, that he regarded the book as "the one important matter of my life."

For Tolstoy everything in turn was the one important matter. "Whatever I may do," he said in another letter to Alexandra, "I at least always feel convinced that forty centuries look down on me from the top of the Pyramids and that the world will perish if I ever stand still." He was almost never still in the four years after *War and Peace*, while the Russians were waiting for another novel from the man they already regarded as their greatest author. He made war on the pedagogues who had condemned his *ABC Book*. He bought another large estate—more than ten square miles—in Samara Province, east of the Volga. He reopened his school for peasant children at Yasnaya Polyana. Affronted by a local magistrate, he thought of emigrating to England. He went back to his novel about Peter the Great and amassed a huge store of material. After beginning the novel in twenty different fashions—by count of the manuscripts—he decided that he couldn't go on with it, since it would never fire his imagination. Would he have to stand still and would the world perish?

One evening in March, 1873, he found a volume of tales by Pushkin in the living room and began reading passages aloud to his wife. He was struck by the opening sentence of one tale: "The guests arrived at the country house." "That's the way for us to write," he exclaimed to Sonya. "Anyone else would start by describing the guests, the rooms, but he jumps straight into the action." Later that same evening, Tolstoy went to his study and started *Anna Karenina*.

The story of the adulterous woman had grown and ripened in his mind since he first thought of it in 1870. At first the writing went rapidly for Tolstoy, and in twelve months he accumulated a great pile of manuscript, besides a finished version of Part One. (There would be eight parts in all. Usually he rewrote each of them five or six times before sending it to the printer, and every new version was copied in a fair hand by Sonya.) It has always seemed to me that this first part, though not his greatest writing, is the absolute summit of Tolstoy's craftsmanship. He jumps straight into the action and it never flags as he moves from one character or episode to another; the transitions are masterly. In almost pure narrative, with only a necessary minimum of description and exposition, he presents all his leading actors not only as striking individuals but also in their family groups, with children and retainers; he puts the plot in motion; he gives us three of his marvelous "set pieces," including the ball at which Kitty's heart is broken; he carries us from Moscow to Levin's

untry estate and then to St. Petersburg, his other principal
ttings; and he prepares us for the distant end of the story.
art One is a model that other novelists have never ceased to
nitate, though none has equaled it.

Tolstoy himself was not impressed, or pretended not to be.
astead of a superb craftsman, he wanted to be a teacher, a
aint, a prophet; he was looking for a faith to protect him
om the utter nihilism to which he reverted in moments of
ejection. After Part One the novel went more slowly, with
atervals when nothing was written. Partly that was because of
Iness and death in the family; in a little more than two
ears, Tolstoy lost three of his children, besides a niece
nd two beloved aunts. There was, however, a stronger rea-
on for the delay. Rebelling at the task of being an artist, he
ent back to writing textbooks and propounding theories of
eaching, he started a stud farm on his Samara estate, he made
usiness trips to Moscow, and in fact he seized upon almost
ny excuse to stay away from his desk. It was not until 1875
aat the novel began appearing in a new magazine, *The Rus-
ian Messenger*, where instalments continued for more than
wo years. The magazine refused to publish Part Eight, which
xpressed dangerous opinions about the Serbo-Turkish War,
nd Tolstoy had it printed at his own expense. Then he re-
ised all the parts once more, and the book appeared as a
vhole in 1878, when the author was fifty years old. It was
ven more highly praised, if possible, than *War and Peace*.
Dostoevsky ran about in Petersburg "waving his hands and
alling Tolstoy 'the god of art.'" As for Tolstoy himself,
e was in the midst of a religious crisis and could hardly
ring himself to read the reviews. Two years later he wrote
o an admirer, "Concering *Anna Karenina*: I assure you
hat this abomination no longer exists for me, and I am only
exed because there are people for whom this sort of thing
s necessary."

There are still people, including myself, for whom this
ort of thing is necessary and who regard Tolstoy the artist
s a more admirable figure than Tolstoy the prophet. For
uch people *Anna Karenina* is one of the very great novels
f the nineteenth century. How does it stand in comparison
with *War and Peace*? A little below it, I think, and here the
neasurement is justified, since these are works by the same
uthor. But what about *The Brothers Karamazov* or *Great
Expectations* or *Moby Dick* or *The Red and the Black*?

Given the separate natures of these works, the question is impossible to answer. Is a whale better than an elephant and for what, sperm oil or ivory? Of what value is a list of the Five Greatest or Ten Greatest if it makes no distinction between running, swimming, and flying creatures?

Judged in its own terms, *Anna Karenina* is not a perfect novel after Part One. There are dull passages, especially in Part Three, and Levin the hero—who of course is Tolstoy himself—expresses too many opinions about burning issues that were quenched long ago. A worse fault is Tolstoy's attitude toward the heroine. He keeps implying that Anna should be pitied not condemned, that judgment is in God's hands, but one suspects the novelist of confusing himself with the God of Moses. One also suspects him of hating Anna for being dark-haired and passionate, whereas Kitty is blonde, perhaps a little frigid, and therefore not to be feared. Yet the author loves Anna too, he brings her alive before flinging her under a train, and the great quality of the novel is this sense of vivid and abounding life, as revealed not only by her but by all the other characters. In its own genre, which is that of the domestic novel raised to an epic scale, *Anna Karenina* is unsurpassed.

In statistical terms, it is a book of 400,000 words divided into eight parts, each of which, except the last, is the length of a short novel. There are seven principal characters, all belonging to the Russian nobility, and more than 160 minor figures, including other nobles but also their servants, a few of their peasants, two artists, a merchant, and a setter bitch. Most of the characters are grouped either around Levin and Kitty, whose courtship is based on that of Tolstoy and his wife, or else around Anna, her husband, and her lover. The stories of these two groups, coming together at moments, but usually separate, move forward in a sort of counterpoint; thus, Anna commits suicide almost on the same day that Kitty is giving birth to her first child. All the events described are contemporary with the writing of the novel; apparently the story begins in the winter of 1874, and it ends in the summer of 1876, shortly after the outbreak of the Serbo-Turkish War.

But what are the differences between *Anna Karenina* and the new novels—especially those by younger writers—that are being admired today?

Perhaps I am asking the question too soon. At this point it might simply lead to the old picture of a giant standing among pygmies or the even older contrast of a golden past with a drab present. That isn't at all what I wanted to suggest. I realize that the question is unfair if only for the reason that Tolstoy was a genius—in other words, something that seldom appears in any century—whereas the best of the younger writers have so far revealed nothing more than unusual talent. Genius is energy—mental energy first of all, but sometimes this is combined, as in Tolstoy's case, with physical, emotional, and sexual energy. Genius is vision, often involving the gift of finding patterns where others see nothing but a chance collection of objects. Genius is a memory for essential details. Genius is "the transcendent capacity for taking trouble," as Carlyle said; it is the capacity for brooding over a subject until it reveals its full potentialities; but that again is a form of energy. Genius is also a belief in oneself and the importance of one's mission, without which the energy is dissipated in hesitations and inner conflicts.

Tolstoy had all these forms of genius and he also had a social advantage that is not enjoyed, so far as I know, by any novelist of our own day. By birth he belonged to the small owning and governing class of Czarist Russia. He was not, it is true, one of its richer members. Besides the title of count—more proudly held in Russia than that of prince —his father had left him an estate of 5400 acres, with 350 serfs and their families grouped in four small villages around Yasnaya Polyana, but the estate yielded an income of only 5000 rubles a year. Though he couldn't live richly on that, even as a bachelor, the estate and the title gave him a feeling of assurance. Usually that feeling is bad for novelists. We are told that the novel is a middle-class form, and the fact is that no great novelist except Tolstoy has come from the true governing class of any country. Even Bulwer-Lytton, not a great novelist, was the *first* Baron Lytton; he earned his peerage by writing. Great novels about the aristocracy, like *Remembrance of Things Past,* are likely to be written by persons half in and half out of it, so that their perceptions are sharpened by their ambiguous position. The true aristocrat seldom becomes a novelist; he takes too much for granted.

That Tolstoy has been the one exception was owing partly to his genius, or energy, and partly to the terrible need he felt for being loved. Having lost his mother when he was two, he kept looking everywhere for affection. He burst into tears of joy if he was petted, and tears of rage if anyone scolded him. This need for love—and also for admiration —gave him a lover's clairvoyance, and he was never indifferent to people; everyone was charged for him with positive or negative electricity. I think this continual watchfulness helps to explain his fictional talent. Once the talent had been displayed, his noble birth became an advantage to the writer; it enabled him to write from within the governing circle, as no other novelist could do, and it gave a feeling of centrality to his work, a sense of its existing close to the seats of power.

But none of this leads to the contrast I wanted to make. We shall have to put aside Tolstoy's noble birth—as he himself never put it aside even when he was dressing and working like a peasant—and we shall also have to put aside his genius, while not forgetting it. Besides the genius, however, he also had talent, in the sense of technical skill, self-critical ability, notions about how to present a character, and effectiveness in telling a story; on that level he can be compared quite fairly with recent writers. And so we return to the original question: What are the differences between *Anna Karenina* and the freshly written novels that are being admired today?

The first difference to strike me is that Tolstoy was a primary writer, whereas the new men are secondary; they write in a given fashion because they are following someone else or trying hard to be different from someone else. Tolstoy writes as if *Anna Karenina* were the first novel ever published. To be more accurate, he writes as if there are other novels and he has read them, but doesn't need to bother about them, being perfectly convinced that he can do better. He doesn't let other novelists frighten him away from any subject, no matter how grand or trivial it is or how frequently described in fiction. What he prefers, what he describes with the boldest color and deepest conviction, are the primary events of human life: a proposal, a wedding, a lingering death, a religious conversion, a suicide, and the birth of a first child. He also likes to describe social functions, including many that younger novelists would avoid as being commonplace: a ball, a dinner at a fashionable restaurant, a dinner party at home, an evening at a noblemen's club, and the rite of social excommunication as performed at the opera; always he finds details to give them fresh life. There are still other set pieces in which he describes men's relation to animals or to growing crops, and in these he reveals a feeling of closeness to nature that is one more mark of the primary writer; nature has disappeared from many recent novels.

A second difference between *Anna Karenina* and most contemporary fiction is Tolstoy's method of presenting characters so as to give them substantiality. I can't think of a recent book that gives one such a sense of looking at people in the round, so that one can touch them on all sides and know them not merely as striking individuals but as members of a family and a social order. We are told how they spend their days and where their money comes from. If they have an opinion about social or intellectual problems of any sort, they don't hesitate to express it—sometimes at too great length, as in Levin's case, where we suspect that Tolstoy is using him as a mouthpiece, but usually with dramatic pertinence. The situation is different in recent novels, where characters are likely to be presented merely in relation to the story. We are told about their sex lives when the story deals with sex, as it usually does, and about their artistic lives when it deals with art, but we miss their connection with groups and institutions. If they are teachers, they don't teach; if they are merchants, they don't buy or sell; and if they are intellectuals, they don't talk about ideas, they don't even think but merely feel; and they sometimes read but we don't know what. Tolstoy was interested in everything, told everything, and made everything contribute to the roundedness of his people.

A third difference concerns the familiar matter of values. Tolstoy was writing for a traditional society in which there was no question who were "the right people"; therefore it was easy for him to surround poor Anna with glamor simply by mentioning some of her titled friends. He was also writing for a society that regarded some deeds as inherently sinful and believed all sins should be punished; therefore Anna's fate was accepted as the just outcome of a tragic situation. Today, with the weakening or confusion of moral codes, her story seems more pitiful than justly and inevitably tragic. We are inclined to sympathize with Anna more than Tolstoy intended, while suspecting the author of self-righteousness. Moreover, if the change in values has affected a nineteenth-century classic, it has created still greater problems for the novelists of our own time. How are they going to make us feel that their characters are truly important persons when there is no fixed society against which to measure them? How are they going to construct a tragic situation without using the notion of guilt and punishment?

A last difference—or the last I shall mention—lies in the field of fictional technique. Here there have been real advances in the last eighty years, and most of our younger novelists have learned the Henry Jamesian method of reporting the action through the eyes of a single observer—or sometimes two or three observers, but always as few as possible. It is a most effective method, one that conceals the author and carries the reader directly into the action, but still it raises some awkward questions. How is the author going to convey a simple piece of information that his chosen observer would be unlikely to know or mention? How is he going to describe a social function at which more is happening than one man is likely to comprehend? Tolstoy is never bothered by problems of the sort. His general method is old-fashioned—that of the omniscient author—but he doesn't hesitate to change it as often as necessary, sometimes reporting a scene as if from a high balcony, sometimes entering one mind and sometimes another (even that of the setter bitch), sometimes shifting his point of view two or three times in a chapter, but without confusing the reader, and sometimes inventing a new method to meet a special situation: for example, the four chapters leading to Anna's suicide are perhaps the first prolonged use of interior monologue. He devotes ten or twelve chapters to the events of a single day, as witnessed by a single character, and then in a last short paragraph he gallops through a month or a season. In other words, he writes with perfect freedom, always adapting the method to the material, which he tries to make broadly human, and always conveying that sense of abundant life. For novelists of our own rather timid day, *Anna Karenina* might serve as an example of courage.

I am glad that the novel is being republished in Joel Carmichael's new translation. Besides being more direct than earlier translations and closer to current speech, it has the great advantage of simplifying the Russian names, so that the reader is no longer confused by all the -evnas and -oviches and can give his full attention to the story, as Tolstoy wanted us to do.

# ANNA KARENINA

*"Vengeance is mine; I will repay, saith the Lord."*

*Romans 12:19*

**NOTE:** On the name *Anna Karenina*

The form of the name, Karenina, does not agree with the system of nomenclature in this translation; it is used out of respect for the traditional title of this novel.

# PART ONE

## I

HAPPY families are all alike; every unhappy family is unhappy in its own way.

Everything at the Oblonskys' was topsy-turvy. Oblonsky's wife had found out that he had been having an affair with the French governess who used to live with them, and told him she could no longer stay under the same roof with him. This was the third day things had been this way, and not only the married couple themselves, but the family and the whole household were painfully aware of it. Everyone in the house felt that there was no sense in their living together, and that people who had casually dropped into any inn would have more connection with each other than they, the Oblonsky family and household. Oblonsky's wife refused to leave her rooms; he himself hadn't been home for three days. The children were running around the house as though lost; the English governess had had a quarrel with the housekeeper and written to a friend of hers asking her to look out for a new job for her; the day before the cook had picked dinnertime to go out; the kitchen maid and coachman had given notice.

The third day after the quarrel Prince Stephen Arkadyevich Oblonsky—Stiva, as he was called in society—woke up at his usual time, that is, eight in the morning, not in his wife's bedroom but in his own study, on the leather-covered sofa. He twisted his plump, well-kept body on the springy sofa as though he wanted to plunge into a long sleep again; he hugged the pillow on the other side and pressed his cheek against it; then he suddenly jumped up, sat down on the sofa, and opened his eyes.

Now, what was that again? he thought, recalling a dream. What was it? Of course! Alabin was giving a dinner in Darmstadt, no, not in Darmstadt—somewhere in America. But that's where Darmstadt was, in America. So Alabin was giving a dinner, on glass tables—and the tables were singing "Il mio tesoro," though not "Il mio tesoro" but something better, and then there were some little decanters around and they were really women, he remembered.

Oblonsky's eyes sparkled merrily; he smiled to himself as he sat there thinking: Yes, it was great fun, all right. There were a lot of other good things too, but you can't put them into words, or catch hold of them at all when you're awake.

He noticed a streak of light that had slipped in at the side of one of the blinds; he cheerfully stretched his legs off the sofa and felt about with his feet for the bronze kid slippers his wife had embroidered for his last year's birthday present; out of a nine-year-old habit he stretched out his arm without getting up toward where his dressing gown hung in the bedroom. It was just then that he suddenly recalled why he wasn't sleeping in his wife's bedroom, but in his study; the smile vanished from his face and he frowned.

"Oh, oh, oh!" he groaned, remembering everything that had happened. And again all the details of the quarrel with his wife, his impossible position and, most painful of all, his own guilt sprang to his mind.

No, she'll never forgive me! She can't forgive me. And the most terrible thing about it is that it's all my own fault, I'm to blame, though I'm not really to blame either. That's the whole tragedy of it, he thought. "Oh dear, oh dear," he muttered in despair, recalling the most painful points of the quarrel.

What had been most disagreeable of all was the first moment when, on coming back cheerful and satisfied from the theater with a huge pear for his wife in his hand, he had not, to his surprise, found her in the drawing room or in his study, but finally saw her in her bedroom holding the unlucky note that had revealed everything.

There was his Dolly, whom he thought of as constantly harried and simple-mindedly bustling about, sitting motionless with the note in her hand, looking at him with an expression of horror, despair, and fury.

"What is this? This?" she asked, indicating the note.

As he remembered this Oblonsky was tormented, as often

happens, not so much by the event itself as by his response to his wife's question.

What happened then was what happens to people who are caught at something shameful. He couldn't manage to put on the right expression for his situation with respect to his wife now that his guilt was exposed. Instead of acting offended, making denials or excuses, asking forgiveness, or even remaining indifferent—anything would have been better than what he did do!—his face quite involuntarily (a reflex of the brain, he thought; he was fond of physiology) suddenly took on its usual goodhearted and therefore silly smile.

It was this silly smile that he couldn't forgive himself. When she saw it Dolly shuddered as though in physical pain, burst out with her characteristic violence in a torrent of bitter words and rushed out of the room. Since then she had refused to see him.

That stupid smile is to blame for everything, Oblonsky thought. But what can I do? What is there to do? he said to himself in despair, without finding an answer.

## II

OBLONSKY was honest with himself. He could not deceive himself by telling himself that he repented of his conduct. He could not feel repentant that he, a handsome, amorous man of thirty-four, was not in love with his wife, the mother of five living and two dead children, who was only a year younger than he. He only regretted that he hadn't been able to conceal things from her better. But he felt the full gravity of his position and was sorry for his wife, their children, and himself. He might have been able to hide his misconduct from his wife better if he had expected the news to have such an effect on her. He had never thought the matter over clearly, but had vaguely imagined that she had long since guessed he was unfaithful to her and was shutting her eyes to it. He even thought that a completely undistinguished woman like her, worn out, aging, already plain, just a simple goodhearted mother of a family, ought to have been indulgent, out of a feeling of fairness. What had happened was just the opposite.

Terrible, just terrible! Oblonsky kept saying to himself, without finding any solution. And how well everything was going until now! What a splendid life we had! She was contented and happy with the children, I never bothered her in the least, and left her to do as she pleased with the children and the house. Of course, it's not so good that *she* was a governess right here in the house. That was bad! There's something banal and vulgar in making love to your own governess. But what a governess! (He vividly recalled Mlle. Roland's teasing black eyes and her smile.) But as long as she was here in the house I never allowed myself to do a thing. And the worst of it all is that she's already . . . The whole thing had to happen just for spite! Oh, dear! But what on earth can I do?

There was no answer to this beside the usual answer life gives to the most complicated and insoluble problems, which is: you must live according to the needs of the day, that is, forget yourself. He couldn't forget himself in sleep, at least not until nighttime; he could not yet return to the music being sung by the little decanter women, so he had to look for forgetfulness in the dream of living.

Well, we'll see, Oblonsky said to himself; he got up, put on his gray dressing gown with the blue silk lining, knotted the girdle, and taking a deep breath of air into his broad chest, went over to the window with his usual robust stride, turning out his feet, which carried his full body so lightly; he raised the blind and rang loudly.

The bell was answered immediately by his old friend and valet, Matthew, who came in with his clothes, boots, and a telegram. He was followed by the barber with the shaving things.

"Any papers from the office?" Oblonsky asked, taking the telegram and sitting down in front of the mirror.

"On the table," Matthew answered, with a questioning, sympathetic look at his master, and after a moment added with a sly smile: "They've sent someone from the livery stables."

Oblonsky said nothing, merely gazing at Matthew in the mirror; it was plain from the glance they exchanged that they understood each other very well. Oblonsky's look seemed to say: "Why tell me that? As though you didn't know!"

Matthew put his hands into the pockets of his jacket, put out his foot, and looked at his master in silence, with a slight, good-humored smile.

"I ordered him to come back next Sunday, and till then not to bother either you or himself for no reason," he said, evidently getting off a prepared sentence.

Oblonsky saw Matthew was joking to draw attention to

himself. He tore open the telegram and read it, guessing at the words, misspelt as usual, and his face brightened.

"Matthew, my sister Anna will be here tomorrow," he said, momentarily stopping the barber's shiny plump hand that was clearing a rosy path between the long curly whiskers.

"Thank God!" said Matthew, showing that he understood just as well as his master the meaning of the visit, that is, that Oblonsky's beloved sister Anna might bring about a reconciliation between husband and wife. "Alone, or with her husband?" he asked.

Oblonsky couldn't answer, since the barber was busy on his upper lip, and raised one finger. Matthew nodded into the mirror.

"Alone. Should one of the upstairs rooms be got ready?"

"Ask Princess Oblonsky."

"Princess Oblonsky?" repeated Matthew doubtfully.

"Yes, tell her. Here, take the telegram with you and tell me what she says."

Oh, you want to sound her out, was how Matthew understood this, but all he said was: "Yes, sir."

Oblonsky had already washed, and his hair was brushed; he was about to get dressed when Matthew, walking slowly in his creaking boots, came back into the room holding the telegram. The barber had already gone.

"Princess Oblonsky has instructed me to say that she is going away. Let him do as he likes, that is, you, sir," he said, laughing with his eyes only; putting his hands in his pockets and his head to one side, he gazed at his master.

Oblonsky was silent, then a kind and somewhat pathetic smile appeared on his handsome face.

"Ah, Matthew, well?" he said, shaking his head.

"Don't worry, sir, it will all turn out all right," said Matthew.

"All right?"

"Exactly, sir."

"D'you think so? But who's that?" asked Oblonsky, hearing the rustle of a woman's dress outside the door.

"It's me, sir," said a firm, agreeable female voice, and Matrona, the children's nurse, thrust her stern, pock-marked face into the doorway.

"Well, what is it, Matrona?" asked Oblonsky, going over to her.

Though Oblonsky was completely at fault with respect to his wife and felt this himself, almost everyone in the house,

even the nurse, who was Princess Oblonsky's best friend, was
on his side.

"Well, what?" he said dejectedly.

"You must go to her, sir, and admit your guilt once again.
Perhaps God will help! She's in terrible torment; for that
matter everything in the house is at sixes and sevens. You
must take pity on the children, sir. Admit you were wrong,
sir—what else can you do? If you put your hand in the fire—"

"But you know she won't see me—"

"Do your own part. God is merciful, sir. Pray to God—
pray, sir!"

"Very well then, you can go now," said Oblonsky, suddenly
blushing. "And now I must get dressed," he said, turning to
Matthew and energetically throwing off his dressing gown.

Matthew was already holding out, like a horse's collar, the
shirt he had got ready; he blew an invisible speck off it and
with obvious satisfaction enveloped his master's well-cared-
for body in it.

## III

WHEN he was dressed Oblonsky sprinkled some scent on
himself, adjusted his cuffs, and with a mechanical gesture
distributed in various pockets his cigarettes, his wallet,
matches, and watch with its double chain and bunch of
charms, shook out his handkerchief, and, feeling clean,
fragrant, healthy, and physically cheerful in spite of his misfortune, went out with a slight bounce at each step into the
dining room, where coffee was waiting for him, with some
letters and papers at the side.

He read the letters. One of them was extremely disagreeable—from a dealer who was buying a forest on his wife's
property. This forest had to be sold; but just now, until he
and his wife were reconciled, it couldn't be spoken about.
The most unpleasant thing about it was the introduction of
a money interest into the question of the forthcoming reconciliation with his wife. He was vexed by the idea that he
might be governed by this interest, and seeking a reconciliation with his wife in order to sell off the forest.

After finishing the letters Oblonsky reached for the papers
from the office, quickly leafed through two files, made a few
notes with a big pencil and pushed them aside to begin on

his coffee. Over the coffee he unfolded the still damp morning paper and began reading it.

Oblonsky subscribed to and read a liberal newspaper, not extremist, but the one most people went by. In spite of his having no particular interest in science, or art, or politics, he was firmly guided in all these subjects by the views that most people and the newspaper held; he only changed them whenever most people did, or rather, he did not change them—they imperceptibly changed within him of their own accord.

Oblonsky never selected either his opinions or his point of view; opinions and points of view slipped into him automatically, just as he did not choose the fashion of his hats or coats but took whatever was being worn. Since he lived in a certain society and had a desire for some intellectual activity, such as usually develops with maturity, it was just as vital for him to have opinions as to have a hat. If there was any reason why he preferred liberalism to conservatism, which was also the point of view of many in his set, it was not because he thought liberalism more reasonable, but because it suited his style of life better. The liberal group said that everything in Russia was bad, and as a matter of fact Oblonsky had a great many debts, and definitely not enough money. The liberals thought marriage was an obsolete institution and had to be reformed, and as a matter of fact family life gave Oblonsky very little satisfaction and obliged him to lie and to pretend, which was contrary to his nature. The liberals said, or rather suggested, that religion was only a check on the barbarous part of the population, and as a matter of fact Oblonsky could not bear standing through even a short church service without his feet hurting, and could not understand the point of all those terrible, highfalutin words about the other world when it would be very gay to live in this one too. At the same time Oblonsky, who liked a merry joke, found it agreeable to startle the simple-minded by saying that if you were going to take pride in your ancestry why stop at Prince Rurik and deny your first ancestor—the ape?

Thus liberalism had become a habit of Oblonsky's; he liked his newspaper, as he did his after-dinner cigar, for the slight cloud it produced in his head. He read the leading article, which explained that it was a complete waste of time in our age to raise the cry that radicalism was threatening to swallow up all conservative elements or that the government had to take steps to crush the hydra of the revolution: on the contrary, "in our opinion the danger lies not in the imaginary hydra of revolution but in the obstinacy of the traditional attitude, which is a brake on progress," etc. He also read the financial article, which talked about Bentham and Mill and got off a few jibes at the administration. With his characteristic acuteness he got the point of each jibe; who made it, whom it was directed at and why, and as usual this gave him a certain amount of satisfaction. But his satisfaction was spoiled today by the thought of Matrona's advice, and by the trouble in the house. He also read that there was a rumor about Count Beust going to Wiesbaden, that gray hair was going to be ended, that a light carriage was up for sale, that a young person was offering her services: but these items did not give him the tranquil, ironical pleasure they would have before.

After finishing the paper and a second cup of coffee with a buttered roll, he got up and flicked some crumbs off his waistcoat; expanding his broad chest, he gave a joyful smile, though not because there was anything specially pleasant on his mind—the joyful smile was produced by a first-rate digestion.

But now this joyful smile brought everything back to mind; he grew pensive.

Two childish voices made themselves heard outside the door; Oblonsky recognized them as the voices of his little boy Grisha and of Tanya, his oldest daughter. They had been dragging something along and had knocked it over.

"I told you not to put the passengers on the roof," Tanya shouted in English. "Now pick them up!"

Everything's all mixed up, thought Oblonsky, there are the children running around by themselves. He went to the door and called them in. They put aside a box that was supposed to be a train and came to their father.

Tanya, her father's favorite, ran in boldly, embraced him and swung laughing from his neck, delighted as usual by the familiar aroma of his whiskers. Kissing his face, flushed with stooping and radiant with tenderness, the girl unclasped her hands and was about to run off, but he held her back.

"How is Mama?" he asked, passing his hand over his daughter's smooth, delicate little neck. "Good morning," he said with a smile, at his little boy's greeting.

He was aware of liking the little boy less, and always tried to be fair; but the little boy felt this and did not respond with a smile to the chilly smile of his father.

"Mama? She's up already," Tanya answered.

Oblonsky sighed: that means she hasn't slept all night again, he thought.

"Well, is she in a good mood?"

Tanya knew that her father and mother had had a quarrel, that her mother could not be in a good mood, that her father must have known this, and that it was all pretense, his asking her about this so lightly. She blushed for him. He saw this at once and blushed also.

"I don't know," she said. "She didn't tell us to have our lessons, but to take a walk with Miss Hull to Grandmama's."

"Well, go along then, my darling little Tanya. Oh, but wait," he said, holding her back anyhow and stroking her delicate little hand.

He took a box of sweets down from the mantelpiece, where he had put it the day before, and picked out her two favorites, a chocolate and a colored cream.

"For Grisha?" said the little girl, holding out the chocolate.

"Yes, yes." He stroked her little shoulder once again, kissed the nape of her neck and let her go.

"The carriage is ready," said Matthew. "Also, some woman is here to see you about something," he added.

"Has she been here long?" asked Oblonsky.

"About half an hour."

"How often have you been told to announce things at once!"

"But you have to have time to finish your coffee," said Matthew in the companionable, coarse tone it was impossible to get angry at.

"Very well, have her come in immediately," said Oblonsky, frowning with annoyance.

The woman—the widow of a petty official by the name of Kalinin—was asking for something that was impossible and senseless; but Oblonsky had her sit down and listened to her attentively as usual, without interrupting, until she was finished, then gave her detailed advice on whom to apply to and how; in a brisk, efficient way he even gave her a little note, in his heavy, sprawling, elegant and legible handwriting, to someone who might be able to help her. After getting rid of her Oblonsky took his hat and paused, trying to recall whether he had forgotten anything. It turned out that he had forgotten nothing except what he had wanted to—his wife.

Yes, of course! His head sank, and his handsome face took on a distracted expression. Should I see her now or not? he said to himself. And an inner voice said to him that there was no need to see her, that nothing could come of it but deceit, that it was impossible to improve or patch up their relations because it was impossible to make her attractive again or exciting, or to turn him into an old man incapable of love. Nothing could come of it now but deceit and lies; and deceit and lies were contrary to his nature.

But sooner or later I'll have to; things can't be left this way after all, he said, trying to give himself courage. He straightened up, lighted a cigarette, and started smoking; he took two puffs and threw it into a mother-of-pearl ashtray, strode rapidly through the gloomy drawing room and opened the other door into his wife's bedroom.

## IV

DOLLY, her once thick and beautiful hair now scanty and done up with hairpins at the nape of her neck, and her large, frightened eyes protruding from her emaciated face, was standing there in a dressing jacket. Things were scattered about the room in front of an open wardrobe she was taking something out of. When she heard Oblonsky's steps she stopped, looking at the door and making a futile attempt to put on an expression of stern disdain. She felt she was afraid of him, and afraid of the prospect of a talk. She was only trying to do what she had been trying to do now for the tenth time during the past three days: to sort out her own and the children's things, which she was going to take to her mother's —and now again she could not make up her mind to it; now as before she was saying to herself that things couldn't stay that way, that she had to do something to punish and humiliate him, to revenge herself if only for a small part of the pain he had inflicted on her. She still kept on saying that she was going to leave him, but she could not get out of the habit of considering him her husband and of loving him.

Aside from this she felt that if she could scarcely manage to take care of her five children here, in her own house, it would be still worse where she meant to take them. For that matter the youngest had fallen ill because he had been fed a bad broth, while the others had scarcely had any dinner the day before at all. She felt it was impossible to leave, but, deceiving herself, she kept sorting things out anyhow and pretending she would.

When she saw Oblonsky she thrust her hand into a drawer of the wardrobe as though looking for something, and only looked round at him when he had come all the way over to her. But her face, on which she was trying to put an expression of severe determination, looked bewildered and anguished.

"Dolly!" he said in a soft, shy voice. He lowered his head and tried to look pathetic and submissive, while radiating freshness and health nevertheless.

With a swift glance she took in his figure, shining with freshness and health, from head to toe. Yes, she thought, he's happy and contented! And me? . . . And that repulsive good nature of his, which everyone likes and praises him so much for; that good nature of his—I hate it!! she thought. She pursed her lips, and a muscle on the right side of her pale, nervous face started twitching.

"What d'you want?" she said quickly, in a high unnatural voice.

"Dolly!" he repeated, his voice trembling. "Anna's coming today."

"What's that to do with me? I can't receive her!" she cried.

"But really, Dolly, you must, after all—"

"Go away, go away, go away!" she cried out without looking at him, as though the cry were squeezed out of her by physical pain.

Oblonsky could be calm when he thought about his wife, he could hope that things would turn out "all right," as Matthew put it, and could calmly read the paper and drink his coffee; but when he saw her suffering face and heard that sound of her voice, resigned to fate and hopeless, he gasped, a lump rose up in his throat, and his eyes glistened with tears.

"My God, what have I done! Dolly! For God's sake! After all—" He couldn't go on; his throat choked up with sobs.

She slammed the wardrobe shut and looked at him.

"Dolly—what can I say? Only—forgive me, forgive me . . . Remember . . . surely nine years of our lives ought to atone for a few moments . . . a few moments . . ."

She looked down and listened, waiting for what he would say, as though imploring him to make her change her mind somehow.

"A few moments of infatuation . . ." he got out, and wanted to continue, but at this word her lips tightened again as though in physical pain, and again the cheek muscle on the right side of her face began twitching.

"Go away—go away from here!" she cried out in a still more strident voice, "and don't say a word to me about your infatuations and your beastliness!"

She started to go out, but staggered and caught hold of the back of a chair for support. His face grew broader, his lips swelled, and his eyes filled with tears.

"Dolly!" he said, by now sobbing. "For God's sake, think of the children, it's not they who are to blame. I'm the one to blame; punish me, make me atone for my sin. I'll do anything I can, I'm ready for anything! I'm the guilty one, words can't express my guilt! But—Dolly, forgive me!"

She sat down. He could hear her loud, heavy breathing, and he felt inexpressibly sorry for her. She tried to say something several times, but was unable to. He waited.

"You remember the children when you want to play with them, Stiva, but I remember them and I know that now they're ruined," she said, obviously repeating one of the phrases she had said to herself more than once during the past three days.

She had said "Stiva"; he looked at her gratefully and reached for her hand, but she moved away from him with revulsion.

"I think of the children and would do anything in the world to save them; but I don't know myself how I can—by taking them away from their father, or by leaving them with a debauched father—yes, a debauched father . . . So, tell me yourself, after this—after what has happened, will we be able to go on living together? Can we? Tell me, will it be possible?" she repeated, raising her voice. "When my husband, the father of my children, starts an affair with the governess of his own children . . ."

"But what's to be done? What's to be done?" he said in a pathetic voice, not knowing himself what he was saying, and sinking his head lower and lower.

"You're hateful to me—repugnant!" she cried out, getting more and more excited. "Your tears are just—water! You never loved me; you have no heart, no honor! To me you are loathsome, hateful, and a stranger—yes, a complete stranger!" She pronounced the word *stranger,* which horrified herself, with anguish and hatred.

He looked at her, and the expression of hatred on her face frightened and startled him. He did not understand that his pity infuriated her. What she saw in his eyes was pity, but not love.

No, he thought, she hates me; she'll never forgive me. "This is horrible—horrible!" he muttered.

Just then a child, who had probably fallen down, began crying in the other room; Dolly listened; all at once her face softened. She seemed to be collecting herself, as though she didn't know where she was or what she had to do; then she got up quickly and moved toward the door.

But after all, she loves my child, he thought, noticing how her face changed when the baby cried; *my* child, so how can she hate me?

"Dolly, just one more word," he said, following her.

"If you follow me, I'll call the servants, the children! Everyone will know what a scoundrel you are! I'll leave today, and you can live here with your mistress!"

She went out, slamming the door.

Oblonsky sighed, wiped his face and stepped softly out of the room. Matthew says things'll turn out all right, but how? I don't even see how it's possible. Oh dear, how horrible it all is! And what a vulgar way to shout, he said to himself, recalling her screaming and the words "scoundrel" and "mistress." Why, the maids might have heard her! Terribly vulgar, terribly! Oblonsky stood alone for a few seconds, wiped his eyes, sighed, and straightening up went out of the room.

It was a Friday, and the German clockmaker was winding the clock in the dining room. Oblonsky recalled a joke of his about this accurate, bald-headed clockmaker—about the German himself "being wound up his whole life in order to wind up clocks," and smiled. Oblonsky liked a good joke. But maybe things will turn out all right! There's a nice word, he thought, *turn out;* I'll have to use that.

"Matthew!" he called. "You and Mary arrange everything for my sister Anna in the little sitting room," he said when Matthew appeared.

"Yes, sir."

Oblonsky put on his fur coat and went out onto the front steps.

"Won't you be home for dinner, sir?" said Matthew, accompanying him.

"I'll see. Here, take some money," he said, taking a ten-ruble bill out of his wallet. "Will that be enough?"

"Enough or not, that's what we'll have to get along on,

that's plain," said Matthew, closing the carriage door and stepping back onto the steps.

Meanwhile Dolly, after soothing the child and realizing from the sound of the carriage that he had left, went back to her bedroom. This was the only refuge she had from the cares of the house, which enveloped her the moment she came out. Even now, during the few minutes she had gone out to the nursery, the English governess and Matrona had managed to ask her a few questions that couldn't be put off and that she alone could answer: "What walking clothes should the children put on?" "Ought they to have some milk?" "Should a new cook be sent for?"

"Oh, leave me alone, just leave me alone!" she cried, and went back to her bedroom. There she sat down where she had spoken to Oblonsky; she locked her thin hands, with the rings that had slipped down on her bony fingers, and began sorting out in her mind the conversation she had just had with him.

So he's gone! But how did he finish with *her*? she thought. Surely he's not seeing her? Why didn't I ask him? No, no, we'll never be able to make up! Even if we stay together in the same house—we're strangers. Strangers forever! she repeated, with special emphasis once again on the word she found so terrible. And oh, how I loved him! My God, how I loved him! But don't I love him now too? Don't I love him more than before? And the most terrible thing is—she began, but cut short her thought because Matrona put her head in the door.

"Why not send for my brother?" she said; "after all, he can make a dinner, or else the children won't have anything to eat until six o'clock, like yesterday."

"All right, I'll be right out and see to it . . . But has the fresh milk been sent for?"

And Dolly plunged into her daily worries, and for a time drowned her grief.

v

THANKS to his abilities Oblonsky had done well at school, though he was lazy and mischievous and consequently one of the last in his class. But in spite of his chronic dissipation, his minor appointments, and his youth, he occupied a respectable and well-paid post as head of one of the government boards in Moscow. He had gotten it through his sister Anna's husband, Alexis Alexandrovich Karenin, who held one of the most important positions in the ministry the board was part of; but if Karenin hadn't nominated his brother-in-law to this post hundreds of other people—brothers, sisters, relations, cousins, uncles, aunts—would have gotten Stiva Oblonsky this post or one like it, at some 6000 rubles a year, which he needed since in spite of his wife's respectable fortune his affairs were in a bad way.

Half Moscow and Petersburg were relatives or friends of Oblonsky's. He was born among those people who were or had become the powers of this world. A third of the men in the official world, the older ones, had been friends of his father's and had known him in swaddling clothes; another third were on intimate terms with him, and the rest knew him very well. Consequently those who hand out the good things of this world, in the shape of government posts, grants, concessions, and such things, were all friends of his; they could not overlook one of their own people. Oblonsky did not have to exert himself particularly to get a profitable position; all he had to do was not to be difficult, envious, quarrelsome, or quick to take offense, which for that matter, being good-tempered by nature, he never was. It would have seemed absurd to him if he had been told he would not obtain a post with the salary he needed, especially since he was not demanding anything out of the ordinary: he only wanted the same thing as everyone else like him, while he was capable of filling such an office no worse than anyone else.

Oblonsky was not only liked by everyone who knew him, because of his good nature, gaiety, and unquestionable honesty, but something about him, in his handsome radiant looks, his beaming eyes, black hair and eyebrows, his pink and white face, had a physical effect of kindliness and merriment on anyone who ran into him. "Ah, Stiva! Oblonsky! There he is!" almost everyone he met said with a joyful smile. Even if it sometimes happened that after talking to him it turned out that nothing particularly joyful had happened, still, the next day and the day after that everyone was just as delighted to meet him as before.

By his third year as head of this government board in Moscow, Oblonsky had won not only the affection but the esteem of his colleagues, subordinates, chiefs, and everyone who had anything to do with him. The principal qualities that had won him this general respect in his office were first of all an extreme indulgence toward people, based on an awareness of his own shortcomings; secondly, his utter liberalism, not the liberalism he read about in the newspapers but the one he had in his blood, which made him behave in an absolutely equal and identical way with everyone, whatever their rank or status; thirdly—and chiefly—a total indifference to the business he was engaged in, because of which he never got excited or made mistakes.

When he arrived at his office Oblonsky, deferentially followed by the doorkeeper carrying his portfolio, went to his little private study, put on his uniform and went out into the board room. The clerks and attendants all got up, and gave him a cheerful, respectful bow. As usual Oblonsky quickly walked over to his seat, shook hands with the members, and sat down. He did as much joking and chatting as was proper, then turned to business. No one was abler at finding the boundary between freedom, simplicity, and formality which was necessary for the pleasant carrying on of business. A secretary with a cheerful, respectful look, like everyone else in Oblonsky's office, came over with some papers and remarked, in the easy, familiar tone Oblonsky was responsible for:

"We've got hold of that information from the Penza Provincial Government after all. Here, if you don't mind—"

"So you finally got it?" said Oblonsky, holding the paper down with his finger. "Well, gentlemen—" And the sitting began.

If they only knew, Oblonsky thought, inclining his head with an important look as he listened to a report, what a shamefaced little boy their chairman was half an hour ago! And his eyes twinkled as the report was read. Business was not supposed to be interrupted before two o'clock, when there was a break for lunch.

It was not yet two o'clock when the great glass doors of the board room suddenly opened and someone came in. All the members sitting beneath the Tsar's portrait or behind the emblem of justice, looked round at the door, glad of a distraction; but the guard turned the intruder out at once and closed the glass door behind him.

After the report was read Oblonsky got up, stretched himself, and in tribute to the liberalism of the period took out a cigarette in the board room and went to his own office. Two of his colleagues—Nikitin, a veteran functionary, and Grinevich, a Gentleman of the Bedchamber—went out with him.

"We'll be able to finish after lunch," said Oblonsky.

"Easily," said Nikitin.

"That Fomin must be an absolute rascal," said Grinevich, referring to one of the figures in the case under consideration.

Oblonsky frowned at this remark of Grinevich's, to convey the view that it was improper to form a premature judgment, and did not answer.

"Who was that who came in?" he asked the doorkeeper.

"Someone slipped in without permission, Your Excellency, when my back was turned. He was asking for you. So I said, 'When the members go out, then—'"

"Where is he?"

"He may have gone out into the corridor, or else he's still walking about here. That's the one," said the doorkeeper, indicating a powerfully built, broad-shouldered man with a curly beard and a sheepskin cap on, who was swiftly and light-footedly running up the worn-down steps of the stone staircase. A thin official with a portfolio, on his way down, stopped and threw a disapproving glance at the feet of the running man, then glanced questioningly at Oblonsky.

Oblonsky was standing on the top of the stairs. His good-humored face, shining over the gold-laced collar of his uniform, beamed even more as he watched the man coming up.

"So it's you, Levin! At last!" he said with a friendly, ironical smile, as he gazed at Levin approaching him. "How is it you deign to look me up in this den?" said Oblonsky, embracing his friend as well as shaking him by the hand. "Have you been here long?"

"I've just arrived. I very much want to see you," Levin answered, looking round with constraint, and at the same time irritably and uneasily.

"Well, let's go to my study," said Oblonsky, who was familiar with his friend's self-conscious and irascible shyness; he took Levin by the hand and led him along as though he were guiding him past some danger.

Oblonsky was on intimate terms with almost everyone he knew: men of sixty, boys of twenty, actors, ministers of state, tradesmen, and Lords in Waiting, so that a great many of those who were intimate with him stood at the two extremes of the social ladder, and would have been very surprised to learn that through Oblonsky they had something in common. He was on familiar terms with everyone he drank champagne with, and he drank champagne with everyone; consequently, when he met any of his disreputable pals, as he jok-

ingly called a great many of his friends, when he was with
his subordinates, he was able with his characteristic tact to
minimize the disagreeable impression on them. Levin was not
a "disreputable pal," but with his tact Oblonsky felt that
Levin thought that he might not wish to express his intimacy
with him in front of his subordinates; this was why he
hurried him off to his private room.

Levin was almost the same age as Oblonsky, and was on
intimate terms with him not through champagne alone. Levin
had been his comrade and friend since early youth. They
were attached to each other in spite of differing characters
and tastes, as friends are who meet in early youth. But in
spite of this, as often happens between people who have
chosen different careers, each of them, even though justifying each other's activity in any argument, despised it at
heart. It seemed to each of them that the life he himself
was leading was the only real life, while his friend's life was
a mere phantom. Oblonsky could not refrain from a slight
ironical smile at the sight of Levin. How many times had he
not seen him arriving in Moscow from the country, where
he was doing something or other, though just what Oblonsky
could never quite understand; nor was he interested. When
Levin arrived in Moscow he was always excited, in a hurry,
slightly shy, and vexed by this shyness, and generally with a
completely novel, unexpected view of things. Oblonsky
laughed at this, and liked it. In just the same way Levin at
heart despised both his friend's urban style of life and his
official duties, which he considered nonsense and ridiculed.
But the difference was that when Oblonsky did what everyone else did he laughed in a self-assured and good-humored
way, while Levin did so without assurance and sometimes
angrily.

"We've been expecting you for some time," Oblonsky said,
going into his private room and releasing Levin's arm, as
though indicating that there all dangers were past. "I'm very,
very glad to see you," he went on. "Well, what are you up
to? How are you? When did you get here?"

Levin was silent, looking at the unfamiliar faces of Oblonsky's two colleagues, and especially at the hands of the elegant Grinevich, who had such long white fingers, and such
long yellow fingernails tapering at the ends, and such huge
glittering cuff links that they plainly absorbed his whole attention and gave him no freedom to think. Oblonsky noticed
this at once and smiled.

"Oh, of course, let me introduce you," he said. "My colleagues—Philip Nikitin and Michael Grinevich," then, turning to Levin, "an active member of his District Council, one of the new kind, a gymnast who can lift a hundred-and-eighty-pound weight with one hand, a cattle breeder and hunter, and my friend—Constantine Levin, Sergius Koznyshov's brother."

"Delighted," said the elderly official, Nikitin.

"I have the honor of knowing your brother Koznyshov," said Grinevich, holding out his slender hand with the long fingernails.

Levin frowned, shook hands coldly, then turned at once to Oblonsky. Although he had great regard for his half-brother, a writer well known throughout Russia, he could not endure being treated not as Constantine Levin but as the brother of the famous Koznyshov.

"No, I'm not on the District Council any longer. I've quarreled with all of them and I've stopped going to meetings," he said, addressing Oblonsky.

"That was quick!" said Oblonsky with a smile. "But why? What happened?"

"It's a long story, I'll tell it to you some time," said Levin, but began telling it at once. "The long and the short of it is that I've become convinced that the District Council doesn't do anything, and can't do anything," he began, speaking as though someone had just offended him. "On the one hand it's just a game, they play at parliament, and I'm neither young enough nor old enough to be entertained by games; on the other hand"—he hesitated—"it's a means of graft for the provincial coterie. Before there used to be guardianships and magistracies, now there's the District Council; it's not a bribe, but it means unearned salaries." He spoke as heatedly as though one of those present were contesting his opinion.

"Aha! So I see you're in a new phase once again, a conservative one," said Oblonsky. "But we'll talk about that later."

"Yes, later. But I had to see you," said Levin, staring at Grinevich's hand with loathing.

Oblonsky smiled slightly.

"Didn't you once say you'd never wear European clothes again?" he said, looking at Levin's new suit, evidently made by some French tailor. "Yes, I see: a new phase!"

Levin suddenly blushed, but not the way adults blush, very slightly, hardly aware of it themselves, but as little boys

blush, feeling absurd because of their shyness and therefore
ashamed of themselves and blushing even more, to the point
of tears. It was so strange seeing this intelligent, virile face in
such a childish state that Oblonsky turned his eyes away.

"But where can we see each other? I really must talk to
you," said Levin.

Oblonsky seemed to reflect: "Here, why don't we go to
Gurin's for lunch, and talk there. I'm free until three."

"No," said Levin, after a moment's thought, "I have to go
somewhere."

"Well, all right, then let's have dinner."

"Dinner? But I really have nothing special in mind, just a
word or two, there's something I want to ask you. We can
have a talk some other time."

"Well, say your two words right now and we'll chat over
dinner."

"The two words are these," said Levin, "but it's really
nothing in particular."

His face took on a look of rage, from his effort to overcome his own shyness.

"What are the Shcherbatskys up to?" he asked. "Is everything the same as usual?"

Oblonsky, who had known for a long time that Levin was
in love with Kitty Shcherbatsky, Oblonsky's sister-in-law,
gave a barely perceptible smile, and his eyes sparkled gaily.

"You said two words, but I can't answer you in two words,
because—Excuse me a moment."

The secretary had come in, familiarly deferential, and with
that certain modest awareness, common to all secretaries, of
superiority to their superiors in their knowledge of affairs,
came over to Oblonsky with some papers and, in the form of
a question, began explaining some difficulty. Oblonsky did
not let him finish, but amiably placed his hand on his sleeve:

"No, do it the way I told you to," he said, softening the
remark with a smile, and briefly explaining his view of the
matter handed the papers back and said: "So do it that way,
please."

The embarrassed secretary went off. Levin, who had quite
recovered from his confusion during the conference with
the secretary, stood leaning with both arms against a chair;
his face had an expression of mocking attentiveness.

"I don't understand, I just don't understand," he said.

"What don't you understand?" said Oblonsky, smiling as

cheerfully as ever and taking out a cigarette. He was expecting some extravagance from Levin.

"I don't understand what you're doing," said Levin, shrugging his shoulders. "How can you take all that seriously?"

"Why not?"

"Because there's nothing to it."

"That's what you think, but actually we're overwhelmed by work."

"Paper work. Well, of course, you have a gift for it," added Levin.

"You mean you think I'm deficient in something?"

"That may be too," said Levin. "But I admire your grandeur all the same, and I'm proud to have such an important fellow as a friend. But you haven't answered my question," he added, making a desperate effort and looking straight into Oblonsky's eyes.

"All right! All right! Just wait a bit and you'll find yourself coming to it too. It's all very well for you, with your six thousand acres in the Karazin District, and muscles like yours, you're as fresh as a twelve-year-old girl—but you'll be coming over to us someday too. But as to what you were asking about, there haven't been any changes, though it's a pity you stayed away so long."

"But why?" asked Levin, frightened.

"Oh, nothing," Oblonsky answered. "We'll talk about it later. But just what did you come for this time?"

"Oh, we'll talk about that later too," said Levin, once again blushing to the roots of his hair.

"Well, all right then, it's only natural," said Oblonsky. "You know I'd like to ask you over, but my wife hasn't been feeling very well. Though wait, if you want to see them they're sure to be at the Zoo today from four to five. That's where Kitty skates. You go along there, I'll pick you up and we can have dinner together."

"Fine! Then I'll see you later."

"Just watch out, after all, I know you—you'll forget or else suddenly dash back to the country!" Oblonsky shouted after him with a laugh.

"Don't worry!"

And Levin left the room, only remembering when he was already at the door that he had forgotten to say good-by to Oblonsky's colleagues.

"He must be a very energetic fellow," said Grinevich, after Levin had left.

"Yes, my dear boy," said Oblonsky, shaking his head. "Now there's a lucky fellow! Six thousand acres in the Karazin District, everything ahead of him, and as lively as could be! Not like one of ourselves."

"But what have you to complain of, Oblonsky?"

"Oh, things are awful, terrible," said Oblonsky, with a heavy sigh.

## VI

WHEN Oblonsky had asked Levin just why he had come to Moscow, Levin had blushed and been furious with himself for blushing, because he could not reply: "I've come to propose to your sister-in-law," though that was his only reason for coming.

The Levins and the Shcherbatskys were two old noble Moscow houses; they had always been on intimate and friendly terms with each other. This relationship had become still stronger during the time Levin had been a student. He had prepared for and entered the university together with young Prince Shcherbatsky, the brother of Dolly and Kitty. During this period Levin spent a great deal of time frequenting the Shcherbatsky house; he had fallen in love with the entire family. However strange it might seem, he had fallen in love with the house itself and with the Shcherbatsky family, especially the female half. Levin himself could not remember his own mother, and his only sister was older than he, so that it was in the Shcherbatsky house that he saw for the first time the home life of an old, noble, cultivated and upright family, which the deaths of his father and mother had deprived him of. All the members of this family, and especially the female half, seemed to him to be enveloped in some mysterious, poetic veil; not only did he see no shortcomings in them, but under the poetic veil that covered them he imagined the loftiest feelings and every possible perfection. Just why these three young ladies had to speak French one day and English the next; why they took turns at certain hours playing the piano, the sounds of which penetrated to the brother's room upstairs, where the students were busy; why all those teachers of French literature, music, drawing, and dancing kept coming; why at certain hours all three young ladies, together with Mlle. Linon, took a carriage to the Tverskoy Boulevard in their satin cloaks—Dolly in a long one, Natalie in a medium long one, and Kitty in a very short one, so that her shapely little legs in the tightly drawn red stockings were quite visible; why they had to promenade along the Tverskoy Boulevard escorted by a footman with a gilt cockade in his hat—all of this, and a great deal more that was in that secret world of theirs, remained completely incomprehensible to him, but he knew that everything done there was magnificent, and he was in love with just this mystery of everything that was going on.

While a student he had very nearly fallen in love with the eldest, Dolly, but she was quickly married off to Oblonsky. Then he began falling in love with the second. He seemed to feel that he had to fall in love with one of the sisters; the only thing was, he couldn't make up his mind which one. But Natalie too got married to a diplomat, Lvov, the moment she came out. Kitty had still been a child when Levin left the university. Young Shcherbatsky, who had gone into the Navy, was drowned in the Baltic, and Levin's relations with the Shcherbatskys, in spite of his friendship with Oblonsky, became less close. But that same year, at the beginning of winter, when Levin came back to Moscow after a year in the country and saw the Shcherbatskys, he understood which one of the three he was really destined to fall in love with.

Nothing would have seemed simpler than for him, a man thirty-two years old, of good family and rich rather than poor, to propose to Princess Shcherbatsky; in all likelihood he would instantly have been acknowledged as a first-rate match. But Levin was in love, and because of this it seemed to him that Kitty was such perfection in every way, a being far above everything else on earth, while he was a lowly, earthy creature, that it was absolutely unthinkable for others and herself to regard him as worthy of her.

Having spent two months in Moscow as though bemused, meeting Kitty almost every day in society, which he began to frequent in order to see her, Levin abruptly decided that the whole thing was out of the question and went back to the country.

Levin's conviction that it was impossible was based on his not being a good or worthy match for the delightful Kitty, from the point of view of her family, while Kitty herself could never love him. In the eyes of her family he did not have a conventional, well-defined occupation or position in society, whereas his classmates, when he was thirty-two, were already either a colonel and aide-de-camp, or a professor, or a director of banks and railroads, or the chairman of a government board like Oblonsky. He, on the other hand—he was well aware of how he must appear to others—was a landowner, taken up with breeding cows, shooting snipe, and putting up buildings; that is, an untalented fellow who had come to nothing and according to the views of society was only doing whatever people did who were not fit for anything else.

The mysterious, delightful Kitty herself could never love such a plain fellow as he thought himself, especially one so simple and undistinguished. Aside from that his former relationship to Kitty—the relationship of an adult to a child, because of his friendship with her brother—seemed still another obstacle to love. A plain, goodhearted fellow, such as he considered himself, might be loved as a friend, he thought, but to be loved the way he loved Kitty a man had to be handsome, and above all—someone special.

He had heard that women often loved plain, simple men, but he didn't believe it, since he judged by himself and he himself could only love beautiful, mysterious, and exceptional women.

But after he spent two months alone in the country he became convinced that this time he was not in love as he had been when he was very young; that this feeling did not give him a moment of rest; that he could not live without having settled the question of whether she was going to be his wife or not; and that this despair was simply due to his own imagination, and that he had no proof that he would be rejected. And he had now come to Moscow firmly resolved to make a proposal and to get married if he was accepted . . . Or else—But he could not think of what would happen to him if he were refused.

VII

HAVING reached Moscow by the morning train, Levin went to stay at his older half-brother's, Koznyshov, and after changing went to see him in his study, with the intention of telling him at once why he had come and to ask his advice; but his brother was not alone. There was a well-known professor of philosophy sitting with him, who had come from Kharkov just to clear up a misunderstanding that had arisen between them on a highly important philosophical problem. The professor was carrying on a heated polemic against the materialists, which Koznyshov had been following with interest; after reading the professor's latest essay he had written him a letter with his objections; he had reproached the professor with having made too many concessions to the materialists. The professor had come along at once to talk things over. They were discussing a fashionable question: Was there a line of demarcation between psychic and physiological phenomena in human behavior, and if so, where was it?

Koznyshov greeted his brother with the same chilly, affable smile he gave everyone, introduced him to the professor, and went on with the conversation.

The professor, a small sallow man with spectacles and a narrow forehead, broke off the discussion for a moment to shake hands, then went on speaking without paying any attention to Levin. Levin sat down to wait for the professor to leave, but quickly grew interested in what they were talking about.

Levin had come across the articles in the newspapers they were discussing, and had read them because of his interest in the evolution of the principles of natural science, which he had specialized in at the university, but he had never associated these scientific deductions as to the animal origin of man, reflex actions, biology, and sociology, with all those questions about the meaning of life and death, which had lately been coming to his mind more and more often.

Listening to his brother's conversation with the professor, he noticed that they connected scientific with spiritual questions, and several times almost went as far as the latter, but each time, the moment they approached the most important thing, as it seemed to him, they immediately hastened to retreat and again plunged into the domain of fine distinctions, qualifications, quotations, allusions, and references to authorities, so that he found it difficult to grasp what it was all about.

"I cannot admit," said Koznyshov, with his characteristic clarity and precision of expression and elegance of diction, "I cannot under any circumstances agree with Keiss that the entire conception of the external world is based on impressions. The most fundamental concept, that of existence, is not derived from the senses, since there is not even a special organ for the transmission of such a concept."

"Yes, but Wurst, Knaust, and Pripasov would all reply that your consciousness of existence derives from the merging of all your sensations, and that this consciousness of existence is the result of the sensations. Wurst even says straight out that without sensations there would be no concept of existence."

"I should say the opposite—" Koznyshov began, but here it seemed to Levin once again that after moving close to the most important thing they were withdrawing again, and he decided to ask the professor a question.

"Consequently, if my feelings are destroyed, if my body dies, then there can't be any existence at all?" he asked.

The professor, annoyed and as though in intellectual pain at the interruption, looked round at the strange questioner, who looked more like a barge man than a philosopher, and glanced at Koznyshov, as though asking: What's there to say to *that*? But Koznyshov, who spoke with far less exertion and one-sidedness than the professor, and who had enough space left over in his head both to answer the professor and at the same time to understand the simple and natural point of view from which the question had been asked, smiled and said:

"We do not yet have the right to answer that question . . .".

"We lack the data," the professor affirmed, and went on with his arguments. "No," he said, "I should like to point out that even if, as Pripasov says quite clearly, sensation is based on impressions, we must still rigorously distinguish between the two concepts . . ."

Levin stopped listening and waited for the professor to leave.

VIII

AFTER the professor had gone Koznyshov turned to his brother.

"I'm very glad you've come. Will you be staying long? How's the farming?"

Levin knew his older brother didn't have much interest in farming and had only asked him about it out of politeness, so he merely told him about the sale of some wheat and about money matters.

Levin wanted to tell his brother about his intention of getting married and to ask his advice, and had even made up his mind to do so, but after seeing his brother and listening to his conversation with the professor, and then hearing the involuntarily patronizing tone in which his brother asked him about business (their mother's estate had not been divided between them, and Levin managed it as a unit) Levin felt that for some reason he couldn't start talking to his brother about his decision to get married. He felt his brother wouldn't look at it as he would wish him to.

"And your District Council, how is all that?" asked Koznyshov, who was very interested in District Councils and thought them extremely important.

"Actually, I don't know . . ."

"What? But aren't you a member of the board?"

"Not any longer; I've resigned," Levin answered, "I don't go to the meetings any more."

"What a pity!" said Koznyshov, frowning.

In self-defense Levin began talking about what went on at the meetings in his district.

"But that's how it always is!" Koznyshov interrupted him. "That's how we Russians are. For that matter it may be a good trait—this ability to see our own shortcomings, but we overdo it, we console ourselves with the irony that's always at the tip of our tongue. All I can say to you is that if you gave the same rights we have in our rural institutions to any other European country—the Germans and the English would have gotten their freedom out of them, but all we do is laugh."

"But what can be done?" said Levin guiltily. "That was my last attempt. And I kept trying with all my heart. I can't do it; I'm not suited to it."

"It's not that you're not suited," said Koznyshov. "You don't have the right attitude."

"That may be," Levin answered dejectedly.

"And d'you know, brother Nicholas is back again."

Nicholas was Levin's older brother, and a half-brother of Koznyshov's; he was a ruined man who had squandered most of his fortune, mingled with the most peculiar and worst society, and quarreled with his brothers.

"What's that?" cried Levin horrified. "How do you know?"

"Prokofy saw him in the street."

"Here, in Moscow? Where is he? D'you know?" Levin got up from the chair as though about to leave at once.

"I'm sorry I told you," said Koznyshov, shaking his head at his younger brother's excitement. "I wrote to find out where he's living, and sent him the promissory note he'd given Trubin, which I'd paid off. This is his answer."

Koznyshov handed his brother a note he took from under a paperweight.

Levin read the strange familiar handwriting: "I humbly beg to be left in peace. That is the only thing I demand of my charming brothers. Nicholas Levin."

Levin read this and holding the note in his hands stood in front of Koznyshov without raising his head.

There was a struggle going on in his heart between his desire to forget all about his unfortunate brother and the awareness that this would be despicable.

"He's evidently trying to offend me," Koznyshov went on. "But he cannot. I should like to help him with all my heart, but I know that's impossible."

"Yes, yes," said Levin, "I understand and I appreciate your attitude toward him; I'll go to see him myself."

"Go if you like, but I don't advise it," said Koznyshov. "That is, as far as you're concerned I'm not afraid of anything, he won't be able to set us against each other; but from your own point of view I advise you not to go; he can't be helped. But do as you please."

"Perhaps he can't, but I feel, especially at this moment—but that's something else again—I feel I won't be able to be at ease otherwise."

"Now that I don't understand," said Koznyshov. Then he added: "But there's one thing I do understand: it's been a lesson in humility. Ever since brother Nicholas became what he is I've begun to look differently, more indulgently, on what is called rascality. You know what he did—"

"Oh, it's an awful business, awful!" Levin repeated.

Having gotten his brother's address from Koznyshov's footman, Levin was about to start off to see him at once, but after thinking it over decided to postpone it till that evening. Before anything else, in order to have some peace of mind, what he had to do was settle what he had come to Moscow for. Levin had left his brother to go to Oblonsky's office, and after hearing about the Shcherbatskys from him he drove off to the place where he had been told he could find Kitty.

## IX

AT four o'clock Levin stepped out of a hired sleigh at the Zoo and, feeling his heart pounding away, went down the path leading to the ice hills and the skating pond, sure of finding her there, since he had seen the Shcherbatskys' carriage at the entrance.

It was a clear frosty day. Rows of carriages, private sleighs, sleighs for hire, and mounted police were standing about at the entrance. Well-dressed people, their hats shining in the bright sunshine, were crowding in at the gates and along the clean-swept narrow paths between the little Russian chalets with their carved eaves; the bushy old birches of the Zoological Gardens, their boughs all weighed down with snow, seemed to be freshly decked out in festive garments.

He followed the path to the skating pond and said to himself: I must calm down, I mustn't be excited . . . What's the matter with you? What is it? . . . Be quiet, jackass! he kept saying to his heart. And the more he tried to calm himself the more his breathing grew labored. An acquaintance saw him and called out to him, but Levin did not even recognize him. As he approached the ice hills, he heard the clatter of the chains dragging up the toboggans or letting them down, the rumble of the toboggans, and the sounds of gay voices; a few more steps and the skating pond opened up in front of him. He instantly picked her out of all the skaters.

He knew she was there by the joy and the terror that laid hold of his heart. She was standing talking to some woman at the opposite end of the pond. There seemed nothing special either about her dress or her attitude; but for Levin it was as easy to pick her out of the throng as a rose among nettles. Everything was lit up by her. She had a smile that made everything radiant round about. Could I go on to the ice, he thought, and go up to her? The place she was standing on seemed to him an unapproachable shrine, and there was a moment when he was on the verge of leaving, he was so filled with fear. He had to make an effort and reflect that all sorts of people were passing around her, and that he might have come there to go skating himself. He stepped down, avoiding a long look at her, as though she were the sun, but he saw her, just like the sun, even without looking.

On this day of the week and at this time of the day the people who met at the ice pond were all of one set, and all acquainted with each other. There were both expert skaters showing off their skill, beginners holding onto the backs of chairs with shy, awkward movements, little boys, and old people who went skating for reasons of health; to Levin they all seemed fortune's favorites because they were there, close to her. It seemed that everyone on skates was catching up with and passing her with utter indifference, and even speaking to her; they were all amusing themselves quite independently of her as they took advantage of the excellent ice and the fine weather.

Nicholas Shcherbatsky, Kitty's cousin, in a short little jacket and tight trousers, was sitting on a bench with his skates on; when he saw Levin he called out to him:

"Well, Russia's champion skater! Been here long? The ice is wonderful, get your skates on!"

"I haven't got any," Levin answered, astonished by such boldness and easy manners in her presence, and not losing sight of her for a second, even though he wasn't looking at her. He had the feeling that the sun was coming near him. She was in the corner, and keeping her slender little feet close together in their high boots, with obvious timidity, was skating toward him. A little boy in Russian costume, violently waving his arms and stooping down very low, was catching up with her. She was not skating very steadily; taking her hands out of the little muff that was hanging by a cord, she held them out in readiness, and looking at Levin, whom she had recognized, she smiled at him and at her own fears. When she finished making her turn she gave herself a push with her resilient little foot and skated straight up to Shcherbatsky; holding onto him with one hand she nodded her head at Levin with a smile. She was more beautiful than he had imagined her.

Whenever he thought about her, he was able to form an image in his mind of everything about her, especially the charm of her small, fair head and face with its expression of childlike clarity and sweetness, so freely poised on the shapely, girlish shoulders. Her childlike expression together with the delicate beauty of her figure made up her special charm, which he remembered very well; but what would always strike him about her, quite unexpectedly, was the expression in her eyes, soft, serene, and straightforward, and especially her smile, which always carried Levin off to some enchanted world where he felt softened and filled with tenderness, as he remembered feeling on some rare occasions in early childhood.

"Have you been here long?" she said, giving him her hand. "Oh, thank you," she added, as he picked up a handkerchief that had dropped out of her muff.

"I? Not long, I got here yesterday—I mean, today," Levin replied; in his excitement he didn't understand her question at first. "I meant to come and see you," he said, and then, as he recalled his purpose in looking for her, he grew confused at once and blushed. "I didn't know you could skate, and skate so well."

She gazed at him attentively, as though trying to see why he was so confused.

"Your compliments are worth a good deal. There's a tradition here that you're the best skater," she said, flicking some hoar-frost crystals off her muff with a little black-gloved hand.

"I used to be a passionate skater; I wanted to achieve perfection."

"I think you do everything passionately," she said with a smile. "I should so like to see how you skate. Why don't you put your skates on—let's skate together."

Skate together! thought Levin, looking at her; it's not possible!

"I'll put them on right away," he said, and went off to rent some skates.

"It's a long time since we've seen you here, sir," said the attendant, holding up Levin's foot to bore a hole in the boot. "Since you left none of the gentlemen are experts. Would that be all right?" he said, tightening the strap.

"Fine, fine, please just hurry," Levin answered. He found it difficult to hold back a grin of happiness that involuntarily spread over his face. Yes, he thought, this is what life is, this is happiness! *"Together,"* she said, *"let's skate together!"* Should I tell her right now? But that's why I'm afraid to tell her just now, when I'm happy, happy if only because of hoping. . . . And what about later? But I really must! I must! Away with weakness!

Levin got up, took off his overcoat, and taking a running start over the rough ice near the hut onto the smooth ice, he skated effortlessly along, seeming to speed up, slow down, and guide his course by will alone. He grew timid as he approached her, but her smile calmed him once again.

She gave him her hand, and they went off together, increasing their speed, and the faster they went the harder she pressed his hand.

"I would learn faster with you; for some reason I trust you," she said to him.

"And I trust myself when you lean on me," he said, but this frightened him at once and he blushed. And in fact, the moment he said these words, suddenly, as the sun hides behind a cloud, her face lost its kindness, and Levin recognized the familiar play of her features, indicating a mental effort: a little wrinkle appeared on her smooth forehead.

"Is anything the matter with you? But I don't have the right to ask," he said quickly.

"Why should there be? . . . No, there's nothing the matter with me," she replied coldly, and added immediately: "Have you seen Mlle. Linon?"

"Not yet."

"Go over to her, she's so fond of you."

What can that mean? thought Levin; I've annoyed her! Help me, O Lord! And he hurried over to the old Frenchwoman with gray curls, who was sitting on a bench. Showing her false teeth in a smile, she greeted him as an old friend.

"Yes, here we are growing up," she said to him, indicating Kitty with a glance, "and getting older. 'The Little Bear' is a big one already!" the Frenchwoman went on with a laugh, reminding him of his joke about the three girls, whom he used to call the Three Bears, from the fairy tale. "D'you remember when you used to call them that?"

He remembered nothing of the sort, but she had been laughing over this joke for ten years and was attached to it.

"Well, be off with you, go on skating. But hasn't our Kitty turned out to be a good skater?"

When Levin hurried back to Kitty again her expression was no longer severe, her eyes looked just as straightforward and sweet as ever, but it seemed to Levin that there was something special, a note of deliberate calm in this sweetness. He felt sad. After talking about her old governess and her oddities, she asked him about his life.

"Surely you must be bored in the country in winter?" she said.

"No, I'm not bored, I'm too busy," he said, feeling that she was making him fit in with her serene tone, which he lacked the strength to depart from, just as it had been at the beginning of the winter.

"Will you be here long?" Kitty asked him.

"I don't know," he answered, not thinking of what he was saying. The thought crossed his mind that he was surrendering to her tone of serene friendliness, and that he would leave again without having settled anything; he decided to rebel.

"You don't know?"

"I don't know. That depends on you," he said, and was instantly horrified by his own words.

Whether she heard what he said or refused to hear, she seemed to stumble, thrust her foot out twice, and hurriedly skated away from him. She skated up to Mlle. Linon, said something to her, and went off to the little house where the women took off their skates.

My God, what have I done! Help me, O Lord, tell me what to say! Levin prayed, at the same time feeling a need for violent movement; he picked up speed and started doing inside and outside turns at full speed.

Just then a young man, the best of the new skaters, came out of the café with his skates on and a cigarette in his mouth; he took a running start and came leaping down the steps on his skates with a clatter. He then flew down the slope, and without even changing the easy set of his arms glided out on the ice.

"Ah, a new trick!" said Levin, and immediately ran up the slope to try it out.

"Watch out—you have to have practice!" Nicholas Shcherbatsky called out to him.

Levin mounted the steps, got up as much speed on top as he could, and then came down, keeping his balance in the unaccustomed motion by means of his arms. He tripped on the last step, but barely grazing the ice with his hand, he made a violent effort, caught himself and skated off laughing.

What a wonderful fellow he is, and how nice! thought Kitty, who was just coming out of the little house with Mlle. Linon, looking at him with a smile of sweet affection, as though at a beloved brother. Am I really to blame, have I really done something terrible? People call it flirting; I know he's not the one I love, all the same I have a good time with him, and he's so wonderful. But why did he say that? she thought.

When he saw Kitty going out with her mother, who had met her on the steps, Levin, flushed by his violent exercise, paused for a moment's thought. He took off his skates and caught up with the mother and daughter at the way out of the Zoological Gardens.

"Delighted to see you," said the Princess. "We're at home on Thursdays, as usual."

"You mean today?"

"We shall be very pleased to see you," said the Princess drily.

This dryness of hers upset Kitty; she could not refrain from a desire to smooth over her mother's chilliness. She turned her head and said with a smile: *"Au revoir!"*

Just then Oblonsky, his hat tilted to one side, with radiant face and eyes, came into the Gardens like a happy conqueror. But on going up to his mother-in-law he answered her questions about Dolly's health with a mournful, guilty expression. After talking with his mother-in-law in a quiet, dejected way, he straightened up and took Levin by the arm.

"Well, shall we go?" he asked. "I've been thinking about you the whole time, and I'm very pleased you came," he said, looking him importantly in the eye.

"Yes, yes, let's go!" answered Levin happily, still hearing that voice in his ears, saying *"Au revoir"* and seeing the smile with which it had been said.

"The Angleterre, or the Hermitage?"

"It's all the same to me."

"Then the Angleterre," said Oblonsky, who chose the Angleterre because he owed more money there than at the Hermitage, and thought it wrong to avoid it. "Have you got a sleigh? Wonderful! I've sent my carriage home."

The two friends were silent all the way. Levin was thinking about what the change of expressions on Kitty's face had meant; first he assured himself that there was some hope, then he fell into despair and saw clearly that his hopes were senseless, but all the while he felt a completely different man, quite different from what he had been before her smile and the words *"Au revoir!"*

Oblonsky was composing the menu on the way.

"You like turbot, don't you?" he said to Levin as they arrived.

"What's that?" asked Levin. "Turbot? I *love* turbot."

x

As they entered the restaurant Levin could not help noticing something special in Oblonsky's expression, a sort of restrained radiance about his face and whole figure. Oblonsky took off his overcoat, and with hat to one side he went on into the dining room, giving orders to the Tatars in swallowtails with napkins, who clustered around him. Bowing right and left to acquaintances of his who as usual were delighted to see him here as anywhere else, he made his way to the buffet, tossed down some vodka over a bit of fish to begin with, and said something to the painted, beribboned Frenchwoman in lace and ringlets sitting behind the little counter, that made even this Frenchwoman burst into a sincere laugh. As for Levin, he did not drink any vodka just because this Frenchwoman was offensive to him; she seemed to him constructed completely out of false hair, rice powder, and toilet water. He hurried away from her as though from some filthy place. His whole soul was swimming in thoughts of Kitty, and his eyes shone with a smile of triumph and happiness.

"This way, please, Your Excellency, this way—Your Excellency won't be disturbed here!" said an old, specially eager whiteheaded Tatar, with broad hips and coattails separating over them. "Please, Your Excellency," he said to Levin, as a sign of respect to Oblonsky that he was paying special attention to his guest also.

In a flash he had spread a fresh tablecloth on a round table already covered with a cloth, under a bronze chandelier; he moved up some velvet chairs to the table and stood there in front of Oblonsky with a napkin and the menu in his hand, waiting for their orders.

"If Your Excellency would like it, a private room will be free immediately: Prince Golitsyn's, with a lady. We have some fresh oysters, sir."

"Aha! Oysters!"

Oblonsky lost himself in thought.

"A change of plan, Levin?" he said, holding his finger on the menu. His face actually expressed a genuine perplexity. "The oysters, though—are they good? Look out now!"

"From Flensburg, Your Excellency, there are none from Ostend."

"Flensburg, that's all very well, but are they fresh?"

"Just came in yesterday, sir."

"Well now, shouldn't we just begin with the oysters, and then go on and change our whole plan? Eh?"

"I don't care at all. What I should like most of all is cabbage soup and porridge, but of course they don't have that here."

"Some porridge *à la russe*, sir?" said the Tatar, bending over Levin like a nurse over a child.

"No, seriously, whatever you order, that'll be fine. I've been skating and I feel like eating. And don't think for a moment," he added, noticing an expression of discontent on

Oblonsky's face, "that I won't appreciate whatever you select. I'll be delighted to have a good dinner."

"I should hope so! No matter what you say that's one of life's pleasures," Oblonsky said. "Well then, my good fellow, let us have two—no, that's too little—three dozen oysters, vegetable soup—"

*"Printanier,"* murmured the Tatar, but it was plain that Oblonsky had no desire to give him the pleasure of naming the dishes in French.

"—vegetable, you know, then the turbot with a thick sauce, then . . . roast beef, but make sure it's all right, and then capon, eh? Oh yes, and stewed fruit, too."

The Tatar, taking note of Oblonsky's way of not referring to the dishes according to the French menu, did not repeat what he said, but gave himself the satisfaction of repeating the entire order according to the menu: *"Potage printanier, turbot sauce Beaumarchais, poularde à l'estragon, macédoine de fruits . . ."* then instantly, as though on springs, he put aside one menu in a cardboard cover and took up another, the wine list, which he held out to Oblonsky.

"What should we have to drink?"

"Whatever you please, but not too much—champagne!" said Levin.

"What, to begin with? But of course, please, let's. D'you like the white seal?"

*"Cachet blanc,"* the Tatar chimed in.

"Well, let's have that with the oysters, then we'll see."

"Yes sir. And the table wine, sir, what would you like?"

"Let's have the *Nuits.* No, the classic Chablis—that would be better."

"Yes sir. And your own special cheese, sir?"

"Why yes—the Parmesan. Or would you like something else?"

"No, it doesn't matter at all," said Levin, who couldn't help smiling.

The Tatar darted off, his coattails flying; five minutes later he flew back with a dish of opened oysters in their pearly shells and a bottle between his fingers.

Oblonsky crumpled his starched napkin, put it inside his waistcoat, and settling his arms comfortably on the table set about the oysters.

"Not bad at all," he said, tweaking the quivering oysters out of their pearly shells with a silver fork and gulping them down one after another. "Not bad at all," he repeated, raising his moist, glistening eyes first toward Levin, then toward the Tatar.

Levin ate the oysters, though he liked white bread and cheese more. But he was admiring Oblonsky. Even the Tatar, as he adjusted his white tie after drawing the cork and pouring the sparkling wine into the thin, wide glasses, looked at Oblonsky with a smile of obvious pleasure.

"And don't you like oysters?" asked Oblonsky, emptying his wineglass. "Or are you worried about something, eh?"

He wanted Levin to be cheerful. It was not that Levin was not cheerful, but he felt ill at ease. With everything his heart was full of he felt awkward and uncomfortable in this eating place, with its private rooms where ladies were dining, among all this hustle and bustle; everything there, the bronzes, the mirrors, the gaslights, the Tatars—it was all offensive to him. He was afraid of sullying what his heart was brimming over with.

"Me? Yes, I'm preoccupied; but aside from that all this makes me feel uncomfortable," he said. "You cannot imagine how strange all this seems to me, straight from the country. It's like the fingernails of that fellow I saw at your place."

"Yes, I noticed how fascinated you were by poor Grinevich's nails," said Oblonsky, laughing.

"I can't help it," Levin replied. "Try it yourself, pay me a visit; look at it from the point of view of someone who lives in the country. In the country we try to fix our hands so they'll be easy to work with; we trim our nails and sometimes roll up our sleeves. Here people let their nails grow indefinitely on purpose and put on cuff links the size of small saucers so that doing anything with their hands is out of the question."

Oblonsky smiled merrily. "Yes, that's a sign that he doesn't have to do any coarse labor. With him it's his mind that does the work . . ."

"That may be. Still it seems strange to me, just as it seems strange to me that in the country we do our best to eat as quickly as possible in order to be in condition to do what we have to, while here you and I try to put off finishing our meal as long as possible and so order oysters to eat."

"Well, of course," Oblonsky agreed. "But isn't that the object of education: getting pleasure out of everything?"

"Well, if that's the object I'd rather be a savage."

"You are one anyhow. All you Levins are savages."

Levin sighed. He recalled his brother Nicholas, and

scowled, feeling ashamed and distressed; but Oblonsky started talking about a subject that distracted him at once.

"Well, are you coming to see us this evening, I mean the Shcherbatskys," he said, his eyes glittering portentously as he pushed back the rough, empty oyster shells and drew over the cheese.

"I'm definitely going," Levin replied. "Though it seemed to me that the Princess was reluctant to invite me."

"What are you talking about! What nonsense! That's the way she is . . . And now what about the soup, my good fellow? . . . That's her way, the *grande dame*," said Oblonsky. "I'm going too, but I have to turn up at a musical rehearsal at Countess Banin's first. But really, how odd you are! How can you explain your suddenly vanishing from Moscow? The Shcherbatskys kept on asking me about you without stopping, as though I were supposed to know. The only thing I know is that you're always doing what nobody else ever does."

"Yes," said Levin slowly and agitatedly. "You're right, I am peculiar. But the oddity is not in my having gone away, but in my coming back now. I've come back now—"

"What a lucky fellow you are!" Oblonsky interrupted, looking straight into Levin's eyes.

"What for?"

" 'I know a fine steed  By the marks of his breed,  And a young man in love—By his eyes!' " Oblonsky declaimed. "Everything lies ahead of you!"

"Don't tell me that for you everything lies behind?"

"No, but even though it's not behind me you have a future while I have a present—and even that's only so-so."

"What d'you mean?"

"Yes, things are not too good . . . But I don't want to talk about myself, and for that matter it's impossible to explain it all," said Oblonsky. "Why did you come back to Moscow anyhow? . . . Here, take all this away!" he called out to the Tatar.

"Can't you guess?" answered Levin, a light shining deep in his eyes as he gazed steadily at Oblonsky.

"I can, but I'm not the one who ought to start speaking about it. That alone should be enough to tell you whether I've guessed right or not," said Oblonsky, looking at Levin with the suggestion of a smile.

"Well then, what do you say about it?" said Levin in a

trembling voice, feeling that every muscle in his face was twitching. "What do you think of it?"

Oblonsky slowly drained his glass of Chablis, without taking his eyes off Levin.

"I?" he said, "There's nothing I could wish for more—nothing. It's the best thing that could happen."

"But aren't you making a mistake? D'you know what we're talking about?" said Levin, his eyes boring into Oblonsky's. "You think there's a chance?"

"I do. Why shouldn't there be?"

"No, really, d'you think there is? No, you must tell me exactly what you think! And what if—suppose—I'm refused? . . . For that matter I'm sure—"

"But why do you think that?" said Oblonsky, smiling at his excitement.

"That's how it seems to me sometimes. That would be awful, after all, both for me and for her."

"Oh, for a girl in any case there's nothing so awful about it. All girls take pride in being proposed to."

"All girls, yes, but not her."

Oblonsky smiled. He understood this feeling of Levin's very well, he knew that for him all the girls in the world were divided into two kinds: one kind was—all the girls in the world except her, and those girls had every human frailty and were very commonplace girls; the other kind was—she alone, with no frailties at all and far beyond all mankind.

"Wait a second, you must have some of this sauce," he said, keeping Levin's hand from pushing the sauce away.

Levin obediently helped himself to the sauce, but did not give Oblonsky a chance to eat.

"No, now you listen—listen!" he said. "You can understand that for me this is a question of life or death. I've never spoken about it to anyone. And I can't speak about it to anyone as I can with you. You and I, after all, are completely different from each other in every way: different tastes, opinions, everything; but I know you're fond of me and understand me, and because of that I'm terribly fond of you. But for God's sake you must be absolutely frank!"

"I'm telling you what I think," said Oblonsky with a smile. "But I'll tell you something else: my wife is the most amazing woman . . ." Oblonsky sighed as he recalled his relations with his wife; after a moment's silence he went on: "She can foresee things. She can see through people completely; but that's the least of it, she knows what's going to happen, especially about marriages. For instance, she prophesied that the Shakhovskoy girl was going to marry Brenteln. No one would believe it, but that's how it turned out. And—she's on your side."

"How do you mean?"

"Just that it's not only that she likes you, she says that Kitty is sure to become your wife."

When Levin heard this his face was lit up by the sort of smile that is close to tears.

"She says that!" Levin cried. "I've always said what an angel your wife is! But enough, that's enough talk about that," he said and got up.

"Very well, but just sit down."

But Levin couldn't sit still. He paced back and forth in the little cage of a room twice with his vigorous stride, blinking his eyes to hold back the tears, and only then sat down at the table again.

"You must understand," he said, "that this isn't love. I've been in love, but this isn't it. This is not a feeling of my own, it's some sort of external power that's taken possession of me. You see I went away because I'd made up my mind that it could never happen, that it was happiness unknown on earth; but I've wrestled with myself and I see that without it life is impossible. And it must be settled—"

"Then why did you go away?"

"Just a moment! Oh, there's such a crowd of ideas! There's so much to ask! Listen: of course you can't imagine what you've done for me by telling me that. I'm so happy I've even become mean; I've forgotten everything. I just learned today that my brother Nicholas—you know he's here—I've forgotten all about him too. It seems to me he's happy too, it's a sort of madness! But there's one terrible thing . . . Now you're married, you know that feeling . . . The terrible thing is, that—we older men, with a past . . . not of love, but of sin . . . suddenly we come close to a pure, innocent being; that's what's disgusting, that it's impossible not to feel oneself unworthy."

"But you haven't had many sins."

"All the same," said Levin, "all the same: 'reading back my life with horror, I curse it all atremble and bitterly regret—' Yes, that's so."

"But what can be done about it, that's the way the world is," said Oblonsky.

"My one consolation, like that prayer I've always liked so much, is—'Forgive me not for my deserts, but out of lovingkindness.' And that's the only way she'll be able to forgive me."

## XI

LEVIN emptied his wineglass, and they fell silent.

"There's one thing I ought to tell you. D'you know Vronsky?" Oblonsky asked Levin.

"No—why do you ask?"

"Let's have another bottle," said Oblonsky, turning to the Tatar, who kept filling their glasses and hovering about them just when he wasn't wanted.

"Why should I know Vronsky?"

"The reason you should know Vronsky is because he's one of your rivals."

"Who is he?" said Levin, and suddenly the expression of childlike rapture, which Oblonsky had just been admiring, vanished from his face; he looked malevolent and disagreeable.

"Vronsky is one of the two sons of Count Cyril Vronsky, and one of the finest examples of Petersburg's gilded youth. I met him in Tver when I was stationed there; he had come on a recruiting mission. Terribly rich, handsome, great connections, an Imperial aide-de-camp and—on top of all that—a very nice, good-natured chap. But he's more than just a nice chap; I've come to know him here; he's both cultivated and very able. He's a man who's going far."

Levin scowled in silence.

"Well then, he turned up here shortly after you, and I gather he's head over heels in love with Kitty; you understand that her mother—"

"Excuse me, but I don't understand a thing," said Levin, frowning morosely. All at once he recalled his brother Nicholas and how odious he had been to forget him.

"Just hold on a moment," said Oblonsky, smiling and touching Levin's arm. "I've been telling you what I know, and I repeat—in this delicate and emotional matter it seems to me that as far as can be guessed the chances are on your side."

Levin leaned back in his chair; his face was white.

"But I should advise you to settle the matter as quickly

as possible," Oblonsky continued, filling Levin's glass.

"No, thank you, I can't drink any more," said Levin, pushing his glass away. "I'll get drunk . . . Well now, how are you getting along?" he went on, plainly wishing to change the subject.

"Just one more word: in any case I advise you to decide the question quickly. Not today, I don't think," said Oblonsky. "Go there tomorrow morning, in the classic manner, propose, and may the Lord prosper you. . . !"

"You've always said you wanted to come for a shoot with me, why not come this spring?" said Levin.

With all his heart he now regretted having begun this conversation with Oblonsky. The *special* feeling he had was offended by the talk of the rivalry of some Petersburg officer and by Oblonsky's advice and suggestions.

Oblonsky smiled. He understood what was going on in Levin's heart.

"I'll come some time," he said. "Yes, my boy, women are the pivot everything turns round on. Look at me—I'm in a bad way too, very bad. And all because of women. Now, tell me frankly," he went on, taking out a cigar and holding his glass with one hand, "you must give me some advice."

"But what about?"

"Here it is. Let's say you're married, you love your wife, but you're attracted by another woman."

"Excuse me, but I absolutely cannot understand that— exactly as I couldn't understand how after eating my fill here I could go past a bakery and steal a roll."

Oblonsky's eyes glistened more than usual.

"And why not? A roll sometimes has a smell you just can't resist. 'What bliss it is, when I have conquered My own earthbound desires But even if I fail, at least, I've had me that much pleasure!' "

Oblonsky said this with a subtle smile. Levin too could not help smiling.

"No, but seriously," Oblonsky went on, "you can understand it—a sweet woman, a gentle, loving creature, poor and alone, who sacrifices everything. Now that it's all done already—you understand—surely she can't be deserted? Let's say one should separate from her, so as not to destroy one's family life, but surely not without pitying her, doing something for her, making things easier?"

"Well, there you must excuse me. You know that for me there are only two kinds of women . . . Or rather, not that, but . . . there are women, and then there is . . . I've never seen any charming fallen creatures, nor will I ever, but ones like that painted Frenchwoman behind the counter out there, with her curls, are an abomination to me—and that's the way all fallen women look to me."

"But what about the one in the Gospels?"

"Oh stop it! Christ would never have uttered those words if he had known how they would be abused. Out of the whole Gospel those words are the only ones ever remembered. Anyhow, I'm not saying what I think, but what I feel. I feel repelled by fallen women. You're afraid of spiders and I of abominations like that. In all probability you've never studied spiders and don't know their habits; it's just the same for me."

"It's easy for you to talk that way—just like that character in Dickens who tossed all difficult questions over his right shoulder with his left hand. But denying a fact is no answer. What am I to do—tell me, what should I do? One's wife is getting old, and oneself is full of life. You hardly have a chance to look round before you feel that you can no longer love your wife, I mean *love*, no matter how you respect her. And then, all of a sudden, love pops up, and you're lost, lost!" said Oblonsky in somber despair.

Levin smiled.

"Yes, lost," Oblonsky continued. "But what is there to do now?"

"Don't steal rolls."

Oblonsky burst out laughing. "Ah, the moralist! But you can understand, there are two women: one of them insists only on her rights and those rights are your love, which you can't give her, while the other sacrifices everything for you and demands nothing. What should you do? How should you act? It's a dreadful tragedy."

"If you want my real opinion about this, I must tell you I don't believe in the tragedy of it, and this is why: in my opinion, love—both kinds of love, which you remember Plato defines in his *Symposium*—both these kinds serve as a touchstone for people. Some people understand only one kind, others the other. It's futile for those who understand only non-Platonic love to talk about tragedy. In love like that there can be no tragedy. 'Thank you kindly for the pleasure, good-by!—there's your whole tragedy. And there can't be any tragedy in Platonic love because in such love everything is clear and pure, because—"

Just at this moment Levin recalled his own sins, and the inner struggle he was undergoing; he added unexpectedly:

"Though perhaps you may be right. It's very possible . . . But I don't know, I really don't know."

"There, you see," said Oblonsky. "You're very consistent. It's both your virtue and your defect. You yourself are a consistent character and you want all the facts of life to be consistent, but that's not how it is. You despise public service because you want work to correspond invariably with its goal, but that's not how it is. You always want everyone's activity to have a goal, too, and love and family life always to be one and the same. And that's not how it is. All the diversity, all the charm, all the beauty of life is made up of light and shade."

Levin sighed and was silent. He was thinking of himself and not listening to Oblonsky.

And suddenly they both felt that even though they were friends, even though they had been dining together and drinking wine, which should have brought them still closer together, each of them was thinking only of himself, and neither had anything to do with the other. Oblonsky had already had this experience more than once, of the extreme estrangement instead of intimacy that takes place after a dinner, and he knew what had to be done.

"The bill!" he shouted, and went out into the neighboring room where he immediately met some aide-de-camp he knew and started up a conversation about some actress and the man who was keeping her. And in the conversation with the aide-de-camp Oblonsky instantly felt relief and relaxation after his conversation with Levin, who always forced him into too much intellectual and spiritual concentration.

When the Tatar appeared with a bill for twenty-six rubles and some change, plus a tip, Levin, whose rustic soul would have been horrified some other time at paying the fourteen rubles or so of his share of the bill, now paid no attention to it and paid up. He went home to dress and to go on to the Shcherbatskys', where his fate was to be decided.

## XII

PRINCESS Kitty Shcherbatsky was eighteen years old. This was the first winter she had come out, and her success had been greater than that of both her older sisters and even greater than her mother had expected. Not only were nearly all the young men who danced at the Moscow balls in love with Kitty, but that very first winter two serious suitors had presented themselves: Levin and, directly he had left, Count Vronsky.

Levin's appearence at the beginning of the winter, his frequent visits, and his obvious love for Kitty, gave rise to the first serious conversations and arguments between her parents about her future.

The Prince was on Levin's side; he said he wished nothing better for Kitty. But the Princess, with the characteristic feminine habit of circling round a question, said that Kitty was too young, that Levin had not indicated in any way that his intentions were serious, that Kitty was not attached to him, and so on; but she didn't mention the chief things—that she was expecting a better match for her daughter and that she didn't like Levin or understand him. When Levin went off so abruptly the Princess was delighted; she said to her husband triumphantly: "You see, I was right!" And when Vronsky appeared she was still more pleased; it fortified her opinion that Kitty ought to make not simply a good match but a brilliant one.

For the mother there could be no comparison at all between Vronsky and Levin. The mother disliked both Levin's strange and bitter judgments and his awkwardness in society, which she thought based on pride, as well as the peculiar life, from her point of view, that he led in the country, busy with cattle and peasants; she also disliked particularly his coming to the house for six weeks in a row while in love with her daughter, when he seemed to be waiting for something and kept looking around as though afraid he would be doing them too great an honor if he proposed, not understanding that when he frequented a house with an unmarried girl in it he had to explain himself. Then suddenly, without declaring himself, he had left. It's a good thing that he's so unattractive, and that Kitty didn't fall in love with him, her mother thought.

Vronsky satisfied all the mother's wishes. Very rich, able, distinguished, launched on a brilliant career in the Army and at Court, and an enchanting man. Nothing better could have been hoped for.

At the balls Vronsky was openly attentive to Kitty; he danced with her and came to the house, so it was impossible to have any doubt as to the seriousness of his intentions.

Nevertheless her mother had been in a state of terrible anxiety and agitation all that winter.

The Princess's own marriage, thirty years before, had been arranged by an aunt. The young man, whom everything was known about beforehand, had come, looked at the girl, and was looked at by the family; then the aunt who was arranging the match found out and passed on the impression that had been made on each side; the impressions were good; on an appointed day the expected proposal was then made to the parents and accepted. Everything had taken place very easily and simply; at least so it seemed to the Princess. But with her own daughters she had the feeling that the business of giving daughters away in marriage, which seemed so ordinary, was not at all easy or simple. How many anxieties had been lived through, how many ideas had to be thought over, how much money had been spent, how many arguments with her husband there had been over the marrying off of the two older ones, Dolly and Natalie! Now that the youngest had come out, there were the same anxieties, the same doubts and even more serious quarrels with her husband than about the older ones. The old Prince, like all fathers, was especially punctilious about the honor and purity of his daughters; he was irrationally jealous of his daughters, especially of Kitty, who was his favorite; at every step he made his wife a scene for compromising their daughter. The Princess had got used to this with her first two daughters, but now she felt that the Prince's punctiliousness had greater justification. She saw that social customs had been changing a great deal lately, and that a mother's responsibilities had become still more difficult. She saw that girls Kitty's age formed societies of some kind, went off to lecture courses, saw men freely and drove about the streets alone. A great many of them never curtsied, and, above all, were completely convinced that choosing a husband was their business and not their parents'. "Nowadays girls are not given away in marriage as they used to be," all these young girls thought and said, and so did even all the older people. But how marriages were managed nowadays the Princess could not find out from anyone. The French custom—parents deciding their children's fate—was not accepted; it was condemned. The English custom—complete liberty for girls—was also not accepted; it was impossible in Russian society. The Russian custom of matchmaking was considered monstrous somehow, and was laughed at by everyone, including the Princess. But how a girl had to get married, or be given in marriage, no one knew. Everyone the Princess discussed it with said the same thing: "You know, in our days it's high time we gave up all these old-fashioned customs. After all, it's the young people who marry, not the parents; therefore the young people must be left to make their own arrangements as best they can." But it was all very well to speak this way for those who had no daughters; the Princess knew her daughter might fall in love with someone she was seeing a lot of, and it might be someone who didn't want to marry, or who would make an unsuitable husband. And no matter how often it was suggested to the Princess that "in our days" young people ought to arrange their own futures, she could not believe it, any more than she would have been able to believe that the best toys for five-year-old children could ever be loaded pistols. This was why the Princess was more anxious about Kitty than she had been about her older daughters.

Now she was afraid that Vronsky might limit himself to a mere flirtation. She saw that her daughter was already in love with him, but consoled herself with the thought that he was an honorable man and would not do that. But at the same time, with manners as free as they were, she knew how easy it was to turn a young girl's head, and what a light view men generally take of such a misdeed. The week before Kitty had told her mother of a conversation she had had with Vronsky during a mazurka. This conversation calmed the Princess to some extent; but she could not feel entirely at ease. Vronsky had told Kitty that both he and his brother were so used to doing whatever their mother wanted that they would never decide on anything important at all without consulting her. "I'm looking forward with special pleasure now to Mama's arrival from Petersburg," he had said.

Kitty had reported this without attaching any special meaning to it. But her mother understood it differently. She knew the old lady was expected from one day to the next, she knew she would be happy over her son's choice, and it seemed strange to her that for fear of hurting his mother he did not make a proposal; but she so much wanted the marriage itself, and, above all, longed for relief from her anxiety, that she believed it. Painful as it was for her now to witness the unhappiness of her oldest daughter Dolly, who was preparing to leave her husband, the Princess's anxiety about her youngest daughter's fate, now about to be decided, absorbed all her emotions. Levin's arrival that day had given her an additional cause for alarm. She was afraid that Kitty, who had seemed to have some feeling for Levin at one point, might refuse Vronsky out of an excessive sense of honor, and that Levin's arrival would confuse and delay things just as they were about to be concluded.

"Has he been back long?" asked the Princess when they got home, referring to Levin.

"He got here today, Mama."

"There's one thing I want to say . . ." the Princess began, and by her serious and intent look Kitty guessed what it would be about.

"Please, Mama," she said, blushing and turning to her quickly, "please don't say anything about that. I know—I know all about it."

She wanted the same thing her mother did, but the reasons for her mother's wishes wounded her.

"I only wanted to say that having held out hopes to one—"

"Mama, darling, for Heaven's sake don't say it. It's so terrible to talk about it."

"I won't then, I won't," said the mother, seeing the tears in her daughter's eyes, "but there's one thing, my darling: you promised me once you wouldn't keep any secrets from me. Will you?"

"Never, Mama, none at all," Kitty answered, blushing and looking straight into her mother's eyes. "But I have nothing to tell you just now. I . . . I . . . even if I wanted to, I wouldn't know what to say, or how to say it . . . I don't know. . . ."

No, with eyes like that she couldn't tell a lie, thought her mother, smiling at her excitement and happiness. The Princess was smiling at how enormous and important the poor girl must think what was going on in her own soul.

## XIII

AFTER dinner, and before the evening party began, Kitty experienced a feeling like that of a young man going into combat. Her heart was pounding heavily, and her thoughts could not settle on anything.

She felt that this evening, when both men were going to

meet for the first time, was bound to decide her future. She kept imagining them to herself over and over again, sometimes separately and sometimes together. When she thought of the past she dwelt with contentment and tenderness on the memories of her relations with Levin. The recollections of her childhood, and the recollections of Levin's friendship with her dead brother, lent a special, poetic charm to her relations with him. His love for her, which she was sure of, flattered her and made her happy; it was easy for her to think about Levin.

But something disquieting was mixed in with her thoughts of Vronsky, though he was extremely well bred and calm; it was as though there were something fraudulent there—not in him, he was very simple and goodhearted—but in herself, whereas with Levin she felt completely simple and clear.

On the other hand, the moment she thought of a future with Vronsky a brilliantly happy prospect rose up before her, while with Levin the future seemed dim and vague.

When she went upstairs to dress for the evening party and looked into the mirror, she saw with joy that she was in one of her good days, in full possession of all her powers. This was necessary for what lay ahead: she felt herself to be outwardly serene, and her movements free and graceful.

At half-past seven, just as she came down into the drawing room, the footman announced, "Constantine Dmitrich Levin." The Princess was still in her room; the Prince had not yet come down.

Well, thought Kitty, that's that; all the blood rushed to her heart. She glanced at the mirror and was terrified at her pallor.

Now she was absolutely sure that this was why he had come earlier, in order to find her alone and propose. And it was only now, for the first time, that the entire affair appeared to her in a new and different light. She understood only now that the question did not concern herself alone—whom she was going to be happy with and whom she would love—but that at that very moment she would have to hurt a man she loved. And hurt him cruelly . . . And why? Because he, the darling, loved her, because he was in love with her! But there was no help for it—what was necessary had to be done.

Oh my God, she thought, surely I don't have to tell him myself? And what can I tell him? Can I tell him I don't love him? That would be a lie. Then what will I tell him? That I love someone else? No, that's impossible. I'll go away, just go away!

She was already near the door when she heard his footsteps. No, that's dishonest! What is there for me to be afraid of? I haven't done anything wrong. Come what may, I'll tell the truth! For that matter it's impossible to feel ill at ease with him. There he is . . . she said to herself, as she saw his powerful, diffident figure in front of her, and his blazing eyes fixed on her. She looked straight into his eyes, as though begging him for forgiveness, and held out her hand.

"I think I've come at the wrong time, I'm too early," he said, looking round at the empty drawing room. When he saw that his expectations had been realized, and that nothing was there to prevent his speaking out, his face took on a gloomy look.

"Oh no," said Kitty, and sat down at the table.

"But that's all I wanted, to find you alone," he began, not sitting down and not looking at her, in order not to lose heart.

"Mama will be down in a moment. She was rather tired yesterday. Yesterday . . ."

She spoke without knowing herself what her lips were saying, and without turning her imploring, tender gaze away from him.

He looked at her; she blushed and fell silent.

"I told you I didn't know whether I would stay long . . . that it depended on you . . ."

She lowered her head more and more, not knowing herself how she was going to respond to what was approaching.

"That it depended on you," he repeated. "I meant . . . I meant . . . The reason I came . . . was . . . that . . . to be my wife!" he said, not knowing what he was saying himself; then, feeling that the most terrible part had been got through, he stopped and looked at her.

She was breathing heavily, not looking at him. She was filled with rapture. Her soul was brimming over with happiness. She had not in the least expected that the expression of his love would have such a violent effect on her. But this lasted for only an instant; she remembered Vronsky. She raised her clear, truthful eyes to Levin and, seeing his despairing face, answered hurriedly:

"It's impossible . . . Forgive me."

How close she had been to him just a moment before, how

important for his life! And how strange and remote she had now become!

"It could not have been otherwise," he said, without looking at her.

He bowed and turned to go.

### XIV

JUST then the Princess came in. A look of horror came over her face when she saw the two of them alone, and their distracted expressions. Levin bowed to her and said nothing. Kitty was silent, her eyes cast down. Thank God, she's refused him! thought the mother, and her face lit up with the habitual smile with which she greeted her Thursday-evening guests. She sat down and began asking Levin questions about his life in the country. He sat down again, waiting for the other guests to arrive so that he might leave unnoticed.

Five minutes later Countess Nordston, a friend of Kitty's who had married the winter before, came in.

She was a dried-up, sallow, nervous, sickly woman with glittering black eyes. She was fond of Kitty, and her affection for her, like the affection all married women have for un-married girls, was expressed in her desire to marry Kitty off in accordance with her own ideal of happiness, which was being married to Vronsky. She had always disliked Levin, whom she had often met there at the beginning of the winter. Her constant and favorite reaction whenever she met him consisted of making fun of him.

"I love it when from the height of his majesty he looks down at me: either he cuts short his intelligent conversation because I'm stupid, or else he patronizes me. That's what I adore—he patronizes me! I'm simply delighted that he can't bear me," she would say about him.

She was right; Levin actually couldn't bear her; he de-spised her because of just the thing she prided herself on and regarded as a merit—her nervousness, and her refined contempt for and aloofness from everything coarse and common.

Between Levin and Countess Nordston a relationship had grown up that is seen quite frequently in society, when two people outwardly remaining on friendly terms despise one another to such a point that they cannot treat the other seriously and cannot even be offended by each other.

Countess Nordston pounced on Levin instantly.

"Ah, Levin! You've come back to our depraved Babylon," she said, holding out her tiny yellow hand to him and recalling something he had once said at the beginning of the winter, about Moscow being Babylon. "Is it that Babylon has reformed or that you've been spoiled?" she added with a sneer, looking over at Kitty.

"I'm extremely flattered, Countess, at your remembering my remark," Levin retorted; he had had time to recover his self-possession and immediately entered into their relationship of malicious banter. "It obviously had a powerful effect on you."

"I should think so, I jotted it all down! Well, Kitty, have you been skating again?"

And she began talking to Kitty. Awkward as it was for Levin to leave now, it was at any rate easier to do that than to stay the whole evening looking at Kitty, who seldom looked at him and kept avoiding his eye. He was about to get up when the Princess, noticing his silence, turned toward him and said:

"Are you staying on in Moscow? But aren't you busy with the District Council, I thought, and can't stay away too long?"

"No, Princess, I've given up the District Council," he said. "I've just come for a few days."

There's something odd about him, thought Countess Nordston, looking at his severe, earnest face; for some reason he's not launching into one of his harangues. But I'll draw him out—I simply adore making a fool out of him in front of Kitty, and I'll do it, too!

"Levin," she said to him, "will you please explain to me what this means—you know all about it—on our Kaluga estate all the peasant men and women have drunk up everything they had, and now they won't pay us anything. What does it mean? You're always praising the peasants so much."

Just then another woman came into the room, and Levin got up.

"You must forgive me, Countess, but I really don't know anything about it and can't tell you anything," he said, and glanced over at the officer who was following the lady in.

That must be Vronsky, Levin thought, and to make sure he looked at Kitty. She had already got in a look at Vronsky and then turned back to Levin. And solely by the look in her eyes, which involuntarily lit up, Levin understood that she loved Vronsky, understood it just as surely as though she had told him in words. But what kind of a man was he?

Rightly or wrongly Levin could not help staying on now; he had to discover the sort of man she loved.

There are people who on meeting a successful rival are instantly ready to disregard everything good about him and see nothing but the bad; there are others, on the contrary, who want more than anything else to discover those qualities that have enabled their lucky rival to win out over them, and with an aching pain in their heart look for nothing but the best in him. Levin was one of the latter. But it was not difficult for him to see what was good and attractive in Vronsky. It leaped to the eye at once. Vronsky was a dark, solidly built man of medium height, with a good-natured, handsome, and extraordinarily serene, resolute face. In his face and figure, from the closely cropped black hair and freshly shaven chin to his loosely fitting, brand-new uniform, everything was simple and at the same time elegant. Stepping aside to make way for a lady, Vronsky came over to the Princess and then to Kitty.

As he moved toward her his fine eyes gleamed with particular tenderness, and with a scarcely discernible, happy, and modestly triumphant smile (as it seemed to Levin) he carefully and respectfully bent over her and held out his small, though broad hand.

After greeting everyone and saying a few words he sat down, without once looking over at Levin, who had not taken his eyes off him.

"Let me introduce you," said the Princess, indicating Levin. "Constantine Dmitrich Levin, Count Alexis Kirilovich Vronsky."

Vronsky got up and with a friendly look into Levin's eyes shook his hand.

"I think I was to have dined with you earlier this winter," he said, with his simple, open smile, "but you went off to the country unexpectedly."

"Levin hates and despises the city and us city dwellers," said Countess Nordston.

"My words must have had a powerful effect on you for you to remember them so well," said Levin, and remembering he had made the same remark before he blushed.

Vronsky looked at Levin and at Countess Nordston and smiled.

"But do you always live in the country?" he asked. "I should think it must be boring in winter."

"It's not boring if you have something to do, and for that matter it's not boring by yourself," Levin answered sharply.

"I like the country," said Vronsky, noticing Levin's tone and pretending not to.

"But I hope, Count, that you would never agree to live in the country all the time," said Countess Nordston.

"I don't know, I've never tried it for long. I once had a very strange feeling," he went on. "I never had such a longing for the country, for the Russian countryside with its peasants and their bark shoes, as when I spent a winter with my mother in Nice. Nice is a bore in and for itself, you know. Even Naples and Sorrento are only good for a short time, and that is just where your thoughts turn to Russia, and especially the country. They seem to. . . ."

He spoke to both Kitty and Levin, turning his calm, friendly gaze from one to the other, and evidently saying just what he thought.

Noticing that Countess Nordston wished to say something, he stopped without finishing what he had started, and began listening to her attentively.

The conversation did not flag for a second, so that the old Princess, who in case of a shortage of topics always had two heavy cannon in reserve—classical versus modern education, and general conscription—did not have to move them up, and Countess Nordston did not find a chance to bait Levin.

Levin wanted to enter into the general conversation but was unable to: every other minute he said to himself, Now's the time to go, but he kept waiting for something and didn't leave.

The conversation touched on table-turning and spirits, and Countess Nordston, who believed in spiritualism, began relating the miracles she had seen.

"Ah Countess, you must take me there without fail; for goodness' sake take me to him! I've never seen anything extraordinary, though I'm constantly on the lookout for it," said Vronsky with a smile.

"Very well, next Saturday then," she replied; "and are you a believer, Levin?"

"Why do you ask me? You know quite well what I would say."

"But I want to hear your opinion."

"My opinion is simply this," Levin answered, "that

these turning tables prove that our so-called cultivated society is no higher than the peasants. They believe in the evil eye, spells, and witches, while we—"

"What, you don't believe?"

"I cannot, Countess."

"But if I've seen them myself?"

"The peasant women also say they've seen goblins with their own eyes."

"Then you think I'm not telling the truth?" And she broke into a mirthless laugh.

"But of course not, Masha, Levin is saying that *he* can't believe," said Kitty, blushing for Levin; he saw this and getting even more annoyed was about to reply when Vronsky, with his cheerful, open smile instantly came to the rescue of the conversation, which was threatening to become disagreeable.

"You absolutely refuse to admit that's possible?" he asked. "But why? We admit the existence of electricity, which we don't understand; so why mightn't there be a new force, which we still don't understand, and which—"

"When electricity was discovered," Levin broke in quickly, "what was discovered was simply a phenomenon; its cause and effects were unknown, and centuries passed by before anyone thought of applying it. But the spiritualists, on the contrary, began with the tables writing for them and spirits coming to them, and it was only then that they began saying that there was some unknown force there."

Vronsky listened attentively to Levin, as he always listened, showing a manifest interest in what he was saying.

"Yes, but the spiritualists say that we don't know now what kind of a force it is, but that it is a force, and these are the conditions in which it functions. Let the scientists discover what the force consists of. No, I don't see just why this might not be a new force, if it—"

"Because," Levin interrupted, "in electricity every single time you rub some resin against wool a certain phenomenon is produced, while with the other it doesn't happen every time, therefore it's not a natural phenomenon."

Doubtless feeling that the conversation was taking on a character that was too serious for a drawing room, Vronsky made no objection; in an effort to change the subject he smiled gaily and turned to the ladies.

"Let us try it now, Countess—" he began, but Levin wanted to finish saying what he thought.

"I think," he went on, "that the attempt on the part of the spiritualists to explain their miracles by some new force is a complete fiasco. Though they definitely speak of a spiritual force, they want to subject it to a material test."

Everyone was waiting for him to finish, and he felt it.

"I think you'd be an excellent medium," said Countess Nordston. "There's something ecstatic about you."

Levin opened his mouth and was about to reply, but blushed and said nothing.

"Let us try some table-turning now, Princess Kitty, please," said Vronsky. "Would you permit us?" he said to her mother.

Vronsky stood up, glancing about for a table.

Kitty got up to fetch a table, and as she passed by Levin their eyes met. She was sorry for him from the bottom of her heart, all the more so since she pitied him for the misfortune she herself had been the cause of. If it's possible to forgive me, forgive me, her eyes said, I'm so happy!

I detest everyone, including you and myself! his eyes said in reply, and he took up his hat. But he was not destined to leave. Just as they were about to arrange themselves around a table, and Levin was about to leave, the old Prince came in and after greeting the ladies turned to Levin.

"Aha!" he said happily, "been back long, my boy? I didn't even know you were here. I'm delighted to see you!"

The old Prince sometimes talked to Levin as an intimate, sometimes not. He embraced him and while talking to him did not notice Vronsky, who had got up and was calmly waiting for the Prince to address him.

Kitty felt that after what had happened her father's amiability was oppressive to Levin. She also saw with what chilliness her father finally answered Vronsky's bow, and how Vronsky looked at him in good-natured perplexity, trying to understand, and failing to, why anyone should not have had a friendly attitude toward him, and she blushed.

"Prince, do let us have Levin," said Countess Nordston. "We want to try an experiment."

"What experiment? Table-turning? Forgive me, ladies and gentlemen, but in my opinion quoits are more amusing," said the old Prince, looking at Vronsky and guessing that it was he who had started it. "After all, there's some sense in quoits."

Vronsky gave the Prince a startled look with his steady eyes, and smiling very slightly he immediately started up a conversation with Countess Nordston about the great ball that was taking place the following week.

"May I hope you'll be there?" he said, turning to Kitty.

The moment the old Prince turned away from him Levin went out unnoticed, and the last impression he took with him from this evening party was Kitty's smiling, happy expression as she answered Vronsky's question about the ball.

## XV

WHEN the party was over Kitty reported her conversation with Levin to her mother; in spite of all her compassion the thought that she had been *proposed to* delighted her. She had no doubt of her having behaved properly, but for a long time she could not fall asleep. There was one impression that pursued her relentlessly—Levin's face, his eyebrows knit together and the mournful look in his kind eyes as he stood listening to her father and glancing at her and at Vronsky. And she began to feel so sorry for him that tears came to her eyes. But then at once she thought of the one she had taken instead. She vividly imagined that resolute, virile face, that noble serenity, and the kindness he always showed everyone in everything; she recalled the love for herself of the one she loved, and joy filled her heart once again as she lay back on the pillow with a smile of happiness. Such a pity, such a pity, she said to herself; but what can I do? It's not my fault. But an inner voice said something else. Whether she regretted having lured Levin on, or having refused him, she had no idea. But her happiness was poisoned by doubts. Lord have mercy, Lord have mercy, Lord have mercy! she repeated to herself until she fell asleep.

All this time one of the frequently repeated scenes between the parents about their favorite daughter was going on downstairs, in the Prince's little study.

"What? This is what!" the Prince shouted, flinging his arms out and then instantly wrapping his squirrel-lined dressing gown around him. "That you have no pride, no dignity, you disgrace your daughter, you ruin her by all this vile, idiotic matchmaking!"

"But please, for God's sake, Prince, what is it I've done?" said the Princess, on the verge of tears.

Contented and satisfied after her conversation with Kitty, she had come to say good night to the Prince as usual, and though she had had no intention of telling him about Levin's proposal and Kitty's refusal, she hinted to him that she thought the Vronsky situation was completely settled and would be decided the moment his mother arrived. At these words the Prince exploded there and then and began shouting out all sorts of indecent words.

"What have you done? First of all this: you've been enticing a suitor, and all Moscow is going to talk about it, and rightly so. If you're going to give evening parties invite everyone, and not only hand-picked suitors. Invite all the whippersnappers"—as the Prince called the young men of Moscow—"get in a pianist, and let them dance around, not the way you did it tonight—suitors and pairing everyone off! It's horrible, horrible, for me to see that sort of thing, and now you've had your way and turned the child's head. Levin is a thousand times the better man. As for that Petersburg fop, they make them on a machine, they're all according to the same pattern, and all trash! And even if he were a Prince of the Blood, Kitty doesn't need him!"

"But what did I do?"

"Just this—" the Prince cried out furiously.

"I know that if I were to listen to you," the Princess interrupted, "we'd never get Kitty married off! If that's so we'll have to go to the country."

"That would be better."

"Just a moment—you think I'm ensnaring them, but it's not so in the least: a young man, a very fine young man, has fallen in love, and I think she—"

"So you think! And what if she falls in love too, while he has about as much idea of marrying her as I? Oh, if only I hadn't seen it with my own eyes!—'ah, spiritualism, ah, Nice, ah, the ball—!' " And at each word the Prince, pretending to imitate his wife, gave a curtsey. "And what if we really ruin little Kitty, and she really does take it into her head to—"

"But why do you think that?"

"I don't think it, I know it; women don't have eyes for that, but we do. I see a man whose intentions are serious

—Levin; then I see a popinjay like that popinjay, whose only thought is his own amusement."

"Oh well, once you get something into your head—"

"And you'll remember it, but then it'll be too late, just as it was with poor little Dolly."

"All right then, very well, let's not talk about it," the Princess stopped him, at the thought of the unfortunate Dolly.

"Splendid, good night!"

And making the sign of the cross over each other as they kissed, but each one feeling that they were clinging to their separate opinions, they separated for the night.

At first the Princess had been firmly convinced that that evening had settled Kitty's future, and that there could be no doubt about Vronsky's intentions; but what her husband said upset her. When she reached her own room, terrified at the uncertainty of the future, she repeated to herself several times, just as Kitty had: Lord have mercy, Lord have mercy, Lord have mercy!

### XVI

VRONSKY had never known what family life was. His mother had been a brilliant society woman in her youth, and during her marriage and especially afterward had had a great many love affairs, which everyone knew about. He could scarcely remember his father, and had been educated in the Corps of Pages.

Leaving school a very young and brilliant officer, he immediately fell into the circle of rich Petersburg officers. Although occasionally he frequented Petersburg society all his love interests lay outside it.

In Moscow, for the first time, after the coarse and luxurious life of Petersburg, he experienced the delight of friendship with a sweet, innocent society girl who was in love with him. It never even entered his head that there might be anything wrong about his relations with Kitty. At balls he danced chiefly with her; he went calling on the family. He talked the usual society talk with her; all sorts of nonsense, but nonsense that he involuntarily put a special meaning into for her. In spite of his saying nothing to her that he might not have said in public, he felt that she was growing more and more dependent on him, and the more he felt this the pleasanter it was for him, and the more tender his own feeling grew for her. He did not know that his behavior toward Kitty had a certain name, that he was leading a young girl into temptation with no intention of marrying her, and that this seduction was one of the evil actions habitual among brilliant young men like himself. He thought himself the first to discover this pleasure, and he enjoyed his discovery.

If he had been able to hear what her parents were saying that night, if he had been able to adopt the point of the family and had learned that Kitty would be unhappy if he didn't marry her, he would have been very surprised, and would have refused to believe it. He could not have believed that something that gave such a great deal of harmless satisfaction to him, and above all to her, could be wrong. Still less could he have believed that he ought to get married.

Marriage had never entered his mind as a possibility. Not only did he not like family life, but in accordance with the general opinion of the bachelor world he lived in, he regarded a family, and especially a husband, as something alien, hostile, and above all—ridiculous.

But as Vronsky left the Shcherbatskys' that evening, though he did not even suspect what her parents were saying, he had the feeling that the secret spiritual bond that existed between him and Kitty had been strengthened that evening with such force that he had to do something about it. But he had no notion what could or should be done.

That's what's so delightful about it, he thought, as he left the Shcherbatskys', taking with him as always an agreeable sensation of purity and freshness, partly due to his not having smoked the whole evening, together with a novel feeling of tenderness at her love for him—the delightful thing is that nothing was said by her or by me, but we understood each other so well, in the invisible conversation of looks and overtones, that tonight it was clearer than ever that she told me she loves me. And so sweetly, so simply, above all so trustingly! I myself feel better, purer. I feel that I have a heart and that there's a great deal of good in me. Those sweet loving eyes! When she said, "*and very much . . .*"

But then what? Well, nothing . . . It's all right for me, and it's all right for her. And he began thinking of how he might finish off the evening.

He turned over in his mind the places he might go to. The Club? A game of bezique, champagne with Ignatov? No,

not there. Château des Fleurs? Oblonsky'll be there—
French couplets, the cancan . . . No, I'm sick of it. That's
just why I like the Shcherbatskys' so much, I change for
the better there. I'll just go home.

He went straight to his rooms at the Hotel Dussot, ordered
some supper, and, after undressing, he had scarcely laid his
head on the pillow before he fell into a deep, undisturbed
sleep as usual.

## XVII

THE next day, at eleven in the morning, Vronsky drove
to the station to meet his mother, arriving on the Petersburg
train; the first person he ran into on the broad flight of steps
was Oblonsky, who was expecting his sister on the same
train.

"Aha, Your Excellency!" exclaimed Oblonsky. "Whom are
you here for?"

"My mother," Vronsky answered, smiling as everyone did
who met Oblonsky; he shook hands with him and they
went up the steps together. "She's due in from Petersburg
today."

"I waited for you till two last night. Where did you go
on to after the Shcherbatskys'?"

"Home," Vronsky answered. "To tell the truth I was in
such a good mood last night after the Shcherbatskys' that
I didn't feel like going anywhere."

" 'I know a fine steed by tumty-tum of his breed, and a
young man in love—by his eyes!' " Oblonsky declaimed,
just as he had before with Levin.

Vronsky smiled, as though not denying this, but he
changed the subject at once.

"And whom are you meeting?" he asked.

"I? A lovely woman," said Oblonsky.

"Well, well!"

"*Honi soit qui mal y pense!* My sister Anna."

"Ah! You mean Madame Karenin?" Vronsky said.

"I suppose you know her?"

"I think so. Or perhaps not . . . Actually I don't remember," Vronsky answered distractedly, vaguely imagining something stiff and boring at the mention of Karenin.

"But you surely know my famous brother-in-law, Alexis
Karenin. Everyone knows him."

"Well, I've heard of him and I know him by sight. I know he's able, learned, and devout, or something . . . But you know, that's not—*not in my line*," said Vronsky in English.

"Yes, he's a very remarkable fellow; something of a conservative, but a fine chap," Oblonsky remarked, "a very fine chap."

"So much the better for him," said Vronsky with a smile. "Ah, there you are," he said, turning to a tall, aged footman of his mother's who was standing by the door. "Come in here."

Aside from Oblonsky's general amiability, Vronsky had lately been feeling even closer to him because he was associated in his mind with Kitty.

"Well, are we giving that supper for the diva next Sunday?" he said to him, smilingly taking him by the arm.

"Definitely. I'm collecting subscriptions. Oh, did you meet my friend Levin last night?" asked Oblonsky.

"Of course, but I think he left quite early."

"He's a splendid chap," Oblonsky went on. "Didn't you think so?"

"I don't know why," Vronsky replied, "but there's something prickly about everyone in Moscow, except of course for present company," he put in jokingly. "For some reason they're always getting on their high horse and losing their tempers, as though they wanted to stir you up . . ."

"There's something in that, there really is," said Oblonsky, smiling merrily.

"Is there much more of a wait?" said Vronsky to a porter.

"The train's signaled already," the porter answered.

The approach of the train was becoming more and more evident as a result of the preparatory bustle in the station, the scurrying of porters, the appearance of gendarmes and attendants, and the arrival of people meeting people. Through the frosty vapor workmen in short sheepskins and soft felt boots could be seen crossing the curving rails. The whistle of the locomotive in the distance and the sound of something heavy approaching could be heard.

"No," said Oblonsky, who had a great desire to tell Vronsky about Levin's intentions concerning Kitty. "You're not quite right about Levin. It's true that he's very nervous and often disagreeable, but he makes up for it sometimes by being extremely nice. He has an honest, straighforward nature, and a heart of gold. But last night there were special reasons," Oblonsky went on with a meaningful smile, completely forgetting the sincere compassion he had felt for his friend the day before, and feeling the same thing now, though this time for Vronsky. "Yes, there was a reason why he might have been either specially happy, or specially unhappy."

Vronsky stopped and asked him point-blank: "Now what d'you mean? Did he propose to your sister-in-law last night?"

"Perhaps," said Oblonsky. "Something of the kind was the way it seemed to me yesterday. So if he went away early and was still out of sorts, that was it . . . He's been in love for such a long time, I'm very sorry for him."

"So that's it! . . . But I think she can count on a better match," said Vronsky, and straightening up he started moving forward again. "Though I don't know him," he added. "What a painful situation! That's why most people make such a point of knowing tarts. With them a failure only proves you didn't have enough money, and here—it's your pride that's in the scales. But here's the train."

And in fact the whistle of the locomotive could be heard in the distance. A few minutes later the platform started shaking, and the locomotive came puffing in, the steam driven downward by the frost, the piston of the middle wheel slowly and evenly pushing and pulling, and the muffled-up engine driver covered with frost, leaning over; the tender, which made the platform tremble more and more slowly and heavily, was followed by the baggage car, with a dog whining in it; finally, the passenger cars, shuddering to a halt, came up.

The sprightly conductor whistled and jumped off while the train was still moving; one by one some of the impatient passengers began getting off after him: a Guards officer, bolt upright and glaring about sternly; a fidgety little tradesman with a bag, smiling cheerfully, and a peasant with a sack across his shoulder.

Vronsky, standing side by side with Oblonsky, watching the cars and the people coming out, had forgotten his mother completely. What he had just heard about Kitty had excited him and made him happy. He squared his chest unconsciously; his eyes shone. He felt like a conqueror.

"Countess Vronsky is in this compartment," said the smart-looking conductor, coming up to him.

The conductor's words aroused him and made him think of

his mother and their forthcoming meeting. At heart he had no respect for his mother, and without admitting it to himself did not love her, but in accordance with the ideas of the circle he lived in and because of his upbringing, he could not imagine any other relationship with his mother but one of the most respectful obedience, and the more respectful and obedient he was in appearance the less he respected and loved her at heart.

## XVIII

VRONSKY followed the conductor into the car, and stopped on the threshold of the compartment to make way for a woman coming out. With the instinctive reaction of a man of the world, Vronsky, with one glance at this woman's appearance, placed her as belonging to the best society. He apologized and was about to go on into the carriage, but he felt it necessary to glance at her once again—not because she was very beautiful, nor because of the elegance and demure grace visible in everything about her, but because there was something particularly tender and caressing in the expression of her sweet face as she passed by him. When he looked around she also turned her head. Her shining gray eyes, which because of their thick lashes seemed dark, paused with friendly attentiveness at his face as though she recognized him, and then swept on at once to the passing crowd as though looking for someone. In this short glance Vronsky had time to notice the subdued vitality that played over her face and fluttered between her shining eyes, and the scarcely perceptible smile that curved her rosy lips. It was as though an excess of something so filled her whole being that it expressed itself against her will, sometimes in the brilliance of her gaze, sometimes in her smile. She deliberately tried to extinguish that light in her eyes, but it blazed out against her will in that faint smile.

Vronsky entered the car. His mother, a dried-up old woman with black eyes and ringlets, screwed up her eyes as she looked at her son; she smiled slightly with her thin lips. She got up from the seat, gave her handbag to the maid, and held her dry little hand out to her son to kiss; then she raised his head and kissed his face.

"You got my telegram? Are you all right? Thank God."

"Have you had a good trip?" said her son, sitting down

beside her and listening involuntarily to a woman's voice outside the door. He knew it was the voice of the woman he had met as he entered the carriage.

"Just the same I don't agree with you," the voice was saying.

"A Petersburg point of view, Madame."

"Not Petersburg, just a woman's," she replied.

"Well, allow me to kiss your hand."

"Good-by then, Monsieur. Take a look round for my brother, and send him to me," said the woman, just outside the door; then she came back into the compartment again.

"Well, did you find your brother?" said Vronsky's mother to her.

Vronsky realized now that this was Karenin's wife Anna.

"Your brother is here," he said, getting to his feet. "Forgive me, I didn't recognize you; for that matter our acquaintance was so brief," said Vronsky, bowing, "that you surely don't remember me."

"Oh no, I should have recognized you; I think your mother and I spent the entire trip talking of nothing but you," she said, finally allowing the liveliness that had been trying to shine through to show itself in a smile. "But anyhow my brother isn't here."

"Go and call him, Alexis," said the old Countess.

Vronsky went out onto the platform and shouted: "Oblonsky! Over here!"

But Anna did not wait for her brother; when she saw him she stepped out of the carriage with a firm, light tread. As soon as Oblonsky came up to her she flung her left arm around his neck with a motion that surprised Vronsky by its firmness and grace, pulled him toward her quickly and kissed him heartily. Without turning his eyes away Vronsky looked at her and smiled; he didn't know why himself. But he remembered that his mother was waiting for him and went back into the carriage.

"Very sweet, isn't she?" said the Countess about Anna. "Her husband put her into my compartment, and I was delighted. We chatted together the whole way. And as for you, they say—*vous filez le parfait amour. Tant mieux, mon cher, tant mieux.*"

"I have no idea what you're referring to, *maman*," her son answered coldly. "Well, shall we go?"

Anna came into the carriage again to say good-by to the Countess.

"There, Countess, you've met your son, and I my brother," she said gaily. "And all my little stories are exhausted; there would have been nothing else to tell."

"Oh no," said the Countess, taking her by the hand. "I could travel all around the world with you and never be bored. You're one of those delightful women it's a pleasure both to talk to and to be silent with. And please don't think about your son any more; it's impossible never to be separated, after all."

Anna stood there motionless, holding herself very erect and smiling with her eyes.

"Anna has a little son, eight years old, I think," the Countess explained to Vronsky. "She's never been separated from him and keeps worrying about having left him."

"Yes, the Countess and I spent the whole time talking, she about her son and I about mine," said Anna, and once again a smile lit up her face, a caressing smile due to him.

"You must have been awfully bored," he said, instantly catching in midflight the ball of coquetry she had tossed him. But apparently she did not feel like continuing the conversation in this tone; she turned to the old Countess:

"I'm very grateful to you. I scarcely noticed how the day passed. Good-by, Countess."

"Good-by, my dear," the Countess answered. "Let me kiss your charming face. As an old woman all I can do is tell you straight out that I've fallen in love with you."

However casual the phrase, Anna plainly believed it from her heart and was delighted by it. She blushed, bent over a little and held out her face to the Countess's mouth; then she straightened up again and with the same smile hovering between her eyes and lips gave Vronsky her hand. He pressed the small hand held out to him; the energetic pressure with which she firmly and boldly shook his hand, as though it were something special, delighted him. She went out with the rapid stride that carried her rather full body with such peculiar lightness.

"Very sweet," said the old lady.

Her son thought the same. His eyes followed her as long as her graceful figure was still visible, and a smile lingered on his lips. Through the window he watched her go up to her brother, put her arm through his and in a lively way start telling him something that obviously had nothing to do with Vronsky, who found this annoying.

"Well, *maman*, how are you? Are you quite well?" he repeated, turning to his mother.

"Everything is all right, splendid. Alexander was terribly sweet. Marie has become very pretty. She's very interesting."

She began talking once again about what interested her most of all, her grandson's christening, which was the reason for her trip to Petersburg, and about the special favor the Tsar had shown her eldest son.

"There's Lavrenty at last," said Vronsky, looking through the window. "Shall we go now? If it's all right with you."

The old major-domo who had been traveling with the Countess appeared in the carriage to report that everything was ready; the Countess stood up to go.

"Let's go, there are not so many people now," said Vronsky.

The maid took the handbag and the little dog; the major-domo and the porter carried the other bags. Vronsky took his mother by the arm; but when they had left the carriage a number of people with frightened faces suddenly ran past. The stationmaster with his peculiar colored cap also ran past them.

It was evident that something unusual had happened. The people who had left the train were running back.

"What is it?" "What?" "Where?" "Jumped in front!" "Run over!" the passers-by could be heard shouting.

Oblonsky, with his sister on his arm, both of them also looking frightened, came back and to avoid the crowd stood beside the carriage.

The women went into the carriage, while Vronsky and Oblonsky followed the crowd to find out the details of the accident.

A guard, either because he was drunk or too bundled up against the severe cold, had not heard a train being shunted and had been run over.

Even before Vronsky and Oblonsky had come back the women had learned these details from the major-domo.

Oblonsky and Vronsky had both seen the mangled corpse. Oblonsky was visibly distressed. His face was puckered up; he seemed ready to burst into tears.

"How horrible! Oh Anna, if you'd only seen! Oh, how horrible!" he kept repeating.

Vronsky was silent; his handsome face was grave but quite calm.

"Oh, if you had only seen it, Countess," said Oblonsky. "And his wife is there . . . It's horrible to see her . . . She flung herself on the body. They say he was the sole support of a huge family. Horrible!"

"But isn't it possible to do something for her?" said Anna in an agitated whisper.

Vronsky looked at her, and left the carriage at once. "I'll be back immediately, *maman*," he remarked, turning in the doorway.

When he came back a few minutes later Oblonsky was already chatting with the Countess about a new singer; the Countess was glancing impatiently at the door, waiting for her son.

"We can go now," said Vronsky, coming in.

They left together. Vronsky went on ahead with his mother, followed by Anna and her brother. At the exit Vronsky was overtaken by the stationmaster.

"You gave my assistant two hundred rubles. Would you be so kind as to tell me whom you meant them for?"

"For the widow," said Vronsky with a shrug. "I don't understand what there is to ask about."

"Did you give something?" exclaimed Oblonsky from behind, and pressing his sister's arm he added: "Very kind, really very kind! Isn't he a splendid chap? Well, Countess, my respects."

Oblonsky and his sister stayed behind, looking for her maid. By the time they left, the Vronskys' carriage had already driven off. The people coming out were still talking about what had happened.

"What a horrible death!" said someone passing by. "They say he was cut in two."

"On the contrary, I think it's the easiest, it's instantaneous," said someone else.

"How can they be so careless!" said a third.

Anna sat down in the carriage; to his astonishment Oblonsky saw that her lips were trembling and that she was only holding back her tears with difficulty.

"What's the matter with you, Anna?" he asked, after they had gone a few hundred yards.

"It's a bad omen," she said.

"What nonsense!" said Oblonsky. "The main thing is that you've come. You can't imagine how I'm counting on you."

"Have you known Vronsky long?" she asked.

"Yes. You know we're hoping he'll marry Kitty."

"Oh?" said Anna softly. "Well, now let's talk about you," she added, shaking her head as though trying to drive away

physically something superfluous that was bothering her.
"Let me hear about your troubles. I got your letter and
here I am."

"Yes, everything depends on you," said Oblonsky.

"Well, tell me all about it."

And Oblonsky began his story.

When they got home Oblonsky helped his sister out, sighed,
pressed her hand and drove to the office.

## XIX

WHEN Anna came into the room Dolly was sitting in the
little drawing room with a plump, little fair-haired boy,
already very like his father, listening to his French reading
lesson. The little boy was reading aloud; he kept twisting and
trying to pull off a button that was hanging loosely from his
jacket. His mother moved his plump little hand away several
times, but it kept creeping back again to the button. She
pulled it off and put it in her pocket.

"Stop moving your hands, Grisha," she said, and again
took up the rug she was knitting, a piece of work begun long
before that she always busied herself with at difficult moments; she was knitting nervously now, looping the wool
over the needle and counting the stitches. Though the day
before she had sent word to her husband that she did not
care whether his sister came or not, she had gotten everything ready for Anna's arrival and was waiting for her with
agitation.

Dolly was undone by her distress, entirely consumed by it.
But she recalled that her sister-in-law was the wife of one of
the most important people in Petersburg, and a Petersburg
*grande dame*. Because of this circumstance she had not done
what she had told her husband, that is, she had not forgotten her sister-in-law was arriving. After all, it isn't Anna's
fault, thought Dolly; I don't know anything but good things
about her, and as far as I'm concerned she's always shown
me affection and friendship.

As far as Dolly could recall her impression in Petersburg
of the Karenins, to be sure, she disliked their house itself;
there was something false in the whole style of their family
life.

But why shouldn't I receive her? thought Dolly; as long as
she doesn't think she's going to console me! All these con-

solations, exhortations, and Christian forgivenesses—I've gone over them a thousand times, none of it's any good.

All these days Dolly had been alone with the children. She did not want to talk about her misery, but with this misery on her mind she was unable to talk about anything unimportant. She knew that one way or another she was going to tell Anna everything; sometimes she was happy at the thought of telling her, and sometimes irritated at having to speak of her humiliation to her, his sister, and listen to her get off some pat expressions of consolation and exhortation.

As often happens, while looking at the clock and expecting her any minute Dolly let slip by just the moment when her guest arrived, by not hearing the bell ring.

When she heard the rustle of a dress and light footsteps already in the doorway, she looked around, with an involuntary expression not of pleasure but of astonishment on her drawn face. She got up and embraced her sister-in-law.

"What, are you here already?" she said, kissing her.

"Dolly, I'm so glad to see you!"

"So am I," said Dolly with a feeble smile, trying to see by Anna's expression whether she knew or not. She must know, she thought, as she noticed the look of compassion on Anna's face. "Come, let me show you to your room," she continued, trying to postpone the moment of explanation as long as possible.

"Isn't that Grisha? Heavens, how he's grown!" said Anna, and after kissing him, without taking her eyes off Dolly, she stood there blushing. "No, please, let's not go anywhere."

She took off her shawl and hat, and catching it in her black and very curly hair she shook her head to get it loose.

"But you're just radiating joy and health!" said Dolly, almost with envy.

"I? Yes . . ." said Anna. "But goodness, there's Tanya! The same age as my little Seryozha," she added, turning to the little girl who was running in. She took her in her arms and kissed her. "My sweet little darling! Now show me all of them."

She mentioned them all; she recalled not only their names, but the years, and the months they were born, the characters and the illnesses of all the children. Dolly could not help appreciating this.

"Well, let's go up to see them," she said. "Vasya's asleep now, what a pity."

After seeing the children they sat down to coffee by themselves in the drawing room. Anna took hold of the tray, then pushed it aside.

"Dolly," she said, "he's told me."

Dolly looked at her coldly. She was expecting a few hypocritically compassionate remarks now; but Anna said nothing of the sort.

"Dolly, darling!" she said. "I don't want to defend him, or console you: that's impossible. Dearest, I'm simply sorry for you, sorry from the bottom of my heart!"

Under her thick lashes her shining eyes suddenly filled with tears. She moved closer to Dolly and with her own energetic little hand took hold of hers. Dolly did not draw away from her, but the dry expression on her face did not change. She said: "It's not possible to console me. All is lost, after what's happened, all is lost!"

All at once, the moment she said this, her expression softened. Anna raised Dolly's dry, thin hand, kissed it, and said:

"But Dolly, what's to be done? What can be done? What's the best thing to do in this horrible situation? That's what we have to think about."

"Everything's over with, and that's all," said Dolly. "And the worst of it all is, you understand, that I can't leave him; the children—I'm tied hand and foot. And I cannot live with him, it's torture for me to see him."

"Dolly darling, he's told me, but I want to hear it from you—tell me everything."

Dolly looked at her questioningly. Anna's face showed only unfeigned sympathy and love.

"If you like," she said abruptly. "But I'll tell it from the beginning. You know how I was when I got married. With *maman*'s bringing up I was not only innocent, I was stupid. I didn't know a thing. I know people say husbands tell their wives about their former life, but Stiva"—she corrected herself—"but Stephen told me nothing. You won't believe me but until now I thought I was the only woman he'd known. That's how I've lived for eight years. You understand I not only didn't have any suspicions of infidelity, I thought it was impossible, and then, just imagine, with notions like that to find out suddenly all the horror, all the vileness! . . . You understand me—to be completely sure of your happiness, then suddenly"—Dolly went on, holding back her sobs—"receiving a letter—his letter to his mistress, my governess. No, it's too horrible!" She hastily snatched out a handkerchief and buried her face in it. "I could understand an infatuation," she went on after a moment's silence, "but to deceive me so deliberately, so slyly, and with whom? To go on being my husband, together with her—it's horrible! You can't understand—"

"Oh no, Dolly darling, I do understand, I do!" said Anna, squeezing her hand.

"And d'you think he understands the utter horror of my position?" Dolly went on. "Not in the least. He's happy and contented."

"Oh no!" Anna interrupted her quickly. "He's pitiful, he's eaten up by remorse . . ."

"Is he capable of remorse?" Dolly interrupted, giving Anna a searching look.

"Yes, I know him. I couldn't look at him today without pity. We both know him. He's kindhearted, but he's proud, and now he's so humiliated. The thing that touched me most of all"—here Anna guessed what it was that could touch Dolly most of all—"is that he's tormented by two things: he's ashamed of himself because of the children, and then, because he loves you—yes, yes, he loves you more than anything in the world"—she hurriedly stopped Dolly, who was about to protest—"and he hurt you, because he shattered you. 'No, no, she'll never forgive me,' he keeps on saying."

Dolly meditatively looked past her sister-in-law, listening to what she was saying.

"Yes, I understand that his situation is dreadful; it's worse for the guilty than for the innocent," she said, "if he feels that his guilt is the cause of the whole calamity. But how can I forgive him, how can I live with him again after her? Living with him now would be torture, just because I still love him as I did before . . ."

Sobs prevented her saying anything further.

But as though on purpose every time she softened she began to speak once again of what irritated her.

"After all, she's young, she's beautiful," she went on. "Can you understand, Anna, my youth and good looks have been taken away, and by whom? By him and his children. I have served him, and in serving him everything I had has vanished, and now of course a fresh, vulgar little creature is far more agreeable to him. They probably spoke together about me, or—what's even worse—kept quiet. You understand?" Again her eyes smoldered with hatred. "And afterward, if he were to tell me anything . . . Would I believe him? Never. No, everything's finished, everything, my only consolation, the reward for all my labors, all my sufferings . . . Would you believe it, I've just been giving Grisha a lesson. Before it used to be a joy, now it's torture. Why should I make an effort, go to any trouble? What use are the children? The terrible thing is that my heart has suddenly been transformed, and instead of love and tenderness for him all I have is rage, yes, rage. I could kill him, and—"

"Dolly, dearest, I understand, but don't torture yourself. You're so hurt, so upset that there's a great deal you don't see quite as it is."

Dolly subsided; for a moment or two they were both silent.

"What should I do, Anna? Think, help me. I've thought the whole thing over and I can't see any way out."

Anna could not think of anything, but her heart responded directly to every word, to every expression on Dolly's face.

"I'll say one thing," Anna began. "I'm his sister, I know his character, his capacity for forgetting everything, everything"—she made a gesture in front of her forehead—"his capacity for being carried away completely, but on the other hand for repenting completely. He doesn't believe, he doesn't understand, now, how he could do what he did."

"No, he understands, he understood!" interrupted Dolly. "But what about me? You're forgetting me, you don't suppose it's any easier for me?"

"Just a moment. When he spoke to me I'll confess to you I didn't understand the full horror of your position. All I saw was him, and the family being broken up; I was sorry for him, but after speaking to you, I as a woman see something else; I see how you're suffering, and I can't tell you how sorry I am for you! But Dolly, dearest, I completely understand your suffering, there's only one thing I don't know: I don't know . . . I don't know how much love there is still left in you for him. That you know—whether there's enough left for you to forgive him. If there is—then forgive him!"

"No," Dolly began, but Anna interrupted her, kissing her hand once again.

"I know the world more than you do," she said. "I know how people like Stiva look on this. You say he spoke about you to *her*. That could never happen. Such people may be unfaithful, but their homes, their wives, are holy things for them. Somehow such women go on being despised by them and don't interfere with the family. They draw some sort of an inviolable line between their families and women like that. I don't understand it, but that's how it is."

"Yes, but he kissed her—"

"Dolly, dearest, just a moment. I saw Stiva when he was in love with you. I remember the time he came to see me and burst into tears speaking about you, about what poetic loftiness you presented for him, and I know that the longer he lived with you the loftier you became for him. We used to laugh at him, you know, the way he would begin every remark by saying: 'Dolly's an amazing woman.' For him you were always a goddess, and you've remained so, this infatuation did not touch his soul—"

"But what if the infatuation repeats itself?"

"I understand it couldn't . . ."

"But you—would you forgive?"

"I don't know, I can't judge . . . No, I can," said Anna, after a moment's thought: after taking the situation in and weighing it, she added: "Yes, I can—I can. Yes, I would forgive. I wouldn't be the same afterward, but I would forgive, and would forgive in such a way that it would be as though nothing at all had happened, absolutely nothing."

"Well, of course," Dolly interrupted her quickly, as though saying something she had often thought, "or else it wouldn't be forgiveness. If you're going to forgive, it must be completely, completely. But let me take you to your room," she said, getting up. On their way she embraced Anna. "My dearest, I'm so happy you've come. I feel easier, much easier."

xx

ANNA spent that whole day at home, that is, at the Oblonskys', and didn't receive anyone: some people she knew had actually found out about her arrival already and called on her the same day. Anna spent the whole morning with Dolly and the children. She only sent a note to her brother, for him to dine at home without fail. "Come," she wrote. "God is merciful."

Oblonsky dined at home: the conversation was general, and his wife spoke to him familiarly as "Stiva," which had not been so before. There was still the same alienation between husband and wife, but there was no longer any question of separation; Oblonsky saw there was a chance for explanation and reconciliation.

Kitty came in directly after dinner. She knew Anna, though not at all well, and was coming to her sister's now full of fears as to how she would be received by this Petersburg society woman whose praises were being sung by everybody. But Anna liked her—Kitty saw that at once. Anna plainly admired her beauty and youth, and Kitty had not even recovered her poise before she felt not only under Anna's influence, but infatuated with her, in the way young girls are capable of falling in love with older married women. Anna was not at all like a society woman, or like the mother of an eight-year-old son, but would rather have resembled a twenty-year-old girl in the suppleness of her movements, her freshness, and the vivacity that played about her face and kept breaking through in a smile or a look, if it had not been for the grave and occasionally sad expression in her eyes, which struck Kitty and attracted her. Kitty felt that Anna was completely simple and hid nothing, but that she had within her another, higher world of interests, complex and poetical, that were beyond Kitty's reach.

After dinner, when Dolly went to her own room, Anna got up quickly and went over to her brother, who was just lighting a cigar.

"Stiva," she said to him with a gay twinkle in her eye, making the sign of the cross over him as she indicated the door with a glance, "go along now, and may God help you!"

He understood, threw aside his cigar, and vanished through the door.

When Oblonsky had gone out she went back to the sofa, where she had been sitting surrounded by the children. Either because the children saw their mother loved this aunt, or because they themselves were aware of some special charm in her, first the two older ones, and then the smaller ones too, as it often is with children, had begun clinging to their new aunt even before dinner and would not leave her. And between them all something like a game sprang up, which consisted in sitting as close as possible to Anna, touching her, holding her little hands, kissing her, playing with her ring, or at least touching the frills of her dress.

"Well, now, how were we sitting before?" Anna said, sitting in her own place again.

And again Grisha slipped his head underneath her arm, leaned it against her dress, and beamed with pride and happiness.

"And now, when is the ball?" she said, turning to Kitty.

"Next week, it's going to be a splendid one. One of those balls that are always gay."

"And are there any that are always gay?" said Anna with tender irony.

"It's strange, but there are. It's always gay at the Bobrishchevs', at the Nikitins' too, while at the Meshkovs' it's always boring. Surely you've noticed it?"

"No, my dear, for me there are no such balls any longer where it's always gay," said Anna, and in her eyes Kitty saw that special world that was closed to her. "For me there are only balls which are less difficult and boring . . ."

"But how can a ball be boring for *you*?"

"But why shouldn't it be boring for *me* at a ball?" asked Anna.

Kitty noticed that Anna knew what the answer to this would be.

"Because you're always prettier than anyone else."

Anna had a capacity for blushing. She blushed and said: "In the first place, that's never so; secondly, even if that were to be so what use would it be to me?"

"Are you going to this ball?" asked Kitty.

"I think it'll be impossible not to. Here, take it," she said to Tanya, who was pulling off a loosely fitting ring from her white, slender, tapering finger.

"I should be very glad if you came. I should so much want to see you at a ball."

"If I have to go at least I'll be consoled by the thought of its giving you some satisfaction . . . Grisha, please don't pull so hard, they're all in a tangle as it is," she said, rearranging a loose lock of hair Grisha was playing with.

"I imagine you at the ball in lilac."

"But why must it be lilac?" asked Anna smiling. "Well, children, run along now, go on. Don't you hear? Miss Hull is calling you to tea," she said, tearing the children away from her and sending them into the dining room.

"But I know why you're asking me to go to this ball. You're expecting a lot from it, and you would like everyone to be there, and everyone to take part in it."

"How do you know? That's right."

"Oh, what a wonderful age you are," Anna went on. "I remember very well that sort of blue mist, like the mist on the Swiss mountains. That mist that envelops everything in that blissful time when childhood is just coming to an end, and out of that vast circle, happy and gay, a path takes shape that keeps getting narrower and narrower, and you go on into this lane gaily and fearfully, even though it looks bright and lovely . . . Who hasn't passed through that?"

Kitty smiled without a word. But how did *she* pass through that? How I long to know all about her romance, thought Kitty, recalling the unpoetical looks of Anna's husband.

"I know something—Stiva's told me, and I congratulate you, I like him very much," Anna went on. "I met Vronsky at the station."

"Oh, was he there?" asked Kitty, reddening. "But what did Stiva tell you?"

"Stiva babbled out everything to me. I should be very happy about it too.

"I made the trip yesterday with Vronsky's mother," she went on, "and she kept talking to me about him without a stop; he's her favorite. I know how biased mothers are, but—"

"But what did his mother tell you?"

"Oh, such a lot! I know he's her favorite, but even so it's obvious how chivalrous he is . . . For instance, she told me he wanted to give up his entire fortune to his brother, and that as a child he did something else that was very unusual, he saved a woman from drowning. In one word—a hero," said Anna, smiling and thinking about the two hundred rubles he had given away at the station.

But she said nothing about the two hundred rubles. For some reason she found it unpleasant to think of. She felt there was something about it that concerned her, the sort of thing it shouldn't have been.

"She insisted that I go to visit her," Anna went on. "I'd be glad to see the old lady, I'm going to see her tomorrow. But thank God, Stiva's been with Dolly in the study a long time," Anna added, changing the subject and getting up, dissatisfied with something, Kitty thought.

"No, I'm first!" "No, me!" the children shouted, rushing to see Aunt Anna, finishing their tea.

"All together!" said Anna, running to meet them with a laugh; she put her arms around this whole cluster of children, struggling and shrieking for joy, and tumbled them on the floor.

## XXI

DOLLY came out of her room for the grownups' tea. Oblonsky did not come out; doubtless he had left his wife's room by the back door.

"I'm afraid you'll be cold upstairs," remarked Dolly to Anna. "I'd like to move you downstairs, we can be closer to each other."

"Oh really, please don't worry about me," Anna replied, scrutinizing Dolly's face to see whether or not there had been a reconciliation.

"There'll be too much light for you here," answered her sister-in-law.

"I assure you I always sleep like a dormouse anywhere."

"What's all this?" Oblonsky asked his wife as he came out of his study.

By his tone both Kitty and Anna knew at once that there had been a reconciliation.

"I want to move Anna downstairs, only the curtains have to be changed. No one else can do it, I'll have to myself," Dolly answered, turning to him.

Heaven only knows whether they're completely reconciled, Anna thought when she heard Dolly's tone, chilly and composed.

"Oh Dolly, come now, always looking for trouble," said Oblonsky. "If you like I'll do the whole thing myself . . ."

Yes, they must have made up, Anna thought.

"I know the way you'll do everything," answered Dolly. "You'll tell Matthew to do something that can't be done and then go out yourself, while he gets everything mixed up." Dolly's usual ironical smile crinkled up the corners of her mouth as she said this.

But they've made up completely, thought Anna, absolutely completely, thank God! and delighted at having been the cause of this she went over to Dolly and kissed her.

"Not in the least, why do you despise Matthew and me so much?" said Oblonsky to his wife, with a slight smile.

The whole evening Dolly was slightly ironical toward her husband, as usual, while Oblonsky was contented and gay, but just enough not to indicate that he had forgotten his guilt now that he was forgiven.

At half-past nine a particularly gay and agreeable family

conversation around the Oblonskys' tea table was spoiled by what seemed to be a perfectly simple incident; for some reason this simple incident seemed peculiar to everyone. In the midst of a chat about common acquaintances in Petersburg, Anna suddenly got up.

"I've got a photo of her in my album," she said. "And while I'm at it I'll show you my Seryozha too," she added with a proud mother's smile.

Toward ten o'clock, when she usually said good night to her son and often tucked him in bed herself before going to a ball, she had grown sad at being so far away from him; and no matter what was being talked about her thoughts kept returning to her curly-headed Seryozha. She longed to look at his picture and talk about him. Taking advantage of the first pretext that came up, she got up and went off for the album with her light, firm step. The flight of steps going up to her room went up off the landing of the big, well-heated front staircase.

As she was going out of the dining room there was a ring at the door.

"Who can that be?" said Dolly.

"It's too early for anyone to come for me, and too late for anyone else," Kitty remarked.

"Must be some office papers," said Oblonsky, and while Anna was crossing the landing on the staircase a footman ran up to announce the new arrival, who was standing under the lamp; looking down, Anna recognized Vronsky instantly, and a peculiar feeling of pleasure mixed with fear suddenly stirred in her heart. He was standing there with his overcoat on, getting something out of his pocket. Just at the moment she was halfway up the top flight he lifted his eyes and saw her; an expression of something like embarrassment and fright passed over his face. She nodded slightly and went on; behind her she heard Oblonsky's loud voice calling him to come in, and Vronsky's low, soft, tranquil voice refusing.

When Anna came back with the album he was already gone, and Oblonsky was saying that he'd driven over to find out about a dinner they were giving the next day to some visiting celebrity.

"And he wouldn't come in for anything. What an odd fellow he is," Oblonsky added.

Kitty blushed. She thought she was the only one who understood why he had called and then not come in. He was at our house, she thought, didn't find me there and thought I'd be here; but he didn't come in because he thought it was too late, and because Anna was here.

They all glanced round at each other without a word, and began looking at Anna's album.

There was nothing either unusual or peculiar about someone calling on a friend at half-past nine to inquire about the details of a projected dinner and then not coming in; but it seemed peculiar to all of them. And to Anna more than anyone it seemed peculiar and not right.

### XXII

THE ball had only just begun when Kitty and her mother started up the broad staircase, flooded with light and decked out with flowers and powdered footmen in red liveries. From the rooms there came a steady hum of movement as from a beehive, and while they were arranging their coiffures and gowns in front of a mirror on the landing between the plants, they could hear the accurate, measured sounds of the violins starting up the first waltz. A little old man in civilian dress and smelling of scents, who was smoothing the gray hair at his temples in front of another mirror, jostled them on the stairs, and stepped aside, obviously admiring Kitty, whom he didn't know. A beardless youth, one of those young society men whom old Prince Shcherbatsky referred to as "whippersnappers," with an unusually low-cut waistcoat, who was adjusting his white tie as he went along, bowed to them, and after hurrying past them turned back and asked Kitty for a quadrille. She had already promised Vronsky the first quadrille, and was bound to give this young man the second. An officer buttoning his glove stood aside for them at the door, and stroking his mustache drank in the sight of the rosy Kitty.

In spite of all the great trouble and thought her toilette, coiffure, and all the preparations for the ball had cost her, Kitty now entered the ballroom in her complicated tulle dress over its pink slip as easily and simply as though all these bows and laces and all the details of her toilette had not cost her and her household a moment's attention, as though she had been born in this tulle and lace, and in the high coiffure with the rose and two leaves on top.

When the old Princess was about to adjust a twisted end of her sash, just before going into the ballroom, Kitty drew back slightly. She felt that everything ought to look beautiful and graceful on her just as it was, and that there was no need to adjust anything at all.

Kitty was having one of her happy days. The dress was not tight anywhere, her lace bodice did not slip, the bows did not crumple or tear off; her pink slippers with their high curved heels did not pinch her little feet, but gladdened them. Her thick braids of fair hair held up on her small head as though they had grown there naturally. All three buttons on each of her long gloves, which did nothing to change the shape of her hands, were fastened and hadn't snapped off. The black velvet ribbon of her locket clung to her throat with special tenderness. This ribbon was delicious; when she was looking at herself in the mirror at home Kitty had felt that the ribbon was actually speaking. There might have been some doubt about everything else, but the ribbon was delicious. Here at the ball too Kitty smiled as she looked at it in the mirror. Her bare shoulders and arms gave her a feeling of chilled marble, a feeling she particularly liked. Her eyes sparkled and her red lips, aware of their own seductiveness, could not help smiling.

She had not had time to enter the room and go over to the throng of ladies, all tulle, ribbons, lace and flowers, who were waiting to be asked to dance—Kitty never stayed long in a crowd like that—before she had been asked for a waltz, and asked by the best partner there, the head of the dancing hierarchy, the celebrated master of ceremonies and ball director, George Korsunsky, a handsome, stately married man. He had just left Countess Bonin, with whom he had danced the first round of waltzes, and looking around at his domain, that is, the handful of couples who had started dancing, he saw Kitty coming in and hurried over to her with that special, free-and-easy amble peculiar to ball directors. He bowed; without asking whether she wanted to he held out his arm to encircle her slender waist. She looked around for someone to hand her fan to, and the hostess, smiling at her, took it.

"How wonderful that you arrived on time," he said putting his arm around her waist. "Such a bad habit, being late."

Bending her left arm she put it on his shoulder, and her little feet in their pink slippers started moving swiftly, lightly, and rhythmically over the slippery floor in time with the music.

"What a relaxation it is to waltz with you," he said to her, sliding into the first, unhurried steps of the waltz. "What bliss —such lightness, such *precision!*" he said to her, as he said to almost everyone he knew well.

She smiled at his praise, and went on looking around the room over his shoulder. She was not a girl coming out the first time, for whom all the faces at a ball fuse together into one impression of enchantment; nor was she a girl who had been dragged from one ball to another until all the faces were so familiar they bored her. She was somewhere in between the two; she was excited, but at the same time she had enough control of herself to be able to keep everything under observation. She saw the cream of society grouped in the left corner of the room. Korsunsky's wife Lida, the beauty, was there, bare to the point of impossibility; the hostess was there; Krivin, bald head radiant, who was always wherever the élite were, was there; youths not bold enough to go over kept looking toward them; there her eyes found Stiva, and then she saw the lovely figure and head of Anna in a black velvet gown. *He* was there, too. Kitty had not seen him since the night she had refused Levin. Kitty's farsighted eyes recognized him immediately; she even noticed that he was looking at her.

"What about another round? You're not tired?" said Korsunsky, puffing slightly.

"No, thank you."

"Where shall I bring you?"

"I think Madame Karenin's over there . . . take me to her."

"Wherever you say."

And Korsunsky waltzed off directly toward the throng in the left corner of the room, slowing down and repeating *"Pardon, mesdames, pardon, pardon, mesdames,"* tacking about in the sea of lace, tulle, and ribbons; and without touching a feather, he turned Kitty round so sharply that her slender ankles in their openwork stockings were exposed as her train spread out like a fan and covered Krivin's knees. Korsunsky bowed, squared his open shirt front, and held his arm out to take Kitty over to Anna. Kitty flushed and took her train off Krivin's knees; a little dizzy, she looked around in search of Anna. Anna was not in lilac, which Kitty had set her heart on, but in a black, low-cut velvet dress that showed off her full shoulders and bosom, which looked carved out of old ivory, her rounded arms and tiny slender hands. Her dress was completely trimmed in

Venetian lace. In her black hair, all her own, she wore a small garland of pansies, which were also in the black band of her sash, among the white lace. Her coiffure did not catch the eye; the only thing noticeable about it were the willful little tendrils of curly hair that always escaped at her temples and the nape of her neck, and added to her beauty. There was a string of pearls around her sturdy, chiseled neck.

Kitty had been seeing Anna every day, was in love with her, and invariably imagined her in lilac. But now, when she saw her in black, she felt she had never realized her full charm before. She saw her now as something completely new and unexpected. Now she realized that Anna could never be in lilac, and that her charm consisted of just that—she always stood out from her dress; it was never conspicuous. The black dress with its rich lace was also unnoticeable on her: it was merely a frame, what was visible was only herself, simple, natural, elegant, and at the same time gay and full of life.

She held herself very erect as usual; she was talking to the host, with her head turned toward him slightly, when Kitty came over to the group.

"No, I shan't be the one to throw the first stone," she was saying in answer to something he had said. "Although I don't understand it," she went on, shrugging her shoulders; then with a tender protecting smile she turned at once to Kitty. Taking in her dress with a swift feminine glance, she made a motion with her head, scarcely perceptible but understood by Kitty, in approval of her dress and her beauty.

"You even come dancing into the room," she said.

"She's one of my most faithful assistants," said Korsunsky, bowing to Anna, whom he had not yet seen. "The Princess is a great help in making a ball gay and beautiful. A waltz, Madame?" he said, bending toward Anna.

"Oh, d'you know each other?" asked the host.

"Whom do we not know? My wife and I are like white wolves, everyone knows us," Korsunsky replied. "A waltz, Madame?" he said again.

"I don't dance, whenever it's possible not to," Anna said.

"Tonight it's not possible," Korsunsky answered.

Just then Vronsky came over.

"Well then, if it's impossible not to dance tonight, let us be off," she said, disregarding Vronsky's bow and quickly putting her hand on Korsunsky's shoulder.

Why is she so annoyed with him, thought Kitty, who had noticed Anna's intentional disregard of Vronsky's bow. Vronsky came over to Kitty: he reminded her that he had the first quadrille and regretted not having had the pleasure of seeing her for such a long time. Kitty, full of admiration, watched Anna waltzing while she listened to him. She was expecting him to ask her for a waltz, but he did not: she glanced at him in surprise. He flushed and hurriedly asked her to waltz, but he had no sooner put his arm around her slender waist and taken the first step when the music suddenly stopped. Kitty looked at his face, which was so close to her, and for a long time afterward, for several years, that look full of love that she gave him then and that he did not respond to, cut her to the heart in an agony of shame.

"*Pardon! Pardon!* A waltz, a waltz!" Korsunsky called out from the other side of the room; seizing the first girl within reach he started dancing himself.

## XXIII

VRONSKY and Kitty waltzed around the room several times. After the waltz Kitty went over to her mother, and had scarcely enough time to say a few words to Countess Nordston before Vronsky followed her for the first quadrille. During the quadrille nothing important was said; there was a spasmodic conversation first about the Korsunskys, husband and wife, whom he described very entertainingly as sweet forty-year-old children, then about a projected public theater; only once did the conversation touch her to the quick—when he asked about Levin, whether he was there, and added that he liked him very much. But Kitty did not really expect any more from the quadrille. What she was waiting for, her heart sinking, was the mazurka. It seemed to her that the mazurka ought to settle everything. His not asking her for the mazurka during the quadrille did not alarm her; she was sure she was going to dance the mazurka with him, as she had at previous balls, and she refused five other partners by saying she was already taken. For Kitty, until the final quadrille, the whole ball was a magic dream of joyous flowers, sounds, and movements. She only stopped dancing when she felt too tired and asked for a rest.

But as she was dancing the final quadrille with one of the boring young men it was impossible to refuse, she happened to find herself facing Vronsky and Anna. She had not been together with Anna since the very beginning; now she suddenly saw her again, this time in a new and unexpected light. She saw in her the elation with success she knew so well. She saw that Anna was drunk with the wine of the rapture she had aroused. Kitty knew this feeling and knew its signs, and she saw them in Anna—the quivering light flashing in her eyes, the smile of happiness and elation that curled her lips involuntarily, and the graceful precision, accuracy and lightness of her movements.

But who is it? Kitty asked herself: everyone—or just one? Without giving any help to the distressed young man she was dancing with, who had lost the thread of the conversation and couldn't pick it up again, and seemingly under the spell of the merry, resounding, peremptory cries of Korsunsky, who first ordered everyone to form a *grand rond*, then a *chaîne*, she kept watching, and her heart sank more and more.

No, she thought, it's not the admiration of the crowd that's gone to her head, it's the enthusiasm of one man— but who is he? Surely *he's* not the one?

Every time Vronsky spoke to Anna a joyous light flared up in her eyes, and a smile of pleasure curved her red lips. She seemed to be making an effort to hide these signs of joy, but they passed over her face of their own accord. Kitty looked at him in horror: But what's happening to *him*? What Kitty saw so clearly in the mirror of Anna's face she saw in him too. What had become of his unchangeably calm, firm manner, and the calm nonchalance of his expression? No— now, whenever he spoke to her he bowed his head a little as though he wanted to fall down in front of her; in his eyes there was nothing but an expression of submission and terror. "I don't wish to be offensive," that expression seemed to keep saying, "but I want to save myself and I don't know how." There was a look on his face Kitty had never seen before.

They were talking about people they both knew, and carrying on the most trivial conversation, but it seemed to Kitty that every word they said was decisive for their fate and hers. What was strange was that even though they really were speaking about how ridiculous Ivan Ivanovich was with his French accent, or whether a better match might be found for the Eletsky girl, nevertheless these words meant something to them, which they felt just as Kitty did. The entire ball, the entire world—everything was overlaid by a mist in Kitty's heart. Only the strict school of training she had gone through propped her up and forced her to do what was required of her, that is, dance, answer questions, talk, and even smile. But before the mazurka began, when chairs were already being set out for it and several couples had moved from the small to the large ballroom, a moment of despair and terror laid hold of her. She had refused five men who had asked for the mazurka, and now she was not in it. There was not even a hope of her being asked, just because she had had too great a success and it could never have entered anyone's head that she had not already been asked. She ought to have told her mother she was feeling ill and then gone home, but she lacked the strength. She felt shattered.

She went off to the far end of the small drawing room and sank into an easy chair. Her airy skirts stood out like a cloud from her slender figure; one thin, bare, delicate girlish arm dropped nervelessly and was lost in the pink folds of her tunic; the other held a fan with which, with rapid, short strokes, she fanned her glowing face. But though she looked like a butterfly that had just settled on a blade of grass and was about to flutter off at any moment and spread its rainbow wings, her heart was crushed by a frightful despair.

But I may be wrong, perhaps it wasn't that way. And again she recalled everything she had seen.

"Kitty, what does this mean?" said Countess Nordston, coming over on the carpet to her soundlessly. "I don't understand."

Kitty's lower lip quivered; she got up quickly.

"Kitty, aren't you dancing the mazurka?"

"No—no," said Kitty, her voice tremulous with tears.

"He asked her for the mazurka in front of me," said Countess Nordston, knowing Kitty would understand who "he" and "she" were. "She said, 'Aren't you dancing with Princess Shcherbatsky?' "

"Oh! It's all the same to me!" Kitty replied.

No one but herself understood her position, no one knew that she had just refused a man whom she may have loved, and refused him because she had trusted another.

Countess Nordston found Korsunsky, whom she was to dance the mazurka with, and told him to ask Kitty instead.

Kitty danced in the first pair; luckily for her she did not have to speak, since Korsunsky kept running back and forth managing his domain. Vronsky and Anna were sitting almost opposite her. She saw them with her farsighted eye and she saw them close by as well, when they met in the figures; the more she saw them the more she was convinced that her unhappiness was complete. She saw that in this crowded room they felt by themselves. And on Vronsky's face, which was always so resolute and self-possessed, she saw that expression of bewilderment and submission which had startled her, an expression like that of an intelligent dog when it feels guilty.

Anna smiled, and the smile passed on to him. She became thoughtful, and he turned serious. Some supernatural force drew Kitty's eyes to Anna's face. In her simple black gown Anna was enchanting; enchanting were her full arms with their bracelets, enchanting her strong neck with its pearl necklace, enchanting the straying curls of her loose hair, enchanting the graceful light movements of her small feet and hands, enchanting her beautiful, animated face: but there was something terrifying and cruel in her enchantment.

Kitty admired her even more than before, and suffered more and more. Kitty felt crushed, and her face showed it. When Vronsky came across her in the course of the mazurka he did not recognize her at first—she had changed so much.

"What a splendid ball!" he said to her, just to say something.

"Yes," she replied.

In the middle of the mazurka, as they were repeating a complicated figure newly invented by Korsunsky, Anna went out into the center of the circle, chose two men, and summoned Kitty and another woman to join her. As Kitty went over to her she looked at her with fright. Half-closing her eyes Anna looked at her and smiled, squeezing her hand. But when she saw that Kitty responded to her smile only with an expression of despair and astonishment, she turned away from her and began talking cheerfully to the other woman.

Yes—there is something strange, devilish, and enchanting about her, thought Kitty.

Anna did not wish to stay on to supper, but the host tried to persuade her.

"Come, Madame," Korsunsky began, drawing her bare arm under his sleeve. "What an idea I have for a cotillion—*un bijou!*"

He moved forward a little, trying to draw her along. The host smiled approvingly.

"No, I'm not staying," Anna answered smilingly; but in

spite of her smile both Korsunsky and the host understood by the resolute tone of her answer that she was not staying.

"No, even as it is I've done more dancing in Moscow, at this one ball of yours, than I have the whole winter in Petersburg," said Anna, glancing round at Vronsky, who was standing next to her. "I must rest before my journey."

"And are you definitely leaving tomorrow?" Vronsky asked.

"Yes, I think so," Anna answered, as though surprised by the boldness of his question; but the irrepressible, shimmering brilliance of her eyes and smile inflamed him as she said this.

She did not stay to supper, but went off.

## XXIV

YES, there is something in me that's loathsome and repellent, thought Levin, leaving the Shcherbatskys' and setting off for his brother's on foot. I don't fit in with other people. Pride, they call it. But I'm not even proud. If it were a matter of pride I should never have put myself in such a position.

He imagined to himself Vronsky—happy, kindhearted, intelligent, and serene, who had surely never been in the terrible position Levin had been in that evening.

Yes, she was bound to choose him; it had to be that way, and I have no reason to complain of anyone or anything. It's my own fault. What right did I have to think she would want to unite her life with mine? Who am I? And what am I? An insignificant fellow wanted by no one and of no use to anyone.

He recalled his brother Nicholas, and dwelt on the recollection happily.

"Isn't he right, that everything in the world is evil and base? We've hardly judged Nicholas fairly. Of course from the point of view of Prokofy, who saw him in a ragged coat and drunk, he's contemptible; but I know him differently. I know his soul, I know we resemble each other. And instead of going off to look for him, I went out to dinner, and went there.

Levin went over to a lamppost, read his brother's address, which he had in his wallet, and hailed a sleigh. All the long way to his brother's Levin vividly called to mind everything he knew about what had happened to Nicholas. He recalled how his brother, at the university and for a year afterward, in spite of the mockery of his friends, lived like a monk, strictly observing all the religious rites, attending services, fasting, and avoiding any pleasures, especially women; then, when he suddenly broke loose, he had become intimate with the vilest people and sank into the wildest debauchery. Then he recalled the story of the little boy his brother had brought from the country to educate, and whom, in a fit of rage, he had beaten so badly that he was brought up on charges of mayhem. Then he recalled the story of a sharper his brother had lost money to, given a promissory note and then prosecuted on a claim of fraud. (That was the money Koznyshov had paid.) Then he recalled the night Nicholas had spent in jail for disorderly conduct. He remembered the scandalous suit he had begun against their brother Koznyshov, whom he had accused of not paying him his share of their mother's estate; and finally, the time he left for a post in one of the western provinces and had been brought to court there for assaulting a village Elder . . . All this was terribly disgusting, but to Levin it did not seem at all so base as it must seem to those who did not know Nicholas Levin, did not know his whole story, or what was in his heart.

Levin recalled that during the time Nicholas had been in a period of piety, fasting, visiting monks, and going to church, when he was seeking in religion some help to bridle his passionate nature, not only did no one give him any support, but everyone, including himself, laughed at him. He was teased, called "Noah," and "the Monk"; when he broke loose no one helped him, but everyone turned aside in horror and disgust.

Levin felt that his brother Nicholas at heart, in the very depths of his soul, in spite of all the depravity of his life, was no more in the wrong than those who despised him. He was not to blame for having been born with his uncontrollable temperament, and a kink in his mind. He had always wanted to be good.

I'll tell him everything, I'll make him tell me everything, and I'll show him I love him and that's why I understand him, Levin decided, as he drove up at eleven o'clock to the hotel shown by the address.

"Upstairs, twelve and thirteen," the hall porter replied to Levin's question.

"Is he there?"

"Must be."

The door to Room 12 was half-open, and from within, in a streak of light, dense fumes of bad, weak tobacco came out; Levin heard some voice he didn't know, but he knew at once his brother was there; he could hear his cough.

As he went through the doorway the unknown voice was saying: "It all depends on how intelligently and rationally the affair is managed."

Levin glanced into the room and saw that the speaker was a young man with a huge shock of hair, in a workman's coat, and that a young, pock-marked woman in a woollen dress without collar or cuffs was sitting on a sofa. He couldn't see his brother. It gave Levin a pang of distress to think of his brother living in the midst of such strangers. No one had heard Levin, who, taking off his galoshes, could over-hear what the man in the workman's jacket was saying. He was talking about some business enterprise.

"Oh, devil take the privileged classes!" said his brother's voice, with a cough. "Masha! Get us some supper; bring some wine if there's any left, if not send for some."

The young woman got up, came out from behind the partition in the room, and saw Levin.

"There's some gentleman here, Mr. Nicholas," she said.

"Whom d'you want?" said Nicholas Levin's voice angrily.

"It's me," said Levin, coming forward into the light.

"Who's me?" Nicholas's voice repeated still more angrily. Levin could hear him getting up quickly and catching against something; then in the doorway in front of him he saw the gigantic, thin, stooping figure of his brother, with his great frightening eyes, so familiar but always so startling because of his weirdness and sickliness.

He was even thinner than he had been three years before, the last time Levin had seen him. He was wearing a short coat; his hands and broad bones seemed even more immense; his hair had become thinner; the same straight mustaches drooped from his lips and the same eyes gazed strangely and naïvely at Levin.

"Ah—Kostya!" he said suddenly, as he recognized his brother, and his eyes lit up with joy. But at this very moment he looked round at the young man and made a convulsive movement with his head and neck that was so familiar to Levin, as though his necktie were strangling him, and an utterly different look, wild, tormented, and cruel, settled on his haggard face.

"I wrote both you and Sergius that I don't know you and don't want to. What is it? What d'you want?"

He was completely different from the way Levin had imagined him. The worst part of his character, and the most oppressive, which made all relations with him so difficult, had been forgotten by Levin when he thought of him. Now, when he saw his face, and especially that convulsive movement of his head, he remembered it all.

"I didn't want to see you for any particular reason," he answered meekly, "I simply came to see you."

His brother's meekness plainly softened Nicholas; his lips quivered.

"Oh, is that it?" he said. "Well, come in and sit down. D'you want some supper? Masha, get supper for three. No— wait a moment. D'you know who this is?" he said, turning to his brother and indicating the young man in the workman's jacket. "This is Mr. Kritsky, a friend of mine ever since Kiev, a most remarkable fellow. The police are after him, of course, since he's not a scoundrel."

And he glanced around at everyone in the room in his usual way. When he saw that the woman, standing in the doorway, was about to go out he shouted at her: "Wait a minute, I said." And with the incoherence and inability to express himself that Levin knew so well, glancing around again at everyone, he began telling his brother Kritsky's story: how he had been expelled from the university for starting a society to help destitute students, and also Sunday schools, how he had later become a teacher in an elementary school, and then been expelled from that, and how he had been tried afterward on some charge or other.

"Were you at Kiev University?" said Levin to Kritsky, in order to break the awkward silence that followed.

"Yes, I was there," Kritsky said with an angry frown.

"And this woman," Nicholas Levin interrupted him with a nod at her, "is my life's companion, Masha Nikolayevna. I took her out of a whorehouse"—his neck jerked as he said this—"but I love and respect her, and I beg all those who wish to know me," he added, raising his voice and scowling, "to love and respect her too. She's exactly the same as my wife, exactly the same. So now you know whom you have to deal with. And if you think you're lowering yourself— well, here's the floor and there's the door."

And again his eyes glanced round questioningly at everyone.

"But why should I be lowering myself? I don't understand," said Levin.

"So go get the dinner, Masha: three portions, some vodka and wine . . . No, wait a minute . . . No, never mind . . . Go on."

## XXV

So you see," Nicholas Levin went on, painfully wrinkling his forehead and twitching. It was evidently difficult for him to think of what to say and do. "There, you see—" He indicated a bundle of iron rods tied together with string in a corner of the room. "D'you see that? That's the beginning of a new business we're going into. It's going to be a Productive Association . . ."

Levin scarcely listened. He kept looking into his brother's sickly, consumptive face, and felt more and more sorry for him; he could not force himself to listen to what his brother was telling him about the Association. He saw that it was simply an anchor to save him from despising himself. Nicholas went on speaking:

"You know that capital has oppressed the workers. Our workers, the peasants, bear the whole burden of labor, and they're so situated that no matter how hard they work they cannot get out of their bestial condition. All the profits on their labor, by which they might improve their situation, get some leisure and thus some education, all this surplus value is taken away from them by the capitalists. Society is set up in such a way that the more they work the richer the merchants and landowners will become, while they remain beasts of burden forever. This system must be changed," he concluded, looking at his brother questioningly.

"Yes, of course," said Levin, looking at the flush that had come over his brother's prominent cheekbones.

"So we're starting a Locksmiths' Association, where everything produced, the profits and instruments of production as well, everything, will belong to everyone."

"Where is the business going to be?" asked Levin.

"In the village of Vozdrema, Kazan Province."

"But why in a village? It seems to me there's a lot of work in the country as it is. Why have a Locksmiths' Association in a village?"

"Because the peasants are slaves now just as they've always been, and that's why you and Sergius don't like it when anyone tries to take them out of their slavery," said Nicholas, irritated by the objection.

Levin sighed as he looked round the gloomy, filthy room. This sigh seemed to annoy Nicholas still more.

"I know the aristocratic views you and Serguis have. I know that he uses all the force of his mind to justify the existing evils."

"But why are you talking about Sergius?" said Levin with a smile.

"Sergius? This is why!" Nicholas suddenly shouted at the mention of Sergius' name. "This is why—but what's the use of talking? There's just one thing—why did you come to see me? You despise the whole thing, very well then, just be off with you, be off!" he shouted. "Go away! Go away!"

"I don't despise anything in the least," said Levin meekly. "I'm not even arguing about it."

Just then Masha came back. Nicholas looked around at her angrily. She hurried over to him and whispered something.

"I'm not well, I've grown irritable," said Nicholas, breathing heavily and calming down. "Then you talk to me about Sergius and his article. It's such nonsense, such a fraud, such self-deception! What can a man write about justice who doesn't know anything about it? Have you read his article?" he said to Kritsky, sitting down again at the table and clearing away some half-filled cigarettes to make room.

"No," said Kritsky morosely; he was obviously reluctant to enter into any conversation.

"Why not?" said Nicholas irritably, now turning on Kritsky.

"Because I don't think it necessary to waste any time on it."

"What d'you mean? Just how d'you know you'd be wasting time? The article is too deep for a great many people, it's beyond them. It's different for me, I can see through the way he thinks and I know why it's weak."

They all fell silent. Kritsky slowly got up and reached for his cap.

"Won't you stay to supper? Good-by then. When you come tomorrow bring the locksmith."

As soon as Kritsky had left Nicholas smiled and winked.

"He's no good either," he remarked. "You know I can see—"

Just then Kritsky called to him from the doorway.

"What d'you want now?" said Nicholas and went out into the corridor.

When he was left alone with Masha, Levin said to her, "Have you been with my brother a long time?"

"It's two years already. His health has turned very bad. He drinks a lot," she said.

"What does he drink?"

"Vodka; it's bad for him."

"A lot?" Levin whispered.

"Yes," she said, timidly looking at the door just as Nicholas appeared.

"What were you talking about?" he said, scowling and shifting his frightened eyes from one to the other. "What about?"

"Not about anything," Levin replied, embarrassed.

"If you don't feel like telling me, don't. But you have no business talking to her. She's a tart and you're a gentleman," he muttered, jerking his neck.

"I can see you've understood and weighed everything, and have a compassionate attitude toward my errors," he continued, raising his voice.

"Mr. Nicholas, Mr. Nicholas," Masha whispered again, coming close to him.

"Very well! Very well! And what about supper? Ah, there it is," he said, as a waiter came in with a tray. "Here, put it here," he said angrily; he seized the vodka at once, filled a glass and gulped it down greedily. "Have some, will you?" he said to Levin, cheering up at once.

"Well, enough about Sergius. I'm very happy to see you anyhow. When all's said and done we're not strangers. Go on, have a drink. Tell me, what are you doing?" Nicholas went on, greedily munching a piece of bread and pouring out another glass. "How are you living?"

"I live alone in the country, as I used to, looking after the farming," Levin replied, watching with horror his brother's greediness as he ate and drank, and trying to hide his noticing it.

"Why don't you get married?"

"It hasn't turned out that way," Levin answered, flushing.

"Why not? For me all that is over with! I've ruined my life. I've said it before, and I say it again, that if I had been given my share of the property when I needed it my whole life would have been different."

Levin hastened to change the subject. "Did you know that your little Vanya is now a clerk in my office at Pokrovsk?"

Nicholas jerked his head and grew thoughtful.

"Yes—tell me what's happening at Pokrovsk. Is the house still there, and the birch trees, and our schoolroom? And the gardener, Philip, can he still be alive? How well I remember the gardenhouse, with the sofa! Now mind you don't change anything in the house, just get married soon and set things going again as they used to be. Then I'll come and see you, if your wife is nice."

"But come to stay with me now," said Levin. "What a fine life we'd have there!"

"I would come to you if I knew I wouldn't find Sergius there."

"He won't be there. I live completely independently of him."

"Yes, but no matter what you say you'll have to choose between him and me," said Nicholas, looking shyly into his brother's eyes. This shyness moved Levin.

"If you want to know what I really think about that, I'll tell you—in your quarrel with Sergius I'm not on either your side or his. You're both wrong. You're more in the wrong outwardly, while he is more wrong inwardly."

"Ah! Ah! So you understood that, you understood it?" Nicholas cried out joyfully.

"But personally, if you want to know, I value my friendship with you more, because —"

"Why, because of what?"

Levin couldn't say he valued it because Nicholas was unhappy and needed friendship. But Nicholas realized that that was just what he had meant to say and, frowning, he reached for the vodka again.

"Enough, Mr. Nicholas!" said Masha, stretching out her plump, bare arm toward the bottle.

"Let go! Don't bother me! I'll give you a beating!" he shouted.

Masha gave a shy, kindly smile, which Nicholas responded to, and she took the vodka.

"And d'you think she doesn't understand anything?" said Nicholas. "She understands all this better than any of us. You see there really is something good and sweet about her."

"Have you been to Moscow before?" said Levin to her, for the sake of saying something.

"Don't speak to her so politely. That's what she's afraid of. No one ever spoke to her so politely except the magistrate when she was on trial for attempting to escape from the brothel. God, what madness there is in the world!" he suddenly exclaimed. "All these new institutions, these magistrates, these District Councils—it's all so grotesque!"

And he began talking about his collisions with the new institutions.

Levin listened to him; the condemnation of all social institutions, which he shared with him and often expressed himself, was unpleasant for him to hear now from his brother's mouth.

"In the next world we'll understand it all," he said jokingly.

"The next world? Oh, I dislike the next world, I dislike it!" said Nicholas, fixing his wild, frightened eyes on his brother's face. "Though after all I suppose that leaving all this vileness and confusion, one's own as well as other people's, would be a good thing, but I'm afraid of death, I'm terribly afraid of death." He shuddered. "But have something to drink. D'you want some champagne? Or let's go out somewhere. Let's go to the gypsies! You know I've gotten very fond of the gypsies and of Russian folk songs."

His speech got twisted; he began jumping from one subject to another. With Masha's help Levin talked him out of going anywhere and put him to bed completely drunk.

Masha promised to write Levin if necessary, and to try to persuade Nicholas to go and live with him.

## XXVI

THE next morning Levin left Moscow and arrived home toward evening. In the train on the way he discussed politics and the new railroads with his neighbors, and just as in Moscow he was distressed by his confusion of ideas, by a dissatisfaction with himself, and by a vague sense of shame about something or other. But when he got out at his station, and recognized his one-eyed coachman Ignat, with his coat collar turned up, and when he saw his rug-covered sleigh in the dim light from the station window, and his horses with their plaited tails, and their harness with its rings and tassels, and when Ignat, while putting everything away told him the local news—how the contractor had come, and how Pava had had a calf—he felt his confusion clearing up a little, and his shame and dissatisfaction with himself passing away. He felt this at the mere sight of Ignat and the horses; but when he put on the sheepskin coat that had been brought for him, and sat down well wrapped up in the sleigh and started off turning over in his mind the instructions to be given about the estate and watching the side horse, a former saddle horse from the Don, used up but still spirited, he began to understand what had been happening to him in a completely different way. He felt he was himself again and had no desire to be any different. Now he only wanted to be better than he had been before. First of all he decided that from that day on he would no longer set his hopes on the extraordinary happiness that marriage was to have given him, and therefore would not belittle the present so much. Secondly, he would never permit himself to be carried away by base passion, the recollection of which had tormented him so when he had been making up his mind to propose. Then, recalling his brother Nicholas, he determined that he would never again allow himself to forget him, but would keep track of and watch out for him so as to be ready to help if he was having a hard time. That, he felt, was going to come soon. Then his brother's talk about communism, which he had treated so lightly at the time, now made him reflect. He thought a complete transformation of economic conditions was nonsense, but he had always felt the injustice of his own abundance in comparison with the misery of the people, and now he determined that in order to feel himself completely in the right, even though he had always worked hard and lived frugally, he would now work still harder and allow himself even less luxury. And all this seemed to him so easy to carry out that he spent the whole trip in the most agreeable reverie. Toward nine o'clock in the evening he reached his house, with a robust feeling of hope for a new and better life.

A light from the windows of the room of his old nurse Miss Agatha, who acted as his housekeeper, fell on the snow-covered space in front of the house. She had not yet gone to sleep. Kuzma, whom she had woken up, ran out onto the porch, barefoot and sleepy. Laska, a setter bitch, came bounding out too, almost knocking Kuzma off his feet;

she whined, rubbed up against Levin's knees, and jumped up, longing to put her front paws on his chest but not daring to.

"Well, you didn't stay away long," said Miss Agatha.

"I got tired of it, Miss Agatha. It's all very well to go visiting, but home is better," he answered, and went to his study.

The study was gradually lighted up by a candle that was brought in. The familiar details emerged: the stag's antlers, the bookshelves, the mirror, the stove with its ventilator, long since in need of repair, his father's sofa, the large table with an open book on it, a broken ash tray, and a note-book in his own handwriting. When he saw all this a moment of doubt came over him about the possibility of arranging the new life he had been dreaming about on the way. All these traces of his life seemed to seize hold of him and say: "No, you won't escape from us and you won't be any different, you'll be just as you've always been: full of doubts, perpetually dissatisfied with yourself, with futile attempts at self-improvement followed by lapses, and in constant expectation of the happiness which hasn't been given you and is out of the question for you."

This was what all his belongings said, but there was another voice in his heart that said that there was no need to surrender to the past and that it was possible to do anything you wanted with yourself. And in obedience to this voice he went to the corner and began exercising with the two thirty-six pound dumbbells there, trying to make himself feel vigorous. Footsteps creaked outside the door, and he hastily put down the dumbbells.

His foreman came in and said everything was all right, thank God, but reported that the buckwheat in the new drying kiln had been burned. Levin was irritated by the news. The new drying kiln had been built and partly invented by him. The foreman had always been against it, and was now reporting the burned buckwheat with concealed triumph. But Levin was firmly convinced that if it had been burned it was only because the instructions he had given hundreds of times had not been carried out. He was vexed, and rebuked the foreman. But there was one important and joyful event: Pava, his best and most expensive cow, bought at the cattle show, had had a calf.

"Kuzma, get my sheepskin. And tell them to bring a lantern, I'll go take a look," he said to the foreman.

The stalls for the most expensive cattle were just behind the house. Crossing the yard past the pile of snow near the lilac bush he went over to the cattle shed. There was a warm, steamy smell of dung when the frozen door was opened, and the cows, startled by the unaccustomed light of the lantern, began moving about on the fresh straw. The broad, smooth, black-and-white back of a Frisian cow glistened. The bull, Berkut, was lying down with a ring through his nose; he was about to get up but thought better of it and only snorted a couple of times as they passed by. Pava, a red beauty huge as a hippopotamus had turned her back; she was hiding her calf from the visitors and sniffing it.

Levin went into the stall, examined Pava and raised the red-speckled calf on to its long, tottery legs. Pava got excited and was about to moo, but calmed down when Levin moved the calf toward her; she sighed heavily and began licking it with her rough tongue. The calf, fumbling about, pushed its nose under its mother's belly and flicked its little tail.

"Here, Theodore, get some light over here, bring the lantern," said Levin, examining the calf. "Like the mother! Takes after the father in color, but that doesn't matter. Very fine. Big bones and deep flanks. Well, Vasili, isn't she fine?" he said to the foreman, completely reconciled about the buckwheat by his joy over the calf.

"What could have made her turn out bad? Oh, the contractor Simon came the day after you left. We'll have to settle with him, Mr. Constantine," said the foreman. "I told you before about the machine."

This one question led Levin back into all the details of the estate, which was a big and complicated one, and he went directly from the cattle shed to his office; after a talk with the foreman and with Simon the contractor he returned to the house and went straight upstairs to the drawing room.

## XXVII

The house was big and old-fashioned, and though Levin lived there alone he used and heated the whole of it. He knew this was foolish, and even wrong and contrary to his present new plans, but the house was an entire world for him. It was the world his father and mother had lived and died in. They had lived the life that seemed to Levin the ideal of all perfection, and that he dreamed of renewing together with his own wife and his own family.

Levin scarcely recalled his mother. The thought of her was a sacred memory; in his imagination his future wife had to be a repetition of the enchanting, holy ideal of womanhood that his mother had been for him.

Not only could he not imagine love for a woman outside of marriage, but what he imagined to himself first of all was a family, and only then the woman who was to give him that family. Consequently his ideas about marriage did not resemble those of most of the people he knew, for whom marriage was just one of the many things in life; for Levin it was the chief thing in life, on which all happiness depended. And now he had to renounce it!

When he went into the small drawing room where he always had tea, and settled in his armchair with a book while Miss Agatha brought his tea in with her usual "And now I'll sit down too, Mr. Constantine," and sat down on a chair near the window, he felt that however strange it might be he had not abandoned his dreams, and that without them he would be unable to go on living. Either with her or with someone else—that was what would happen. He read his book, thought over what he was reading, pausing to listen to Miss Agatha, who chattered on tirelessly; meanwhile different images associated with farming and his future family life passed disconnectedly through his mind. He felt that in the depths of his soul something was settling down, adjusting and arranging itself.

He listened to Miss Agatha's talk about how Prokhor had forgotten the Lord and spent on drink all the money Levin had given him to buy a horse with, and had almost beaten his wife to death; he listened and read his book, and recalled the whole stream of ideas evoked by what he was reading. It was a book by Tyndall on heat. He recalled his own condemnation of Tyndall for his self-satisfaction about the cleverness he had performed his experiments with, and his lack of philosophic outlook. Then suddenly a joyful thought floated to the surface; two years from now I'll have two Frisian cows in the herd, Pava herself may still be alive, there'll be three young cows by Berkut, and three others to top it all off—how wonderful! He took up the book again.

Very well then, electricity and heat are the same thing; but can one quantity be substituted for the other to solve an equation? No. Then what follows? The connection between all natural forces can be felt instinctively as it is . . . It'll be specially pleasant when Pava's calf is already a red-speckled cow, and the whole herd, topped off by these three . . .

Wonderful! I'll be going out with my wife and with some guests to have a look at the herd . . . My wife will say: "Kostya and I reared this calf like a baby." Then a guest will say: "But how can all this interest you so much?" "Everything that interests him interests me . . ."

But who will she be? And he recalled what had happened in Moscow . . . Though what can I do about it? It's not my fault. But now everything's going to be different. That's all nonsense about life preventing it, or the past preventing it. You have to struggle to lead a better life, a far better life . . .

He raised his head and sank into thought. Old Laska, who had not yet quite digested her joy at his return and had run out to the yard to bark, came back wagging her tail, bringing with her a smell of fresh air; she came over to him and thrust her head beneath his hand, whining plaintively and begging to be patted.

"The only thing she can't do is talk," said Miss Agatha. "A dog—after all she understands that her master's come back and is feeling depressed."

"Why depressed?"

"But don't you think I can see, Mr. Constantine? It's high time I knew how gentry are; I've grown up among them since I was a child. Never mind, Mr. Constantine; as long as you stay in good health and have a clear conscience."

Levin looked at her intently, surprised at her having understood what was on his mind.

"Should I bring a little more tea?" she said, and went out with the cup.

Laska kept thrusting her head beneath his hand. He stroked her and she curled up at his feet immediately with her head on her outstretched hind paw. And as a sign that now everything was all right and satisfactory she opened her mouth slightly, smacked her sticky lips and settling them around her old teeth lay still in blissful peace. Levin carefully followed this last movement of hers.

That's just how I am too! he said to himself, just the same! Never mind, everything's all right.


### XXVIII

EARLY the next morning after the ball Anna sent her husband a telegram to say she was leaving Moscow the same day.

"No, I must, I really must leave," she said to Dolly, explaining her change of plans in a tone that implied she had recalled so many things she had to do that they couldn't even be enumerated. "It would really be best if I left today!"

Oblonsky was not dining at home, but promised to come by at seven to see her off.

Kitty had not come either, but had sent a note to say she had a headache. Dolly and Anna had dinner alone with the children and the English governess. Whether the children were fickle, or whether they were very sensitive and felt that Anna was not the same that day as she had been when they had fallen so much in love with her, and that she no longer took an interest in them, at any rate they suddenly cut short their games with their aunt and their love for her, and were completely unconcerned by her departure. Anna was busy all morning with preparations for the trip. She wrote notes to her Moscow acquaintances, made up her accounts, and packed. It seemed to Dolly that altogether Anna was not at ease, but was in that mood of anxiety that Dolly knew so well, which does not seize one without a cause and for the most part hides discontent with oneself. After dinner Anna went to her room to change; Dolly followed her.

"How odd you are today!" Dolly said.

"I? D'you think so? I'm not odd, I just feel nasty. That happens to me sometimes. I keep wanting to weep. It's all very silly, but it will go away," Anna said quickly, and she thrust her flushed face into a tiny bag she was packing a nightcap and some cambric handkerchiefs into. Her eyes shone peculiarly and kept filling with tears. "When I left Petersburg I didn't feel like it, and now it's the same leaving here."

"You came here and did a good deed," said Dolly, watching her attentively.

Anna, her eyes moist with tears, looked at her.

"Don't say that, Dolly, I did nothing, there was nothing I could do. I often wonder why people conspire to spoil me. What did I do, and what could I have done? It was you who found enough love in your heart to forgive—"

"Heaven knows what would have happened if it weren't for you! How lucky you are, Anna!" said Dolly. "Your heart is so clear and good."

"Everyone has skeletons of his own in the cupboard, as the English say."

"But what skeletons do you have? Everything about you is so clear."

"But I do have!" Anna said suddenly, and unexpectedly, following her tears, a sly, ironical smile puckered her lips.

"Well, at least they're amusing, your skeletons, not depressing," said Dolly, smiling.

"No, they're depressing. D'you know why I'm leaving today and not tomorrow? I want to confess something to you, something that's been weighing on me," said Anna, resolutely throwing herself back into an armchair and looking straight into Dolly's eyes.

To her astonishment Dolly saw that Anna had flushed up to her ears and the curly black locks on the nape of her neck.

"Yes," Anna continued. "D'you know why Kitty didn't come to dinner? She's jealous of me. I've spoiled—I was the reason the ball was an agony to her, and not a joy. But really, really, I wasn't to blame, or at least not very much," she said, drawling out the "not very much" in a small voice.

"Oh, how like Stiva you said that!" said Dolly, laughing.

Anna was hurt. "Oh no, no! I'm not like Stiva," she said, frowning. "I only told you that because I don't permit myself to have any doubts of myself, even for a second."

But the moment she uttered these words she felt they were untrue; not only did she have doubts of herself, but the thought of Vronsky excited her; she was leaving sooner than she had wanted to in order to avoid seeing him again.

"Yes, Stiva told me you danced the mazurka with him and he—"

"You can't imagine how absurdly it all happened! All I was thinking about was helping the match along and—

suddenly it all came out differently. Perhaps against my will I—" She blushed and stopped.

"Oh, they feel that instantly!" said Dolly.

"But I should be in despair if there were anything serious in it on his side," Anna interrupted her. "And I'm sure it will all be forgotten and Kitty will stop hating me."

"Well, to tell you the truth, Anna, I'm not very anxious for Kitty to marry him. It's much better for it to be broken up, if Vronsky is able to fall in love with you in one day."

"Dear God, that would be so silly!" said Anna, and again a deep flush of pleasure passed over her face at hearing the thought at the back of her mind expressed in words. "So, that's why I'm leaving, after having made an enemy of Kitty, whom I became so attached to. What a darling she is! But you'll smooth things over, Dolly, won't you?"

Dolly could scarcely refrain from smiling. She loved Anna, but it was pleasant for her to see that she too had her weaknesses.

"An enemy? That's impossible!"

"I should so like all of you to love me as I love you; and now I love you all still more," she said with tears is her eyes. "Oh, how silly I am today!"

She dabbed her face with a handkerchief and started dressing.

Oblonsky, rosy, gay, and smelling of wine and cigars, came in only just before she was to leave.

Anna's agitation had infected Dolly; when she embraced Anna for the last time, she whispered: "Remember, Anna— I'll never forget what you did for me. And remember that I love you, and will always love you, as my best friend."

"I don't know why you should," Anna said, kissing her and trying to hold back her tears.

"You understood me, and you understand me now. Good-by, my darling!"

## XXIX

WELL, it's all over, and thank God! was the first thought that came to Anna's mind after she said good-by for the last time to her brother, who had been blocking the entrance to the railway car until the very last bell. She sat down in her lounge beside her maid, Annushka, and peered about in the half-light of the sleeping compartment. Tomorrow, thank

God, I'll be seeing Seryozha and Alexis, and my life will go on in its pleasant, usual way as before.

Still with the same preoccupation she had had that whole day, Anna settled herself in for the trip with satisfaction and deliberation; with her deft little hands she unlocked her red bag, took out a small pillow which she placed on her knees, locked the bag again and carefully wrapping up her feet settled down comfortably. An invalid woman was already going to bed. Two other women started up a conversation with her; the fat old one was wrapping up her feet and making remarks about the heating. Anna said a few words in reply, but not expecting any amusement from the conversation asked Annushka to get her reading lamp; she fastened it to the arm of the seat and took a paper knife and an English novel out of her handbag. For a while she couldn't read. At first she was disturbed by the bustling and walking about; then, when the train started, it was impossible not to listen to the noises; then the snow, beating on the left window and sticking to it, the sight of the conductor passing by, bundled up and covered with snow on one side, and the conversations about what a terrible snowstorm was raging outside, all distracted her attention. Farther on it was just the same; the same jolting and clatter, the same snow beating on the window, the same rapid changes from steaming heat to cold and back again to heat, the same faces gleaming in the semidarkness, and the same voices; Anna began to read and to understand what she was reading. Annushka was already dozing, her broad hands, with one of the gloves torn, holding the red bag on her lap. Anna understood what she was reading, but it was unpleasant for her to read, that is, to follow the reflection of the lives of other people. She had too strong a desire to live herself. If she was reading about the heroine of a novel tending an invalid, she felt like walking inaudibly about the invalid's room; if she read about a Member of Parliament making a speech, she felt like making the speech; if she read about Lady Mary riding to hounds, teasing her sister-in-law and astounding everyone with her boldness, she felt like doing all that herself. But there was nothing to be done, so she forced herself to read, her little hands toying with the smooth paper knife.

The hero of the novel had already begun to attain his English idea of happiness—a baronetcy and estate—and Anna wanted to go to the estate with him, when she suddenly felt that he ought to be ashamed of this, and that she was ashamed of the same thing. But what was there for him to be ashamed of? And what am I ashamed of? she asked herself in indignant surprise. She put down the book and leaned back against the back of the seat, clutching the paper knife firmly in both hands.

There was nothing to be ashamed of. She reviewed her memories of Moscow. They were all good and agreeable. She remembered the ball, remembered Vronsky and his submissive lover's face, remembered their relations with each other —there was nothing to be ashamed of. Nevertheless it was just at this point of her recollection that the feeling of shame grew stronger, as though some inner voice were saying to her, just as Vronsky came to mind: "Warm, very warm, hot!" Well, what of it? she said to herself resolutely, shifting her position on the seat. What can it mean? Surely I'm not afraid to look at this straightforwardly? What of it? Surely there's no question, there can't be any question of anything else in the relations between this boyish officer and myself but what there is between any acquaintances?

She smiled disdainfully and took up her book again, but by now she definitely could not follow what she was reading. She passed the paper knife over the windowpane, then laid its smooth, cold surface to her cheek and very nearly laughed out loud at the delight that suddenly, for no reason, seized hold of her. She felt that her nerves were like strings being stretched tighter and tighter around some sort of rotating pegs. She felt that her eyes were opening wider and wider, her fingers and toes twitching nervously, and that something inside was pressing in on her breathing; all the forms and sounds in the wavering semidarkness struck her with extraordinary vividness. Flitting doubts kept descending on her: Was the train moving forward, backward, or standing still? Was it Annushka next to her or some stranger? What's that on the arm of the chair—a fur coat or some animal? And am I here myself? Am I myself or someone else? She was afraid of surrendering to this delirium. But something seemed to draw her into it, and she could surrender at will or hold back. She stood up to recover herself, threw off her wrap and the cape of her warm dress. For a moment she came to her senses, and realized that the lean peasant who had come in, in the long overcoat with the missing buttons, was the carriage stoker, that he was looking at the thermometer, that the wind and the snow had whirled in at the door behind him; then everything got mixed up again . . . This peasant in the long coat started gnawing something on the wall, the old woman began stretching her legs out the whole length of the carriage and filling it up with a black cloud; then something squeaked and pounded in a terrifying way as though someone were being torn to bits; a scarlet flame blinded her eyes, and everything was hidden by a wall. Anna had felt as though she were falling all the way down. But it wasn't at all terrifying, it was gay. The voice of the bundled-up, snow-covered man shouted something just above her ear. She stood up and came to her senses; she realized that they had come to a station and that this was the conductor. She asked Annushka to hand her the cape she had taken off and a shawl, and putting them on she moved toward the door.

"Do you wish to go out?" Annushka asked.

"Yes, I feel like a breath of air. It's very hot in here."

She started opening the door. The snow and wind whirled toward her and tussled for the door with her. This also struck her as gay. She got the door open and went out. The wind seemed to have been only waiting for her; it whistled joyfully and tried to seize her and carry her off, but she held onto the cold doorpost with one hand and clutching her skirt got down onto the platform and moved behind the carriage. The wind had been strong on the carriage steps, but on the platform, sheltered by the carriages, it was quiet. She inhaled deep breaths of the snowy, frosty air with enjoyment; standing beside the carriage she looked around at the platform and the lighted station.

### XXX

A RAGING storm was roaring and whistling between the wheels of the train, around the columns and behind the corner of the station. The carriages, columns, people, everything visible, was covered with snow on one side, and was being covered more and more. The tempest would subside for a second, then burst out again in gusts it seemed impossible to withstand. Yet some people, exchanging merry remarks, were scurrying over the creaking boards of the station, constantly opening and closing the big doors. The stooping shadow of a man glided past her feet, and she heard the sounds of a hammer on iron. "Give me that telegram!" said an angry voice from the other side, out of the stormy darkness. "Over here, please! Number twenty-eight!" still other

voices shouted, and people wrapped up and covered with
snow went running back and forth. A couple of gentlemen
with cigarettes glowing in their mouths passed by her. She
took another deep breath, to get her fill of fresh air, and
had already taken her hand out of the muff in order to take
hold of the post and go back into the carriage, when someone in a military greatcoat, directly at her side, blocked the
wavering light of the lantern. She glanced round, and instantly recognized Vronsky's face. Putting his hand to his
cap, he bowed to her and asked whether she needed anything, whether he might be of service to her. For quite a long
time she looked at him without saying a word; in spite of
the shadow in which he was standing she saw, or thought she
saw, even the expression of his face and eyes. It was the
same expression of deferential rapture that had had such an
effect on her the night before. During the past few days she
had said to herself more than once, and said it again just a
moment before, that Vronsky was for her just another one of
the hundreds of identical young men she constantly kept
meeting everywhere, and that she would never permit herself
even to think of him; but now, the first moment she met him
again, she was seized by a feeling of joyous pride. There was
no need for her to ask why he was there. She knew it just
as surely as though he had told her he was there in order
to be where she was.

"I didn't know you were coming. Why are you?" she said,
letting fall her hand, with which she was about to hold onto
the post. Her face radiated an irrepressible joy and animation.

"Why am I going?" he repeated, looking straight into her
eyes. "You know I'm going in order to be wherever you are,"
he said. "I cannot do anything else."

Just then the wind, as though it had overcome all obstacles,
scattered the snow from the roofs of the carriages, and set a
loose sheet of iron clattering; the deep whistle of the locomotive in front gave a gloomy, mournful howl. Now all the
terror of the storm seemed to her even more beautiful. He
had said just what her heart wished for, though it was
what her reason feared. She said nothing in reply; he saw a
struggle in her face.

"Forgive me if what I said has displeased you," he said
humbly.

He spoke politely and respectfully, but so firmly and stubbornly that for a moment she could not think of an answer.

"What you said is wrong, and if you are a good man I beg you to forget it, as I shall too," she said at last.

"Not one word of yours, not one movement of yours will I ever forget, and I cannot—"

"Enough! Enough!" she cried out, vainly trying to put a stern expression on her face, which he was avidly gazing into. Taking hold of the chilly post with one hand she mounted the steps and went into the little vestibule of the carriage. But in this tiny vestibule she came to a stop, turning over in her mind what had happened. Without remembering either her own words or his, she understood instinctively that this momentary conversation had brought them terribly close together; she was frightened by this and gladdened. She stood still for a few seconds, went into the carriage and sat down. The state of tension that had tormented her at first was not only renewed but heightened to a point where she was afraid that something in her that was stretched too far would break any minute. She did not sleep all night. But there was nothing gloomy or disagreeable in this tension, or in the visions which filled her imagination; on the contrary, they had something joyful, glowing, and exciting. Toward morning she dozed off sitting up; when she woke it was already bright daylight and the train was approaching Petersburg. At once thoughts of the house, her husband, and her son, and the cares of the coming day and afterward beset her.

In Petersburg, as soon as the train came to a stop and she got out, the first face to draw her attention was her husband's. Heavens! how have his ears got like that? she thought, looking at his cold, dignified figure, and at what struck her now especially—his ears pressing up against the rim of his round hat. When he saw her he came toward her, arranging his lips in his usual mocking smile and looking straight at her with his large, tired eyes. A disagreeable feeling oppressed her heart as she met his unbending, weary gaze, as though she had expected to find him different. She was especially struck by the feeling of dissatisfaction with herself that came over her when she met him. It was a feeling she had been familiar with for a long time: it was like the hypocrisy she had always experienced in her relations with him, though before she never used to notice it, while now she was clearly and painfully aware of it.

"Here he is, as you see, a devoted husband, tender as he was in the first year of marriage, burning with a desire to see you," he said in his slow, high-pitched voice, in the tone he almost always used with her, a tone of mockery of anyone who might really speak that way.

"Is Seryozha well?" she asked.

"And is this all my reward," he said, "for my ardor? He's quite well, quite well. . . ."

## XXXI

VRONSKY did not even try to sleep that night. He sat in his armchair, sometimes staring straight ahead of him, sometimes looking round at the people going in and out, and if even before he had struck and upset people who didn't know him by his look of unshakable serenity, now he seemed even prouder and more self-sufficient. He looked at people as though they were objects. A nervous young man sitting opposite him, a clerk in the local courts, hated him for this look. The young man kept asking him for a light, started talking to him, and even jostled him, in order to make him see that he was a man, not an object, but Vronsky kept looking at him just as he did at the lamp; the young man started grimacing, feeling his self-control dwindling away under the strain of this man who refused to acknowledge his existence.

Vronsky saw nothing and no one. He felt like a king, not because he believed he had made any impression on Anna—he still didn't believe that—but because the effect she had had on him made him happy and proud.

What would come of all this, he did not know, or even think about. He felt that all his previously dissipated, scattered forces were concentrated and directed with terrifying energy toward one blissful aim, and this made him happy. He only knew that what he had told her was true, that he would go wherever she was, that all life's happiness, the sole meaning of life now lay for him in seeing and hearing her. And when he left the carriage in Bologova for a glass of seltzer water, and saw Anna, his first word to her said willy-nilly just what he was thinking. He was happy that he had said this to her, so that now she would know it and think about it. He didn't sleep all night. When he returned to his carriage he kept recalling all the positions in which he had seen her, and everything she had said; in his imagination visions of a possible future floated about, making his heart stand still.

When he left the train in Petersburg he felt lively and

fresh after his sleepless night, as though he had had a cold bath. He stopped outside his own carriage, waiting for her to come out. I'll see her once again, he said to himself, smiling involuntarily, I'll see the way she walks, her face; she'll say something, turn her head round, look over, perhaps smile . . .

But before seeing her he saw her husband, whom the stationmaster was deferentially conducting through the crowd. Yes, of course—"the husband!" Only now for the first time did Vronsky realize clearly that her husband was someone connected with her. He knew she had a husband, but he hadn't believed in his existence; he only believed in it fully when he saw him, with his head and shoulders, and his legs in black trousers; especially when he saw how this husband calmly took her hand with a feeling of ownership.

When he saw Karenin, with his fresh Petersburg face and severe self-confident figure, in a round hat, and his slightly rounded back, Vronsky believed in him, and he had a disagreeable feeling such as a man tormented by thirst might have who has made his way to a spring only to find a dog, sheep, or pig in it, drinking the water and muddying it at the same time. Karenin's gait, his splay feet and waddle, irritated Vronsky particularly. Vronsky acknowledged only his own unquestionable right to love her. But she was still the same, and the sight of her still affected him physically, exhilarating and exciting him, and filling his soul with happiness. He ordered his German valet, who came running over to him from the second class, to take his things and leave, and he himself went over to her. He saw Karenin's first meeting with his wife, and with the insight of someone in love, detected signs of the slight embarrassment with which she talked to her husband. No, he decided in his own mind, she does not and cannot love him.

Even as he was approaching Anna from behind he noticed with joy that she sensed his approach and was about to turn around; then she recognized him and turned back to her husband.

"Did you have a comfortable night?" he said, bowing toward her and Karenin together, and leaving it up to Karenin to assume that the bow was for him as well and to recognize him or not as he chose.

"Very comfortable indeed, thank you," she replied.

Her face looked tired; it lacked the play of animation that shone forth in her smile or eyes; but for an instant something flashed in her eyes at the sight of him, and even though the spark was extinguished immediately he was happy for that instant. She looked at her husband to see whether he knew Vronsky. Karenin looked at him with distaste, absently trying to recall him. Here Vronsky's serene self-assurance struck up against Karenin's chilly self-assurance like a scythe against a stone.

"Count Vronsky," said Anna.

"Ah! I think we know each other," said Karenin, holding out his hand with indifference. "You left with the mother and return with the son," he said, distinctly enunciating every syllable as though releasing one precious thing after another. "I suppose you're back from leave?" he said, and without waiting for an answer he turned back to Anna and said in his bantering tone: "Well, I suppose Moscow was in floods of tears when you left, eh?"

By speaking to Anna in this way he was showing Vronsky that he wanted to be left alone; turning to him again he touched his hat, but Vronsky turned to Anna:

"I hope to have the honor of calling on you."

Karenin glanced at him with his weary eyes.

"Delighted," he said coldly. "We're at home on Mondays." Then dismissing Vronsky once and for all, he said to his wife in the same bantering tone: "And what a good thing it was that I just happened to have half an hour's free time, so that I could meet you and show you all my devotion!"

"You've already made too much of a point of your devotion, I can't appreciate it very much," she said in the same manner. She listened involuntarily for the sound of Vronsky's footsteps behind them. But what is it to me? she thought, and began asking her husband how Seryozha had passed the time without her.

"Oh splendidly! Mariette says he was very sweet and—here I must wound you—didn't miss you at all, not like your husband. But let me thank you once again, my dear, for having given me a day. Our dear Samovar will be in ecstasies." (He called the celebrated Countess Lydia Ivanovna the Samovar because she was always getting excited and heated up about everything.) "She's been asking about you. And you know, if I may make so bold as to give advice, you might go over to see her today. Her heart is always aching about everyone, isn't it? Now she's busy reconciling the Oblonskys in addition to all her own troubles."

Countess Lydia was a friend of Karenin's and the center

of one of the sets in Petersburg society that Anna was most closely connected with through her husband.

"But after all I wrote to her."

"She always has to hear the details. Go and see her, my dear, if you're not too tired . . . Well, Kondraty's brought the carriage for you, and I'll be off to my committee. Now I won't be dining alone again," Karenin went on, no longer facetiously. "You can't imagine how accustomed I am to—"

And with a meaningful smile, and a long-drawn-out squeeze of her hand, he helped her into the carriage.

## XXXII

THE first one to meet Anna at home was her son. He hurtled down the staircase toward her, in spite of his governess's outcry, shouting "Mama! Mama!" in wild rapture. Running up to her he clung round her neck.

"I told you it was Mama!" he shouted to the governess. "I knew it!"

Her son gave Anna a feeling of something like disappointment, just as her husband had. In her imagination he had been better than he really was. She was obliged to descend to reality in order to enjoy him as he was. But he was charming even as he was, with his fair curls, blue eyes, and plump shapely little legs in their tight-fitting stockings. Anna experienced an almost physical enjoyment in feeling his closeness and his caresses, and a moral solace when she met his simplehearted, trustful, loving look, and listened to his naïve questions. She got out the presents sent by Dolly's children and told her son that in Moscow there was someone's daughter called Tanya, and how Tanya could read and even teach children.

"D'you mean I'm worse than she?" Seryozha asked.

"For me, you're the best in the whole world."

"I know," said Seryozha, smiling.

Anna had not had time to finish her coffee before Countess Lydia's arrival was announced. Countess Lydia was a tall, stout woman with an unhealthy, sallow complexion and beautiful, dreamy black eyes. Anna was attached to her, but today for the first time she seemed to see her with all her shortcomings.

"Well now, my dear, did you take the olive branch along?" Countess Lydia asked the moment she came into the room.

"Yes, it's all over with, it wasn't even as important as we thought," Anna replied. "My sister-in-law is altogether too hasty."

But Countess Lydia, who always took an interest in things that didn't concern her, was in the habit of never listening to what did interest her; she interrupted Anna:

"Yes, indeed, there's a great deal of sorrow and wickedness in the world, and today I'm so upset."

"But what is it?" Anna asked, trying to repress a smile.

"I'm beginning to get exhausted by breaking lances in the cause of truth, sometimes I feel quite drained. Those Little Sisters of mine"—this was a philanthropic, religious and patriotic society—"were doing splendidly, but with these gentry it's impossible to get anything accomplished," Countess Lydia added, with an ironical air of surrendering to destiny. "They took up the idea, perverted it and now they're discussing it in such a petty, trivial way! Two or three people, including your husband, understand the full significance of the project, while the others have simply dropped it. I got a letter from Pravdin yesterday. . . ."

Pravdin was a well-known Panslavist who lived abroad; Countess Lydia told Anna about his letter.

Then the Countess reported some other unpleasantnesses, and the intrigues being carried on against the plan for unifying the Churches, and hurried off, since she still had a meeting of some society to go to that day, as well as the Slavonic Committee.

But wasn't it just the same before? Anna said to herself; why did I never notice it? Or is she in a particularly bad mood today? Actually it's just funny: here she is a Christian, all she wants is to do good, yet she's always getting angry, and everyone's an enemy—all enemies in the name of Christianity and doing good!

After the Countess a friend called, the wife of a high official, and reported all the news of the town. At three she left too, promising to come back to dinner. Karenin was at the Ministry. When Anna was left alone she spent the time before dinner keeping her son company while he dined (which he did apart) and arranging her things, reading and answering the notes and letters that had piled up for her on the table.

The feeling of groundless shame she had had during the journey, and her agitation, had completely vanished. In the habitual circumstances of her life she once again felt firm and blameless.

With astonishment she recalled her state of mind the day before. What actually happened? Nothing. Vronsky said something stupid, the sort of thing it's easy to put a stop to, and I gave him the right answer. Mentioning it to my husband is unnecessary and impossible. Talking about it would mean giving it an importance it doesn't have.

She recalled how she had once reported to Karenin what amounted to a declaration of love from one of his subordinates in Petersburg, and how Karenin had replied that every woman living in society was exposed to that sort of thing, that he relied on her tact completely and would never permit himself to lower either himself or her by being jealous. So there's no point in telling him, she said to herself; besides, thank God, there's nothing to tell!

### XXXIII

KARENIN returned from the Ministry at four o'clock, but as often happened did not have enough time to see her. He went into his study to receive some petitioners who had been waiting and to sign a few papers brought by his private secretary. An old cousin of Karenin's, a departmental head and his wife, and one young man recommended for a post under Karenin came to dinner (there were always about three people to dinner at the Karenins'). Anna came into the drawing room to entertain them. At exactly five o'clock the bronze Peter the First clock had not struck the fifth note when Karenin came out in a white tie and evening coat with two stars, since he had to leave directly after dinner. Every minute of Karenin's life was taken up and allocated; in order to have the time to do everything he had to do every day he maintained the strictest punctuality. "Without haste, and without repose," was his motto. He came into the room, greeted everyone, and quickly sat down, smiling at his wife.

"Yes, my solitude is ended. You wouldn't believe how uncomfortable"—he stressed the word *uncomfortable*—"it is dining alone."

At dinner he talked to his wife about Moscow affairs, and with an ironical smile asked about Oblonsky; but the conversation was chiefly general, about official and social affairs in Petersburg. After dinner he spent half an hour with his

guests and, again pressing his wife's hand with a smile, he
went out and left for a council meeting. That evening Anna
did not go either to see Princess Betsy Tverskoy, who had
invited her that evening after learning of her arrival, or to
the theater, where she had a box. The principal reason she
didn't go was that the dress she had been counting on wasn't
ready. Altogether, as she busied herself with her toilette
after the guests had left, she was very put out. Before leaving for Moscow, Anna, who was generally an expert at dressing inexpensively, had given a dressmaker three dresses to be
altered. The dresses had to be altered so as to be unrecog-
nizable, and they were supposed to have been ready three
days before. It had turned out that two of the dresses were
not ready at all, while the third had not been altered properly. The dressmaker had come to make her explanations, maintaining that it would be better that way; Anna had lost her
temper to such a point that she felt ashamed of herself afterward. To calm herself completely she went to the nursery
and spent the whole evening with her son, put him to bed
herself, made the sign of the cross over him, and tucked him
in. She was happy at not having gone anywhere and at having spent the evening so well. She felt lighthearted and serene; she saw so clearly that everything that had seemed to
her so important on the railway trip was just one more commonplace incident of society life and that there was nothing
for her to feel ashamed of herself for either in her own or
in anyone else's eyes. She sat down by the fire with an English novel and waited for her husband. At exactly half-past
nine she heard his ring, and he came into the room.

"At last!" she said, stretching out her hand to him.

He kissed it and sat down next to her. "I can see by everything about you that your trip was a success," he said.

"Very much so," she replied, and began telling him everything from the very beginning: her traveling together with
Countess Vronsky, her arrival, the accident at the station.
Then she spoke of the feeling of compassion she had had,
first for her brother, then for Dolly.

"I don't consider it possible to excuse a man like that,
even though he is your brother," said Karenin sternly.

Anna smiled. She understood that he had said this just to
show that considerations of kinship could not prevent him
from expressing his honest opinion. She was familiar with
this trait of her husband's and liked it.

"I'm happy that everything ended up well and that you're

back," he went on. "Well, what are they saying there about the new decree I carried through the Council?"

Anna had not heard a thing about this decree, and she felt ashamed of herself for having been able to forget so easily something that was so important to him.

"Here, on the contrary, it's kicked up quite a stir," he said with a complacent smile.

She saw that Karenin wanted to tell her something about this that pleased him, and by her questions she led him on to tell her what it was. With the same complacent smile he told her about the ovations he had received as a result of the enactment of this decree.

"I was very, very pleased. It demonstrates that we are finally beginning to develop a sensible, firm view of the matter."

After finishing his second cup of tea with cream and some bread, Karenin got up and started toward his study.

"But you didn't go anywhere; weren't you bored?" he said.

"Oh no!" she answered, getting up too and accompanying him through the room to his study. "What are you reading now?" she asked.

"I'm reading the Duc de Lille's *Poesie des enfers*," he replied. "A quite remarkable book."

Anna smiled, as one smiles at the foibles of people one is fond of, and putting her arm though his accompanied him to the door of his study. She knew this habit of his, which had become a necessity, of reading in the evenings. She knew that in spite of his official duties, which consumed almost all his time, he considered himself bound to follow anything remarkable that made its appearance in the world of thought. She also knew that what interested him in reality were political, philosophical, and theological works, and that art was completely alien to his nature, but that in spite of, or rather because of this Karenin did not miss anything in the arts that made a sensation, and considered it his duty to read everything. She knew that in the domain of politics, philosophy, and theology Karenin was full of doubts, or groped about, but that in questions of art and poetry, and especially of music, for which he was totally devoid of any understanding, he had the most definite, categorical views. He was fond of talking about Shakespeare, Raphael, and Beethoven, and about the significance of the new schools of poetry and music, which he had all divided up in an extremely lucid, logical way.

"Well, God bless you!" she said at the door to his study, where a shaded candle and a bottle of water had already been set out for him beside his armchair. "I'll go and write a letter to Moscow."

He pressed her hand and kissed it again.

He's a good man nevertheless—honest, kindhearted, and remarkable in his own profession, Anna said to herself, when she had returned to her own room, as though she were defending him against someone who was accusing him and saying it was impossible to love him. But how oddly his ears stick out! Or has he just had a haircut?

Exactly at midnight, as Anna was still sitting at her desk writing Dolly a letter, she heard the even tread of his slippered feet, and Karenin, freshly washed, with his hair brushed and a book under his arm, went over to her.

"Time now, time!" he said with a meaningful smile, and went into the bedroom.

And what right did he have to look at him that way? thought Anna, remembering how Vronsky had looked at Karenin.

She undressed and went into the bedroom, but not only did her face show no trace of the animation that had sparkled from her eyes and smile when she was in Moscow: on the contrary, now all her fire seemed altogether extinguished, or hidden somewhere far away.

## XXXIV

WHEN he had gone to Moscow, Vronsky had left a large apartment he had on Great Morskoy Street to his friend and favorite companion, Petritsky.

Petritsky was a young lieutenant, not particularly noble and not only not rich, but heavily in debt; he was always drunk toward evening and had often been arrested for various escapades, both ludicrous and scandalous, but was very well liked by both comrades and superiors. When he got to his apartment from the station, around noon, Vronsky saw a familiar hired carriage at the front door. He rang and while still outside heard men's laughter, a woman's lisping voice, and Petritsky shouting: "If that's one of the scoundrels don't let him in!" Vronsky told the servant not to announce him, and stepped softly into the first room. Baroness Shilton, Petritsky's friend, radiant in lilac satin, with a rosy little face and flaxen hair, sitting in front of the round table making coffee, filled the whole room with her Parisian chatter like a canary. Petritsky in his greatcoat, and Captain Kamerovský in full uniform, probably straight from duty, were sitting around her.

"Bravo! Vronsky!" Petritsky cried out, leaping up and scuffing his chair back. "The master himself! Baroness, some coffee for him from the new coffeepot. Now this is a surprise! I hope you're satisfied with the new ornament of your study," he said, indicating the Baroness. "Surely you know each other?"

"I should think so!" said Vronsky, smiling gaily and pressing the Baroness's little hand. "What an idea! An old friend."

"You're just home from a trip," said the Baroness, "so I'll bolt. I'll leave instantly if I'm in the way."

"You're at home wherever you are, Baroness," said Vronsky. "Kamerovsky! Hello," he added, coldly shaking hands with Kamerovsky.

"Now you're never able to say such nice things," said the Baroness to Petritsky.

"But why d'you say that? Directly after dinner I'll say things just as good."

"But after dinner it's not worth anything! Then let me give you some coffee; go have a wash and get ready," said the Baroness, sitting down again and carefully turning a small screw on the new coffeepot. "Pierre, pass me the coffee," she said to Petritsky, whom she called Pierre, after his surname, making no bones of her relations with him. "I'll put some more in."

"You'll spoil it."

"No, I won't! Well, and how's your wife?" said the Baroness abruptly, interrupting Vronsky's conversation with his friends. "We've been marrying you off here. Have you brought your wife back with you?"

"No, Baroness. I was born a gypsy and I'll die one."

"So much the better! Give me your hand on that."

And the Baroness, not letting Vronsky go, began telling him her latest plans for the future, interspersed with jokes, and asking his advice.

"He still won't give me a divorce! What on earth can I do?" (*He* was her husband.) "Now I'd like to sue him. What do you advise me to do? Kamerovsky, watch out for the coffee—it's boiling over, can't you see how busy I am! I want to sue him because I need my property. You see what nonsense it all is;

just because I'm supposed to be unfaithful to him," she said contemptuously, "he wants to have the use of my property."

Vronsky listened with pleasure to the gay prattle of this pretty young woman, agreed with her, gave her half-joking advice and in general instantly assumed his habitual way of talking to this kind of woman. In his Petersburg world everyone was divided into two completely opposite kinds. One was the inferior kind: vulgar, stupid, and above all ridiculous people, who believed that a husband should only live with the woman he was married to, that a girl should be innocent, a woman modest and a man manly, self-controlled, and resolute; that you had to bring up your children and earn your living, pay your debts—and various other idiocies like that. That was the old-fashioned and absurd kind of people. But there was a second kind of people, the real ones, to which they all belonged, for whom the main thing was to be elegant, beautiful, generous, bold, and gay, to give way unblushingly to every passion and to laugh at everything else.

It was only for the first moment that Vronsky, after the impressions he had brought back from Moscow of a completely different world, felt startled; instantly afterward, as though he were stepping into an old pair of slippers, he entered his own former gay and agreeable world.

The coffee never did get made, but boiled over and splashed everyone, producing exactly the effect that was needed; that is, it gave an excuse for much noise and laughter and stained the expensive rug and the Baroness's dress.

"Well, good-by now, or else you'll never get washed, and I'll have on my conscience the worst crime a gentleman can commit—griminess. So you advise me to take a knife to his throat?"

"Definitely, and hold it so that your charming hand will be close to his lips. He'll kiss your hand and all will end well," Vronsky replied.

"Till tonight then at the French Theatre!" With a rustle of skirts she vanished.

Kamerovsky got up too, and without waiting for him to leave Vronsky shook hands with him and went off to the bathroom. While he was washing, Petritsky in a few words described the position he was in to the extent that it had changed since Vronsky's trip.

He didn't have a penny; his father had said he wouldn't give him any and wouldn't pay his debts; his tailor wanted to have him arrested, and someone else was definitely threatening him with arrest; his colonel had said that if these scandals weren't put a stop to Petritsky would have to leave the regiment; he was sick and tired of the Baroness, especially since she kept trying to give him money, but there was another one, he'd show her to Vronsky, wonderful, charming, in the severe Oriental style, *genre* "Rebecca the slave girl, you know!" He had also had a quarrel the day before with Berkashev, and intended to send along his seconds, but of course nothing would come of it. So in general everything was splendid and exceptionally gay. Without allowing his friend to enter into any of the details of his own situation, Petritsky launched into an account of all the interesting news. Listening to Petritsky's familiar stories, in the familiar setting of the apartment he had had for three years, Vronsky had the pleasant feeling of returning to his customary, carefree Petersburg life.

"No, it's not possible!" he cried, releasing the pedal of his washstand, under which he was dousing his healthy, ruddy neck. "It's not possible!" he cried out at hearing that Laura had taken up with Mileyev and thrown over Fertinhof. "And is he still as stupid and complacent? And what about Buzulukov?"

"Buzulukov? Oh what a story there is about him—really perfect!" Petritsky shouted. "You know his one passion is for balls, he never misses a single Court ball. He went to a grand ball in a new helmet; have you seen the new helmets? Very nice, they're lighter. Well, there he was standing—No, but listen . . ."

"But I am listening," Vronsky replied, rubbing himself with a bath towel.

"The Grand Duchess was passing by with some ambassador, and it was just his luck that they started talking about the new helmets. The Grand Duchess wanted to show this ambassador one of the new helmets. Well, they saw our boy standing there." (Petritsky imitated the way he stood with his helmet.) "The Grand Duchess asked him for his helmet and—he didn't give it to her! What's this? Everyone winks at him, nods, frowns—hand it over! But he doesn't. He stands there dead on his feet. You can imagine! Then someone—what's his name?—tries to take his helmet off—he still doesn't give it up! The other one snatches it off and hands it to the Grand Duchess. 'And here's one of the new ones,' says the Grand Duchess. She turns the helmet over and—just imagine this! hoppla! out comes a pear and some candy, two pounds of candy! The dear boy had been collecting them!"

Vronsky shook with laughter. And for a long time afterward, when speaking about other things, he would go off into his hearty laugh, showing his strong, closely set teeth, whenever he remembered the helmet.

After hearing all the news Vronsky, with the help of his valet, put on his uniform and went to report. After reporting he intended to go to see his brother, then Betsy, and make a few visits, in order to start moving about in the milieu in which he would be able to meet Anna. As always in Petersburg he left the house not intending to return until late at night.

# PART TWO

## I

AT the end of the winter a consultation took place at the Shcherbatskys'. It was supposed to decide on the state of Kitty's health and on what had to be done to restore her failing strength. She was ill, and with the approach of spring her health grew worse. The family doctor prescribed cod-liver oil, then iron, then nitrate of silver, but since neither the first, second nor third was of any help and he advised her to go abroad in the spring, a famous specialist was called in. The famous specialist, a very handsome man in his prime, made a point of examining Kitty. He seemed to take a special pleasure in insisting that maidenly modesty was merely a relic of barbarism and that nothing could be more natural than for a man who was not yet old to handle a naked young girl. He found this natural because he did it every day and while doing it did not feel or think anything wrong, as it seemed to him, and consequently he regarded modesty in a girl not merely as a relic of barbarism but as an insult to himself.

They had to submit, since though all the doctors had studied the identical books at the same school and knew one science, and though some people said this celebrated physician was no good, in the Princess's house and in her set it was accepted for some reason that this celebrated physician alone knew something special, and was the only one who could save Kitty. After a painstaking examination and tapping away at the patient, distraught and stupefied with shame, the celebrated doctor, having carefully washed his hands, was standing in the living room talking to the Prince. Listening to the doctor the Prince frowned and coughed. The Prince, who was neither stupid nor sickly and had seen a good deal of life, had no faith in medicine and at heart resented this whole farce, all the more so since he was doubtless the only one who fully understood the reason for Kitty's illness. What a windbag, he thought, as he listened to the famous doctor babbling about the symptoms of Kitty's illness. The doctor meanwhile refrained with difficulty from expressing his disdain for this old nobleman, and it was only with an effort that he lowered himself to the level of his understanding. He realized that there was no point in talking to the old man, and that the head of this family was—the mother. It was before her that he intended to scatter his pearls.

It was just at this point that the Princess came into the drawing room, together with the family doctor. The Prince went out, making an effort not to show how ludicrous he thought the whole farce. The Princess was distraught; she did not know what to do next. She felt guilty about Kitty.

"Well, Doctor, it's up to you to decide our fate," said the Princess. "Tell me everything." What she wanted to ask was, Is there any hope? but her lips quivered and she was incapable of putting this question to him. "Well, Doctor?"

"In just a moment, Princess, I shall have a consultation with my colleague, and then I shall have the honor of giving you my opinion."

"Should we leave you then?"

"As you like."

With a sigh the Princess went out.

When the doctors were left alone, the family doctor deferentially began expressing his opinion, which was that there was an incipient tubercular condition but . . . and so on. While listening to him the celebrity glanced at his heavy gold watch.

"Yes, yes," he said, "but . . ."

The family doctor respectfully stopped talking in the middle of a sentence.

"As you know we cannot determine the inception of a tubercular condition; nothing is definite until the cavities appear. But we may be able to suspect it. There are some indications—bad appetite, nervous excitability, and so on. The question is this: If a tubercular condition is suspected what must be done to maintain nutrition?"

"But as of course you know there are always some psychic causes behind it all," the family doctor permitted himself to interpolate with a subtle smile.

"That, of course, goes without saying," the celebrated specialist replied, glancing at his watch once again. "Excuse me, but has the bridge over the Yauza been repaired, or does one still have to drive all the way round?" he asked. "Ah—so it's repaired! Then I can get there in twenty minutes. As we were saying, the question is this: How to maintain nutrition and improve the nerves. One thing is connected with the other, and we must treat both things at once."

"And what about a trip abroad?"

"I'm rather hostile to trips abroad. Remember—if there is an incipient tubercular condition, which is something we cannot tell, a trip abroad won't help. What is essential is some means of maintaining nutrition without doing any harm."

And the celebrity explained his plan of therapy by means of Soden waters, which the chief reason for prescribing was evidently that they could do no harm.

The family doctor listened with respectful attention.

"But what I should emphasize in favor of a trip abroad," he said, "is that it would be a complete change and take her away from circumstances full of associations. Besides which her mother would like it."

"Oh! Well, in that case why shouldn't they go? Only those German quacks are going to do a great deal of harm . . . They'll have to be made to follow my instructions . . . Well, let them go . . ."

He looked at his watch again. "High time for me to go," he said, moving toward the door.

The celebrated specialist informed the Princess—a feeling of propriety suggested this—that he would have to see the patient once more.

"What! Another examination!" exclaimed the mother, horror-stricken.

"Oh no, just a few more details to be attended to, Princess."

"As you please, Doctor."

And the mother, accompanied by the doctor, went to see Kitty in the living room. Flushed and emaciated, with a peculiar glitter in her eyes because of the shame she had been through, Kitty was standing in the middle of the room. When the doctor came in she flushed crimson and her eyes filled with tears. Her whole illness and the treatment seemed to her so stupid, even ridiculous! Her treatment seemed to her as absurd as putting the pieces of a broken vase together again. Her heart was broken—why were they trying to dose her with pills and powders? But it was impossible to hurt her mother, especially since her mother considered herself to blame.

"Please sit down, Princess," said the celebrity.

With a smile he sat down opposite her, took her pulse, and began to ask boring questions again. In the midst of answering them she suddenly lost her temper and stood up.

"I beg your pardon, Doctor, but this is really leading nowhere. You keep asking me the same thing over and over."

The celebrity was not offended.

"Morbid excitability," he said to the Princess after Kitty had gone out. "In any case I had finished . . ."

And the doctor gave the Princess, as though she were an exceptionally intelligent woman, a scientific diagnosis of the young Princess's condition, concluding with directions for taking the useless waters. At the question as to whether they should go abroad, the doctor began pondering profoundly, as though solving a difficult problem. The answer was finally given: they were to go abroad, and not believe what the quacks told them, but refer to him about everything.

When the doctor had gone it was just as though something gay had happened. The Princess was much more cheerful when she went back to her daughter, and Kitty pretended she was more cheerful too. She often, almost always, had to pretend now.

"I'm really perfectly well, *maman*. But if you'd like to take a trip, then let us go!" she said, and trying to show she was interested in the forthcoming journey she began talking about the preparations for it.

## II

JUST after the doctor had left Dolly came in. She knew there was supposed to be a consultation that day, and in spite of her just having gotten up from a confinement—she had given birth to a daughter at the end of the winter—and in spite of her having a great many troubles and worries of her own, she had left her baby and a sick daughter to come and hear Kitty's fate, which was now being decided.

"Well, what is it?" she said, coming into the drawing room without taking off her hat. "You're all very cheerful; is everything all right then?"

They made an attempt to report to her what the doctor had said, but it turned out that although he had spoken very fluently and at great length it was quite impossible to transmit what he had said. The only thing of interest was that a trip abroad had been decided on.

In spite of herself Dolly sighed. Her best friend, her sister, was going away. And her own life was not gay: her relations with Oblonsky after their reconciliation had become humiliating. The soldering accomplished by Anna had proved defective; once again the harmony of the family had broken at the same point. There was nothing definite, but Oblonsky was almost never home, there was almost never any money, and suspicions of infidelity tormented Dolly constantly; afraid of undergoing the pangs of jealousy she herself tried to cast them off. The first explosion of jealousy, once experienced, could no longer be repeated, and even the revelation of some infidelity could no longer have the same effect on her as it had the first time. Now such a revelation could only deprive her of her family habits, and she allowed herself to be deceived, despising him and above all herself for this weakness. On top of which the cares of a large family tormented her without letup: either something went wrong with the feeding of the baby, or the nurse left, or, as now, one of the children fell ill.

"Well, and how are all of you?" asked her mother.

"Oh *maman*, you have so many troubles of your own! Lili's fallen ill, I'm afraid it's scarlet fever. I've just come over now to see how things are, because if it is scarlet fever——God forbid!——then I'll be shut up without being able to come out at all."

After the doctor left the old Prince also came out of his study, and after holding out his cheek to Dolly and exchanging a few words with her, he turned to his wife:

"Well, what's been decided? Are you going? And what are you thinking of doing with me?"

"I think you should stay behind, Alexander," said his wife.

"Just as you please."

"But *maman*, why shouldn't Papa come along with us?" said Kitty. "It'll be more cheerful for him as well as for us."

The old Prince got up and stroked Kitty's hair. She raised her head and forcing a smile looked at him. It had always seemed to her that although he never said very much to her he understood her better than anyone else in the family. As the youngest she was her father's favorite, and it seemed to her that his love for her had given him a great deal of insight. As her gaze now met his blue, kindly eyes, looking at her steadily, it seemed to her that he saw through her completely and understood all the misery inside her. She bent toward him blushing, expecting a kiss, but he only patted her hair and said:

"What absurd chignons! It's impossible to get at your real daughter, all you can do is stroke the hair of some dead old woman. Well, Dolly darling," he said, turning to his oldest daughter, "and what's your young prodigal up to?"

"Nothing at all, Papa," Dolly replied, seeing he referred to Oblonsky. "He's always going out. I hardly ever see him," she could not help adding with an ironical smile.

"Hasn't he gone to the country yet to sell the forest?"

"No, he keeps marking time."

"Is that so! And shall I have to stop marking time? Well, at your service," he said to his wife as he sat down. "And as for you, Kitty," he said to his youngest daughter, "one fine day you must wake up some time and say to yourself, 'But I'm completely well and cheerful after all, and can go out again for a walk with Papa in the frost early in the morning.' Eh?"

What her father said seemed very simple, but at these words Kitty felt confused and disconcerted, as though she were a criminal caught in the act. Yes, she thought, he knows everything, he understands the whole thing and this is how he's telling me that even though I feel humiliated I must get over it.

She could not gather together enough energy to say anything in reply. She started to, but suddenly burst into tears and rushed out of the room.

"All these jokes of yours!" the Princess lashed out at him. "You're always—" And she began making her usual speech of reproach.

For quite a long time the Prince listened to his wife's reproaches in silence, but he began frowning more and more.

"She's so pathetic, the poor little thing, just pathetic, and you don't feel how painful she finds any reference to the cause of it. Oh—to be so mistaken about people!" said the Princess, and by the change in her tone Dolly and the Prince understood that she was talking about Vronsky. "I can't understand why there aren't laws against such vile, ignoble people."

"I really can't listen to all this!" said the Prince morosely, getting up from his armchair as though about to leave, but stopping in the doorway: "There are such laws, my dear, and since you've put it up to me let me tell who's to blame for the whole thing: you—just you, and you alone. There have always been laws against such young bucks and there still are! Yes, and if anything had been done that ought not to have been, then old as I am I would have challenged him to a duel —that fop! Now go on in and dose her and keep calling in all those quacks!"

The Prince seemed to have a great many other things to

say, but the moment the Princess heard this tone of his, which is what always happened in serious matters, she instantly gave in and took everything back.

"Alexander, Alexander," she whispered, moving closer and beginning to weep.

The moment she started crying the Prince also calmed down. He went over to her.

"Well, that's enough now, enough! I know how hard it is for you too. It can't be helped. There's no great harm done. God is merciful . . . Be thankful . . ." he said, no longer knowing himself what he was saying, and responding to the Princess's moist kiss which he felt on his hand; then he went out of the room.

Even at the moment Kitty had left the room in tears Dolly had instantly seen, with her maternal, family habit of mind, that there was some woman's business to be done here, and she prepared to do it. She took off her hat, and mentally rolling up her sleeves, prepared for action. During her mother's attacks on her father she had tried to restrain her as far as her filial respect allowed her. During the Prince's explosion she kept silent; she had a feeling of shame on her mother's behalf and of tenderness toward her father for his instant return to kindness; but when her father went out she prepared to do the chief thing that was necessary—go to Kitty and soothe her.

"I've been meaning to ask you for a long time, *maman*—d'you know whether Levin wanted to propose to Kitty the last time he was here? That's what he told Stiva."

"Well, what of it? I don't quite see—"

"Then it may be that Kitty refused him? Didn't she tell you?"

"No, she didn't say a thing about either one of them, she's too proud. But I know the whole thing is due to that—"

"Yes, but just think, if she refused Levin—and she wouldn't have refused him if it hadn't been for the other, I know. And then the other deceived her so horribly."

It was too terrible for the Princess to think of how much she was to blame concerning her daughter, and she lost her temper.

"Oh, I don't understand anything at all any more! Nowadays every girl wants to make up her own mind about everything, they never tell their mothers anything, and then—"

"*Maman*, I'll go to her now."

"Go along then—am I stopping you?" said her mother.

## III

WHEN she went into Kitty's little boudoir, a pretty pink room decorated with old Dresden figures, as pretty, pink and merry as Kitty herself had been only two months before, Dolly remembered how they had both arranged the little room the year before, with what gaiety and love. Her heart froze when she saw Kitty sitting on the low chair nearest the door, staring at a corner of the carpet with fixed eyes. Kitty looked up at her sister without any change in her cold, rather severe expression.

"I'm going home now and I'll be shut up there, and you won't be able to visit me," said Dolly, sitting down beside her. "I want to talk to you."

"What about?" asked Kitty quickly, raising her face apprehensively.

"About your trouble, what else?"

"I have none."

"Now, Kitty, enough of that. You don't think I can help knowing? I know all about it. And believe me, it's so trivial . . . All of us have gone through the same thing."

Kitty said nothing; there was a stern expression on her face.

"He's not worth your suffering because of him," Dolly continued, going straight to the point.

"No, because he made a fool of me," said Kitty in a shaking voice. "Don't speak about it! Please don't speak about it!"

"But who told you that? No one's ever said that. I'm sure he was in love with you and still is, it's just that—"

"Oh, the most horrible thing about it all is this commiseration," cried Kitty, suddenly losing her temper. She turned round on the chair, blushed, and began rapidly moving her hands about, clutching first with one hand then with the other at the buckle of a belt she was holding. Dolly knew this habit of her sister's of fingering things when she was excited; she knew that Kitty was capable of forgetting herself in a heated moment and of saying a great many excessive and disagreeable things; she tried to quiet her, but it was already too late.

"Just what d'you want me to feel—what?" said Kitty quickly. "That I was in love with someone who wouldn't have anything to do with me, and that I'm dying for love of him? And I hear this from my own sister who thinks that . . . that she's sympathizing with me! I hate all this compassion and hypocrisy!"

"Kitty, you're not being fair."

"Why are you tormenting me?"

"On the contrary, I . . . I see you're upset . . ."

But Kitty was so excited she wasn't listening to her.

"There's nothing for me to feel brokenhearted or be consoled about. I'm proud enough never to permit myself to love a man who doesn't love me."

"But I'm not even saying that—There's just one thing—tell me the truth," Dolly went on, taking her by the hand, "tell me—did Levin speak to you?"

The mention of Levin seemed to deprive Kitty of her last bit of self-control; she jumped up from her chair and, flinging the buckle on the floor and gesticulating rapidly with her hands, she broke out:

"What's Levin got to do with it all? I can't understand why you have to torment me. I said it before and I say it again, I have some pride and I would never, *never* do what you're doing—go back to a man who has deceived you, and been in love with another woman. I can't understand that, I just can't understand it! You may be able to do it, but I never could!"

Having said this, she looked at her sister, and when she saw that Dolly was silent, her head drooping sadly, Kitty sat down by the door instead of leaving the room as she had meant to; covering her face with a handkerchief she bowed her head.

The silence continued for a moment or two. Dolly was thinking of herself. The humiliation she was constantly aware of was peculiarly painful when she was reminded of it by her sister. She had not expected such cruelty from Kitty, and she was angry with her. But suddenly she heard the rustle of a dress and at the same time a burst of suppressed sobbing. A pair of arms encircled her neck from below. Kitty was kneeling in front of her.

"Oh Dolly, darling, I'm so terribly unhappy!" she whispered remorsefully. And her sweet tear-stained face hid itself in Dolly's skirts.

The tears seemed to be the lubricant that was indispensable if the machinery of sisterly relations was to run properly. After their tears the sisters did not talk about what was on their minds, but by speaking of secondary matters they understood each other. Kitty understood that what she had said in anger about the infidelity of Dolly's husband and her hu-

miliation had wounded her poor sister to the depths of her
being, but that Dolly forgave her. For her part Dolly found
out everything she wanted to; she was convinced that her
guesswork had been right and that Kitty's grief, her incurable
grief, was due to just this fact of Levin's having proposed to
her and to her having refused him, while Vronsky had deceived her, and that she was ready to fall in love with Levin
and to hate Vronsky. Kitty did not say a word about this;
she simply spoke of her state of mind.

"I have no troubles at all," she said after she calmed
down. "But you can see how everything came to seem vile,
repulsive, and coarse to me, myself above all. You can't imagine what vile thoughts I have about everything."

"But what sort of vile thoughts could you have?" asked
Dolly, smiling.

"The nastiest, the nastiest and the coarsest; I can't tell you
what they are. It's not unhappiness, or depression, but much
worse. It's as though everything that had been good in me,
everything, is hidden away, and the only thing left is vileness. How can I explain to you?" she went on, seeing a look
of perplexity in her sister's eyes. "Papa started speaking to
me just now—it seems to me the only thing he's thinking
about is that I have to get married. Mama takes me to a ball—
I have the impression she's only taking me so that I can get
married as quickly as possible and she can be rid of me. I
know that's not so, but I can't drive these notions away. I
can't bear seeing any so-called eligible men. It seems to me
they're just sizing me up. Going anywhere in a ball gown
used to be plain and simple pleasure for me, I was delighted
with myself. Now I feel ashamed, ill at ease. What d'you
think? That doctor—well . . ."

Kitty hesitated: she wanted to go on and say that ever since
this change had taken place in her Oblonsky had become unbearably disagreeable to her and that she couldn't see him
without having the coarsest and most monstrous fancies.

"There you are, I see everything in the coarsest, vilest
light," she went on. "That's what my illness is. Perhaps it will
go away . . ."

"And you don't think that—"

"I can't help it. It's only with the children that I feel all
right, only with you."

"What a pity you can't come to stay with us."

"But I will come. I've had scarlet fever, and I'll talk
*maman* into it."

Kitty insisted on having her own way and moved over to Dolly's, where she nursed the children through the whole attack of scarlet fever that actually did take place. The two sisters saw all six children safely through it. But Kitty's health did not improve and in Lent the Shcherbatskys went abroad.

IV

THERE was actually just one topmost set in Petersburg: everyone in it knew and even visited everyone else. But this large circle had its own subdivisions. Anna had friends and close connections with three different groups. One was the official, career group of her husband's, which consisted of his colleagues and subordinates, connected in the most variegated and capricious way and separated by their social circumstances. It was only with difficulty that Anna could now recall the feeling of almost religious veneration she had had toward these people at first. Now she knew them all as people know each other in a provincial town; she knew who had which habits and weaknesses; where the shoe pinched this foot or that; she knew their relationships with each other and with the topmost center; she knew who backed whom, how and by what each one supported himself and who agreed or disagreed with whom about what; but in spite of Countess Lydia's urging, this circle of governmental masculine interests never interested Anna and she avoided it.

The second circle that was close to Anna was the one through which Karenin had made his career. The center of this circle was Countess Lydia. It was a group of elderly, plain, philanthropic, and devout women, and able, learned, and ambitious men. One of the able men who belonged to this circle called it the "conscience of Petersburg society." Karenin had the greatest esteem for this little circle, and during the first period of her life in Petersburg, Anna, who had a great capacity for getting along with everyone, had found friends even here. But now, after her return from Moscow, this little group had become unbearable. It seemed to her that both she and they were all pretending, and it became so boring and uncomfortable in this group that she called on Countess Lydia as rarely as possible.

The third group, finally, where Anna had connections, was in society proper—the society of balls, dinner parties, and brilliant gowns, a society that clung to the Court with one hand in order not to sink down into the demimonde, whom the members of this circle thought they despised, though their tastes were not only similar but identical. Anna was connected with this set through the wife of her cousin, Princess Betsy Tverskoy, who had an income of 120,000 rubles a year and from Anna's very first appearance in society had taken a great fancy to her, shown her all sorts of attentions and had drawn her into her own circle, making fun of Countess Lydia's set.

"When I'm old and ugly I'll be just like that," Betsy said, "but for you, for a young and beautiful woman, it's still too early for that charity ward."

In the beginning Anna had avoided this world of Princess Tverskoy's as much as she could, since it was beyond her means and she preferred the first set sincerely as well; but when she came back from Moscow a change for the opposite took place. She avoided her moral friends and went into grand society. She would meet Vronsky there; it gave her a disturbing joy whenever they met. She would meet him most often at Betsy's, who was a Vronsky by birth and a cousin of his. Vronsky went wherever he might meet Anna, and whenever he could he spoke to her about his love. She never gave him any encouragement, but each time she met him the same feeling of animation surged up in her heart that had overcome her that day in the train when she had seen him for the first time. She felt joy lighting up her eyes and curving her lips into a smile whenever she saw him, and she was unable to hide the expression of this joy.

At first Anna sincerely believed that she was annoyed by his allowing himself to pursue her, but very soon after her return from Moscow, when she went to an evening party where she had thought she was going to meet him and he wasn't there, she saw clearly, by the sadness that overwhelmed her, that she was deceiving herself, and that his pursuit was not only not disagreeable to her but constituted the whole interest of her life.

A famous singer was singing for the second time, and the whole of high society was at the Opera House. When he saw his cousin from his seat in the front row, Vronsky went over to her box without waiting for the intermission.

"How is it you didn't come to dinner?" she said to him. "I'm amazed at the clairvoyance of lovers!" she added with a smile, in a tone that only he could hear. "She wasn't there! But come along after the opera."

Vronsky looked at her questioningly. She nodded. He thanked her with a smile and sat down beside her.

"And how I remember the way you joked about others!" said Betsy, who took a special satisfaction in following the progress of this passion. "Where has all that gone to! You're caught, my dear boy!"

"That's the only thing I wish for, to be caught," Vronsky replied with his calm, good-natured smile. "The only thing I have to complain about is that I'm not caught enough, to tell the truth. I'm beginning to lose hope."

"But what hope could you have?" said Betsy, offended on behalf of her friend. "Let's not fool each other!" But there were little sparks flickering in her eyes that said she understood very well indeed, just exactly as he did himself, what it was that he might hope for.

"None at all," said Vronsky, laughing and showing his close-set teeth. "Excuse me," he added, taking her opera glasses from her hand and intently scanning the opposite row of boxes over her bare shoulder. "I'm afraid I'm becoming ridiculous."

He knew perfectly well that he was running no risk of being ridiculous in the eyes of Betsy and of all the people in society. He knew perfectly well that in the eyes of these people the role of anyone who was the disappointed lover of a girl, or of any free woman generally, might be ridiculous; but that the role of a man pursuing a married woman and staking his whole life on involving her in adultery at all costs —*that* role had something about it that was beautiful, and could never be ridiculous, and because of this there was a proud, happy smile lurking under his mustache as he put the opera glasses down and looked at his cousin.

"But why didn't you come to dinner?" she said admiringly.

"I must tell you about that. I was busy, and with what d'you think? I'll give you a hundred guesses, a thousand— you'd never find out. I was making peace between a husband and someone who had offended his wife. Yes, really!"

"And did you make peace?"

"Practically."

"You'll have to tell me all about it," she said, getting up. "Come back in the next intermission."

"I can't; I'm going to the French Theatre."

"What, from Neilson?" Betsy asked horror-stricken,

though she couldn't have told Neilson's voice from a chorus girl's.

"What can I do? I have an appointment there, all in connection with my peacemaking mission."

"Blessed are the peacemakers, for they shall be saved," said Betsy, recalling something like she had once heard someone say. "Well sit down then and tell me; what is it all about?"

She sat down again.

## V

ITS a little on the indecent side, but it's so charming I have a terrible longing to tell it," said Vronsky, looking at her with laughing eyes. "I shan't mention any names."

"Then I'll guess them, so much the better."

"Well, listen: two gay young fellows were out driving—"

"Officers of your regiment, of course?"

"I'm not saying officers, just two young fellows who'd been lunching—"

"In other words drinking."

"Perhaps. They were driving off to a friend's for dinner, in the gayest of spirits. They saw a pretty woman passing them in a hired sleigh looking around at them and—at any rate so it seemed to them—laughing and nodding to them. Naturally they went after her, galloping at full speed. To their surprise the beauty stops at the entrance to the very house they were going to themselves. The beauty runs up to the apartment on the top floor. All they can see are red lips under a short veil and lovely little feet."

"You tell the story with such feeling it seems to me you were one of the two."

"And what did you say to me just now? Well, the young fellows went into their friend's flat, he was giving a farewell dinner. There actually they may have drunk rather too much, which is what always happens at farewell dinners. At dinner they asked who lived on the topmost apartment in that house. No one knew, only their host's footman, when they asked whether there were any 'girls' living at the top, answered that there were a great many of them about. After dinner the young fellows went into their host's study and wrote a note to the unknown beauty. They wrote a passionate letter, a declaration of love, and took the letter upstairs themselves to explain anything that might not have seemed quite clear in the letter."

"Why d'you tell me such horrible things? Well?"

"They rang. A maid opened the door, they handed over the letter and assured the maid that they were both so much in love that they were going to expire then and there in the doorway. The baffled maid carried on the negotiations. Suddenly a gentleman, red as a lobster, with whiskers like sausages, appeared and told them no one lived there but his wife and kicked them out."

"But how d'you know he had whiskers 'like sausages,' as you call them?"

"Just listen. Today I went over to reconcile them."

"And what happened?"

"Now this is the most interesting part. It turns out that the happy couple are a Titular Councilor and a Titular Counciloress. The Titular Councilor has made a complaint, and now I'm turning into a peacemaker—and what a peacemaker! I assure you Talleyrand wouldn't hold a candle to me."

"But what's the difficulty?"

"You'll soon hear. We apologized quite properly: 'We're in utter despair, we beg your forgiveness for an unfortunate misunderstanding.' The Titular Councilor with the sausage-shaped whiskers begins to thaw, but he also wants to express his own feelings, and the moment he starts expressing them he starts getting hot under the collar and making insulting remarks, so once again I have to set all my diplomatic talents in motion. 'I agree they behaved badly, but I beg you to take into consideration its having been a misunderstanding, their youth; after all the young men had just been dining. You can understand that. They repent from the bottom of their hearts, and beg you to forgive their misconduct.' The Titular Councilor starts softening up again. 'I quite agree, Count, and I am prepared to forgive them, but you must understand that my wife, my wife, a respectable woman, has been subjected to the persecution, insults, and insolence of some young louts, these rasc—' And you understand, one of these young louts is standing there, and I have to make peace between them. Once again I set my diplomacy in motion, and once again, just when the only thing that has to be done is to finish the whole business my Titular Councilor gets hot again, turns red, his sausages stick out, and again I dissolve in diplomatic subtleties."

"Oh, you really must hear this!" laughed Betsy, turning to

a woman who was just entering the box. "He's just told me the funniest thing!"

"Well, good luck," she added, giving Vronsky a finger that wasn't holding her fan, and with a movement of her shoulders letting down the bodice of her dress, which had risen a little, so that she might be properly nude when she went into the front of the box in the gaslight for everyone to see.

Vronsky went to the French Theatre, where he actually did have to see his colonel, who never missed a show there, in order to discuss his peacemaking, which he had been busy and amused with for the past three days. Petritsky, whom he was fond of, was mixed up in this business, as well as young Prince Kedrov, a splendid fellow and first-rate companion who had recently joined the regiment. But above all it was the interests of the regiment that were involved.

Both of them were in Vronsky's squadron. The colonel had been approached by the functionary, the Titular Councilor Wenden, with a complaint against his officers for having insulted his wife. According to Wenden's story his young wife —he had been married six months—had been in church with her mother, and suddenly feeling unwell through being in a certain condition, could not stand up any longer and had gone home in the first sleigh she could find, a smart-looking one. The officers had immediately raced after her; she had been frightened, and feeling more unwell than ever had run home upstairs. Wenden himself, who had come back from the office, had heard the bell ringing and then some voices, had gone out and, on seeing some drunken officers with a letter, had thrown them out. He demanded severe penalties.

"You can say what you like," said the colonel to Vronsky, whom he had invited to his house, "Petritsky is becoming impossible. Not a week goes by without some scandal. This official won't leave things alone, he's going to go further."

Vronsky saw what a bad business the whole thing was: a duel was out of the question; everything had to be done in order to mollify the Titular Councilor and hush things up. The colonel had called Vronsky in because he knew him to be an honorable, able man, and above all, one who valued the honor of the regiment. They talked things over and decided that Petritsky and Kedrov had to go along with Vronsky to see the Titular Councilor and apologize. The colonel and Vronsky both understood that Vronsky's name and rank as Imperial aide-de-camp were bound to be a great help in mollifying the Titular Councilor. Actually these two factors had proved partially effective, but the result of the peacemaking was still in doubt, as Vronsky had explained.

When he got to the French Theatre, Vronsky went out into the lobby with the colonel and reported to him his success, or lack of it. After turning it all over in his mind the colonel decided to do nothing further about the entire matter, but then, for pleasure, started questioning Vronsky concerning the details of his interview, and for some time was unable to refrain from laughing as he listened to Vronsky's story about how the Titular Councilor, after calming down, would suddenly flare up again as he recalled the details of what had happened, and how Vronsky, at the final hint of a reconciliation had maneuvered a retreat, pushing Petritsky out in front of him.

"A disgraceful scandal, but side-splitting. Kedrov really can't fight the fellow! So he got terribly excited, did he?" the colonel repeated, laughing. "And what did you think of Clare this evening? Magnificent!" he said, referring to the new French actress. "No matter how often you see her she's different every day. Only the French are capable of that."

## VI

PRINCESS Betsy left the Opera House without waiting for the end of the last act. She scarcely had time to go to her dressing room, put some powder on her long white face and rub it off again, tidy herself up and order tea to be served in the big drawing room before carriages began arriving one after the other at the entrance to her huge house on Great Morskoy Street. As the guests passed beneath the broad portico a stout hall porter, who read his newspaper in the morning behind the glass door to the edification of the passers-by, noiselessly opened this enormous door to admit them.

Almost at the same moment the hostess, her coiffure rearranged and her face freshened up, came out of one door and the guests out of another into the large drawing room with dark walls, thick carpets, and brightly lighted table, its white tablecloth, silver samovar and translucent china gleaming in the candlelight.

The hostess sat down at the samovar and took off her gloves. Moving their chairs forward with the help of unobtrusive footmen, the company took their places, dividing up into two parts—near the samovar together with the hostess, and, at the opposite end of the drawing room, around the wife of an ambassador, a beautiful woman with sharply drawn black eyebrows dressed in velvet. In both circles the conversation kept wavering—as it always does for the first few minutes, being interrupted by recognitions, greetings, and offers of tea—as though looking for something to settle on.

"She's an exceptional actress; it's obvious she's studied Kaulbach," said a diplomatic attaché in the circle around the ambassador's wife. "Did you notice how she fell—"

"Oh please, let's not talk about Neilson! It's impossible to say anything new about her," said a stout, red-faced, fair-haired woman in an old silk dress, who had no eyebrows and no chignon. This was Princess Myagky, famous for her simplicity and down-to-earth manners and nicknamed the *enfant terrible*. She was sitting in between the two circles listening in on and slipping into the conversations first of one then of the other. "Three different people made exactly the same remark to me today about Kaulbach, as though it had been agreed on. They all seemed delighted with it, I don't know why."

This comment cut short the conversation; it was necessary to think up some new topic again.

"Tell us something entertaining, but not malicious," said the ambassador's wife, a great expert in the elegant conversation the English call "small talk," turning to the diplomatic attaché who was also at a loss as to how to begin now.

"That's said to be very difficult, only malice is amusing," he began with a smile. "But I'll try. Just give me a theme—everything depends on the theme. Once a theme is given there's no trouble at all in embroidering on it. I often think the famous talkers of the last century would find it difficult nowadays to talk cleverly. Cleverness has become so tiresome . . ."

"And that was said a long time ago," said the ambassador's wife, interrupting him laughingly.

The conversation had begun amiably, but just because it was now too amiable it came to a halt again. It was necessary to resort to the one sure and never-failing resource—gossip.

"Don't you think Tushkevich has something Louis XV about him?" he said, indicating with his eyes a handsome, fair-haired young man standing by the table.

"Oh yes! He's in the same style as the drawing room, that's why he's here so often."

This conversation was sustained, since what was being

spoken of by allusions was just what it was impossible to mention in this room, that is, Tushkevich's relations with their hostess.

The conversation around the hostess and her samovar, which had also been vacillating for a little while between the three inevitable topics of the latest public news, the theater, and neighborly malice, had also settled on the last theme, that is, backbiting.

"Have you heard that the Maltishchev woman—not the daughter, the mother—is also having a *diable rose* costume made for herself?"

"It's not possible! No, but really, how delicious!"

"I'm astonished that with her mind—after all, she's not stupid—she doesn't see how ridiculous she's being."

Each one had something disparaging or derisive to say about the luckless Maltishchev woman, and the conversation crackled along gaily like a kindling bonfire.

Princess Betsy's husband, a stout good-natured fellow, who was a passionate collector of engravings, having learned his wife was entertaining some people, came into the drawing room before going off to his club. Silently, across the thick rug, he came over to Princess Myagky.

"How did you like Neilson?" he said.

"Oh, how can you creep up on me like that? How you frightened me!" she answered. "Please don't talk to me about the opera, you haven't the slightest understanding for music. It would be better if I lowered myself to your level and started talking to you about your majolica and engravings. Well, what treasures have you been buying lately at the flea market?"

"Would you like to see them? But you don't know anything about it."

"Just let me see them. I've been learning from those, what's their name?—the bankers, they have some magnificent engravings, they showed them to us."

"What? Have you been to the Schützburgs?" asked the hostess from her place at the samovar.

"We have, *ma chère*. They invited my husband and myself to dinner, and told me that the sauce alone at the dinner cost a thousand rubles," said Princess Myagky in a loud voice, feeling that everyone was listening to her, "and it was an absolutely vile sauce, something green! I had to invite them back; I made a sauce for eighty-five kopecks, and they all loved it. I can't make thousand-ruble sauces."

"She's unique!" said the hostess.

"Marvelous!" said someone else.

The effect produced by whatever Princess Myakgy said was always the same; its secret consisted of her saying simple things that made sense, even when, as now, they were not quite to the point. In the society she lived in remarks like this had the effect of the wittiest jokes. Princess Myagky didn't understand why they had this effect, but she knew they did and exploited it.

Since everyone had been listening to Princess Myagky and the conversation around the ambassador's wife had come to a stop, the hostess tried to unify the whole company: she turned to the ambassador's wife:

"Are you quite sure you don't want any tea? You should come over and join us."

"No, we're really very comfortable here," answered the ambassador's wife smilingly, and went on with the conversation that had begun.

This conversation was very agreeable. The Karenins, husband and wife, were being run down.

"Anna's changed a great deal since her trip to Moscow. There's something odd about her," said a woman who was a friend of hers.

"The principal change is that she's brought the shadow of Alexis Vronsky back with her," said the ambassador's wife.

"And why not? You know the Grimm fairy tale, 'The Man without a Shadow.' It's a punishment for something or other. I never could understand why it was a punishment. But it must be unpleasant for a woman to be without a shadow."

"Yes, but women with a shadow usually end badly," said Anna's friend.

"Bad cess to your tongue," Princess Myagky, hearing this remark, said suddenly. "Anna is a wonderful woman. I don't like her husband, but I like her very much indeed."

"But why don't you like her husband? He's such a remarkable man," said the ambassador's wife. "My husband says there are very few statesmen like him in Europe."

"My husband tells me the same thing, but I don't believe it," said Princess Myagky. "If our husbands didn't tell us that we would see things as they are, and to my mind Karenin is simply stupid. I say this only in a whisper . . . Doesn't that clear everything up? Before, when I was ordered to consider him intelligent, I kept on trying to and I considered myself stupid for not seeing how intelligent he was;

but the moment I said, 'he's stupid,' but said it in a whisper, everything became quite clear. Isn't that so?"

"How malicious you are today!"

"Not in the least. I have no other way out. One of the two of us is stupid. Well, as you know, it's never possible to say that about yourself."

"No one is satisfied with his fortune, but everyone is satisfied with his wit," said the attaché, quoting some French verse.

"That's just it," said Princess Myagky, turning to him quickly. "But the point is I'm not going to let you have Anna. She's so wonderful, so charming! What can she do if everyone falls in love with her and follows her around like a shadow?"

"But I wasn't thinking of condemning her," said Anna's friend, to justify herself.

"If no one follows us about like a shadow that doesn't prove we have the right to condemn anyone else."

And having properly disposed of Anna's friend, Princess Myagky got up and together with the ambassador's wife went over to the table where a general conversation was going on about the King of Prussia.

"Whom were you running down over there?" asked Betsy.

"The Karenins. The Princess was giving us a sketch of Karenin," said the ambassador's wife with a smile, as she sat down at the table.

"What a pity we didn't hear it," said the hostess, glancing round at the door. "Ah, there you are at last!" she said to Vronsky with a smile as he came in.

Vronsky not only knew everyone, but he saw everyone he met here every day, and so he came in with the calm manner with which one rejoins people in a room one has only just left.

"Where am I coming from?" he said in answer to a question from the ambassador's wife. "There's no escape, I'll have to confess. From the Opéra Bouffe. I think it must be the hundredth time I've seen it, and each time it gives me fresh pleasure. Heavenly! I know it's scandalous, but at the opera I go to sleep, while at the Bouffe I sit it out to the last minute, and it's always gay. Today—"

He mentioned a French actress and was about to tell some story about her, but the ambassador's wife stopped him with mock horror.

"Please don't tell us all those horrid things!"

"All right, then, I won't, all the more since everyone knows all about those horrid things!"

"And everyone would go there if it were as accepted as the opera," put in Princess Myagky.

<br>

VII

SOME steps were heard at the entrance, and Princess Betsy, knowing they were Anna's, glanced over at Vronsky. He looked at the door, and his face took on a strange, new expression. He was looking joyfully, insistently, yet timidly at the woman coming in, as he slowly rose from his seat. Anna came into the room. Holding herself very erect as usual, and with that swift, firm and light step that distinguished her from other society women, without changing the direction of her eyes, she crossed the short space to her hostess, shook her hand, smiled, and with the same smile looked round at Vronsky. Vronsky made a low bow and drew up a chair for her.

She responded only by inclining her head; she blushed and frowned. Then, quickly nodding to acquaintances and pressing the hands extended toward her, she immediately turned to the hostess.

"I was at Countess Lydia's and tried to come earlier, but I couldn't get away. Sir John was there. Very interesting."

"Isn't he the missionary?"

"Yes, he was telling us some very interesting things about life in India."

The conversation that had been interrupted by her entrance flared up again like the flame of a lamp that has been blown about.

"Sir John! Of course, Sir John. I've seen him. He's a very good talker. The older Vlasyev girl is completely infatuated with him!"

"And is it true that the younger one is going to marry Topov?"

"Yes, it's said to be quite settled."

"I'm surprised at her parents. It's said to be a love match."

"A love match? What antediluvian ideas you have! Who talks about love nowadays?" said the ambassador's wife.

"What can be done? That preposterous old fashion still hasn't died out," said Vronsky.

"So much the worse for those who follow the fashion.

The only happy marriages I know are based on reason."

"Yes, but to make up for that, how often the happiness of marriages based on reason flies away like dust just because of the appearance of the passion that was never acknowledged," said Vronsky.

"But what we call 'marriages based on reason' are those in which both have already sown their wild oats. It's like scarlet fever, it's something you have to go through."

"Then they'll have to find a way to give an inoculation of love, like a vaccination."

"When I was young I was once in love with a deacon," said Princess Myagky. "I don't know whether that helped me any."

"No, I think, quite seriously, that in order to know what love is you have to make a mistake and then correct it," said Princess Betsy.

"Even after marriage?" said the ambassador's wife archly.

"It's never too late to mend," said the attaché, quoting the English proverb.

"That's just it," Betsy put in, "you have to make a mistake and correct it. What do you think about all this?" she said to Anna, who with a scarcely noticeable fixed smile on her lips, was listening to this conversation in silence.

"I think," said Anna, toying with a glove she had removed, "I think that—if there are as many minds as there are heads, then there are also just as many kinds of love as there are hearts."

Vronsky had been looking at Anna, waiting with a sinking heart for what she would say. He sighed as though some danger were past when she said this.

Anna suddenly turned to him. "But I've just received a letter from Moscow. It says that Kitty Shcherbatsky is very ill."

"Really?" said Vronsky with a frown.

Anna looked at him sternly. "Doesn't that interest you?"

"On the contrary, very much indeed. Just what do they write, if I may ask?" he said.

Anna got up and went over to Betsy.

"A cup of tea," she said, stopping behind Betsy's chair.

While Princess Betsy was pouring the tea, Vronsky went over to Anna. "But what did they write you?" he repeated.

"I've often thought men never understand what honor is, though they're always talking about it," said Anna, without answering him. "I've been meaning to tell you for a long time," she added, moving off a few steps and sitting down at a side table covered with albums.

"I don't quite grasp the meaning of that," he said, handing her the cup of tea.

She glanced at the sofa next to her, and he instantly sat down.

"Yes, I've been meaning to tell you," she said without looking at him, "you've behaved badly, very badly indeed."

"D'you suppose I don't realize that I've behaved badly? But who is responsible for my behavior?"

"Why do you tell me that?" she said, looking at him sternly.

"You know why," he answered boldly and happily, meeting her gaze without lowering his eyes.

It was not he, but she who grew confused.

"That merely proves you have no heart," she said. But her look told him that she knew he had a heart, and it was because of it that she was afraid of him.

"What you were speaking of just now was a mistake, it wasn't love."

"Remember that I've forbidden you to pronounce that word, that loathsome word," said Anna shuddering; but at once she felt that by that one word alone, "forbidden," she was indicating that she claimed certain rights over him and by that very fact was spurring him on to speak of love. "I've meant to tell you this for a long time," she went on, looking resolutely into his eyes, her face a blaze of crimson. "I came here purposely today because I knew I'd meet you. I came to tell you that this must come to an end. I've never had to blush before anyone, but you are making me feel as though I were guilty of something or other."

He looked at her, struck by the new, spiritual beauty of her face.

"What do you want me to do?" he said simply and gravely.

"I want you to go to Moscow and ask Kitty to forgive you," she said.

"You can't want that," he said.

He saw she was saying something she had to force herself to say, not what she wanted to.

"If you love me as you say," she whispered, "allow me to be at peace."

His face lit up. "Surely you know that for me you are all of life; but I don't know how to give you peace and cannot do it. All of me, love—yes. I'm incapable of thinking of you and of myself separately. For myself you and I are one. And I cannot foresee any possibility of peace either for myself or for you. I see a possibility of despair, of unhappiness—or I see a possibility of happiness, and of what happiness! Surely that is possible?" he added with his lips alone, but she heard him.

She bent all the power of her mind to say what she ought to say; but instead of that she fixed her eyes on him, full of love, and said nothing.

At last! he thought, enraptured. Just when I was beginning to despair, when it seemed as though the end would never come—at last! She loves me! She admits it!

"Then do this for me, never say such things to me, and let us be good friends," she said, in words, though her eyes said something quite different.

"We can never be friends, you know that yourself. But whether we shall be the happiest or the unhappiest people in the world—all that depends on you."

She was about to say something, but he stopped her.

"After all, there's only one thing I'm asking for, I'm asking for the right to hope, to torment myself, as I am now; or, if even that's not possible, then order me to disappear, and I'll disappear. You shall never see me again, if my presence upsets you."

"I don't want to drive you away anywhere."

"Just don't change anything. Leave everything as it is," he said, his voice trembling. "Here comes your husband."

Karenin, with his unhurried, clumsy walk, was actually just coming into the drawing room.

Glancing over at his wife and Vronsky, he went over to the hostess and, sitting down for a cup of tea, began saying something in his deliberate, never indistinct voice, making fun of someone in his usual bantering tone.

"Your Rambouillet is in full muster," he said glancing round the whole company. "Graces and Muses."

But Princess Betsy could not bear this tone of his, which she called "sneering" in English, so, like an able hostess, she immediately led him into a serious conversation about universal military service. Karenin was immediately carried away by the conversation and now very earnestly began defending the new law against Princess Betsy, who attacked it.

Vronsky and Anna remained sitting at the little table.

"This is becoming indecent," whispered a woman, indicating Anna, Vronsky, and Karenin with a glance.

"What did I tell you?" replied Anna's friend.

But it was not these women alone, almost everyone in the drawing room, even Princess Myagky and Betsy herself, kept glancing over at the couple who had taken themselves out of the general circle, as though they were disturbed by it. Karenin alone did not look over toward them, and was not distracted from his interest in the conversation that was now in full swing.

Having noticed the unpleasant impression this was making on everyone, Princess Betsy slipped some one else into her place to listen to Karenin and went over to Anna.

"I never fail to be astonished by the clarity and precision with which your husband expresses himself," she said. "The most transcendental ideas become quite easy for me whenever he talks about them."

"Oh yes!" said Anna, smiling radiantly with happiness, not understanding a word of what Betsy was telling her. She went over to the large table and joined in the general conversation.

Karenin, having stayed a half hour, went over to Anna and proposed that they go home together; but without looking at him she answered that she was staying on to supper. Karenin bowed to the company and left.

The Karenins' fat old Tatar coachman, in his shiny leather coat, was finding it difficult to restrain the near gray horse, which was freezing and rearing up in the portico. The footman stood there, holding open the carriage door. The hall porter stood there, holding open the outer door. With her nimble little hand Anna was disentangling the lace on her sleeve from a hook on her fur coat, and with bent head was listening with delight to what Vronsky was saying to her as he accompanied her.

"You haven't said a thing; let's agree that I demand nothing either," he said, "but you know that it's not friendship I need, the only happiness in life that's possible for me is that word you dislike so much, yes . . . love . . ."

"Love . . ." she repeated slowly, in a musing voice, and suddenly, while disentangling the lace, she added: "The reason I dislike the word is because it means such a great deal to me, far more than you can understand." She looked into his face. *"Au revoir!"*

She held out her hand to him and with her brisk, elastic step went past the hall porter and vanished into the carriage. Her glance, the touch of her hand, had inflamed him. He kissed the spot on the palm of his hand where she had touched him, and went home, happy in the knowledge that he had drawn closer to the attainment of his goal that evening than he had during the previous two months.

## VIII

KARENIN did not see anything peculiar or improper in his wife's sitting together with Vronsky at a separate table and having a lively chat with him, but he noticed that this seemed peculiar and improper to the others in the drawing room, and so it seemed improper to him too. He decided he would have to mention it to Anna.

When he got home he went into his study as he usually did, sat down in an armchair, opened a book on the papacy at the place marked by the paper knife, and read until one o'clock, as he usually did; only occasionally he would rub his high forehead and shake his head as though driving something away. At his usual hour he got up and made his preparations for bed. Anna still wasn't there. With the book under his arm he went upstairs; but tonight, instead of his usual thoughts and reflections about his official affairs, his mind was filled with his wife, with something unpleasant that had happened concerning her. Contrary to his habit he did not go to bed, but started pacing back and forth through the rooms with his hands clasped behind his back. He could not lie down; he felt he had to think over beforehand this new circumstance that had arisen.

When Karenin had made up his mind that it was necessary to talk things over with his wife, it had seemed to him very easy and simple; but now, as he began thinking over this new circumstance that had arisen, it seemed to him very complicated and difficult.

Karenin was not a jealous man. It was his conviction that jealousy was an insult to one's wife, and that one ought to have confidence in one's wife. Just why one should trust one's wife, that is, have complete confidence that his young wife was always going to love him, he never asked himself: but he felt no distrust, because he had confidence and told himself that it was necessary to have it. But now, even though his conviction that jealousy was a shameful feeling and that it was necessary to have confidence was not destroyed, he felt

that he was standing face to face with something illogical
and irrational, and he did not know what to do.

Karenin was standing face to face with life, with the possibility of his wife's loving someone else, and this seemed to
him extremely irrational and incomprehensible, because it
was life itself. He had spent his entire life working in official
circles dealing with reflections of life. Each time he had
knocked up against life itself he had stepped out of its way.
Now he was undergoing a feeling such as a man would have
who was calmly crossing a bridge over a chasm and suddenly
saw that the bridge was broken and the abyss was there. This
abyss was life itself—the bridge was that artificial life Karenin had been living. For the first time questions arose in
his mind about the possibility of his wife's falling in love with
someone, and this horrified him.

Without undressing he paced back and forth with his even
step across the resounding parquet floor of the dining room,
lighted by only one lamp, across the carpet of the dark drawing room where some light was reflected only on the large
portrait that had recently been done of himself and hung
over the sofa, and on through her sitting room, where there
were two candles burning, lighting up the portraits of her
relatives and friends and the pretty knickknacks on her writing table he had known so well so long. He walked through
her room to the door of the bedroom and turned back again.

At each section of his walk, for the most part on the parquet of the lighted-up dining room, he would stop and say to
himself: Yes, I must make a decision and stop it, and express
my opinion of it and my decision. Then he would turn back
again. But just what should I express? What decision? he
would say to himself in the drawing room, and not find an
answer. After all, he would ask himself before turning into
his study, just what has happened? Nothing. She talked to
him a long time—well, what of it? Aren't there a great many
men in society a woman can talk to? Besides, being jealous
means degrading both myself and her, he would say to himself as he entered her sitting room; but this consideration,
which had had such weight for him before now had no weight
and meant nothing. At the bedroom door he would turn back
again into the room, and the moment he had gone back into
the dark drawing room some voice would say to him that
that was not so, and that if others had noticed it, it meant
that there was something there. Then in the dining room he
would say to himself again: Yes, it's necessary to make a de-

cision and stop it, and express my opinion . . . And once again he would ask himself in the dining room before turning back, But what decision? Then he would ask himself, But what happened? He would answer, Nothing, and recall that jealousy was a feeling that was an insult to one's wife, but in the drawing room he would convince himself again that something had happened after all. His thoughts as well as his body went round in a full circle without encountering anything new. He noticed this, rubbed his forehead, and sat down in her sitting room.

There, as he looked at her table with the malachite cover on the blotting paper and an unfinished note on the top of it, his thoughts suddenly changed. He began to think about her—what she was thinking and feeling. For the first time he vividly pictured to himself her own personal life, her thoughts, her desires, and the idea that she might and must have a life of her own seemed to him so terrifying that he hastily drove it away. This was the abyss he was terrified of looking into. To transfer himself by thought and feeling into another being was a spiritual activity that was alien to Karenin. He regarded it as a harmful and dangerous abuse of fancy.

And the most terrible thing about it all, he thought, is that just now, just when my work is almost finished—he was thinking of a project he was busy with—when I need complete calm and all my mental powers, this senseless anxiety descends on me. But what can I do? I'm not one of those people who can endure anxiety and agitation without having the strength to face up to them.

"I must think things over, make a decision, and put it out of my mind," he muttered aloud.

Questions about her feelings, about what has been taking place or may take place in her soul—that's none of my business, that's the business of her conscience and concerns religion, he said to himself, with a feeling of relief at the awareness of having found a juridical point on which he could duly hang the circumstance that had arisen.

Consequently, Karenin said to himself, questions concerning her feelings and all that—are questions for her conscience, which cannot be any of my business, while my own duties are clearly defined. As the head of a family, I am the person who is bound to guide her and therefore is partly responsible; I must point out the danger I see, warn her, and even make use of my authority. I must speak to her plainly.

And in Karenin's mind everything he was now going to say to his wife took on a clear form. As he turned over in his mind what he was going to say he regretted having to put his time and his intellectual powers to such obscure domestic use; nevertheless the form and sequence of his forthcoming statement took shape in his mind clearly and distinctly, like an official report. What I must point out is the following: first of all, I must indicate the importance of public opinion and propriety; secondly, explain the religious significance of marriage; thirdly, indicate if necessary the misfortune that may come about for our son; fourthly, refer to her own misfortune.

And interlacing his fingers, palms facing down, he stretched them until the joints cracked.

This gesture, a bad habit he had of putting his hands together and cracking his knuckles, always soothed him and brought him back to that precision of mind he needed so much now. The sound of a carriage drawing up was heard at the entrance. Karenin stood still in the middle of the room.

A woman's steps were heard coming up. Karenin, ready for his speech, was standing pressing his interlocked fingers together seeing whether one joint or another would not crack. One of them did.

Even as he heard the sound of her light footsteps on the staircase he sensed her approach, and although he was satisfied with his speech he grew frightened about the forthcoming interview.

IX

ANNA came in with her head bowed, toying with the tassels of her hood. Her face shone with a bright glow, but it was not a cheerful glow—it suggested the terrible glow of a fire on a dark night. When she saw her husband, Anna raised her head and smiled, as though just waking up.

"Aren't you in bed? How extraordinary!" she said, throwing off her hood and going on into her dressing room without stopping. "Time, Alexis, time!" she added from behind the door.

"Anna, I must have a talk with you."

"With me?" she said, surprised, coming out of the door and looking at him. "What does that mean? What about?" she asked, sitting down. "Well, let's have a talk then, if it's so necessary. Though it would be better to go to sleep."

Anna said the first thing that came to her tongue; she herself was astonished at her capacity for lying. How simple and natural her words were, and how it really seemed as though she were simply sleepy! She felt clothed in an impenetrable armor of lies. She felt that some unseen force was helping her and propping her up.

"Anna, I must give you a warning," he said.

"A warning?" she said. "About what?"

She was looking at him so simply, so cheerfully, that no one who didn't know her as he did would have been able to notice anything unnatural in either the sounds or the sense of what she said. But for him, who knew her, who knew that when he went to bed five minutes late she would notice it and ask the reason, for him who knew that she would immediately tell him all her joys, pleasures, and worries instantly—for him to see now that she did not want to notice his state, did not want to say a word about herself, meant a great deal. He saw that the depths of her soul, which had always been open to him before, were now closed. That was the least of it: by her tone he saw that she was not even embarrassed at this, but seemed to be saying to him straight out: Yes, it is closed, and that's how it ought to be and will be from now on. Now he had a feeling such as a man might have, on returning home and finding his own house locked up. But perhaps the key can still be found, Karenin thought.

"I should like to warn you," he said in a low voice, "that through recklessness and light-mindedness you may be giving people an occasion to discuss you. Your excessively lively conversation today with Count Vronsky"—he pronounced the name firmly, with quiet deliberation—"has attracted some attention."

He said this and looked into her laughing eyes, terrifying to him now because of their impenetrability, and as he spoke he felt the utter uselessness and futility of his own words.

"That's how you always are," she replied, as though not understanding him at all, and deliberately understanding, out of everything he had said, only the last part. "First you're displeased when I'm bored, then you're displeased when I'm cheerful. I was not being bored. Does that offend you?"

Karenin shivered, and bent his hands to crack his knuckles.

"Oh please don't crack your knuckles, I dislike it so!" she said.

"Anna—is this you?" said Karenin, silently making an effort to control himself and keeping his hands still.

"But what's all this about?" she said, in a tone of comical surprise and sincerity. "What d'you want me to do?"

Karenin said nothing; he rubbed his forehead and eyes. He saw that instead of saying what he had wanted to, that is, warning his wife against making a mistake in the eyes of the world, he had involuntarily gotten excited about something that concerned her own conscience, and was struggling against some barrier set up by his imagination.

"This is what I intend to say," he went on coldly and calmly, "and I ask you to listen to me. As you know, I consider jealousy an offensive and degrading feeling, and will never permit myself to be guided by it; but there are certain rules of propriety which cannot be broken with impunity. Today it was not I who noticed, but judging by the impression made on the company, everyone noticed that your action and behavior were not quite all that could be wished for."

"Really, I don't understand a thing," said Anna, shrugging her shoulders. It's all the same to him, she thought, but it was noticed in public, and that's what upsets him! "You're not well, Alexis," she added, getting up and starting through the door, but he moved forward as though wishing to stop her.

His face looked ugly and morose, as Anna had never seen it before. Anna stopped and, bending her head backward and sideways, began taking out her hairpins with her quick hands.

"Well, I'm still listening for what's to follow," she said calmly and mockingly. "I'm actually interested, since I'd like to know what it's all about."

She said this and was surprised by her natural, tranquil, genuine tone, and her choice of words.

"I do not have the right to go into the details of your feelings; in general I consider that useless and even harmful," Karenin began. "When we dig into our own souls we often dig up something that might have gone on lying there unnoticed. Your own feelings are a matter for your own conscience; but before you, before myself, and before God I am bound to point out to you your duties. Our lives are joined together, and joined together not by man but by God. Only a crime can break this bond, and a crime of that kind entails a severe punishment."

"I don't understand a thing. Oh dear, and I'm so sleepy on

top of it!" she said, quickly shaking out her hair and looking for any pins that were left.

"Anna—for God's sake don't talk that way," he said mildly. "It may be that I'm making a mistake, but believe me that I'm saying what I am just as much for my own sake as for yours. I am your husband, and I love you."

For an instant her head had drooped, and the mocking glint in her eye had died away, but the word "love" aroused her again. She thought: Love? As though he were capable of love! If he hadn't heard that there is such a thing he would never even have used the word. He doesn't even know what it is!

"Alexis, I honestly don't understand," she said. "Explain what it is you—"

"Allow me to finish. I love you. But I'm not speaking of myself; the chief persons involved in this are our son and you yourself. It may very well be, I repeat, that what I'm saying may appear to you to be completely idle and out of place; it may be that it has arisen through an error of mine. In that case I ask you to forgive me. But if you yourself feel that there is even the slightest ground for it, then I ask you to reflect, and if your heart prompts you to tell me . . ."

Without noticing it himself Karenin was saying something quite different from what he had prepared.

"I have nothing to say. And I—" she suddenly said quickly, holding back a smile with difficulty, "really it's high time to go to bed."

Karenin sighed; without saying another word he went into the bedroom.

When she came into the bedroom he was already lying down. His lips were sternly pressed together, and he did not look at her. Anna lay down in her own bed and kept expecting him momentarily to start speaking to her once more. She was both afraid of his speaking and eager for it. But he was silent. She lay motionless for a long time, having already forgotten about him. She was thinking of the other, she saw him and she felt her heart filling with excitement and guilty joy at the thought. Suddenly she heard an even, tranquil nasal whistling. For a moment Karenin seemed to have been frightened by his own snoring and stopped, but after waiting a couple of breaths the snoring started again with a new, calm regularity.

"It's late, it's late, it's already late," she whispered with a smile. For a long time she lay motionless with her eyes open; it seemed to her she could see their gleam in the darkness herself.

## X

FROM this time on a new life began for Karenin and for his wife. Nothing in particular happened. As usual Anna went out into society, visited Princess Betsy especially often and met Vronsky everywhere. Karenin saw this, but there was nothing he could do. To all his efforts to draw her into explanations she counterposed an impenetrable wall of a sort of cheerful perplexity. Outwardly everything was the same, but their intimate relations had completely changed. Karenin, who was so powerful a figure in his governmental life, felt powerless here. Like an ox, his head submissively lowered, he waited for the poleax he felt hanging over him. Each time he began thinking about it he felt that it was necessary to make one more attempt, that through kindness, tenderness, and persuasion there was still a hope of saving her, of making her come to her senses, and each day he prepared for a talk with her. But each time he began talking to her, he felt that the same spirit of evil and deceit which possessed her also took possession of him, and he did not say anything like what he meant to or strike the right note. Involuntarily he spoke to her in his usual half-bantering tone, of making fun of anyone who would speak that way. And in that tone it was impossible to say what had to be said to her . . .

## XI

WHAT had been for Vronsky the sole and exclusive desire of his life for almost a whole year, taking the place of all previous desires, and what had been for Anna an impossible, terrifying and so all the more enchanting dream of happiness —this desire had been fulfilled. Pale, his lower jaw trembling, he was standing in front of her begging her to calm herself, without knowing himself why or how.

"Anna! Anna!" he said in a trembling voice. "Anna—for God's sake!"

But the louder he spoke the lower drooped her once proud and gay, but now shame-stricken head; writhing she slipped off the sofa and was sitting on the floor, at his feet; she would have fallen on the carpet if he had not held her.

"My God! Forgive me!" she said sobbing, pressing his hand to her breast.

She felt so sinful, so guilty, that the only thing left for her to do was to humble herself and beg to be forgiven; now she had no one in her life but him, so she addressed her plea for forgiveness to him too. As she looked at him she felt her own humiliation physically, and could say nothing further. But what he felt was what a murderer must feel looking at the body he has deprived of life. The body he had deprived of life was their love—the first period of their love. There was something horrifying and repulsive in the recollection of what had been paid for this dreadful price of shame. The shame she felt at her own spiritual nakedness crushed her, and communicated itself to him. But in spite of all the murderer's horror in the face of the murdered body, that body had to be cut in pieces and hidden away; the murderer had to make use of what he had gained by the murder.

And just as the murderer, in a fury, as though with passion, flings himself on the body and drags it along, hacking away at it, so Vronsky too covered her face and shoulders with kisses. Yes—it was these kisses that had been bought with this shame. Yes, and this hand of his, which will always be mine, is the hand of my accomplice. She lifted his hand and kissed it. He knelt down and tried to see her face; but she hid it and said nothing. At last, as though making an effort to control herself, she sat up and pushed him aside. Her face was still just as beautiful, but it was all the more pathetic.

"Everything is finished," she said. "I have nothing but you now. Remember that."

"I cannot fail to remember what to me is life itself. For one moment of happiness like this—"

"What happiness!" she said with revulsion and horror, and her horror was involuntarily communicated to him. "For the love of God, not a word, not one more word."

She quickly got up and moved away from him.

"Not one more word," she repeated, and with an expression of frigid despair that was strange to him she left. She felt that at that moment she was incapable of expressing in words the feeling of shame, joy, and horror at this entry of hers into a new life; she did not want to speak about it, she did not want to vulgarize the feeling by vague, imprecise words. But

afterward too, on the next day and the next, she could not
only not find words to express all the complexity of these
feelings of hers, but could not even find the thoughts with
which she would have been able to reflect on everything that
was going on in her soul.

She said to herself: No, I can't think about it now—later,
when I've calmed down. But that calm for reflection never
came; every time the thought came to her about what she had
done. and what was going to become of her, and what she
ought to do, she was seized with horror, and drove these
thoughts away.

Later, she said to herself, later—when I'm calmer.

But in dreams, when she had no power over her own
thoughts, her situation appeared to her in all its monstrous
nakedness. Almost every night there was one dream that
kept returning to her. She dreamed that both of them together were her husbands, and that both lavished their caresses on her. Alexis Karenin was weeping as he kissed her
hands, and saying: How wonderful it is now! And Alexis
Vronsky was also there, and he was her husband too. And
she, astonished that this had used to seem impossible to her,
was explaining to them with a laugh that this was far simpler
and that now they were both pleased and happy. But this
dream weighed on her like a nightmare, and she would wake
up horrified.

### XII

EVEN just after Levin's return from Moscow, when he still
started and blushed every time he recalled the shame of having been refused, he said to himself: I blushed and started in
just the same way, and thought everything was over with,
when I flunked physics and had to stay on in the second
class; in just the same way I thought myself ruined when I
bungled that business of my sister's that was put in my charge.
And what of it? Now that years have gone by whenever I
recall it I'm astounded that it could have upset me so. It'll be
the same with this trouble too; as time goes by I'll be indifferent to the whole thing.

But three months had gone by and he had still not grown
indifferent, and it was just as painful for him to think of it as
it had been at first. He could not be at peace, because after
having dreamed for so long about a family life, and having

felt that he was ripe for it, nevertheless he was still not married and was farther away from marriage than ever before. He himself felt painfully just what everyone else around him felt too, that it was unwholesome for a man of his age to live alone. He recalled how, just before leaving for Moscow, he had once said to his cattleman Nicholas, a naïve peasant he liked to talk to: "Well, Nicholas, I want to get married," and how Nicholas had promptly answered, as though it were something there could be no doubt about, "And high time too, Mr. Constantine."

But marriage was farther away from him now than ever before. The place was taken; now, when in his imagination he would put some other girl he knew into it he felt it was completely impossible. In addition, the memory of her refusal and of the role he had played in it tormented him with shame. No matter how much he told himself that he was not in the least to blame, the recollection of it, together with other shameful memories, would make him start and blush. In his past, as in every man's, there had been actions he knew were wrong, for which his conscience should have tormented him; but the memory of these bad actions of his did not torment him nearly so much as these trivial, but shameful memories. Such wounds never closed up. And among these recollections there now stood her refusal, and the pathetic figure he must have cut in the eyes of the others that evening. But time and work had their effect. The painful memories became more and more covered up in his mind by the commonplace but important events of country life. With each week that went by he thought about Kitty less and less often. He was impatiently waiting for the news that she had already been married or was about to be, hoping this news would completely cure him, like the pulling of a tooth.

Meanwhile spring had come, a splendid, steady spring, without any of the expectations and disappointments of spring, one of those rare springs that plants, animals, and people rejoice in equally. This splendid spring roused Levin still more and confirmed him in his intention of renouncing everything in the past in order to arrange his solitary life firmly and independently. Although many of the plans he had come back to the country with had not been put into effect, nevertheless he had held to the most important thing—living a pure life. He did not undergo any of the shame that usually tormented him after a lapse, and he could look people boldly in the eye. By February he had already received a letter from Masha saying that his brother Nicholas's health had got much worse, but that he refused to be treated; because of this letter Levin went to see his brother in Moscow and succeeded in persuading him to see a doctor and go to a spa abroad. He was so successful in persuading his brother, and in lending him some money for the trip without annoying him, that in this respect he was very pleased with himself.

Aside from the farming, which demanded special attention in springtime, and aside from his reading, Levin had begun something else that winter—writing a book on farming, the basis of which consisted in taking the character of the farm worker as an absolute datum, like climate and soil, so that in consequence all the conclusions of agricultural science should be drawn not only from the data of climate and soil, but from the data of climate, soil, and a certain fixed character in the laborer. Thus, in spite of his solitude, or because of it, his life was exceptionally full, and it was only rarely that he felt an unsatisfied desire to communicate some of the ideas roving about in his mind to someone beside Miss Agatha, though with her too he would often find himself discussing physics, theories of agriculture and especially of philosophy—philosophy was Miss Agatha's favorite subject.

The spring had a slow start. During the last weeks of Lent the weather had been clear and frosty. There was a thaw in the daylight sunshine, but at night the temperature sank to sixteen degrees Fahrenheit; the snow was crusted over so hard that carts did not have to stay on the roads. Easter took place under the snow. Then suddenly, on Easter Monday, a warm wind began blowing, clouds came up, and for three days and three nights a warm, stormy rain poured down. On Thursday the wind died down and a dense gray mist came up as though to hide the secrets of the changes that were taking place in nature. The melted snow rushed down beneath the mist, the river ice began cracking and moving forward, and the turbid, foaming torrents began flowing more rapidly; the following Monday, from evening on, the mist dissolved, the clouds broke up into fleecy cloudlets, the sky cleared, and the real spring had come. In the morning the bright sun quickly sucked up the thin ice on the water, and the warm air all around throbbed with vapors from the awakening earth. The old grass grew green, as well as the young grass that pushed up in needle points; the buds swelled on the guelder-rose and the currant bush, and the birch trees were sticky with sap; honey bees began buzzing among the golden catkins of the willow. Unseen larks burst into song above the velvety green and the frozen stubble, pewits began crying above the lowlands and marshes where the water brought down by the storm was not yet absorbed; and cranes and geese flew high above giving their springtime call. The cattle, their winter coats still only gone in patches, began to low in the meadows, crook-legged lambs began frisking about their bleating mothers, just losing their wool; nimble-footed children began rushing about the quickly drying paths marked with the imprints of bare feet, the merry voices of women bleaching linen began chattering by the ponds, and the axes of the peasants getting their wooden plows and harrows ready began ringing out in the yards.

The real spring had come.

## XIII

LEVIN put on his high boots and, for the first time, not a fur coat but a cloth jacket, and started out through the farm, stepping through the streams that dazzled the eyes in the sunshine, crossing a stretch of ice first, then of sticky mud.

Spring is a time for making plans and resolutions. As Levin went into the yard, and like a tree that in springtime still doesn't know just where and how its young shoots and twigs, still imprisoned in their buds, are going to turn out, he himself had no very clear idea of just what he was going to start doing now on his beloved farm, but he felt himself full of the finest plans and resolutions. First of all he went over to the cattle yard. The cows had been let out into the paddock; warmed by the sun, their smooth new coats gleaming, they were mooing away, asking to be let into the fields. After admiring his cows, which he was familiar with down to the tiniest detail, Levin ordered them driven into the fields and the calves let out into the paddock. The cowherd ran off happily to get ready for the fields. The dairymaids, picking up their petticoats and splashing through the mud with their naked, white legs, not yet sunburned, began running around with their sticks driving the mooing calves, mad with the joy of spring, out into the yard.

After admiring the new calves born that year, which were exceptionally fine—the older calves were as big as a peasant cow, and Pava's three-month-old was the same size as the yearlings—Levin ordered a trough to be put outside for them and some hay put into the racks. But it turned out that the racks that had been made in the autumn and had been in the paddock which was never used in the wintertime, were broken. He sent for the carpenter, who according to his contract was supposed to be working on the threshing machine. But the carpenter turned out to be repairing the harrows, which should have been ready by the week before Lent. This annoyed Levin very much. What was annoying was the repetition of this constant slovenliness in farm work, against which he had been struggling with all his might for so many years. He found out that the racks, of no use in wintertime, had been taken into the work horses' stable, which was where they had been broken, since they had been lightly made, for calves. In addition, as a result of this, it became apparent that the harrows and all the agricultural tools that orders had been given to examine and repair back in the winter, and that three carpenters had been taken on for specially, had not been repaired, and that the harrows were only now being repaired, when the harrowing had to be done. Levin sent for the foreman, but then went out at once himself to look for him. The foreman, who was as radiant as everything else that day, was coming from the threshing ground in an astrakhan-trimmed coat, breaking a piece of straw in his hands.

"Why isn't the carpenter at the threshing machine?"

"Oh, I meant to tell you yesterday—the harrows have to be repaired. Plowing time, you know."

"And in the winter—why wasn't it done then?"

"But what d'you need the carpenter for?"

"Where are the racks from the calves' yard?"

"I've given orders for them to be put in their places. What can you do with people like that!" said the foreman, with a wave of his hand.

"Not with people like this, but with a foreman like this!" Levin exclaimed, flaring up. "What do I keep you on for!" he shouted. Then, reminding himself that this wouldn't be any help, he stopped short in the middle of a sentence and merely sighed. "Well, what about it; can we begin sowing?" he asked after a moment's silence.

"With Turkino it'll be possible tomorrow or the day after."

"And the clover?"

"I've sent Vasili and Mishka, they're sowing. But I don't know whether they'll get through—it's sticky."

"How many acres?"

"Sixteen."

"But why not the whole place?" shouted Levin.

He was even more annoyed at the clover's being sown on only sixteen acres and not on fifty. Planting clover, both in theory and according to his own experience, was only successful when it was done as early as possible, practically while the snow was still there. And Levin had never been able to get this done.

"We haven't the people for it. What can you expect with people like that? Three of them haven't shown up. And now Simon—"

"Then you should have let the straw wait."

"But I did."

"Then where are the men?"

"Five of them are turning the compott"—he meant compost—"four are shifting the oats, they might spoil, Mr. Constantine."

Levin knew perfectly well that this "they might spoil" meant that his English seed oats were already ruined—again his orders hadn't been carried out.

"But didn't I tell you as far back as Lent, use the ventilators!" he shouted.

"Don't worry, we'll get it all done in time."

Levin waved a hand angrily, went to the barn to look at the oats, and went back to the stable. The oats were not yet spoiled, but the men were turning them over with shovels, though it was possible to let them drop into the lower granary directly. After giving orders for it to be done that way, and taking two of the men away to do some clover planting, Levin got over his annoyance with the foreman. For that matter it was such a fine day it was impossible to stay angry.

"Ignat!" he called to the coachman, who with sleeves rolled up was washing a carriage at the pump. "Saddle me—"

"Which one, sir?"

"Well—why not Kolpik?"

"Yes, sir!"

While the horse was being saddled Levin, in order to make it up with the foreman, who was hovering about in sight, called him over again, and began talking to him about the spring work that was coming up and about his farming plans.

Carting the manure had to be started earlier, so that everything was finished before the first hay harvest; the far field would have to be worked with plows uninterruptedly so as to keep it fallow; the hay harvests would have to be gathered in by hired laborers, not on a profit-sharing basis.

The foreman listened attentively; he was plainly making an effort to approve of his master's proposals; but he still had that hopeless, dejected look that was so familiar to Levin and had always annoyed him. The look said: That's all very well but—God willing!

Nothing distressed Levin as much as this manner. But it was a manner that was common to all the foremen he had ever had. They had all had the same attitude toward his proposals, so he no longer got angry, but distressed; he felt even more stimulated for a struggle against this sort of elemental power, the only name for which he could find was "God-willingness", and which was constantly opposing him.

"Well," said the foreman, "we'll see if we can manage it."

"But why shouldn't you be able to manage it?"

"We absolutely have to hire another fifteen men. You see they don't come. Some came along today, they were asking for seventy rubles each for the summer."

Levin was silent. Once again that force was opposing him. He knew that no matter how they tried they had never been able to hire more than forty, or thirty-seven, or thirty-eight laborers at the right price; forty would be hired, but never any more. Yet all the same he could not help but keep struggling.

"Send over to Sury and to Chefirovka, to see whether any'll come. We have to look for them."

"If you want me to send for them I'll send for them," said the foreman dejectedly. "But the horses have been getting weak too."

"We'll buy some more. Of course I know you always want less of everything and worse," he added laughing, "but this year I'm not going to let you have things your own way. I'm going to do everything myself."

"But I don't think you sleep much as it is. It's much more cheerful for us when you keep your eye on us."

"So they're sowing the clover in the Birch Valley? I'll go over and take a look," said Levin, mounting the little light bay horse Kolpik that the coachman had led up.

"You won't be able to get across the streams, Mr. Constantine," the coachman called out.

"Then I'll go through the woods."

And Levin rode through the muddy yard out of the gates and into the field at a brisk pace, his good little horse, which had been standing about too long, snorting at the puddles and straining at the bridle.

If Levin had felt cheerful in the cattle sheds and farmyard he felt even more so in the fields. Gently swaying to his good little horse's pace, inhaling the warm smell with the freshness of snow and air in it, as he rode through the woods over the crumbling sinking snow that melted with each footstep, he was delighted by the sight of each tree of his, with the moss reviving on its bark and the buds swelling up. When he had passed through the woods a vast expanse of even velvety-green carpet stretched out before him, without one bare spot or bog, and only stained here and there by patches of thawing snow. Nor was he irritated by the sight of a peasant's horse and colt trampling the young growth (he told a peasant he met to drive them off) or by the jeering, silly answer he got from a peasant, Ipat, whom he came across and asked: "Well, Ipat, time to sow soon?" "Plowing first, Mr. Constantine," Ipat replied. The farther he rode the gayer he became; plans for the farm kept coming to mind, each one better than the next: planting willows in all the fields in lines facing south, so that the snow would not linger under them; dividing up the fields, tilling six and keeping three under grass; building a cattle yard at the farther end of one field, digging a pond and making movable pens for the cattle for manuring. Then he would have eight hundred acres of wheat, three hundred of potatoes, and four hundred of clover without exhausting a single acre.

Dreaming along this way, and carefully guiding his horse along the borders of the fields so as not to trample the young growth, he rode up to the laborers who were sowing the clover. The seed cart was not standing on the side but in the middle of a field of winter wheat, which was being cut up by the wheels and trampled by the horse. Both men were sitting on the border, probably sharing a pipe. The earth in the cart, which the seeds were mixed with, had not been pulverized, but was crushed or frozen into lumps. When they saw Levin the laborer Vasili moved toward the cart, while Mishka began sowing. This was a bad business, but Levin seldom got angry at the workers. When Vasili came over Levin told him to lead the horse over to the border.

"It doesn't matter, sir, the wheat will recover," answered Vasili.

"Please don't argue," said Levin, "just do as you're told."

"Yes, sir," Vasili answered, taking the horse's head. "But

the sowing is the best yet, Mr. Constantine," he said ingratiatingly. "Just the walking is terrible. You drag along fifty pounds on each boot."

"And why hasn't that earth been sifted?" Levin asked.

"Oh, we crumble it up," answered Vasili, taking up some seed and rubbing the earth between his palms.

Vasili wasn't to blame for having been brought unsifted earth, but it was annoying anyhow.

Having more than once tried out a method he knew for swallowing his anger and righting anything that seemed wrong, Levin made use of this method now. He watched Mishka striding along swinging the huge clods of earth that stuck to each foot, dismounted, took the seed basket from Vasili and moved forward to begin sowing.

"Where did you stop?"

Vasili pointed to a mark with his foot, and Levin started off, scattering the seeds as best he could. Walking was as difficult as in a quagmire, and after finishing a row Levin stopped, drenched in sweat, and handed back the seed basket.

"Now when summer comes, sir, you mustn't blame me for that row!" said Vasili.

"Why not?" said Levin gaily, already feeling how effective his method had been.

"You'll see when summer comes. It'll stand out. Just take a look where I did the sowing last spring—how I worked! After all, Mr. Constantine, I don't think I could try any harder if it was for my own father. I don't like bad work myself and I see that others don't do any either. If it's good for the master it's good for us. Just look over there now," said Vasili, pointing out at the field, "it does your heart good."

"It's a fine spring too, Vasili."

"A spring like this, the old people can't remember. I've been home, one old man there has sown wheat too, about an acre of it. He was saying you couldn't tell it from rye."

"And have you been sowing wheat long?"

"But it was you who taught us to sow it, the year before last; it was you who gave me a bushel of seed. We sold a quarter of it and sowed the rest."

"Well, be sure you crumble the lumps," said Levin, going over to his horse. "And watch out for Mishka. If the crop turns out all right you'll get half a ruble for every acre."

"Thank you kindly. We're all very grateful to you anyhow."

Levin mounted his horse and rode off into a field where

there was some of last year's clover, and to another that had been prepared for the spring wheat by deep plowing.

The clover was coming up magnificently. It was already reviving and all steadily growing green among the last year's wheat stubble. The horse sank up to its fetlocks into the mud, and as each foot was pulled out of the half-thawed ground it made a smacking noise. In the plowed field riding was out of the question altogether: the earth held up only where there was ice, and in the thawing furrows the horse's legs sank all the way in. The plowed land was first rate; in two more days it would be possible to harrow and sow it. Everything was beautiful, everything full of joy. On the way back Levin rode through the streams, hoping that the water would have gone down. And as a matter of fact he did get across, frightening two ducks. There must be some snipe too, he thought, and just as he turned off for his house he met the forester, who confirmed what he had thought about the snipe.

Levin rode on home at a trot, so as to have enough time for dinner and to get his gun ready for the evening.

## XIV

As Levin, in the highest spirits, was approaching his house, he heard the tinkle of a bell coming from the side of the chief entrance.

Yes, that must be someone from the station, he thought; this is just when the Moscow train comes in. . . . Who could it be? Nicholas? He did say: "I might go to the spa, or I might come to stay with you." At first he was annoyed, and afraid that his brother Nicholas's presence would destroy this happy springtime mood of his. But then he grew ashamed of this feeling, and instantly it was though he stretched out his spiritual arms and with a melting joy expected and with all his soul now wished it to be his brother. He spurred on his horse and after passing the acacia tree saw the sleigh from the station, with a man in a fur coat in it. It was not his brother. Oh, if only it's someone agreeable I can talk to! he thought.

"Ah!" he cried, joyfully raising both arms. "Now here's a guest! Oh, how glad I am to see you!" he exclaimed as he recognized Oblonsky.

Now I'll know for certain whether she's married or when she will be, he thought. On this magnificent spring day he felt that the memory of her was not in the least painful to him.

"You didn't expect me, did you?" said Oblonsky, climbing out of the sleigh, with mud on his nose, cheek and eyebrows, but radiant with gaiety and health. "I came to see you—first," he said, embracing and kissing Levin. "To do some shooting—second, and to sell the Yerzushovo forest—third."

"Splendid! And what a spring! How did you manage to get here in a sleigh?"

"On wheels it would have been even worse, Mr. Constantine," put in the driver, whom Levin knew.

"Well, I'm really very, very glad to see you," said Levin, with a sincere, childishly joyful smile.

Levin led his visitor into a room for guests, where Oblonsky's things were also taken—a bag, a gun in a gun case, and a cigar case; leaving him to wash and change, Levin went off to the office to give orders about the plowing and the clover. Miss Agatha, who was always very concerned for the honor of the house, met him in the hall with questions about dinner.

"Do just as you please, but be quick about it," he said, and went out to see the foreman.

When he came back Oblonsky, washed, combed, and beaming, was just coming out of his room; they went upstairs together.

"Well, I'm delighted at having got to you! Now I'll be able to understand all those mysterious things you're up to here. Actually I do envy you. What a house, and how splendid everything is—so bright and gay," said Oblonsky forgetting it was not always springtime and bright weather. "And what a charmer your old nurse is! A pretty little housemaid in an apron would be preferable, but this one goes very well with your monastic life and dour style."

Oblonsky gave him a great deal of interesting news, including something that was of particular interest to Levin—that his brother Sergius Koznyshov intended to come and stay with him in the country that summer.

Oblonsky did not say a single word about Kitty or about the Shcherbatskys generally: he only conveyed his wife's regards. Levin was grateful to him for his tact, and was delighted with his being there. As usual in his solitude a huge mass of thoughts and feelings had been accumulating that he could not communicate to those around him, and now he poured out over Oblonsky both the lyric joy of spring, his failures and his farming plans, his ideas and comments about the books he had been reading, and especially the idea of his own book, the basis of which, though he didn't notice this himself, consisted of a critique of all previous works on agriculture. Oblonsky, who was always sweet-tempered and understood everything from the slightest hint, was especially sweet-tempered on this visit, and Levin noticed in him a new trait that was flattering to himself—respect and a sort of tenderness.

The only effect of the efforts of Miss Agatha and the cook to make it a particularly good dinner was that the two famished friends, sitting down to the first course, ate their fill of bread and butter, smoked goose, and pickled mushrooms, in addition to which Levin ordered the soup to be served without the pasties the cook had wanted to astound the visitor with particularly. But Oblonsky, even though accustomed to very different dinners, thought everything magnificent—the herb brandy, the bread, the butter, and especially the smoked goose, and the little mushrooms, the nettle soup, the chicken in white sauce, and the white Crimean wine: it was all magnificent and delicious.

"Splendid, splendid," he said, lighting a thick cigarette after the roast. "It's just as though I'd landed on a peaceful shore here after the noise and jolting of a steamer. So you say that the laborer as such should be an element to be studied and used as a guide in the choice of agricultural methods. Of course I'm just a layman in all this, but it seems to me that the theory and its application will have an effect on the laborer too."

"Yes, but wait: I'm not talking about political economy, but about agricultural science. That ought to be like the natural sciences and should study the given phenomena and the laborer from the point of view of his economic, ethnographic—"

Just then Miss Agatha came in with some jam.

"Well, Miss Agatha," Oblonsky said to her, kissing the tips of his plump fingers, "what smoked goose you have, and what herb brandy! . . . But don't you think it's time, Kostya?" he added.

Levin glanced through the window at the sun, which was just setting beyond the bare treetops of the forest.

"Yes, it is, high time," he said. "Kuzma, get the gig ready!" And he ran downstairs.

Oblonsky went down and carefully took the canvas cover off the varnished case himself, opened it and began assembling his expensive gun, which was of a new type. Kuzma, already scenting a large tip, would not leave Oblonsky's side, putting on both his stockings and his boots for him, which Oblonsky willingly allowed him to do.

"Kostya, if that dealer Ryabinin comes—I told him to come today—leave word for him to be asked in and wait for me."

"But you aren't going to sell Ryabinin the forest?"

"Yes. D'you know him?"

"Of course I do. I've had some dealings with him absolutely and positively."

Oblonsky laughed: "absolutely and positively" were the dealer's favorite words.

"Yes, it's wonderfully comic, the way he talks. She knows where her master's off to!" he added, patting Laska, who was whining and jumping around Levin, licking first his hand, then his boots or his gun.

When they went out the gig was already standing at the door.

"I told them to bring the gig round, though it's not far, or should we walk?"

"No, let's drive," said Oblonsky, going over to the gig. He got in, wrapped his legs in a tiger-skin rug, and lighted a cigar. "How is it you don't smoke! A cigar is not only a pleasure, it's the crown and hallmark of delight. This is the life! How delightful! Now this is just how I'd like to live!"

"But who's stopping you?" said Levin, smiling.

"No, you're a lucky fellow. You've got everything you like here. You like horses—you have them; dogs—you have them; hunting—you've got that; farming—you've got that too."

"Perhaps it's because I'm glad of what I have and don't grieve about what's missing," said Levin, thinking of Kitty.

Oblonsky understood; he glanced over at him but said nothing.

Levin was grateful to Oblonsky for saying nothing about the Shcherbatskys after noticing, with his invariable tact, that Levin was afraid of talking about them; though by now Levin already felt like finding out what was tormenting him so he dared not start speaking.

"Well, how are things with you?" Levin said, recollecting how wrong it was to be thinking only of himself.

Oblonsky's eyes twinkled merrily.

"After all, you don't admit that it might be possible to like rolls when you've got your full ration of bread—you think that's a crime; but I don't believe you can live without love," he said, understanding Levin's question in his own way. "There's no help for it, that's how I'm made. And really, it does so little harm to anyone and gives oneself so much pleasure—"

"What's that, or is it something new again?"

"There is, my boy! You know Ossian's type of woman, don't you, the kind of woman you see in dreams? Well, there are women like that—and such women are terrible! Woman, you see, is the sort of subject that no matter how much you study it is always completely different."

"Then it would be better not to study it at all."

"No—some mathematician once said the pleasure was not in the discovery of the truth but in the search for it."

Levin listened in silence; in spite of all his exertions he was quite unable to find his way into his friend's soul and understand his feeling, or the charms of studying women of that kind.

### XV

THE place they were going to shoot from was not far away, by a stream amidst young aspen. When they reached the wood Levin got down and led Oblonsky into a corner of a mossy, marshy glade that was already free from snow. He himself went back to a forked birch on the other side and, leaning his gun against the fork of a dead lower branch, took off his coat, tightened his belt, and worked his arms to test their freedom of movement.

Laska, old and gray, who had been following close on his heels, watchfully sat down in front of him and pricked up her ears. The sun was sinking beyond the dense forest, and the little birches scattered among the aspen, with their drooping boughs and swollen buds ready to burst open, stood out clearly against the sunset glow.

From the thicket, where there was still some snow left, came the scarcely audible sound of water still running in narrow little twisting rivulets. Small birds were chirping; now and then they flew from tree to tree.

In the intervals of utter silence the rustling of last year's leaves could be heard, set in motion by the thawing of the earth and the growth of the grass.

Why, you can see and hear the grass growing! Levin said to himself, noticing a wet, slate-colored aspen leaf moving beside a shoot of young grass. He was standing up, listening and looking down, first at the moist, mossy earth, then at Laska, all ears, then at the sea of bare treetops stretching out in front of him at the foot of the hill, then at the darkening skies streaked with fleecy clouds. A hawk, its wings beating slowly, was flying high above the distant forest; another just like it was flying in the same direction, then it vanished. The birds were twittering more and more loudly and fussily in the thicket. Not far off an owl hooted, and Laska, starting up, took a few cautious steps forward; bending her head to one side she began listening intently. A cuckoo could be heard from beyond the streamlet. It made its usual cuckoo-call twice, then grew hoarse, started going too fast and broke down.

"Why—it's the cuckoo already!" said Oblonsky, coming out from behind a bush.

"Yes, I hear it," answered Levin, irritably breaking the silence of the forest by the sound of his own voice, which he himself found disagreeable. "In a moment now . . ."

Oblonsky's figure went behind the bush again; Levin saw only the bright flare of a match followed by the red glow of a cigarette and a spiral of blue smoke.

Click! Click! came the clack of Oblonsky's gun being cocked.

"But what's that scream?" asked Oblonsky, drawing Levin's attention to a long-drawn-out cry, in a high thin voice, like a colt whinnying in play.

"Don't you know? That's a hare. But enough talking! Listen—they're flying!" Levin almost shouted, cocking his gun.

A thin, far-off whistling could be heard and after a precise interval of two seconds, so familiar to hunters, there was a second, then a third whistle; by the third a hoarse cry could be heard.

Levin looked right and left about him; there before him, in the dull-blue sky over the blurred mass of tender aspen shoots, a flying bird appeared. It was flying straight toward him: the sound of its honking close at hand, like that of dense cloth being steadily torn across, could be heard just above his ear; the bird's long beak and neck were already quite visible, and just as Levin was taking aim a red flash came from behind the bush where Oblonsky was standing: the bird dropped like an arrow, then fluttered up again.

There was another flash followed by the sound of a hit, and its wings threshing about as though trying to stay up in the air the bird stopped, hung there a moment, and plummeted down on the marshy ground with a heavy thud.

"Not a miss, was it?" shouted Oblonsky, who couldn't see through the smoke.

"Here it is!" said Levin, pointing at Laska, who with one ear raised, proudly wagging the tip of her fluffy tail, stepping softly as though wishing to draw out the pleasure, and seeming to smile, was bringing the dead bird over to her master. "Well, I'm glad you got it," said Levin, at the same time already feeling a twinge of envy at not having managed to kill the snipe himself.

"An awful miss with the right barrel," answered Oblonsky, reloading. "Sh-sh—they're flying!"

And in fact they heard two piercing whistles in swift succession. Two snipe playfully racing each other and whistling, but not crying, flew directly over the heads of the hunters. Four shots rang out, and the snipe wheeled swiftly like swallows and vanished from sight . . .

The shooting was splendid; Oblonsky killed two more birds and Levin two, one of which was lost. It began turning dark. Low in the west Venus, bright and silvery, was already gleaming delicately through beyond the young birches; high in the east flickered the red fire of dim Arcturus. Above his head Levin located and lost again the Great Bear. The snipe had already stopped flying, but Levin decided to wait until Venus, which he could see beneath a birch bough, would rise above it and all the stars of the Great Bear would be visible. Venus had already risen above the birch bough, and the car of the Great Bear together with its shaft was already completely visible in the dark-blue sky, but he kept on waiting.

"Isn't it time to go?" said Oblonsky.

It was already silent in the forest; not a single little bird stirred.

"Let's stay a little while longer," Levin replied.

"Just as you like."

They were now standing about fifteen yards apart.

"Stiva!" Levin said, suddenly and unexpectedly. "Why haven't you told me whether your sister-in-law is married, or when she's going to be?"

Levin felt himself to be so firm and serene that no possible answer could upset him. But he didn't in the least expect the reply Oblonsky gave him.

"She never thought of getting married, and she's not thinking of it now, she's very ill and the doctors have sent her
abroad. They're even afraid for her life."

"What's that!" cried Levin. "Very ill? What has she got?
How is she—"

While they were both talking, Laska, pricking up her ears,
looked up at the sky and then at them, full of reproach.

Now's the time they find for chattering, she thought, and
here they come flying . . . Yes, there it is, they'll miss it,
thought Laska.

But just then they both suddenly heard a piercing whistle
that seemed to flick them by the ear; they both seized their
guns, there were two flashes of lightning, and two shots rang
out at the same moment. A high-flying snipe folded its wings
instantly and fell into the thicket, bending down the slender
young shoots.

"Wonderful! Both of us got it!" cried Levin, and ran off
to the thicket with Laska to look for the snipe. Oh yes, wasn't
there something unpleasant? he thought: of course—Kitty,
she's ill . . . What can be done about it, such a pity, he
thought.

"Got it? There's a clever dog," he said, taking the warm
bird out of Laska's mouth and putting it inside the gamebag,
which was almost full. "I've found it, Stiva!" he called out.

## XVI

ON the way home Levin asked Oblonsky for all the details
of Kitty's illness and the plans of the Shcherbatskys, and
though he would have been ashamed to admit it he liked
what he found out. He liked it both because there was still
hope, and even more because the one who had made him
suffer was now suffering herself. But when Oblonsky began
talking about the causes of Kitty's illness and mentioned
Vronsky's name, Levin stopped him.

"I have no right to hear such family details, and to tell
the truth I'm not interested either."

Oblonsky gave a slight smile as he caught the instantaneous change he knew so well on Levin's face, which turned
just as morose as it had been cheerful a moment before.

"Have you completely finished the deal with Ryabinin about
the forest?" Levin asked.

"Completely. I've got a wonderful price, thirty-eight thousand. Eight down and the rest spread over six years. I've been having a lot of trouble with it for a long time. No one wanted to pay any more."

"Well, you've given it away for nothing," said Levin glumly.

"Why for nothing?" said Oblonsky with a good-natured smile; he knew Levin would find fault with everything now.

"Because the forest is worth at least a hundred and eighty-five rubles an acre," Levin replied.

"You landowners!" said Oblonsky jocularly. "That's just your contempt for everyone from the city! But when there's some business to be done we always do it better. Believe me, I've figured it all out," he said, "the forest is being sold very profitably, I'm afraid he might even turn it down after all. You know it's not timber wood," said Oblonsky, hoping the word "timber" would convince Levin completely that his doubts were unfair, "but mostly firewood. It won't run to more than thirty-five yards of fagots per acre, and he's paying me at the rate of seventy rubles an acre."

Levin smiled contemptuously. How well I know that style, he thought, it's not just his, everyone who lives in the city and comes to the country twice every ten years has it too; he picks up two or three country words, and uses them whether they fit or not, totally convinced they've learned everything already. *"Timber," "Runs to yards of fagots per acre"* . . . Just words—he doesn't understand a thing himself.

"I wouldn't start teaching you whatever you write about at the office," he said, "but if I had to I'd ask you. Now you're so sure you know everything there is to know about forests: it's quite difficult. Have you counted the trees?"

"How can you count trees?" said Oblonsky, laughing, still trying to get his friend out of his bad temper. " 'Count the sands, and planets' rays, even though some lofty mind were able—' "

"Well, Ryabinin's lofty mind is able to. There's not a single dealer who would buy anything without counting, unless it's given to him for nothing, as you're doing now. I know that forest of yours; I go shooting there every year. Your forest is worth a hundred and eighty-five rubles an acre cash, and he's giving you seventy in installments. That means you've made him a present of about thirty thousand rubles."

"Now, don't let yourself be carried away," said Oblonsky pathetically. "Why didn't someone make the offer then?"

"Because he's fixed it up with the dealers, he's bought them off. I've done business with them all, and I know them.

They're not dealers, after all—they're profiteers. He wouldn't even go into a deal that brought him ten per cent profit, or fifteen, he waits until he can buy something for a fifth of its value."

"Go on now, you're just in a bad temper."

"Not in the least," said Levin morosely, as they drove up to the house.

A little gig, tightly bound with leather and iron, and with a well-fed horse in broad, tightly stretched straps harnessed to it, was already standing at the porch. Ryabinin's foreman, red-faced and tightly belted, who also acted as coachman, was sitting in it. Ryabinin himself was already in the house, and met the two friends in the hall. He was a tall, lean, middle-aged man with mustaches and a clean-shaven, prominent chin, and murky, bulging eyes. He was wearing a long-skirted blue coat with buttons low down in the back, high boots clinging to his calves and wrinkled around the ankles and covered on top by big galoshes. He wiped his face all around with a handkerchief, and smoothing his coat, which even without that hung very well, greeted the newcomers with a smile, holding his hand out to Oblonsky as though he were trying to catch something.

"So you've come," said Oblonsky, shaking hands with him. "Splendid."

"I didn't dare disobey Your Excellency's commands, though the roads were really very bad. I positively came the whole way on foot, but I got here on time. Mr. Constantine, my respects," he said, turning to Levin and trying to catch up his hand too. But Levin frowned, and pretending not to see his hand, began taking the snipe out. "Has it amused you to go out shooting? Now what kind of bird would that be?" Ryabinin added, looking contemptuously at the snipe. "Something tasty, I suppose." And he wagged his head disapprovingly, as though very much in doubt that the results could have been worth all the bother.

"D'you want to go into my study?" Levin, scowling morosely, said to Oblonsky in French. "Go on into the study, you'll be able to talk there."

"Quite so, wherever you please, sir," said Ryabinin with contemptuous dignity, as though wishing to make it clear that while others might find it difficult to get along with people, he never had the slightest difficulty.

When he entered the study Ryabinin, out of habit, looked around for the icon, but after finding it didn't cross himself.

He looked at the bookcases and shelves, and with the same doubtful air he had shown about the snipe smiled contemptuously and wagged his head disapprovingly, now no longer even admitting any doubt that here the results could have been worth the bother.

"Well, have you brought the money?" asked Oblonsky. "Do sit down."

"There will be no difficulty about the money. I've come to see you, to talk things over."

"What's there to talk about? But do sit down."

"To be sure," said Ryabinin, sitting down and leaning his elbow on the back of the armchair in the most painful way possible. "You'll have to concede me something, Prince. It wouldn't be right. Though the money is absolutely ready, to the last kopeck. There'll be no delay about the money."

Levin, who had meanwhile put his guns away in a cupboard, was just going out of the door, but when he heard the dealer's words he stopped.

"As it is you're getting the forest for nothing," he said. "He came to me too late, or else I'd have told him what the price was."

Ryabinin stood up and, smiling without a word, looked Levin over from his head to his feet.

"A very close fist has Mr. Constantine," he said with a smile, turning to Oblonsky. "It's positively impossible to buy anything from him. I've been bargaining with him for his wheat, offering a very good price."

"Why should I give you something of mine for nothing? I didn't find it lying around on the ground, or steal it."

"Dear me, nowadays it's positively impossible to steal. The jury is absolutely everything nowadays, everything is done honestly, there's no way of stealing anything. We're just talking things over in all honesty. The forest costs too much, there'll be no making ends meet. I'm asking for a concession, if only a trifle."

"But is the deal settled between you or not? If it's settled, there's no use bargaining, but if it's not," said Levin, "I'll buy the forest myself."

The smile vanished abruptly from Ryabinin's face. A hawk-like, greedy, cruel expression settled on it. His bony fingers swiftly unbuttoned his coat, displaying his braided shirt, brass waistcoat buttons, and a watch chain; he quickly got out a thick, old wallet.

"If you please, the forest is mine," he said, quickly crossing himself and holding out his hand. "Take the money, the forest is mine. That's how Ryabinin does business, no haggling over kopecks," he said, frowning and brandishing his wallet.

"If I were you I shouldn't be in any hurry," said Levin.

"What d'you mean?" said Oblonsky in surprise. "After all, I've given my word."

Levin went out, slamming the door. Ryabinin, looking at the door, shook his head with a smile.

"Just youth—positively nothing but childishness. On my honor, believe me, I'm buying it simply for the glory of the thing, so that Ryabinin and no one else will have bought the Oblonsky forest. But as for making ends meet it's all in the hands of God. Trust in the Lord. Please sir, the agreement must be in writing . . ."

An hour later the dealer, carefully straightening out his coat and fastening the hooks of his overcoat, with the agreement in his pocket, got into his tightly covered gig and drove home.

"Gentry!" he said to his foreman. "What a lot!"

"That's so," answered the foreman, handing him the reins and buttoning the leather apron of the gig. "And the deal, Mr. Michael?"

"Well, well . . ."

## XVII

Oblonsky went upstairs, his pockets bulging with the notes the dealer had given him in payment for three months in advance. The business with the forest was finished, he had the money in his pocket, the shooting had been wonderful, and Oblonsky was in the most cheerful mood; consequently he had a particular desire to dispel the ill-temper that had descended on Levin. He felt like finishing the day over supper as pleasantly as it had begun.

Levin really was in a bad mood, and in spite of all his desire to be affectionate and amiable to his charming guest he was unable to control himself. The intoxication of the news that Kitty had not married was gradually beginning to have an effect on him.

Kitty was not married, and was ill, ill for love of a man who had slighted her. This slight seemed to rebound on him. Vronsky had slighted her, while she had slighted him, Levin.

Consequently, Vronsky had the right to despise Levin and therefore was his enemy. But Levin did not think all this. He had a confused feeling that there was something insulting to him in all this; he was not angry now because of what had upset him, he simply found fault with everything that presented itself to him. The stupid sale of the forest, the fraud that Oblonsky had been a prey to and that had been perpetrated in his own house, all irritated him.

"Well, have you finished?" he said when he met Oblonsky upstairs. "D'you want some supper?"

"I wouldn't mind. What an appetite I have in the country, it's amazing! How is it you didn't offer Ryabinin anything to eat?"

"He can go to hell!"

"Really, how you treat him!" said Oblonsky. "You didn't even shake hands with him. Why not shake hands with him?"

"For the same reason I don't shake hands with the footman, and the footman is a hundred times better."

"But what a reactionary you are! And what about the merger of the classes?" said Oblonsky.

"Anyone can merge as much as he likes—good luck to him! I find it repulsive."

"I see you definitely are a reactionary."

"Actually, I've never thought about what I am. I'm—Constantine Levin, that's all."

"Constantine Levin who's in a rotten mood," said Oblonsky, smiling.

"Yes, I'm in a bad mood, and d'you know why? Forgive me, but it's because of that stupid sale of yours . . ."

Oblonsky frowned good-humoredly, like a man being set upon and railed at for no fault of his own.

"Come off it!" he said. "When has anyone ever sold anything without everyone telling him the minute the sale was over, 'It was worth much more'? But when you're selling something no one makes an offer . . . No, I see you've got it in for that unfortunate Ryabinin."

"That may be too. But d'you know why? You'll call me a reactionary again, or some other terrible thing; but it irritates and offends me nevertheless to see on all sides the impoverishment of the nobility, to which I belong, and to which in spite of the merger of the classes I'm very happy to belong. And the impoverishment is taking place not because of any extravagance—that would be nothing, living like a nobleman is a nobleman's business, only the nobility can do it.

Now the peasants around us are buying up land—that doesn't offend me. The squire does nothing, the peasant labors and squeezes out the idlers. That's as it should be, and I'm very glad of it for the peasant's sake. But I find it offensive to see this impoverishment taking place because of— How shall I put it?—because of a kind of simple-mindedness. A Polish leaseholder here has just bought a magnificient property at half its value from some lady who lives in Nice. Elsewhere land worth five rubles an acre is leased to a dealer for less than half a ruble. Now you've just made a present of thirty thousand rubles to that swindler without the slightest reason for it."

"But what should I have done? Counted every tree?"

"They must be counted! You didn't count them, but Ryabinin did. Now Ryabinin's children will have the means to live and educate themselves, and yours may not have!"

"Well, forgive me, but there's something mean about all this counting. We have our own occupation and they have theirs, they have to make profits. Anyhow, the thing's done, and there's an end to it. But here come the fried eggs, just the way I like them best. And Miss Agatha's going to give us some of that marvelous herb brandy . . ."

Oblonsky sat down at the table and began joking with Miss Agatha, assuring her that for a long time he hadn't had such a dinner or supper.

"Well, at least you say nice things about it," said Miss Agatha. "But as for Mr. Constantine, no matter what you give him, even if it's only a crust of bread, he just eats it and goes off."

In spite of all Levin's efforts to master himself, he was morose and silent. There was one question he had to ask Oblonsky, but he felt quite unable to, and couldn't find either the right form for it or the right moment to put it to him. Oblonsky had already gone to his room downstairs, undressed, washed again, put on a frilled nightshirt, and gotten into bed, while Levin was still dawdling about in the room with him, talking about various trivialities and unable to ask him what he wanted to.

"How remarkable it is, the way they make soap," he said, examining and unwrapping a scented cake Miss Agatha had prepared but which Oblonsky had not used. "Just look at it, why it's a work of art."

"Yes, everything's been brought to a pitch of perfection nowadays," said Oblonsky, with a moist, blissful yawn.

"The theaters, for instance, and those amusement places —a-a-a-h!" he yawned. "Electric light now, it's everywhere . . . a-a-a-h!"

"Yes, electric light," said Levin. "To be sure. Well, and where's Vronsky now?" he asked, suddenly putting down the soap.

"Vronsky?" said Oblonsky, cutting short his yawns. "He's in Petersburg. He left shortly after you and since then hasn't been back to Moscow once. And d'you know, Kostya, I'll tell you the truth," he went on, leaning his elbow on the table and propping up his rosy, handsome face, from which his moist, good-natured, sleepy eyes shone like stars. "It was all your own fault. You were afraid of a rival. As I told you at the time, I myself didn't know whose chances were better. Why didn't you just go at it head-on? I told you at the time that—" He yawned without opening his mouth, just with his jaws.

Does he know or doesn't he that I proposed? thought Levin, looking at him. Yes, there's something sly, diplomatic in his expression. And feeling that he was blushing, Levin silently looked Oblonsky straight in the eye.

"If there was anything on her side at the time, it was only through being carried away by appearances," Oblonsky continued. "You know, it was just his being such a perfect aristocrat and his future position in society that had an effect—not on her but on her mother."

Levin frowned. The insult of the refusal he had lived through burned in his heart like a fresh wound he had just received. But he was at home, where even the walls are a help.

"Just one moment," he began, interrupting Oblonsky. "You talk about his being an aristocrat. But let me ask you just what does this aristocracy of Vronsky's or of anyone else's consist of, for me to be slighted because of it? You regard Vronsky as an aristocrat, but I don't. A man whose father crawled up from nothing, through intrigues, and whose mother has had affairs with God knows how many people — Forgive me, but I consider myself an aristocrat and people like me, who can point to three or four honorable generations in their family in the past, who are on the highest level of cultivation—talent and brains, that's a different matter—and who have never cringed before anyone, who've never depended on anyone, the way my father and my grandfather lived. I know a great many people like that.

It seems base to you when I count trees in a forest, and you make Ryabinin a ' present of thirty thousand rubles, but you're getting an income from your lands and I don't know what else, which I'm not getting, consequently I put some value on what I have by birth and hard work. We're the ones who are the aristocrats, and not those who can only exist by the bounty of the powers of this world and who can be bought for a piece of brass."

"But whom are you aiming at? I agree with you," said Oblonsky sincerely and cheerfully, though he felt that when Levin referred to those who could be bought for a piece of brass he also meant him. Levin's vehemence genuinely pleased him. "Whom d'you mean? Though a great deal of what you say about Vronsky isn't true I'm not talking about that. I tell you candidly that in your place I'd go back with me to Moscow and—"

"No, I don't know whether you know it or not, but it's all the same to me now. I will tell you—I proposed and was refused, and Kitty is now an oppressive and shameful memory to me."

"Why? But that's nonsense!"

"Let's not discuss it. Please forgive me if I've been disagreeable to you," said Levin. Now that he had spoken his mind he became once again what he had been that morning. "You won't be angry with me, will you, Stiva? Please don't be," he said, and took Oblonsky smilingly by the hand.

"Of course not, not in the least, nor for anything. I'm glad we've talked things out. And d'you know, a morning shoot is generally first rate. Shouldn't we do one? I wouldn't go to sleep again afterward but go straight off from there to the station."

"A wonderful idea."

## XVIII

THOUGH Vronsky's whole inner life was filled with his passion, his outward life unalterably and irresistibly kept running along its former, customary rails of social and regimental connections and interests. The interests of his regiment took up an important place in his life, both because he was devoted to his regiment and even more because it was devoted to him. The regiment was not only fond of Vronsky, it respected him and took pride in him; it was proud that this enormously rich man, with a splendid education and capacities, for whom the road to all kinds of success, both of ambition and of vanity, lay open, disregarded all this and of all the interests in his life took most to heart the interests of the regiment and of his comrades. Vronsky was aware of his comrades' view of him, and aside from his liking for the life considered himself bound to justify it.

It goes without saying that he never mentioned his love to any of his comrades, and never revealed himself even in the wildest drinking bouts (though he never got drunk enough to lose his self-control), and would silence any of them who were light-minded enough to try hinting at his affair. But in spite of his love affair's being known to the whole town—everyone had guessed more or less correctly at his relations with Anna—most of the young men envied him for just what was the most tiresome thing about it all—Karenin's lofty position and the consequent publicity given the affair in society.

Most of the young women who envied Anna, who for a long time had been bored by her being referred to as *virtuous*, were delighted at what they had been surmising, and were only waiting for the reversal in public opinion to be confirmed before turning on her with the full weight of their disdain. They were already preparing the little lumps of mud they would fling at her when the time came. Most of the older people, and those in high positions, were displeased by the public scandal that was maturing.

At first Vronsky's mother, who had learned about the affair, was pleased, both because according to her notions nothing gave a brilliant young man such a finishing touch as an affair in the best society, and because Anna, whom she had liked so much and who had talked so much about her own son, was nevertheless just the same as all other beautiful, respectable women, according to Countess Vronsky's views. But lately she had found out that Vronsky had turned down a post offered him that was important for his career, merely in order to stay on in the regiment, where he could keep meeting Anna; Vronsky's mother found out that various highly placed personages were annoyed with him because of this, and she changed her mind. What also displeased her was that according to everything she heard about the affair it was not one of those brilliant, elegant worldly affairs she would have approved of, but some sort of desperate, Werther-like passion, as she was told, that might involve him in some stupidity or other. She had not seen him since his unexpected departure from Moscow, and through her elder son she asked for him to come to see her.

Vronsky's older brother was also displeased with him. He didn't analyze what kind of love affair it was—great or small, passionate or not passionate, guilty or pure (though he had some children he kept a ballet girl, and so felt indulgent), but he knew it was a love affair that displeased people who had to be pleased, and consequently he disapproved of his brother's conduct.

Aside from his regimental and social occupations Vronsky had one other occupation—horses, which he was passionately devoted to.

That year a steeplechase for officers had been scheduled. Vronsky put down his name, bought an English thoroughbred mare, and in spite of his love affair was passionately, though reservedly, caught up by the forthcoming races.

These two passions did not interfere with each other. On the contrary, he needed an occupation and distraction independent of his love, in which he could refresh himself and find rest from the feelings that agitated him too violently.

## XIX

THE day of the Krasnoye Selo steeplechase Vronsky came to the regimental mess for his beefsteak earlier than usual. There was no need for him to follow strict training, since his weight came in just under the regulation hundred-sixty pounds; but he had to avoid getting fat too, and he avoided sweet and starchy food. He was sitting there with his coat unbuttoned over a white waistcoat, both elbows leaning on the table, and while waiting for the beefsteak he had ordered he was looking into a French novel on his plate. He was looking at the book only in order to avoid talking to the officers who were coming and going: he was thinking.

He was thinking of Anna's promise to see him that day after the races. He hadn't seen her for three days, and because of her husband's return from abroad didn't know whether it would be all right for that day or not, and didn't know how to find out. The last time he had met her was at his cousin Betsy's country house. As for the Karenins' country house, he went there as seldom as possible. He wanted to go there now, and was turning over in his mind the question of how to do it.

Of course! I'll just say Betsy sent me to ask whether she was coming to the races. Of course I'll go, he decided, lifting his eyes from the book. And as he vividly imagined the joy of seeing her his face lit up.

"Have someone go over to my house and get the troika ready as quickly as possible," he said to the waiter who brought him his beefsteak on a hot silver plate; drawing up the plate he began eating.

From the neighboring billiard room he could hear the click of balls, conversation, and laughter. Two officers came in at the door: one was a young fellow with a weak, refined face who had recently joined the regiment from the Corps of Pages, the other was a plump, elderly officer with little, sunken eyes and a bracelet around his wrist.

Vronsky glanced at them and frowned; looking down at his book as though he hadn't noticed them he began eating and reading at the same time.

"What? Building up your strength for the job?" said the plump officer, sitting down beside him.

"As you see," Vronsky replied, frowning and wiping his mouth without looking at him.

"And you're not afraid of getting fat?" said the other, turning a chair around for the young officer.

"What?" said Vronsky angrily, making a grimace of disgust and showing all his close-set teeth.

"Aren't you afraid of getting fat?"

"Waiter, some sherry!" said Vronsky without replying, and moving his book to the other side he went on reading.

The plump officer took up the wine list and turned to the young officer.

"You pick out something for us to drink," he said, handing him the list and looking at him.

"Some Rhine wine, perhaps?" said the young officer, trying to catch hold of his barely sprouting mustaches and timidly glancing over at Vronsky. When he saw Vronsky was not turning round he got up.

"Let's go to the billiard room," he said.

The plump officer stood up submissively and they started toward the door.

Just then Yashvin, a tall captain with a fine figure, came

into the room, and giving a contemptuous backward nod to the two officers came over to Vronsky.

"So there you are!" he exclaimed, giving him a hearty slap on the shoulder strap with his big hand. Vronsky looked up angrily, but his face lit up at once with the look of serene firm kindliness that was peculiar to him.

"Very sensible, Alexis," said the captain in a loud baritone. "Eat now, then drink one small glass."

"But I don't feel like eating."

"There go the inseparables," added Yashvin, glancing scornfully at the two officers, who were just leaving the room. He sat down beside Vronsky, drawing up his legs in their tight riding breeches, which were too long for the height of the chair, in a sharp angle at the hips and knees. "How is it you didn't come to the Red Theatre last night? *La* Numerov wasn't bad at all. Where were you?"

"I stayed on at the Tverskoys'," Vronsky replied.

"Aha!" said Yashvin.

Yashvin—a gambler and rake who was not only without principles, but whose principles were vicious—was Vronsky's best friend in the regiment. Vronsky was fond of him because of his unusual physical strength, which he demonstrated principally by being able to drink like a fish and never going to sleep without being affected by it in the least, because of his great strength of character, which he demonstrated in his relations with his superiors and comrades, attracting their fear and respect, and also because of his card playing, when he would stake tens of thousands of rubles and invariably, in spite of all the wine he had drunk, play with such skill and dash that he was considered the best player in the English Club. Vronsky respected and liked him especially because he felt that Yashvin liked him not for his name and fortune, but for himself. And among all the men Vronsky knew it was only he whom he would have liked to talk with about his love. He felt that in spite of Yashvin's apparent contempt for all feeling he was the only one—the only one, it seemed to Vronsky—who was capable of understanding the intense passion that now filled his whole life. Aside from this he was certain that Yashvin in any case would be sure to take no pleasure in gossip and scandal, but would have a proper understanding of this feeling of his, that is, he would realize and believe that this love was not a joke, not a pastime, but something more serious and important.

Vronsky did not speak about his love to him, but he knew Yashvin knew everything, understood everything properly, and it was pleasant for him to see all this in his eyes.

"Ah yes!" he said on hearing Vronsky had been at the Tverskoys'; his black eyes twinkled and he plucked at his left mustache, twisting it into his mouth, a bad habit he had.

"And what did you do last night? Did you win?" asked Vronsky.

"Oh well, eight thousand. But three of ‛them shaky, he probably won't pay up."

"Then you can afford to lose on me," said Vronsky, laughing. (Yashvin had placed a large bet on Vronsky.)

"There's not a chance of losing. The only danger is Makhotin."

And the conversation turned to the prospects of the day's race, which was the only thing Vronsky could even think about now.

"Let's go, I've finished," said Vronsky; he stood up and moved toward the door. Yashvin also got up, stretching his great legs and long back.

"It's still too early for me to dine, but I must have a drink. I'll be along directly. Hey there, wine!" he shouted in his rich voice, for which he was celebrated on the drill ground and which was enough to make the glasses rattle. "No, never mind," he shouted again immediately. "You're going home so I can go with you."

He and Vronsky went out together.

XX

VRONSKY'S quarters were in a spacious clean Finnish hut that was divided in two by a partition. Petritsky lived with him in camp too. Petritsky was asleep when Vronsky and Yashvin came into the hut.

"Get up, you've done enough sleeping," said Yashvin, going in behind the partition and giving the tousled Petritsky, his nose buried in the pillow, a prod on the shoulder.

Petritsky jumped up suddenly on to his knees and looked round.

"Your brother's been here," he said to Vronsky. "He woke me up, blast him, and said he'd be coming back." Drawing up his blanket he flung himself into his pillow again. "Leave me alone now, Yashvin," he said, getting angry at Yashvin, who was pulling the blanket off him. "Stop it!" He turned and opened his eyes. "You'd better tell me what to drink, I've got such a horrible taste in my mouth that—"

"Vodka's the best thing," said Yashvin in his deep voice. "Tereshchenko! Some vodka and pickles for your master!" he shouted, evidently delighted with his own voice.

"Vodka, you think? Eh?" asked Petritsky, blinking and rubbing his eyes. "And will you have a drink? Let's have one together! Vronsky, will you have one?" said Petritsky, getting up and wrapping a tiger-skin rug under his arms.

He went over to the partition door, raised his arms, and began singing in French: " 'There was once a king in Thu-u-ule.' Vronsky, will you have a drink?"

"Go away now," said Vronsky, putting on a coat his servant had handed him.

"Where are you off to now?" Yashvin asked him. "There's the troika," he added, seeing the carriage driving up.

"To the stable, then I'll have to go on to Bryansky's about the horses," said Vronsky.

Vronsky actually had promised to go to see Bryansky, who lived seven miles outside Peterhof, and pay him for the horses; he wanted to have enough time to go there too. But his friends understood at once that that wasn't the only place he was going to.

Petritsky, still singing, winked and pursed his lips, as though saying, We all know just which Bryansky *that* is!

"Make sure you're not late!" was all Yashvin said, and to change the subject he asked, "How's my roan? Behaving all right?" looking out the window at the middle horse, which he had sold Vronsky.

"Wait!" Petritsky shouted to Vronsky, who was already on his way out. "Your brother left a letter for you and a note. Wait now, where are they?"

Vronsky stopped. "Well, where are they then?"

"Where are they? Now that's the question!" said Petritsky solemnly, moving his index finger up above his nose.

"Come, tell me—this is stupid!" said Vronsky, smiling.

"Now I haven't lighted the fire. They're here somewhere."

"Enough joking! Where's that letter?"

"No, I've really forgotten. Or did I see it all in a dream? Wait now, wait! Why get angry? If you had knocked back four bottles as I did last night you'd forget the bed you were lying in. Just wait, I'll remember it in a second!"

Petritsky went behind the partition and lay down on his bed.

"Now wait! This is how I was lying, and this is how he was standing. Yes, yes, yes . . . Here it is!" and Petritsky took a letter out from under the mattress where he had hidden it.

Vronsky took the letter and his brother's note. It was just what he had expected—the letter was from his mother; it was full of reproaches for his not having gone to see her, and the note was from his brother, saying they had some things to talk over. Vronsky knew it was all about the same thing. What business is it of theirs! he thought, and crumpling up the letters he pushed them in between the buttons of his coat, in order to read them attentively on the way. In the entrance to the hut he met two officers, one from his own and the second from some other regiment.

Vronsky's quarters were always the haunt of all the officers.

"Where are you off to?"

"I have to go to Peterhof."

"Has the mare come from Tsarskoye?"

"Yes, but I haven't seen her yet."

"They say Makhotin's Gladiator has gone lame."

"Nonsense!" said the other, "but how are you going to race in all this mud?"

"Here are my saviors!" Petritsky cried out, seeing the newcomers. The orderly was standing before him with vodka and some pickles on a tray. "Yashvin here has ordered me to have a drink to brighten me up."

"Well, you let us have it last night all right," said one of the newcomers. "You didn't let us sleep the whole night."

"But how we finished up!" said Petritsky. "Volkov climbed out on to the roof and said he felt mournful. So I said: 'Let's have some music! A funeral march!' And that's how he went to sleep on the roof, to the sound of a funeral march!"

"Drink up now, you must drink the vodka, then some seltzer water with lots of lemon," said Yashvin, standing over Petritsky like a mother forcing her child to take some medicine, "and after that a little champagne, let's say a small bottle."

"Now that's sensible. Wait, Vronsky, let's have a drink."

"No, gentlemen, good-by. I'm not drinking today."

"What, are you getting fat? Well, we're on our own then. Let's have some seltzer and lemons."

"Vronsky!" one of them shouted as he was already going out.

"What?"

"You ought to get a haircut, it'll be getting too heavy, especially on top."

As a matter of fact Vronsky was getting prematurely bald. He laughed gaily, showing his closely set teeth, and drawing his cap over the bald spot went out and got into the carriage.

"To the stables!" he said and was about to get out the letters to read, then he changed his mind and decided not to be distracted before he inspected his horse. Later! he thought.

## XXI

THE temporary stable, a shed made of boards, had been built beside the race course itself, and his horse was to have been brought there the day before. He had not yet seen her. During the last few days he had not taken her out himself but had entrusted her to the trainer; he did not have the slightest idea of what condition she was in now or when she had arrived. He had barely stepped out of the carriage before his groom, the so-called "stable boy," having recognized it while still some distance off, called out the trainer. A dried-up Englishman in high boots and a short jacket, with only a tuft of beard left under the chin, came out to meet him, with the clumsy rolling walk of a jockey, his elbows sticking out.

"Well, how's Frou-Frou?" asked Vronsky in English.

"All right, sir," said the Englishman's voice from all the way inside his throat. "Better not go in," he added, touching his cap, "I've put a muzzle on her, she's all excited. Better not go in, it'll upset her."

"No, I'm going in. I feel like taking a look at her."

"Let's go then," said the Englishman with a frown, still keeping his mouth closed; he went on in front with his limber gait, his elbows waving.

They went into a little yard in front of the shed. A brisk, neat young stable boy holding a broom met them coming in and followed them. In the shed there were five horses standing in their stalls; Vronsky knew that his chief rival, Makhotin's sixteen-hand chestnut Gladiator, ought to have been brought there that same day and was also there. He felt like seeing Gladiator, whom he hadn't seen, even more than his own horse, but he realized that according to the etiquette of horse racing it was not only impossible to see him, but improper even to ask about him. While he was walking along the passage the stable boy opened the door to the second stall on the left, and Vronsky glimpsed a powerful chestnut with white feet. He knew this was Gladiator, but with the feeling of someone turning away from someone else's open letter he turned round and went over to Frou-Frou's stall.

"That's the horse belonging to Mak—Mak . . . I can never get that name straight," said the Englishman over his shoulder, pointing his big, black-nailed thumb at Gladiator's stall.

"Makhotin's? Yes, that's the only serious rival I have," said Vronsky.

"If you were riding him," said the Englishman, "I'd bet on you."

"Frou-Frou's more nervous, she's more powerful," said Vronsky, smiling at the compliment to his riding.

"In a steeplechase the whole thing depends on skill and pluck," said the Englishman.

Vronsky not only felt he had enough pluck (that is, energy and boldness) but—what was far more important—he was firmly persuaded that no one in the whole world could have any more.

"And are you quite sure no more training was necessary?"

"Yes," the Englishman replied. "Not so loud, sir, please, she's getting excited," he said, nodding at the closed stall they were standing in front of, in which they could hear hoofs trampling around in the straw.

He opened the door, and Vronsky entered the stall, which was dimly lighted by one small window. In the stall stood a muzzled, dark-bay horse shifting from one foot to the other in the fresh straw. Looking round him in the half-light of the stall, Vronsky automatically took in again all the points of his favorite horse in one comprehensive glance. Frou-Frou was of medium size, and not faultless technically. She was small-boned all over; even though her chest was well arched it was narrow. Her hindquarters dropped somewhat, and her fore-legs, and her hindlegs even more, were perceptibly curved inward. Neither fore- nor hindlegs were particularly muscu-lar; on the other hand, she was exceptionally broad in girth which was specially striking now that she was lean from training. The bones of her legs below the knees, seen from in front, seemed no thicker than a finger, but looked at from the side were extraordinarily broad. Except for her ribs she seemed all pinched in at the sides and stretched out in depth.

But she had one quality in the highest degree: it made you forget all her shortcomings. This was the quality of *blood*, the blood that *tells*, as the English put it. The muscles, standing out sharply under the network of sinews, covered with delicate, mobile skin as smooth as satin, seemed to be as hard as bone. Her lean head, with prominent, bright, sparkling eyes, broadened out at her muzzle into the flaring blood-red nostrils. In her whole appearance, and particularly about her head, there was a clear-cut, energetic, and at the same time tender expression. She was one of those animals who seem unable to speak only because the physical construction of their mouths does not allow them to.

At any rate it seemed to Vronsky that she understood everything he was now feeling.

The moment Vronsky came in she drew a deep breath and rolling back her bulging eyes so that the whites turned bloodshot, looked at the newcomers from the other side, shaking her muzzle and shifting lightly from one foot to the other.

"Now you see how excited she is," said the Englishman.

"What a darling! A-a-ah!" said Vronsky, stepping toward the mare trying to soothe her.

But the nearer he came the more excited she got. It was only when he reached her head that she suddenly calmed down, her muscles quivering beneath the fine, delicate coat. Vronsky stroked her powerful neck, straightened a lock of her mane that had got on to the wrong side of her sharp withers, and moved his face close to her flaring nostrils, as delicate as a bat's wing. She noisily inhaled and exhaled some air from her distended nostrils, started, pricked up a sharp ear, and stretched out a firm black lip toward Vronsky, as though trying to catch him by the sleeve. But as she remembered her muzzle she gave it a jerk, and once again began shifting from one finely chiseled foot to the other.

"Quiet now, beauty, quiet!" he said, stroking her again on the flank, and left the stall with the happy feeling that the mare was in the best possible condition.

The horse's excitement had infected Vronsky too; he felt the blood rushing to his heart, and just like the horse he wanted to move and bite: it was both terrifying and joyful.

"Well, I'm counting on you," he said to the Englishman. "Be there at six-thirty."

"All right," said the Englishman. "And where are you off to, my lord?" he asked unexpectedly, saying "my lord," which he hardly ever did.

Vronsky raised his head in astonishment and stared, as he knew how to, not into the Englishman's eyes but at his forehead, startled by the boldness of his question. But realizing that the Englishman, in putting this question to him, was looking at him not as an employer but as a jockey, he replied:

"I have to see Bryansky, I'll be home in an hour."

How many times I've been asked that question today! he said to himself, and blushed, which he seldom did. The Englishman looked at him attentively. Then, as though he knew where Vronsky was going, he added:

"The main thing before a race is to keep cool," he said. "Don't get upset about anything, or get into a bad mood."

"All right," Vronsky replied with a smile, and jumping into his carriage he ordered the man to drive to Peterhof.

He had not driven more than a few yards before the clouds, which had been threatening rain since morning, descended; there was a downpour.

Not so good! thought Vronsky, raising the hood of the carriage; it was muddy even before this, now it'll be an absolute swamp.

Sitting alone in the closed carriage he got out his mother's letter and the note from his brother and began reading them.

Yes—it was all the same thing over and over again. All of them—his mother, his brother, everybody—thought they had to interfere in the affairs of his heart. This interference aroused his anger, a feeling he seldom had. What business is it of theirs? Why does everyone consider it his duty to worry about me? And why do they keep after me? Because they see it's something they can't understand. If this were an ordinary, vulgar society love affair they would leave me in peace. They feel that it's something else, that it's not a game, that this woman is more precious to me than life itself. That's what they find incomprehensible and therefore annoying. Whatever our fate is now or is going to be, we are responsible for it, and we won't complain about it, he said to himself, using the word "we" to unite himself with Anna. But no, they have to teach us how to live. They haven't the slightest conception of what happiness is, they don't realize that without this love of ours there is neither happiness nor unhappiness for us—there would be no life, he thought.

He was angry with all of them for interfering just because he felt at heart that they—all of them—were right. He felt

that the love that bound him to Anna was not a momentary
infatuation which would pass away, as society love affairs
pass away without leaving any trace in the life of either one
or the other except agreeable or disagreeable memories. He
felt the full torment of her position and his own, all the
difficulty of hiding their love, exposed as they were to the
eyes of the whole world, of lying and deceiving; and of lying,
deceiving, scheming, and thinking of others just when the
passion that bound them together was so powerful that both
of them were oblivious of everything but their love.

He vividly recalled all the often-repeated incidents in
which lies and deceit, so repugnant to his character, were
unavoidable; he recalled most vividly of all the feeling he
had noticed more than once in her of shame at the necessity
of deceit and lying. And he had the strange feeling that had
occasionally affected him ever since his affair with Anna. It
was a feeling of disgust with something—whether with
Karenin, or himself, or the whole world, he was not quite
sure which. He always drove this strange feeling away, and
now too he shook himself and went on with his train of
thought.

Yes, she was unhappy before, but she was proud and
serene; while now she cannot be serene or dignified, even
though she doesn't show that. Yes, it will have to be put an
end to, he decided.

And for the first time the thought came clearly into his
mind that all this lying had to be stopped, the sooner the
better.

She and I will have to give up everything, and hide ourselves away alone somewhere with our love, he said to
himself.

## XXII

THE downpour did not last long, and by the time Vronsky
arrived, with his center horse in full gallop pulling along the
side horses through the mud with the reins loose, the sun
was looking out again. The roofs of the country houses and
the old lime trees in the gardens on both sides of the main
road were glistening with the moisture; the branches were
dripping gaily and the water ran off the roofs. He was no
longer even thinking about the downpour spoiling the race
course, but was now delighted because thanks to the rain he

was sure to find her at home alone, since he knew that Karenin, who had only recently returned from a spa abroad, had not moved from Petersburg.

Hoping to find her alone, Vronsky did what he always did in order to attract less attention: he got out before crossing the little bridge and walked. He did not go up the steps from the street, but went into the court.

"Has your master returned?" he asked a gardener.

"No sir. The mistress is at home. But you can go in up the steps, the servants are there, they'll open up," the gardener answered.

"No, I'll go through the garden."

Having assured himself that she was alone, and wanting to catch her by surprise, since he hadn't promised to visit her that day and she was certainly not expecting him to come in before the races, he went ahead, holding up his sword and stepping warily along the sand-strewn path, bordered by flowers, to the terrace overlooking the garden. Vronsky had now forgotten everything he had thought on the way about the oppressiveness and difficulty of his position. He was thinking of one thing only—that he was about to see her not in his imagination alone but alive, all of her, just as she was in reality. He was already going up the shallow steps of the terrace, stepping on the whole of his foot so as not to make any noise, when he suddenly recalled something he always forgot, which was the thing that constituted the most painful part of his relations with her—her son, with his questioning and, as it seemed to him, hostile eyes.

This little boy was more of an obstacle to their relations than anyone else. When he was there neither Vronsky nor Anna not only did not permit themselves to speak about anything they might not have repeated in public, but they did not allow themselves even to hint at anything the boy would not understand. They had not come to an agreement about it; it had come about of itself. They would have considered it humiliating to themselves to deceive this child. In his presence they would talk to each other like acquaintances. But in spite of this watchfulness Vronsky often saw an attentive and perplexed look directed at him by the child, and a peculiar timidity, a sort of capriciousness alternating between affection and chilly reserve, in the boy's attitude toward him. It was as though the child felt that there was some sort of important relationship between his mother and this man that he could not understand.

As a matter of fact the boy did feel that he could not grasp this relationship; he tried but could not clarify to himself the feeling he ought to have toward this man. With a child's sensitivity for the display of feeling he saw clearly that his father, his governess, and his nanny—all of them—not only did not like Vronsky, but regarded him with repugnance and fear, even though they said nothing about him, while his mother looked on him as her best friend.

What can it mean? What is he? How should I feel toward him? If I can't understand it's my fault, either I'm stupid, or a bad boy, thought the child; this was what caused the probing, questioning, and partially hostile expression, and the timidity and capriciousness that so embarrassed Vronsky. The presence of this child never failed to arouse in Vronsky the peculiar feeling of groundless disgust he had been having lately. In both Vronsky and Anna the presence of the child evoked a feeling like that of a sailor who sees by the compass that the direction in which he is swiftly moving is far off the right course, but that he is incapable of stopping, that every minute is taking him farther and farther away from the right course, and that to acknowledge that he is off course would be just the same as acknowledging that he is undone.

This child, with his naïve view of life, was the compass that indicated to them the degree of their divergence from what they knew to be the right course but refused to admit.

This time Seryozha was not home and she was quite alone, sitting on the terrace waiting for the return of her son, who had gone out for a walk and been caught by the rain. She had sent a man and a maidservant out to look for him and was sitting there expectantly. Wearing a white dress trimmed with wide embroidery, she was sitting behind some plants in a corner of the terrace and did not hear him. Bowing her dark curly head she was pressing her forehead against a cold watering can that was standing on the parapet, and was holding the can in both her beautiful hands, with the fingers he knew so well. The beauty of her whole figure, her head, neck, and arms always struck Vronsky as a surprise. He stopped and gazed at her with rapture. But no sooner was he about to take a step toward her than she was already aware of his nearness; she pushed aside the can and turned her flushed face toward him.

"What's the trouble? Are you ill?" he said in French, as he went toward her. He wanted to run over to her, but as he recalled that there might be some people around he looked over at the balcony door and blushed, as he always did when he felt that he had to be fearful and circumspect.

"No, I'm quite well," she said, getting up and tightly squeezing his outstretched hand. "I wasn't expecting you."

"Good God! what cold hands!" he said.

"You frightened me," she said. "I'm alone, waiting for Seryozha. He's gone out for a walk; they'll be coming back this way."

But though she tried to look calm her lips were quivering.

"Forgive me for having come, but I couldn't get through the day without seeing you," he continued in French, which he always spoke to her in order to avoid saying the Russian *you*, which was impossibly cold, or the dangerously intimate Russian *thou*.

"What is there to forgive? I'm so happy!"

"But you're ill or upset," he went on, bending over her without releasing her hand. "What were you thinking about?"

"Still about the same thing," she said with a smile.

She was telling the truth. No matter when, at whatever moment, if she were asked what she was thinking about she could reply quite correctly—one thing, her happiness and her unhappiness. This is what she was thinking about just now, when he found her. Why was all this easy for everyone else, for Betsy, for instance (she knew of Betsy's secret affair with Tushkevich) and for her such agony? Today this idea, for a number of reasons, was particularly painful to her. She asked him about the races. He answered and seeing that she was excited, and trying to distract her, he began telling her in a very matter-of-fact way the details of the preparations for the races.

Should I tell him or shouldn't I? she thought, looking into his serene tender eyes. He's so happy, so taken up with his races, he won't understand it as he should, he won't understand its full importance for us.

"But you haven't told me what you were thinking about when I came in," he said, breaking off his account, "Tell me, please!"

She made no reply, and bowing her head a little, she gave him a questioning sidelong look, her eyes shining under their long lashes. Her hand, which was toying with a leaf she had pulled, was shaking. He noticed this and his face took on the expression of submissiveness, of slavish devotion, that captivated her so.

"I see something has happened. Can I be calm for even a

moment when I know you have a sorrow I'm not sharing? Tell me, for the love of God!" he repeated imploringly.

No, I won't forgive him if he doesn't see just how important it is. It would be better to say nothing; what's the point of putting him to the test? she thought, still looking at him in the same way and feeling that her hand with the leaf was trembling more and more.

"For God's sake!" he repeated, taking her hand in his.

"Shall I?"

"Yes, yes, yes . . ."

"I'm pregnant," she said softly and slowly.

The leaf in her hand trembled still more violently, but she didn't lower her eyes from his, in order to see how he would take it. He turned white, started to say something, but stopped himself; he released her hand and lowered his head. Yes, he's understood the full meaning of it, she thought, and gratefully pressed his hand.

But she was mistaken about his having understood the importance of the news just as she, a woman, did. At hearing it he felt with tenfold force an attack of the strange feeling of disgust he kept having; at the same time he realized that the crisis he had wished for was now upon them, that it was impossible to conceal things from the husband any longer, and that it was necessary to put a quick finish to this unnatural position in one way or another.

But aside from this her agitation communicated itself to him physically. He looked at her with moved, devoted eyes, kissed her hand, got up and began pacing back and forth on the terrace in silence.

"Yes," he said, resolutely going over to her. "Neither I nor you regarded our relationship as a plaything, and now our fate is decided." He looked around and said: "We must put an end to this lie we're living in."

"An end? But how can we end it, Alexis?" she said quietly. She was calm now; her face was radiant with a tender smile.

"By your leaving your husband, and our joining our lives."

"But they're joined as it is," she answered, scarcely audibly.

"Yes, but now they must be utterly, utterly."

"But how, Alexis—tell me, how?" she said with mournful irony at the hopelessness of her position. "Is there any way out of such a position? Am I not a wife with a husband?"

"There's a way out of every situation. We must make a decision," he said. "Anything is better than the situation

you're living in. D'you suppose I don't see how you're torturing yourself about everything—people, your son, your husband?"

"Oh—not really about my husband," she said with simple
irony. "I don't know about him and I never think about him.
He doesn't exist."

"You're being sincere. I know you. You torment yourself
about him too."

"But he does not even know," she said, and suddenly her
face flushed crimson; her cheeks, her forehead, her neck and
throat turned red, and tears of shame came into her eyes.
"But let's not talk about him."

XXIII

VRONSKY had already made a few attempts, though not
with such determination as now, to bring her to a discussion
of her own position, and each time he had come up against
the same superficiality and light-mindedness that was shown
now by her answer to his challenge. It was as though there
were something she could not or would not clarify to herself;
as though the moment she began talking about it she—the
real Anna—would retreat somewhere into herself and some
other, strange and alien woman would emerge, whom he did
not love and was afraid of, and who resisted him. But today
he had made up his mind to put everything into words.

"Whether he knows or not," Vronsky said in his usual
firm, calm voice, "whether he knows or not doesn't concern
us. We cannot—you cannot go on this way, especially now."

"But what can we do, according to you?" she asked in
the same tone of light irony. After having been afraid he
would take her pregnancy lightly, she was now annoyed by
his drawing the conclusion that something had to be done
about it.

"Tell him everything and leave him."

"Very well: let's say I do that," she said. "D'you know
what will happen? I'll tell you in advance," and a malicious
gleam came into her eyes, which a second before had been
full of tenderness. " 'Ah, so you love someone else and
have entered on a guilty relationship with him?' " (In imitating her husband she did just as he did and came down
heavily on the word "guilty.") " 'I have given you warning
about the consequences from the religious, the civil, and the

family points of view. You failed to heed me. Now I cannot allow my name to be dishonored—' " ("And that of my son," she had meant to say, but she could not make a joke of her son.) " '—my name to be dishonored,' and something else of that sort," she added. "In short he'd say, with his full official manner lucidly and precisely, that he cannot release me but will take every means in his power to stop a scandal. And he will do, calmly and accurately, just what he says. That's what will happen. He's not a man, but a machine, and a spiteful machine, when he gets angry," she added, thinking as she said this of Karenin with every detail of his figure, his manner of speaking and his character, and in her guilt setting against him everything bad she was able to find in him, and forgiving him nothing because of the terrible sin toward him that she herself was guilty of.*

"But Anna," Vronsky said in a persuasive, mild voice, attempting to calm her, "he'll have to be told in any case, and then it'll be time for us to be guided by whatever he decides to do."

"What—run away?"

"And why not run away? I don't see the possibility of continuing this. And not for myself—I can see how you're suffering."

"Yes, run away—and I'd become your mistress," she said spitefully.

"Anna!" he murmured, with reproachful tenderness.

"Yes," she went on, "become your mistress and ruin all—"

Again she had meant to say "my son," but she could not get the words out.

Vronsky could not understand how Anna, with her strong, honest character, was able to endure this situation of fraud without wanting to get out of it; but he never guessed that the chief reason for this was just this word "son" that she was incapable of uttering. Whenever she thought of her son and of his future attitude toward the mother who had left his father, she grew so afraid of what she had done that she no longer reasoned but like a woman merely tried to soothe herself with false arguments and words so that everything

---

* In Russia before the revolution only the innocent party could obtain a divorce, and then with difficulty. The guilty party could not remarry, and lost custody of any children. (*Translator's note.*)

would stay as it had been and she would be able to forget about the dreadful question of what would happen to her son.

"I beg you, I implore you," she suddenly said in a completely different voice, sincerely and tenderly, taking him by the hand, "never speak to me about that!"

"But, Anna—"

"Never! Leave it to me. I know the full degradation, the full horror of my position; but it's not so easy to decide as you think. Leave it to me, and listen to me. Never speak to me about it. Promise me? No, no—promise!"

"I promise everything, but I cannot be at peace, especially after what you've said. I cannot be at peace when you cannot be—"

"I!" she repeated. "Yes, sometimes I do torment myself, but that will pass, if you never speak to me about that. It's only when you speak to me about it that it torments me."

"I don't understand," he said.

"I know"—she interrupted him—"how painful it is for your truthful nature to lie, and I pity you. I often think of how you've ruined your life for my sake."

"I was thinking the same thing just now," he said, "how you could sacrifice because of me. I cannot forgive myself for your being unhappy."

"Unhappy—I?" she said, coming close and looking at him with a rapturous smile of love, "I—am like someone starving who's been given something to eat. It may be that he's still cold, and his clothes are torn, and he's ashamed of himself, but he's not unhappy. I unhappy? No—this is my happiness—"

She heard the voice of her son, who had come back, approaching, and glancing swiftly around the terrace she got up hurriedly. Her eyes kindled with the fire he knew so well; with a swift motion she raised her beautiful hands, covered with rings, seized his head, gave him a long look, and putting her face, with parted smiling lips, near his, she rapidly kissed his mouth and both eyes, then pushed him away. She was about to go but he held her back.

"When?" he whispered, gazing in rapture at her.

"Tonight, at one," she whispered, and giving a heavy sigh she walked off with her light, quick step to meet her son.

Seryozha had been caught by the rain in the park, and he and his nurse had sat it through in a pavilion.

"*Au revoir*, then," she said to Vronsky, "we'll have to hurry now for the races. Betsy has promised to pick me up."

Vronsky looked at his watch and hurried off.

### XXIV

WHEN Vronsky had looked at his watch on the Karenins' balcony he had been so agitated and preoccupied by his own thoughts that all he had seen was hands on a dial, without realizing what time it was. He went into the highroad, and carefully stepping through the mud made his way to the carriage. He was so full of feeling for Anna that he didn't even think of the time or whether he would still be able to go to see Bryansky. As often happens all he retained was an external faculty of memory that indicated the next thing he had intended to do. He went up to his coachman, who had dozed off on the box in the shadow, already lengthening, of a thick lime tree, admired the swaying columns of midges hovering over the sweating horses, woke him up and jumped in, ordering him to drive to Bryansky's. It was only after he had driven some five miles that he recovered himself to the extent of looking at his watch and realized that it was already half-past five. He was late.

There were to be a number of races that day: a Mounted Guards' race, then a mile-and-a-half for officers, a three-mile, and then the race he was in himself. He was able to get to his own race in time, but if he went to Bryansky's he would only just make it, and would arrive after the whole of the Court was already there. That was bad. But he had given Bryansky his word and so he decided to go on, ordering the coachman not to spare the horses.

He arrived at Bryansky's, spent five minutes with him, and drove back at a gallop. The rapid drive calmed him. The full oppressiveness of his relations with Anna, the vagueness that remained after their conversation—it had all slipped out of his mind; now he was thinking, with joyful excitement, of the race—that he would be able to get there on time in spite of everything, and occasionally the thought of the blissful meeting awaiting him that night flared up in his imagination with a bright light.

The feeling of the coming race took possession of him more and more as he entered farther and farther into the atmosphere of the races, overtaking the carriages that were on their way there from country houses and from Petersburg.

No one was left in his quarters by the time he got there—everyone was at the races, and his valet was waiting for him at the gate. While he was changing, the valet told him that the second race had already begun, that a great many gentlemen had been asking about him, and that the boy had run over twice from the stables.

Having changed without haste (he never hurried and never lost control of himself) Vronsky was driven to the stables. From the stables a sea of carriages, pedestrians, and soldiers surrounding the race course was visible, as well as the stands swarming with people. The second race was probably on already, since he heard a bell just as he was going into the stables. On his way he met Makhotin's white-footed chestnut Gladiator, who was in a blue-bordered orange horse-cloth, his ears trimmed with blue and looking enormous, being led out to the race course.

"Where's Cord?" he asked the groom.

"In the stables, she's being saddled."

Frou-Frou, in her open stall, was already saddled. She was about to be led out.

"Am I late?"

"All right, all right!" said the Englishman. "Don't get excited."

Vronsky once again took in at a glance the fascinating, beloved shape of the mare, whose whole body was trembling, and wrenching himself away from the sight with difficulty he left the stable. He went over toward the stands just at the moment that was most favorable for not attracting anyone's attention. The one-and-a-half mile race had just finished, and all eyes were fixed on an officer of the Horse Guards in front and a Light Hussar behind, who were urging the horses on to the limits of their strength and nearing the winning post. From inside the ring and outside everyone was pressing closer to the winning post, and a group of soldiers and officers from the Horse Guards with loud cheers were expressing their joy at the expected victory of their officer and comrade. Vronsky slipped unnoticed into the thick of the crowd just at about the same moment the bell rang announcing the end of the race, and a tall mud-splashed Horse Guards officer, who had come in first, had leaned over in his saddle, and begun slacking up on the reins of his heavily panting, sweat-darkened, gray stallion.

The stallion, straightening its legs with an effort, reduced the speed of its great body, and the Horse Guards officer looked round him like a man waking up from a deep sleep and forced himself to smile. He was surrounded by a throng of friends and strangers.

Vronsky deliberately avoided the select and fashionable crowd moving around and chatting with reserved freedom in front of the stands. He found out Anna was there, and Betsy, and his brother's wife, and to avoid being distracted he purposely did not go over to them. But he kept running into acquaintances who stopped him, reported the details of the races that had already been run, and asked him why he was late.

Just when the winners were being called to the Imperial Pavilion to be awarded the prizes, and everyone was looking that way, Vronsky's older brother Alexander, a colonel with heavy epaulets, of medium height and as sturdy as Alexis but handsomer and ruddier, with a red nose and a drunken, open face, came over to him.

"Did you get my note?" he said. "You can never be reached anywhere."

In spite of Alexander Vronsky's dissolute, and more particularly drunken life for which he was well known, he was an unquestioned familiar of the Court circle.

Now, speaking to his brother about a matter that was extremely unpleasant for him and knowing that many eyes might be fixed on them, he had a smiling expression, as though he were joking with him about some trifle.

"I got it, but really I don't see what *you're* so worried about," said Vronsky.

"What I'm worried about is that a remark has been made to me just now that you weren't here and that you'd been seen in Peterhof on Monday."

"There are some things that should only be discussed by those directly concerned; the thing you're so worried about is one."

"Yes, but then you shouldn't be in the Army, you shouldn't—"

"I'm asking you not to interfere, that's all."

Vronsky's scowling face turned pale, and his prominent lower jaw quivered, which happened rarely with him. He was very kindhearted and seldom got angry, but when he did, and when his chin quivered, then, as Alexander Vronsky knew, he was dangerous. Alexander Vronsky smiled gaily.

"All I wanted to do was transmit Mother's letter. Answer her and don't get upset before the race. Good luck!" he added, smiling, and went away.

Just then another friendly greeting stopped Vronsky.

"Now you're cutting your friends! How are you, dear boy," said Oblonsky, with his rosy face and glistening well-brushed whiskers shining even here, amidst all the glamour of Petersburg, no less than in Moscow. "I got here yesterday; I'm delighted I'm going to be watching your triumph. When can we see each other?"

"Come to the mess tomorrow," said Vronsky, and apologetically pressing the sleeve of Oblonsky's overcoat he went off to the center of the race course, where horses were already being led out for the great steeplechase.

The sweating, exhausted horses who had already run were being led away by their grooms, and one after another the new ones appeared for the forthcoming race, fresh horses, for the most part English, who with their hoods and tightly girthed stomachs looked like strange, gigantic birds. At the right Frou-Frou, lean and beautiful, was being led up and down, stepping on her rather long and elastic pasterns as though on springs. A little way off the horse blanket was being taken off lop-eared Gladiator. The stallion's powerful, exquisite, completely symmetrical shape, with its magnificent rump and unusually short pasterns starting just above the hoofs, arrested Vronsky's attention in spite of himself. He was about to go over to his own horse, but once again was stopped by someone he knew.

"Ah, there's Karenin!" said the acquaintance he was talking to. "He's looking for his wife, but she's in the middle of the stands. Did you see her?"

"No," Vronsky replied, and without even looking around at the stand where Karenin had been pointed out to him he went over to his horse.

Vronsky had not had time to examine the saddle, which called for some adjustment, before the riders were summoned to the pavilion to draw their numbers and places. With stern, grave faces, many of them pale, seventeen officers assembled at the stand and picked their numbers. Vronsky got number 7. A cry rang out: "Mount!"

Feeling that together with the other riders he constituted a focus toward which all eyes were turned, Vronsky, in the state of tension in which he usually made all his movements deliberate and calm, went over to his horse. In honor of the races Cord had put on his gala clothes—a black, buttoned-up coat, a stiffly starched collar which propped up his cheeks, a bowler hat, and top boots. He was calm and dignified, as he always was, and standing in front of the horse was holding both reins himself. Frou-Frou continued to tremble, as though she had a fever. An eye full of fire glanced sideways at Vronsky as he came up. Vronsky thrust a finger under the girth. The horse rolled her eyes more violently, showed her teeth and laid back an ear. The Englishman pursed his lips, to express a smile at anyone testing his saddling.

"You'd better mount, you'll be less excited."

Vronsky glanced round for the last time at his rivals. He knew that as soon as the race began he would not even see them. Two of them were already riding ahead toward the starting point. Galtsin, a friend of his and one of the dangerous competitors, was circling around a sorrel stallion that would not let him mount. A little Hussar in tight breeches was galloping along hunched over like a cat, trying to look English. Prince Kuzovlyov, white-faced, was sitting on his thoroughbred mare from the Gravov stud farm, which an Englishman was leading by the bridle. Vronsky and all his friends knew Kuzovlyov and his peculiarity—weak nerves and terrible vanity. They knew he was afraid of everything, afraid of riding even an Army horse, but now, just because it was frightening, because people broke their necks and because a doctor, an ambulance with a red cross sewn on it, and a nurse were standing at each obstacle, he had determined to ride. Their eyes met, and Vronsky gave him a friendly, approving wink. There was only one he didn't see, his principal rival—Makhotin on Gladiator.

"Don't hurry," Cord said to Vronsky, "and remember one thing: don't hold her back at the obstacles and don't urge her—let her take them the way she wants to."

"All right, all right," said Vronsky, taking the reins.

"If possible get out in front, but even if you're behind don't lose hope till the very last minute."

Before the mare had time to budge, Vronsky had stepped into the notched steel stirrup with a supple powerful movement, and lightly and firmly seated his compact body in the creaking leather saddle. Putting his right foot in its stirrup he straightened out the double reins with a practiced gesture, and Cord let go. As though not knowing which foot to put first, Frou-Frou, stretching out the reins with her long neck, started off as though on springs, balancing the rider on her supple back. Cord quickened his pace and walked after them. The excited mare, trying to deceive her rider, stretched out the reins first from one side then from the other; Vronsky vainly tried to soothe her by voice and gesture.

They were already approaching the dammed-up stream on their way to the starting point. Some of the riders were in front and some behind, when suddenly Vronsky heard the sounds of a horse galloping up behind him in the mud of the path, and he was overtaken by Makhotin on his white-footed, lop-eared Gladiator. Makhotin smiled, showing his long teeth, but Vronsky shot an angry look at him. He had always disliked him in any case, and now he regarded him as his most dangerous rival; he was annoyed with him for galloping past and getting Frou-Frou excited. Frou-Frou flung her left foot into a canter, gave two bounds, and getting angry at the tightening reins went back into a jerky trot that jolted Vronsky. Cord frowned too, and almost broke into a run after Vronsky.

### XXV

SEVENTEEN officers in all were in the steeplechase, which was supposed to take place over the large three-mile ellipse in front of the pavilion. There were nine obstacles arranged over the course: a brook, a big barrier, nearly five feet high, in front of the Imperial Pavilion itself, a dry ditch, a water jump, an incline, an Irish bank (one of the most difficult obstacles) consisting of an embankment piled high with brushwood, beyond which there was another ditch, which the horses couldn't see, so that a horse had to clear both obstacles or kill itself; then there were two more water jumps and one dry ditch. The finishing line was just opposite the pavilion. But the race was to be begun not in the ring, but some two hundred yards or more to one side of it, and the first obstacle was in this space—the dammed-up brook seven feet across, which the riders were free either to jump or ford.

The riders lined up three times, but each time someone's horse broke out and they had to line up again. The starter, Colonel Sestrin, an expert, was already beginning to lose his temper when finally the fourth time, he shouted "Go!" and they were off.

Every eye and every binocular was trained on the vari-colored little group of riders as they got into line.

"They're off!" "They've started!" could be heard on all sides after the hush of expectation.

People started running singly and in groups from one place to another in order to see better. In the very first minute the group of riders began stretching out, and could be seen approaching the brook in twos and threes, one behind the other. To the onlookers they seemed to have started all together, but for the riders there were seconds of difference that were very important.

The excited and overnervous Frou-Frou lost in the start, and a number of horses took off ahead of her, but even before they reached the brook Vronsky, who with all his strength was holding back the mare tugging at the reins, had easily overtaken three, leaving ahead of him only Makhotin's chest-nut Gladiator, whose rump was moving lightly and regularly just in front of him; in front of them all was the exquisite Diana carrying Kuzovlyov, who was more dead than alive.

For the first few moments Vronsky still had not gotten control either of the mare or of himself. Until he got to the first obstacle, the brook, he was unable to guide her movements.

Gladiator and Diana were approaching it together and almost at the identical instant; simultaneously they rose above the brook and soared over it on to the other side; lightly, as though on wings, Frou-Frou soared up behind them but at just the same moment Vronsky felt he was in the air he suddenly saw, almost beneath the hoofs of his own horse, Kuzovlyov, floundering around with Diana on the other side of the brook (Kuzovlyov had let go the reins after the jump, and the horse had sent him flying over her head). It was only later that Vronsky learned these details; what he saw now was only that directly beneath Frou-Frou's legs, just where she had to alight, Diana's leg or head might turn up. But like a falling cat Frou-Frou exerted her legs and back during the jump and clearing the other horse hurtled on.

Oh the darling! thought Vronsky.

After the brook he gained complete control of the mare and began holding her in, intending to jump the big barrier behind Makhotin, and then try to overtake him at once on the following five-hundred yard flat.

The big barrier stood right in front of the Imperial Pavilion. The Tsar, the whole Court, and crowds of people —they were all looking at them, at him and at Makhotin riding a horse's length ahead of him as they approached the Devil (as the solid barrier was called). Vronsky felt these eyes fixed on him from all sides, but he saw nothing except the ears and neck of his own horse, the ground rushing toward him, and Gladiator's rump and white feet swiftly beating time in front of him, always keeping just the same distance ahead. Gladiator soared up, without touching anything, flicked his short tail, and vanished from Vronsky's sight.

"Bravo!" said a single voice.

That same second the boards of the barrier flashed before Vronsky's eyes, directly in front of him. Without the slightest change in her movements the mare soared up under him; the boards vanished, there was just a knock of something behind him. Excited by Gladiator moving ahead of her the mare had jumped too soon in front of the barrier and had struck it with a hind hoof. But her pace did not change, and Vronsky, as he was hit in the face by a lump of mud, realized that he was once again the same distance behind Gladiator. Again he saw in front of him his rump, short tail, and again the same flashing white feet keeping the same distance.

Just at the same moment Vronsky thought Makhotin now, had to be passed, Frou-Frou herself, who already grasped what was in his mind, without the least urging, put on a substantial burst of speed and began closing in on Makhotin on the best side, the side of the rope. Makhotin would not let her pass on that side. Then, no sooner had Vronsky thought it would be possible to pass on the outside as well, Frou-Frou shifted her gait and began passing him on the same side. Frou-Frou's shoulder, already darkening with sweat, was drawing level with Gladiator's rump. For a few strides they moved together. But as they approached the obstacle, Vronsky began working the reins in order not to take the outer circle, and swiftly overtook Makhotin on the slope itself. He caught a flash of his mud-bespattered face; it even seemed to him he was smiling. He passed Makhotin, but felt him immediately behind, and constantly heard just behind his back the regular thudding of Gladiator's hoofs and his rapid and still completely fresh breathing.

The next two obstacles, a ditch and a fence, were taken easily, but Vronsky began hearing Gladiator's thudding and snorting coming closer. He urged on the mare; he joyfully felt her increasing her speed with ease, and the sound of Gladiator's hoofs began to be heard again at their former distance.

Vronsky was now in the lead, which was just what he had wished and what Cord had advised him; now he was sure of winning. His excitement, his delight, and his tenderness for Frou-Frou kept growing stronger and stronger. He felt like looking behind him, but he dared not; he tried to keep calm and not urge on the mare, in order to let her keep the same reserves he felt Gladiator still had. There was only one obstacle left, the most difficult one; if he passed it ahead of the others he would come in first. He was galloping up to the Irish bank. Together with Frou-Frou he saw this bank while still far away, and a moment of doubt came to both of them together, to him and to the mare. He noticed some indecisiveness in the set of the mare's ears, and raised his whip, then he felt instantly that his doubts were groundless: the mare knew what had to be done. She increased her speed and soared up evenly, exactly as he had thought she would, and as she bounded off the ground surrendered to the force of inertia, which carried her far beyond the ditch; and in the very same rhythm, effortlessly, from the same foot, Frou-Frou continued her gallop.

"Bravo, Vronsky!" he heard the voices of a cluster of people standing near this obstacle—he knew they were those of his regiment and friends. Yashvin's voice was unmistakable, though he didn't see him.

Oh my darling! he thought of Frou-Frou, as he listened to what was happening behind him. He's over it! he thought, hearing Gladiator galloping behind him. The only thing left was the last water jump, a yard and a half across. Vronsky did not even look at it, but wishing to win by a large margin he began sawing on the reins with a circular movement, raising and lowering the mare's head in time with her gait. He felt she was using her last reserves; not only were her neck and shoulders wet, but on her withers, her head, and her sharp ears the sweat was coming out in drops; she was breathing in short, harsh gasps. But he knew her reserves were enough to last out the remaining five hundred yards, It was only because he felt nearer the ground, and because of the special smoothness in her movements, that Vronsky knew how much his mare had increased her speed. She soared over the water jump as though unaware of it. She soared over it like a bird; but at just this moment Vronsky, to his horror, felt he had failed to keep up with her motion; without even understanding how it had happened himself, he had made a terrible, unforgivable movement of his own by letting himself drop back in the saddle. His position changed suddenly; he realized something horrible had happened. Before he was able to understand just what it was the white feet of the chestnut stallion flashed by directly alongside him, and Makhotin passed him at a fast gallop. Vronsky was touching the ground with one foot; his mare was falling over on it; he scarcely had time to free his leg before she sagged, over on one side; snorting heavily and making futile efforts with her delicate sweat-soaked neck to pick herself up, she floundered on the ground at his feet like a wounded bird. Vronsky's clumsy movement had broken her spine. But he didn't understand this until later; what he saw now was only that Makhotin was swiftly vanishing in the distance, while he, staggering, was standing alone on the muddy motionless ground with Frou-Frou, panting heavily, lying in front of him and stretching out her head toward him, looking at him with her beautiful eyes. Still not understanding what had happened, Vronsky pulled at her reins, and again she twisted her whole body like a fish, making the saddle flaps creak; she thrust out her forelegs, but incapable of raising her hindquarters she collapsed at once and fell on her side again. His face distorted by passion, pale, his lower jaw quivering, Vronsky kicked her in the stomach with his heel and began tugging at the reins again. But she didn't move; thrusting her muzzle into the ground she only looked at her master with her eloquent eyes.

"A-a-ah!" groaned Vronsky, clutching his head. "A-a-ah, what have I done!" he cried. "The race lost! And my own fault, shameful, unforgivable! And this exquisite, unlucky mare ruined! A-a-ah, what have I done!"

People were running over toward him—a doctor, an attendant, officers of his regiment. To his misfortune he felt he was whole and unhurt. The mare had broken her back; it was decided to shoot her. Vronsky could not answer any questions, or talk to anyone. He turned away and without picking up the cap that had fallen from his head, he walked off the race course, without knowing where he was going. He was miserable. For the first time in his life he had experienced the bitterest misfortune—misfortune that was irremediable and that he was to blame for himself.

Yashvin overtook him with his cap and led him home; half an hour later Vronsky was himself again. But for a long time the thought of this race remained in his heart as the bitterest and most agonizing memory of his life.

### XXVI

KARENIN'S outward relations with his wife were the same as they had been before. The only difference consisted of his being more busy than ever. With the coming of spring he went to a spa abroad, as he had used to, to recover his health, which was upset each year by his intensive work during the winter; as usual he returned in July and at once took up his customary work with increased energy. And as usual his wife moved to the country house while he remained in Petersburg.

From the time of their conversation after the evening at Princess Tverskoy's he never spoke to Anna about his suspicions or jealousy; his habitual tone of bantering mimicry could not have been better suited to their present relations. He was somewhat colder toward her. It seemed simply as though he were slightly dissatisfied with her for that first night's talk which she had evaded. There was a shadow of annoyance in his relations with her, but no more. You didn't want to talk things over with me, he seemed to be saying to her in his mind, then so much the worse for you. Now you'll be the one to ask me, but I won't talk things over. So much the worse for you, he said mentally, like a man who after trying in vain to put out a fire is infuriated by his vain exertions and says: "Go on and burn then—it's your own fault!"

This man, who was intelligent and subtle in his official duties, failed to understand the utter insanity of such an attitude toward his wife. He did not understand it because he was too afraid of understanding his real position, and in his heart he had closed, locked, and sealed the box in which he kept his feelings toward his family—that is, his wife and his son. Though he was an attentive father, from the end of that winter on he became particularly chilly toward his son, and had the same bantering attitude toward him as toward his wife. "Aha! Young man!" was the way he would talk to him.

Karenin thought and said that he had never had so much official work to do as this year; but what he was not aware of was that it was he himself who kept thinking up things to do that year, that this was one of the ways he had of not opening up the box containing his feelings toward his wife and family and his thoughts about them, which were becoming more and more dreadful the longer they lay there. If anyone had had the right to ask Karenin what he thought about his wife's behavior, Karenin, mild and peaceable, would not have replied but would have flown into a rage at the man who asked him. Because of this too there was something haughty and stern in Karenin's expression when he was asked about his wife's health. Karenin did not want to think about his wife's behavior and feelings, and as a matter of fact he never did.

Karenin's permanent country house was in Peterhof, where Countess Lydia as a rule also lived in summer, close by Anna and in constant relations with her. This year Countess Lydia refused to live in Peterhof, didn't visit Anna once, and hinted to Karenin at the unsuitability of Anna's friendship with Betsy and Vronsky. Karenin sternly cut her short, after expressing the thought that his wife was above suspicion; from then on he began avoiding Countess Lydia. He did not want to see and did not see that many people in society were already looking at his wife askance; he did not want to understand and did not understand why his wife had particularly insisted on moving to Tsarskoye Selo, where Betsy lived and which was not far from where Vronsky's regiment was stationed. He did not allow himself to think about it and he did not; but at the same time, in the depths of his heart, without ever expressing it to himself and without having not only any proofs but even suspicions, he knew without a doubt that he was a cuckold, and because of this he was deeply unhappy.

How often during the course of his eight years of happiness with his wife, in looking at the unfaithful wives and deceived husbands of others, had Karenin not said to himself: How could they let it go so far? How is it they don't put a stop to this revolting situation?

But now, when the disaster had fallen on his own head, not only did he not think of putting a stop to this situation,

but he refused to recognize it at all. He refused to recognize
it just because it was too dreadful, too unnatural.

Since returning from abroad Karenin had been at the country house twice. Once he dined there, the other time he spent
an evening with guests, but he never once stayed the night as
he had been in the habit of doing before.

The day of the races was a very busy one for Karenin; but
while laying out his day in the morning he decided to go to
the country house to see his wife immediately after an early
dinner, and go from there to the races, which would be attended by the entire Court and where he had to put in an appearance. He was going to see his wife because he had
decided to do so once a week for the sake of propriety. Aside
from this he had to give his wife the housekeeping money on
he fifteenth of the month, according to their routine.

Having considered all this about his wife, with his usual
control over his own thoughts he didn't allow these thoughts
to stray on to anything else concerning her.

His morning was very busy. The day before Countess Lydia
had sent him a pamphlet by some famous traveler in China
who was passing through Petersburg, together with a letter
asking him to receive the traveler himself, who for various
reasons was extremely interesting and useful. Karenin had not
had time to read the pamphlet in the evening, and had to
finish it in the morning. Then he received petitioners, and
began hearing reports, giving audiences, assigning posts, ordering dismissals, apportioning rewards, pensions, salaries,
and attending to correspondence—the daily grind, as he
called it, that took up so much time. Then came his personal
business—a visit from his doctor and from the manager of
his property. The manager did not take up much time. He
merely gave Karenin some money he needed together with a
short report on the state of his finances, which were not in
very good condition; it turned out that since they had been
away from home very often that year expenses had been
greater and there was a deficit. But the doctor, a famous
Petersburg physician who was on friendly terms with Karenin, took up a lot of time. Karenin was not even expecting
him that day; he was surprised by his arrival and still more
by his questioning him very attentively about his condition,
sounding his chest, and tapping and feeling his liver. Karenin
did not know that his friend Countess Lydia had noticed that
his health was bad that year and had asked the doctor to

visit his patient and examine him. "Do it for my sake," Countess Lydia had said.

"I shall do it for the sake of Russia, Countess," the doctor replied.

"A priceless man!" said Countess Lydia.

The doctor was very dissatisfied with Karenin. He found that his liver was substantially enlarged, his digestion slack: the spa had done him no good at all. He prescribed as much more physical activity as possible and as much less intellectual strain as possible, and above all no worries of any kind—that is, something that was just as impossible for Karenin as not breathing; and he went off, leaving Karenin with the disagreeable feeling that something was wrong with him, and that it was impossible to put it right.

On leaving Karenin, the doctor ran into an old acquaintance of his on the stairs, Slyudin, Karenin's manager. They had been friends at the university and though they seldom met they respected each other and were on good terms; the doctor would not have expressed a frank opinion of his patient to anyone but Slyudin.

"I'm delighted that you've been to see him," said Slyudin. "He's not well and I have the impression that—Well, what is it?"

"I'll tell you," said the doctor, signaling over Slyudin's head for his coachman to drive up. "I'll tell you," said the doctor, taking a finger of his kid gloves in his white hands and stretching it. "If you try to snap a cord that's slack it's very difficult, but stretch it as far as possible and lay the weight of a single finger on the strained cord—and it'll snap. Because of his zeal and conscientiousness he's strained to the utmost degree, and there's also some pressure from outside, which is heavy too," the doctor concluded, raising his eyebrows significantly. "Will you be at the races?" he added, going down to the carriage that had drawn up.

"Yes, yes, of course, it takes up a lot of time," said the doctor in answer to something Slyudin said which he hadn't quite caught.

The doctor, who had taken so much time, was followed by the famous traveler, and Karenin, by merely making use of the pamphlet he had just read and his own former knowledge of the subject, impressed the traveler with the depth of his own knowledge of the subject and the breadth and enlightenment of his views.

Together with the traveler the arrival was announced of a

provincial Marshal of the Nobility, who had turned up in Petersburg and with whom Karenin had some things to discuss. After his departure Karenin had to finish his routine business with his private secretary, then had to drive over to see one more important personage on a grave and important matter. Karenin did not manage to come back until five o'clock, his dinnertime, and having dined with his private secretary invited him to go off to his country house together with him and then to the races.

Without acknowledging it to himself Karenin now looked for an opportunity to have a third person present whenever he saw his wife.

## XXVII

ANNA was upstairs, standing in front of the mirror and with Annushka's help pinning a final bow to her dress, when she heard the sounds of wheels crushing the gravel at the entrance.

It's still too early for Betsy, she thought, and glancing through the window she saw the carriage and sticking out of it a black hat and Karenin's familiar ears. Now that's a piece of luck! Can he be staying overnight? she thought, and everything that might come of this seemed so terrifying and horrible to her that without a moment's reflection she went out to meet him with a gay and radiant face, and feeling within her the presence of the now familiar spirit of lies and deceit she instantly surrendered to this spirit and began talking without realizing herself what she was saying.

"But how delightful!" she said, giving her husband her hand and greeting Slyudin with a smile as a member of the household. "I hope you'll be staying the night, won't you?" was the first thing the spirit of deceit suggested to her. "Now we can go together. Only it's a pity I promised to go with Betsy; she's picking me up."

Karenin frowned at the mention of Betsy.

"Oh, I should never separate the inseparables," he said in his usual bantering tone. "I'll go with Slyudin. The doctors have also ordered me to take walks. I'll walk part of the way and imagine I'm taking the waters."

"There's no hurry," said Anna. "Would you like some tea?" She rang. "Bring some tea and tell Seryozha his father's arrived. Well, how is your health? Slyudin, you haven't been

here before, just see how pleasant it is out on my terrace,"
she said, turning first to one then the other.

She spoke very simply and naturally, but too much and too
quickly. She felt this herself, especially since she noticed by
the inquisitive way Slyudin was looking at her that he seemed
to be watching her.

Slyudin got up at once and went out onto the terrace.

She sat down beside her husband. "You're not looking altogether well," she said.

"Yes," he said, "the doctor came to see me today and
took up an hour's time. I have the feeling one of my friends
sent him to me—that's how precious my health is—"

"No, but what did he say?"

She questioned him about his health and what he was
doing, trying to persuade him to take a rest and move out to
the country with her.

She said all these things gaily, quickly, and with a peculiar
sparkle in her eyes; but Karenin no longer ascribed any meaning now to this tone of hers. All he heard was what she said,
which he understood in its direct sense only. And he replied
to her simply, even though banteringly. The whole conversation was perfectly commonplace, but afterward Anna could
never recall this whole brief scene without an agonizing
twinge of shame.

Seryozha came in accompanied by his governess. If Karenin
had allowed himself to observe anything he would have
noticed the timid, confused way the child looked first at his
father then at his mother. But he did not want to see anything and he saw nothing.

"Aha! Young man! He's grown. He's really turning into
quite a man. How d'you do, young man."

And he gave the frightened Seryozha his hand.

Even before Seryozha had been timid with his father, and
now that Karenin had begun calling him "young man,"
and the problem of whether Vronsky was a friend or an
enemy had entered his mind, he avoided his father. He
glanced round at his mother as though asking for protection.
It was only with his mother that he felt at ease. But while
Karenin was speaking with the governess he held on to his
son's shoulder, and Seryozha felt so painfully uncomfortable
that Anna saw he was about to burst into tears.

When Anna, who had blushed the moment her son came in,
noticed how uncomfortable he felt, she jumped up quickly,
took Karenin's hand off the boy's shoulder, gave her son a

kiss and led him out to the terrace, going back immediately.

"Well, now it's time to leave," she said, looking at her watch. "I wonder what's happened to Betsy!"

"Yes," said Karenin, getting up; he interlaced his hands and cracked his knuckles. "I've also come to bring you some money. Since 'fables won't feed nightingales,'" he said, "I should think you need some."

"No, I don't—or rather I do," she said, not looking at him and blushing to the roots of her hair. "But I suppose you'll be coming here from the races."

"Oh yes!" Karenin replied. "And here's the pearl of Peterhof, Princess Tverskoy," he added, looking through the window at the approaching carriage, of English make, with the tiny body set very high up. "What elegance! Ravishing! Well, we'll be off too."

Princess Tverskoy did not get out of the carriage; only her footman, in his black hat, cape, and gaiters jumped down at the entrance.

"I'm going, good-by!" said Anna, and after giving her son a kiss she went over to Karenin and held out her hand to him. "It was very sweet of you to come."

Karenin kissed her hand.

"*Au revoir* then. So you'll be coming back for tea, how wonderful!" she said and went out gay and radiant. But the moment she could no longer see him she felt the spot on her hand which his lips had touched and shuddered with loathing.

### XXVIII

BY the time Karenin appeared at the races Anna was already sitting in the pavilion at Betsy's side, in the stand where all the highest society had assembled. She caught sight of her husband quite far off. Two men, her husband and her lover, were the two centers of her life, and without the help of her external senses she was aware of their presence. While he was still quite far off she felt her husband approaching, and followed him involuntarily among the surging throng he was making his way through. She watched him approaching the pavilion, sometimes replying condescendingly to obsequious bows, or greeting his equals in a friendly, absent-minded way, or assiduously trying to catch the eye of the powers of this world and raising his large round hat that pressed down the tips of his ears. She was familiar with all these ways of his, and loathed every one of them. Nothing but ambition, nothing but a desire to get ahead!—that's the only thing he has in his soul, she thought, and all his lofty ideas, his love of enlightenment, religion, all of it is nothing but a means of getting ahead!

She could tell by the way he kept looking at the Ladies' Pavilion (he was looking straight at her, but could not distinguish her in the sea of muslins, ribbons, feathers, sunshades, and flowers) that he was trying to find her; but she purposely disregarded him.

"Karenin!" Princess Betsy called out to him, "I'm sure you can't see your wife—there she is!"

He smiled his chilly smile.

"There's so much glamour here my eyes are dazzled," he said, going over to the pavilion. He smiled at Anna as a husband ought to who has just seen his wife, and greeted the Princess and other acquaintances of his, giving each one their due—that is, making jokes with the women and exchanging greetings with the men. An adjutant general Karenin respected, well known for his intelligence and cultivation, was standing at the foot of the pavilion; Karenin started speaking to him.

There was an interval between races, so there was nothing to interfere with conversation. The adjutant general condemned racing, and Karenin protested in their defense. Anna listened to his high, measured voice, without missing a single word; every word seemed to her false and grated painfully on her ear.

When the three-mile steeplechase was about to begin she leaned forward and did not take her eyes off Vronsky as he approached his horse and mounted, and at the same time she could hear her husband's untiring, repulsive voice. She was tormented by fears for Vronsky, but was even more tormented by the incessant sound, as it seemed to her, of her husband's high voice with its familiar intonations.

I'm a bad woman, a ruined woman, she thought, but I dislike lying, I can't bear lying, while *he* (her husband) lives on lies. He knows everything, sees everything; what can his feelings be if he can speak so calmly? If he killed me, if he killed Vronsky, I'd respect him. But all he wants is lies and propriety, Anna said to herself, without thinking of just what it was that she wanted from her husband, or how she would have liked him to be. Nor did she understand that this peculiar talkativeness of Karenin's, which annoyed her so much, was merely the expression of his inner anxiety and restlessness. Just as a hurt child skips about and moves his muscles in order to deaden a pain, so Karenin needed mental activity in order to deaden the thoughts about his wife that in her presence and Vronsky's, and because of the constant repetition of his name, kept thrusting themselves on his attention. Just as it is natural for a child to skip about, so it was natural for him to speak intelligently and well. He was saying:

"In Army, that is, cavalry races, danger is an indispensable condition of racing. If England is able to point to the most brilliant cavalry exploits in military history it is only thanks to her having developed this ability historically both in her men and in her animals. To my mind sport is extremely important, and as usual all we see is the superficial side of things."

"There's nothing superficial about it at all," said Princess Tverskoy. "They say one of the officers has broken two ribs."

Karenin smiled his usual smile, which showed his teeth but expressed nothing beyond that.

"Let us grant, Princess, that that's not superficial, but profound. Though that's not the point," and he turned back to the general with whom he was carrying on a serious conversation. "Don't forget that those racing are Army men, who have chosen this career; we must admit that every profession has its good and bad points. This is all directly part of an Army man's duties. The monstrous sports of fisticuffs or Spanish bullfighting are a sign of barbarism. But a specialized sport is a sign of progress."

"No, I'll never come again; it gets me too upset," said Princess Betsy. "Isn't that so, Anna?"

"It's upsetting, but you can't tear yourself away," said some other woman. "If I'd been a Roman I should never have missed a single gladiatorial show."

Anna said nothing; without putting down her binoculars she kept looking at one spot.

Just then a high-ranking general made his way through the pavilion. Interrupting his speech, Karenin hastily but with dignity stood up, and made him a low bow as he passed by.

"You're not racing?" said the general jokingly.

"My race is a more difficult one," Karenin answered respectfully.

And though this reply meant nothing the general took on a look as though he had heard an intelligent remark from an intelligent man and completely understood the point of it.

"There are two sides to it," Karenin resumed, "that of the performers and that of the spectators; now a love for these spectacles is the surest sign of an inferior development on the part of the spectators, I quite agree, but—"

"Princess, a bet!" came Oblonsky's voice from below, addressing Betsy. "Whom are you backing?"

"Anna and I are betting on Prince Kuzovlyov," Betsy replied.

"I'm for Vronsky. A pair of gloves?"

"You're on!"

"But what a wonderful sight, isn't it?"

Karenin was silent while the others around him were talking, then began again immediately.

"I agree, but manly sports—" he said, about to continue.

But just then the riders were started and all conversation stopped. Karenin also fell silent, and everyone rose and faced the brook. Karenin was not interested in racing and so he didn't look at the riders, but began taking in the spectators absent-mindedly with his tired eyes. His gaze settled on Anna.

Her face was white and stern. It was plain that she saw nothing and nobody, except for one. Her hand clutched her fan convulsively; she was holding her breath. He looked at her and hastily turned away to look at the others.

Yes, that woman too and the others are also very excited, it's all quite natural, Karenin said to himself. He did not want to look at her, but his eyes were involuntarily drawn to her. Once again he looked into her face, trying not to read what was so clearly written in it, and against his will, with horror, he read in it the very thing he did not want to know.

The first fall—Kuzovlyov's at the brook—excited everyone, but Karenin saw clearly in Anna's pale, triumphant face that the one she was watching had not fallen. And after Makhotin and Vronsky had jumped the big barrier, when the officer following them had fallen on his head and been knocked unconscious, and a murmur of horror passed through the whole crowd, Karenin saw that Anna did not even notice this and only understood with difficulty what those around her started talking about. But he kept looking at her more and more often, and more intently. Anna, completely consumed by the sight of Vronsky racing, felt the gaze of her husband's cold eyes directed at her from the side.

She glanced over for a second, looked at him questioningly, then turned away again with a slight frown.

What do I care? she seemed to be saying to him, and from then on did not once look at him again.

It was an unlucky steeplechase; of the seventeen officers more than half were thrown and hurt. By the end of the race everyone was in a state of agitation, which was heightened by the fact that the Tsar was displeased.

## XXIX

EVERYONE was loudly protesting his disapproval, everyone was repeating a phrase someone had made—"all we need are lions and gladiators"—and everyone was full of horror, so that when Vronsky fell and Anna groaned aloud there was nothing unusual about it. But then a change came over Anna's face that was really improper. She completely lost command of herself. She began to flutter like a captive bird: first she would get up to go somewhere, then she would turn to Betsy.

"Let us go, let us go!" she said.

But Betsy did not hear her. Leaning over she was talking to a general who had come up to her.

Karenin went over to Anna and politely offered her his hand.

"Come, if you like," he said in French; but Anna was listening to what the general was saying and didn't notice her husband.

"He's also broken a leg, they say," said the general. "This really does beat everything."

Without answering her husband, Anna raised her binoculars and looked at the spot where Vronsky had fallen; but it was so far away and there were so many people crowding around that it was impossible to make anything out. She lowered the binoculars and was about to go, but just then an officer galloped up and started reporting something to the Tsar. Anna craned forward to listen.

"Stiva! Stiva!" she called to her brother.

But her brother didn't hear her, and again she was on the point of leaving

"Let me offer you my hand once again, if you would like to go," said Karenin, touching her arm.

She drew back from him with revulsion, and without looking him in the face replied: "No, no, leave me alone, I'm staying on."

Now she could see an officer running through the crowd to the pavilion from the place Vronsky had fallen. Betsy waved her handkerchief at him. The officer brought the news that the rider had not been hurt but that the horse had broken its back.

When she heard this Anna sat down quickly and covered her face with the fan. Karenin saw that she was weeping and could not hold back not only her tears, but the sobs that made her bosom heave. Karenin screened her with his own person to give her time to recover herself.

"For the third time I offer you my arm," he said, turning to her a moment later. Anna looked at him, not knowing what to say. Princess Betsy came to her rescue.

"No, I brought Anna and I promised to take her back," Betsy said, intervening.

"Forgive me, Princess," he said, smiling politely, but looking her firmly in the eyes, "but I see Anna's not quite well and I should like her to come with me."

Anna looked about her frightened, then got up docilely and put her hand on her husband's arm.

"I'll send someone to see him, find out what's happened and let you know," Betsy whispered to her.

As they left the pavilion Karenin spoke to those he met as he always did; Anna was also supposed to speak and make conversation as usual, but she was completely beside herself and walked on holding her husband's arm as though in a dream.

Is he hurt or not? Is it true? Will he come or not? Will I see him tonight? she thought.

She got into Karenin's carriage in silence and in silence drove out of the crowd of vehicles. In spite of everything he had seen Karenin nevertheless refused to allow himself to think of his wife's real situation. All he saw were the outward signs. He saw that she had behaved improperly, and regarded it as his duty to tell her that. But it was very difficult for him to say only that and nothing more. He opened his mouth to tell her that she had behaved improperly, but in spite of himself said something quite different.

"Really, how prone we all are to these cruel spectacles," he said. "I notice—"

"What? I don't understand," said Anna contemptuously.

He was offended, and at once began telling her what he had wanted to.

"I must tell you—" he began.

Here it is—a scene! she thought; she felt frightened.

"I must tell you, that your behavior today was improper," he said to her in French.

"In what way was it improper?" she said in a loud voice, quickly turning her head toward him and looking him straight in the eyes, but now no longer with her former mask of gaiety but with an air of determination underneath which she had difficulty hiding her fear.

"Don't forget him," he said, indicating the open window behind the coachman. Rising slightly he put up the window.

"What was it you found improper?" she repeated.

"The despair you were unable to conceal when one of the riders fell."

He waited for her to protest; but she looked ahead of her in silence.

"I've already asked you to behave in public in such a way that malicious tongues would be unable to say anything against you. There was a time when I spoke of inner relations—I'm not speaking of them now. What I'm speaking of now is external relations. You behaved improperly, and I do not wish it to happen again."

She did not hear half of what he was saying; she was afraid of him, and wondering whether it was true that Vronsky had not been hurt. Was he the one they were speaking about, who was all right, but whose horse had broken its back? She merely smiled with feigned irony when Karenin stopped talking, and said nothing in reply, since she had not heard what he had been saying. Karenin had begun speaking boldly, but when he clearly grasped what it was that he was talking about her fear communicated itself to him. He saw this smile of hers, and a strange delusion laid hold of him.

She's smiling at my suspicions! Yes, she's going to tell me at once what she told me that other time—that I have no reason to be suspicious, that it's ridiculous!

Now that a disclosure of the whole thing was hanging

over him he wished for nothing so much as for her to reply to him just as mockingly as before by saying that his suspicions were ridiculous and baseless. What he knew was so dreadful that now he was ready to believe anything. But the expression on her sullen, frightened face now no longer promised even deception.

"I may be mistaken," he said. "In that case I beg you to forgive me."

"No, you're not mistaken," she said slowly, looking in desperation at his cold face. "You are not mistaken. I was in despair and I cannot help being in despair. I'm listening to you and thinking about him. I love him, I'm his mistress, I can't bear it, I'm afraid—I hate you . . . You can do whatever you like with me!"

And flinging herself into a corner of the carriage she burst into sobs, hiding her face in her hands. Karenin did not stir, and did not stop looking straight ahead of him. But his whole face suddenly took on the stately motionlessness of a corpse, and this expression did not change throughout the drive to the country house. When they drew up to the house he turned his head toward her, still with the same expression.

"Very well! But I demand that the external conditions of .propriety be observed until"—his voice trembled—"I take steps to safeguard my honor, and communicate them to you."

He got out first and helped her out. In front of the servants he pressed her hand in silence, got back into the carriage and drove off to Petersburg.

After he had left, a footman arrived from Princess Betsy with a note for Anna:

*"I've inquired about Alexis's health; he's written me that he's well and unhurt, but in despair."*

Then he *will* come! thought Anna; how wonderful that I've made a clean breast of everything.

She looked at her watch. There were three hours left, and the memories of their last time together set her blood on fire.

Heavens, how light it is! It's dreadful, but I love looking at his face, and I love this fantastic light . . . Karenin! Oh yes—well, thank God it's all over with him!

## XXX

As always happens wherever people gather together, so at the little German spa the Shcherbatskys went to there took place the usual crystallization as it were of society that assigns each one of its members a definite and unalterable niche. As definitely and unalterably as a drop of water in the cold takes on a certain form of snow crystal, so each new person arriving at a spa instantly and with the same precision settles into his own special place.

"Prince Shcherbatsky together with wife and daughter," by virtue of the lodgings they took, their name, and the people they knew whom they found there, instantly crystallized into a definite place predestined for them.

At the spa that year there was a genuine German Princess, with the result that the crystallization of society took place even more energetically. Princess Shcherbatsky was determined to present her daughter to the German Princess, and performed this rite on the very day after their arrival. Kitty made a low and graceful curtsey in the "very simple," that is, extremely fashionable summer dress ordered from Paris for her. The German Princess said: "I hope the roses will soon return to that pretty little face," and instantly a definite path was laid down for the life of the Shcherbatskys in which any deviation was out of the question. The Shcherbatskys made the acquaintance of the family of an English lady, of a German Countess and her son, who had been wounded in the last war, of a Swedish scholar, and of a Monsieur Canut and his sister. But in spite of themselves the company they kept most consisted of a Moscow lady, Madame Rtishchev and her daughter, who irritated Kitty because of her having fallen ill for the same reason as herself, for love, and of a Moscow colonel whom Kitty had seen and known since childhood in a uniform and epaulets, and who here, with his little eyes, open neck, and colored necktie looked exceptionally ridiculous, and was also a bore, since it was impossible to get rid of him. When all this had been firmly established it became very boring for Kitty, especially since Prince Shcherbatsky left for Carlsbad and she was left alone with her mother. She had no interest in the people she knew, feeling quite sure nothing novel would emerge from them. Thus her chief private interest at the spa now consisted of watching those she didn't know and speculating about them. It was a trait of Kitty's character always to expect the most splendid things in people, particularly in those she didn't know. And now, as she speculated about who was who, what sort of people they were and what relationship they had to each other, Kitty imagined the most astonishing, splendid characters for them, which she found confirmation for in her observations. Among such people she was especially interested in a Russian girl who had come to the spa together with a Russian invalid whom everyone called Madame Stahl. Madame Stahl belonged to the highest society, but she was so ill she could not walk; it was only on the fine days, which were rare, that she would appear at the springs in a bath chair. But it was not because of illness but pride, as Kitty's mother explained, that Madame Stahl was unacquainted with any of the Russians there. The Russian girl looked after Madame Stahl and was besides, as Kitty observed, on friendly terms with all the serious invalids, whom there were a great many of at the waters, and looked after all of them in the most natural way. According to Kitty's observations this Russian girl was not related to Madame Stahl, nor was she a paid companion. Madame Stahl called her "Varenka"; others called her "Mademoiselle Varenka." Quite apart from Kitty's interest in observing the relationship of this girl to Madame Stahl and to other people she wasn't acquainted with, Kitty felt an inexplicable attraction toward this Mlle. Varenka, which often happens, and when their eyes met she felt the girl liked her too.

Mlle. Varenka was not exactly past her first youth, but seemed a being beyond youthfulness—you might think her nineteen years old, or thirty. If her features were analyzed she was rather prettier than she was plain, in spite of her unhealthy complexion. She would also have had a good figure if she hadn't been far too dried up, with a head that was too large for her medium height; but she couldn't have been attractive to men. She was like a beautiful flower, which though its petals were all there had already withered and had no scent. Besides which she couldn't have been attractive to men because she didn't have enough of what

Kitty had too much of—a repressed flame of vitality and the awareness of her own attractiveness.

She always seemed to be absorbed in work that left no room for doubt, and therefore seemed incapable of taking an interest in anything outside it. It was this contrast with herself that particularly attracted Kitty. Kitty felt that it was in her, and in her manner of life, that she would find a model for what she was now painfully looking for: interest in life, values in life, beyond the worldly relations between girls and men, which were repugnant to Kitty now and seemed to her no more than a shameful display of merchandise awaiting a buyer. The more Kitty observed her unknown friend the more she grew convinced that this girl was the creature of perfection she imagined her to be, and the more she wanted to meet her.

Both girls crossed each other's path several times a day, and at every encounter Kitty's eyes would say: Who are you? What are you? Can it really be that you're the wonderful creature I imagine you are? Though for Heaven's sake don't think—her glance would add—that I would allow myself to pick people up: I simply admire you and love you. I love you too, the unknown girl's eyes would answer, you're very, very charming. If I had the time, I should love you even more.

And as a matter of fact Kitty saw that she was constantly occupied: either she would be taking the children of some Russian family home from the springs, or fetching a shawl for some sick woman and wrapping her up in it, or trying to divert some irritable patient, or picking out and buying biscuits for someone's coffee.

Soon after the Shcherbatskys arrived, two new people who aroused general disapproval began turning up at the springs in the morning. One was a very tall, round-shouldered man with enormous hands and with black eyes that were naïve and terrifying at the same time, wearing an old overcoat that was too short for him, and a slightly pock-marked woman with a sweet expression, very badly and tastelessly dressed. As soon as she saw they were Russians, Kitty's imagination began making up a beautiful, touching romance about them. But her mother, after learning from the guest list that they were Nicholas Levin and Masha, explained to her what a bad man this Levin was, and all her dreams about them vanished. Not so much because of what her mother told her as because it was Constantine's brother, these two people suddenly came to seem extremely unpleasant to Kitty. Because of his habit of jerking his head this Levin now aroused in her an insurmountable feeling of disgust.

It seemed to her that his dreadful great eyes, which kept following her insistently, expressed a feeling of hatred and mockery, and she tried to avoid meeting him.

## XXXI

IT was a foul day; it had been raining all morning and the invalids with their umbrellas had crowded into the arcades.

Kitty was walking with her mother and the Moscow colonel, who was cheerfully strutting along in his European coat, bought ready-made in Frankfurt. They were walking along one side of the arcades, trying to avoid Levin, who was walking on the other side. Varenka, in her dark dress and black hat with a turned-down brim, was walking up and down the entire length of the arcade with a blind Frenchwoman, and whenever she met Kitty they would exchange friendly looks.

"May I speak to her, Mama?" said Kitty, gazing after her unknown friend; she had noticed she was going over to the spring and thought they might meet there.

"Well, if you want to so much I'll inquire about her first and speak to her myself," her mother replied. "What d'you find about her that's so special? She must be some little companion. If you like I'll arrange to meet Madame Stahl. I knew her sister-in-law," the Princess added, raising her head proudly.

Kitty knew that her mother was offended because Madame Stahl seemed to avoid meeting her, and did not insist.

"What a wonderfully sweet thing she is!" she said, looking at Varenka, who was handing the Frenchwoman a glass. "Just look how simply and sweetly she does that."

"I really find your infatuations very funny," said the Princess. "Come, we'd better turn back," she added, as she noticed Levin coming toward them with his companion and a German doctor, whom he was talking to in a loud, angry voice.

They were just turning around to go back when they suddenly heard voices, not merely loud talk but actual shouting. Levin had stopped and was yelling, and the doctor had also gotten excited. A crowd was collecting around them. Kitty and her mother hastily withdrew, while the colonel joined the crowd to find out what it was all about.

A few minutes later the colonel caught up with them.

"What was it?" asked the Princess.

"Shameful! Scandalous!" replied the colonel. "The only thing to be afraid of is running into Russians abroad. That tall fellow has been bickering with the doctor and flinging insults at him for not giving him the right treatment; he began waving his stick at him. It's simply scandalous!"

"How disagreeable!" said the Princess. "Well, how did it end?"

"Luckily that—that girl with a hat like a mushroom intervened. I think she's Russian," said the colonel.

"Mlle. Varenka?" asked Kitty, delighted.

"That's it. She recovered herself before anyone else, took that fellow by the arm and led him away."

"There, Mama," said Kitty to her mother. "And you were surprised at my admiring her."

The next day, as she was watching her unknown friend, Kitty noticed that Mlle. Varenka was already on the same terms with Levin and his young woman as she was with her other protégés. She would go up to them, talk to them, and serve as interpreter for the young woman, who spoke nothing but Russian.

Kitty began entreating her mother even more insistently to let her make friends with Varenka. And however disagreeable it was for the Princess to seem to be taking the first step in her desire to get to know Madame Stahl, who allowed herself such haughty airs, she made inquiries about Varenka and after learning particulars that enabled her to conclude there was nothing bad in this acquaintance, though nothing good either, the Princess herself approached Varenka first and introduced herself.

Choosing a time when her daughter had gone to the spring and Varenka had stopped in front of the baker's, the Princess went over to her.

"Allow me to introduce myself," she said with her dignified smile. "My daughter has quite lost her heart to you," she said. "Perhaps you don't know me, I am—"

"It is more than mutual, Princess," Varenka answered hurriedly.

"How kind you were yesterday to our poor fellow countryman!" said the Princess.

Varenka blushed. "I don't remember, I don't think I did anything," she said.

"But you saved this Levin from some unpleasantness."

"Well, you see his companion called me over and I tried to calm him; he's very ill and he's not satisfied with the doctor. I'm used to looking after invalids like that."

"Yes, I've heard you live in Mentone with your aunt, I think, Madame Stahl. I used to know her sister-in-law."

"No, she's not my aunt. I call her *maman* but I'm not related to her; I was brought up by her," replied Varenka, blushing again.

This was said so simply, the honest, frank expression on her face was so sweet, that the Princess realized why her Kitty had fallen in love with her.

"And what about this Levin?"

"He's leaving," Varenka replied.

Just then, radiant with joy at her mother's having struck up an acquaintance with her unknown friend, Kitty came over from the spring.

"Well, Kitty, your intense desire to make friends with Mademoiselle—"

"Varenka," prompted Varenka with a smile. "That's what everyone calls me."

Kitty flushed with delight, long and silently pressing her new friend's hand, which did not return the pressure but lay motionless in Kitty's hand. Mlle. Varenka's hand did not return the pressure, but her face radiated a quiet, joyful though also somewhat mournful smile, which displayed large but beautiful teeth.

"I've wanted this for a long time myself," she said.

"But you're so busy—"

"Oh, on the contrary, I have nothing to do at all," replied Varenka, but at that very moment she had to leave her new acquaintances because two little Russian girls, the daughters of one of the invalids, ran over to her.

"Varenka, Mama's calling for you!" they shouted.

And Varenka went off with them.

### XXXII

THESE were the details the Princess had learned about
Varenka's past and about her relationship to Madame
Stahl, and about Madame Stahl herself.

Madame Stahl, of whom some people said that she had
tormented her husband to death, while others said he had
tormented her by his immoral conduct, had always been a
sickly and hysterical woman. When she gave birth to a new
child, after already being divorced from her husband, the
child had died at once, and Madame Stahl's relatives,
knowing her sensitivity and afraid the news would kill
her, replaced her dead child with one born that same night
in the same house in Petersburg, the daughter of a baker
at the Palace. This was Varenka. Later on Madame Stahl
had found out that Varenka was not her daughter but she
had gone on bringing her up, especially since very soon
afterward Varenka lost all her relatives.

Madame Stahl had been living abroad in the south constantly for more than ten years already, without ever
getting out of bed. Some said Madame Stahl had established
herself socially as a philanthropic, extremely devout woman;
others said that at heart she really was the highly moral
creature, living only for the welfare of her fellows, that she
posed as. No one knew what her religion was—Roman Catholic, Protestant, or Greek Orthodox—but one thing was incontestable: she was on friendly terms with the most exalted
personages of all the churches and denominations.

Varenka constantly lived with her abroad, and everyone
who knew Madame Stahl, knew and was fond of Mlle.
Varenka, as they all called her.

After learning all these details the Princess saw nothing
objectionable in an intimacy between her daughter and
Varenka, especially since Varenka's manners and education were excellent: she spoke very good English and French,
and what was most important she conveyed Madame Stahl's
regret that it was her illness that deprived her of the pleasure
of making the Princess's acquaintance.

After meeting Varenka, Kitty grew more and more fascinated by her; she discovered new virtues in her every
day.

The Princess, learning that Varenka sang well, invited her to come and sing to them one evening.

"Kitty plays, and we have a piano, a bad one, to be sure, but you will give us a great deal of pleasure," said the Princess with her affected smile, which was particularly disagreeable for Kitty now because she noticed that Varenka did not feel like singing. But Varenka came that evening bringing her music with her. The Princess had invited Madame Rtishchev, her daughter, and the colonel.

Varenka seemed quite indifferent to the presence of people she didn't know, and went over to the piano immediately. She could not accompany herself, but she sang wonderfully well by sight. Kitty, who played well, accompanied her.

"You have exceptional talent," the Princess said to Varenka, after she had sung her first song extremely well.

Madame Rtishchev and her daughter thanked and complimented her.

"Just see what a crowd has collected to listen to you," said the colonel, looking through the window. In fact a rather large crowd had gathered beneath the windows.

"I am very glad it gives you pleasure," replied Varenka simply.

Kitty looked at her friend with pride. She was enraptured by her talent, by her voice, by her face, but above all she was enraptured by the way in which it was evident that Varenka thought nothing of her own singing and was completely indifferent to compliments: all she seemed to be asking was: Shall I have to sing some more or is that enough?

If I were she, thought Kitty to herself, how proud I should be! How delighted I'd be to see that crowd beneath the windows! But to her it's all the same. She's only moved by her desire not to refuse and to please Mama. But what is it in her? What gives her the strength to disregard everything, and to be so calm and independent? How I should like to know, and to learn it from her, thought Kitty, looking into her serene face. The Princess asked Varenka to sing something else, and Varenka sang another song just as smoothly, distinctly, and well, standing at the piano and keeping time on it with her thin, brown hand.

The next piece in the music book was an Italian song. Kitty played the prelude and glanced at Varenka.

"Let's skip that one," said Varenka, blushing.

Kitty fixed a frightened, questioning look on Varenka's face.

"Some other one, then," she said hastily, turning over the pages, having instantly understood that something or other was associated with this song.

"No," Varenka answered, putting her hand on the music and smiling, "no, let's do that one." And she sang just as serenely, coldly, and well as she had before.

After she finished everyone thanked her again and went off for tea. Kitty and Varenka went out into the little garden next to the house.

"Is there some memory associated with that song?" said Kitty. "Don't talk about it," she hastened to add, "just tell me whether it's so?"

"No, why not? I'll tell you," said Varenka simply, and without waiting for an answer went on: "Yes, there is a memory, and at one time it was a bitter one. I was in love with someone and used to sing it to him."

Kitty, moved, silently gazed at Varenka with great wide eyes.

"I loved him and he loved me; but his mother was against it and he married someone else. He lives not far from us now; sometimes I see him. You didn't think I'd had a romance too?" she said, and on her handsome face there flickered a spark of the fire Kitty felt had once lit up her whole being.

"Why should I have thought that? If I were a man I shouldn't be able to love anyone else after knowing you. I just don't understand how he was able to forget you and make you unhappy to please his mother; he must have been heartless."

"Oh no, he's a very good man, and I'm not unhappy; on the contrary I'm very happy. Then we're not going to sing any more today?" she added, starting toward the house.

"How good you are, how good you are!" exclaimed Kitty, and stopping her she gave her a kiss. "If I could only be just a little bit like you!"

"Why should you be like anyone? You're perfectly all right as you are," said Varenka, with her gentle, weary smile.

"No, I'm not good at all. Now, tell me—Wait a moment, let's sit down again," said Kitty, pulling Varenka down on a little bench beside her. "Tell me, isn't it humiliating to think that a man has slighted your love? That he didn't want to—"

"But he didn't slight me; I believe he loved me, but he was an obedient son—"

"But what if he hadn't done it because of his mother's wishes, but just so, of his own accord?" said Kitty, feeling that she had given away her secret and that her face, crimson with shame, had already betrayed her.

"Then he would have behaved badly, and I shouldn't want him," replied Varenka, evidently understanding that it was no longer a question of herself but of Kitty.

"But the humiliation?" said Kitty. "It's impossible to forget the humiliation, impossible!" she said, recalling her own look during that last ball, when the music had paused.

"Where is the humiliation? You didn't do anything wrong, did you?"

"Worse than wrong—it was shameful."

Varenka shook her head and put her hand on Kitty's.

"But how could it have been shameful?" she said. "After all, you couldn't tell a man who was indifferent to you that you loved him?"

"No, of course not; I never said a single word, but he knew. No, no, there are looks, there are things you do. If I live to be a hundred I'll never forget it."

"But why not? I don't understand. The question is whether you love him now or not," said Varenka, calling everything by its name.

"I hate him; I can't forgive myself."

"But why?"

"The shame, the humiliation."

"Oh dear, if everyone were like you—so sensitive . . ." said Varenka. "There isn't a girl who hasn't gone through that. All of that is so unimportant."

"What is important then?" asked Kitty curiously, looking into her face with surprise.

"Oh, lots of things are important," said Varenka with a smile.

"But what?"

"Lots of things are more important," Varenka answered, not knowing what to say. But just then they heard the Princess's voice from the window:

"Kitty—it's getting chilly! Either get a shawl or come inside."

"Yes, it's time!" said Varenka, getting up. "I still have to drop in on Madame Berthe; she asked me to."

Kitty held her by the hand; in passionate curiosity and entreaty her eyes were asking: But what is it, what is it that's so important, that makes you so calm? You know —tell me!

But Varenka didn't even understand what Kitty's eyes were asking about. All she was thinking of was that she still had to visit Madame Berthe that day and get home in time for *maman*'s midnight tea. She went inside, collected her music, and saying good-by to everyone, prepared to leave.

"Allow me to accompany you," said the colonel.

"Yes, how can you go about alone now at night?" agreed the Princess. "Let me send Parasha with you, at least."

Kitty saw that Varenka was only with difficulty holding back a smile at the idea that she had to be escorted.

"No, I always walk about alone, nothing ever happens to me," she said, taking her hat. She kissed Kitty once again and without saying what it was that was important strode off briskly, her music under her arm, and vanished into the half-darkness of a summer night, carrying with her the secret of what was important and what gave her that enviable dignity and calm.

<br>

### XXXIII

KITTY also met Madame Stahl, and this acquaintance, together with her friendship for Varenka, not only had a strong influence on her but consoled her in her grief. She found this consolation in the fact that, thanks to this acquaintance, an entirely new world was opened up to her that had nothing in common with her past, an exalted, noble world from the heights of which she calmly looked down upon this past. What Kitty discovered was that aside from the life of instinct that she had hitherto given herself up to there was a life of the spirit. This life was disclosed to her through religion, but it was a religion that had nothing in common with what Kitty had known since childhood, which had found its expression in Mass and vespers at the private chapel of the Widows' Almshouse where you met everyone you knew, and in learning old

Slavonic texts by heart with the priest; this was a lofty, mystical religion that was bound up with beautiful thoughts and feelings that you could believe in not only because you had been ordered to, but because you could love it.

Kitty did not learn all this from words. Madame Stahl spoke to Kitty as though she were a charming child you looked on with pleasure as a reminder of your own youth; she said only once that consolation in all human sorrows could be given only by love and faith, and that there are no sorrows too trivial for Christ's compassion; then she immediately changed the subject. But in every one of her movements, in every word she said, in every "heavenly" look of hers, as Kitty called it, and especially in the whole story of her life, which Kitty learned of through Varenka, in everything, Kitty discovered "what was important," which until then she had not known.

But however exalted Madame Stahl's character, however moving her whole history, however lofty and tender her words, Kitty could not help noticing some traits in her that troubled her. She noticed that when Madame Stahl questioned her about her relatives she smiled contemptuously, which was contrary to Christian kindness. She noticed also that when she once met a Roman Catholic priest at her house Madame Stahl had assiduously kept her face behind the lamp shade and smiled in a peculiar way. However trivial these two observations were they troubled her, and she felt doubts about Madame Stahl.

But to make up for it Varenka, all alone, without family or friends, with her sad disappointment, who wished for nothing and regretted nothing, was just that embodiment of perfection Kitty had only allowed herself to dream of. Because of Varenka she understood the value of simply forgetting yourself and loving others, in order to be serene, happy, and good. And that was what Kitty wanted to be. Now that she clearly understood *the most important thing,* Kitty was not satisfied with being enthusiastic about it, but instantly surrendered with all her heart to this newly disclosed life. On the basis of what Varenka told her about the work of Madame Stahl and of others she mentioned, Kitty made up a plan for her future life. Just like Madame Stahl's niece Aline, whom Varenka told her a great deal about, Kitty, no matter where she lived, was going to seek out the unfortunate, help them as much as possible, spread the Gospel and read it to the sick, to criminals, to the dying. The idea of reading the Gospel to criminals, as Aline did, was particularly fascinating to Kitty. But all these were secret dreams, which Kitty did not speak of either to her mother or to Varenka.

But while waiting for a time when she could carry out her plans on a large scale, Kitty even now, at the spa where there were so many sick and unhappy people, easily found an opportunity to apply her new rules, in imitation of Varenka.

At first all the Princess noticed was that Kitty was under the powerful influence of her new infatuation, as she called it, for Madame Stahl and especially for Varenka. She saw that not only did Kitty imitate Varenka in her activities, but involuntarily imitated her in the way she walked, talked, and blinked her eyes. But then the Princess noticed that independently of this fascination some serious spiritual upheaval was taking place in her daughter.

The Princess saw that in the evenings Kitty would read the Gospels in French, given her by Madame Stahl, which she had never used to do; that she avoided society acquaintances and spent time with the invalids who were under Varenka's protection, and particularly with the impoverished family of a sick painter by the name of Petrov. It was plain that Kitty took pride in performing the duties of a sister of mercy for this family. This was all very well, and the Princess had nothing against it, especially since Petrov's wife happened to be a lady and the German Princess, having noticed Kitty's activities, praised her and called her a ministering angel. All this would have been perfectly all right, if it were not exaggerated. But the Princess saw that her daughter was going to extremes, and she told her as much.

"One must never exaggerate," she said to her.

But Kitty said nothing in reply; in her heart she merely thought it was impossible to speak of exaggeration when it was a question of Christianity. For how could there be any exaggeration in following a teaching that instructs you when you are hit on one cheek, to turn the other, and to give away your coat if your cloak is taken? But the Princess disliked this exaggeration, and disliked still more what she felt was Kitty's unwillingness to open up her whole heart to her. As a matter of fact Kitty did hide her new ideas and plans from her mother. She hid them not because she did not respect and love her mother, but simply because it was her mother. She would have revealed them to anyone sooner then to her.

"It seems some time since Madame Petrov has come to see us," the Princess said once, about the painter's wife. "I've invited her, but somehow she didn't seem pleased."

"No—I haven't noticed anything, *maman*," said Kitty, flushing.

"Have you seen them recently?"

"We're arranging to go for an outing in the mountains tomorrow," Kitty replied.

"Well, go, of course," answered the Princess, looking into her daughter's embarrassed face and trying to guess what lay behind it.

Varenka came to dinner that same day and reported that Anna Petrov had changed her mind about going to the mountains the next day. The Princess noticed that Kitty blushed once again.

"Kitty, has there been some falling out with the Petrovs?" said the Princess when they were alone. "Why has she stopped sending over the children and coming to visit us?"

Kitty replied that nothing had happened between them and that she was quite at a loss to understand why Anna Petrov seemed to be displeased with her. Kitty was quite truthful: she did not know why Anna Petrov had changed toward her, but she could guess. What she guessed at was something she could not tell her mother or admit to herself. It was one of those things you know but can't admit even to yourself: it was so terrible and shameful to be mistaken about.

Again and again she turned over in her mind all her relations with this family. She recalled the simple pleasure on Anna Petrov's round, good-natured face whenever they met; she recalled the secret conversations they had had about the sick man, their plots to lure him away from work, which he was forbidden to do, and take him for walks; the attachment of the youngest boy, who called her "my Kitty" and didn't want to go to bed without her. How wonderful everything had been! Then she recalled the thin, the terribly thin figure of Petrov, with his long neck, in his brown coat; his sparse curly hair, his inquiring blue eyes she had thought so dreadful at first, and his sickly efforts to appear

vigorous and lively in her presence. She remembered her
own struggle in the beginning to conquer the revulsion she
felt for him, as she did for all consumptives, and the efforts
she had made to think up something to say to him. She
recalled the timid look, full of emotion, he had given her,
and the strange feeling of compassion and awkwardness,
followed by the consciousness of her own benevolence,
she had experienced because of it. How wonderful it had
all been! But all that had been in the beginning. And now,
a few days before, everything had suddenly been spoiled.
Anna Petrov would meet Kitty now with feigned amiability
and keep her husband and her under constant observation.

Surely this touching joy of his at her approach could not
be the reason for Anna Petrov's coolness?

Yes, she remembered, there was something unnatural in
Anna Petrov, quite unlike her own kindness, when she said
so irritably the day before yesterday, "There, he's just kept
waiting for you, he wouldn't drink his coffee without you,
though he's grown terribly weak." Yes, and perhaps she
was also annoyed by my giving him the rug. It was such a
simple thing, but he accepted it so clumsily, he thanked me
at such length I began to feel uncomfortable myself. Then
that portrait of me, which he did so well. And the main
thing—that look, so confused and tender! Yes, yes, that's
it! Kitty repeated to herself horrified. No, it cannot, it must
not be! He's so pathetic! she said to herself afterward.

This doubt poisoned the delight of her new life.

### XXXIV

JUST before the end of the season Prince Shcherbatsky,
who had gone on to Baden and Kissingen after Carlsbad
to see some Russian friends and to drink in some Russian
spirit, as he said, rejoined his family.

The Prince and the Princess had views on living abroad
that were completely opposed. The Princess thought everything splendid, and in spite of her established position in
Russian society she tried when abroad to imitate a Continental lady, which, being thoroughly Russian, she was not.
Because of this her behavior was artificial, which made her
feel somewhat uncomfortable. The Prince, on the contrary,
thought everything abroad detestable and Continental life

oppressive; he clung to his Russian habits and purposely tried to show himself less European when abroad than he actually was.

The Prince returned thinner, the skin bagging loosely on his cheeks, but in the most cheerful state of mind. His cheerful temper was heightened still further when he saw Kitty completely recovered. The news of Kitty's friendship with Madame Stahl and Varenka, and the observations the Princess passed on to him of some sort of change that had taken place in Kitty, upset him; they aroused his usual feeling of jealousy of anything that drew his daughter away from him, and of fear that she might slip out from under his influence into regions beyond his reach. But these disagreeable reports were soon submerged in the sea of good humor and gaiety that was always within him and had been particularly reinforced by his taking the waters at Carlsbad.

The day after his arrival the Prince, in his long overcoat, his Russian wrinkles and baggy cheeks propped up by a starched collar, went off to the springs with his daughter, in the gayest of moods.

It was a magnificent morning: the neat, cheerful houses with their little gardens, the sight of the German housemaids working merrily away, red-faced, red-armed, and beer-soaked, and the bright sunshine cheered your heart up; but the closer they came to the springs the more often they encountered invalids, who amidst the customary conditions of well-organized German life looked even sadder. By now Kitty was no longer struck by this contrast. The bright sunshine, the merry glitter of the greenery, the sound of music, were the natural background of all these people she knew, and of the changes, for better or for worse, that she kept track of; but to the Prince the brightness and brilliance of a June morning and the sound of the orchestra that was playing a fashionable gay waltz, and especially the sight of the sturdy housemaids, seemed something indecent and monstrous in conjunction with these melancholy corpses collected from every corner of Europe.

In spite of his feeling of pride and as it were renewed youth, as he walked arm in arm with his favorite daughter, he now felt ill at ease and ashamed because of his own vigorous stride, his massive full-blooded limbs. He almost felt like a man with no clothes on in public.

"Now introduce me, you must introduce me to your

new friends," he said to his daughter, pressing her arm with his elbow. "I've even grown attached to this vile Soden of yours because it's done you so much good. But it's mournful here, very mournful! Now who is that?"

Kitty told him the names of the people they met, acquaintances and others. Just at the entrance to the garden they met blind Madame Berthe and her guide, and the Prince was delighted at the tender expression on the old Frenchwoman's face when she heard Kitty's voice. With the excessive amiability of the French she immediately started talking to him, praising him for having such a lovely daughter, and in Kitty's presence praising her to the skies, calling her a treasure, a pearl, and a ministering angel.

"Then she must be the second angel," said the Prince, smiling. "The one she calls angel number one is Mlle. Varenka."

"Oh! Mlle. Varenka—now there's a real angel after all," Madame Berthe agreed.

In the arcade they met Varenka herself. She hurriedly came over toward them, carrying an elegant little red bag.

"See—Papa's come!" Kitty said to her.

Varenka made a motion somewhere between a bow and a curtsy, simply and naturally, as she did everything, and started talking to the Prince as she talked to everyone, naturally and simply.

"I know you of course, know you very well," the Prince said to her with a smile, from which Kitty saw with delight that her father liked her friend. "But where are you off to in such a rush?"

"Mama is here," she said, turning to Kitty. "She couldn't sleep the whole night and the doctor advised her to go out. I'm bringing her her work."

"So that's angel number one," said the Prince when Varenka had gone.

Kitty saw that he felt like making fun of Varenka, but couldn't because he liked her.

"Well, now let's see all these friends of yours," he added, "Madame Stahl as well, if she deigns to recognize me."

"But did you used to know her, Papa?" asked Kitty in alarm, noticing a spark of mockery lighting up in her father's eyes at the mention of Madame Stahl.

"I used to know her husband, and her too, a little, before she joined the Pietists."

"What are the Pietists, Papa?" asked Kitty, already frightened by the fact that there was an actual name for what she esteemed so much in Madame Stahl.

"I don't really know myself. I only know she thanks God for everything, for every misfortune; she even thanks God for her husband's death. Of course that looks a little absurd, since they got on badly. . . . Over there now—who's that? What a pathetic face!" he asked, noticing sitting on a bench an invalid, rather short, in a brown coat and white trousers, that fell in strange folds over his fleshless legs.

This man raised his straw hat above his sparse curly hair, displaying a high forehead with a sickly flush on it from the hat.

"His name is Petrov; he's a painter," said Kitty, blushing. "And that's his wife," she added, indicating Anna Petrov, who, just as they were approaching, it seemed on purpose, had started off after a child that was running away down the path.

"What a pathetic fellow, and what a nice face he has!" said the Prince. "Why didn't you go over to him? He wanted to speak to you."

"Let's go back then," said Kitty, turning round resolutely. "How are you feeling today?" she asked Petrov.

Petrov got up, supporting himself on his cane, and timidly glanced at the Prince.

"This is my daughter," said the Prince. "Allow me to introduce myself."

The painter bowed and smiled, showing peculiarly brilliant white teeth.

"We were expecting you yesterday, Princess," he said to Kitty.

He staggered as he said this, then staggered again to show he had done it on purpose.

"I wanted to come, but Varenka said your wife had sent word you weren't going."

"What—not going?" said Petrov, blushing and immediately breaking into a cough, as he looked around for his wife. "Annetta, Annetta!" he said in a loud voice, and the thick veins stretched out along his thin white neck like cords.

Anna Petrov came over.

"How was it you sent word to the Princess that we weren't going!" he said to her in an irritated whisper, his voice failing.

"Good morning, Princess," said Anna Petrov with the forced smile that was so unlike her former manner. "Delighted to meet you," she said to the Prince. "You've been expected for some time, Prince."

"How was it you sent word to the Princess we weren't going?" the painter whispered hoarsely to her once again, still more angrily, and plainly annoyed even more because his voice had betrayed him and he couldn't speak as he wished to.

"Dear me, I thought we weren't," his wife answered in annoyance.

"But how could you when——" He started coughing and waving a hand.

The Prince lifted his hat and moved off with Kitty.

"Dear, dear," he sighed deeply. "Oh, what poor things!"

"Yes, Papa," Kitty answered. "But you must realize they have three children, no servants, and almost no money. He gets something from the Academy——" she went on animatedly, trying to stifle the agitation that had risen in her because of the peculiar change in Anna Petrov's attitude toward her.

"And here's Madame Stahl too," said Kitty, indicating a bath chair in which something in gray and blue, propped up on pillows, was lying under a sunshade.

This was Madame Stahl. A morose-looking, robust German laborer who pushed the chair was standing behind her. Beside her was a fair-haired Swedish Count whom Kitty knew by name. A number of invalids were lingering near by looking at Madame Stahl as though she were something extraordinary.

The Prince went over to her, and Kitty instantly observed that spark of mockery in his eyes that upset her so. He went up to Madame Stahl and began talking to her in the excellent French so few people speak any longer, extremely politely and amiably.

"I don't know whether you remember me, but I feel bound to recall myself to your mind in order to thank you for your kindness to my daughter," he said to her, raising his hat and not putting it on again.

"Prince Alexander Shcherbatsky," said Madame Stahl, raising toward him her heavenly eyes, in which Kitty detected some displeasure. "Delighted. I've grown so fond of your daughter."

"Are you still in bad health?"

"Oh I've grown quite used to it," said Madame Stahl, and introduced the Prince to the Swedish Count.

"But you've changed very little," the Prince said to her. "I haven't had the honor of seeing you for the past ten or eleven years."

"Yes, God gives us a cross and also the strength to bear it. It's often surprising, why life drags on—The other side!" she said, turning irritably to Varenka, who was not wrapping her legs in the rug quite properly.

"Doubtless so that we can do good," said the Prince, laughing with his eyes.

"That is not for us to judge," said Madame Stahl, catching the shade of expression on the Prince's face. "So you'll send me that book, dear Count? I'm very grateful to you," she said, turning to the young Swede.

"Ah!" exclaimed the Prince, seeing the Moscow colonel standing near by; with a bow to Madame Stahl he went off together with Kitty and the Moscow colonel.

"That's our aristocracy, Prince!" said the Moscow colonel, intending to sound scornful; he had a grudge against Madame Stahl for refusing to meet him.

"She's still the same," answered the Prince.

"And did you know her before her illness, Prince, that is, before she took to her bed?"

"Yes, I knew her just when she was taking to her bed."

"They say she hasn't stood up on her feet for the past ten years—"

"She doesn't get on her feet because her legs are so short. She has a very bad figure."

"Papa, it's not possible!"

"That what wicked tongues say, my love. But your Varenka does catch it," he added. "Oh, these invalid women!"

"Oh no, Papa," Kitty protested warmly. "Varenka worships her. And then she does so much good! Just ask anyone! Everyone knows her and Aline Stahl."

"That may be," he said, pressing her arm with his elbow. "But it would be better if it were done so that if you asked anyone they wouldn't know about it."

Kitty fell silent, not because she had nothing to say, but because she didn't want to disclose her secret thoughts to her father either. But the strange thing was that in spite of her having determined not to submit to her father's opinions, and not to allow him to enter into her inmost sanctuary, she felt that the divine image of Madame Stahl, which she had been carrying about in her heart for a whole month, had vanished beyond recall, just as a figure formed by some clothes flung aside vanishes the moment you understand that is only the way the clothes happen to be lying. What was left was only a short-legged woman who kept lying down because she had a bad figure and who nagged at poor patient Varenka for not wrapping the rug around her properly. By no effort of the imagination was it possible to restore the former Madame Stahl any longer.

## XXXV

THE Prince communicated his cheerful mood to his household, his acquaintances, and even the German landlord of the place where they were stopping.

After returning from the springs with Kitty and inviting the colonel, Madame Rtishchev and Varenka for coffee, the Prince ordered the table and chairs to be taken out into the garden under the chestnut tree to be set for breakfast there. Both landlord and servants were enlivened by his cheerfulness. They knew how openhanded he was; and in half an hour the sick German doctor who lived upstairs was gazing enviously through the window out at the merry Russian party of healthy people gathered under the chestnut tree. Beneath the quivering shadows of leaves, at the table covered with a white tablecloth and set with coffeepot, bread, butter, cheese, and cold game, sat the Princess in a cap with lilac handing out cups of coffee and sandwiches. The Prince was sitting at the other end of the table eating heartily and talking in a loud, jolly voice. He had spread out everything he had bought in front of him: carved caskets, knickknacks, paper cutters of all kinds, which he had bought quantities of at all the spas, and he gave them away to everyone, including Lieschen the housemaid, and the landlord, with whom he joked away in his comical broken German, assuring him that it was not the waters that had cured Kitty but his own excellent cooking, especially his plum soup. The Princess laughed at her husband's Russian manners, but was more animated and cheerful than she had ever been at a spa before. The colonel smiled as usual at the Prince's jokes, but with respect to Europe, which he thought he had made a careful study of, he took the side of the Princess. The good-natured Madame Rtishchev rocked with laughter at every absurd thing the Prince said, and Varenka, in a way Kitty had never seen before, succumbed to feeble but infectious laughter, inspired by the Prince's jokes.

All this cheered Kitty up, but she could not help feeling troubled. She could not solve the problem her father had unconsciously set her by his jocular view of her friends and of the life she had begun to love so much. This problem was added to by the change in her relations with the Petrovs, which had been expressed that day so obviously and disagreeably. Everyone felt gay, but Kitty could not; this tormented her still more. She had a feeling somewhat similar to what she had felt as a child when she was locked into her room as a punishment and listened to the merry laughter of her sisters.

"Now what did you buy all this stuff for?" said the Princess with a smile, handing her husband a cup of coffee.

"Well, if you go out walking you come to a shop and they ask you to buy something: 'Eminence,' 'Excellency,' 'Serene Highness.' Well, by the time they've got to 'Serene Highness' I can't hold out any longer—and ten thalers are gone."

"It's all because of boredom," said the Princess.

"Of course it's boredom. It's so boring, my dear, you don't know which way to turn."

"How can you be bored, Prince? There are so many interesting things now in Germany," said Madame Rtishchev.

"But I know all about these interesting things: I know about plum soup, and I know about pea sausages. I know all about it."

"No, but say what you like, Prince, they have interesting institutions," said the colonel.

"Now what's interesting about them? They're all as satisfied as a lot of brass pennies—they've conquered everyone. But what should I be so satisfied about? I haven't conquered anyone, instead I have to take my own boots off and even put them outside the door myself. I get up in the morning, get dressed right away, and go into the dining room for some rotten tea. How different it is at home! You get up without rushing, get angry at something, grumble, recover yourself properly, turn things over in your mind—all without rushing!"

"But time is money, you're forgetting that," said the colonel.

"It depends on the time! There are times you'd give a whole month away for a kopeck, and times you wouldn't give away a half-hour for anything. Isn't that so, Kitty? But what's the matter with you? Why so glum?"

"I'm all right."

"Now where are you off to?" he said, turning to Varenka. "Stay a little longer."

"I must go home," said Varenka, getting up and bursting into a laugh again. When she had recovered she said goodby and went into the house to get her hat. Kitty followed her. Even Varenka looked different to her now. She was no worse, but she was different from the way Kitty had imagined her to be before.

"Heavens, it's a long time since I've laughed so much!" said Varenka, collecting her sunshade and bag. "What a darling your papa is!"

Kitty said nothing.

"When shall we see each other?" asked Varenka.

"Mama wanted to call on the Petrovs. Will you be there?" said Kitty, sounding her out.

"Yes," Varenka answered. "They're getting ready to leave. I promised I'd help them pack."

"Then I'll come too."

"But no, what are you thinking of?"

"Why not? Why not? Why not?" Kitty began, opening her eyes wide and clutching at Varenka's sunshade to prevent her leaving. "No, wait a moment, why not?"

"Nothing. Because your papa's arrived—and then they feel embarrassed when you're there."

"No, you must tell me why you don't want me to spend so much time at the Petrovs'. You don't, do you? Why not?"

"I didn't say that," said Varenka quietly.

"No, please tell me!"

"Tell you everything?" asked Varenka.

"Everything, everything!"

"Actually there's nothing special, it's just that Petrov had wanted to leave before, and now he doesn't want to go at all," said Varenka, smiling.

"Well?" Kitty urged her, looking at her darkly.

"Well, for some reason his wife said he doesn't want to leave because you're here. Of course that was silly, but because of that they've had a quarrel about you. And you know how irritable these sick people are."

Kitty, frowning more and more, said nothing; only Varenka spoke, trying to mollify Kitty and soothe her; she saw an explosion was about to take place—either tears or words, she didn't know which.

"So it's better for you not to go there . . . You understand, there's no reason to be offended—"

"It serves me right, it serves me right!" Kitty cried quickly, snatching the sunshade out of Varenka's hand and looking past her friend's eyes.

Varenka, looking at her friend's childish anger, felt like smiling, but she was afraid of offending her.

"Why does it serve you right? I don't understand . . ." she said.

"It serves me right because all of it was pretense, it was all made up, it didn't come from the heart. Why should I have had anything to do with a stranger? This is the result, that I started a quarrel and did something no one asked me to do. Because it was all pretense! Pretense—pretense!"

"But what was the point of the pretense?" said Varenka softly.

"Oh how stupid, how hateful! There was no need for me to—It was all pretense!" she said, opening and shutting the sunshade.

"But what was the point of it?"

"The point was to seem better to people, to myself, to God; to deceive anyone! No—I'll never give in to that again! Even if I'm bad, at least I won't be a liar, a fraud!"

"But who's being a fraud?" Varenka said reproachfully. "You talk as though—"

But Kitty was in one of her fits of passion; she wouldn't let her finish.

"I'm not talking about you, not talking about you at all. You're just perfect. Yes, yes, I know you're utterly perfect; but how can I help it if I'm bad? None of that would have happened if I hadn't been bad. So just let me be as I am, without pretending. What have I got to do with Anna Petrov? Let them live the way they want to, and I'll do the same. I can't be any other way . . . But it's not that, it's not that at all!"

"What isn't what at all?" said Varenka, perplexed.

"All of it. The only way I can live is according to my

heart, and you live by rules. I loved you just so, but you probably loved me in order to save me, to instruct me!"

"You're being unfair," said Varenka.

"But I'm not talking about anyone else, just about me."

"Kitty!" came her mother's voice, "come over here and show Papa your corals."

With a haughty look, and without making peace with her friend, Kitty took the little box with the corals from the table and went over to her mother.

"What's the matter with you? Why are you so red?" her mother and father both said to her in unison.

"It's nothing," Kitty replied. "I'll be right back." She ran after Varenka.

She's still here! she thought. Dear God, what can I say to her? What have I done? What did I say? Why did I hurt her? What can I do? What can I tell her? Kitty thought, and stopped in the doorway.

Varenka, with her hat on, was sitting at the table holding the sunshade and examining its spring, which Kitty had broken. She raised her head.

"Varenka—forgive me, forgive me!" whispered Kitty, going over to her. "I don't remember what I said. I—"

"Really, I never wanted to hurt your feelings," said Varenka, smiling.

Peace was made. But with her father's arrival the whole world Kitty had been living in changed for her. She did not renounce everything she had learned, but she realized that she had been deceiving herself in thinking she could be what she wanted to be. It was as though she had recovered consciousness; she felt the whole difficulty of maintaining herself, without hypocrisy or boastfulness, on the heights she had wanted to raise herself to. In addition she felt the whole dreariness of that world of sorrow, and of sick and dying people, in which she had been living; the efforts she had made to like it now seemed to her agonizing, and she longed to get away as soon as possible, to some fresh air, to Russia, to Yergushovo, where, as she had learned from a letter, her sister Dolly was moving with the children.

But her love for Varenka did not weaken. When she said good-by Kitty tried to persuade her to come to stay with them in Russia.

"I'll come after you get married," said Varenka.

"I'll never marry."

"Well, I'll never come then."

"Then that's the only reason I'll get married. Now remember, don't forget your promise!" said Kitty.

The doctor's forecast had proved right. Kitty came home to Russia quite cured. She was not as carefree and merry as before, but she was tranquil. Her Moscow sorrows became a memory.

# PART THREE

## I

KOZNYSHOV wanted to take a rest from his intellectual labors: instead of going abroad as usual he went to stay with Levin in the country at the end of May. He was convinced life in the country was the best life, and he was going to his half-brother's now in order to enjoy it. Levin was delighted, especially since he no longer expected his brother Nicholas that summer. But in spite of his affection and respect for Koznyshov, Levin felt ill at ease with him in the country. His brother's attitude made him uncomfortable: it even annoyed him. For Levin the country was a place for living, that is, for joys, suffering, and work; for Koznyshov it was on the one hand a place to rest from working, and on the other a useful antidote to depravity, an antidote he took with satisfaction, conscious of its usefulness. For Levin the country was good because it constituted a domain for labor that was unquestionably useful; for Kozynshov it was good especially because nothing could or should be done there. Also, Koznyshov's attitude toward the peasants irritated Levin somewhat. Koznyshov would say he liked the common people and knew them; he would often chat with peasants, which he was able to do well, sincerely and without affectation, and from every such conversation he would draw general conclusions in favor of the common people, as a proof of how well he knew them. Levin disliked this sort of attitude toward the common people. For him the peasants were merely the principal partner in a joint enterprise, and though sometimes, as their partner, he would be filled with enthusiasm for their strength, meekness, and fairness, he would very often be furious with them, when other qualities were demanded, for their heedlessness, sloppiness, drunkenness, and lying. This was in spite of all the respect and love for them that he had in his blood, doubtless sucked in, as he said himself, with the milk of his peasant nurse. If Levin had been asked whether he liked the peasants he would certainly have been at a loss for an answer. He both liked the peasants and did not like them, just as he did people in general. Of course since he was kind-hearted he liked people more than he disliked them, and so too the peasants. But as for liking or not liking the peasants as though they were something special, he was incapable of this, because not only did he live with the peasants, not only were all his interests bound up with the peasants, but he considered himself part of them; he did not regard himself or the peasants as having any special qualities or shortcomings, and could not contrast himself with them. Aside from this, though for a long time he had lived in the most intimate relations with the peasants as master, arbiter, and above all counselor (the peasants trusted him and would walk thirty miles to ask his advice), he had no definite opinions about them, and would have found it just as difficult to answer the question whether he knew the peasants as he would whether he liked them. Saying he understood the peasants would have been just the same as saying he understood people. He was constantly observing and learning about all sorts of different people, including peasants, whom he considered good and interesting, and was constantly observing new traits in them, changing his previous opinions and forming others.

It was just the contrary with Koznyshov. Just as he liked and praised life in the country by way of contrast to the life he disliked, so he liked the peasants by way of contrast with a class of people he disliked, and understood peasants as something contrasted with people in general. Peasant life had been clearly classified by his methodical mind into definite categories, drawn partly from peasant life itself but primarily from its contrast with other ways of life. He never changed his mind about the peasants or his sympathetic attitude toward them.

Whenever the two brothers got into disagreements about the peasants Koznyshov would always convince Levin precisely because he had such definite conceptions about the peasants, their characters, qualities, and tastes; whereas Levin did not have a definite and unchangeable conception, so that in these arguments he was always caught contradicting himself.

For Koznyshov his younger half-brother was a splendid fellow, *with his heart in the right place* (as he expressed it, in French) but with a mind that even though quick enough was subject to the impressions of the moment and so was full of contradictions. With the condescension of an older brother he would sometimes explain the meaning of things, but he could find no satisfaction in arguing with him since he beat him too easily.

Levin looked on his half-brother as a man of enormous intellect and education, who was noble in the loftiest sense of the word and had the gift of being able to work for the common welfare. But in the depths of his soul, the older he got and the better he came to know his brother, the more often the thought came into his head that this capacity of working for the common welfare, which he felt himself to be completely devoid of, might not be and was not so much a quality as the contrary, a lack of something. It was not a lack of kind, honorable, noble desires and tastes but of some vital force, of what is called heart, of that impulse that forces a man to choose, out of the countless ways of life presented to him, just one, and to desire that one alone. The more he came to know his brother the more he noticed that both Koznyshov and many others who worked for the common welfare had not been brought by their hearts to this love of the common welfare, but had intellectually reasoned that it was good to occupy oneself with it, and this was the only reason they did so. This conviction of Levin's was strengthened still further when he noticed that his brother did not take questions about the general welfare or about the immortality of the soul any more to heart than he did a game of chess, or the ingenious construction of a new machine.

Aside from this, Levin also felt ill at ease in the country with his brother because in the country, especially in summer, he would be constantly busy with the farming; the long summer days would not be long enough to do everything that had to be done, and Koznyshov would be resting. But even though he was resting, that is, not working on his writing, he was so used to intellectual activity that he was fond of expressing, in an elegant, concise form, the ideas that passed through his head, and he liked to have someone listen to him. And the most usual and natural listener for him was his brother. Thus in spite of the friendly simplicity of their relationship, Levin felt uncomfortable leaving him alone. Koznyshov liked to stretch out on the grass in the sun and lie there basking, lazily chatting.

"You won't believe what a pleasure this bucolic indolence is for me," he would say to his brother. "Not a thought in my head—as empty as a drum."

But it was boring for Levin to sit around listening to him, especially since he knew that while he was absent the ma-

nure was being carted out into the unplowed fields that
weren't ready for it, the men would be dumping it God knows
how unless he kept watch; the plowshares wouldn't be screwed
on but taken off, and then they would say the plows were a
silly invention, there was nothing like the good old peasant
plow and so on.

"Haven't you had enough walking around in the sun?"
Koznyshov would say to him.

"I'll just run round to the office for a second," Levin would
answer, and run off to the fields.

II

At the beginning of June, Miss Agatha, Levin's old
nurse and housekeeper, was carrying a jar of mushrooms
she had just pickled to the cellar when she slipped, fell and
sprained her wrist. The district doctor, a talkative young
man who had just finished his studies, arrived, looked at the
wrist, said it wasn't dislocated and put on compresses; he
stayed to dinner and, obviously enjoying his talk with the
celebrated Sergius Koznyshov, told him all the district gossip in order to display his enlightened view of everything,
and complained of the bad state of affairs in the District
Council. Koznyshov listened attentively, asked questions,
and, inspired by his new audience, grew quite talkative; he
made a number of penetrating and weighty observations,
which were respectfully appreciated by the young doctor;
soon he was in the lively temper, familiar to his brother, that
he usually fell into after a brilliant and animated discussion.
After the doctor had left, Koznyshov felt like going to the
river with his fishing rod. He liked to fish; he seemed to take
pride in being able to like such a stupid occupation.

Levin who had to go to see the plowed land and the meadows, offered to take his brother there in the gig.

It was just that season of the year when the year's harvest
is already assured, when worries begin about next year's sowing, and the mowing is at hand; when the gray-green ears
of rye, formed but not yet bursting, wave gently in the
wind; when the green oats, interspersed with yellow tufts of
grass, stand irregularly on the late-sown fields; when the
early buckwheat has already spread out to cover the ground;
when the fallow land, trodden hard as stone by the cattle, has
been half-plowed leaving the paths that were too hard to

take the plow; when the smell of the dried-out heaps of manure mingles at twilight and dawn with that of the honied grasses; and on the lowlands the riverside meadows are a dense sea of grass awaiting the scythe, with blackening heaps of sorrel stalks scattered through it.

It was the season when there is a short breathing spell in the work of the land, before the beginning of the harvest, which comes every year and every year calls forth every ounce of the peasants' strength. The crop was a splendid one, and the clear hot summer days, with their short dewy nights, had set in.

The two brothers had to pass through a forest in order to get to the meadows. Koznyshov kept on admiring the beauty of the thickly leaved forest, pointing out to Levin first the shadowed side of the old lime tree, about to flower and brightly mottled with yellow buds, then the young shoots of this year's saplings glittering like emeralds. Levin disliked talking and hearing about the beauties of nature. For him words took away the beauty of what he was looking at. He nodded at whatever his brother said, but in spite of himself began thinking about something else. When they had passed through the forest, his whole attention was absorbed by the sight of a fallow field on a slope, here and there yellow with grass, or trampled and checkered with furrows, or dotted with heaps of manure, and some parts even plowed. A string of carts was moving over the field. Levin counted the carts and was pleased that all the manure needed had been brought up, and as he looked at the meadows his thoughts passed on to the question of mowing. When the hay was being harvested he always had a special feeling that touched him to the quick. When they got as far as the meadow Levin stopped the horse.

There was some morning dew still left at the roots of the thick grass, and Koznyshov, to avoid wetting his feet, asked to be driven across the meadow to the clump of willows near which perch could be caught. Though Levin was sorry to crush his grass he drove across the meadow. The high grass twisted softly around the wheels and the horse's legs, leaving its seeds on the wet spokes and hubs.

Koznyshov sat down by the willows, after arranging his fishing tackle, while Levin led away his horse, tethered it, and went off into the vast gray-green sea of the meadow, unruffled by the wind. The grass, silky with the seeds it was scattering, came up almost as high as his waist in the places which had been flooded in springtime.

Crossing the meadow, Levin came out onto the road, where he met an old man with a swollen eye who was carrying a swarm of bees in a skep.

"What? Have you caught a stray swarm, Fomich?" he asked.

"What an idea, Mr. Constantine! If only we don't lose our own! This is the second time a swarm has got away, luckily the boys caught them again. They were plowing your field; they unharnessed the horse and galloped after them."

"Well, Fomich, what d'you think? Should we mow, or should we wait?"

"Well, well! The way we do it is to wait until St. Peter's Day, but you always start mowing earlier. Well, why not, God willing, the grass is fine. The cattle will have more room."

"And the weather, what d'you think about that?"

"That's up to God; maybe the weather'll be fine too."

Levin went back to his brother. Koznyshov hadn't caught anything, but he wasn't bored and seemed to be in the most cheerful spirits. Levin saw that he had been stimulated by the conversation with the doctor and wanted to have a chat. Levin, on the other hand, was anxious to get home quickly to give orders about hiring the mowers for the next day and to make up his mind about harvesting the hay, which greatly preoccupied him.

"Well, let's go," he said.

"But what's the hurry? Let's sit around here for a while. How wet you've got! I haven't caught a thing, but it's very pleasant. Any kind of sport is good because it places you in contact with nature. What a delight this steel-colored water is!" he said. "These riverside banks always remind me of that riddle," he went on, "d'you know it? The grass says to the water, 'We quiver and we quiver' . . ."

"I don't know that one," said Levin dejectedly.

## III

D'YOU know, I've been thinking about you," said Koznyshov. "The things that are going on in your district, according to what that doctor said—and he's far from stupid—are quite incredible. I've told you before and I say it again: it's a bad business, your not attending the District Council meetings, and altogether your keeping aloof from Council business. If decent people keep aloof, of course, heaven knows what will happen. We pay the money, it all goes into salaries, and there are neither schools, nor district nurses, nor midwives, nor pharmacies—nothing."

"But I tried, didn't I?" Levin replied softly and reluctantly, "I can't do it! How can I help it!"

"What d'you mean you can't do it? I confess it escapes me. I won't admit indifference or incapacity—can it be plain laziness?"

"Neither the first, second, nor third. I've tried it and I see there's nothing I can do there," said Levin.

He didn't pay much attention to what his brother was saying. Gazing at the plowed land beyond the river he made out something black but couldn't see whether it was a horse or the foreman on horseback.

"But why can't you do anything? You made an attempt, and according to you it was a failure, and so you just give up. How can you be so lacking in self-respect!"

"Self-respect!" said Levin, stung by his brother's remark. "I don't understand. If they had told me at the university that others understood integral calculus and I didn't that would be a question of self-respect. But in such things you have to be convinced in advance that you must have certain abilities and above all that such things are extremely important."

"Well—isn't it important?" said Koznyshov, piqued in his turn by the fact that his brother considered something that occupied him unimportant and particularly since it was obvious that he was scarcely listening to him.

"It doesn't seem important to me, do what you like, it doesn't grip me," answered Levin, who had made out that what he had been looking at was the foreman, and that the foreman had probably released the peasants from their plowing. They were turning their plows over. Surely they couldn't have finished their plowing? he thought.

"Well, but listen now," said his older brother, with a frown on his handsome, intelligent face, "there are limits to everything. It's all very well to be a crank and an upright fellow and dislike hypocrisy—I know all that; but what you're saying now after all either has no meaning or else has a very wrong meaning. How can you think it unimportant for the common people, whom you claim to be so fond of—"

I never claimed that, thought Levin.

"—simply to die without being given any help? The ignorant midwives murder the babies, the people vegetate in ignorance and remain at the mercy of every village clerk, while you've been given the means to help this, and you don't help because according to you it's not important." And Koznyshov confronted him with a dilemma. "Either you're so undeveloped you don't see everything you could do, or else you don't want to sacrifice your peace of mind, or your vanity—I don't know which—in order to do it."

Levin felt that all that was left for him to do was to give in or acknowledge that he was short on love for the general welfare. This offended and annoyed him.

"Both one and the other," he said resolutely. "I don't see what could be done—"

"What? D'you mean it's impossible, if you distribute money the right way, to provide medical help?"

"Impossible—so it seems to me. To give medical help all over the three thousand square miles of our district, with all our snowstorms, and the deep slush when the snows melt, and the heavy field work, seems to me impossible. Besides I don't believe in medicine in general."

"Really now, that's unfair! I could give you a thousand cases where—and what about schools?"

"What are schools for?"

"What are you talking about! Don't tell me you have doubts about the value of education? If it's good for you it's good for everyone."

Levin felt himself to be morally cornered, so he got excited and in spite of himself expressed his principal reason for being indifferent to social questions.

"Perhaps that's all very well, but why should I concern myself with setting up medical centers I'll never use, schools I'm not going to send my children to and where the peasants don't want to send their children either, and for that matter I don't believe there's any need to send them anyhow," he said.

For a moment Koznyshov was startled by this unexpected objection, but he immediately formed another plan of attack.

He fell silent, took out a line, cast it, then turned to his brother with a smile.

"All right then . . . First of all, a medical center is needed. Didn't we have to send for the district doctor for Miss Agatha?"

"Well, in my opinion her hand's going to stay crooked."

"That's another question . . . Then, a peasant who's literate would be more useful and valuable to you as a laborer."

"No—ask anyone you like," Levin answered firmly, "as a laborer someone who's literate is far worse. They can't repair roads and when they build bridges they steal."

"Nevertheless," said Koznyshov with a frown—he disliked being contradicted, especially when people kept jumping back and forth from one thing to another, incoherently advancing new arguments so that you didn't know which one to answer—"nevertheless, that's not the point. Just a moment—do you admit that education is a good thing for the people?"

"Yes," said Levin without thinking, and was instantly aware that what he had said was not what he thought. He felt that if he admitted that it would be proved to him that he was talking senseless rubbish. He didn't know just how this would be done, but he knew it would be logically demonstrated beyond question; now he waited for this demonstration.

The proof turned out to be far simpler than he had expected.

"If you admit it's a good thing," said Koznyshov, "then as an honest man you cannot help but like and sympathize with such a cause and wish to work for it."

"But I still don't admit it's a good thing," said Levin, reddening.

"What? But you just said—"

"That is, I don't admit it's either good or possible."

"You can't know that without having made the effort."

"Well, let's suppose it is," said Levin, though he didn't think so at all. "I still don't see why I should concern myself with it anyhow."

"What d'you mean?"

"Well, since we're going to talk about the whole thing just explain it to me from the point of view of philosophy," Levin said.

"I don't see what philosophy has to do with it," said Koznyshov, in a tone Levin took to mean he didn't acknowledge his brother's right to discuss philosophy. This irritated Levin.

"This is what!" he started heatedly. "I think that in any case the motive of all our actions is personal happiness. In the District Council at present I, as a nobleman, see nothing that would contribute to my welfare. The roads are no better, and can't be better; my horses can get me through the bad ones too. I don't need doctors or medical centers, and I don't need a magistrate; I never apply to one and I never will. Not only don't I need any schools, they actually harm me, as I've told you. As far as I'm concerned the District Council simply means a tax of a few pennies an acre, having to go to town and spend the night with some bedbugs and listen to all sorts of nonsense and meanness, but it's not personal interest that makes me do it!"

"Just a moment," Koznyshov interrupted him with a smile, "it was not personal interest that prompted us to work for the emancipation of the serfs, but we did."

"No!" Levin stopped him, more and more excited. "The emancipation of the serfs was something else again. There was a personal interest there. We wanted to throw off a yoke that had been weighing us all down, all right-minded men. But to be a Town Councilor, to discuss how many street cleaners are required, and how to lay out the drains in a town I don't live in; to be on a jury and try a peasant for stealing a ham, and to sit for six hours on end listening to all the rubbish being babbled by the counsel and the prosecutor, and hear the president asking my simple-minded old Alyosha: 'Prisoner at the bar, do you plead guilty to the charge of having stolen a ham?' 'What's that?' "

Levin was carried away by now, and began to imitate the prosecutor and simple-minded Alyosha: it seemed to him that it was all perfectly relevant.

But Koznyshov shrugged his shoulders.

"Well, what are you trying to show?"

"I'm only trying to show that I'll always be ready to defend the rights that concern me—my interests, with all my strength; when I was a student once and we were all searched and the gendarmes read our letters, I was ready to defend those rights with all my strength, defend my right to education and freedom. I can understand conscription, which touches the fate of my children, my brothers, and myself; I'm ready to discuss whatever concerns me; but as for debating the disposition of forty thousand rubles of Council funds, or sitting in judgment on simple-minded Alyosha—I don't understand it and I can't do it."

Levin spoke as though a dam holding back his words had burst. Koznyshov smiled.

"Let's say you're going to be tried tomorrow; well, would you prefer being tried in the old-fashioned Criminal Court?"

"I'm not going to be tried. I'm not going to cut anyone's

throat, so I won't have to be. Now all those District Councils of ours!" he went on, once again leaping off to something completely irrelevant, "all that business is like those little birch boughs we stick in the ground on Trinity Sunday in order to imitate the woods that grow naturally in Europe— I can't water those birches or believe in them!"

Koznyshov simply shrugged his shoulders to express his surprise at how birch trees had suddenly popped up in their argument, though he instantly understood what his brother had meant.

"Just a moment: it's impossible to reason that way, you know," he remarked.

But Levin felt like vindicating this shortcoming he was aware of in himself—his indifference to the general welfare —and he went on:

"I don't think any activity can be effective," he said, "if it is not based on personal interest. This is a general truth—a philosophical truth," he said, resolutely repeating the word *philosophical* as though he wanted to show that like every one else he also had the right to discuss philosophy.

Koznyshov smiled once more. He's also got some philosophy or other in the service of his inclinations, he thought.

"Well now, why not leave philosophy out of it," he said. "The principal task of philosophy throughout the ages has been to discover the necessary connection between personal and social interests. But that's not the point; the point is that all I have to do is correct your illustration. The birches are not simply stuck in: some of them are planted, and others are sown, and those are the ones that have to be tended more carefully. The only nations that have a future, the only nations that can be called historic, are those that have a sense of what is important and meaningful in their institutions, and that cherish them."

And Koznyshov shifted the argument into the domain of philosophy and history, which was inaccessible to Levin, and showed him how thoroughly unsound his ideas were.

"As for your not liking it, forgive me, but that's just the result of our Russian laziness, our seignioral style, and I'm sure that in your case it's only a temporary error and will pass."

Levin was silent. He felt he was beaten on all points, but at the same time he felt that his brother had not understood what he meant. The only thing he didn't know was just why this wasn't understandable—whether it was because he was incapable of expressing clearly what he meant, or because his brother didn't want to or couldn't understand him. But he didn't go into these notions more deeply; without making any objections to his brother he began reflecting on a quite different, personal concern of his.

Koznyshov wound up his last line, untied the horse, and they drove off.

## IV

THE personal concern that had been preoccupying Levin during their conversation was this: The year before, when he had once come to a field while it was being mown and had lost his temper with the foreman, Levin had resorted to a remedy of his own in order to calm himself—he had taken a scythe from one of the peasants and begun mowing himself.

He liked this work so much that he went mowing several times; he had mowed the whole meadow in front of the house, and as soon as spring came this year he had made his plans—he was going to devote several whole days to mowing, together with the peasants. Ever since his brother came he had been in two minds—should he go mowing or not? He felt uncomfortable at leaving his brother alone for days at a time, and he was afraid he would make fun of him for it. But as he walked across the meadow he recalled the impression mowing had made on him, and had very nearly made up his mind that he would go. Now, after his irritating conversation with his brother, he recalled this intention again.

I need some physical exercise or else my character will definitely go bad, he thought, and he decided to go mowing now no matter how ill at ease it would make him feel in front of his brother and the peasants.

In the evening Levin went to the office; he gave orders about the work to be done and sent out to the villages to tell the mowers to come the next day to mow the Kalina meadow, his best and biggest.

"And please send my scythe to Titus to be sharpened; have it at the meadow tomorrow, I may go mowing myself," he said, trying not to look embarrassed.

The foreman smiled and said, "Very well, sir."

At tea that evening Levin said to his brother, "It looks as

though the weather's settling. Tomorrow I'm starting in to mow."

"I like that work very much," said Koznyshov.

"I'm terribly fond of it. I've sometimes gone mowing with the peasants myself, and tomorrow I want to spend the whole day mowing."

Koznyshov raised his head and looked at his brother curiously.

"How d'you mean? All day long—like the peasants?"

"Yes, it's very agreeable," said Levin.

"It's splendid physical exercise, but surely you won't be able to keep it up?" said Koznyshov, with no trace of irony.

"I've tried it, it's hard at first but you work yourself into it after a while. I don't think I'll fall behind—"

"What an idea! But tell me, how do the peasants take it? They must make fun of their master for being such a crank."

"I don't think so; but it's such a cheerful kind of work, and at the same time so strenuous that there's no time to think."

"But how can you dine with them? It would be a bit awkward, sending you some claret and roast turkey, and a bottle of Lafitte, out there."

"No, I'll just come home at the same time they take their rest."

The next morning Levin got up earlier than usual, but the instructions he had to give about the farm delayed him and by the time he got to the field the mowers were already well into their second swath.

Even while on the hill he could already see the meadow below, part of it in the shadow, already mown, with the green rows and the black piles of coats the mowers had taken off at the point where they had begun their first swath.

As he approached he saw more and more peasants, following one another in a long row, each one swinging his scythe in his own way, some of them in coats and some only in their shirts. He counted forty-two of them.

They were slowly moving forward over the uneven bottom of the meadow, where there had been an old dam. Levin recognized several of them. There was old Yermil, wearing a very long white Russian shirt and bending over as he swung the scythe; young Vaska was there, who had been one of Levin's coachmen; he took the whole width of the swath with each sweep. Titus was also there; he was a short, thin little peasant who was Levin's mowing teacher. He was walk-

ing along out in front without bending, cutting in a very wide
arc as though in play.

Levin dismounted and, tethering his horse by the wayside, went over to join Titus, who got another scythe from
behind a bush and handed it to him.

"It's ready, sir; it's like a razor, it cuts by itself," said
Titus, smilingly taking his cap off as he handed him the
scythe.

Levin took the scythe and began trying it. The mowers
who had finished their swaths came out onto the road one
after the other, sweaty and cheerful, and laughingly greeted
their master. They all looked at him, but no one said anything until one tall old man with a wrinkled beardless face,
wearing a short sheepskin coat, stepped out on to the road
and started speaking to him.

"Watch out now, sir, once you start you'll have to finish!"
he said; Levin heard some reserved laughter among the
mowers.

"I'll try to," he said, stepping into place behind Titus and
waiting for the signal to begin.

"Watch out now!" repeated the old man.

Titus cleared a spot, and Levin started in behind him. It
was short roadside grass there, and Levin who had not done
any mowing for a long time and was embarrassed by everyone staring at him, mowed badly at first, though his swing
was powerful. He could hear voices behind him:

"He's not holding it right; too high; look at him stooping
too much," one said.

"Ought to keep the heel lower," said another.

"Never mind, it's all right, he'll work into it," the old
man went on. "See—there he goes . . . Swath's too wide,
he'll strain himself . . . He's the master, he has to, he's
working for himself! Look how uneven it is! We'd catch it
if we did that!"

The grass started turning softer, and Levin, listening to
everything but making no reply, and straining himself to
mow as well as possible, followed Titus. They did about a
hundred paces. Titus was going on ahead, without stopping
or showing the slightest fatigue; but Levin was already growing afraid he would not be able to hold out, he was so tired.

He felt he was at the end of his tether, and decided to ask
Titus to stop. But just then Titus himself stopped; he bent
over, picked up some grass, wiped the scythe and started
whetting it. Levin straightened up with a sigh and looked

around. There was a peasant behind him who was plainly just as tired, because without coming even with Levin he had stopped instantly and started whetting his scythe too. Titus whetted his own scythe and Levin's, and they began mowing again.

It was the same at Levin's second try. Titus was moving on, sweep after sweep, without stopping and without tiring. Levin followed him, trying not to fall behind. It was growing more and more difficult for him; a moment came when he felt he had no more strength left, but just then Titus stopped again and began whetting his scythe.

That was how they got through their first row. This long row seemed to Levin particularly difficult, but to make up for it, after they finished the row and Titus, shouldering his scythe, strode slowly back over the tracks made by their boot heels on the mown surface, and Levin also went back along his own swath, then, though the sweat poured down his face in streams, dripped off his nose, and drenched his whole back as though he were soaking, he felt wonderful. What made him especially glad was that he knew now he would hold out.

His satisfaction was poisoned only by the poorness of his swath. I ought to swing less with my arms and more with my whole body, he thought, comparing Titus's swath, which looked as though it had been cut out along a line, with his own uneven row of irregularly lying grass.

Levin noticed that the first row had been done by Titus especially rapid, probably with a desire to try out his master; it had happened to be a long one. The following rows were already easier, nevertheless Levin had to exert all his strength in order not to fall behind the peasants.

He thought of nothing and wished for nothing, except not to fall behind the peasants and to do his work as well as possible. Behind him he heard only the swishing of the scythes and ahead of him he saw only the receding figure of Titus, the convex half-circle of the mown piece in front of him, the flower heads and grass slowly and rhythmically falling around the blade of his scythe, and ahead of him the end of the swath that would bring him rest.

Suddenly, as he worked, he had a pleasant sensation of cold on his hot, sweating shoulders, without understanding what it was or where it came from. He looked up at the sky while whetting his scythe. A low, heavy cloud had come up, and fat raindrops were falling. Some of the peasants went over to their coats and put them on; others, and Levin too, merely wriggled their shoulders joyfully up and down beneath the delightful freshness.

They did another, and still another row. They went on mowing—long rows and short rows, with good grass and bad. Levin lost all awareness of time; he had absolutely no idea whether it was late now or early. A change had begun to take place in his work now that gave him an enormous amount of pleasure. In the midst of his work moments would come over him when he would forget what he was doing; it became easy for him, and during these same moments his row would come out almost as even and as good as Titus's. But the instant he would recall what he was doing he would feel the full burdensomeness of toil, and the swath would come out badly.

After finishing another swath he was about to start another, but Titus stopped; going up to the old man he whispered something softly to him. Both of them looked at the sun. What are they talking about, why don't they start another swath? Levin thought, not thinking that the peasants had been mowing for at least four hours already without stopping and that it was time for them to have their lunch.

"Lunch, sir," said the old man.

"Is it time already? Well—lunch then."

Levin handed his scythe to Titus and walked toward his horse over the swaths of the spacious stretch of meadow, slightly sprinkled by the rain, together with the peasants who were going off to fetch the bread in their coats. It was only then that he recalled that he had guessed wrong about the weather, and that the rain was wetting his hay.

"It's going to ruin the hay," he said.

"Never mind, sir, mow in the rain, rake in the sun!" said the old man.

Levin untethered his horse and rode home for coffee. Koznyshov had only just got up. Levin rode back to the mowing again after his coffee, before Koznyshov had had time to get dressed and come down to the dining room.

v

AFTER lunch Levin did not go back to his old place in the line but found himself between a humorous old man, who invited him to be his neighbor, and a young peasant, who had just got married the autumn before and was out for his first summer's mowing.

The old man, holding himself erect, was walking on ahead, taking regular, long strides with his turned-out feet, and as though playing, with a precise regular movement that didn't seem to cost him any more effort than swinging his arms while walking, was laying back the grass in a high level ridge. It was as though it were not he but the sharp scythe alone that was whizzing through the juicy grass.

Young Mishka was walking behind Levin. His pleasant young face, with a twist of fresh grass bound round his hair, was straining with the effort, but the moment anyone looked at him he smiled. It was obvious that he would sooner have died than admit it was hard.

Levin was walking between them. In the heat of the day the mowing did not seem so difficult to him. The sweat he was soaked in cooled him off, and the sun that burned his back, head, and arms, bare to the elbow, lent him firmness and tenacity; more and more frequently those moments of unconsciousness would come on him when you didn't have to think about what you were doing. The scythe sliced away of its own accord. Those were happy moments. Even more joyful were the moments when on reaching the river where the swaths ended up the old man would wipe his scythe with some wet grass, rinse the blade in the fresh river water, ladle out a little in his whetstone box and offer it to Levin.

"How about some home-brew? Good, eh?" he said with a wink.

And as a matter of fact Levin had never had a better drink than this warm water with green stuff floating in it and the rusty taste of the tin box. Then came the slow blissful walk back, with his hand on the scythe, during which you could wipe off the streams of sweat, take a deep, deep breath, and watch the long line of mowers and everything happening round about, in the woods and fields.

The longer Levin kept mowing the more often he would feel the moments of oblivion when it would no longer be his arms that were swinging the scythe, but the scythe itself, like a body full of life and self-consciousness, would move forward of its own accord, and the work would perform itself, accurately and carefully, as though by magic, without a thought being given to it. These were the most blissful moments.

It was difficult only when this automatic, unconscious

movement had to be stopped and thought about; when a hillock had to be mowed round, or a space which hadn't been cleared of sorrel stalks.

The old man did this easily. The hillock would come along, he would change his movement and in short jabs, sometimes with the point of the scythe and sometimes with its heel, would mow all around the hillock from both sides. And while doing this he would keep on looking ahead of him and noticing everything he was advancing toward: sometimes he would pick a wild berry and eat it, or offer it to Levin; sometimes he would flick a twig out of the way with the point of his scythe, or examine a quail's nest that the hen would fly out of right under the scythe; or he would catch a snake crossing his path, fork it up with the scythe, show it to Levin and toss it away.

Both Levin and the young fellow behind him found these shifts of movement difficult. Both of them, having gotten into the swing of one unvarying movement, were in a fever of exertion, and were unable to alter their movements while at the same time noticing what lay ahead of them.

Levin took no notice of how the time passed. If he had been asked how long he had been mowing he would have said half an hour, when actually it was almost noon already. Just as they were starting on another swath the old man drew Levin's attention to the little girls and boys who, scarcely visible, were coming toward the mowers from all sides, through the tall grass and along the road, carrying jugs of kvass stopped up with rags, and bundles of bread that strained their little arms.

"Look at the midges crawling along!" he said, pointing to them, and shading his eyes to look at the sun.

They finished two more swaths, then the old man stopped.

"Now, sir, dinnertime!" he said firmly. As they reached the river the mowers made their way back through the swaths to their coats where the children who had brought their meal were sitting and waiting for them. The peasants began to assemble—those from some distance away under their carts, those from nearby beneath a willow shrub they threw some grass under.

Levin sat down with them; he did not feel like going away.

Any constraint in front of their master had long since vanished. The peasants began getting ready for their dinner. Some of them washed; the young children bathed in the river; others arranged a spot for a rest, unfastened their bags of bread and unstoppered their jugs of kvass.

The old man broke some bread into a bowl, mashed it up with the handle of a spoon, poured some water from the whetstone box over it, broke some more bread into it, and sprinkling some salt over it turned to the east and began saying a prayer.

"Now, sir, have some of my dinner," he said, kneeling in front of the bowl.

The bread and water tasted so good that Levin changed his mind about going home for dinner. He had his meal with the old man and chatted with him about the latter's domestic affairs; he took the liveliest interest in them and told him about himself, with all the details that might interest him. He felt closer to him than to his own brother; involuntarily he smiled because of the tenderness he felt for him. When the old man had gotten up again, said a prayer, and then lay down again at once under the shrub, putting some grass under his head for a pillow, Levin did the same; in spite of the clinging flies that were so tenacious in the sunshine and the midges that tickled his sweating face and body, he fell asleep at once, and did not wake up until the sun had passed over to the other side of the shrub and begun to reach him. The old man had been awake for a long time; he was sitting there whetting some of the young boys' scythes.

Levin looked around and did not recognize the place, everything had changed so much. A vast stretch of the meadow had been mown and was shining with a new and peculiar brilliance, its swaths already exhaling their aroma in the slanting rays of the setting sun. The river-side shrubs that had been cut down, and the river itself, which had been invisible before but now had a steely gleam along its bends, the people getting up and moving around, and the steep wall of still uncut grass, the hawks circling above the bare meadow—it was all completely new. When he was fully conscious Levin began thinking how much had been mown already and how much more could still be done that day.

What had been finished was exceptional for forty-two men. The whole of the larger meadow, which in the days of serfdom had taken thirty mowers two days, was already completed. The only thing left uncut was some corners where the rows were short. But Levin felt like mowing as much as possible that day; he was annoyed with the sun for setting so soon. He felt no fatigue at all; all he felt like doing was getting to work again as soon as he could and finishing as much as possible.

"Well, what d'you think—can we still finish Mashkin hill?" he said to the old man.

"God willing!—but the sun is low. Perhaps a little vodka for the boys?"

During the next break, when they were sitting down again and those who smoked were lighting their pipes, the old man announced to the young men: "If Mashkin hill is mown—there'll be some vodka!"

"Well, why not! Get to it, Titus! We'll finish it in no time! We can eat our fill tonight! Let's go!" different voices cried out, and the mowers started off to their places, finishing their bread as they went.

"All right, boys, keep it up!" said Titus, and started off ahead almost at a trot.

"Get along, get along!" said the old man, hurrying after him and easily catching up with him. "Watch out—I'll mow you down!"

Both the old men and the younger ones started mowing as though they were competing with one another. But no matter how much they hurried they never spoiled the grass; the swaths were laid back just as tidily and accurately as ever. A small patch left in a corner was mown in five minutes. The last mowers were finishing their swaths while the ones in front had slung their coats over their shoulders and crossed the road to Mashkin hill.

The sun was already sinking beyond the trees when, their whetstone boxes rattling, they entered the wooded ravine of Mashkin hill. In the middle of the ravine the grass was waist-high; it was delicate, soft, and bushy, and speckled with wild pansies here and there among the trees.

After a brief consultation—whether to mow lengthwise or crosswise—Prokhor Yermilin, also a famous mower, a huge, swarthy peasant, took the lead. He went a swath ahead, turned back, and started off; they all started lining up behind him, going downhill along the hollow and back up to the very fringe of the wood. The sun had set behind the wood. The dew had already fallen, and only the mowers who were on top of the hill were in the sunshine, while below, where the mist was rising, and on the other side they were moving in cool, dewy shade. The work went ahead at a great clip.

The rich-smelling grass, cut with a juicy sound, was laid

down in high rows. The mowers, crowding together from all sides along the short swaths, rattling their tin boxes, their scythes ringing whenever they touched, their whetstones hissing on the blades, shouting to one another gaily, kept urging one another on.

Levin was still mowing between the old man and the young fellow. The old man, who had put on his short sheepskin, was just as gay, full of jokes, and limber as ever. Among the trees their scythes kept on cutting wood mushrooms, swollen fat in the juicy grass. But the old man, whenever he came across a mushroom, would bend over, pick it up, and put it inside his jacket. "Another treat for my old woman," he would say.

But though it was easy to mow the wet, limp grass, it was hard going up and down along the steep slopes of the ravine. But this didn't bother the old man. Swinging his scythe just as usual, taking short steps in his roomy bark-lined shoes, he slowly climbed the slope; though his whole body shook and his breeches hung out below his shirt, he did not pass by a single blade of grass or a mushroom on his way, and kept on joking with the other peasants and Levin as usual. Levin walked behind him; he often thought he was bound to fall as he carried his scythe up a steep slope which would have been difficult to climb even without a scythe; but he climbed up and did all that had to be done. He felt that some external force was moving him forward.

## VI

THEY mowed the Mashkin hill, finished off the final swaths, put on their coats and gaily went off home. Levin regretfully said good-by to them and rode off home, too. He looked back from the top of the hill: in the fog rising from the lowlands he couldn't see them, and could hear only their merry rough voices, laughter, and the sound of clanking scythes.

Koznyshov had long since had his dinner, and was in his room drinking ice water with lemon, looking through the newspapers and reviews that had just come by post, when Levin, his tousled hair sticking to his sweaty forehead, and his back and chest dark with dampness, burst into the room full of good cheer.

"Well, we finished the whole meadow! It was wonderful,

amazing! And how have you been getting on?" said Levin, who had completely forgotten the disagreeable conversation of the night before.

"Good God, what a sight!" said Koznyshov, looking at his brother with annoyance for a moment. "The door, the door! Shut it!" he cried. "You must have let in a full dozen!"

Koznyshov could not bear flies; he would open the windows in his room only at night and painstakingly keep doors shut.

"Not one, I'll swear. And if I let any in I'll catch them. You won't believe what a pleasure it was! How did you spend the day?"

"Very well indeed. But don't tell me you've been mowing the whole day? I should think you're as hungry as a wolf. Kuzma has got everything ready for you."

"No, I don't feel like eating. I ate down there. But I'll go have a wash."

"Well, well, go along then, I'll be along in a moment," said Koznyshov, shaking his head as he looked at his brother. "Be quick about it," he said smiling, and collecting his books he prepared to go along. He had suddenly turned cheerful himself and didn't want to be separated from his brother. "And where were you during the rain?"

"What rain? A few drops—no more. I'll be back right away. So you've had a good day, what? Wonderful!" And Levin went off to dress.

Five minutes later the brothers met in the dining room. Though Levin had really thought he didn't feel like eating, and just sat down to the meal only in order to avoid offending Kuzma, as soon as he began eating the meal seemed to him extraordinarily delicious. Koznyshov smiled as he looked at him.

"Oh yes, there's a letter for you," he said. "Kuzma, please fetch it, it's downstairs. But make sure you close the door."

The letter was from Oblonsky. Levin read it aloud. Oblonsky was writing from Petersburg: " 'I've had a letter from Dolly, who's in Yergushovo; everything seems to be going wrong there. Please go and see her, and help her out with some advice; you know about everything. She'll be so happy to see you. The poor thing's completely alone. My mother-in-law is still abroad with everyone.'

"Now that's splendid! I'll definitely ride over," said Levin. "And you'll come along. She's such a wonderful woman, isn't she?"

"Then they're not far from here?"

"A little over twenty-five miles, maybe thirty. But it's a first-rate road. It'll be a fine drive."

"I'll be delighted," said Koznyshov, still smiling.

The sight of his younger brother always put Koznyshov in a cheerful temper.

"What an appetite you have!" he said, looking at his sun-burned ruddy face and neck bent over the plate.

"Wonderful! You won't believe what an effective remedy it is for all sorts of foolishness. I'd like to enrich medical science with a new term—work cure."

"I shouldn't think you'd need it."

"No, but various nervous cases would."

"Yes, it ought to be tried out. You know I was about to come and watch you mowing, but the heat was so unendurable I didn't get any farther than the woods. I sat there for a while, then went through the woods to the village, met your old wet nurse and sounded her out about what the peasants think of you. It was my understanding that they don't approve of all this. She said, 'It's no business for a gentleman.' In general it appears to me that the people have a very clear-cut view of what they require in the way of what they call a 'gentleman's' activity. And they won't allow the gentry to deviate from the lines laid down in their minds."

"That may be: but after all this was a pleasure I've never experienced in my whole life. And there's nothing bad in it either, is there?" Levin replied. "What can be done about it, if they don't like it! But I think it's all right anyhow, eh?"

"In general," said Koznyshov, "I see you're delighted with your day."

"Delighted. We mowed the entire meadow! And what an old man I made friends with there! You can't imagine what a charming fellow he is!"

"So you're delighted with your day. So am I. First of all, I solved two chess problems, one of which is very pretty, it's a pawn gambit. I'll show it to you. And then I thought over our conversation yesterday."

"What? Our conversation yesterday?" said Levin, who was blissfully blinking and puffing after the meal he had finished and was quite incapable of recalling just what they had been talking about the day before.

"I find that you're partly right. Our disagreement consists of this: you consider personal interest the incentive, whereas I take the view that an interest in the general welfare ought to be present in every man on a certain level of education.

It may well be that you are right, and that activity based on material interest would be more desirable. In general you have an impulsive nature, *primesautière*, as the French say: you want passionate, energetic activity, or nothing at all."

Levin listened to his brother without understanding a single thing or wanting to. He was only afraid his brother might ask him some question that would make it plain he hadn't been paying any attention.

"So that's what it is, my dear boy," said Koznyshov, touching him on the shoulder.

"Yes, of course. But what's the difference, I'm not fighting for my own opinion," answered Levin with a guilty, childlike smile. What could I have been arguing about? he thought; it stands to reason that I'm right and he's right and everything is wonderful. Now I just have to go to the office and leave some instructions.

He got up, stretching and smiling.

Koznyshov smiled too. "D'you want to take a walk? Let's go together," he said; he didn't want to leave his brother, who was radiating such freshness and vigor. "Come on, we can drop in at the office if you have to."

"Good Heavens!" Levin cried out, in such a loud voice that Koznyshov was frightened.

"What's the matter?"

"Miss Agatha's arm!" said Levin, slapping his head. "I'd forgotten all about her!"

"It's much better."

"Well, I'll just run in to see her anyhow. I'll be back before you have time to put on your hat."

And he ran downstairs, clattering his heels like a rattle.

## VII

OBLONSKY had gone to Petersburg in order to perform a most natural and essential duty, which every official is familiar with and every outsider finds incomprehensible—to remind the Ministry of his existence. Without this, life in government service is impossible. Having taken practically all the money away from the household to perform this duty he spent his time gaily and agreeably at the races and in country houses. Dolly had moved to the country with the children in order to cut down expenses as much as possible. She had gone to Yergushovo, the estate that had come with her dowry, where the forest had been sold that spring and that was about thirty-five miles away from Levin's Pokrovsk.

The big old house at Yergushovo had been pulled down long since, and the lodge had been done up and built on to by the old Prince himself. Twenty years before, when Dolly was a child, the lodge had been roomy and convenient, though like all lodges it stood facing away from the entrance drive and the south. But now it was old and dilapidated. When Oblonsky had driven down that spring to sell the forest Dolly had asked him to examine the house and order whatever repairs were necessary. What he thought necessary was to upholster all the furniture with cretonne, put up curtains, clean out the garden, build a bridge by the pond, and plant flowers; but he had forgotten a great many other indispensable things, whose absence tormented Dolly later.

No matter what pains Oblonsky took to be an attentive father and husband, he was simply incapable of recalling that he had a wife and children. He had the tastes of a bachelor; he could not think in any other terms. On his return to Moscow he had proudly declared to his wife that everything was prepared, that the house would be a little jewel, and that he strongly advised her to go there. For Oblonsky his wife's departure for the country was extremely agreeable from all points of view: it was healthful for the children, it cost less money, and it gave him more freedom. As for Dolly, she considered moving to the country in the summer vital for the children, especially the little girl, who couldn't seem to recover after her scarlet fever, and finally in order to escape the petty humiliations, the petty debts to the fuel man, fishmonger, cobbler, which tormented her. On top of all this she also wanted to go away because she was dreaming of luring her sister Kitty, who was supposed to return from abroad in the middle of the summer and had been ordered to bathe, to stay with her in the country. Kitty had written to her from the spa that nothing beckoned to her so much as spending the summer together with Dolly in Yergushovo, which for both of them was full of childhood memories.

At first country life was very hard for Dolly. When she had lived in the country she had been a child, and an impression had stayed with her that the country was a haven from all the disagreeable things in town, and that life there, though far from elegant (Dolly easily reconciled herself to that) was cheap and comfortable; everything was there, everything was cheap, everything was available, and it was good for the children. But now, coming to the country as mistress of a house, she realized it was all quite different from what she had thought.

The day after they arrived there was a tremendous downpour, and at night the rain trickled through into the passage and into the nursery, so that the children's beds had to be carried out into the drawing room. There was no kitchen maid; of the nine cows some, the dairywoman said, were about to calve, others had one calf, still others were old, and the rest were hard-uddered; there was no butter or milk to be gotten even for the children. There were no eggs. It was impossible to get a chicken; they had to boil and roast tough, stringy, purple old roosters. It was impossible to get any peasant women to wash down the floors—they were all out planting potatoes. It was impossible to go for a drive; one of the horses was jittery and intractable. There was no place to go swimming—the whole river bank was trampled over by cattle and exposed to the road; it was even impossible to go for a walk, because the cattle came into the garden through the broken fence and there was one terrifying bull that kept bellowing and therefore might doubtless gore someone. There were no clothes closets. The ones there were didn't shut and would open by themselves when anyone walked by. There were no big pots or pans, no boiler in the washhouse and not even an ironing board for the maids.

When Dolly first encountered what seemed to her these horrifying difficulties, instead of tranquillity and repose, she was in despair. She bustled about with all her strength, feeling the situation to be completely hopeless, and constantly holding back the tears that welled up in her eyes. The manager, a former noncommissioned officer whom Oblonsky had taken a liking to and promoted from hall porter because of his handsome, respectful appearance, took no share at all in Dolly's calamities; he would say deferentially: "It's all quite impossible, these people are simply abominable." He gave not the slightest help.

The situation seemed hopeless. But in the Oblonskys' house, as in all family houses, there was one inconspicuous yet most important and useful person—Matrona. She soothed her mistress and assured her that it would all *turn out all right* (this was her phrase, which Matthew had learned from her), and without hurrying or getting excited set to work herself.

She immediately got together with the foreman's wife; on the very first day she had tea with her and the foreman beneath the acacias and discussed everything. Matrona's club was quickly established beneath the acacias; then and there, because of this club, which consisted of the foreman's wife, a village Elder, and the office clerk, the difficulties of life gradually began to subside. By the time a week had passed everything had in fact *turned out all right*. The roof was repaired, a kitchen maid—a relative of the Elder's—was found, hens were bought, the cows began to give milk, the garden was fenced in with poles, a mangle was made by the carpenter, hooks were put into the closets, which no longer opened of their own accord; an ironing board covered with army cloth was laid across the arm of a chair and the chest of drawers, and a smell of hot irons filled the maids' room.

"There you are! And you were completely in despair!" said Matrona, pointing to the board.

A bathing house was even built, out of straw mats. Lili started to go swimming, and at least part of Dolly's expectations began to be realized; life in the country was at least comfortable, if not restful. For Dolly, with six children, there was no question of rest. One of them would be sick, another might be sick, there was not enough of something for a third, a fourth was showing signs of bad character, and so on and so forth. Rarely, very rarely, there would be a brief period of repose. But these cares and anxieties were the only kind of happiness possible for Dolly. If not for them she would have been left alone with her thoughts about her husband, who didn't love her. But aside from that, no matter how painful the fear of illness was for a mother, as well as the illnesses themselves and the worry about the signs of bad character in her children, the children themselves were already beginning to repay her now in small joys for all her troubles. These joys were so small they were imperceptible, like grains of gold in sand, and at bad moments she saw nothing but her troubles —nothing but the sand; but there were also wonderful moments when she saw nothing but the joys, nothing but the gold.

Now, in the isolation of the countryside, she began to grow aware of these joys more and more often. In looking at her children she would often make every effort possible to persuade herself that she was making a mistake, that as a mother she was biased in their favor; all the same she couldn't

help telling herself that she had charming children, all six of
them, each one in a different way but all of them rarities—
and she was happy in them and proud of them.

VIII

At the end of May, when everything was now more or less
settled down, she received an answer from her husband to
her complaint concerning the chaotic state of the country
house. He wrote to ask her forgiveness for his failure to have
thought of everything and promised to come out the first
chance he could. This chance did not present itself, and,
until the beginning of June, Dolly was still living in the
country without him.

On the Sunday before St. Peter's Day, Dolly drove to Mass
for all her children to take communion. In her intimate talks
with her sister, mother, and friends, Dolly often astounded
them by her freedom of thought concerning religion. She had
her own peculiar religion of metempsychosis, in which she
firmly believed, caring very little about the dogmas of the
Church. But within the family she carried out strictly all
the demands of the Church—not only to show an example,
but with all her heart—and she was very uneasy over the
children's not having been to communion for about a year.
With the full approval and sympathy of Matrona she had decided to attend to this now, in the summer.

A few days beforehand she had thought over how to dress
all the children. Dresses were made, altered, and washed,
hems and frills were let down, buttons were sewn on and ribbons got ready. A dress for Tanya, which the English governess had undertaken to alter, gave Dolly a great deal of anxiety. In altering it the governess had put the seams in the
wrong place, made the holes for the arms too big, and completely spoiled the dress. It was so tight around Tanya's
shoulders it was painful to see. But Matrona had the inspiration of putting in some gussets and making a little cape for
it. Things were put right, though what was very nearly a
quarrel almost broke out with the English governess. But by
morning everything was all right, and by nine o'clock—the
hour the priest had been asked to defer the service to—the
children, beaming with happiness in their new clothes, were
standing in front of the carriage on the steps, waiting for
their mother.

Instead of the jittery Raven, the foreman's Brownie had been harnessed to the carriage on Matrona's authority, and Dolly, who had been delayed by concern for her own toilette, came out in a white muslin dress and got into the carriage.

Dolly had dressed and done her hair with anxiety and excitement. She had used to dress for herself, in order to be beautiful and attractive; later on, the older she grew, the more disagreeable it became for her to get dressed—she saw she was losing her looks. But now she dressed once again with pleasure and excitement. Now she was no longer dressing for herself, not for her own beauty, but, as the mother of these treasures, just in order not to spoil the general effect. And, when she looked at herself in the mirror for the last time, she was satisfied with herself. She looked lovely—not lovely as she had used to want to look at a ball, but lovely for the object she now had in mind.

There was no one in the church except peasants, domestics, and their womenfolk. But Dolly saw, or thought she saw, the enthusiasm generated by her children and herself. The children were not only beautiful in their little holiday dresses, but were charming because they behaved so well. Alyosha, it is true, did not stand very well, he kept turning around trying to see his own jacket from behind; but he was extraordinarily charming anyhow. Tanya was standing like a grownup and looking after the little ones. But the little one, Lili, was ravishing because of her naïve astonishment at everything, and it was difficult not to smile when, as she took the sacrament, she said in English: "Please, some more."

After returning home the children felt that something solemn had taken place, and were very quiet.

Everything went well at home too, except that at lunch Grisha began whistling, and what was worst of all would not obey the governess, and was not given any pudding. On a day like this Dolly would not have permitted any punishments, if she had been there, but it was necessary to back up the governess's orders, and she confirmed her decision not to let Grisha have any pudding. This somewhat spoiled the general gaiety.

Grisha wept, saying that Nikolinka had also whistled but no one was punishing him, and that it wasn't because of the pudding that he was crying—it was all the same to him!—but because of the unfairness. This was really too sad, and Dolly made up her mind to persuade the governess to forgive Grisha and went to find her. But on her way she saw a scene that filled her heart with such joy that tears came into her eyes and she forgave the culprit herself.

The culprit was sitting in the dancing room at the corner window; Tanya was standing beside him with a plate. Under the pretext of wanting to feed her dolls, she had asked the governess for permission to take her own portion of pudding into the nursery, and had brought it to her brother. Still weeping over the injustice he had had to endure, he ate the pudding that had been brought him and through his sobs he kept mumbling: "Eat some too—we'll eat it—together—together . . ."

Tanya had been affected at first by pity for Grisha, then by the consciousness of her own virtuous behavior, and tears came to her eyes too; but she did not refuse, and ate her share.

When they saw their mother they were frightened, but when they looked at her face they saw that what they were doing was all right and burst out laughing; their mouths full of pudding, they began wiping off their smiling lips with their hands and smeared their radiant faces with tears and jam.

"Heavens! The new white dress! Tanya! Grisha!" said Dolly, trying to save the dress while smiling a blissful, rapturous smile with tears in her eyes.

The new clothes were taken off, orders were given for the girls to put on their overalls and the boys their jackets, and for Brownie to be harnessed up again, to the foreman's annoyance, in order to drive off for a mushroom hunt and then go to the bathhouse. The sound of rapturous squealing filled the nursery and did not die down until they actually left for the bathhouse.

They collected a whole basketful of mushrooms; even Lili found a wood mushroom. What had used to happen was that Miss Hull would find one and show her; but this time she found a big one all by herself, and there was a rapturous shriek: "Lili found a mushroom!"

Then they drove to the river, put the horses under the birch trees and went to the bathhouse. Terenty, the coachman, tethered to a tree the horses that were swishing their tails to keep off the flies, stamped down the grass, stretched out in the shadow of a birch, and smoked his pipe, while there came to him from the bathhouse the incessant joyous squealing of the children.

Even though it was a nuisance to look after all the children and stop their pranks, though it was difficult to remember, without mixing them up, all these little stockings, drawers, and shoes from different feet, and to untie and unbutton, then fasten up again all the tapes and buttons, Dolly, who had always liked bathing and considered it useful for the children, enjoyed nothing so much as this bathing together with all the children. To go over all these chubby little legs, pull their little stockings over them, to take all these naked little bodies into her arms and dip them into the water, to hear them squeal, sometimes with delight, sometimes in fright; to watch her cherubs gasping and splashing about, with eyes wide open, frightened, yet joyful, was a great delight for her.

When half the children were already dressed, some peasant women in holiday dress, who had been out picking herbs, came up to the bathhouse and stopped there shyly. Matrona called one of them over to give her a sheet and a blouse to dry that had fallen into the water, and Dolly started a conversation with them. The women, who had been giggling behind their hands at first without understanding questions, soon grew bolder and began to talk, immediately winning Dolly over because of the sincere admiration they showed for the children.

"What a little beauty, just look, as white as sugar," said one of them, admiring Tanya and shaking her head. "But so thin—"

"Yes, she was ill."

"So you've been in swimming too?" said another to the baby.

"No, he's only three months old," Dolly answered proudly.

"Goodness!"

"And have you any children?"

"There were four, two are left; a boy and a girl. I weaned her in the spring."

"But how old is she?"

"Why, two years old."

"Why did you nurse her so long?"

"That's our custom: for three fasts . . ."

The conversation became extremely interesting for Dolly: What sort of confinement had she had? What was the matter with the boy? Where was her husband? Did he come home often?

Dolly did not feel like leaving the peasant women, her conversation with them was so interesting, and their interests were so completely identical. What was most pleasant of all for Dolly was that she saw clearly that what all these women admired most of all was that she had so many children and

that they were all so pretty. The women amused Dolly and offended the English governess, who was the cause of laughter that she found incomprehensible. One of the younger
women kept staring at the Englishwoman, who was dressing after everyone else, and when she had put on her third
petticoat could not refrain from remarking: "Look at her!
Wrapping, wrapping, and she still hasn't wrapped herself up
enough!" And all the women burst out laughing.

IX

SURROUNDED by all the children, their heads wet from
their swim, Dolly, a kerchief around her head, was already
near the house when the coachman said: "Some gentleman is
coming by, I think the one from Pokrovsk."

Dolly looked out in front and was delighted to see the familiar figure of Levin, in a gray hat and a gray coat, coming
toward them. She was always glad to see him, but now she
was particularly glad because he was seeing her in all her
glory. No one could understand her splendor better than
Levin.

Seeing her, he found himself confronted by one of the pictures of the future family life of his dreams.

"You're just like a hen with her brood, Dolly!"

"Oh, how happy I am to see you!" she said, holding her
hand out to him.

"Happy, but you didn't even let me know. My brother's
staying with me. It was from Stiva I finally heard you were
here."

"From Stiva?" asked Dolly in surprise.

"Yes, he wrote you were moving out and thought you
might allow me to help you somehow or other," said Levin,
and after saying this he suddenly got embarrassed. He
stopped speaking and walked on beside the gig in silence,
snapping off shoots from the lime trees and biting them in
two. He was embarrassed because it had occurred to him
that it might be unpleasant for Dolly to be helped by an outsider in something that ought to have been done by her husband. As a matter of fact Dolly did not like this habit of Oblonsky's of forcing his family affairs on strangers, and she
saw at once that Levin understood this. It was just this refinement of perception of Levin's, this delicacy, that made
Dolly fond of him.

"Of course I understood that all he meant was that you wanted to see me, and I'm delighted," said Levin. "After running a house in town I should imagine you find everything out here primitive, and if I can be of any use I'm entirely at your service."

"Oh now!" said Dolly. "It was uncomfortable at first, but everything is going splendidly now, thanks to my old nurse," she said indicating Matrona, who understood they were talking about her and gave Levin a cheerful friendly smile. She knew him and knew he would make a good husband for her young miss, and she wanted the matter to come off.

"Please get in, sir, we'll move closer together," she said to him.

"No, I'll walk. Children, who's for racing the horses with me?"

The children scarcely knew Levin and didn't remember when they had seen him last, but they did not have toward him that strange feeling of embarrassment and repugnance children so often have for hypocritical adults, and for which they are so often and so painfully punished. Hypocrisy in anything at all may deceive the most intelligent, shrewdest man, but the dullest child recognizes it no matter how skillfully it is concealed and is repelled by it. Whatever Levin's shortcomings, there was not a trace of hypocrisy in him, so the children showed him the same friendliness they saw on their mother's face. At this invitation of his the two oldest jumped out and ran off with him just as simply as though they were running with their nurse, or Miss Hull or their mother. Lili also began begging to go with him, and her mother handed her over to him; he put her on his shoulder and ran off with her.

"Don't be afraid, don't be afraid!" he said to Dolly, smiling at her gaily. "There's not a chance of my hurting or dropping her."

And as she watched his strong, agile, watchfully careful and ultracautious movements, Dolly was reassured and gave him a cheerful approving smile.

Here, in the country, with the children and with Dolly, whom he got along with very well, Levin fell into the mood of childlike gaiety that often came upon him and that Dolly liked so much. He ran around with the children, taught them acrobatics, amused Miss Hull with his broken English and told Dolly everything he had been doing in the country.

After dinner, when Dolly was sitting alone with him on the balcony, she started speaking about Kitty.

"Did you know, Kitty's arriving and is going to spend the summer with me?"

"Really?" he said, turning crimson; in order to change the subject he said at once: "Then I'll send you two cows. If you want to settle up for them you can pay me five rubles a month, if it doesn't make you ashamed of yourself."

"No, thank you. We're getting on all right now."

"Then I'll just take a look at your cows; if you like I'll leave instructions about how to feed them. It's all a question of feeding."

And Levin, simply in order to deflect the conversation, expounded to Dolly his theory of dairy farming, which was that the cow is merely a machine for converting fodder into milk and so on.

He was saying this while passionately longing, yet dreading to hear some details about Kitty. He was afraid the peace of mind he had acquired with such toil would be dissipated.

"Yes, but all that would have to be kept track of, and who's going to do it?" Dolly answered unwillingly.

She had now gotten her household running so smoothly with Matrona's help that she didn't feel like making any changes; also, she had no confidence in Levin's knowledge of agriculture. Arguments about a cow being a machine for the manufacture of milk were suspect to her. It seemed to her that this kind of reasoning could only be an obstacle to farming. The whole thing seemed far simpler to her: as Matrona had explained, all that was necessary was to give Spotty and Whiteside more to eat and drink, and to stop the cook from taking the garbage over to the laundress's cow. That was clear, while arguments about cereal and grass fodders were dubious and obscure. But the main thing was that she longed to talk about Kitty.

X

Kitty writes me that she wants nothing so much as solitude and quiet," said Dolly after a pause.

"And her health—is it better?" asked Levin agitatedly.

"She's completely recovered, thank God. I never believed there was anything the matter with her lungs."

"Oh, I'm so glad!" said Levin, and there was something

touching and helpless in his face, Dolly thought, as he said this and gazed at her.

"Listen to me, Constantine," said Dolly, with her kind, somewhat ironic smile. "Why are you angry with Kitty?"

"I? I'm not angry," said Levin.

"Yes, you are. Why didn't you call either on us, or on them, when you were in Moscow?"

"Dolly," he said, blushing to the roots of his hair, "I'm astonished that you, with all your kindness, haven't felt what the reason was. How is it you have no pity for me, if nothing else, when you know that—"

"When I know what?"

"You know that I proposed and was refused," muttered Levin, and all the tenderness he had felt for Kitty a moment before was replaced in his heart by a feeling of anger at her insult to him.

"But why do you think I knew that?"

"Because everyone does."

"Now there you're surely mistaken; I didn't know, though I had suspected as much."

"Ah! Well, now you know."

"All I knew was that something had happened that tormented her dreadfully, and that she asked me never to speak of it. And if she didn't tell me she didn't tell anyone. But what did happen between you? Tell me."

"I've told you what happened."

"When was it?"

"The last time I was at your house."

"Let me tell you something," said Dolly. "I'm terribly, terribly sorry for her. You're suffering from nothing but pride—"

"That may be," said Levin, "but—"

She stopped him. "But I'm terribly, terribly sorry for *her,* the poor little thing. Now I understand everything."

"Well, you must excuse me," he said, getting up. "Good-by and *au revoir!*"

"No, wait a moment," she said, catching him by the sleeve. "Wait a moment, do sit down."

"Please, I beg of you, let's not discuss it," he said, sitting down with the feeling that a hope he had thought dead and buried was stirring and rising in his heart.

"If I were not fond of you," Dolly said, the tears coming to her eyes, "if I did not know you as I do—"

The feeling he had thought dead was reviving more and

more; it was rising up and taking possession of Levin's heart.

"Yes, now I understand it all," Dolly went on. "You can't understand this: for you men, who are free to do your own choosing, it's always clear whom you love. But a girl who's in a state of expectation, with her feminine, girlish modesty, a girl who sees you men only from a distance, takes everything on trust—a girl may, and does, have feelings that make it impossible for her to know what to say."

"Yes, if the heart doesn't tell her—"

"No, the heart does tell her, but just think: you men have intentions concerning a girl, you visit the house, you get to know her, you observe her, wait to see whether you've found in her something to love, then when you're sure you're in love you propose—"

"Well, it's not like that entirely."

"Never mind, you propose when your love has ripened, or when the balance falls in favor of one of two choices. But a girl isn't asked. She's supposed to choose for herself, but she can't choose, all she can answer is 'yes' or 'no.' "

Yes, a choice between me and Vronsky, thought Levin, and the dead hope that had revived died once again and only weighed painfully on his soul.

"That's how you pick a dress, or something else you buy, but not love," he said. "The choice has been made, and so much the better . . . There can't be any repetition."

"Oh that pride! That pride!" said Dolly, as though despising him for the baseness of this feeling in comparison with the other feeling, which only women can know. "At the time when you were proposing to Kitty she happened to be in just that situation in which she couldn't give an answer. She was hesitating: hesitating between you and Vronsky. She was seeing him every day, but you she hadn't seen for a long time. Supposing she had been older—if I had been in her place, for instance, there couldn't have been any hesitation. He's always been repulsive to me, and that's how it turned out too."

Levin recalled Kitty's answer. She had said, *"It's impossible . . ."*

"I value your confidence in me," he said drily, "but I think you're mistaken. Whether I'm right or wrong, that pride you despise so much has made any thought of your sister impossible for me—you understand, completely impossible."

"I'll say just one more thing. You understand that I'm

speaking about a sister whom I love as much as my own children. I'm not saying she loved you, all I mean is that her refusal at just that moment proves nothing."

"I don't know!" exclaimed Levin, jumping up. "If you knew how much pain you're causing me! It's just as though a child of yours had died, and people were to tell you, Now this is how he would have been, or this, and he might have lived, and you would have been rejoicing in him, and all the while he's dead, dead, dead . . ."

"How absurd you are," said Dolly with a melancholy smile, in spite of Levin's agitation. "Yes, I understand it now more and more," she went on reflectively. "So you won't be coming to see us when Kitty's here?"

"No, I won't. Of course I shan't avoid your sister, but whenever I can I'll try to relieve her of the unpleasantness of my company."

"You're quite, quite absurd," Dolly repeated, gazing tenderly into his face. "Very well, then, we'll act as though we had never spoken of it. What are you doing here, Tanya?" Dolly said in French to her little girl who had just come in.

"Where's my spade, Mama?"

"I'm speaking French and you must too."

The little girl tried to say it in French, but had forgotten the word for spade; her mother prompted her and then told her in French where to look for it. This struck Levin disagreeably.

Now nothing in Dolly's house or about her children seemed to him even remotely as charming as before.

Why does she talk to the children in French? he thought. How unnatural and false! And the children feel it. Teach them French and unteach them sincerity, he thought to himself, not knowing that Dolly had thought the whole thing over dozens of times and decided it was necessary to teach her children in this way even to the detriment of their sincerity.

"But where are you off to? Stay a little longer."

Levin stayed to tea, but his gaiety had all gone; he felt uncomfortable.

After tea he went out into the hall to order the horses driven up; when he came back he found Dolly in a state of agitation, with a distraught look and tears in her eyes. While Levin had been gone something had happened that had suddenly destroyed all the joy and pride Dolly had been feeling that day. Grisha and Tanya had had a fight about a ball.

Dolly, hearing cries in the nursery, hurried in and found them looking dreadful. Tanya was holding Grisha by the hair while he, his face distorted with rage, was pummeling her with his fists wherever he could. When Dolly saw this something snapped in her heart. It was as though a shadow came over her life: she realized that these children of hers, whom she took such pride in, were not only perfectly ordinary, but were even bad and ill bred, with coarse, bestial inclinations—vicious children.

She could not speak or think of anything else and could not help telling Levin her misfortune.

Levin saw she was unhappy, and tried to soothe her by saying it didn't show anything bad and that all children had fights; but as he said this he thought in his heart: No, I won't put on airs and talk French to my children, but I won't have children like that either; all you have to do is not to spoil children or pervert them, and they'll be charming. No, I won't have children like that!

He said good-by and left; she did not try to keep him.

## XI

In the middle of July an Elder from Levin's sister's village, fifteen miles from Pokrovsk, came to see him with a report on business and the hay harvest. His sister's estate derived its chief income from the meadows, which were flooded every spring. Before the hay used to be harvested by the peasants for seven rubles an acre. When Levin had undertaken the management of the estate he came to the conclusion, after examining the harvest, that it was worth more, and fixed a price of eight rubles. The peasants would not pay so much, and Levin suspected they were also keeping off other buyers. Then he went there himself and arranged to have the harvest gathered in by paying partly in cash and partly in kind. His own peasants used every means in their power to hinder this innovation, but the plan worked and in the very first year the meadows brought in almost twice as much. The previous year, the third, the peasants continued their opposition, and the harvest was gathered in the same way. This year the peasants had gathered in the whole harvest in return for a third of it in payment, and now the village Elder had come to announce that the harvest was all gathered and that he, for fear of rain, had invited the office clerk over, divided everything up in his presence, and already piled up eleven stacks of Levin's share. The Elder's vague answers to the question about how much hay there had been on the principal meadow, his haste in dividing the hay up without asking, his whole tone made it clear to Levin that there was something fishy about this division of the hay, and he made up his mind to drive over to check it himself.

Arriving at the village for dinner, Levin left his horse with an old man who was a friend of his, the husband of his brother's wet nurse, and since he wanted to find out the details of the harvest he went to see the old man at his bee-hives. Parmenich, a talkative, well-built old man, greeted Levin joyfully, showed him over his whole farm and told him all the details of his beekeeping and the swarming of the bees that year; but in answer to Levin's questions about the harvest talked vaguely and reluctantly.

This was a further confirmation of Levin's surmise. He went to the meadow and examined the haystacks. There could not have been more than fifty loads in each stack, and in order to catch out the peasants Levin ordered the carts that were carrying the hay to be brought up on the spot, for one stack to be loaded and carried to the barn. The stack gave only thirty-two loads. In spite of the Elder's assurances that the hay had been loose and had settled down in the stacks, and in spite of his swearing that everything had been done "in the fear of the Lord," Levin insisted on his point that the hay had been divided up without any orders from him, and that therefore he would not accept this hay at an estimate of fifty loads per stack. After long-drawn-out bickering the argument was settled by having the peasants accept these eleven stacks as their share, at an estimate of fifty loads apiece, and by starting a new calculation for Levin's share. The argument and the allocation of the haystacks lasted until it was time for the evening meal. When the last of the hay was divided up Levin entrusted the rest of the supervision to the office clerk and sat down on a haystack marked with a willow branch, looking on with pleasure at the meadow teeming with peasants.

Beyond a marsh in front of him, within a bend of the river, a line of gaily dressed peasant women was moving along, merrily chattering away in their loud voices, while the scattered hay was quickly forming into gray, winding rows over the pale green stubble of the meadow. The women were followed by the peasants with pitchforks, and these rows were built up into broad, high, fluffy stacks. At the left carts were rattling along the part of the meadow that was already cleared; one after another the stacks, loaded on in tremendous forkfuls, were vanishing, and in their places heavy cartloads of fragrant hay drooping over the horses' rumps were piling up.

"Make hay while the sun shines! Then you'll have hay!" said the old beekeeper, sitting down beside Levin. "It's tea, not hay! Scattering grain for ducklings, that's how they pick it up!" he added, pointing to the stacks piling up. "Since dinnertime they've carted off a good half."

"That's the last one, what?" he shouted to a young peasant boy driving by, who was standing up in the front of a cart flicking the tips of his hemp reins.

"The last one, Papa!" the boy yelled back, holding in the horse; he looked round with a smile at the rosy, gay young woman sitting inside the cart and also smiling, and drove on.

"Who's that? Your son?" asked Levin.

"My youngest," said the old man with an affectionate smile.

"What a fine boy!"

"Not so bad."

"Married already?"

"Two years last St. Philip's Day."

"Any children?"

"What children? For a whole year he didn't understand a thing himself, and bashful too he was," the old man answered. "Hay now! Real tea!" he repeated, wanting to change the conversation.

Levin looked more attentively at Ivan Parmenich and his wife. They were loading the hay not far from him. Ivan was standing on the load, taking in, leveling off and stamping down the enormous heaps of hay that his young and beautiful wife was adroitly passing up to him, first in armfuls, then in forkfuls. The young woman was working easily, cheerfully, and skillfully. The densely packed hay could not be taken up all at once by the pitchfork. She would loosen it first with the prongs, then stick them in, lean her whole weight on the fork with a springy, rapid movement and at once, bending her red-sashed back, straighten up again, her full bosom thrust forward beneath the white smock, and deftly turning the fork in her hands toss a swatch of hay high into the cart. Ivan, obviously trying to save her every minute of superfluous labor, would hurriedly catch the bundle of hay in his out-stretched arms and spread it evenly in the cart. When she had passed the last of the hay to him with a rake, the young woman shook off the chaff that sprinkled her neck, and adjusting a red handkerchief that had slipped from her white, unsunburned forehead, crawled under the cart to fasten down the load. Ivan was showing her how to tie the cord up to the crosspiece, and at something she said burst out laughing. Strong, young, newly awakened love shone in both their faces.

### XII

THE load was fastened. Ivan jumped down and led away the gentle well-fed horse by the bridle. His wife tossed the rake onto the load and swinging her arms strode off vigorously to join the other women who had gathered in a circle. Ivan, coming out onto the road, fell into line with the other loaded carts. Resplendent in their brightly colored dresses, rakes on their shoulders, the women walked along behind the carts, chattering in their loud merry voices. One wild, rough woman's voice started a song and sang it through, and fifty healthy voices, coarse or fine, took it up simultaneously and sang the same song through in unison from the beginning.

The singing women were coming closer to Levin, and it seemed to him as though a thundercloud of gaiety were advancing on him. The cloud advanced and enveloped him, the haystack he was lying on, the other haystacks and wagon and the entire meadow together with the distant fields—everything seemed to be throbbing and heaving to the strains of this wildly gay song with its shouting, whistling, and clapping. Levin grew envious of this healthy gaiety; he felt like taking part in the expression of this joy in life. But there was nothing he could do and he had to keep lying down, looking and listening. When the singing throng had vanished, out of sight and hearing, a painful feeling of yearning because of his solitude, his physical idleness, and his alienation from the world seized hold of him.

Some of the same peasants who had quarreled with him about the hay more than the others, those whom he had offended or who had tried to cheat him, these same peasants had bowed to him, and had obviously not had or could have had any ill will toward him; they were not only not repentant but had totally forgotten they had ever tried to cheat him. All that had been swallowed up in the sea of their joyful common toil. God gave the day and God gave the strength for it. Both the day and the strength for it were devoted to labor, and that was its own reward. And whom was the labor for? What would its fruits be? Such considerations were irrelevant and trivial.

Levin had often admired this life, and had often experienced a feeling of envy for the people who lived it, but today for the first time, especially under the impact of what he had seen of the relations between Ivan Parmenich and his young wife, the thought came into Levin's mind that it was up to him to exchange the far too wearisome, idle, artificial, and selfish life he was living for this pure, delightful social life full of work.

The old man who had been sitting with him had long since gone home; the peasants had all scattered. The ones who lived nearby had driven off home, while those from a distance had gathered together to have their supper and spend the night in the meadow. Unnoticed Levin continued lying on the haystack, looking, listening, and thinking. The peasants who were staying in the meadow overnight did not go to sleep almost the whole of the short summer night. At first he could hear the general gay conversation and laughter over their meal, then again singing and laughing.

The whole of the long working day had left no trace in them of anything but merriment.

Before dawn everything died down. All that could be heard were the night sounds of the ceaselessly croaking frogs and of the horses snorting in the morning mists rising in the meadow. Coming to, Levin got up from the haystack and looking at the stars realized the night was over.

Well, then what am I going to do? How am I going to do it? he said to himself, trying to give expression to all the thoughts and feelings he had had that short night. All his reflections and feelings were divided into three separate trains of thought. One was the renunciation of his old life, his useless knowledge, his completely futile education. This renunciation gave him pleasure; it was easy and simple for him. His other ideas and thoughts touched on the life he now wanted to live. He felt the simplicity, purity, and rightness of this life clearly, and was convinced he would find in it that satisfaction, serenity, and dignity whose absence he was so painfully aware of. But a third series of thoughts revolved around the question of how to effect this transition from the old to the new life. Here nothing came to his mind that was at all clear. Get married? Start working and having to work? Leave Pokrovsk? Buy land? Join a peasant commune? Marry a peasant girl? Just how will I do it? he asked himself again without finding an answer. But I didn't sleep all night long, now I can't keep things straight, he said to himself. I'll clear things up later. One thing is certain—tonight decided my fate. All my former dreams of family life are nonsense, all wrong, he said to himself. This is all much simpler and better . . .

How beautiful! he thought, looking at the strange mother-of-pearl-colored shell of white fleecy clouds hanging just over his head in the center of the sky. How exquisite everything is on this exquisite night! And when did this shell have time to form? I looked up at the sky a moment ago, there was nothing there—just two white streaks. Yes—just like that, imperceptibly, my ideas about life have also changed!

He left the meadow and walked off along the highroad to the village. A slight breeze had sprung up; it had become gray and sullen; the gloomy moment had come that usually precedes the dawn, the full triumph of light over darkness.

Shivering with the cold, Levin walked rapidly, gazing at the ground. Now what's that? Who's coming there? he thought, hearing a tinkle of bells and lifting his head. Coming toward him some forty paces away a four-horse carriage with baggage on the top was being driven along the grassy highroad he was walking on. The shaft horses were pressing against the shaft because of the ruts, but the skillful coachman, sitting sideways on the box, kept the shaft going over the ruts so that the wheels ran along the smooth part.

This was all Levin noticed, and without thinking of who it might be driving along he absent-mindedly glanced into the carriage.

An old woman was dozing in a corner, while a young girl who had obviously just awakened was sitting at the carriage window holding the ribbons of a white nightcap in both hands. Bright and pensive, full of an elegant, complex interior life that was alien to Levin, she looked across him toward the glow of the sunrise.

Just at the moment when this vision was already vanishing, the candid eyes glanced at him. She recognized him, and her face was lit up by joyful astonishment.

He could not have been mistaken. There were no eyes on earth like those. There was only one creature on earth able to focus all the light and meaning of life for him. That was she —Kitty. He supposed she was on her way from the railroad station to Yergushovo. And everything that had agitated Levin that sleepless night, all the decisions he had made—everything—suddenly vanished. He recalled with revulsion his dreams of marrying a peasant girl. Only there, in that swiftly receding carriage that had crossed to the other side of the road, there and only there was there a chance of solving the riddle of his life that had lately been weighing on him so agonizingly.

She didn't look out again. The sound of the springs faded away, the tinkling of the bells was scarcely audible. The barking of dogs indicated that the carriage had passed through the village too—all that was left was the empty fields round about, the village lying ahead, and he himself, isolated and alien to everything, walking along the deserted highroad alone.

He glanced at the sky, hoping to see there the shell he had looked at with such pleasure, which embodied for him the whole course of his thoughts and feelings that night. There was no longer anything in the sky that looked like a shell. There in the unattainable heights above some mysterious change had already taken place. There was not even a trace of the shell; a quilt of cloudlets, growing tinier and tinier, was evenly spread out over a whole half of the sky. The sky had turned blue and bright: it answered his questioning look with the same tenderness, but with the same unfathomability.

No, he said to himself, no matter how good that simple and laborious life is, I can't return to it. I love *her*.

## XIII

No one but those closest to him knew that Karenin, apparently cold and rational, had one weakness that contradicted the general trend of his character. He was incapable of listening to or looking at the tears of a child or a woman with indifference. The sight of tears threw him into a state of perplexity; he completely lost any capacity for thought. The chief of his staff and his secretary knew this and would warn women petitioners on no account to start crying if they did not want to spoil their case. "He'll get angry and stop listening to you," they would say. And in such circumstances, as a matter of fact, Karenin would get so upset by tears that he would fly into a rage. "I can do nothing, absolutely nothing for you! Kindly leave at once!" he would usually shout in such cases.

When Anna, on her return from the races, had told him of her relations with Vronsky, burst into tears immediately afterward and hidden her face in her hands, Karenin, in spite of the fury this had aroused in him, had felt at the same time an upsurge of the emotional disturbance tears always produced in him. Knowing this and knowing that any expression of his feelings at that moment would be out of keeping with the situation, he tried to suppress any display of life, and so he neither moved nor looked at her. This was what had brought about the peculiar, deathlike expression on his face that had so struck Anna.

When they had driven home he had helped her out of the carriage and by making an effort to control himself had said good-by to her with his customary politeness and uttered a few words that committed him to nothing—he had said he would inform her of his decision the following day.

His wife's words, which confirmed his worst suspicions, had given him bitter pain. This pain was heightened still further by the strange feeling of physical pity which had been evoked by her tears. But when he was left alone in the carriage, to his own surprise and joy, he felt utterly liberated both from his pity and from the doubts and jealous anguish that had been tormenting him lately.

He felt like someone who has just had a tooth extracted after a long-drawn-out toothache. After dreadful pain, and a sensation of something vast, larger than his head, being pulled out of his jaw, the sufferer suddenly, still not believing in his own good fortune, feels that the thing that has been poisoning his life for so long and preoccupying his whole attention, no longer exists, and that once again he can live, think, and be interested in something beside his tooth alone. This was Karenin's feeling. The pain had been strange and terrible, but now it was past; he felt that once again he could live and think about something beside his wife.

No honor, no heart, no religion—a depraved woman! I've always known and always seen it, though in my pity for her I tried to deceive myself, he thought. And it really did seem to him that he had always seen it; he recalled details of their past life together that had never seemed to him wrong in any way before—now these details were a plain proof that she had always been depraved. I made a mistake in linking my life to hers, but there was nothing wrong in my mistake, so I can't be unhappy. It's not I who am to blame—he said to himself—but she. She is no longer any concern of mine. For me she doesn't exist . . .

Whatever might happen to her and to their son, toward whom his feelings had changed just as they had toward her, lost all interest for him. The only thing that preoccupied him now was the question of what would be the best and most decent way, the way that was the most convenient for him and therefore the fairest, of shaking off the filth she had bespattered him with in her own fall, and of continuing to proceed along the path of his own active, honorable, and useful life.

I cannot be unhappy simply because a despicable woman has committed a crime; the only thing I must do is find the best way out of the painful position she has placed me in. And I will find it—he said to himself, frowning more and more—I'm not the first, nor will I be the last. And without even thinking of historical instances, beginning with Menelaus and La Belle Hélène, freshly revived recently in everyone's memory, a whole series of cases of wives' infidelities in the highest society sprang to Karenin's mind.

Daryalov, Poltavsky, Prince Karibanov, Count Paskudin, Dram—yes, Dram too, such an honest, businesslike fellow —Semyonov, Chagin, Sigonin . . . Karenin recalled. It's true that somehow or other these people are all made to look ridiculous, but I've never seen anything but unhappiness there and have always been sympathetic, Karenin said to himself, though that wasn't true either—he had never sympathized with unfortunates of this kind but had always had a higher opinion of himself the more often he heard of cases of wives deceiving their husbands. It's a misfortune that can happen to anyone, and now it's happened to me. The only question is what is the best way to endure the position. And he began to go over in his mind the details of the manner in which people who had found themselves in the same position as himself had reacted.

Daryalov had fought a duel. . . .

In his youth Karenin had been particularly attracted by the idea of dueling just because he was physically timid and very well aware of it. Karenin could not think of a pistol being aimed at him without being terrified; he had never used a weapon in his life. In his youth this terror had often forced

him to think about dueling and measure himself up against
a situation in which it was necessary to endanger his life.
Once he had achieved success and an established position in
life he had long since forgotten about it, but this old ingrained feeling now reasserted itself, and even now the fear of
his own cowardice proved to be so powerful that for a long
time Karenin lovingly considered from all points of view the
idea of a duel, though he knew in advance that under no circumstances would he ever fight one.

There's no doubt that our society is still so primitive (not
like England) that a great many people—this "great many"
including those whose opinion Karenin particularly esteemed
—take a favorable view of dueling; but what would be the
result of it? Let's suppose I challenge him to a duel—Karenin
went on to himself; vividly picturing the night he would spend
after the challenge and the pistol aimed at himself he shuddered and realized that he would never do it—let's suppose I
challenge him to a duel. Let's suppose they show me how to
do it—he went on thinking—put me in position, I squeeze the
trigger—he said to himself, closing his eyes—and it turns out
I've killed him—he shook his head to drive away such stupid
thoughts. What would be the sense of killing a man in order
to define one's own relations with a guilty wife and with one's
son? In any case I should have to decide what's to be done
with her. But what's even more likely, and what would undoubtedly happen—I would be killed or wounded. There I'd
be, an innocent man, victimized—killed or wounded. That's
even more senseless. But that's the least of it: challenging
him to a duel would be dishonest behavior on my own part.
Don't I know in advance that my friends would never permit
me to engage in a duel—would never permit the life of a
statesman needed by Russia to be placed in jeopardy? Then
what would happen? What would happen would be that I,
knowing in advance that things would never get so far as
real danger, simply wanted to acquire a certain false glamour
by means of such a challenge. That's dishonest, it's hypocritical, it would be deceiving both others and oneself. A duel
is unthinkable, and no one expects it of me. My aim is to
safeguard my reputation, which I need in order to continue
my career unhindered.

His professional career, which had been very important in
Karenin's eyes even before, now seemed to him overwhelm-
ingly so.

Having considered a duel and rejected it, Karenin turned to

the idea of a divorce, another way out that had been taken by some of the husbands he recalled. Turning over in his mind all the known cases of divorce (there were a great many in the highest society, which he was well acquainted with), Karenin could not find a single one where the purpose of the divorce had been what he himself had in mind. In all these cases the husband had yielded up the wife or sold her, and the very party who through being in the wrong had no right to enter into a marriage, entered into fictitious, pseudo-legal relations with a new spouse. But in his own case Karenin saw that it would be impossible to get a legal divorce, that is, one in which the guilty wife would simply be cast off. He saw that the complex circumstances of the life he was leading excluded the possibility of any of the coarse proofs demanded by the law in order to establish the wife's guilt; he saw that a certain refinement taken for granted in that life would not even permit such proofs to be brought forward even if there were any, and that resorting to them would lower his reputation more than it would hers.

An attempt at divorce could only lead to a scandalous trial that would give his enemies a heaven-sent opportunity to slander him and undermine his exalted position in society. Thus his chief objective—the clarification of the position with the least possible disturbance—could not be achieved through a divorce either. Aside from this, if there was a divorce, or even an attempt at a divorce, it was obvious that the wife would break off relations with her husband and be united with her lover. And at the bottom of Karenin's heart, in spite of what he thought was his utter, contemptuous, indifference toward his wife, there was one feeling he still had toward her—a disinclination for her to be united with Vronsky unhindered, so that her crime would prove advantageous to her. The mere thought of this irritated Karenin so much that just by imagining it he groaned aloud with inner pain, leaned forward and shifted his place in the carriage, and for some time he sat there scowling, wrapping his bony, easily chilled legs in the fluffy rug.

Besides a formal divorce it might be possible to do what Karibanov, Paskudin, and that nice fellow Dram did—that is, just separate, he went on thinking after he had calmed down; but this step also had the same disadvantages with respect to scandal as a divorce, and the main thing was that it would throw his wife into Vronsky's arms in exactly the same way as a formal divorce, "No, that's impossible,

impossible!" he said aloud, wrapping the rug around his legs again; I cannot be unhappy, but neither she nor he ought to be happy.

The feeling of jealousy that had tormented him during the period of his uncertainty had passed away the moment the tooth was painfully extracted by his wife's words. But that feeling had been replaced by another: by a desire not only for her not to triumph but for her to be paid back for her crime. He never acknowledged this feeling, but at the bottom of his heart he wanted her to suffer for having destroyed his peace of mind and his honor. And, running once more through the conditions of a duel, of a divorce and of a separation and once more rejecting them, Karenin persuaded himself that there was only one way out—to keep her, hiding from the world what had happened and taking all the steps needed to cut short her liaison, and above all —this he did not acknowledge to himself—to punish her. I must inform her of my decision that, after reviewing the painful position in which she has placed the family, any other solution would be worse for both parties than the *status quo* for the sake of appearances, which I should agree to observe, though under the strict condition that she carries out my wishes, that is, breaks off relations with her lover.

In support of this decision, after it was already definitely taken, a further weighty consideration came to Karenin's mind. It is only by such a decision that I can act in accordance with religion, he said to himself. It is only by such a decision that I shall not be casting off a guilty wife but shall be giving her a chance to improve herself and—however painful it may be for me—shall be able to devote a part of my energies to her improvement and redemption.

Even though Karenin knew he could never have any moral influence over his wife, and that nothing but lies would come of this whole attempt at redemption; even though while living through all those bitter moments he had never once thought of seeking guidance in religion, now, when his decision coincided with what seemed to him to be the demands of religion, this religious sanction of his decision gave him complete satisfaction and partial consolation. It made him happy to think that even in such an important crisis in his life no one would be in a position to say that he had not acted in accordance with the rules of the religion whose banner he had always borne aloft amidst the general coolness and indifference. In reflecting on the further details, Karenin did not even see why his relations with his wife should not be able to remain the same, almost, as before. He would of course never again be able to revive his esteem for her; but there was and could be no reason for him to disrupt his own life and suffer because of her being a bad and unfaithful wife. Yes, time will pass, time which mends everything, and the old conditions will be restored—Karenin said to himself—that is, they will be restored insofar as I shall not feel this disturbance any further in the course of my life. She ought to be unhappy, but I'm not to blame and so I cannot be unhappy.

## XIV

BY the time he arrived in Petersburg, Karenin had not only completely determined to carry out his decision, but he had composed in his head a letter he was going to write his wife. Going into the hall porter's room he glanced at the letters and papers that had come from the Ministry and ordered them to be brought to him in his study.

"Have the horses unharnessed and don't admit anyone," he said in answer to the hall porter's question, emphasizing the word "admit" with a certain satisfaction that indicated his pleasant frame of mind.

In his study Karenin paced back and forth twice, halted beside a huge writing desk, on which six candles had already been lighted by his valet who had preceded him, cracked his knuckles, sat down and arranged his writing things. Putting his elbows on the desk, he leaned his head to one side, thought for a moment, and began writing without a moment's hesitation. He wrote with no salutation and in French, using the plural pronoun "*vous*," not so chilly as the same form in Russian.

*In our last conversation I expressed to you my intention of informing you of my decision concerning the subject of that conversation. I have thought everything over carefully and am now writing you with the object of fulfilling that promise.*

*My decision is the following: Whatever your conduct may have been, I do not consider myself justified in breaking the bonds by which a higher power has united us. A family must not be destroyed at the caprice, the arbitrary discretion, or even the crime of one of the partners, and our life must go on as before. This is necessary for myself, for you, and for our son. I am quite confident that you have repented and are repenting the act that has served as the occasion of the present letter, and that you will co-operate with me in eradicating the cause of our discord and in forgetting the past. Otherwise you can imagine for yourself what awaits you and your son. I hope to discuss all this in greater detail face to face. Since the summer season is coming to an end I should like to ask you to move back to Petersburg as soon as possible: not later than Tuesday. All necessary preparations for your return will be made. I beg you to observe that I ascribe particular importance to the execution of this request of mine.*

A. KARENIN

*P.S. I am enclosing some money, which may be needed for expenses.*

He read the letter through and was satisfied with it, especially with his having remembered to enclose the money; there was not a cruel word or a reproach in it, but neither was it indulgent. The main thing was that it was a golden bridge for her to return by. After folding the letter, smoothing it out with a massive ivory paper knife and putting it into an envelope together with the money, he rang the bell with the satisfaction that handling his well-arranged writing things always gave him.

"Give this to the messenger, for him to bring to Madame Karenin tomorrow, in the country," he said and got up.

"Yes, Your Excellency. Would you like to have tea served in the study?"

Karenin ordered tea brought to the study, and toying with the paper knife sat down in an armchair, near which a lamp had been placed ready for him and a French book he had begun on the Eugubine Tables. Above the armchair hung a magnificiently painted, oval portrait of Anna in a gold frame, by a famous artist. Karenin looked at it. The impenetrable eyes gazed down at him ironically and insolently, as they had that last evening they had had it out together. The sight of the black lace on her head, wonderfully painted by the artist, the black hair and the beautiful white hand with the fourth finger covered with rings, made an unbearably insolent and challenging impression on him.

He looked at the portrait for a moment, then shuddered; his lips trembled and made a sound like "b-r-r," and he turned away. Sitting back in the armchair he hastily opened his book. He made an attempt to read, but was quite incapable of reviving the intense interest he had always had in the Eugubine Tables before. He was looking at the book and thinking about something else. He was not thinking about Anna but about some complication that had recently arisen in his official activity and now constituted the chief interest of his work. He felt that he had now penetrated into this complication more profoundly than ever before, and that what he could call without flattering himself a capital idea had occurred to him that ought to disentangle the whole business, promote his career, lay low his enemies and consequently be of the greatest value to the State. The moment the servant had left, after putting down the tea, Karenin got up and went over to his desk. He moved the portfolio of current business to the center of the desk, and with a scarcely perceptible smile of satisfaction took a pencil from the stand and plunged into a study he had sent for of the impending complicated affair.

The complication was this: Karenin's special trait as a statesman, the trait of character peculiar to him, which every prominent functionary has, the trait that together with his tenacious ambition, his reserve, his honesty, and his self-confidence had made his career, consisted of a disdain for red tape, a curtailment of correspondence, and as direct a relationship as possible to essentials and thriftiness. Now it had happened that the famous Commission of June 2 had had brought up before it the question of irrigation in the Zaraysk Province, which was under Karenin's Ministry and constituted a blatant example of wasteful expenditure and a red-tape approach to the problem. Karenin knew this was so. The question of the irrigation of the Zaraysk Province had been initiated by Karenin's predecessor. In fact an enormous amount of money had been and was being spent on this business, quite unproductively, too, and it was obvious that the whole business was bound to lead to nothing. Karenin had realized this at once when he had entered the service and had been about to try to lay his hands on the project; but in the beginning, when he had still felt unsure of himself, he realized that this was injudicious, since it would affect too many interests; later on, when he was preoccupied with other things, he simply forgot about it. This project, like all such projects, moved along of its own accord, by the force of inertia. (It supported a great many people, and one extremely moral and musical family in particular: all the daughters played stringed instruments. Karenin was acquainted with this family: he had stood godfather at the wedding of one of the older daughters.)

The raising of this question by a hostile Department was in Karenin's opinion dishonest, because there were projects in every Department that were not quite right and that in accordance with well-known rules of official etiquette no one ever brought up. But now, once the gauntlet had been thrown down before him, he was going to pick it up boldly: he would demand that a special commission be appointed to study and report on the labors of the Board of Irrigation of Zaraysk Province; but just because of this he was not going to make any concessions to these gentry. He was also going to demand the appointment of still another special commission to study the National Minorities situation. The National Minorities question had been accidentally raised in the June 2 Committee and energetically insisted on by Karenin as a matter of priority in view of the wretched condition of the National Minorities. In the Committee this question had led to some wrangling between several Ministries. The Ministry that was hostile to Karenin had argued that the position of the National Minorities was exceptionally prosperous and that the projected reorganization might destroy their prosperity, and that if there was anything wrong it was due only to the failure of Karenin's Ministry to carry out the measures prescribed by the law.

Now Karenin intended to insist: First of all, that a new commission be set up that would be intrusted with the investigation on the spot of the condition of the National Minorities; secondly, if it were to turn out that the position of the National Minorities was really what it appeared to be according to the official data in the hands of the Committee, that still another scientific commission be appointed to investigate the reasons for this deplorable state of affairs among the National Minorities from the following points of view: (a) politics, (b) administration, (c) economics, (d) ethnology, (e) material conditions, and (f) religion; thirdly, that the hostile Ministry be requested to make a full report of the measures it had taken during the preceding ten years to forestall the deplorable situation in which the

National Minorities now found themselves; and fourthly
and finally, that this Ministry be requested to give an
explanation of why it had acted directly counter to the sense
of the fundamental and organic law, Vol.—, Article 18, and
the footnote to Article 36, as was evident from Reports Nos.
17015 and 18308, dated respectively December 5, 1863 and
June 7, 1864, which had been submitted to the Committee.

A flush of animation covered Karenin's face as he swiftly
wrote out a summary of these ideas for his own use. Having
covered a sheet of paper he got up, rang the bell and sent a
note to his chief secretary asking him to get the necessary
references for him. He got up and as he walked about
the room he glanced at the portrait once again, frowned and
smiled contemptuously. He opened the book on the Eugubine
Tables again, his interest in it having revived once more,
and at eleven o'clock he went off to bed; when he now
recalled as he lay there what had happened with his wife
he no longer took such a gloomy view of it.

XV

THOUGH Anna had stubbornly and angrily contradicted
Vronsky when he had said that her position was impossible
and tried to persuade her to disclose everything to her
husband, at the bottom of her heart she considered her
position false and dishonest, and longed with all her heart
to change it. Though it was in a moment of agitation that
she had told Karenin everything on the way back with him
from the races, in spite of the pain it had given her she
was glad she had. After Karenin had left her she told herself that she was happy, that now everything would become
definite, and that at least there would be no more lying and
deceit. She had no doubt that now her position would be
cleared up for good. It might be bad, this new position of
hers, but it would be definite; there would be no vagueness
or falsehood. The pain she had caused her husband and
herself by saying those words would be compensated for
now, she thought, by everything being clarified. She saw
Vronsky that same evening, but did not tell him what had
taken place between her husband and herself, though that
was necessary if the situation were to be clarified.

When she woke up the next morning the first thing that
came to her mind was the words she had said to her husband;

these words seemed to her so dreadful that she could not understand now how she could have made up her mind to pronounce them, these coarse, strange words, and couldn't imagine what was going to come of it. But the words had been said, and Karenin had left without saying anything.

I saw Vronsky and didn't tell him, she thought: just at the moment he was going out I wanted to call him back and tell him, then I changed my mind, because it was so strange I hadn't told him the very first moment. Why did I want to tell him, but didn't?

And in answer to this question a burning flush of shame spread over her face. She realized what had held her back: she realized she had been ashamed. Her position, which the night before had seemed to be cleared up, now suddenly looked to her not only not cleared up, but hopeless. She had come to be in dread of disgrace, which she had never even thought of before. The moment she thought of what her husband would do the most terrifying thoughts came into her head. It occurred to her that his manager would come any moment to drive her out of the house, and that her shame would be proclaimed to the whole world. She asked herself where she would go when she was driven out of the house, and could not find an answer.

When she thought of Vronsky it appeared to her that he did not love her, that he was already beginning to find her burdensome, and that she could not offer herself to him; because of this she felt hostile to him. It seemed to her that the words she had spoken to her husband and kept going over and over again in her imagination had also been said to everyone, that everyone had heard them. She couldn't make up her mind to look into the eyes of the people she was living with. She couldn't make up her mind to call for the maid, still less to go down and see her son and his governess.

The maid, who had been listening at the door for some time, came in of her own accord. Anna looked into her eyes questioningly and blushed with alarm. The maid apologized for having come in and said she thought she had heard the bell. She had brought in a dress and a note. The note was from Betsy. Betsy was reminding her that Lisa Merkalov and the Baroness Stolz were coming to see Betsy that morning together with their admirers, Kaluzhsky and old Stremov, for a game of croquet. *"Do come, if only to contemplate it as a study in manners. I'll be expecting you,*" she wrote in conclusion.

Anna read the note and sighed heavily.

"I don't need anything, anything at all," she told Annushka, who was moving bottles and brushes around on the dressing table. "You can go, I'll dress at once and be right down. I don't need anything, not a thing."

Annushka went out; Anna did not begin dressing but kept sitting in the same position, her head and arms drooping. Every now and then her whole body would quiver, as though she wanted to make some gesture, say something or other, only to sink back lifeless again. She kept repeating over and over again: "Oh my God! My God!" But neither "my" nor "God" had any meaning for her. The idea of looking to religion for help in her position was for her, in spite of her never having had any doubts about religion, in which she had been brought up, just as alien as looking for help to Karenin himself. She knew beforehand that religion could help her only on condition that she renounce what constituted the whole meaning of her life. Not only was she miserable, but she was beginning to feel afraid because of her new state of mind, which she had never been in before. She felt that in her soul everything was beginning to look double, as objects may look double to tired eyes. Sometimes she had no idea of what it was that she was afraid of and what she wanted. Whether she was afraid of what had happened, and wanted that, or of what was going to happen, and wanted that, or just what it was that she wanted, she had no idea.

Oh, what am I doing! she said to herself, as she suddenly felt a pain in both sides of her head. She recovered, and saw she was clutching the hair on her temples with both hands, pulling it. She jumped up and began walking back and forth.

"Coffee is ready; Mademoiselle and Seryozha are waiting for you," said Annushka, who had come in again only to find Anna in the same position.

"Seryozha? What about Seryozha?" asked Anna, suddenly livening up as she remembered her son's existence for the first time that whole morning.

"I think he's done something naughty," Annushka answered smiling.

"What d'you mean, naughty?"

"You had some peaches lying about in the corner room; I think he ate one of them on the sly."

Suddenly the thought of her son pulled Anna out of her hopelessness. She recalled the partially sincere though largely exaggerated role of a mother living for her son that she had taken on during the past few years, and she joyfully felt that in her situation she had one prop that was independent of her relation to her husband and to Vronsky. That prop was her son. Whatever position she might fall into she could not desert her son. Let her husband put her to shame and drive her away, let Vronsky grow cold toward her and go on living an independent life of his own (she thought of him once again with bitter reproachfulness), she could not leave her son. Her life had a goal. And it was necessary to act, *act*, in order to secure her position with respect to her son, so that they would not take him away from her. She even had to act quickly, as quickly as possible, before they took him away. She must take her son and leave. That was the only thing she had to do now. She must calm down and get out of this agonizing situation. The idea of direct action bound up with her son, of leaving somewhere instantly together with him, served to calm her.

She dressed quickly, went downstairs, and with determined steps went into the drawing room where coffee was waiting for her together with Seryozha and his governess. Seryozha, all in white, was standing by the table under a mirror, doing something with some flowers he had brought in, his back and head bent and looking intensely concentrated, an expression that she was very familiar with and that made him resemble his father.

The governess was looking exceptionally stern. Seryozha cried out in a strident voice, as he often did, "Mama!" and stood still, undecided whether to throw down the flowers and go over to his mother to greet her, or to finish the garland and take it to her.

The governess greeted Anna and began telling her a long detailed story about Seryozha's misconduct, but Anna wasn't listening to her: she was thinking about whether she should take her along or not. No, I won't take her, she decided, I'll leave alone, together with my child.

"Yes, that's very wicked," said Anna, and taking her son by the shoulder she looked at him not with a severe but with a timid expression, which confused and gladdened the boy, and gave him a kiss. "Leave him with me," she said to the astonished governess, and she sat down at the breakfast table without letting go of his hand.

"Mama! I—I—didn't . . ." he said, trying to see by her expression what he had to expect on account of the peach.

"Seryozha," she said the moment the governess left the room, "that was wrong, but you're not going to do it again, are you? Do you love me?"

She felt tears coming into her eyes. How can I help loving him? she said to herself, gazing into his frightened yet delighted face. And how could he take sides with his father in order to punish me? How can he help but pity me?

The tears were already about to stream down her cheeks; to hide them she jumped up abruptly and almost ran out to the terrace.

After the thunderstorms of the past few days the weather had turned fine and cold. In the bright sun that filtered through the rain-soaked leaves the air was chilly.

She shivered, both because of the cold and because of her inner terror that had clutched with renewed violence in the fresh air.

"Off with you now, go to Mariette," she said to Seryozha, who had been about to follow her outside; she began pacing back and forth over the straw matting of the terrace. How can they help but forgive me? Won't they understand that there was no other way for it all to happen? she said to herself.

Stopping and looking out at the crown of an aspen tree trembling in the wind, with its soaked leaves brightly gleaming in the chilly sunshine, she realized that they would not forgive her, that from now on everything and everyone was going to be just as merciless as that sky, as those green trees. And once again she felt everything in her soul was becoming unfocused. No thinking, no thinking, she said to herself; I must make preparations. Where to? When? Whom should I take along? Yes—to Moscow by the evening train: Annushka and Seryozha, and only the barest necessities. But first I have to write them both.

She quickly went back into the house to her sitting room, sat down at the table and wrote to Karenin:

> *After what has happened I can no longer remain in your house. I am leaving and taking our son along. I don't know anything about law and so I don't know which one of the parents a child ought to be with: but I'm taking him along because without him I cannot go on living. Be generous—leave him with me.*

Up to now she had been writing quickly and naturally, but this appeal to his generosity, which she did not believe in, and the necessity of concluding the letter with something that would sound touching made her pause.

*As for my speaking about my guilt and my remorse, I am incapable of it, because—*

Once again she stopped, having lost the connection between her ideas. No, she said to herself, that's all that's needed. She tore up the letter and rewrote it, leaving out the reference to his generosity, and sealed it.

Another letter had to be written to Vronsky. *"I have told my husband,"* she started in, and then sat for a long time, incapable of continuing. That was so coarse, so unfeminine. Besides, what can I write him? she said to herself. Once again a flush of shame covered her face at the recollection of his serenity, and a feeling of vexation with him made her tear up the sheet with this phrase on it into tiny bits. There's no need for anything at all, she said to herself, and closing her blotting pad she went upstairs, told the governess and the servants that she was leaving that evening for Moscow, and set to work at once packing.

## XVI

IN every room of the country house porters, gardeners, and footmen were walking back and forth carrying things out. Cupboards and chests of drawers were open: someone rushed off to the shop twice for cord; the floor was strewn with newspapers. Two trunks, some bags, and some strapped-up rugs were carried out into the hall. The carriage and two hired cabs were waiting at the steps. Anna, who had forgotten her inner agitation in the labor of packing, was standing in front of the table in her sitting room packing her hand bag when Annushka drew her attention to the sound of a carriage driving up. Anna looked through the window and saw Karenin's messenger on the steps ringing the front door bell.

"Go and see what it's about," Anna said, serenely prepared for anything. She sat down in an armchair, her hands folded in her lap. The footman brought in a thick envelope addressed in Karenin's handwriting.

"The messenger has been ordered to bring back an answer," he said.

"Very well," she said, and the instant the servant left she ripped open the letter with trembling fingers. A packet of new banknotes in a paper band fell out. She disengaged the letter and began reading it from the end first. *"All necessary preparations for your return will be made. I ascribe particular importance to the execution of this request of mine,"* she read. She ran on further, backward, read it all, and once again read the whole letter from the beginning. When she had finished she was chilled through, and felt that a dreadful misfortune, altogether unexpected, had descended on her.

That morning she had repented of what she had told her husband, and all she had wanted was those words to have remained unsaid. Now this letter was assuming these words to be unsaid, and giving her what she had wanted. But this letter appeared to her to be more horrifying now than anything she could have imagined.

He's right, he's right! she muttered. Of course, he's always in the right, he's a Christian, he's magnanimous! Oh what a mean, horrible creature! And no one but me understands that or ever will; and I can't explain it. They'll say, What a religious, ethical, honorable, intelligent man! but they'll never see what I've seen. They don't know how he's been smothering my life for eight years, smothering everything in me that was alive, that he never once even thought of me as a living woman who needed to be loved. They don't know how he wounded me at every turn and was still satisfied with himself. Didn't I try, try with all my might, to find some justification for my life? Didn't I struggle to love him, and to love my child by the time it was no longer possible to love my husband? Then the time came when I realized that I could no longer deceive myself, that I was alive, that I wasn't to blame, that God made me so that I needed love and life. And now? If he killed me, if he killed him, I could bear it all, I'd forgive everything, but no! He—

How was it I didn't guess what he would do? He could only do what's natural to his mean character. He'll remain in the right, and as for me, who am already ruined, he'll drive me still further, still lower into ruin . . .

"You can imagine for yourself what awaits you and your son—" She remembered the words from the letter. He's threatening to take my son away; according to their stupid law that's probably possible. But don't I know why he's saying that? He doesn't believe in my love for my son either, or else he despises that feeling of mine (he was always sneering at it) he despises that feeling of mine, but he knows I won't abandon my child, that I can't abandon my child, that without my child there won't be any life for me even with the man I love, but that if I abandon my child and run away from him I would be behaving like the most shameful, the most contemptible of women —he knows I won't have the strength to do that.

"Our life must go on as before." She recalled another phrase from the letter. Even before that life was agony, and lately it's been horrible. Then what would it be now? He knows all that, he knows that I can't repent breathing, loving; he knows that nothing will come of it but lies and deceit; but he has to go on torturing me. I know him—I know he's like a fish in water in falsehood, he swims in it with delight. But no, I'm not going to give him that delight, I'll tear apart the web of lies he wants to entangle me in; come what may, anything is better than lies and deceit!

But how? My God! My God! Was any woman ever so unhappy as I?

"No, I'll tear it apart, tear it apart!" she cried out, jumping up and forcing back her tears. She went over to the writing desk to write him another letter. But at the bottom of her heart she was already feeling that she lacked the strength to tear apart anything, lacked the strength to escape from her former position, however false and dishonorable it was.

She sat down at the desk, but instead of writing she folded her arms on the desk, put her head on them and burst into tears, sobbing away with her bosom heaving, the way a child cries. She was crying because her dream of having her position clarified and defined was destroyed forever. She knew in advance that everything would stay just as it had been, and even be worse than before. She knew that the position that she enjoyed in society and that had seemed to her so trivial that morning, was precious to her, and that she would not have the strength to change it for the shameful position of a woman who has left her husband and child to join her lover; that no matter how she tried she would never be stronger than herself. She would never experience the freedom of love but would always remain a criminal wife threatened with exposure at every moment, who was deceiving her husband for the sake of a shameful liaison with a man who was alien to her and independent, and with whom she could not live a life together. She knew that this was what was going to happen; at the same time it was so horrible that she could not even imagine to herself how it would end. And she wept without restraint, like a child that has been punished.

The sound of the footman's steps forced her to recover herself; hiding her face she pretended to be writing.

"The messenger is asking for the reply," the footman announced.

"The reply? Yes," said Anna, "let him wait, I'll ring."

What can I do? she thought. What can I decide by myself? What do I know? What do I want? What do I love?

Again she had the feeling that things were beginning to lose their focus in her soul. She was frightened once again by this feeling and clutched at the first pretext for action that presented itself to her and that could distract her from thoughts about herself.

I must see Alexis (this was how she referred to Vronsky in her thoughts), he's the only one who can tell me what I ought to do. I'll go to Betsy's, perhaps I'll see him there, she said to herself, having completely forgotten that only the evening before, when she had told him she wasn't going there he had said that in that case he wouldn't go either. She went over to the desk and wrote her husband: *"I have received your letter. A."* She rang, and gave the note to the footman.

"We're not going," she said to Annushka, who had just come in.

"Not going at all?"

"No, but don't unpack till tomorrow, and let the carriage stay there. I'm going to the Princess's."

"What dress shall I lay out?"

## XVII

The croquet party Princess Tverskoy had invited Anna to was to consist of two ladies and their admirers. These two ladies were the chief representatives of a select new Petersburg coterie, which in imitation of some imitation of something called itself "the seven wonders of the world." While the coterie these ladies belonged to was, to be sure, higher than that frequented by Anna, it was completely hostile to it. Aside from which old Stremov, one of the influential persons in Petersburg and Lisa Merkalov's admirer, was one of Karenin's enemies in the service. For all these reasons

Anna did not want to go, and it was this refusal of hers that Betsy had been referring to in her note. But now Anna decided to go in the hope of seeing Vronsky.

Anna arrived at Betsy's ahead of the other guests.

Just as she was going in, Vronsky's footman, with side whiskers combed out so that he looked like a Gentleman of the Bedchamber, was also entering. He stopped in the doorway and, taking off his cap, let her pass. Anna recognized him, and it was only then that she recalled what Vronsky had said to her the evening before about his not coming. This was probably why he was sending a note.

As she took off her outdoor things in the hall she heard the footman, who even pronounced his *r*'s like a Gentleman of the Bedchamber, say "From the Count to the Princess," as he handed over the note.

She wanted to ask him where his master was; she wanted to turn back and send him a letter, for him to come to see her or for herself to go to his place. But both things were out of the question: she could already hear her arrival being announced by the ringing of bells ahead of her, and Betsy's footman was already standing half-turned toward her in the doorway, waiting for her to enter the inner rooms.

"The Princess is in the garden; she will be informed at once. Would Madame care to go into the garden?" said another footman in the next room.

Her state of indecision and uncertainty was still the same as at home; it was even worse, since it was impossible to do anything, impossible to see Vronsky, and she had to stay here in company that was alien to her, contrary to her mood; but she was wearing a dress that she knew suited her: she was not alone, but surrounded by this habitual setting of luxurious idleness, and she felt more at ease here than at home. She did not have to think of what she had to do; everything took place of its own accord. When she met Betsy coming toward her, strikingly elegant in a white dress, Anna smiled at her as usual. Betsy was accompanied by Tushkevich and a young girl who was a relative of hers and who, to the great delight of her provincial parents, was spending the summer with the famous Princess.

There was probably something odd about Anna; Betsy commented on it.

"I slept badly," answered Anna, glancing at the footman coming toward them who she supposed was carrying Vronsky's note.

"I'm so glad you've come," said Betsy. "I'm tired; I was just longing to have a cup of tea before the others got here. But won't you take Masha to the croquet ground," she said, turning to Tushkevich, "and try it out? Where the grass is cut. You and I can have a heart-to-heart talk over tea, we'll have a cozy chat, won't we?" she said with a smile to Anna, in English, pressing the hand Anna was holding her sunshade with.

"Especially since I can't stay with you long, I absolutely must go over to see old Countess Vrede, I promised her ages ago," said Anna, for whom lying, which was contrary to her nature, was not only simple and natural for her in society but even gave her pleasure.

Just why she had said this, which a second before she hadn't even thought of, she would have been quite incapable of explaining. She said it for the simple reason that since Vronsky was not going to be there she had to insure her own freedom and try to see him somehow. But just why she happened to mention the aging Countess Vrede, an old Lady in Waiting to whom she owed the same sort of visit she owed many others, she would have been unable to explain, while at the same time, as it turned out later, if she had been thinking up the most cunning means of arranging to see Vronsky she couldn't have thought of anything better.

"No, I'm not going to let you go for anything," replied Betsy, gazing intently into Anna's face. "Really, I should be hurt if I were not so fond of you. It's just as though you were afraid of being compromised by my society. Please let us have our tea in the little drawing room," she said to the footman, half-closing her eyes as she always did when speaking to a footman. She took the note from him and read it. "Alexis has played us a mean trick," she said in French. "He writes that he can't come," she added in the most natural simple tone of voice, as though it could never even have entered her head that Vronsky had any interest for Anna other than as a croquet player.

Anna knew Betsy knew everything, but when she heard her mention Vronsky in her presence she was always persuaded for a moment that she didn't know anything.

"Ah!" said Anna indifferently, as though scarcely interested, and continued to smile. "How could your society compromise anyone?" This playing with words, this hiding of secrets, had immense charm for Anna as indeed it does for all women. And it was not the need for hiding anything or the purpose of the hiding that she found fascinating, but the process itself. "I can't be more Catholic than the Pope," she said. "Stremov and Lisa Merkalov—the cream of the cream of society! Besides, they're received everywhere, and *I*"—she laid special stress on the *I*—"I've never been strict or intolerant. I simply don't have the time."

"No, but perhaps you don't care to meet Stremov? Let him and your husband break lances in committee, it's no concern of ours. But in society he's the most agreeable man I know, and a passionate croquet player. You'll soon see. And in spite of his ludicrous position as a lovesick suitor of Lisa's, at his age, you simply must see how he carries this ludicrous position off! He's terribly sweet. D'you know Sappho Stolz? Absolutely the latest thing."

Betsy kept on saying all this, but meanwhile Anna saw by her gay, intelligent look that she understood her situation to some extent and was contriving something. They were in a small sitting room.

"But I shall have to write Alexis," said Betsy; she sat down at a table, jotted down a few lines, and put the paper in an envelope. "I'm writing to ask him for dinner; I've one woman too many. Just take a look and see whether it's convincing. Forgive me now, I must leave you for a moment. Would you just seal the envelope and send it?" she said from the doorway, "there are some instructions I must give."

Without thinking for an instant Anna sat down at the table with Betsy's letter and without reading it added beneath it: *"I must see you. Come to Vrede's garden; I'll be there at six o'clock."* She sealed it; Betsy came back and sent it off in her presence.

As a matter of fact the two women started up a "cozy chat," just as Betsy had promised before the other guests arrived, over their tea, which was brought to them in the cool little drawing room on a little tea-table. They went over everyone who was expected; the conversation settled on Lisa Merkalov.

"She's very sweet, I've always liked her," said Anna.

"You must like her; she raves about you. She came to see me yesterday after the races and was simply in despair at not finding you. She says that you're a real heroine in a novel, and that if she were a man she would have committed a thousand follies for your sake. Stremov tells her that that's what she does in any case."

"But tell me, please, there's something I've never been

able to understand," said Anna, after a short silence, and in
a tone of voice that indicated clearly that she wasn't asking
an idle question, but one that was more important for her
than it should have been: "Tell me please, just what is her
relationship with Prince Kaluzhsky, the one they call Mishka?
I've hardly ever met them. Just what is it between them?"

Betsy's eyes twinkled; she looked at Anna keenly.

"It's a new style," she said. "They've all taken it up.
They've kicked over the traces, though there are ways and
ways of doing that."

"Yes, but what are in fact her relations with Kaluzhsky?"

Betsy unexpectedly broke into a merry unrestrained peal
of laughter, which seldom happened with her.

"Now you're taking over Princess Myagky's territory.
That's a question for an *enfant terrible!*" Betsy, obviously
trying to hold herself in but unable to, broke out in the
infectious laughter peculiar to people who seldom laugh.
"You'll have to ask them," she said, through tears of
laughter.

"Now you're laughing," said Anna, who couldn't help also
being infected by her laughter, "but I've never been able
to understand it. I don't understand the role of the husband in it all."

"The husband? Lisa Merkalov's husband carries her rugs
around after her and is always at her service. And as for
anything further that may be going on no one wants to
know about it. You know that in good society there are
even certain details of the toilette that are not talked about
or thought of. That's how this is too."

"Are you going to the Rolandaki party?" asked Anna, to
change the subject.

"I don't think so," Betsy answered; without looking at her
friend she began carefully pouring the aromatic tea into
the little translucent cups. Moving the cup over to Anna she
got out a cigarette, put it into a silver holder and lighted it.

"You see, I'm in a fortunate position," she began holding
the cup and not laughing now at all. "I understand you and
I understand Lisa. Lisa is one of those naïve people who
when they're children have no idea of what's good or what's
bad. At any rate she didn't understand it when she was
very young. Now she knows that this incomprehension of
hers suits her. It may be that now she deliberately fails to
understand," Betsy said with a subtle smile. "But in any
case it suits her. Don't you see, it's possible to look at one

and the same thing tragically, and turn into a torment, or look at it simply and even gaily. It may be that you're inclined to look at things too tragically."

"How I should long to know others as I know myself," said Anna seriously and pensively. "Am I worse than others, or better? I think I'm worse."

"An *enfant terrible*, an *enfant terrible*," repeated Betsy. "But here they come."

## XVIII

FOOTSTEPS and a man's voice were heard, then a woman's voice and laughter; these were followed by the expected visitors coming in: Sappho Stolz and a young man radiant with a superabundance of health, the so-called Vaska. It was obvious that he had been flourishing on a diet of rare beefsteak, truffles, and Burgundy. Vaska bowed to the ladies and looked at them, but only for a second. He came into the drawing room after Sappho and once there walked behind her as though he were tied to her; he kept his glittering eyes glued to her as though he wanted to devour her. Sappho Stolz was a blonde with black eyes. She came in with short, brisk steps, on high-heeled slippers, and shook hands with the women like a man.

Anna had never met this new celebrity before, and she was struck by her beauty, by the extravagance of her dress, and by the boldness of her manners. Her delicately gilded hair, both false and her own, was built up into such a superstructure that her head was just as large as her shapely, well-developed and extremely exposed bust. Her stride was so impetuous that the shape of her knees and her upper thighs stood out beneath her dress at each step, and the question involuntarily rose to one's mind just where, in this piled-up swaying mountain of material in back, her own real, small and shapely body, which was so exposed above and so hidden behind and below, actually ended.

Betsy hastened to introduce her to Anna.

"Just imagine! We very nearly ran over two soldiers," she began at once, twinkling and smiling as she threw back her train which she had jerked too far over to one side. "I was driving with Vaska—oh, of course, you don't know each other." And she introduced the young man by his surname, blushing as she burst out laughing over her mistake, that is, at her having referred to him as Vaska in the presence of a stranger.

Vaska bowed to Anna once again, but said nothing to her. He turned to Sappho: "You've lost the bet, we were the first ones to arrive. You must pay up," he said smiling.

Sappho laughed still more gaily. "But not now," she said. "It doesn't matter at all, I'll get it later."

"All right, all right. Oh yes!" she said suddenly, turning to Betsy. "But how silly of me! I'd completely forgotten— I've brought along a visitor. Here he is!"

But the unexpected young visitor whom Sappho had brought along and forgotten all about was such an important personage that in spite of his youth both women stood up to be introduced to him.

He was Sappho's new admirer. Like Vaska he dogged her footsteps.

A moment later Prince Kaluzhsky arrived, as well as Lisa Merkalov together with Stremov. Lisa Merkalov was a thin brunette with a lazy Oriental cast of face and beautiful eyes that everyone referred to as unfathomable. The style of her dark costume (which Anna instantly noticed and appreciated) was in complete harmony with her beauty. She was just as soft and languid as Sappho was abrupt and concentrated.

But to Anna's taste she was far more attractive. In speaking about her to Anna, Betsy had said she had adopted the pose of an ingenuous child, but when Anna saw her she felt this was wrong. She really was an ingenuous and spoiled, though sweet and irresponsible woman. Her manner was just the same as Sappho's, to be sure; she was followed about just as Sappho was by two admirers, one young and one old, who seemed stitched to her and kept devouring her with their eyes; but there was something about her that was superior to everything that surrounded her—she had all the brilliance of a real diamond among bits of glass. This brilliance shone out of her beautiful eyes, which really were unfathomable. The weary yet passionate gaze of these eyes of hers, encircled by dark rings, was striking because of its utter honesty. After looking into these eyes it seemed to everyone that they knew her through and through, and knowing her could not help loving her. When she saw Anna her whole face suddenly lit up with a joyful smile.

"Oh, how happy I am to see you!" she said, going over to her. "At the races yesterday I was just trying to get over to you, but you had left. Yesterday especially, I had been longing to see you. It was dreadful, wasn't it?" she said, looking at Anna with eyes that seemed to reveal her whole soul.

"Yes, I hadn't the least idea it was so exciting," said Anna, blushing.

Everyone got up just then to go into the garden.

"I'm not coming," said Lisa, smiling and sitting down beside Anna. "Are you staying here too? Really, who wants to play crouquet!"

"Oh, I like it," said Anna.

"Now how do you manage not to get bored? Just looking at you is enough to make anyone cheerful. You're full of life, while I always feel bored."

"But how can you be bored? Yours is the gayest circle in Petersburg," said Anna.

"It may be that the people we don't see are still more bored; though we're not gay, certainly I'm not, but dreadfully, dreadfully bored."

Sappho lighted a cigarette and went out into the garden with the two young men. Betsy and Stremov stayed at the tea-table.

"What d'you mean, bored?" said Betsy. "Sappho says they all couldn't have been gayer at your house yesterday."

"Sheer anguish!" said Lisa. "After the races we all went back to my place. The same people, over and over again! And the same thing, over and over! We spent the whole evening lolling about on sofas. What's gay about that? No really, how *do* you manage not to be bored?" she said to Anna again. "All one has to do is look at you to see a woman who can be happy or unhappy—but never bored. Show me how you do it!"

"I don't do anything," Anna replied, blushing at these searching questions.

"Now that's the best way," Stremov put in.

He was a man of about fifty, turning gray; he was still fresh, very plain, but with an intelligent face full of character. Lisa was a niece of his wife's, and he spent all his free time with her. Though an enemy of Karenin's in the service, as an intelligent man of the world he made a special effort when he met Anna to be particularly amiable to her as his enemy's wife.

" 'Don't do anything,' " he repeated, with a subtle smile. "That's the best method. I've been telling you for a long time," he said to Lisa, "that in order to avoid being bored all you have to do is not to think you're going to be bored. It's just the same as not being afraid you won't be able to fall asleep if what you're afraid of is sleeplessness. That's just what Madame Karenin has been saying."

"I should be delighted if I had said that," said Anna, smiling, "because it's not only clever, it's the truth."

"No, but you tell us—why is it impossible to sleep and impossible not to be bored?" said Lisa.

"In order to fall asleep you have to work, and to feel gay you have to work, too."

"But why should I work when no one needs my work? I'm incapable of deliberately pretending to, and I don't want to."

"You're incorrigible," said Stremov without looking at her, and turned to Anna again.

Since he met Anna rarely there was nothing he could say to her but commonplaces, but he voiced these commonplaces—about when she was going to Petersburg, about how fond of her Countess Lydia was—with an expression indicating that he longed wholeheartedly to please her, to demonstrate his respect and even more.

Tushkevich came in to say everyone was waiting for the croquet players.

"No, please, don't go!" Lisa begged, when she heard Anna was leaving. Stremov joined in.

"It's too great a contrast to go from the company here to old Countess Vrede's," he said. "Besides, for her you'll simply be an occasion for talking scandal, whereas here you only give rise to the highest feelings of exactly the opposite kind," he said to her.

For a moment Anna wavered, undecided. The flattering remarks of this clever man's, the naïve and childlike affection Lisa Merkalov showed her, the whole of this social setting she was so used to—it was all so easy for her here, while what was awaiting her was so difficult that for a moment she was undecided whether to stay and put off still further the painful moment of explanation. But when she recalled what was waiting for her alone at home, if she did not make some decision, and recalled her gesture of clutching her hair in both hands, which even in recollection filled her with horror, she said good-by and left.

## XIX

VRONSKY, in spite of his apparently frivolous social life, was a man who hated disorder. While still in the Corps of Pages in his early youth he had once been humiliated by a refusal of a loan he had asked for when hard up, and ever since then he had never again put himself in such a position.

In order to keep his affairs going in an orderly way he would shut himself up alone some five times a year, more or less frequently, depending on circumstances, and clear up all his affairs. He called this having a wash-up or doing the laundry.

He woke up late the morning after the races; without shaving or taking a bath he put on a linen tunic and distributing money, bills, and letters on the table set to work. When Petritsky, who knew that he was generally bad tempered at this time, woke up and saw his friend at the desk, he dressed quietly and went out without disturbing him.

Every man who is familiar to the smallest detail with the full complexity of his own circumstances involuntarily imagines that the complexity of these circumstances and the difficulty of clearing them up is merely a personal, accidental peculiarity of his own; it never occurs to him that others are steeped in the same complexity as himself. So it seemed to Vronsky. He thought, not without pride at heart and not without reason, that anyone else would long since have gotten into a mess and been forced to behave badly if he had been in a situation that was as difficult. He felt that this was just the time it was necessary to look into and clarify his position in order to avoid getting into a mess.

The first thing he set about, as the easiest, was his financial position. Having jotted down on a small sheet of notepaper everything he owed, in his small handwriting, he added it up and found that he owed 17,000 rubles, with a few hundred over that he struck out for the sake of clarity. He counted his money, plus what he had in his bankbook, and found he had left 1800 rubles, while there was nothing to anticipate before the new year. He read over the list of debts and divided them into three catagories, which he listed separately. The first category contained the debts that had to be paid at once, or at any rate that money had to be kept in readiness for so that there could not be a moment's hesitation

in paying them on demand. Such debts amounted to around
4000 rubles: 1500 for the horse, 2500 as security for
Venyovsky, a young friend of his who had lost that much to
a sharper in Vronsky's presence. Vronsky had wanted to
pay out the money then and there (he had it on him),
but Venyovsky and Yashvin insisted that they would pay
and not Vronsky, who had not even been playing. This was all
very well, but Vronsky knew that in this filthy business,
even though his only connection with it had been his verbal
guarantee for Venyovsky, he had to have 2500 rubles on
hand to fling at the sharper and have no further conversation with him. Thus, for this first and most important category he had to have 4000 rubles.

The second list contained less important debts, some
8000 rubles. These were chiefly debts to the race-course
stables, the oats and hay dealer, the English trainer, the sad-
dler, and so on. On these debts he also had to pay out some
2000 in order to feel quite at ease. The last category—
debts to shops, hotels, and the tailor—was one there was
no need to bother about. So all he needed was at least
6000 for current expenses, and he had only 1800. For a man
who had 100,000 rubles a year, which is what everyone set
Vronsky's fortune at, it would have seemed that such debts
could not have been troublesome, but the point was that
he was far from having this 100,000. His father's vast fortune, which alone had brought in as much as 200,000 a year,
had not been divided between the brothers. When his older
brother, who had had a pile of debts, had married Princess
Varya Chirkov, the daughter of a penniless Decembrist,
Vronsky had given up to his older brother his entire income from his father's fortune, reserving for himself only
25,000 a year. At that time Vronsky had told his brother
that that would be enough money for him until he got
married, which in all probability would never happen. His
brother, who was in command of one of the most expensive
regiments and had only just married, could not help but
accept this gift. Their mother, who had her own private
fortune, gave Vronsky another 20,000 every year in addition to the 25,000 agreed on, and he spent it all. Lately his
mother, having quarreled with him because of his love
affair and his leaving Moscow, had stopped sending him
this money. Because of all this Vronsky, who had already
fallen into the habit of living on 45,000 and had only
received 25,000 this year, was now in difficulties. He could

not ask his mother for money in order to get out of them.

Her last letter, which he had received the day before, had particularly irritated him because of the way it hinted at her readiness to help achieve success in society and in his career, but not in a life that scandalized all of good society. This wish of his mother's to bribe him offended him to the depths of his soul and made him feel still colder toward her. But he could not go back on the generous promise he had made, even though he now felt, dimly foreseeing some consequences of his affair with Anna, that this generous promise had been given light-mindedly, and that though unmarried he might need the whole 100,000 a year. But it was impossible to go back on it: he had only to think of Varya, his brother's wife, who was so wonderful and sweet, and recall how she kept reminding him at every possible opportunity that she had never forgotten his generosity and appreciated it, to realize the impossibility of taking back what he had given. It was as impossible as striking a woman, stealing, or lying. There was only one possible and obligatory way out, which Vronsky decided on without a moment's hesitation: to borrow 10,000 rubles from a moneylender, which there would be difficulty about, cut down on his debts in general, and sell his race horses. After deciding this he wrote a note at once to Rolandaki, who had offered more than once to buy his horses. Then he sent for the English trainer and for the moneylender, and allocated the money he had among the various bills. When he had finished all this business he wrote a chilly, sharp answer to his mother's letter. Then, getting three of Anna's notes out of his wallet, he reread and burned them, and, recalling the conversation he had had with her the night before, sank into a reverie.

## XX

VRONSKY'S life was especially happy because he had a code of principles that defined beyond question everything that ought and ought not to be done. This code of rules took up a very small circle of contingencies, but to make up for it the rules were beyond discussion, and Vronsky, who never went outside this circle, never hesitated for a moment to do what had to be done. These rules laid it down beyond question that a card sharper had to be paid, while a tailor did not, that you must not lie to men, but that you could to women, that you could not deceive anyone, but that you could a husband, that you could not forgive insults but that you could insult others, and so on. All these rules might be irrational and bad, but they were beyond question; in carrying them out Vronsky felt that he was at ease and could carry his head high. It was only recently, because of his relations with Anna, that he had begun to feel that his code of rules did not completely cover all situations, and that difficulties and doubts would be coming up in the future for which he would find no guiding thread at all.

His present relationship to Anna and to her husband was simple and clear for him. It was simply and precisely defined in the code of rules he was guided by.

She was a respectable woman who had given him her love, and he loved her; therefore she was for him a woman who was worthy of just as much respect as a legitimate wife and even more. He would have let his hand be cut off before allowing himself not only to insult her by a word or a hint, but not to show her all the respect any woman could look for.

His relationship toward society was also clear. Everyone might know or suspect what was going on, but no one ought to dare speak about it. Otherwise he was ready to force the speaker to be silent and to respect the nonexistent honor of the woman he loved.

His relationship toward Karenin was clearest of all. From the moment Anna gave Vronsky her love he had regarded only his own claim on her as unassailable. Her husband was merely a superfluous hindrance. There was no doubt of his being in a pitiable situation, but what could be done about it? The only thing the husband had a right to was to demand satisfaction, weapon in hand, and from the very first moment on Vronsky had been ready for this.

But lately new inner relationships between himself and her had been appearing that frightened Vronsky by their vagueness. Only the night before she had told him she was pregnant. And he felt that this news, and what she expected of him, demanded something that was not completely defined by the code of rules his life was guided by. As a matter of fact he had been taken by surprise, and the first moment she had told him about her condition his heart had prompted him to ask her to leave her husband. He had said this, but having thought it over he now saw clearly that it would be better to manage without that; yet while saying this to himself he felt apprehensive—mightn't it be wrong?

If I said she should leave her husband that meant uniting herself with me. Am I ready for that? How can I take her away now, when I have no money? Suppose I could manage to—But how can I take her away when I'm in the service? If I said that I must be ready for it, that is, I'd have to have money and leave the service.

He pondered. The question of leaving the service or not led him to another, secret interest of his, which only he knew of and which was almost the chief though secret interest of his whole life.

Ambition was his old dream in childhood and youth, a dream that he did not acknowledge to himself but that was so powerful that even now the passion was there to contend with his love. The first steps he had taken in society and in the service had been successful, but two years before he had made a gross blunder. In a desire to display his independence and to be promoted, he had refused a post that had been offered him, hoping that this refusal would enhance his value; but it turned out that he had been too bold and he was passed over. Having willy-nilly put himself in the position of an independent man he carried it off, behaving with great subtlety and intelligence, as though he were not angry with anyone, had not been offended by anyone, and only wished to be left in peace since he was having a good time. Actually though, he had stopped having a good time even the year before, when he had left for Moscow. He felt that this independence on the part of a man who could do everything but did not want anything, was already beginning to pall, that many people were beginning to think that he could not even do anything but be an honest good-natured fellow. His affair with Anna, which had created such an uproar and attracted general attention, had for a while, by giving him a new glamour, stilled the worm of ambition gnawing at him, but a week before this worm had reawaked with renewed force. Serpukhovskoy, a childhood playmate, of the same milieu and same society, and a comrade of his in the Corps of Pages who had finished at the same time as himself and whom he had always vied with in the classroom, at gymnastics, in playing pranks, and in dreams of glory, had just returned from Central Asia, where he had been promoted twice and won a distinction seldom awarded to a general so young.

As soon as he returned to Petersburg he began being talked about as a rising star of the first magnitude. Though a messmate of Vronsky's and the same age, he was a general expecting an appointment that might influence the course of state affairs, while Vronsky, though independent, brilliant, and the lover of a beautiful woman, was merely a cavalry captain who was being allowed to remain as independent as he pleased.

Of course I'm not envious of Serpukhovskoy, I couldn't be, thought Vronsky, but his advancement shows me that if a man like me watches for a chance his career can be made very quickly. Three years ago his position was the same as mine. If I resign I'll be burning my boats; if I stay in the service I shan't be losing anything. She herself said she didn't want to change her situation, and since I have her love I can't envy Serpukhovskoy.

Slowly twisting his mustache he got up from the table and began pacing up and down the room. His eyes were shining with a special brightness; he felt himself to be in that resolute, serene, and joyful state of mind that always came over him after he had put things in order. Everything was pure and clear, as it always had been before after a stock-taking. He shaved, took a cold bath, dressed, and went out.

## XXI

I'VE come to fetch you. Your laundry's taken a long time today," said Petritsky. "Is it finished?"

"Finished," Vronsky replied, laughing with his eyes alone and twisting the tips of his mustache as cautiously as though after the order that had been imposed on his affairs any overbold or rapid movement might upset it.

"Afterward you always look as though you'd just stepped out of a bath," said Petritsky. "I've just come from Gritsky's" —their name for their colonel—"they're expecting you."

Vronsky, his thoughts elsewhere, looked at his friend without answering.

"Is that where the music is?" he said, listening to the familiar sounds that were floating over to him of brass instruments playing polkas and waltzes. "Why the celebration?"

"Serpukhovskoy's arrived."

"Ah!" said Vronsky. "I had no idea."

The smile in his eyes gleamed still brighter.

Once he had decided in his own mind that he was happy in his love and that he was going to sacrifice his ambition to it—or at any rate had assumed this role—Vronsky could no longer feel either any jealousy of Serpukhovskoy or any annoyance with him for not having called on him first when he came to see the regiment. Serpukhovskoy was a good friend and he looked forward to seeing him.

"I'm delighted!"

Dyomin, the colonel, had taken a large country house. Everyone was gathered together on the spacious lower balcony. The first thing that leaped to Vronsky's eye in the courtyard was a group of singers in white linen coats standing beside a keg of vodka, and the hale, jovial figure of the colonel surrounded by officers; he had gone out onto the top step of the balcony and in a loud voice that rose above the music (one of Offenbach's quadrilles) was giving orders and gesticulating at some soldiers standing on one side. A group of the men, a master sergeant and a few non-commissioned officers, went up to the balcony together with Vronsky. The colonel went back to the table, then out again onto the steps with a champagne glass, and announced a toast: "To the health of our old comrade, the gallant General Prince Serpukhovskoy! Hurrah!"

Serpukhovskoy, holding a glass and also smiling, came out after the colonel.

"You keep getting younger, Bondarenko," he said turning to a red-cheeked, smart-looking sergeant, serving his second term, who was standing directly in front of him.

Vronsky had not seen Serpukhovskoy for three years. He was more mature and had grown whiskers, but he was still just as well built; he was striking not so much by his looks as by the gentleness and nobility of his face and bearing. The only change Vronsky noticed in him was that serene unflagging radiance that settles on the faces of people who are successful and are sure of everyone's acknowledging it. Vronsky was familiar with this radiance and noticed it instantly in Serpukhovskoy.

As he went down the stairs Serpukhovskoy saw Vronsky. A smile of joy lit up his face; he jerked his head backward and raised his glass to salute Vronsky, showing by this gesture that he could not help going first to the sergeant, who had drawn himself up and was already puckering his lips for a kiss.

"So there he is!" cried the colonel. "And Yashvin told me you were in your black mood."

Serpukhovskoy kissed the sprightly sergeant on his moist, fresh lips, and wiping his mouth with a handkerchief went over to Vronsky.

"Well, I am delighted!" he said, pressing his hand and taking him aside.

"You look after him!" the colonel shouted to Yashvin, nodding at Vronsky, and went below to the soldiers.

"Why weren't you at the races yesterday? I expected to see you there," said Vronsky, surveying Serpukhovskoy.

"I got there late. Excuse me," he added, turning to his adjutant. "Please have this divided up among the men equally, whatever it comes to."

He hurriedly took three one-hundred-ruble notes out of his wallet and blushed.

"Vronsky! D'you want something to eat or drink?" asked Yashvin. "Hey, get the Count something to eat! And here, drink this!"

The carousing at the colonel's went on for some time.

Everyone drank a great deal. Serpukhovskoy was tossed up and caught several times. Then the colonel was tossed and caught. Then the colonel went into a dance with Petritsky, to the accompaniment of the singers. Then the colonel, by now weakening somewhat, sat down on a bench in the courtyard and began demonstrating to Yashvin Russia's superiority to Prussia, especially in the cavalry charge, and the revelry subsided for a moment. Serpukhovskoy went inside to the bathroom to wash his hands, and found Vronsky there drenching his head with water. He had taken off his coat and put his hairy red neck under the washstand tap, and was dousing it and his head with his hands. After washing Vronsky sat down beside Serpukhovskoy, right there on a little sofa, and a conversation started up that was of great interest to them both.

"I've been hearing all about you from my wife," said Serpukhovskoy. "I'm glad you've been seeing her so often."

"She's a friend of Varya's, and they're the only women in Petersburg I find it a pleasure to see," replied Vronsky with a smile. He was smiling because he foresaw the theme the conversation was going to turn to, and was pleased.

"The only ones?" asked Serpukhovskoy, smiling.

"And I kept hearing about you, but not only from your wife," said Vronsky, forbidding this allusion by a severe look. "I was delighted by your success, but not surprised in the least. For that matter I'd been expecting more."

Serpukhovskoy smiled. He was plainly pleased by this opinion of himself and thought it unnecessary to conceal it.

"I, on the contrary—I admit it frankly—expected less. But I'm pleased, very pleased indeed. I'm ambitious, it's a weakness of mine and I admit it."

"Perhaps you wouldn't admit it if you hadn't been successful," said Vronsky.

"I don't think so," said Serpukhovskoy, smiling again. "I'm not saying life wouldn't be worth living without it, but it would be boring. Of course I may be mistaken, but it seems to me that I have some ability in the field of activity I chose, and that if I had power in my hands, whatever it was, it would be better than in the hands of a great many people I know," said Serpukhovskoy radiantly aware of his own success. "That's why the closer I am to it the more pleased I am."

"That may be so for you, but not for everyone. I thought the same thing, but here I am alive and I don't think it's worth living just for that," said Vronsky.

"There it comes!" said Serpukhovskoy, laughing. "I began by saying I'd heard about you and about your turning down that promotion . . . Of course I was all for you. But there's a way of doing everything; I think what you did was right, but you didn't do it the way you should have."

"What's done is done; you know I never go back on what I've done. Besides, I'm doing splendidly."

"Splendidly—for a while. But you won't stay satisfied with that. I wouldn't say this to your brother, he's a sweet child, just like this host of ours here. There he is now!" he added, cocking an ear at a shout of *Hurrah!*—"He's always merry, but that's not what would keep you satisfied."

"I'm not saying it would."

"That's not the only thing. People like you are needed."

"By whom?"

"By whom? By society. Russia needs men, needs a party, or else everything will go and is going to the dogs."

"What d'you mean? Bertenev's Party? To stand off the Russian Communists?"

"No," said Serpukhovskoy, frowning with annoyance at being suspected of such stupidity. "That's all just nonsense. That's always been and always will be. There are no Communists. But intriguers have always found it necessary to think up some pernicious, dangerous party. It's an old trick. No, what's needed is a strong party made up of independents like you and me."

"But why?" Vronsky named a few people in power. "Now why aren't they independent?"

"Simply because they haven't got or weren't born with independent means; they had no names, they weren't born close to the sun as we were. They can be bought, either by money or by flattery. To stay in power they have to think up some policy. And they put out some idea or other, some policy that they don't believe in themselves and that may be harmful; the whole policy is just a way of keeping their government quarters and a salary. It's as simple as that, if you take a look at their cards. I may be worse than they are, or more stupid, though I don't see why I should be worse, but you and I definitely have one important advantage—we're harder to buy. People like that are needed now more than ever."

Vronsky listened carefully, but he was not absorbed so much by the content of what Serpukhovskoy was saying as by his attitude to the matter; Serpukhovskoy was already thinking of contending with the regime, in which he had his own likes and dislikes, while Vronsky's interests in the service did not go beyond his squadron. Vronsky also realized how powerful Serpukhovskoy might become through his incontestable capacity for thinking things through and understanding them, through his intellect and the talent he had for speaking, which was so rarely met with in the milieu he lived in. However ashamed he was of himself, Vronsky envied him.

"Nevertheless there's one principal thing I lack for that," he replied. "I lack the desire for power. I had it, but now it's gone."

"Forgive me, but that's not true," said Serpukhovskoy with a smile.

"No, it's true, it's true!—now, to be frank," Vronsky added.

"Yes, it's true *now*, that's something else again; but this *now* isn't going to last forever."

"Perhaps," Vronsky answered.

"You say 'perhaps,'" Serpukhovskoy went on, as though he had guessed Vronsky's thoughts, "but I say to you 'surely.' That's why I wanted to see you. You were right to behave the way you did. I understand that, but you mustn't—*keep it up.* I'm simply asking you for a blank check. I'm not going to take you under my wing—though on the other hand why shouldn't I? How often you took me under yours! I hope our friendship is worth more than that. Yes," he said, smiling at Vronsky tenderly like a woman, "give me a blank check, leave the regiment, and I'll advance you imperceptibly."

"But you must understand that I don't want anything," said Vronsky, "except that everything should stay as it is."

Serpukhovskoy got up and stood in front of him. "You say everything should stay as it is. I understand what that means. But listen to me: we're both the same age, you may have known a greater number of women than I"—Serpukhovskoy's smile and gesture indicated that Vronsky need have no fear, that he was going to touch the sore spot tenderly and cautiously—"but I'm married, and believe me, when you've known only your own wife, as someone once wrote, and love her, you know more about all women than if you had known them by the thousands."

"We'll be right there!" Vronsky cried out, to some officer, sent by the colonel to call them, who was looking into the room.

Vronsky felt like hearing him finish, to find out what he was going to tell him.

"Here's my opinion for you. Women are the chief stumbling block in a man's career. It's hard to love a woman and do anything else. There's only one way to love in comfort and without hindrance—marriage. How can I express it, and tell you what I think? Wait a bit, wait a bit!" said Serpukhovskoy, who liked similes. "Yes, it's like carrying a load and trying to do something with your hands—it's only possible when the load is tied to your back—that's what marriage is. That's what I felt when I got married. Suddenly my hands had been freed. But to drag this load around with you without being married—you'll have your hands so full you won't be able to do anything at all. Look at Mazankov, or Krupov. They ruined their careers because of women."

"But what women!" said Vronsky, recalling the little Frenchwoman and the actress the two men had been involved with.

"The more established a woman's position is in society the worse it is. It's no longer even a question of carrying a load with your own hands, but of wrenching it away from someone else."

"You've never been in love," said Vronsky softly, looking straight ahead and thinking of Anna.

"Possibly. But remember what I've told you. And one more thing: women are all more materialistic than men. We turn love into something vast, but they're always down to earth."

"Coming, coming!" he said to a footman who had come. But the footman had not come to call them again, as he had thought: he was bringing Vronsky a note.

"Your man brought this. From Princess Tverskoy."

Vronsky opened the letter and turned crimson. "A headache's just come on, I'm going home," he said to Serpukhovskoy.

"Well, good-by then. Are you giving me a blank check?"

"We'll talk about it later, I'll look you up in Petersburg."


## XXII

IT was already six o'clock and in order to get there on time without using his own horses, which were well known, Vronsky got into Yashvin's hired carriage; he told the coachman to go as fast as possible. It was an old four-seater with lots of room. He sat down in a corner, put his legs up on the seat in front and sank into thought.

A vague consciousness of the order his affairs had been brought into, a vague recollection of Serpukhovskoy's friendliness and flattering regard for him as a man who was needed, and most of all the anticipation of the reunion before him—all this was fused into a general, joyous feeling of life. This feeling was so strong that he smiled involuntarily. He put his legs down, crossed them, took one of them in his hand and felt the resilient muscle of the calf that had been bruised in his fall the day before, then threw himself back and took a number of deep breaths.

Delightful! Just delightful! he said to himself. Before too he had often felt a joyful awareness of his own body, but he had never loved himself, and his body, so much as now. It gave him pleasure to feel the slight pain in his powerful leg, pleasure to feel the muscles of his chest moving as he breathed. The same bright and chilly August day that had made Anna feel so hopeless seemed to him excitingly invigorating, and refreshed his face and neck, still glowing from his brisk rubdown. The aroma of the brilliantine on his mustache seemed to him particularly agreeable in this fresh air. Every-

thing he saw through the window of the carriage, everything
in this cold pure air in the pale light of the setting sun, was
just as fresh, gay, and vigorous as he was himself—the house
roofs gleaming in the rays of the setting sun, the sharp outlines of the fences and corners of buildings, the figures of
the occasional pedestrians and carriages that were met with,
the motionless greenery of the trees and grass, and the fields
with their evenly laid out ridges of potatoes, the slanting
shadows falling from the houses, the trees, and the bushes,
and from the very potato ridges themselves. It was all beautiful, like a lovely landscape just painted and varnished.

"Faster, faster!" he leaned out of the window and said to
the coachman; he got a three-ruble note out of his pocket
and thrust it into the hand of the coachman who had looked
round. The coachman's hand fumbled with it under the lamp,
the whip hissed, and the carriage whirled swiftly along the
level highway.

I don't need anything, anything at all but the happiness I
have, he thought, looking at the ivory knob of the bell between the windows and visualizing Anna as he had seen her
the last time. The longer it goes on the more I love her. Ah—
the garden of the Vrede house! Now just where will she be?
How will I find her? Why did she tell me to meet her here,
and use Betsy's letter? he thought now for the first
time; but there was no longer any time for thought. He
stopped the coachman before driving as far as the avenue and
opened the door; he jumped out of the carriage while it was
moving and went into the avenue that led to the house.
There was no one there, but he looked over to the right and
saw her. Her face was covered with a veil, but with a joyful
glance he took in the special way of walking, holding her
shoulders and poising her head that was peculiar to her
alone, and it was as though an electric current had instantly
pulsed through his body. With renewed strength he was aware
of himself, from the springy movements of his legs to the
movement of his lungs as he breathed, and something tickled
his lips.

When she came up to him she squeezed his hand hard.

"You're not angry I asked you to meet me? I had to see
you," she said, and the sight of the grave and severe set of
her lips beneath her veil changed his mood instantly.

"Angry? I! But how did you get here? Where can we go?"

"It doesn't matter," she said, putting her hand on his arm.
"Come, we must talk things over."

He realized that something had happened, and that this meeting was not going to be cheerful. In her presence he lost his will power: without knowing the reason for her agitation he already felt that he too was being infected involuntarily by the same agitation.

"What is it? What's the matter?" he asked, squeezing her hand with his elbow and trying to read her thoughts in her face.

She took a few steps in silence, gathering her courage; suddenly she halted.

"I didn't tell you last night," she began, breathing quickly and heavily, "that when I went home together with Karenin I told him everything—I told him that I could no longer be his wife, that—I told him everything!"

He listened to her, involuntarily leaning toward her with his whole body as though trying to soften the painfulness of her situation. But the moment she said this he suddenly straightened up and his face took on a proud, stern expression.

"Yes—yes, that's better, a thousand times better! I realize how hard it was," he said.

But she paid no attention to what he was saying; she could read his thoughts by the way he looked. She had no way of knowing that the expression on Vronsky's face was due to the first idea that crossed his mind—that a duel could no longer be avoided. The idea of a duel had never even entered her mind, so she had another explanation for his momentary expression of sternness.

When she had received Karenin's letter she already knew at the bottom of her heart that everything was going to stay just as it had been, that she would be incapable of disregarding her own situation, deserting her son and joining her lover. The morning she had spent at Betsy's made her even more certain of this. Nevertheless this meeting was exceptionally important for her. She hoped it would alter their situation and rescue her. If on hearing this news he had said to her, firmly, passionately, without an instant's hesitation: "Give up everything and run away with me!" she would desert her son and go away with him. But the news did not have the effect on him she had expected—he simply looked as though he had been offended by something.

"It wasn't hard at all. It happened by itself," she said irritably. "Here—" She pulled her husband's letter out of her glove.

"I understand, I understand," he interrupted her, taking the letter but not reading it and trying to soothe her: "I wanted only one thing, I was only asking for one thing—to end this situation so that I could devote my life to your happiness."

"Why are you saying that to me?" she said. "Could I be in doubt about that? If I doubted that—"

"Who's that coming?" Vronsky said abruptly, indicating two women coming toward them. "They may know us," and he hurriedly moved toward a little side path, drawing her along after him.

"Oh I don't care!" she said. Her lips were trembling; it seemed to him that her eyes were gazing at him from under the veil with a peculiar malevolence. "As I was saying that's not the point, I don't doubt that—but look at what he wrote me. Read it . . ." She halted once again.

Once again, just as when he had heard of her rupture with her husband, Vronsky in reading the letter involuntarily succumbed to the natural feeling that was aroused in him by his relationship to the injured husband. Now, as he held his letter in his hands, he involuntarily pictured the challenge he would doubtless find waiting for him at home that very day or the day after, and the duel itself, during which, after firing in the air, he would stand there with the same cold, haughty expression his face bore at that very moment, and await the injured husband's shot. At the same instant the thought flashed through his mind of what Serpukhovskoy had just told him and which he had been thinking himself that morning—about its being better not to tie oneself down; he knew this was a thought he could not communicate to her.

After reading the letter he raised his eyes to hers; his gaze was not firm. She understood instantly that he had already considered this himself just before. She knew that whatever he told her he would not be telling her everything he thought. She realized that her last hope had been betrayed; this was not what she had been expecting.

"You see what kind of a man he is," she said, her voice trembling; "he—"

"Forgive me, but it makes me happy," Vronsky interrupted. "For God's sake let me finish," he added, imploring her with his eyes to give him time to make his words clear. "It makes me glad because things cannot, they simply cannot stay the way he imagines."

"But why can't they?" Anna murmured, holding back her tears, obviously no longer attributing the slightest importance to what he was saying. She felt her fate had been decided.

Vronsky had meant to say that after the duel, which he thought inevitable, things could no longer go on as before, but he said something else.

"They can't go on that way. I hope you'll leave him now. I hope," he grew confused and blushed, "that you'll permit me to arrange and think out our life. Tomorrow—" he began.

She didn't let him finish.

"And what about my son?" she cried. "Did you see what he wrote? I would have to leave him, and that I can't and won't do!"

"For God's sake, which is better? To leave your son or to continue in this humiliating position?"

"Whom is the position humiliating for?"

"For everyone, and for you most of all."

"You say 'humiliating.' Don't say that—words like that have no sense for me," she said in a trembling voice. She did not want him to say something false now. All she had left was his love, and she wanted to love him. "You must understand that from the day I fell in love with you everything was transformed. There's only one thing left for me, just one thing—your love. If I have that I feel myself so exalted, so unshakable, that nothing can be humiliating for me. I am proud of my position, because—proud because—proud—" She couldn't finish saying what it was that she was proud of: Tears of shame and desperation stifled her voice. She stood still and burst into sobs.

He too felt something welling up in his throat, and a twitching in his nose; for the first time in his life he felt on the verge of weeping. He would have been unable to say just what it was that moved him so; he pitied her, and he felt that he couldn't help her, and at the same time he knew that he was to blame for her misery, that he had done something wrong.

"Surely a divorce is possible?" he said feebly. She shook her head without answering. "Couldn't you take the boy away, and still leave him?"

"Yes, but it all depends on him. Now I must go back to him," she said drily. Her premonition that everything was going to remain as before had not deceived her.

"I'm going to Petersburg on Tuesday, everything will be decided."

"Yes," she said, "but let's not talk any more about it."

Anna's carriage, which she had sent away with instructions to come round to the little gate of the Vrede garden, drove up; she said good-by to Vronsky and drove home.

## XXIII

ON Monday the usual sitting of the Commission of June 2 took place. Karenin entered the meeting room, greeted the members and the chairman as usual, and took his seat, resting his hand on the papers lying ready in front of him. These included the references he needed and a draft of the statement he intended making. But he didn't require the references. He remembered everything and thought it unnecessary to go over in his mind what he was going to say. He knew that when the time came and when he saw before him the face of his opponent, vainly trying to put on a look of indifference, his speech would flow out by itself better than he could prepare himself for it now. He felt that the import of his speech was of such magnitude that every single word of it would be weighty.

Meanwhile, listening to the usual report he had the most innocent and inoffensive air. No one would have thought, looking at his white hands with their swollen veins and long fingers, toying so delicately with the two edges of the sheet of white paper lying before him, or at his head, leaning over to one side with an expression of weariness, that words would be pouring out of his mouth in a moment which would create a fearful storm and make the members start shouting and interrupting each other, so that the chairman would have to call them to order.

When the report was over, Karenin, in his quiet, high-pitched voice, announced that he had a number of considerations to submit concerning the Commission for the Reorganization of the National Minorities. Attention centered on him. He cleared his throat, and without looking at his opponent but picking out, as he always did when making a speech, the first person sitting in front of him—a peaceful little old man who had never had any opinion to express in the Commission—he began to expound his views. When he got to the point about the fundamental and organic law his opponent leaped to his feet and started protesting. Stremov, who was also a member of the Commission and had also been stung to the quick, began defending himself—and the meeting became tempestuous generally. But Karenin triumphed; his motion was carried; three new Commissions were appointed, and the following day nothing but this meeting was talked about in a certain Petersburg circle. Karenin's success was even greater than he had expected.

When he woke up the next morning, Tuesday, he recalled his victory of the day before with satisfaction, and though he wanted to appear indifferent he could not help smiling when his chief secretary, in order to flatter him, reported the rumors that had come to him about what had happened in the Commission.

Immersed in business with the secretary, Karenin had completely forgotten it was Tuesday, the day he had designated for Anna's return, and he was disagreeably surprised and shocked when a servant entered to 'announce her arrival.

Anna had got to Petersburg early in the morning; the carriage she had wired for had been sent to meet her, so Karenin might have known of her arrival. But he didn't come out when she arrived. She was told he hadn't left yet and was busy with his secretary. She left orders for him to be told she had arrived, went to her boudoir and started unpacking, expecting him to come in to see her. But an hour passed without his coming in. She went into the dining room on the pretext of giving some instructions, and purposely spoke in a loud voice, expecting him to come out there; but he didn't come out, though she heard him accompanying his secretary out of his study. She knew it was his custom to leave soon for his office, and she wanted to see him beforehand so that their relations might be clearly defined.

She crossed the drawing room and resolutely went in to see him. When she entered his study he was in his official uniform, evidently ready to leave, with his elbows on a little table, looking glumly in front of him. She saw him first, and realized he was thinking about her.

When he saw her he started to get up, but changed his mind; then his face flushed, something Anna had never seen before, and he swiftly got up and came toward her, not looking into her eyes but higher up, at her forehead and hair. He came up to her, took her hand, and asked her to sit down.

"I'm very glad you've come," he said, sitting down beside her; he evidently wanted to tell her something, but he stammered instead. He tried to speak a number of times, but kept stopping. In spite of her having schooled herself while preparing for this interview to despise and reproach him, she didn't know what to say; she felt sorry for him.

Thus the silence lasted quite some time. "Is Seryozha well?" he said, and without waiting for an answer he added: "I shan't be dining at home today, and I have to leave in a moment."

"I meant to go away to Moscow," she said.

"No, you were right, quite right to come," he said, and fell silent again.

Seeing that he was incapable of beginning himself she started to speak herself.

"Alexis," she said, looking at him without lowering her eyes under the stare he kept directing at her hair, "I'm a sinful woman, and a bad woman, but I'm the same as I was, and as I told you at the time; I've come to tell you that I cannot change anything."

"I haven't asked you about that," he said, suddenly looking resolutely and full of hate into her eyes. "That is just what I thought." It was plain that his anger had completely restored all his faculties. "But as I said to you at the time and wrote you," he went on in a shrill voice, "and as I repeat once again, I'm not obliged to know all that. I am ignoring it. Not all wives are as kind as you are, in hastening to inform their husbands of such a *pleasant* piece of news." (He laid special emphasis on the *pleasant*.) "I shall go on ignoring it as long as the world is unaware of it, as long as my name has not been dishonored. Therefore I am merely warning you that our relations must remain what they have always been, and that I shall only take steps to safeguard my honor in the event that you let yourself be *compromised*."

"But our relations cannot be what they were before," Anna began in a timid voice, looking at him in dismay.

When she saw these serene gestures of his once again and heard that piercing, childish, sarcastic voice, her loathing destroyed the pity she had felt, and she was simply afraid; but whatever happened she wanted to clarify her position.

"I cannot be your wife, when I—" she began again.

He gave a vindictive, chilly laugh.

"The style of life you've chosen must have affected your principles. I have so much respect or contempt for both— I respect your past and despise your present—that the interpretation you gave my words was far from my thoughts."

Anna sighed and hung her head.

"But I don't understand how anyone with as much independence as you have," he went on more and more heatedly, "after informing your husband of you infidelity, without seeming to find anything reprehensible in it, then find it reprehensible to perform a wife's obligations toward her husband."

"Alexis! What do you want of me?"

"What I want is not to see that man here; I want you to conduct yourself so that neither *society* nor the *servants* should be *able* to reproach you—I want you not to see him. It seems to me that's not much. In return you will enjoy the rights of a faithful wife without having to fulfill her obligations. That is all I have to say to you. It's time for me to go now. I won't be dining in."

He got up and started toward the door. Anna also got up. He bowed silently and let her pass.

## XXIV

THE night Levin had spent on the haystack did not pass without having some effect on him. The farming he had been doing disgusted him now; he lost all interest in it. In spite of the splendid harvest he had never, at any rate he thought he had never had so many mishaps or so much ill feeling between him and the peasants till this year, and the reason for these mishaps and this ill feeling now seemed to him completely understandable. The delight he had felt in the actual labor, because of his greater intimacy with the peasants, the envy he felt for them and for their life, the desire to enter into that life, which during that night had no longer been a dream for him but an intention whose details he had been thinking through—all this had so changed his view of the way his farm was being run that he was quite incapable of taking his former interest in it any longer; he could not help but perceive the unpleasantness of his attitude toward the laborers, which was the basis of it all. The herd of improved cows like Pava, the land all dressed and plowed, the nine level fields hedged round with willows, the 240 heavily manured acres, the seed drills and so on—that was all splendid if it had been brought about by himself alone or by himself and some friends together, people who were in sympathy with him. But now he saw clearly (working on his book about agriculture, in which the laborer was supposed to be the chief element in farming, had helped him a lot here) that the farming he was doing was merely a cruel and stubborn contest between himself and the laborers, in which on one side—his side—there was a bitter, strenuous, constant attempt to remodel everything according to a pattern accepted as the best, while on the other side there was the natural order of things. In this struggle he saw that, with the greatest expenditure of effort on his part, and without any effort even intended on the part of the others, the only thing accomplished was that the farming pleased no one, and first-rate tools, and first-rate cattle and land were ruined to no avail. But the main thing was that not only was the energy directed into this completely wasted, but that now he could not help feeling, once the meaning of his farming was laid bare, that the goal of his efforts was most unworthy. At bottom what was the struggle about? He was fighting for every penny (which he couldn't help, since the moment he slackened his efforts he wouldn't have enough money to pay the laborers off) while all they were fighting for was to work calmly and pleasantly, that is, just as they were accustomed to. It was to his interest for each laborer to finish as much work as possible, while at the same time keeping his mind on it, trying not to break the winnowing machines, the horse rakes, and the threshing machines, and paying attention to what he was doing. But what the laborer felt like doing was working as agreeably as possible, with breaks for a rest, and above all in a carefree way, without worrying or thinking.

That summer Levin saw this at every turn. He gave orders to mow the clover for hay, after picking out the bad acreage that was overgrown with grass and hemlock unfit for seed; what they cut down was all the best seed clover, defending themselves by claiming that that was what the foreman had ordered and consoling him with assurances that the hay would be wonderful; but he knew they had done it only because these acres were easier to mow. He sent out the horse rake to turn the hay: it was broken in the very first rows, because the peasant found it tiresome to sit on the seat under the rotating wings. Then he was told: "Don't worry, sir, the women will toss it all in no time!" The plows turned out to be useless, because it never entered the peasant's head to raise the plowshare at the turn, and when he did it by force he strained the horses and ruined the ground; then Levin was asked to be calm. The horses were let out into the wheat because none of the peasants wanted to be night watchman, and in spite of the orders against it they all took turns on night duty, and Vanka, after working all day, fell asleep and confessed his guilt, saying: "I'm completely in your hands, sir."

Three of the best calves died from overfeeding, through being turned out into the clover where it had been cut without having been watered; the peasants simply refused to believe the clover had blown them up, but to console him told him stories about a neighbor of his who had lost 112 head of cattle in three days. None of this happened because anyone wished to hurt Levin or his farming; on the contrary he knew they liked him and thought him a straightforward gentleman (their highest praise); all this happened only because they wanted to work merrily and without any worries, and his interests were not only alien and incomprehensible to them but were inevitably opposed to their own entirely justified interests.

For a long time now Levin had been feeling dissatisfied with his attitude toward farming. He had seen that the boat was leaking, but he had not found or even looked for the leak, perhaps through deliberate self-deception. But now he could no longer deceive himself. His farming was not only of no interest to him any longer, it was repugnant and he could no longer give his mind to it.

Added to this was the presence not more than twenty miles away of Kitty Shcherbatsky, whom he wanted to see and couldn't. When he had been at Dolly's she had asked him to call: to call in order to propose once again to her sister, who, she had given him to understand, would now accept him. Levin himself realized after having seen Kitty that he hadn't stopped loving her, but he couldn't visit the Oblonskys knowing she was there. The fact of having proposed to her and been refused set up an insurmountable barrier between them.

I can't ask her to marry me just because she can't marry the man she wanted, he said to himself. The thought of this made him cold and hostile toward her. I'll be incapable of speaking to her without feeling reproachful, of looking at her without malice, and she'll only grow to hate me even more—and quite right too. Besides, after what Dolly said to me how can I visit them now? How can I help but show that I know what she told me? And to go there magnanimously to forgive her, pity her! I'd be playing the role in front of her of someone who forgives her and honors her with his love!

Why did Dolly tell me that? I might have been able to see her by accident; then everything would have happened by itself, but now it's impossible, impossible!

Dolly sent him a note asking him for a sidesaddle for Kitty. "*I was told you had a saddle,*" she wrote, "*I hope you'll be able to bring it over yourself.*"

This was more than he could stand. How could an intelligent, tactful woman humiliate her sister so? He wrote out ten notes, tore them all up, and sent the saddle over with no reply at all. It was impossible to write he was going to come, because he couldn't come; to write that he couldn't come because he was taking a trip was still worse. He sent off the saddle without an answer, conscious that he had done something shameful; the next day, after putting all the farming, which had become so disagreeable to him, into the hands of his foreman, he set off for a remote district to visit his friend Sviyazhsky, who had some splendid snipe marshes near him and had written him not long before asking him to keep a long-standing promise to pay him a visit. The snipe marshes in the Surovsky District had long since been beckoning to Levin, but he had kept putting off the trip because of his farm work. But now he was delighted to go away both from the Shcherbatskys' proximity and most of all from the farm, especially to go shooting, which had always served as his best consolation whenever he was troubled.

## XXV

THERE was no railway or stagecoach to the Surovsky District, and Levin drove there in his own leather-topped four-wheeler.

Halfway there he stopped at a rich peasant's to feed his horses. A bald, fresh-faced old man with a red beard turning gray around the cheeks, opened the gates, squeezing up against the post to let the three horses pass through. After showing the coachman to a place in a lean-to in the big, clean, tidy new yard where some charred old-fashioned plows were standing, the old man invited Levin indoors. A young woman in a clean dress with galoshes on her bare feet was bending over washing the floor in the new passageway. She was frightened by Laska, who ran in behind Levin, and gave a shriek, but immediately burst out laughing at her own fright when she was told the dog wouldn't hurt her. She pointed out the door to Levin with her bare arm and bending over she hid her pretty face once again and went on scrubbing.

"D'you want a samovar?" she asked.

"Yes, please."

The main room was large, with a Dutch stove and a partition. Under the icons stood a table with painted patterns, a bench and two chairs. A little cupboard with crockery stood by the door. The shutters were closed, there were very few flies, and it was so clean that Levin took care that Laska, who had been running along the highway rolling in the puddles, did not muddy up the floor, and he told her to lie down in a corner by the door. After looking the room over Levin went out into the backyard. The good-looking young woman in galoshes swinging two empty pails on a wooden yoke ran out ahead of him to the well for water.

"Look lively now!" the old man shouted out after her gaily, and came over to Levin. "Well, sir, are you off to see Nicholas Sviyazhsky? He stops at our place too," he began garrulously, leaning his elbows on the railing of the steps.

In the middle of the old man's story about his friendship with Sviyazhsky the gates creaked open once again and the laborers with their plows and harrows came into the yard from the fields. The horses harnessed to the plows and harrows were massive and well fed. The laborers obviously belonged to the household. Two were young men wearing print shirts and peaked caps; the other two were hired men with homespun shirts, one of them an old man, the other a young fellow. Moving off from the steps the master of the house went over to the horses and began unharnessing them.

"What have they been plowing?" asked Levin.

"They've been plowing between the potatoes. We also rent a little land. You, Fedot, don't let the gelding out, lead him to the trough, we'll harness another . . ."

"Say, Father, have those plowshares I ordered been delivered?" asked the young fellow, tall and robust, and plainly the old man's son.

"Over there in the passage," answered the old man, winding the reins up into a ring and throwing them on the ground. "Put them on while they're having their dinner."

The good-looking young woman with the full pails dragging at her shoulders, came into the passage. Some other women also turned up from somewhere, young and pretty, middle-aged, old and plain, with children and without.

The water in the samovar was beginning to sing; the laborers and the family, having disposed of the horses, came in for their dinner. Levin, who had gotten his supplies from his carriage invited the old man to have some tea with him.

"Well, I've already had some today," said the old man, accepting the invitation with obvious pleasure. "Just to keep you company, perhaps."

Over tea Levin heard the whole story of the old man's farm. Ten years before he had rented three hundred acres from the woman who owned them, the year before he had bought them and was renting another seven hundred from a neighboring landowner. He had let out a small part of the land—the worst part—while he cultivated a hundred acres himself together with his family and two hired hands. The old man complained of how badly things were going. But Levin saw that he was simply complaining for the sake of propriety, and that his farm was flourishing. If it had been in a bad way he would not have bought land at thirty-five rubles an acre, would not have married off three of his sons and a nephew, and would not have rebuilt his house twice after fires, improving it each time. In spite of the old man's grumbling it was plain that he was rightly proud of his prosperity, proud of his sons, his nephew, his sons' wives, his horses, his cows, and especially of the fact that the whole enterprise held together.

Levin gathered from the conversation that the old man was not against innovations either. He had planted a great many potatoes, and his potatoes, which Levin had seen while driving up, had already flowered and were forming fruit, while Levin's own potatoes were just beginning to flower. He had plowed the potato land with an English plow, borrowed from the neighboring landowner, and had sowed wheat. One little detail about how the old man, in thinning out his rye, had used the thinnings of the rye as fodder for the horses, struck Levin especially. How often Levin, seeing this splendid fodder going to waste, had wanted to gather it, but it had always seemed to him impossible. Now this peasant had had this done, and he couldn't say enough in praise of it as fodder.

"What is there for the young women to do? They carry the heaps out onto the road, then a cart comes for them."

"There you are; landlords like us are always getting into trouble with our laborers," said Levin, handing him a glass of tea.

"Thank you," said the old man, taking the glass but refusing the sugar, pointing to the little nibbled lump he had left. "How can a farm be run with hired hands?" he said. "They're just ruination. Take Sviyazhsky now: we know the soil he has, black as poppy seed, yet his harvests are nothing to sing about. It's just not looked after right!"

"But you use hired hands too on the farm?"

"Yes, but we're all peasants. We do everything ourselves. Anyone who's no good—out! We'll get along by ourselves."

"Father, Finogen wants some tar fetched," said the young woman in galoshes, coming in.

"Well, sir, that's how it is!" said the old man, getting up; he crossed himself several times, thanked Levin and went out.

When Levin went into the back room to call his coachman he saw all the men of the peasant's family at table. The women served the table standing up. The robust young son, his mouth full of porridge, was telling a funny story, and they were all guffawing, the young woman in the galoshes with special gaiety as she refilled his bowl with cabbage soup.

It may very well be that the good-looking face of the young woman in the galoshes contributed a great deal to the impression of well-being this peasant household made on Levin, but this impression was so strong that Levin could never quite rid himself of it. The whole way over to Sviyazhsky's from the old man's his thoughts kept returning to this farm as though there were something in this impression that claimed his special attention.

## XXVI

SVIYAZHSKY was Marshal of the Nobility for his district. He was five years older than Levin and had been married a long time. His young sister-in-law, whom Levin liked very much, lived in his house. Levin knew that Sviyazhsky and his wife were very anxious to have him marry this girl. He knew this beyond any question, as all so-called eligible young men always know it, though he could never have brought himself to say this to anyone; he also knew that in spite of his wanting to get married, and in spite of the fact that according to everything about her this extremely attractive girl ought to make a splendid wife, he could no more marry her, even if he hadn't been in love with Kitty Shcherbatsky, than he could fly to the moon. This knowledge poisoned the pleasure he hoped to find on this visit to Sviyazhsky.

On receiving Sviyazhsky's letter inviting him to go shooting, Levin thought about this at once, but in spite of it he made up his mind that these intentions of Sviyazhsky's concerning him were no more than a completely unfounded surmise of his own, and that therefore he would go anyhow. Besides this, at the bottom of his heart he felt like trying himself out, testing his feelings for the girl again. The domestic life of the Sviyazhskys was extremely agreeable, and Sviyazhsky himself, the best type of locally active man Levin knew, had always been of exceptional interest to him.

Sviyazhsky was one of those people—always a source of astonishment to Levin—whose judgment, perfectly logical, though never original, goes along one line while their lives, extremely definite and unwavering in direction, go along another, completely independent of and almost always in contradiction with their judgment. Sviyazhsky was an extreme liberal. He despised the nobility and considered the majority of noblemen secretly in favor of serfdom and merely too timid to speak out. He considered Russia a doomed country on the order of Turkey, and the Russian Government so bad he never allowed himself even to bother criticizing its actions seriously. At the same time he had an official position, and was a model Marshal of the Nobility; when he traveled he always put on a cockade and a red band on his cap. He thought you could only live like a human being abroad, which is where he went to stay whenever he could, while at the same time he carried on a very complicated and advanced system of farming and kept track of everything in Russia with extreme interest. He thought the Russian peasant stood on some intermediate level of evolution between the ape and man, yet at district elections no one shook hands with the peasants or listened to their opinions more gladly than he. He didn't believe in either God or the devil, but he was very concerned with the question of improving the condition of the clergy and of the reduction in the number of parishes, and also took special pains to keep the church in his own village.

On the Woman's Question he was on the side of the extreme partisans of the complete emancipation of women, especially of their right to work, but he lived with his wife in such a way that everyone admired their friendly childless family life, and he arranged his wife's life so that she never did or could do anything but share her husband's efforts to pass time as gaily as possible.

If Levin had not had the trait of putting the best interpretation on people, Sviyazhsky's character would not have presented the slightest doubtfulness or difficulty for him; he would have said to himself, A fool or a knave, and it would all have been clear. But he couldn't call him a fool, since Sviyazhsky was undoubtedly not only very intelligent, but very cultivated, and he bore his cultivation with unusual simplicity. There was not a subject he didn't know; but he only displayed his erudition when he was forced to. Still less could Levin call him a knave, since Sviyazhsky was unquestionably honorable, kindhearted, and able, constantly engaged, actively and cheerfully, on work that was highly esteemed by everyone around him, and certainly never did anything or could do anything consciously that was bad.

Levin kept trying to understand this but never did; he always contemplated Sviyazhsky and his life as though they were a living enigma.

He and Levin were friends, so Levin would allow himself to sound him out and try to probe to the very foundations of his views on life; but it was always futile. Every time Levin attempted to penetrate further than the reception rooms of Sviyazhsky's mind that were open to everyone, he noticed that Sviyazhsky became slightly disconcerted. A scarcely perceptible look of alarm would pass over his face, as though he were afraid Levin might understand him, and he would give him a cheerful, good-humored rebuff.

Now that Levin had been disappointed in farming he found it especially agreeable to visit Sviyazhsky. Apart from the cheerful effect it had on him to see these happy doves in their well-built nest, satisfied with themselves and with everyone, he now wanted, in his dissatisfaction with his own life, to get at the secret that gave Sviyazhsky's life such clarity, definiteness, and gaiety. Aside from this Levin knew he would see some neighboring landowners at Sviyazhsky's, and he was particularly interested now in talking about farming and listening to all those conversations about crops, laborer's wages, and so on, that Levin knew were conventionally sneered at but that now seemed to him important.

They may not have been important under serfdom, or they may not be important in England, Levin thought; in both cases the conditions themselves were or are fixed; but here in Russia, when that has all just been transformed and is only just settling down, the question of how these conditions are going to be established is the only important question.

The shooting turned out to be worse than Levin had expected; the marsh had dried out, and there were no snipe at all. He walked around the whole day and came back with only three, but to make up for it he brought back, as he always did after a day's shooting, a splendid appetite, a splendid mood, and the state of intellectual excitement that always accompanied any violent physical exercise. Even while out shooting, when nothing would have seemed to be on his mind, he kept thinking again and again of the old peasant and his family, and the impression they had made on him not only seemed to call for attention, but also for the solution of something it was bound up with.

Over tea in the evening, in the presence of two landowners, who had come in on some guardianship business, a very interesting conversation sprang up, just as Levin had expected.

Levin was sitting beside his hostess at the teatable and had to keep up a conversation with her and her sister, who was sitting opposite him. His hostess was a short, fair, round-faced woman all radiant with dimples and smiles. Levin tried to find out through her the answer to the riddle, represented by her husband, which was so important for him; but his thoughts were not entirely free, since he was agonizingly ill at ease. This was because her sister was sitting opposite him in what seemed to him to be a dress specially put on for him, with a particularly low, square-cut décolletage showing her white bosom. This quadrangular cut, in spite of the extreme whiteness of the bosom or just because of it, made it impossible for Levin to think freely. He imagined to himself, doubtless mistakenly, that this square cut had been made for his benefit; he thought he had no right to look at it and kept trying not to, but he felt guilty if only because that was the way it had been cut. It seemed to him that he was deceiving someone, that he ought to be making some sort of explanation, but that any explanation was completely out of the question, and because of this he kept constantly blushing and was awkward and ill at ease. This awkwardness of his infected the sister as well, but the hostess did not seem to notice it and purposely kept bringing her into the conversation.

"You were saying," the hostess continued, "that my husband can't find anything Russian interesting. On the contrary, though he's happy when he's abroad it's never the same as it is here. When he's here he feels he's where he should be. There are so many things for him to do, and he has the gift of being able to take an interest in everything. Oh——have you been to see our school?"

"I've seen it . . . Isn't it a little ivy-covered house?"

"Yes, that's what Nastya does," she said, indicating her sister.

"Do you teach yourself?" asked Levin, trying to look past the décolletage, but feeling that no matter where he looked in that direction he would see it.

"Yes, I've been teaching there and still am, but we have a first-rate schoolmistress now. We've introduced gymnastics too."

"No thank you, no more tea for me," said Levin, and feeling he was being rude, but no longer capable of keeping up this conversation, he got up blushing. "I've heard something very interesting being said over there," he added, and moved to the other end of the table, where Sviyazhsky was sitting with the two landowners. He was sitting sideways at the table, leaning one elbow on it and turning his cup round with that hand while he kept gathering his beard up with the other; he would lift his beard to his nose as though sniffing it, then let it down again. His black eyes shining, he was looking directly at the landowner with the gray mustache, who was getting excited, and obviously finding some amusement in what he was saying. The landowner was complaining about the peasants. It was clear to Levin that Sviyazhsky had an answer to the landowner's grumbling that would instantly annihilate the point of what the latter was saying, but that because of his position he couldn't produce this answer and was listening to the landowner's absurd remarks with a certain satisfaction.

This landowner with the gray mustache was obviously a die-hard believer in serfdom, and a passionate farmer who was an old hand at living in the country. Levin saw the signs of this both in the way he dressed—he was wearing an old-fashioned shiny coat he was evidently not used to—his intelligent deep-set eyes, his excellent Russian, his commanding tone of voice, evidently ingrained from long use, and the decisive movements of his large, handsome, sunburned hands, the right one of which had an old engagement ring on the little finger.

### XXVII

IF it weren't such a pity to throw away everything that's been set in motion . . . a lot of work's gone into it . . . I'd shrug my shoulders, sell it all and be off, like Sviyazhsky, and hear *La Belle Hélène*," said the landowner, a pleasant smile lighting up his clever old face.

"Yes, but since you don't throw it all away," Sviyazhsky said, "there must be some advantages."

"Just one—I live in a house of my own, which hasn't been bought or rented. And then one keeps on hoping the peasants will get some sense. As it is you wouldn't believe it—the drunkenness, the debauchery! They keep splitting up all their land, there's not a horse or a cow left. They're all starving, but just hire one of them as a laborer, he'll do his best to smash everything you have, he'll even complain to the magistrate!"

"But you complain to the magistrate in your turn," said Sviyazhsky.

"Complain? I? Not for anything in the world! There'd be so much talk you'd be sorry you ever started! At the works now, they pocketed the advance money and took off. And what did the magistrate do? Why, he acquitted them! Things are only kept going by the village tribunal and the village Elder. He thrashes them in the good old style! If it weren't for that you might as well throw it all up and fly to the other end of the world!"

The landowner was plainly trying to tease Sviyazhsky, though Sviyazhsky not only didn't lose his temper but was obviously amused.

"But here we are carrying on our farming without such measures," he said smiling, "I, Levin, and he."

He nodded at the other landowner.

"Oh yes, Petrovich here manages, but just ask him how! D'you call that rational farming?" said the landowner, manifestly flaunting the word "rational."

"My farm is a very simple one, thank God," said Petrovich.

"The only reason I do any farming is to have some money on hand for the autumn taxes. The peasants come along saying 'Master, help us!' Well, these peasants are still our own people, our neighbors, you feel sorry for them. So you lend them the first third they need, but you say: 'Remember, my boys, I helped you and you'll help me when I need it—sowing the oats, or haymaking, or the harvest.' So you come to an agreement, so much work per family. Of course it's true there are some unscrupulous ones among them too."

Levin, who was very familiar with these patriarchal methods and had been for a long time, exchanged glances with Sviyazhsky; interrupting Petrovich, he addressed the landowner with the gray mustache again.

"Then what's your opinion?" he asked. "How should a farm be managed nowadays?"

"Why, the way Petrovich does it: either pay the peasants in kind or rent the land to them. That can be done—but that's just the way the general welfare of the country is being destroyed. Under serfdom, when I had land, it used to bring in a ninefold yield with good management; when payment is made in kind it brings in threefold. Russia's been ruined by the emancipation!"

Sviyazhsky looked over at Levin with smiling eyes and even made a barely perceptible sign of mockery; but Levin did not think the words of the landowner were ridiculous—he understood them better than he did Sviyazhsky. As for a great deal of what the landowner went on to say in his attempt to prove that Russia had been ruined by the emancipation of the serfs, it even seemed to him very true, novel, and undeniable. It was evident that the landowner was expressing his own ideas, which very seldom happens, and they were ideas that he had been led to not by any desire to find something for an idle mind to do, but that had grown out of the circumstances of his life, which he had brooded over in his rural isolation and reflected on from every angle.

"The fact of the matter is, don't you see, that progress is never accomplished except by authority," he said, obviously wanting to show he had had some education. "Just take the reforms introduced by Peter, or Catherine, or Alexander. Take European history. It's all the more so in agriculture. Even the potato was introduced into Russia by force. Even our wooden plows, after all, haven't always been used. They were brought here, maybe in the earliest days, but no doubt also by force. Now in our own day, we landowners, under serfdom, started in farming with improvements; drying kilns, threshing machines, all sorts of implements—we introduced all that by our own authority; at first the peasants resisted, then they copied us. Now, with the abolition of serfdom, our authority has been taken away, and our farming, which had been raised to a high level, is bound to sink back again to the most barbarous, primitive condition. That's how I look at it."

"But why? If it's rational you'll be able to keep it up with hired labor," said Sviyazhsky.

"Not without authority. Tell me, just tell me: Whom am I to do it with?"

There it is, thought Levin, manpower—the chief element in farming.

"With hired laborers."

"Hired laborers don't want to work well, or work with good tools. The only thing our hired laborers can do is get drunk as pigs, and when they're drunk they ruin everything you give them. They'll water the horses to death, spoil a good harness, sell the tires for drink, and drop bolts into the threshing machine to break it. They hate the sight of anything unfamiliar. That's just why the whole level of agriculture has gone down. Land has been abandoned, or overgrown with weeds, or handed over to the peasants, and where millions of bushels were once raised you get a few hundred thousand now; the wealth of the whole country has decreased. If they had done the same thing but at the same time figured out that—"

And he began developing his own scheme of emancipation, which would have eliminated these shortcomings.

This didn't interest Levin, but after he finished Levin returned to his first proposition and said, turning to Sviyazhsky and trying to make him express his own serious opinion:

"It's perfectly true that there has been a decline in the level of agriculture, and that it's impossible to carry on rational farming profitably with our present attitude toward the peasants," he said.

"I don't think so," objected Sviyazhsky, by now quite serious. "All I see is that we don't know how to farm, and that the level at which we used to farm under serfdom was not too high, on the contrary, it was too low. We have no machines, and no good stock, no real management, and we don't know how to keep accounts. Ask any landowner—he doesn't know what he makes money on and what he doesn't."

"Italian bookkeeping!" said the landowner sarcastically. "No matter how you calculate, if they ruin everything you've got there won't be any profit."

"But why should they ruin everything? They can break one of your miserable threshing machines, or a Russian presser, but they won't break my steam threshing machine. They'll ruin one of your wretched Russian nags, the kind you have to drag along by the tail, but just get in a Percheron, or just a good cart horse, and they won't be harmed. That's how it is with everything. What we have to do is raise the standard of farming even higher."

"Yes, if you can afford it! It's all very well for you, but I'm keeping a son at the university, and I'm paying for my younger ones at the secondary school—*I'm* not going to be able to buy any Percherons."

"That's what banks are there for."

"And wind up being auctioned off? No, thank you!"

"I don't agree that it's possible or necessary to raise the level of farming any higher," said Levin. "I've been trying to, and I have means, but I've never been able to accomplish anything. I don't know who benefits by the banks. At any rate no matter what I've spent money on for farming I've always had a loss: stock—a loss; machinery—a loss."

"Now there's the truth!" said the landowner with the gray mustache, actually laughing with pleasure.

"And I'm not the only one," Levin went on. "I see all the landowners around me who are carrying on a rational farming system; with rare exceptions they're all running at a loss. Well, now you tell us—how is your own farm doing? Is it profitable?" said Levin, and in Sviyazhsky's eyes he instantly noticed that fleeting look of alarm he had always noticed when he tried to penetrate further than the public reception rooms of his mind.

Besides, this question wasn't entirely honest on Levin's part. Over tea his hostess had just told him that they had hired a German from Moscow that summer, an expert bookkeeper, who for five hundred rubles had investigated the management of their farm and discovered that it had been running at a loss of some 3000 rubles and a bit. She couldn't recall just how much it was, but apparently the German had worked it all out to the last fraction of a kopeck.

At the mention of the profit on Sviyazhsky's farm the landowner smiled, evidently familiar with the sort of profits his neighbor and Marshal was likely to have been making.

"It may be unprofitable," Sviyazhsky retorted, "but that simply proves either that I'm a bad manager or that I'm putting in capital in order to increase income."

"Oh—income!" cried Levin in horror. "Land may produce income in Europe, where it's been improved by the labor applied to it, but here in Russia all the land has been getting worse because of the labor put in on it, that is, it's being worked out. As a result there is no income."

"What d'you mean—no income? That's a natural law."

"Then we're outside the law: here rent doesn't explain anything, on the contrary, it's a source of confusion. No, it's up to you to tell us how the doctrine of income can be—"

"Would you like some potcheese and sour cream? Masha, bring us some potcheese and sour cream or raspberries," Sviyazhsky said, turning to his wife. "This year the raspberries are holding out remarkably late."

And in the most excellent spirits Sviyazhsky got up and went out, obviously thinking the conversation had ended at just the point where it seemed to Levin it was only beginning.

Levin went on talking with the landowner, trying to prove to him that the whole difficulty arose out of our own refusal to discover the characteristics and habits of our laborers; but like everyone who thinks by himself in solitude the landowner was impervious to the ideas of others and particularly stubborn about his own. He insisted that the Russian peasant was a hog and loved being one, and that to get him out of his hoggishness you had to have authority, and there was none; you needed a stick, but we had become so liberal that we had suddenly replaced the thousand-year-old stick by some kind of lawyers and model prisons where the stinking, good-for-nothing peasants were fed on good soup and provided with so and so many cubic feet of air.

"What makes you think," said Levin, trying to get back to the point, "that it's impossible to discover a relationship to manpower which would make labor productive?"

"Nothing like that will ever happen with the Russian people! We have no authority," answered the landowner.

"But how can any new conditions be discovered?" said Sviyazhsky, who had eaten his potcheese and sour cream, lighted a cigarette, and was now coming over again to the argument. "Every possible relationship to manpower has been analyzed and studied," he said. "That relic of barbarism, the primitive commune with everything reciprocally guaranteed, is decomposing of itself; serfdom has been abolished;

the only thing left is free labor, in which the forms are defined and ready-made, and must be accepted. The hired hand, the day laborer, the farmer—you can't get away from them."

"But Europe isn't satisfied with this system."

"It's dissatisfied and is looking for new forms. And it will probably find them."

"That's all I'm talking about," answered Levin. "So why shouldn't we look for them for ourselves?"

"Because it would be just the same as inventing new methods for building railroads. They're ready now, all invented."

"But what if they don't suit us, what if they're stupid?" said Levin.

And once again he noticed a look of alarm in Sviyazhsky's eyes.

"Oh yes, we can fling our caps in the air—*we've* found what Europe's been looking for! I know all that, but, forgive me—d'you know what's been done in Europe about the organization of labor?"

"Not very well."

"This question is now preoccupying the best minds in Europe. The Schulze-Delitsch movement—And then there's all that vast literature on the working-class question, of the most liberal Lassalle tendency . . . The Mulhausen system— that's already accomplished, as you doubtless know."

"I've got some notion about it, but it's very vague."

"No, you just talk that way, you probably know it all no worse than I. Of course I'm not a professor of sociology, but it interested me, and really, if it's of interest to you it would be better if you studied it."

"But what conclusion have they come to?"

"Excuse me . . ."

The landowners had gotten up, and Sviyazhsky, having checked Levin once again in his disagreeable habit of prying into what lay beyond the reception rooms of his mind, went to see his guests out.

## XXVIII

LEVIN was unendurably bored that evening with the ladies: he was excited as never before by the thought that the dissatisfaction with farming that he felt now was not a personal mood, but was the general state of affairs in Russia, and that some arrangement for the workers in which they would work as they did for the peasant he had met on his way over was not a dream, but a problem that had to be solved. It seemed to him that this problem could be solved and that an attempt ought to be made to do it.

After saying good night to the ladies and promising to stay on another day in order to ride over to see an interesting landslide in the state forest, Levin went to his host's study before going to sleep to get some books on the working-class question that Sviyazhsky had suggested to him. Sviyazhsky's study was an immense room lined with book cupboards. It had two tables—one of them a massive writing desk in the middle, the other a round one with the latest numbers of various reviews and newspapers in different languages arranged around a star-shaped lamp. Next to the writing desk there was a stand with various business papers in drawers marked by gold labels.

Sviyazhsky got out the books and sat down in the rocking chair.

"What are you looking at?" he said to Levin, who had stopped at the round table and was looking at one of the reviews.

"Oh yes, that's a very interesting article," said Sviyazhsky about the review Levin had in his hands. "It turns out," he added with gleeful animation, "that the chief agent in the partition of Poland was not Frederick at all. It turns out—"

And with his characteristic lucidity he began giving a condensed account of these new and extremely important and interesting discoveries. In spite of Levin's being pre-occupied just now by his thoughts about agriculture more than anything else, he asked himself as he listened to his host: What can be inside of him? And why, *why* is he interested in the partition of Poland?

When Sviyazhsky finished, Levin asked in spite of himself: "Well, what about it?" But there was nothing about it: what was interesting was simply what had "turned out." But Sviyazhsky did think it necessary to explain just why it all interested him.

"Yes, I was very interested in that irritable landowner," said Levin with a sigh. "He's intelligent and was saying a great many correct things."

"Oh, go on! At heart he's a die-hard believer in serf-dom, as they all are!" said Sviyazhsky.

"Whose Marshal you are . . ."

"Yes, except that I marshal them in the opposite direction," said Sviyazhsky, laughing.

"Now this is what I find very interesting," said Levin, "he's right when he says that our method, that is, rational farming, doesn't pay, and that the only farming that works is either one based on moneylending, like that quiet fellow's, or else the simple kind. Whose fault is it?"

"Ours, of course. Besides, it's not true it doesn't pay. Vasilchikov's pays."

"A factory . . ."

"But I still don't understand what surprises you. The people are on such a low level of development, both material and moral, that it's perfectly plain they're bound to resist anything unfamiliar. Rational farming pays in Europe because the people are educated; consequently, what we have to do is educate the people—that's all."

"But how can the people be educated?"

"To educate the people three things are needed—schools, schools, and more schools."

"But you said yourself the people were on a low level of material development; how will the schools help that?"

"You know you remind me of that story about giving advice to a sick man: 'Try a laxative.' 'They gave me one, it's worse now.' 'Try leeches.' 'I have: it's worse.' 'Well, then all you can do is pray to God.' 'I have and that's worse.' It's just the same with you and me. I mention political economy, you say—worse. I mention Socialism—worse. Education—worse."

"But how *will* schools help?"

"They'll give the people other needs."

"Now there's something I've never understood," Levin protested hotly. "How will schools help the people improve their material condition? You say schools and education will give them new needs. That would be so much the worse, since they'll be incapable of satisfying them. As to how a knowledge of addition and subtraction and the catechism is going to help them improve their material condition, I've never been able to understand. The other evening I met a peasant woman with a nursing child and asked her where she was going. She said she was going to see the 'wise woman' because her little boy had convulsions and she was taking him to be cured. I asked her how the wise woman cured convulsions. 'She puts the baby on the perch among the chickens and says something.'"

"But there you say the same thing yourself! For her *not* to take the child to be cured by putting it on a perch in the chicken house," said Sviyazhsky, smiling gaily, "what we need is—"

"Oh no!" said Levin irritably. "For me that cure is just the same as curing the people by means of schools. The peasants are poor and uneducated—we know that just as surely as the peasant woman knows the child has convulsions because it screams. But just how the schools are going to cure this calamity of poverty and ignorance is just as incomprehensible as it is incomprehensible how putting the chickens on a perch is going to cure convulsions. What has to be cured is the source of their poverty."

"Well, there at least you agree with Spencer, whom you dislike so much. He also says that education can be the result of greater well-being and comfort, of frequent ablutions, as he puts it, but not of being able to read and reckon . . ."

"All right, I'm very happy or rather very unhappy to find myself agreeing with Spencer; it's just that I've known that for a long time. The schools won't be any help, the thing that can help is an economic system in which the peasants are richer and have more leisure—and then there will be schools too."

"But throughout Europe now the schools are compulsory."

"And how do you yourself feel about what Spencer says?" asked Levin.

But an expression of fright flashed through Sviyazhsky's eyes; he said with a smile:

"No, really, that convulsion story is magnificent! Did you hear it yourself?"

Levin saw that he was never going to find the connection between this man's life and his thoughts. It was obvious that it was a matter of complete indifference to him what his reasoning led him to: what he required was only the process of reasoning itself. And it was disagreeable when the process of reasoning led him into a blind alley; that was the only thing he disliked, and he evaded it by shifting the conversation to something gay and agreeable.

All the impressions of that day, beginning with the impression of the peasant at the halfway point, which seemed to serve as the foundation for all his inner feelings and thoughts, had violently agitated Levin. There was this charming Sviyazhsky, who kept his opinions only for use in public and who obviously had some other principles of life that were hidden from Levin, while at the same time, together with the throng whose name is legion, he guided public opinion by means of thoughts that were alien to him; and that exasperated landowner, completely correct in his views, painfully wrung out of his life, but wrong in his bitterness against a whole class, which was the best class in Russia; Levin's dissatisfaction with his own activity and the confused hope he had had of finding a general remedy—all this fused into a feeling of inner agitation and the expectation of an imminent resolution.

Left alone in the room he had been given, stretched out on a spring mattress that gave unexpectedly whenever he moved an arm or a leg, Levin could not fall asleep for a long time. Not a single conversation with Sviyazhsky interested him, though a great many things Sviyashsky had said were clever, but the landowner's arguments called for consideration. Involuntarily he recalled everything the landowner had said and in his imagination corrected his own answers.

Yes, I ought to have said to him: "You say that our farming doesn't pay because the peasant hates all improvements and that they have to be introduced by force; now, if farming didn't pay without such improvements you'd be right, but it does pay, and it pays only where the peasant acts in accordance with his own habits, the way it is on that peasant's farm halfway over here. Our common discontent with farming proves that those to blame are either ourselves or the peasants. We've pushed along on our own way, the European way, for a long time, without taking into account the characteristics of our manpower. Let us try looking on our manpower not as abstract man*power*, but as the Russian peasant, with all his instincts, and let us arrange our farming accordingly."

What I ought to have said to him was: "Just imagine that your farming is being carried on like that old man's, that you have found a means of interesting the laborers in the outcome of their labor, and have found a happy medium in the degree of progress which they will recognize—then, without exhausting the soil you will get twice and three times as much as before. Divide everything up equally; give one half to the manpower; the share left for you will be bigger, and manpower will get more. But to do this we must lower the standard of farming and interest the laborers in its results. *How* to do this is a question of detail; but there can be no doubt of its being possible."

This idea violently excited Levin. He couldn't fall asleep half the night, turning over in his mind all the details of implementing it. He hadn't intended leaving the next day, but now he made up his mind to go home early in the morning. Aside from this the sister-in-law in the square-cut bodice produced a feeling in him like that of the shame and repentance due to the commission of a wrong action. But the main thing was that he had to leave at once: he had to get to the peasants in time to propose his new scheme to them, before the winter sowing, so that it could be done on the new basis. He had made up his mind to revolutionize his whole former system of farming.

## XXIX

THE execution of Levin's scheme presented a great many difficulties, but he struggled on as best he could, and though he didn't attain what he had wanted his success was enough for him to enable himself to believe without self-deception that the thing was worth doing. One of the principal difficulties was that farming was already under way, that it was impossible to stop everything and start it all up again from scratch; the machine had to be overhauled while still in motion.

On his return home that same evening, when he told the foreman of his plans, the foreman, with visible pleasure, agreed with that part of what Levin was saying that proved that everything done up to then was nonsensical and pernicious. The foreman said he had been saying as much for a long time, but that no one had wanted to listen to him. As for the proposal made by Levin, that he participate as a shareholder, together with the laborers, in the enterprise of the farm as a whole, the foreman merely expressed great dejection, though no definite opinion, and immediately started talking about the necessity of carting away the last sheaves of rye and starting the second plowing, so that Levin felt that now was not the time to bring up his proposal.

When he started talking to the peasants about the same thing and made them an offer of land on the new conditions, he ran into the same principal obstacle: they were so taken up with the current day's work that they had no time to reflect on the advantages or disadvantages of Levin's proposal.

The naïve peasant Ivan, the cowman, seemed to grasp Levin's proposal fully—to share together with his family in the profits of the dairy farm—and was in complete sympathy with the project. But when Levin hinted at the future profits a look of alarm passed over Ivan's face; he regretted that he couldn't stay to hear the whole thing, and he hurriedly thought up something for himself to do that couldn't be put off: he would seize a pitchfork to remove the hay from the stalls, or run off to fill the troughs or sweep up the manure.

Another difficulty consisted in the invincible disbelief of the peasants that the landowner's aim might consist of anything but the desire to squeeze all he could out of them. They were firmly convinced that his real aim, no matter what he told them, would always be hidden in what he didn't tell them. And they themselves, though they talked a great deal while giving their opinion, never said what their own real aim was. Aside from this (Levin felt that the choleric landowner had been right) the peasants laid it down as a primary and unalterable condition of any agreement that they would not be forced into any new methods of farming or the use of any new implements. They agreed that an English plow did better plowing, that a scarifier did the work more quickly, but they thought up a thousand reasons why it would be impossible for them to use one or the other, and even though Levin was convinced that the level of farming had to be lowered he was sorry to renounce the various improvements whose advantages were so obvious. But in spite of all these difficulties he got his own way, and by autumn his project was under way, or at any rate so it seemed to him.

At first he had thought of putting the whole farm, just as it was, in the hands of the working peasants and the foreman on the new conditions of partnership, but he very soon saw this was impossible, and he decided to divide it up. The dairy farm, the vegetable garden, the orchard, the hay fields, the arable land, divided into several parts, were to constitute separate units. Ivan, the naïve cowman, who it

seemed to Levin understood the project better than anyone else, got together a co-operative association, consisting primarily of his own family, and became a partner
in the dairy farm. The far field, which had lain fallow for
eight years, was taken over, with the aid of an intelligent
carpenter, Theodore Rezunov, by six peasant families on
the new social basis, and a peasant, Shurayev, similarly
took over all the kitchen gardens. Everything else was still
run in the old way, but these three units were the start
of the new order and took up all Levin's time.

To be sure, the dairy farm for the time being was not
running any better than before; Ivan strongly opposed
heating the cowshed and making butter from fresh cream;
he maintained that cows ate less fodder when they were
cold and that butter made from sour cream went further.
He demanded his wages just as before, and didn't have the
slightest interest in the fact that the money he got was not
wages but an advance against profits.

To be sure, Theodore Rezunov's association did not
plow their land twice before sowing, as had been agreed;
they justified this by saying there wasn't enough time. To
be sure, the peasants of this association, even though they
had agreed to carry on the enterprise on the new basis,
never referred to the land as jointly owned, but as land held
for payment in kind, and more than once the peasants,
and Rezunov himself, said to Levin: "If only you'd accept
rent for the land you'd feel better and we'd feel freer." In
addition to this, these peasants kept putting off, on various
pretexts, the agreed on building of a cattle yard and granary
on this land and procrastinated until winter.

To be sure, Shurayev had arranged to sublet his kitchen
gardens to the other peasants in small lots. He had
obviously misunderstood, apparently deliberately, the conditions on which the land had been let to him.

To be sure, Levin would often feel, in speaking with the
peasants and explaining all the advantages of the project to
them, that they were only listening to the sound of his voice
and had it firmly fixed in their minds that no matter what he
said they were not going to let themselves be swindled by
him. He felt this especially whenever he spoke to the most
intelligent of the peasants, Rezunov, and noticed a glint in his
eyes that clearly displayed both his derision of Levin and a
firm conviction that if anyone was going to be swindled it
wasn't going to be Rezunov.

But in spite of all this Levin thought that the project was making headway and that by keeping strict accounts and insisting on his own point of view he would prove to them the advantages of such a system, and then the project would move by itself.

All these things, together with the rest of the farming that was left on his hands, as well as the work at home on his book, took up all Levin's summer to such a point that he scarcely ever went shooting. At the end of August he learned from a servant of theirs who brought back the sidesaddle that the Oblonskys had left for Moscow. He felt that by not having answered Dolly's letter—a piece of rudeness he could not think of without a blush of shame—he had burned his boats and would surely never be visiting them again. This was exactly the way he had behaved with the Sviyazhskys when he had left without saying good-by. But he was never going to visit them either. Now he no longer cared about all that. The reorganization of his farming system preoccupied him as nothing else in his life had before. He read through the books he had gotten from Sviyazhsky, and after ordering the things he lacked he also read through both politico-economic and Socialist books on this subject; as he had expected he found nothing that had any reference to what he was trying to do. In the politico-economic books, in Mill, for instance, which he studied first with immense ardor, hoping to find out at any moment an answer to the problems that preoccupied him, he found a number of laws that had been deduced from the state of European agriculture; but he couldn't see at all why these laws, inapplicable in Russia, were supposed to be universal. He saw the same thing in the Socialist books: either they were lovely phantasies, though inapplicable, that he had been infatuated with while still a student, or else they were improvements or repairs of the state of affairs that Europe had been immersed in and that Russian agriculture had nothing in common with. Political economy said that the laws according to which the welfare of Europe had developed and was developing, were universal and incontestable. Socialist doctrine said that any evolution according to such laws would lead to ruin. And neither one nor the other not only gave no answer, but they didn't give the slightest hint at what he, Levin, and all the Russian peasants and landowners were to do with their millions of hands and acres in order to make them as productive as possible for the common good.

Once he really got his teeth into this project he conscientiously read through everything bearing on his subject; he intended going abroad in the autumn to go on studying this question on the spot, so that the same thing that had so often happened with him in discussing various questions wouldn't happen to him now. What would often happen would be that the moment he began grasping the thought of someone he was talking to and expounding his own he would suddenly be asked: "And what about Kaufmann, and Jones, and Dubois, and Miccelli? You haven't read them? Read them! They've worked it all out."

He now saw clearly that Kaufmann and Miccelli had nothing to tell him. He knew what he wanted. He saw that Russia had magnificent land and magnificent laborers and that in a few cases, such as that of the peasant at the halfway point on the road, the laborers and the land produced a great deal, but that in the majority of cases, when the capital was expended in the European way, they produced very little, and that this was due only to the fact that the workers were willing to work and were working well only in the way that was characteristic of them, and that this resistance was not accidental, but was constant, with its roots in the spirit of the people. He thought that the Russian people, with their mission of deliberately settling and cultivating vast unoccupied territories as long as they remained unoccupied, held to the methods called for by that, and that these methods were far from being as bad as was usually thought. And he wanted to prove this, theoretically, in his book, and practically, in his farming.

## XXX

By the end of September the timber had been brought in for the construction of the cattle yard on the land allotted to the co-operative group, the butter had been sold and the profits split up. Practically speaking the farming project had worked out excellently, or at any rate so it seemed to Levin. Thus, in order to give a theoretical explanation of the whole project and finish his book, which in Levin's daydreams was not only supposed to revolutionize political economy but completely destroy it as a science and lay the foundations of a new science—the relationship of land and people—all that was necessary was for him to go abroad, study on the spot everything being done there along those lines, and find convincing proofs that nothing of what was being done there was what was needed. Levin was only waiting for the wheat to be delivered in order to get his money and go abroad. But the rains set in, making it impossible to gather what remained of the corn and potatoes and stopping all the work and even the delivery of the wheat. Mud made the roads impassable; two mills were carried away by floods, and the weather kept getting worse and worse.

On September 30 the sun showed itself in the morning and, hoping for good weather, Levin began seriously preparing for his departure. He ordered the wheat to be sacked for carting, sent the foreman to the merchant to get the money for it, while he himself went about the farm in order to give final instructions before leaving.

Having finished all his business, drenched with the streams of water that kept trickling down the leather behind his neck or over the top of his high boots, but in the most cheerful and lively temper, Levin returned home in the evening. The bad weather had grown still worse toward evening: the sleet lashed the drenched mare so viciously that she walked sideways, shaking her head and ears, but Levin felt cozy under his hood; he kept cheerfully looking round him, now at the muddy streamlets running in the ruts, now at the drops hanging from every bare twig, now at the white patches of frozen sleet on the planks of the bridge, now at the thick layer of still juicy willow leaves heaped round the naked tree. In spite of the gloom of the natural surroundings he felt particularly elated. His conversations with the peasants in an outlying village showed that they were beginning to get used to their new situation. An old house porter whose hut he had gone to in order to get dry obviously approved of Levin's scheme and offered to join an association to buy cattle himself.

All I have to do is to move stubbornly toward my goal and I'll get my own way, thought Levin; that's something worth working and striving for. This isn't a private business of my own, it's a question of the general welfare. The whole farming system, above all the condition of the entire people, must be completely altered. Instead of poverty there will be general wealth and contentment; instead of hostility there'll be harmony and a union of interests. In a word, it will be a bloodless revolution, but a most grandiose revolution, first in the little circle of our district, then the province, then Russia, then the whole world. A just idea cannot help being fruitful. Yes, that's a goal worth working for. And the fact that I started it, I, Constantine Levin, the same man who went to a ball in a black tie and was refused by Kitty Shcherbatsky, and who seems so pathetic and worthless to himself—none of that proves a thing. I'm sure Benjamin Franklin felt just as worthless and had the same distrust of himself as I when he summed himself up. That means nothing. And doubtless he also had his Miss Agatha whom he confided his dreams to.

Thoughts like these filled Levin's mind when he reached home, by the time it was already dark.

The foreman who had been to the merchant's, had returned with an installment of the money for the wheat. An agreement had been made with the old house porter and on the road the foreman had heard that everywhere the corn was still standing in the fields, so that his own one hundred and sixty shocks still ungathered were nothing compared with what the others were losing.

After dinner Levin sat down as usual in an armchair with a book, and as he read he went on thinking about his forthcoming trip in connection with the book he was writing. The whole significance of his project was particularly clear in his mind today, and whole paragraphs that expressed the essence of his ideas took shape of their own accord. I'll have to write that down, he thought; it ought to form the short introduction I had thought superfluous before. He got up, to go over to the writing desk, and Laska, who was lying at his feet, stretched herself and got up too, looking up at him as though asking where they were off to. But there was no time to write anything, because the peasants' foremen had come for the next day's instructions and Levin went out to see them in the hall.

After giving his instructions for the following day's work and seeing all the peasants who had some business with him, Levin went into his study and set to work. Laska lay down under the table; Miss Agatha took her place with her knitting.

After writing for a while Levin suddenly, with extraordinary vividness, remembered Kitty, her refusal and their last meeting. He got up and began pacing about the room.

"There's no sense feeling so bored," Miss Agatha said to him. "What d'you sit around the house for? You ought to go to some spa, now that you've made all the preparations for a trip."

"That's what I'm doing, the day after tomorrow. I have to finish this business."

"A fine business too! Haven't you done enough for the peasants as it is? They're all saying 'Your master's going to get a medal from the Tsar for it!' And a strange thing it is; why should you bother yourself about the peasants?"

"I'm not bothering myself for them, I'm doing it for myself."

Miss Agatha knew all the details of Levin's farming plans. He had often explained his ideas to her in all their details, argued with her, and didn't agree with her criticisms. But this time she completely misunderstood what he had said to her.

"Yes, you must think of your soul before anything else, it's well known," she said with a sigh. "Look at Parfen Denisich, he may have been illiterate, but he died a death God grant everyone," she said, about a servant who had died recently. "He took the sacraments and all."

"That's not what I'm talking about," he said. "I said I was doing it for my own profit. There's more profit for me if the peasants work better."

"But no matter what you do if someone's a lazy good-for-nothing he'll do everything every which way. If he's got a conscience he'll work, if not there's nothing you can do about it."

"Well, you yourself say Ivan's started looking after the cattle better now."

"There's only one thing I say," replied Miss Agatha, evidently not at random, but in strict logic, "you have to get married, that's what!"

Her mentioning the same thing he had just been thinking about hurt and annoyed him. Levin frowned and without answering her sat down again at his work, repeating to himself everything he had been thinking about its importance. Only occasionally he listened in the silence to the clicking of Miss Agatha's needles, and being reminded of what he didn't want to be reminded of he would frown again.

At nine o'clock they heard a bell, and the heavy lurching of a carriage through the mud.

"There, now you'll have some guests, you won't be bored," said Miss Agatha, getting up and going to the door. But Levin ran out ahead of her. His work was no longer moving and he was glad of any visitor at all.

## XXXI

RUNNING halfway down the stairs, Levin heard a familiar sound of coughing in the hall, but because of the sound of his own footsteps he heard it indistinctly and hoped he had made a mistake. Then he caught sight of the whole long, bony familiar figure; it would have seemed impossible to deceive oneself any longer, nevertheless he kept hoping that he was mistaken and that this gangling man taking off his overcoat and coughing away was not his brother Nicholas.

Levin was fond of his brother, but being together with him was always anguish. And now, when Levin, under the influence of the idea that had come to him and of Miss Agatha's hints, was in a confused state of mind, the forthcoming meeting with his brother seemed to him especially distressing. Instead of a cheerful, healthy stranger who he hoped would divert him in his spiritual confusion he had to see his brother, who understood him through and through and who would summon up in him all his innermost thoughts and force him to give full expression to them. This was just what he didn't want.

Angry with himself for this despicable feeling, Levin ran into the hall. The instant he saw his brother close up this feeling of selfish disappointment vanished at once and was replaced by compassion. Dreadful as Nicholas had been before in his emaciation and sickliness, he was still more emaciated and even weaker now. He was a skeleton covered with skin.

He was standing in the hall, jerking his long, thin neck and drawing off a scarf; he gave Levin a strangely pathetic smile. When he saw this smile, meek and submissive, Levin felt his throat contract convulsively.

"You see I've come to you," said Nicholas in a thick voice, not for a moment lowering his gaze from his brother's face. "I've wanted to for a long time, but my health kept on being bad. But now I'm very much improved," he said, wiping his beard with the thin palms of his big hands.

"Yes, yes!" Levin replied. He was still more terrified when he kissed him and with his lips felt the dryness of his brother's flesh and saw close up his great eyes with their strange glitter.

Levin had written him a few weeks before that a small part

of the property that had not been divided had been sold and that Nicholas could get his share, about two thousand rubles.

Nicholas said he had come to get this money now, and most of all to stay awhile in his own nest and touch the soil, so that like the heroes of old he could gather his strength for the work that lay before him. In spite of his being more round-shouldered than ever, and in spite of his emaciation, which because of his height was so striking, his motions were as swift and jerky as usual. Levin led him to his room.

Nicholas took particular pains with his dressing, which he had never used to do, combed his scanty, lank hair, and went upstairs smiling.

He was in the most affectionate and cheerful mood, as Levin recalled him often in childhood. He even referred to Koznyshov without any spite. When he saw Miss Agatha he joked with her and asked her about the old servants. The news of Parfen Denisich's death had a painful effect on him. A look of fright passed over his face, but he recovered immediately.

"But he was old already, wasn't he?" he said, and changed the subject. "Well, I'll spend a month with you, or two, then I'll be off to Moscow. You know Myagkov has promised me a post, I'm going into government service. I'm going to arrange my life in a completely different way now," he continued. "You know I got rid of that woman."

"Masha? Why, what for?"

"Oh, she's a revolting creature! She gave me no end of trouble." But he didn't say what the trouble had been. He couldn't say that he had turned Masha out because her tea was weak, least of all that she had been tending him as though he were an invalid. "Besides, now I want to change my life completely. Of course, like everyone else, I've done some stupid things, but money's the last thing I think of—I don't regret that. Health is what counts, and mine has improved, thank God!"

Levin listened and tried to think of something to say, but he couldn't. Nicholas probably felt this too; he began questioning Levin about his farming interests, and Levin was glad to talk about himself since he could do this without any pretense. He told Nicholas about his projects and activities.

His brother listened, but was obviously uninterested.

The two men were so akin to each other, and so close,

that the slightest movement, a tone of voice, told them both more than anything that could be said in words.

Both of them had only one idea now, Nicholas's illness and imminent death: it stifled everything else. But neither one dared speak of it; because of this whatever they said without expressing the only thing that preoccupied them was all false. Levin had never been so glad that an evening was over and that it was time to go to bed. He had never been so artificial, so false, with any outsider or on any formal call as he was that evening. And his awareness of this artificiality and remorse because of it made him still more artificial. What he wanted to do was weep over his dying, beloved brother, and he had to listen to and keep up a conversation about how he was going to live.

Since the house was damp and his bedroom was the only room heated Levin put his brother to sleep in his own bedroom, behind a partition.

Nicholas went to bed, but whether asleep or not he kept tossing about like a sick man and coughing, and when he couldn't get his throat clear he would mutter something. Sometimes, when his breathing was painful he said, "Oh my God!" Sometimes, when the phlegm choked him he muttered angrily, "Devil take it!" Levin listened to him for a long time without sleeping. Levin's thoughts were very various, but they all ended up the same way—with death.

Death, the inevitable end of everything, confronted him for the first time with irresistible force. And this particular death, there in his beloved brother, who half-asleep kept groaning and out of habit calling indiscriminately first on God then on the devil, was not at all so far away as it had used to seem to him. It was in himself too—he felt it. If not today then tomorrow; if not tomorrow then in thirty years—wasn't it all the same? As to just what this inevitable death was, not only did he not know, not only had he never even thought about it, but he could not and dared not think about it.

I go on working, I try to do something, and all the while I've forgotten that it's all coming to an end, that there is—death!

He sat on his bed in the dark, crouched over hugging his knees, and holding his breath because of his mental concentration. But the more he concentrated his thoughts the clearer it was to him that that's how it undoubtedly was, that he really had forgotten, had overlooked one tiny circumstance in life—that death was coming, that everything would be ended, that nothing was even worth beginning, and that there was nothing to be done about it. Yes, it was dreadful, but it was so.

But after all I'm still alive; so what can I do now, what can I do? he said despairingly. He lighted a candle, cautiously stood up, went over to the mirror and began examining his face and hair. Yes, there were some gray hairs on his temples. He opened his mouth. The back teeth were beginning to go bad. He bared his muscular arms. Yes, they were very powerful. But Nicholas too, who was breathing there with the remnants of his lungs, also had a healthy body. And suddenly he recalled how as children they had gone to bed and were just waiting for Mr. Theodore to get out of the room to throw pillows at each other, and to laugh and laugh uncontrollably so that even their fear of Mr. Theodore could not stop this overflowing, bubbling consciousness of the joy of life.

And now that hollow, sunken chest . . . And I, with no idea of what's going to happen to me or why . . . !

"Kha! K-h-ha! Ah, the devil take it!" Nicholas coughed. "What are you fidgeting about for, why don't you fall asleep?" he called over to him.

"Oh I don't know, I'm not sleepy."

"And I've had a good sleep, I'm no longer in a sweat. Take a look, feel my shirt. No sweat, is there?"

Levin felt it, went back behind the partition, and put out the candle, but he couldn't get to sleep again for a long time. Just when the question of how to live had become a little clearer to him a new and insoluble problem had presented itself—death.

Well, he's dying, he'll be dead by spring, thought Levin. How can I help him? What can I tell him? What do I know about it? I'd even forgotten there was such a thing . . .

## XXXII

LEVIN had noticed long before that when people make you uncomfortable by being too docile and submissive they very soon become unbearable by being too demanding and quarrelsome. He felt this was going to happen with his brother too. And as a matter of fact Nicholas's meekness did not last long. The very next morning he turned irritable and did his best to pick quarrels with him, pricking him at all his most sensitive points.

Levin felt guilty and could do nothing to correct it. He felt that if they hadn't both been pretending, but had had what is called a heart-to-heart talk, that is, simply told each other just what they were thinking and feeling, then they would just have looked into each other's eyes, and Constantine would only have said: "You're dying, dying, dying!" —while Nicholas would simply have replied: "I know I'm dying, but I'm afraid, afraid, afraid!" That's all they would have said if they'd been talking straight from the heart. But it was impossible to live that way, so Levin tried to do what he'd been trying to do all his life without being able to, what a great many people could do so well, as he observed, and without which life was impossible: he tried to say something different from what he thought, and he always felt it came out false, that his brother caught him out and was irritated by it.

The third day he was there Nicholas challenged Levin to tell him of his project once again; he began not only condemning it but deliberately confused it with communism.

"All you've done is taken someone else's idea, but you've distorted it and you want to apply it in the wrong place."

"But I'm telling you it has nothing in common with it. They deny the justice of private property, capital, and inheritance, while I, without denying that as the chief incentive"—Levin loathed himself for using such words, but ever since he had been engrossed in his own work he had involuntarily begun using foreign words more and more often—"simply want to regulate labor."

"That's right, you've taken someone else's idea, cut away from it everything that constitutes its power, and want to make people believe it's something new," said Nicholas, angrily jerking his neck.

"But my idea has nothing in common with—"

"The other idea," said Nicholas malevolently, with a sarcastic smile, his eyes glittering, "the other idea at any rate has what you might call a geometrical charm—of clarity and definiteness. It may be utopian. But let's admit the possibility of making *tabula rasa* of the past—if there's no property, and no family, then labor would regulate itself anyhow. But you have nothing—"

"Why d'you keep mixing them up? I've never been a Communist."

"But I have; I think it's premature, but it's rational and it has a future, like Christianity in the first centuries."

"I simply think manpower must be looked at from the point of view of natural science, that is, studied, its characteristics ascertained, and—"

"But that's a complete waste of time. Manpower finds a certain form of activity according to the stage of its development: there used to be slaves, then there were villeins; in Russia we have labor paid in kind, leaseholders, and hired laborers—so what are you after?"

Levin suddenly flared up at these words, because in his heart of hearts he was afraid it was true—it was true that he wanted to balance between communism and the established institutions, and that this was scarcely possible.

"What I'm after is a way of working that will be productive both for me and for the worker," Levin retorted hotly. "What I want to do is organize—"

"You don't want to organize anything; it's simply the way you've lived your whole life—you want to be original, and show that you're not simply exploiting the peasants, but have some idea behind it."

"All right, that's what you think—leave me alone then!" answered Levin, feeling a muscle in his left cheek twitching uncontrollably.

"You never had any convictions and you still don't, except in order to console your own vanity."

"All right then, just leave me alone!"

"I certainly will! It's high time too, and you can go to the devil! And I'm very sorry I came!"

No matter how Levin tried to soothe his brother afterward, Nicholas wouldn't listen; he kept saying it was far better to separate, and Levin saw that what his brother found unbearable was simply life itself.

Nicholas had already packed to leave altogether when Levin came to see him once again, and in an artificial way begged his pardon if he had said something to offend him.

"Aha—what magnanimity!" said Nicholas with a smile. "If you feel like being in the right I can give you that pleasure: you're in the right—and I'm leaving anyhow!"

Just before Nicholas left he and Levin embraced, and Nicholas suddenly said, with a strange, earnest look:

"Don't think too badly of me anyhow, Kostya!" And his voice trembled.

These were the only words that were said with sincerity.

Levin understood that what these words meant was: You know and can see that I'm in a bad way, and we may never be seeing each other again. Levin realized this, and tears gushed from his eyes. He kissed his brother once again, but he couldn't speak; he couldn't think of what to say to him.

Three days after his brother had left, Levin went abroad too. He ran into young Shcherbatsky, Kitty's cousin, at the railway station, and astonished him by his moroseness.

"What's the matter with you?" Shcherbatsky asked him.

"Nothing at all; just that there's not much joy in the world."

"What d'you mean—not much joy? Just come to Paris with me instead of going off to Mulhausen or whatever it's called. You'll see how much joy there is!"

"No, I've done with all that; it's time for me to die."

"Now there's something!" said Shcherbatsky laughing. "I'm just getting ready to start living."

"I thought so myself not long ago, but now I know I'll soon be dead."

Levin was saying what he had honestly been thinking lately. He saw death, present or imminent, in everything. But the project he had begun engrossed him all the more. Life had to be lived through somehow, after all, until death came. Everything was covered in darkness for him; but it was just because of this darkness that he felt that the only thread that could guide him through the darkness was his work; he clutched at it and clung to it with every ounce of his strength.

# PART FOUR

### I

THE Karenins, husband and wife, continued living in the same house; they met each other every day, but they were utter strangers. Karenin had made it a rule to see his wife every day so that the servants would not have the right to any conjectures, but he avoided dining at home. Vronsky never came to the house, but Anna saw him outside and Karenin knew it.

The situation was distressing for all three of them; not one of them could have lived through a single day in this situation if it were not for the expectation that it would change, that it was only a painful temporary ordeal that would pass away. Karenin was waiting for this passion to pass away, as everything does, for everyone to forget about it, and for his name to cease being dishonored. Anna, on whom the situation depended and for whom it was more painful than for anyone else, endured it because not only did she expect, she felt absolutely certain that soon it would all be settled and cleared up. She had no idea at all of what was going to settle it, but she was absolutely sure that whatever it was it was going to happen very soon. Vronsky, obedient to her in spite of himself, was also expecting something independent of himself that was sure to clear away all the difficulties.

In the middle of the winter Vronsky had a very boring week. He was appointed to show the sights of Petersburg to a foreign Prince who was on an official visit. Vronsky looked distinguished; he also had the art of conducting himself with respectful dignity, and was used to talking with such personages; this was why he was appointed to attend the Prince. But he found this duty extremely tiresome. The Prince didn't want to miss seeing anything in Russia he might be questioned about at home; for that matter he himself wanted to enjoy as many Russian amusements as possible. Vronsky was obliged to act as his guide for both things. In the morning they drove out sight-seeing; in the evenings they participated in the national amusements. The Prince's health was exceptional even for a Prince; through gymnastics and taking good care of his physique he had increased his fortitude to such a point that in spite of the extremes he went to in his pleasures he was as fresh as a glossy great green Dutch cucumber. The Prince had done a great deal of traveling; he thought one of the chief advantages of the modern ease of communications was the accessibility of the national amusements. He had been in Spain, where he had given serenades and become intimate with a Spanish girl who played the guitar. In Switzerland he had shot chamois. In England he had jumped hedges in a pink coat, and shot two hundred pheasants on a bet. In Turkey he had been in a harem, in India he had ridden an elephant, and now in Russia what he wanted to do was savor all the typically Russian amusements.

It cost Vronsky, who was a sort of chief master of ceremonies for him, a great deal of effort to arrange all the Russian amusements suggested to the Prince by different people. There were trotting races, pancakes, bear hunts, troikas, gypsies, and Russian sprees where the crockery was smashed. The Prince took on the Russian spirit with exceptional facility: he smashed trays full of crockery, sat a gypsy girl on his lap, and seemed to be asking: What else is there? Or is this all the Russian spirit amounts to?

Actually, of all the Russian amusements what the Prince liked best was French actresses, a ballerina, and white-seal champagne. Vronsky was used to Princes, but either because he himself had changed or because he was too close to this particular Prince, the week seemed to him terribly wearisome. Throughout the week, without letup, he had the feeling of a man set in attendance on a dangerous madman, who is afraid of him while because of his proximity having fears for his own sanity. He constantly felt the necessity of not for a moment slackening his tone of severe official deference, in order not to be insulted himself. The Prince's way of treating the people who, to Vronsky's surprise, were prepared to go to any lengths to provide him with Russian amusements, was disdainful. His remarks about Russian women, whom he wanted to study, made Vronsky flush with indignation more than once. But the chief reason Vronsky found the Prince so oppressive was that involuntarily he saw himself in him, and what he saw in this mirror did not flatter his self-esteem. The Prince was very stupid, very self-satisfied, very healthy, and very clean, and nothing more. He was a gentleman—that was true; Vronsky couldn't deny it. He was easy and dignified with his superiors, free and simple with his equals, and condescendingly good-natured with his inferiors. Vronsky was the same way himself, and considered this a great merit; but in relation to the Prince he was an inferior, and this condescendingly good-natured attitude made him indignant.

Stupid ox! Is it possible I'm like that? he thought.

In any case when he said good-by to him on the seventh day, before the Prince's departure for Moscow, and received his thanks, he was happy to have gotten rid of this uncomfortable situation and this unpleasant mirror. He said good-by to him at the station on their return from a bear hunt, where they had seen a demonstration of Russian prowess that had lasted all night.

## II

WHEN he got home Vronsky found a note from Anna: *"I'm ill and miserable. I cannot go out, but I cannot go on any longer without seeing you. Come in this evening. Karenin is going to a Council meeting at seven and will be there till ten."* After wondering for a moment at the strangeness of this forthright invitation to come to see her in spite of her husband's insistence on her not receiving him, he decided to go.

That winter Vronsky had been promoted to colonel, had left the regiment and was living alone. He had lunch and lay down on the sofa immediately afterward. Five minutes later the recollection of the grotesque scenes he had been present at during the preceding week were jumbled up and mingled with images of Anna and of the peasant who had played an important part in the bear hunt as beater. Vronsky fell asleep; he woke up in the dark, trembling with fear, and hastily lighted a candle. What was that? What was it? What was that terrifying thing I saw in the dream? Yes, yes . . . I remember that beater, the peasant, a dirty little fellow with a matted beard, bending over doing something, suddenly he started saying some peculiar words in French. Yes, that was all there was in the dream, he said to himself; but then why was it so horrifying? He vividly recalled the peasant again and the incomprehensible French words he had pronounced; a chill of horror ran down his spine.

What nonsense! thought Vronsky, and looked at his watch. It was half-past eight already. He rang for his servant, hurriedly got dressed and went out on to the front steps, having completely forgotten all about his dream and only worried at being late. As he drove up to the Karenins' entrance he looked at his watch and saw it was ten minutes to nine. A high, narrow carriage with a pair of grays was standing at the entrance. He recognized it as Anna's. She's coming to me, Vronsky thought; it would be better if she did, I dislike going into this house. But it doesn't matter, I can't hide myself, he said to himself, and with the manner, habitual to him since childhood, of someone who has nothing to be ashamed of, Vronsky got out of the sleigh and went to the door. The door opened and the hall porter with a rug on his arm called the carriage. Vronsky wasn't used to noticing details, but now he noticed the expression of surprise with which the hall porter looked at him. In the very doorway he almost collided with Karenin. The gaslight fell directly on Karenin's bloodless, worn face under his black hat, and the white necktie gleaming against the beaver collar of his coat. Karenin's motionless, dull eyes were fastened on Vronsky's face. Vronsky bowed, and Karenin, pressing his lips together, raised a hand to his hat and passed by. Vronsky saw him get into the carriage without looking round, take the rug and pair of opera glasses through the carriage window, and disappear. Vronsky went into the hall; his brows were drawn together in a scowl, and his eyes shone with a malevolent, haughty gleam.

What a situation! he thought. If he were to fight in defense of his honor I'd be able to do something, to express my feelings; but this weakness, or meanness . . . He's putting me in the position of a cheat, which I never wanted to be and still don't!

Since his conversation with Anna in the Vrede garden, Vronsky's ideas had changed a great deal. Involuntarily submitting to the weakness of Anna, who was giving herself up to him entirely and was expecting from him nothing but the settlement of her fate and was ready in advance to accept anything, he had long since stopped thinking that his liaison with her could come to an end as he had thought at one time. His ambitious plans had receded into the background once again, and feeling that he had left the sphere of activity in which everything was defined he was giving all of himself over to his feeling, and this feeling kept binding him to her more and more powerfully.

While still in the hall he could catch the sound of her retreating footsteps. He realized she had been waiting and listening for him, and had now gone back into the drawing room.

"No!" she cried out when she saw him; as soon as she spoke the tears came into her eyes. "No—if things go on this way it will happen much much too soon!"

"What, my dear?"

"What? I keep waiting, in torment, one hour, two . . . No, I won't do it! I can't quarrel with you—probably you couldn't help it. No, I won't do it!"

She put both hands on his shoulders and looked at him for a long time with a profound, passionate and at the same time searching look. She was studying his face to make up for the time she hadn't seen him. She was doing what she always did when she saw him—comparing the image of him in her imagination (incomparably superior, and impossible in reality) with him as he was.

## III

Dᴵᴰ you meet him?" she asked, when they had sat down at a table under the lamp. "Now you're punished for being late!"

"Yes, but how did it happen? Wasn't he supposed to be at the Council?"

"He was there and came back, then he went off somewhere else. But it doesn't matter, don't let's speak of it. Where have you been? With the Prince the whole time?"

She knew all the details of his life. He wanted to tell her he had been up all night and had dropped asleep, but when he looked at her excited happy face he felt ashamed of himself. He said he had to go and report the Prince's departure.

"But now it's finished? He's left?"

"Thank God it's finished! You won't believe how unbearable it was for me."

"But why? After all, that's the way all you young men live," she said, frowning, and taking up her crochet work which was lying on the table she began disentangling the hook without looking at him.

"I left that life a long time ago," he said, surprised by the change of expression on her face and trying to penetrate its meaning. "I admit," he said, showing his closely set teeth in a smile, "I kept seeing myself in a mirror, looking at this life the whole week, and I found it disagreeable."

She was holding her crochet work in her hands, though she wasn't crocheting, but looking at him with strange, glittering, and hostile eyes.

"Lisa came to see me this morning—they're still not afraid to call on me, in spite of Countess Lydia," she put in, "and she told me about your Athenian party. How loathsome!"

"I was just going to say that—"

She interrupted him. "Was the Thérèse you used to know there?"

"I was going to say that—"

"How loathsome you all are, you men! How is it you cannot understand that a woman can't forget such things," she said, growing more and more heated and showing him the reason for her annoyance. "Especially a woman who cannot know what sort of life you're leading. What do I know? What have I ever known?" she said. "Just what you've told me. And how can I be sure you've been telling me the truth—"

"Anna! You're hurting me. Don't you believe me? Haven't I told you there's not a thought in my mind which I'd hide from you?"

"Yes, yes," she said, obviously struggling to drive away her jealous thoughts. "But if you only knew how hard it is for me! I believe you, I believe you . . . Well, what were you saying?"

But he couldn't recall all at once what he had wanted to say. These attacks of jealousy that had recently been coming over her more and more often horrified him; no matter how he tried to hide this they made him feel colder toward her, in spite of his knowing that the reason for her jealousy was her love for him. How often had he not said to himself that her love was his happiness; and here she loved him as only a woman can for whom love outweighs every other good thing in life—and he was much further removed from happiness than when he had left Moscow to follow her. At that time he had considered himself unhappy, but happiness lay ahead; while now he felt that his greatest happiness already lay behind him. She was completely different now from what she had been when he saw her first. Both morally and physically she had changed for the worst. She had broadened out all over, and when she mentioned the actress a malevolent expression passed over her face that distorted it. He looked at her as a man would look at a faded flower he had plucked, recognizing with difficulty the beauty for the sake of which he had plucked and destroyed it. And in spite of this he felt that at the time his love had been stronger he might have torn this love out of his heart if he had had a strong desire to, but that at this moment, when it seemed to him that he felt no love for her at all, he knew that the bond between them could not be broken.

"Well, well—then what did you want to tell me about the Prince? I've driven him away, the Demon," she added. Between them they referred to jealousy as the Demon. "Yes, what was it you had begun telling me about the Prince? Why was it so painful for you?"

"Oh, it was unbearable!" he said, trying to find the thread of the thought he had lost. "He doesn't gain on closer acquaintance. If he were to be defined, it would be as a splendidly fed animal of the kind that gets the first medal at a show—nothing more than that," he said, in an irritable tone that aroused her interest.

"No, really," she protested, "what d'you mean? After all, he's seen a great deal; isn't he very educated?"

"It's quite a different education—that education of theirs. It's obvious he's been educated only for the purpose of entitling him to despise education, as they despise everything but animal pleasures."

"But don't all of you like those animal pleasures?" she said, and once again he noted that morose look of hers which evaded his own.

"But why do you defend him so?" he said with a smile.

"I'm not defending him, it's a matter of complete indifference to me, but I think that if you yourself didn't like such pleasures you would have been able to refuse them. But it gives you pleasure to watch Thérèse dressed as Eve . . ."

"The Demon again, the Demon!" said Vronsky, taking her hand, which she had placed on the table, and kissing it.

"Yes—but I can't help it! You have no idea what I suffer waiting for you! I don't think I'm jealous—I'm not jealous! I believe you when you're here with me, but when you're off somewhere by yourself, leading your own life, which is incomprehensible to me . . ."

She turned away from him, having finally disentangled the hook from the crochet work, and with the help of her index finger she swiftly began drawing the stitches of white wool, glistening in the lamplight, through one another, and her slender wrist began turning nervously and swiftly within her embroidered cuff.

"Well—so what happened? Where did you meet Karenin?" she suddenly asked, with an artificial ring to her voice.

"We ran into each other in the doorway."

"And did he bow to you like this?"

She drew out her face, and half-closing her eyes changed the expression on her face, and folded her hands; suddenly Vronsky saw, in her lovely face, the same expression with which Karenin had bowed to him. He smiled, and she laughed merrily, with the delightful laugh from the chest that was one of her chief charms.

"I find him completely incomprehensible," said Vronsky. "If he had broken with you after your conversation with him at the villa, if he had challenged me to a duel. . . . But this is what I fail to understand: How can he endure such a situation? He's suffering, that's obvious."

"He?" she said sneeringly. "He's absolutely contented."

"Why are we all tormenting ourselves, when everything could be so pleasant?"

"He's not! Don't you think I know him—all that falsehood he's saturated with! D'you think if you felt anything you could live the way he lives with me? He doesn't understand anything, doesn't feel anything! How could a man who feels anything live in the same house with a wife who's unfaithful to him? Could he talk to her? Call her 'my dear'?"

And without meaning to she mimicked him again. *"Ma chère,* my dear Anna!"

"He's not a man, not a human being—he's a doll! No one knows that, but I do! Oh, if I were in his place I should long since have killed a wife like that, I'd have torn her to pieces, but I wouldn't call her *'Ma chère,* my dear Anna!' He's not a human being, he's an official machine. He doesn't understand that I'm your wife, that he's a stranger, a superfluous— But let's stop talking about him!"

"My dear, you are unfair, unfair," said Vronsky, trying to calm her. "But it doesn't matter, let's not talk about him. Tell me what you've been doing. What's the matter with you? What is that illness of yours? What did the doctor say?"

She looked at him with mocking amusement. She had obviously thought of some other ridiculous and grotesque traits of her husband and was waiting for an opportunity to parade them.

But he went on: "It's my guess you're not ill at all, it's your condition. When is it to be?"

The ironical gleam in her eye subsided; a different kind of smile—the knowledge of something he didn't know, and a gentle sadness—changed her expression.

"Soon, very soon. You said our position was agony, that it had to be resolved. If you only knew how painful it is for me, what I would give to be able to love you freely and boldly! I wouldn't be in torment, I wouldn't torment you with my jealousy . . . It's going to be soon, but not in the way we think."

And at the thought of how it was going to happen she seemed so pathetic to herself that tears came into her eyes and she could not go on. She laid her hand, its white skin and rings radiant in the lamplight, on his sleeve.

"It won't be the way we think. I didn't want to tell you this, but you've forced me to. Soon, very soon, everything is going to be solved; we'll all be at peace, all of us, and won't have to torment ourselves any longer."

"I don't understand," he said, though he did.

"You asked—when? Very soon. And I shan't survive it. Don't interrupt me!" she said hurriedly. "I know it, I'm sure of it. I shall die, and I'll be glad to die, and set myself free and you too."

Tears rolled down her cheeks; he bent over her hand and began to kiss it, trying to hide his emotion, which he knew was groundless but could not overcome.

"Yes, it's better that way," she said, squeezing his hand hard. "This is the only thing, the only way left to us."

He recovered and raised his head.

"What rubbish! What senseless rubbish you're talking!"

"No, it's the truth!"

"What's the truth? What?"

"That I'm going to die. I had a dream."

"A dream?" Vronsky repeated; in a flash he recalled the peasant in his own dream.

"Yes, a dream," she said. "A dream I had a long time ago. I dreamed I was running into my bedroom, where I had to get something, or find out something; you know how it is in dreams," she said, her eyes opening wide with horror, "and there was something in the bedroom standing in the corner."

"Oh what rubbish! How can you believe—"

But she didn't let herself be stopped; what she was saying was too important for her.

"This something turned around; I saw it was a peasant with a matted beard, small and terrible-looking. I wanted to run away, but he stooped over a sack and began fumbling about in it with his hands—"

She showed how he fumbled about in the sack. Her face was full of horror, and Vronsky, recalling his own dream, felt the same horror filling his soul.

"He fumbled about and muttered something in French, quickly, quickly, and you know, rolling his r's: 'It must be beaten, the iron, pounded, kneaded.' And I was terrified, and I tried to wake up, wake up, but when I woke up I was still in a dream. I began asking myself what it all meant. And Korney said to me: 'Childbirth, childbirth, you're going to die in childbirth, ma'am.' Then I woke up . . ."

"What rubbish, what rubbish!" said Vronsky, but he felt himself that his voice lacked all conviction.

"But let's not speak of it. Ring, I'll order some tea. And wait, I'm not long now for—"

But suddenly she stopped. The expression on her face changed instantaneously. Her horror and agitation were suddenly replaced by an expression of quiet, grave, and blissful attentiveness. He could not understand the meaning of this change. She was listening to the movement of a new life within her.

IV

AFTER meeting Vronsky on the steps of his own house, Karenin went off to the Italian opera, as he had intended. He sat through the first two acts and saw everyone he should. When he returned home he carefully looked at the coatstand; seeing there was no military greatcoat on it he went to his study as usual. Contrary to his custom, though, he did not go to sleep, but paced back and forth in his study until three in the morning. The feeling of anger with his wife, who did not wish to observe the rules of propriety and live up to the only condition he had set for her—not to receive her lover in his own house—gave him no rest. She had not fulfilled his request, and he ought to punish her and realize his threat—demand a divorce and take away the child. He knew all the difficulties involved in this, but he had said he was going to do it, and now he ought to put his threat into effect. Countess Lydia had hinted to him that that would be the best way out of his position, and the practice of divorce had lately advanced so much that Karenin saw it was possible to overcome the formal difficulties. Besides, misfortunes never come singly; the questions of the Native Minorities and of the irrigation of the Zaraysk Province had brought down on Karenin's head so many official unpleasantnesses that for some time he had been in a state of extreme irritation.

He didn't sleep the whole night; by morning his wrath, which had been increasing in some sort of gigantic progression, had reached its ultimate limits. He dressed hurriedly; as though carrying a cup that was full of wrath and afraid to spill any of it, afraid to lose, together with his wrath, the energy he needed for a scene with his wife, he went to her room the moment he learned she was up.

Anna, who thought she knew her husband so well, was struck by the way he looked as he came into her room. He was scowling, and glowered before him, avoiding her gaze; his lips were tightly and disdainfully pressed together. In his bearing, his movements, the sound of his voice, there was a firmness and decisiveness his wife had never seen in him before. He came into the room and without greeting her went straight over to her writing desk, took up her keys and opened the drawer.

"What do you want!?" she cried.

"Your lover's letters," he said.

"They're not there," she said, shutting the drawer. But this movement of hers showed him that he had guessed right, and thrusting her hand roughly to one side, he quickly snatched a portfolio he knew she kept her most important papers in. She tried to jerk it away from him, but he pushed her aside.

"Sit down! I must talk to you," he said, putting the portfolio under his arm and squeezing it so tightly with his elbow that his shoulder was pushed up.

She looked at him in silence, astonished and intimidated.

"I told you I would not allow you to receive your lover in this house."

"I had to see him to—"

She stopped, unable to think up a reason.

"I shall not enter into the particulars of why a woman has to see her lover."

"I meant, all I wanted was—" she said, turning crimson. This coarseness of his angered her and made her bold. "Don't you feel how easy it is to insult me?" she said.

"An honest man or an honest woman can be insulted, but to tell a thief he's a thief is a mere statement of fact."

"I've never seen this new trait of cruelty in you."

"You call it cruelty for a husband to allow his wife her freedom while giving her the honorable protection of his name, on the one condition that propriety is to be observed. Is that cruelty?"

"It's worse than cruelty—it's baseness, if you really want to know!" Anna cried out in a burst of spite; she got up and was about to go out.

"No!" he shouted in his squeaky voice, which now rose a note higher then usual; seizing her by the wrist with his long fingers so violently that the bracelet he squeezed left red marks on her, he flung her forcibly into a chair. "Baseness? If you want to use the word, what is base is—deserting your husband and your son for a lover, then eating your husband's bread!"

She bowed her head. Not only did she not say what she had said to her lover the day before that *he* was her husband, and that Karenin was superfluous, she didn't even think it. She felt the full justice of what Karenin was saying, and only said softly:

"Nothing you can say about my position can make it worse than I know it to be myself, but why are you saying all this?"

"Why am I saying this? *Why?*" he went on just as furiously. "So that you know that since you haven't obeyed me with respect to the observation of propriety I'm going to take steps to put a stop to this situation!"

"As it is it's going to be over with soon, very soon," she muttered, and again tears came into her eyes at the thought of her approaching death, now so longed for.

"It'll be over with sooner than you and your lover imagine! All you need is the satisfaction of your animal passions—"

"Alexis! That is not only ungenerous—it's dishonorable to hit someone who's down."

"Yes, you can't think of anything but yourself, you think the sufferings of a man who was your husband are uninteresting. You don't care at all about his whole life having been ruined, about all he's suff—suff—suffled."

Karenin was talking so rapidly that his tongue got twisted and he couldn't pronounce the word, which finally came out as "suffled." It struck Anna as funny, then instantly she felt ashamed at being able to think anything funny at a moment like that. For the first time she felt for him for a moment; she put herself in his place and felt sorry for him. But what could she say or do? She lowered her head and was silent. He also fell silent for a little while, then began speaking in a chilly voice, less squeaky now, and emphasizing words at random.

"I came to tell you—" he said.

She glanced at him. No, it only seemed that way to me, she thought, recalling the way he looked when he stumbled over the word "suffered." No—could a man with such dull eyes, with such self-satisfied calmness ever feel anything?

"There's nothing I can change," she whispered.

"I came to tell you that I'm leaving for Moscow tomorrow and shall not be returning to this house; you will be informed of my decision by a lawyer to whom I shall entrust a suit for divorce. My son will go to my sister's," said Karenin, making an effort to recall what he had meant to say about the boy.

"You want Seryozha in order to hurt me," she said, looking up at him from under her brows. "You don't love him . . . Leave me Seryozha!"

"Yes, I've even lost my love for my son because he's associated with my loathing for you. But I shall take him all the same. Good-by!"

He started to go; now it was she who stopped him.

"Alexis, leave me Seryozha!" she whispered once more. "I have nothing more to say. Leave me Seryozha until my—I'm going to have a baby soon, let me have him!"

Karenin turned scarlet; snatching his hand away from her he left the room without a word.

## v

THE famous Petersburg lawyer's waiting room was full when Karenin walked in. Three women: an old lady, a young lady, and a tradesman's wife, and three gentlemen: a German banker with a ring on his finger, a tradesman with a beard, and the third, an irate official in uniform with an order hanging from his neck, had evidently been waiting a long time. Two clerks were writing at tables, their pens scratching. The writing-desk accessories, of which Karenin was a connoisseur, were exceptionally fine; Karenin could not help noticing this. One of the clerks, without getting up, screwed up his eyes and addressed Karenin in a disagreeable tone of voice:

"What d'you want?"

"I have some business with the lawyer."

"The lawyer's busy," replied the clerk severely, indicating with his pen the people waiting, and he turned away to go on writing.

"Couldn't he find some time?" said Karenin.

"He has no free time, he's always busy. Kindly wait."

"Then I must trouble you to give him my card," said Karenin with dignity, seeing it was impossible to maintain his incognito.

The clerk took the card and manifestly disapproving of what was on it passed through the door.

Karenin was in favor of public trials on principle, but he was not completely in sympathy with certain details of their application in Russia, for certain high official reasons, and condemned them insofar as he was capable of condemning anything instituted by the Sovereign's authority. His entire life had been spent in administrative activity; consequently, when he disapproved of something his disapproval was softened by his understanding that mistakes were inevitable and that in any particular case improvements could be made. In the new legal institutions he disapproved of the conditions that applied to the lawyers. But until now he had never had anything to do with a lawyer, and so he disapproved of them only in theory; now, however, his disapproval was heightened by the disagreeable impression he had received in the lawyer's waiting room.

"He'll be coming right away," said the clerk; two minutes later, as a matter of fact, the tall figure of an elderly solicitor who had been consulting the lawyer appeared in the doorway, followed by the lawyer himself.

The lawyer was short, stocky, and bald, with a dark reddish beard, long, light eyebrows, and a bulging forehead. He was all dressed up like a bridegroom, from his cravat and double watch chain to his patent-leather boots. He had a clever, rustic face, but his clothes were dandified and in poor taste.

"If you please," said the lawyer, and gloomily ushering Karenin in before him he closed the door.

"Won't you sit down?" He indicated an armchair beside a writing desk covered with papers, and sat down himself behind the desk, rubbing together his little hands with their short fingers overgrown with fair hairs, and leaning his head over to one side. But he had just settled into this pose of his when a moth flew over the table: with a rapidity it would have been impossible to expect the lawyer unlocked his hands, caught the moth, and again assumed his previous posture.

"Before I begin speaking of my business," said Karenin, who had followed the lawyer's movements with astonished eyes, "I must observe that the business I have to discuss with you must be kept secret."

A slight smile moved the lawyer's drooping reddish mustache.

"I should not be in the law if I were incapable of keeping the secrets entrusted to me. But if you would like some confirmation . . ."

Karenin looked at his face; he saw his intelligent gray eyes were laughing as though they knew the whole thing already.

"Do you know my name?" Karenin continued.

"Like every other Russian I know you and your valuable work," said the lawyer, catching another moth and bowing.

Karenin sighed, gathering his courage. But once he made up his mind he went on in his squeaky voice without timidity or hesitation, emphasizing a word now and then.

"I have the misfortune," Karenin said, "of having an unfaithful wife; I should like to break off relations with her legally, that is, get a divorce, but in such a way that our son will not stay with his mother."

The lawyer's gray eyes tried not to laugh, but they were dancing about with irrepressible glee; Karenin saw that it was not only the glee of a man getting a lucrative piece of business—there was triumph and delight there, and a gleam like the ominous gleam he had seen in his wife's eyes.

"You would like my co-operation in obtaining a divorce?"

"Just so, but I must warn you that I may very well be abusing your attention. I've come merely for a preliminary consultation. I should like a divorce, but the forms in which that is possible are of some importance for me. It may very well be that if the forms do not coincide with my requirements I shall forego my legitimate desire."

"Oh, that's how it always is," said the lawyer, "and that's always open to you."

The lawyer looked down at Karenin's feet, feeling that the

sight of his irrepressible merriment might offend his client. He glanced at a moth flying past his nose and his hand quivered, but out of respect for Karenin's situation he did not catch it.

"Though in a general way I am familiar with our legislation on this subject," Karenin went on, "I should like to be familiarized with the forms in which this type of affair is generally consummated in practice."

"You wish me to lay before you," answered the lawyer without looking up, and adopting his client's style with some satisfaction, "the various methods by which it is possible to carry out your request?"

At Karenin's affirmative nod he went on, occasionally flashing a glance over at Karenin's face, which began coming out in reddish blotches.

"According to our laws," he said with a slight suggestion of disapprobation, "divorce is, as you know, possible in the following cases— Wait a while!" he said, turning to the clerk who had put his head in at the door, but getting up all the same, speaking a few words to him and sitting down again. "In the following cases: physical shortcomings in either party, desertion without communication for a period of five years," he said, crooking a short hairy finger, "and then adultery"—he pronounced this word with obvious satisfaction—"divided into the following categories." He went on crooking his thick fingers, though it was evident that the cases and the categories could not be classified together. "Physical shortcomings in the husband or wife, adultery on the part of the husband or wife." Since by now all the fingers had been used up he straightened them all out again and went on: "This is the view in theory, but I take it you have done me the honor of approaching me in order to learn its practical application. Consequently, guided by the precedents, I must inform you that cases of divorce all come down to the following—I presume it's not a question of physical shortcomings? Or one of absence without communication?"

Karenin nodded.

"Come down to the following: the adultery on the part of one party or the other, and detection of the guilty party by mutual agreement, or by involuntary detection in the absence of such agreement. I ought to inform you that the latter case is seldom met with in practice," said the lawyer, and flashing a glance at Karenin he fell silent, like a pistol salesman who after describing the advantages of one weapon or another was now waiting for his client to make a choice. But Karenin was silent, so the lawyer continued: "The most usual, simple, and sensible course, to my mind, is adultery by mutual agreement. I should never allow myself to express it in that way if I were speaking to some unsophisticated person," said the lawyer, "but I think we understand it."

Karenin was so upset, however, that he failed to grasp instantly the sensibleness of adultery by mutual agreement; he looked perplexed, but the lawyer helped him out at once.

"People can no longer live together—that is a fact. And if both are agreed on that the details and formalities become a matter of indifference. And at the same time that is the simplest and surest method."

Karenin fully understood now. But he had religious scruples that prevented him from accepting such a method.

"In the present case that is out of the question," he said. "There is only one course open—involuntary detection, confirmed by letters in my possession."

At the mention of letters the lawyer pressed his lips together, and gave vent to a high-pitched sound of pity and disdain.

"Please remember," he began, "that matters of this kind are decided, as you know, by the Ecclesiastical Department; the Reverend Fathers are addicted to an investigation of such matters down to the minutest details," he said with a smile that showed his sympathy for the taste of the Reverend Fathers. "There is no doubt that letters can provide partial confirmation; but the evidence must be obtained directly, that is, from eyewitnesses. If you do me the honor of bestowing your confidence on me, you might leave the general choice to me of the means to be made use of. He who desires an end must accept the means."

"If that is so," Karenin, suddenly quite pale, was beginning to say, when just then the lawyer got up and went over again to the doorway, where his clerk had come to interrupt him.

"Tell her there are no cheap goods on sale here!" the lawyer said, and turned back to Karenin.

As he returned to his seat he caught another moth unobserved. A fine state the upholstery's going to be in by summer! he thought frowning.

"You were saying?" the lawyer said.

"I shall inform you of my decision by letter," said Karenin, getting up and leaning on the table. After standing a moment in silence, he said: "On the basis of what you have been saying I may conclude, then, that it is possible to procure a divorce. I would also ask you to inform me of your terms."

"It is all quite possible if you give me complete liberty of action," said the lawyer, not responding to the second point. "When may I depend on hearing from you?" he asked, moving toward the door, his eyes and patent-leather boots glittering.

"In a week. And you will be so kind as to inform me whether you will undertake to act in this case and if so on what terms."

"Surely."

The lawyer bowed deferentially, showed his client out the door, and once he was alone abandoned himself to his glee. He was in such a good temper that contrary to his principles he made a concession to the lady he had been haggling with, and he stopped catching moths; he had definitely made up his mind to have his furniture reupholstered in plush the following winter, like Sigonin's.

## VI

KARENIN had scored a brilliant victory at the Committee meeting on August 17, but the consequences of this victory undermined his position. A new Commission was appointed to investigate the living conditions of the National Minorities from all points of view, and on Karenin's initiative was sent into the field with exceptional speed and energy. Three months later a report was presented. The condition of the National Minorities had been studied from the political, administrative, economic, ethnographic, material, and religious points of view. Splendidly composed answers had been provided to all questions, and the answers were incontrovertible, since they were not a product of human thought, which is always subject to error, but were all the result of official labors. All the answers were based on official data—the reports of governors and bishops, based on the reports of district authorities and ecclesiastical superintendents, based in their turn on the reports of rural administrative officers and parish priests: consequently all these answers were incontrovertible. All the questions, for instance, about why the harvests were bad, or why the natives clung to their own creeds, and so on, questions that except for the convenience of the official machine are not and cannot be solved for ages, were given clear and incontestable solutions. And the decisions made supported Karenin's views.

But when the report of the Commission was received Stremov, who had been stung to the quick at the last meeting, adopted a tactic Karenin had failed to anticipate. Stremov, taking with him a number of other members, all at once shifted to Karenin's side, and not only began heatedly backing the implementation of measures recommended by Karenin, but also proposed others along the same lines that were even more extreme. These measures, which were exaggerated to the point of going beyond what had been Karenin's fundamental idea, were taken, and it was then that Stremov's tactic became manifest. Carried to extremes these measures suddenly proved so stupid that at one and the same moment people in the government, public opinion, clever women, and newspapers—everyone came down on the measures, expressing their outrage both at the measures themselves and at their acknowledged originator—Karenin. Stremov now stepped aside, pretending that he had merely been following Karenin's project blindly and was now astounded and indignant at what had been done.

This undermined Karenin. But in spite of his failing health and his family troubles he didn't give in. There was a split in the Commission; some of the members, led by Stremov, justified their mistake by saying they had put their faith in a report presented by the Revisory Commission under Karenin, and now they said that the report of this Commission was rubbish—nothing but wastepaper. Karenin, together with a party of people who saw the danger of such a revolutionary attitude toward documents, continued to support the data elaborated by the Revisory Commission. In consequence everything got all mixed up in the highest spheres and even in society; in spite of the fact that it was all of intense interest to everyone no one could understand whether the National Minorities were really starving and perishing or thriving. Because of this, and partly because of the general contempt for him due to his wife's infidelity, Karenin's position became extremely shaky. In this position he made an important decision. To the Commission's astonishment he declared that he was going to ask permission to make a trip in order to investigate the question on the spot for himself. Having received permission, Karenin set out for these remote provinces.

Karenin's departure started a lot of talk, especially since

just before he left he formally returned the expense money
advanced him for the twelve horses all the way to his destina-
tion.

"I consider that very noble of him," said Betsy in discussing it with Princess Myagky. "Why pay for post horses when
everyone knows the railroads go everywhere now?"

But Princess Myagky didn't agree; Betsy's view actually
irritated her.

"It's all very well for you to talk," Princess Myagky said,
"with all your I don't know how many millions, but I'm delighted when my husband goes out on inspection tours in the
summer. It's very good for his health and he has a good time,
and we've arranged things so that I can keep a carriage and
coachman on the money he's allowed."

On his way to the remote provinces Karenin stopped three
days in Moscow. The day after his arrival he was driving
back from a call on the Governor-General, and at the corner
of Gazetny Street, where there is always a crush of vehicles,
he suddenly overheard his name being shouted out in such a
loud cheerful voice that he could not help looking round. At
the corner on the pavement, in a short stylish overcoat with a
low-crowned stylish hat tilted to one side, his white teeth
gleaming radiantly between his red lips, gay, youthful, and
beaming, stood Oblonsky, resolutely and insistently shouting
and demanding that he stop. With one hand he was holding
on to the window of a carriage that had stopped at the corner; a woman's head in a velvet bonnet and two little children's heads were thrust out of it. He kept smiling and waving
his other hand at his brother-in-law. The woman was also
smiling sweetly and beckoning to Karenin. It was Dolly, with
her children.

Karenin did not want to see anyone in Moscow, least of all
his wife's brother. He raised his hat and was about to pass on,
but Oblonsky told his coachman to stop and ran over to him
across the snow.

"What a shame you didn't let us know! Have you been
here long? And I was at Dussot's yesterday, I saw 'Karenin'
on the board and it never entered my head it was you!" said
Oblonsky, thrusting his head in at the carriage window. "Or
I would have dropped in on you. I'm delighted to see you!"
he said, kicking his feet together to knock off the snow.
"What a shame not to let us know!" he repeated.

"I had no time to; I've been very busy," replied Karenin
drily.

"Come and speak to Dolly, she's longing to see you."

Karenin unfolded the rug his chilly legs were wrapped up in and, getting out of the carriage, made his way across the snow over to Dolly.

"Really, Alexis, why have you been avoiding us in this way?" said Dolly with a smile.

"I've been extremely busy. I'm very glad to see you," he said in a tone that made it clear he was irritated. "How are you?"

"And how is my darling Anna?"

Karenin mumbled something and started to leave. But Oblonsky stopped him.

"D'you know, here's what we'll do tomorrow—Dolly, invite him to dinner! We'll ask Koznyshov and Pestsov, to entertain him with the Moscow intelligentsia."

"Please, do come," said Dolly. "We'll expect you at five or six, as you like. Well, how is my darling Anna? It's been so long . . ."

"She is well," Karenin mumbled with a scowl. "Delighted!" he said, and started back to his carriage.

"Are you coming?" Dolly cried.

Karenin muttered something which Dolly could not catch in the noise of the traffic.

"I'll come to see you tomorrow!" Oblonsky shouted after him.

Karenin got into his carriage and sat far back in it in order not to see anything or to be seen.

"An odd character!" said Oblonsky to his wife; he glanced at his watch and made a gesture in front of his face that meant a caress for his wife and children and jauntily strode away along the pavement.

"Stiva! Stiva!" Dolly called out, blushing.

He turned round.

"You know I have to buy some coats for Grisha and Tanya; give me some money!"

"Never mind! Just tell them I'll pay!" Gaily nodding to a passing acquaintance he disappeared.

## VII

THE next day was Sunday. Oblonsky went to a ballet rehearsal at the Bolshoy Theatre, and gave Masha Chibisov, a pretty dancer under his protection who was making her first appearance, the coral necklace he had promised her the evening before; backstage, in the midday gloom of the theater, he succeeded in placing a kiss on her pretty little face, radiant over her present. Besides giving her the necklace he had to make a rendezvous with her after the ballet. He explained to her that he couldn't be on hand at the beginning of the ballet, but promised to come in for the last act and take her out to supper. From the theater Oblonsky drove to the market place, where he personally selected the fish and asparagus for dinner and by noon was already at Dussot's, where he had to visit three people, who luckily for him were all there: Levin, who had just returned from abroad and was stopping there, the new head of his department, who had just been promoted to this lofty position and was on a tour of inspection in Moscow, and his brother-in-law Karenin, whom he wanted to make sure of getting for dinner.

Oblonsky liked dinners, and what he liked even more was giving a dinner party, a small one, but very select both for food and drinks as well as for guests. He was very pleased with the menu for his dinner that day: there were going to be perch, brought alive to the kitchen, asparagus, and the main dish—a magnificent, plain roast beef, and all the appropriate wines: so much for food and drink. As for the guests, Kitty and Levin would be there, and to make that unobtrusive there would be another girl, a cousin, and young Shcherbatsky; then the main dish among the guests—Koznyshov and Karenin. Koznyshov was a Muscovite and philosopher, Karenin a Petersburger in public life. He also meant to invite another well-known eccentric and enthusiast, Pestsov, a liberal, a great talker, musician, historian, and the most charming of fifty-year-old boys, who would provide the sauce or the garnish for Koznyshov and Karenin. He would stir them both up and egg them on against each other.

The second installment of the dealer's money for the forest had been received and had not yet all been spent. Dolly had been very sweet and kind lately, and the idea of this dinner delighted Oblonsky from all points of view. He was in a most cheerful mood. There were two slightly unpleasant circumstances, but they were both submerged in the ocean of benevolent gaiety surging about in Oblonsky's heart. These were the two circumstances: the first was that he had noted Karenin's chilly stiffness at his encounter with him on the street the day before, and putting the look on Karenin's face and the fact of his not having called on them or let them know of his arrival together with the rumors that had come to his ears about Anna and Vronsky, Oblonsky guessed that things were not going well between Anna and her husband.

That was one unpleasant thing. The other slightly unpleasant thing was that the new department head, like all new department heads, had the reputation of being a terrible fellow who got up at six in the morning, worked like a slave and demanded as much from his subordinates. In addition this new superior had the further reputation of having the manners of a bear, and was reported to hold views diametrically opposed to those of the former department head, which until now had been held by Oblonsky too. The day before Oblonsky had appeared on official business in a uniform; the new superior had been very amiable and had chatted with Oblonsky as though he were an old acquaintance; consequently Oblonsky considered it his duty to call on him in a morning coat. The thought that the new department head might receive him coldly was this second unpleasant circumstance. But Oblonsky felt instinctively that everything would "turn out" splendidly. They're all human beings, after all, all just people like the rest of us sinners, he thought as he entered the hotel, what's the point of getting angry and quarreling?

"How are you, Vasili?" he said turning to a servant he knew as he walked along a corridor with his hat tilted to one side. "Have you let your whiskers grow? Levin's in number seven, eh? D'you mind showing me the way? Oh, and find out whether Count Anichkin"—the new department head—"will receive me."

"Yes, sir," Vasili answered smilingly. "It's a long time since you've been to see us."

"I was here yesterday, but I came in by the other entrance. Is this number seven?"

Levin was standing in the middle of the room with a peasant from Tver measuring a fresh bearskin when Oblonsky entered.

"Ah—did you kill it?" Oblonsky cried. "What a splendid specimen! Is it a she? Hello there, Arkhip!"

He shook hands with the peasant and sat down beside the table, without taking off his coat or hat.

"But take your things off, stay awhile!" said Levin, taking his hat.

"I haven't time, I just looked in for a second," Oblonsky answered. He threw open his coat, but took it off later and sat about for a whole hour chatting with Levin about hunting, and about the most intimate matters as well.

"Well, please tell me what you did abroad. Where were you?" said Oblonsky when the peasant had left.

"I was in Germany, in Prussia, France, and England, though not in the capitals but in the manufacturing towns; I saw a great many new things. I'm glad I went."

"Yes, I know your idea of settling the labor question."

"Not in the least—there can be no such thing in Russia as a labor question. In Russia it's a question of the relationship of the laboring population to the land; that exists abroad too, but there it's a case of repairing something that's been spoiled, while here . . ."

Oblonsky listened to Levin attentively.

"Yes, yes!" he said. "You may very well be right. But I'm glad you're in such a good temper: bear hunting, working, and full of enthusiasms. Because Shcherbatsky had told me—he ran into you—you were in some sort of depression and kept talking about death the whole time—"

"Well, what of it? I haven't stopped thinking about death," said Levin. "It's true that it's time for me to die. And that all this is nonsense. I'll tell you the truth: I set the greatest value on my ideas and on my work, but when you get right down to it, just think of this: our whole world, after all, is only a speck of mildew that has grown up on a tiny little planet. And we think we can do something tremendous—ideas, actions! It's all just grains of sand."

"But my dear boy, all that's as old as the hills!"

"It may be old, but you know when you understand it clearly somehow everything becomes unimportant. When you realize you're going to die from one day to the next, and nothing will be left, how unimportant it all is! I regard my ideas as being very important, but they would prove to be just as unimportant, even if they were to be carried out, as it was to surround this she-bear. That's how you pass your life, distracting yourself by hunting and by work, simply to avoid thinking about death."

Oblonsky listened to Levin with a subtle, tender smile.

"Well, of course! So there you've come round to my own idea. D'you remember how you jumped on me for seeking pleasures in life? 'Be not, thou moralist, so severe!'"

"No, but what's good in life is—" Levin grew confused. "But I don't really know. All I know is we'll soon be dead."

"But why soon?"

"And d'you know, the charms of life are fewer when you think of death—but it's more peaceful."

"On the contrary, it's even gayer toward the end. In any case I must go now," said Oblonsky, getting up for the tenth time.

"But no, stay awhile!" said Levin, holding him back. "When are we going to see each other again? I'm leaving tomorrow."

"What an idiot I am! That's why I came—you absolutely must come to dinner today. Your brother will be there, and Karenin, my brother-in-law."

"Is he here?" said Levin, and wanted to ask about Kitty; he had heard she had been in Petersburg at the beginning of the winter staying with her other sister, the wife of a diplomat, and didn't know whether she had gone back or not, but he changed his mind about asking. It's all the same to me whether she's there or not, he thought.

"Then you'll come?"

"Of course!"

"Be there at five, not in evening dress."

Oblonsky got up and went downstairs to see his new superior. His instinct had not deceived him: the terrible new department head turned out to be extremely affable; Oblonsky had lunch with him and sat around talking, so that it wasn't until four o'clock that he got to Karenin.

## VIII

AFTER returning from church Karenin had spent the whole morning at home. There were two things he had to do that morning: first, to receive a delegation from the National Minorities who were in Moscow at the time on their way to Petersburg and give them their instructions; secondly, write the lawyer the letter he had promised to. The delegation, even though convoked on Karenin's initiative, presented a great many inconveniences, and even dangers, and Karenin was extremely pleased at having intercepted it in Moscow. The delegates did not have the slightest conception of their role and obligations. They were naïvely certain that all they had to do was explain their needs and the real state of affairs, and ask the government for help; they were quite incapable of realizing that some of their statements and requirements would support the enemy faction and thus ruin their whole case. Karenin had a long-drawn-out tussle with them, wrote out a program for them which they were not to depart from; after dismissing them he wrote some letters to Petersburg concerning the guidance of the delegation. Countess Lydia was to be his chief support. She was a specialist in the question of delegations; no one was abler than she in piloting delegations about and getting them on the right track. When he had finished this he also wrote the lawyer a letter, giving him definite permission to act at his own discretion. He enclosed three of Vronsky's notes to Anna, which he had found in the portfolio he had taken away.

Ever since Karenin had left home with the intention of never returning to his family again, and ever since he had seen the lawyer and told even one man of this intention of his, and especially ever since he had translated this matter of life into a matter of paper work, he had grown more and more accustomed to his own intention and now clearly perceived how it was possible to carry it out.

He was sealing the envelope to the lawyer when he heard Oblonsky's loud voice. Oblonsky was arguing with Karenin's servant and insisting on being announced.

What's the difference, thought Karenin; so much the better, I'll tell him at once of my situation with regard to his sister and explain why I can't dine at his house.

"Ask the gentleman in!" he said in a loud voice, gathering up his papers and placing them inside a blotter.

"Now there, you see, you were lying to me, he is in!" came the voice of Oblonsky in answer to the servant who had been barring his way; taking off his coat as he came, Oblonsky entered the room. "Well, I'm delighted I found you in!" Oblonsky started off gaily, "I hope you'll—"

"I can't come," said Karenin coldly, standing there without offering his guest a seat.

Karenin had thought he would embark at once on the chilly terms he ought to be on with the brother of his wife, against whom he was starting a suit for divorce, but he had not reckoned on the ocean of kindness that overflowed the banks of Oblonsky's soul.

Oblonsky opened wide his bright, shining eyes.

"Why can't you? What d'you mean?" he said in French, perplexed. "But you've already promised; we're all counting on you."

"I mean that I can't come to your house because the family relations that used to prevail between us must be cut short."

"What's that? I mean, why?" said Oblonsky with a smile.

"Because I'm starting a suit for divorce against your sister, my wife. I ought to have——"

But Karenin did not have time to finish what he was saying; Oblonsky did something quite unexpected. He groaned aloud and sat down in an armchair. "No, Alexis, what are you saying!" he exclaimed, with a look of pain.

"It is true."

"Forgive me, I do not and cannot believe it . . ."

Karenin sat down, feeling that his words lacked the effect he had expected, that he could not avoid explaining himself, and that no matter what his explanations were his relations with his brother-in-law would stay the same.

"Yes, I find myself in the painful position of being forced to demand a divorce," he said.

"I want to say one thing, Alexis. I know you to be an excellent and fair-minded man, I know Anna—forgive me, I can't change my opinion of her—to be a fine, splendid woman, and that's why, forgive me, I cannot believe it! There's some misunderstanding there," he said.

"If it were only a misunderstanding——"

"One moment, I understand," Oblonsky interrupted him. "But of course: the only thing is—there's no need to hurry. One shouldn't, mustn't be in a hurry!"

"I have not been in a hurry," said Karenin coldly, "and it's impossible to consult anyone in such a matter. I've made up my mind to it."

"This is awful!" said Oblonsky with a heavy sigh. "There's one thing I should do in your place—I beg you to do it!" he said. "I gather the proceedings have not yet been begun. Before you begin the suit see my wife; talk it over with her. She loves Anna like a sister and is fond of you; she's an astonishing woman. Speak to her, for God's sake! Do me this favor, I beg of you!"

Karenin began considering, and Oblonsky looked at him, full of sympathy, without breaking the silence.

"Will you come to see her?"

"I really don't know. This was why I didn't come to call on you. I imagine our relationship ought to change."

"But why? I don't see that. Allow me to think that quite apart from our family relationship you have at least to some extent the same feelings of friendship as I've always had for you . . . As well as genuine esteem," said Oblonsky, pressing Karenin's hand. "Even if your worst suspicions are justified, I don't take it on myself, and never should, to judge one side or the other, and I see no reason why our relations ought to change. But now, do this: come and see my wife!"

"We look at the matter differently," said Karenin coldly. "But let's not speak of it."

"No, but really, why shouldn't you come? If only to dine today? My wife expects you. Do come, please. And the main thing is to talk it over with her. She's an amazing woman. For Heaven's sake—I implore you on bended knee!"

"If you want me to so much I'll come," said Karenin sighing.

And wishing to change the subject he asked about something that interested both of them—Oblonsky's new department head, who though still young had suddenly received such a high position.

Even before, Karenin had never liked Count Anichkin; they had never had the same opinion on anything. Now, though, he could not repress the feeling of hatred, comprehensible to anyone in government service, of a man who has just sustained a defeat in the service for one who has been promoted.

"Well, have you seen him?" said Karenin with a venomous smile.

"Of course, he came to the meeting yesterday. He seems to know the business very well, and he's very energetic."

"Yes, but what is his energy directed toward?" said Karenin. "Toward doing the job, or simply undoing what's already been done? The curse of the State is the red-tape administration, of which he's a worthy representative."

"I don't actually know what there is to find fault with in him. I don't know what his intentions are, but there's one thing—he's a first-rate chap," Oblonsky replied. "I've just been to see him, and really, he's a first-rate chap. We had lunch and I showed him how to make that drink, you know? —wine and oranges? It's very refreshing. The surprising thing is he hadn't known of it. He liked it very much. No, really, he's a splendid chap."

Oblonsky glanced at his watch.

"Good heavens, it's after four already, and I still have to call on Dolgovushin! Then you will come to dinner? Please! You have no idea how upset my wife and I will be if you don't."

Karenin saw his brother-in-law out in a way that was quite unlike his manner on meeting him.

"I've promised and I'll be there," he answered dejectedly.

"Believe me, I appreciate it, and I hope you won't regret it," Oblonsky answered with a smile.

And putting on his coat as he walked, his hand touched the servant's head; Oblonsky broke into a laugh and went out.

"At five o'clock, and not in evening dress, please!" he called out once more, going back to the door.

## IX

IT was past five and a number of the guests had already arrived before the host himself got home. He came in together with Koznyshov and Pestsov, who had met on the doorstep. These were two of the chief representatives of the Moscow intelligentsia, as Oblonsky referred to them. They were respected both for their character and for their minds. They respected each other, but were completely and hopelessly at variance with each other on almost everything—not because they belonged to opposing tendencies, but just because they were in the same camp (their enemies identified them altogether), though in this camp each one had his own shading. And since there is nothing less likely to be subject to agreement than a conflict of opinion on semi-abstract ideas, they not only never had the same opinions but had long since grown accustomed to deride each other's incorrigible aberrations without losing their tempers.

They were going through the doorway chatting about the weather when Oblonsky overtook them. Prince Alexander Shcherbatsky, Oblonsky's father-in-law, young Shcherbatsky, Turovtsyn, Kitty, and Karenin were already sitting in the drawing room.

Oblonsky saw instantly that things were going badly there without him. Dolly, in her gala gray silk dress, obviously worried both about the children, who had to have their meal by themselves in the nursery, and about her husband's still not being there, had been unable to mix the whole of this company together very well without him. All of them were sitting there like parish priests' wives paying calls, as the old Prince said, obviously puzzled by why they were there and squeezing words out of themselves in order not to be silent. The good-natured Turovtsyn obviously felt out of his element, and the smile of his thick lips with which he greeted

Oblonsky as much as said: "Well my boy, now you *have* landed me with some big brains! Drinking now, or the Château des Fleurs—that would be more in my line." The old Prince was sitting there without a word, his glittering little eyes looking askance at Karenin, and Oblonsky saw that he had already thought up some remark to polish off the state dignitary, whom people were invited to see as though he were a dish of sturgeon. Kitty was glancing at the door, gathering her forces together in order not to blush when Levin came in. Young Shcherbatsky, who had not been introduced to Karenin, was trying to look as though that didn't embarrass him in the slightest. Karenin himself was dressed in a white tie and evening dress in accordance with Petersburg custom at a dinner party with ladies, and Oblonsky saw by his face that he had only come in order to keep a promise and by being in this company was fulfilling a wearisome obligation. Indeed, he was the chief cause of the chill that had been freezing all the guests before Oblonsky's arrival.

Oblonsky apologized as he came into the living room and explained that he had been delayed by the same Prince who was his permanent scapegoat for all his delays and absences; in a second he had reintroduced them all to each other and bringing together Karenin and Koznyshov tossed them the russification of Poland as a topic; together with Pestsov they immediately caught on to it. Clapping Turovtsyn on the shoulder, he whispered something comical into his ear and sat him next to Dolly and the old Prince. Then he told Kitty she was looking very pretty today, and introduced Shcherbatsky to Karenin. In one minute he had kneaded all this social dough so that the drawing room blossomed and there was a lively buzz of voices. Levin was the only one missing. But this was all to the good, since when Oblonsky went into the dining room he saw to his horror that the port and the sherry had been gotten at Depret's and not at Levé's, and after giving orders for the coachman to be sent off to Levé's as quickly as possible he went back to the drawing room.

He met Levin at the door.

"Am I late?"

"As though there were anything else you could be!" said Oblonsky, taking him by the arm.

"Are there a lot of people? Who's here?" asked Levin,

blushing in spite of himself and knocking the snow off his cap with his glove.

"They're all our own people. Kitty's here. But let's go in, I'll introduce you to Karenin."

In spite of all Oblonsky's liberalism he knew that meeting Karenin was sure to be flattering, and so he treated his best friends to the honor. But just now Levin was in no state to feel the full pleasure of this acquaintance. He had not seen Kitty since that unforgettable evening when he had met Vronsky, except for that brief moment on the highway. At the bottom of his heart he had known he was going to see her there that night, though he tried to maintain his freedom of thought by assuring himself he had no idea of it. But now, when he heard she was there, he was suddenly filled with such joy and at the same time such fear, that his breath stopped coming and he couldn't get out what he meant to say.

What is she like now? he thought. The same as she was before, or the same as she was in the carriage? What if Dolly had been telling the truth? And why shouldn't it be the truth?

"Yes, please, introduce me to Karenin," he managed to say with difficulty, and with desperate resolution he strode into the drawing room and saw her.

Kitty was neither the same as she had been before, or the same as she had been in the carriage: she was completely different.

She was frightened, timid, and shame-faced, and consequently even more charming. She saw him the instant he came into the room. She had been waiting for him. She was filled with gladness, and was so embarrassed by her own joy that there was a moment, just as he was advancing toward the hostess and glanced round at her once again, when it seemed to herself, to him, and to Dolly, who saw everything, that she would break down and burst into tears. She flushed, turned pale, flushed again, and sat there rigidly, her lips quivering slightly, waiting for him. He went over to her, bowed, and held out his hand in silence. Except for the slight trembling of her lips and the moisture filling her eyes and making them brighter, her smile was almost calm as she said:

"Such a long time since we've seen each other!" and with despairing determination her cold hand pressed his.

"You didn't see me, but I saw you," said Levin, with a

radiant smile of happiness. "I saw you on your way to Yergushovo from the station."

"When?" she asked in astonishment.

"You were driving to Yergushovo," said Levin, feeling about to burst into sobs with the rapture flooding his heart. How did I dare think of anything that wasn't innocent in connection with this touching creature! Yes, it seems what Dolly said was true, he thought.

Oblonsky took him by the arm and led him over to Karenin.

"Allow me to introduce you." He mentioned their names.

"Delighted to see you again," said Karenin coldly, shaking hands with Levin.

"D'you know each other?" asked Oblonsky, surprised.

"We spent three hours in a train together," said Levin with a smile, "but we left as though it had been a masked ball, full of curiosity; at any rate I was."

"Dear me!" said Oblonsky. "If you please—" and he motioned them all toward the dining room.

The men went to the buffet table, which was set with half a dozen different kinds of vodka and as many kinds of cheese, with and without little silver scoops, and caviar, herring, preserves of various kinds, and plates with thin slices of French bread.

The men stood around the fragrant vodkas and delicacies, and the conversation between Koznyshov, Karenin, and Pestsov about the russification of Poland died down in anticipation of dinner.

Koznyshov, who was unmatched for his ability to terminate the most abstract and serious argument by unexpectedly sprinkling some Attic salt on it and thus changing the mood of the disputants, did this now too.

Karenin had been proving that the russification of Poland could only be accomplished on the basis of the loftiest principles, which had to be introduced by the Russian administration.

Pestsov insisted that one nation could assimilate another only when it was more densely populated.

Koznyshov agreed with both of them, though with reservations. But as they were leaving the drawing room, Koznyshov said with a smile, in order to end the conversation:

"Consequently there's only one way to russify alien nationalities—breed as many children as possible. There my brother and I are behaving worse than anyone else, while you gentlemen, as married men, and especially you, Oblonsky, are

behaving absolutely patriotically: How many have you got?"
he said, smiling genially at the host and holding out a tiny
wineglass to him.

Everyone laughed, Oblonsky most gaily of all. "Yes, that's
the best method all right!" he said, munching on some cheese
and pouring some special kind of vodka into the wineglass.
The conversation actually did end on this joke.

"This cheese isn't bad. May I give you some?" said Oblonsky. "And have you really been doing gymnastics again?"
he went on, turning to Levin, and with his left hand feeling
his muscles. Levin smiled, tightening his arm, and under
Oblonsky's fingers a mound of steel like a round Dutch
cheese rose up beneath the fine cloth of Levin's coat.

"What biceps! A Samson!"

"I suppose it requires great strength to go bear hunting,"
said Karenin, who had the vaguest notions about hunting,
breaking off a slice of bread thin as a wafer and spreading
some cheese on it.

Levin smiled. "Not in the least. On the contrary, a child
can kill a bear," he said, moving over with a slight bow for
the ladies, who were coming over to the buffet table with the
hostess.

"And did I hear you've killed a bear?" said Kitty, vainly
trying to prong a recalcitrant, slippery pickled mushroom on
her fork, and shaking the lace on her sleeve which her white
arm gleamed through. "Are there really bears around your
place?" she added, turning her lovely little head toward him
and smiling.

There seemed to be nothing extraordinary in what she
said, but what inexpressible significance every tone of her
voice held for him, every movement of her lips, eyes, hands,
as she said this! It held a plea for forgiveness, trust in him, a
caress, a tender, shy caress, and promise, and hope, and
love that he could not help but believe in and that smothered
him in happiness.

"No, we went out to Tver Province. On the way back I
met your brother-in-law in the train, or rather your brother-
in-law's brother-in-law," he said with a smile. "It was very
funny."

And he gave a gay and entertaining account of how he
had burst into Karenin's compartment in his sheepskin coat
after not having slept all night.

"In spite of the proverb the guard, who judged me by
my clothes, wanted to put me out, but I instantly started

using highfaultin language and—and—you too," he said, turning
to Karenin and forgetting his proper name, "went by my
sheepskin coat at first and wanted to throw me out, but afterward you backed me up, for which I'm very grateful."

"Passengers' rights in the choice of seats are generally
speaking quite undefined," said Karenin, wiping his fingertips
with a handkerchief.

"I saw you were somewhat undecided about me," said
Levin with a good-natured smile, "but I hastened to start up
an intellectual conversation to make up for my sheepskin."

Koznyshov, who was carrying on a conversation with the
hostess and listening to his brother with one ear, glanced
over at him. What's happened to him today? he thought; he's
like a conqueror. He had no idea that Levin felt as though
he had grown wings. Levin knew she was listening to what
he was saying and that she liked hearing him: that was all
that interested him. Not only in this room alone, but throughout the whole world no one existed but himself, who had
acquired enormous significance and importance, and Kitty.
He felt himself to be on a height that made his head whirl,
and somewhere far, far down below were all these nice, excellent Karenins, Oblonskys, and the whole world.

Quite casually, without looking at them but as though
there were no other place for them to sit, Oblonsky seated
Levin and Kitty side by side.

"Well, you might as well sit here," he had said to Levin.

The dinner was just as good as the china, of which Oblonsky was a connoisseur. The Marie-Louise soup had turned
out magnificently; the tiny patties, melting in your mouth,
were impeccable. Two footmen and Matthew in white ties
did the business of the food and wines unobtrusively, quietly, and quickly. On the material side the dinner was a success,
and no less a success on the nonmaterial side. The conversation, sometimes general, sometimes tête-à-tête, never faltered,
and toward the end of the meal had grown so lively that the
men got up from the table without a pause in their talk;
even Karenin was lively.

## x

PESTSOV liked to bring an argument to a finish; he had not
been satisfied with what Koznyshov had said, all the more so
since he was aware of the fallacy in his own view.

"I didn't mean the mere density of population alone," he said to Karenin over the soup, "but taken in conjunction with basic trends, not as a matter of principle."

"It seems to me," retorted Karenin unhurriedly and languidly, "that it's all one and the same thing. To my mind the only nation that can have an effect on another nation is one that is at a higher stage of development, that—"

"But that's the whole point," Pestsov interrupted in his bass voice. (He was always in a hurry to speak, and always seemed to stake his whole soul on what he was saying.) "How can this superior development be recognized? The English, the French, the Germans—which is at a higher stage of development? Who is going to impose his own nationality on the others? We can see that the Rhine has become French, but that hasn't put the Germans lower down!" he cried. "There's a different law involved!"

"It seems to me that the superior influence is always on the side of true education," said Karenin, raising his eyebrows slightly.

"But how are we to ascertain the signs of true education?" said Pestsov.

"I should think those signs are well known," said Karenin.

"Are they really so well known?" Koznyshov intervened with a subtle smile. "Nowadays it's acknowledged that genuine education can only be purely classical, but we have been witnessing the bitter arguments on both sides, and there's no denying that the opposing camp also have powerful arguments in their favor."

"You're a classicist, Koznyshov. Would you like some red wine?" said Oblonsky.

"I'm not expressing an opinion of my own about one form of education or another," said Koznyshov to him with a condescending smile, as though to a child, as he held out his glass. "I'm simply saying that there are powerful arguments on both sides," he went on, turning back to Karenin. "I've had a classical education myself, but in this debate I personally cannot find my own place. I'm not aware of any clear arguments for giving classical studies priority over nonclassical."

"The natural sciences are just as formative both pedagogically and intellectually," Pestsov chimed in. "Just take astronomy, take botany, or zoology, with their systems of general laws!"

"I cannot quite agree with you there," Karenin replied. "It

seems to me impossible to deny that the very process of acquiring the different forms of language has a particularly beneficial effect on intellectual development. Besides, it must also be acknowledged that the influence of classical authors is in the highest degree moral, whereas unfortunately the study of the natural sciences is associated with those false and pernicious doctrines that are the bane of our times."

Koznyshov started to say something, but Pestsov's heavy bass interrupted him. He heatedly began proving how incorrect this view was. Koznyshov calmly waited for the floor, plainly ready with a crushing objection.

"But one is bound to admit," he said, smiling subtly and turning to Karenin, "that weighing the pros and cons of the various sciences is a difficult business, and that the question of deciding which to favor would not be decided so quickly and conclusively if an education along classical lines did not have the advantage you have just pointed out—that of a moral—let's be frank—and anti-nihilistic influence."

"Unquestionably."

"If the classical studies did not have this advantage of an anti-nihilist influence on their side, we should have considered the question at greater length, we should have weighed the arguments on both sides," said Koznyshov with his subtle smile. "We should have given latitude to both tendencies together. But now we are aware that these pills of a classical education contain the salutary virtue of anti-nihilism, and we boldly recommend them to our patients . . . But what if they lacked that salutary power?" he concluded, sprinkling his Attic salt.

Everyone burst out laughing at Koznyshov's pills, Turovtsyn in especially loud, boisterous tones; at last he had heard the comical remark that was the only thing he had been waiting for throughout the conversation.

Oblonsky had not been mistaken in inviting Pestsov. With him there was no chance of a moment's letup in any intellectual conversation. As soon as Koznyshov terminated one discussion with his quip, Pestsov instantly started another.

"It's impossible to agree that the government even had that in mind," he said. "It's obvious that the government is guided by general considerations while remaining indifferent to any influence that may be exercised by its decisions. The question of women's education, for instance, ought to have been considered pernicious, yet the government has been establishing lecture courses and universities for women."

The conversation switched over to the new topic—the education of women.

Kárenin expressed the view that the education of women was usually confused with the question of women's emancipation, and that this was the only reason for considering it pernicious.

"To my mind, on the contrary, these two questions are indissolubly linked to each other," said Pestsov. "It's a vicious circle. Women are deprived of rights because of inadequate education, while the inadequacy of their education is due to their lack of rights. It must not be forgotten that the subjection of women is so complete, and goes back so far that we often refuse to recognize the abyss that separates them from us," he said.

"You said 'rights'," said Koznyshov, who had been waiting for Pestsov to stop. "The rights of jury duty, of voting on Town Councils, of presiding at local government boards, of entering the civil service, sitting in parliament? . . ."

"Unquestionably."

"But even if women, by way of rare exception, can occupy these positions then it seems to me you were wrong in using the expression 'rights.' It would have been more correct to say 'duties.' Anyone will agree that by performing whatever the functions are of a juryman, Town Councilor, or telegraph clerk we feel that we're performing a duty. That's why it would be more correct to say that what women are seeking is duties, and quite rightly too. One can only sympathize with this desire of theirs to assist men in their social labors."

"Absolutely right," agreed Karenin. "I think the only question is whether they are suited to such duties."

"Probably they would be very suitable," Oblonsky put in, "as soon as education has spread among them. We can see this—"

"And what about the proverb?" said the old Prince, who had been listening to the conversation for some time, his ironic little eyes twinkling; "my daughters won't mind—'long hair, short wits . . .' "

"Just the same thing was thought about the Negroes before their emancipation!" said Pestsov angrily.

"The only thing I find odd is that women should be seeking new duties," said Koznyshov, "when we see men, unfortunately, as a rule avoiding them."

"Duties are bound up with rights: power, money, honors —that's what women are seeking," said Pestsov.

"It's just the same as though I were to seek the right to be a wet nurse and felt offended at women's being paid for it while no one wanted me," said the old Prince.

Turovtsyn burst into a loud laugh; Koznyshov regretted that he hadn't said this himself. Even Karenin smiled.

"Yes, but a man can't nurse a baby," said Pestsov, "while a woman—"

"No, there was an Englishman aboard ship who nursed his own baby," said the old Prince, allowing himself this liberty in his daughters' presence.

"There will be just about as many women officials as there are Englishmen like that," Koznyshov finally said.

"Yes, but what is a girl to do if she has no family?" put in Oblonsky, thinking of Masha Chibisov, whom he had had in mind all along as he sympathized with Pestsov and supported him.

"If you took a good look at the story of that girl you'd find it was she who had left her family, either her own or her sister's, where she might have had woman's work to do," Dolly, entering unexpectedly into the conversation, said irritably, doubtless having guessed which girl Oblonsky had in mind.

"But we are defending a principle, an ideal!" protested Pestsov in a resounding bass. "Women have a right to independence and education. They are hampered and oppressed by their knowledge that that's impossible."

"And I'm hampered and oppressed by not being accepted as a wet nurse in the Foundlings' Hospital," said the old Prince once again, to the great delight of Turovtsyn, who laughed so much he dropped the thick end of the asparagus into the sauce.

## XI

EVERYONE took part in the general conversation except Kitty and Levin. At first, when they had been talking about the influence one country might exercise over another, Levin involuntarily began thinking of what he had to say on the subject: but these ideas, which had used to be very important for him, seemed to flicker through his mind as though in a dream; they did not have the slightest interest for him now. It even seemed strange to him that they were taking such pains to discuss something of no use to anyone. In just the same way it might have seemed that Kitty ought to have been interested in what they were saying about the rights and duties of women. How often had she not thought of that, when the friend she had made abroad, Varenka, came to her mind, and her painfully dependent position; how often she had thought of herself and what would become of her if she didn't get married, and how often she had quarreled about it with her sister! But now it didn't interest her at all. She and Levin were carrying on their own conversation, not a conversation but some sort of mysterious communion, which with every moment bound them more and more closely to each other and gave rise to a feeling of joyful fear in both of them before the unknown they were entering upon.

At first Levin, in answer to Kitty's question about how he could have seen her the year before in the carriage, told her how he had been walking on the highway after the mowing and had met her.

"It was very early in the morning. You had probably just woke up. Your mother was asleep in her corner. It was a wonderful morning. I was walking along and wondering, Who could that be in the four-in-hand? A magnificent team of four, with bells, and in an instant you had flashed by, and there I saw you through the window—sitting just like this and holding the ribbons of your cap in both hands and terribly deep in thought about something," he said smiling. "How I wish I knew what you were thinking about then! Was it something important?"

Wasn't I all mussed up? she thought, but when she saw the rapturous smile these details evoked in his memory she felt, on the contrary, that the impression she had made had been a very good one. She blushed and laughed with joy.

"Really, I don't remember."

"What a splendid laugh Turovtsyn has!" said Levin, looking with pleasure at his moist eyes and shaking body.

"Have you known him long?" asked Kitty.

"Who hasn't!"

"And I see you think he's a bad man?"

"Not bad—insignificant!"

"And that's not true! You must change your mind at once!" said Kitty. "I also had a low opinion of him, but he's utterly sweet and wonderfully kindhearted. He has a heart of gold."

"How were you able to find out about his heart?"

"He and I are great friends. I know him very well. Last winter, soon after—after you came to see us," she said with a guilty and at the same time trustful smile, "all Dolly's children were down with scarlet fever and he happened to call. And can you imagine," she said in a whisper, "he felt so sorry for her that he stayed on and began helping her nurse the children. Really—he stayed in the house for three weeks and looked after the children like a nurse."

"I've been telling Levin about Turovtsyn and the scarlet fever," Kitty said, leaning over toward her sister.

"Yes, it was wonderful, he was so sweet!" said Dolly, glancing over at Turovtsyn, who sensed that he was being spoken about, and giving him a gentle smile. Levin looked at Turovtsyn once again and was astonished at not having perceived the full charm of the man before.

"I'm sorry, very sorry; I'll never think ill of people again!" he said gaily, honestly expressing what he felt at the moment.

## XII

IN the discussion that had sprung up around women's rights there were some questions about the inequality of rights in marriage that were too delicate to be touched on in the presence of ladies. During the dinner Pestsov had hurtled toward these questions a number of times, but Koznyshov and Oblonsky had watchfully headed him off.

But when they had risen from the table and the ladies had gone out, Pestsov did not follow them but turned to Karenin and set about explaining the principal reason for this inequality. In his opinion the inequality between husband and wife consisted of the fact that a wife's infidelity and a husband's infidelity were punished inequitably, both in law and in public opinion.

Oblonsky hastened over to Karenin and offered him a cigar.

"No, I don't smoke," replied Karenin calmly, and as though deliberately wishing to show he was not afraid of this conversation he turned to Pestsov with a chilly smile.

"I think the foundations of this attitude are rooted in the very nature of things," he said, and was about to go into the drawing room, but just then Turovtsyn suddenly and unexpectedly started speaking and turned to him.

"Have you heard about Pryachnikov?" said Turovtsyn, who was exhilarated by the champagne he had drunk and had been waiting for a chance to break the silence, which had been weighing on him. "Vasya Pryachnikov," he said with a kindly smile on his moist red lips, primarily addressing the most important guest, Karenin. "I heard today he had a duel in Tver with Kvitsky and killed him."

Just as it seems that a sore spot always attracts blows on purpose, so now too Oblonsky felt that the conversation unfortunately kept hitting up against Karenin's sore spot. He tried to draw his brother-in-law away again, but Karenin himself asked with curiosity:

"What was Pryachnikov dueling about?"

"His wife: he acted like a man! Challenged him and killed him!"

"Ah!" said Karenin indifferently, and raising his eyebrows he went into the drawing room.

"I'm so glad you came," Dolly said to him with a frightened smile, when she met him in the anteroom. "I must have a talk with you. Let us sit down here."

Karenin, with the same look of indifference, produced by his raised eyebrows, sat beside Dolly and feigned a smile.

"Especially since I wanted to ask you to forgive me for going away immediately," he said. "I must leave Moscow tomorrow."

Dolly was quite certain of Anna's innocence, and she felt herself growing pale and her lips start quivering with anger at this chilly, unfeeling man, who so calmly intended to destroy her innocent friend.

"Alexis," she said, looking straight into his eyes with desperate resolution. "I asked you about Anna, and you didn't answer me. How is she?"

"Well, I think," he answered, without looking at her.

"Alexis, forgive me, I have no right to—but I love and esteem Anna as a sister; I beg of you, I implore you to tell me: What has been happening between you? What do you accuse her of?"

Karenin frowned, half-shut his eyes and lowered his head.

"I presume your husband gave you the reasons I think it necessary to change my former relations with my wife," he said, without looking into her eyes, and irritably watching Shcherbatsky walk through the drawing room.

"I don't believe it, I don't, I can't believe it!" said Dolly, violently clenching her bony hands. She swiftly rose to her feet and placed her hand on Karenin's sleeve. "We'll be disturbed here, please let's sit over there."

Dolly's agitation affected Karenin; he got up and submissively followed her into the schoolroom. They sat down at the table, covered over with a piece of oilcloth all cut up by penknives.

"I don't, I don't believe it!" Dolly said, trying to catch hold of his evasive eye.

"It is impossible not to believe in facts," he said, emphasizing the word "facts."

"But what has she done?" Dolly said. "Just what is it she's done?"

"She has slighted her duties and deceived her husband. That is what she has done," he said.

"No, no, it's not possible! No, for the love of God—you're mistaken!" said Dolly, raising her hands to her temples and shutting her eyes.

Karenin gave a cold smile, with his lips alone; he wished to show both her and himself how firm his conviction was. But this passionate defense of Anna, though it did not shake him, reopened his wound. He began to speak with greater heat.

"It's excessively difficult to be mistaken when a wife herself says as much to her husband. When she says that eight years of life together, and a son—that all that has been a blunder and that she wants to start her life all over again!" he said angrily, with a snort.

"Anna and wrongdoing—I can't associate them, I can't believe it."

"Dolly!" he said, looking straight into Dolly's kind, excited face; he felt his tongue unloosing itself of its own accord. "I should give a good deal to be able to have any further doubts. While I was still in doubt, though it was painful, it was easier for me than it is now. While I was in doubt there was still hope, but now there is no hope left, and I'm still in doubt about everything anyhow. I'm in so much doubt about everything that I detest my son and sometimes believe he's not my own. I am very unhappy."

There was no need for him to say this. Dolly realized it the moment she looked into his face; she felt sorry for him, and her belief in her friend's innocence began wavering.

"Oh it's horrible, horrible! But it *can't* be true that you've decided on a divorce?"

"I've made up my mind to take the final step. There's nothing further for me to do."

"Nothing further to do, nothing to do . . ." she murmured

with tears in her eyes. "No—there *is* something else to do!" she said.

"That's just what's so dreadful in this kind of grief—it's impossible to bear one's cross, as it is in every other kind— in losses, in death—here you have to act," he said, as though guessing her thought. "You must get out of the humiliating position in which you've been placed—it's impossible to live as a trio."

"I understand that, I understand it very well," said Dolly, and she lowered her head. She fell silent, thinking of herself and of her own domestic grief, then suddenly with an energetic gesture she raised her head and clasped her hands beseechingly: "But wait! You're a Christian—think of her! What will become of her if you cast her out?"

"I've thought about that, and thought about it a great deal," said Karenin. His face flushed blotchily, and his dim eyes looked straight at her. By now Dolly pitied him with all her heart. "That is just what I did when I was told of my shame by her herself; I left everything as it had been. I gave her a chance to reform, I tried to save her. And what happened? She paid no attention to the easiest of demands—that she observe the proprieties," he said, growing heated. "It's possible to save someone who doesn't want to be destroyed; but if her whole character is so corrupt, so depraved, that destruction itself seems to her salvation, what can be done then?"

"Anything—*except divorce!*" retorted Dolly.

"But what is anything?"

"No, it's too dreadful! She'll be no one's wife, she'll be ruined!"

"But what can I do?" said Karenin, shrugging his shoulders and raising his eyebrows. The memory of Anna's latest action had irritated him so much that he at once grew chilly again as he had been when the conversation began. "I'm very grateful to you for your sympathy, but I must go now," he said, getting up.

"No—wait! You must not ruin her! Wait: I'll tell you what happened to me. I was married, and my husband deceived me; in my anger and jealousy I wanted to abandon everything, I myself wanted to— But I came to my senses, and with whose help? It was Anna who saved me. And so I've gone on living. The children are growing up, my husband has returned to the family and feels how wrong he was, and is growing purer, better, and—I go on living. I forgave him, and so you must forgive her!"

Karenin was listening, but her words no longer had any effect on him. All the spite he had felt the day he had decided on a divorce had risen up in his soul once again. He shook himself and started speaking in a loud, piercing voice:

"I cannot forgive, I do not wish to, and I consider it wrong. I did everything for that woman; she has trampled it all in the mud that is natural to her. I'm not a malevolent man, I've never hated anyone, but I hate her with all the power of my soul! I cannot even forgive her, I hate her too much, for all the wrong she's done me!" he said, tears of anger in his voice.

"Love them that hate you," Dolly whispered shamefacedly.

Karenin smiled contemptuously; he had known that for a long time, but it couldn't be applied to his own case. "Love them that hate you, but to love them that you hate yourself is impossible. Forgive me for having upset you. Everyone has troubles enough of his own!"

Regaining control of himself, Karenin calmly said goodby and left.

XIII

WHEN everyone was getting up from the table Levin wanted to follow Kitty into the drawing room, but he was afraid she might not like it if his attentions became too obvious. He stayed on with the group of men, taking part in the general conversation; without looking at Kitty he was aware of her movements, her looks, and where she was sitting.

Without the slightest effort he had begun at once to keep the promise he had made her—always to esteem and to love everyone. The conversation had gone on to the village commune, in which Pestsov saw some sort of special principle that he called the "choral" principle. Levin disagreed both with Pestsov and with his brother, Koznyshov, who in his usual way both admitted and didn't admit the significance of the Russian commune. But he spoke to them simply in an attempt to bring them together and soften their differences. He didn't have the slightest interest in what he was saying himself, and still less in what they were saying; all he wanted was for them and everyone else to be in a pleasant, cheerful mood. He now knew the one thing that was important. And this one thing was there, at first in the drawing room, though then it began moving about and came to a stop in the doorway. Without turning around he felt a gaze directed at him and a smile, and he could not help turning around. She was standing in the doorway with Shcherbatsky looking at him.

"I thought you were going over to the piano," he said, moving toward her. "That's what I don't get enough of in the country—music."

"No, we only came over to call you away; thank you for coming," she said, rewarding him with her smile, as though it were a present. "What's the good of arguing? After all, no one ever convinces anyone else."

"That's true," said Levin, "what happens most of the time is that the only reason you argue so heatedly is because you simply can't make out just what your opponent is trying to prove."

Levin had often noticed, in arguments between the cleverest people, that after enormous efforts, and an enormous number of logical subtleties and words, the people who were arguing finally became aware that what they had been taking such pains to prove to each other had long since been known to them, from the very beginning of the argument on, but that they liked different things, and didn't want to mention what they liked in order not to be attacked. He had often had the experience in the midst of an argument of understanding what his opponent liked; he would suddenly get to like it himself and immediately agree, whereupon all arguments fell away, superfluous; sometimes he had the contrary experience: you finally said what it was you liked yourself and why you had been thinking up arguments, and if you happened to express this well and sincerely, then your opponent would suddenly agree with you and stop arguing. He tried to say this now.

She wrinkled her forehead, trying to understand. But the moment he started explaining she had grasped it.

"I see—you have to find out what he's arguing in favor of, what he likes, then you can . . ."

She had completely grasped his badly expressed thought and put it in the right words. Levin smiled joyfully, he was so struck by this transition from the confused, verbose argument with his brother and Pestsov to this laconic, clear, almost wordless communication of the most complicated ideas.

Shcherbatsky left them, and Kitty, going over to a table set out for cards, sat down and taking up a piece of chalk began drawing divergent circles on the new green cloth.

They resumed the conversation started at dinner—about the emancipation of women and their occupations. Levin agreed with Dolly's opinion that a girl who didn't get married would find woman's work for herself in a family. He supported this with the remark that there wasn't a single family that could get along without women to help, and that there were and had to be nurses, either hired ones or relatives, in every family, rich or poor.

"No," said Kitty, blushing, but looking at him with her candid eyes all the more boldly, "a girl may be so situated that she can't enter into a family without humiliating herself, while she herself—"

He understood the allusion.

"Oh yes!" he said, "yes, yes, yes, you're right, you're right!"

And he grasped everything Pestsov had been trying to demonstrate at dinner about women's freedom, simply by seeing in Kitty's heart the fear of humiliation and of spinsterhood, and through loving her he sensed this fear and humiliation and abruptly abandoned all his own arguments.

A silence came over them. She was still drawing with the chalk on the table. Her eyes were glowing softly. Yielding to her mood he felt a constantly growing tension of happiness throughout her whole being.

"Oh—I've scribbled all over the table!" she said, putting down the chalk and moving as though she were about to get up.

How can I stay here alone, without her? he thought horrified, and took up the piece of chalk. "Don't go," he said, sitting down at the table. "I've been wanting to ask you something for a long time."

He looked straight into her tender, though frightened eyes.

"Ask me—please!"

"There," he said, and wrote down the initial letters: w,y,g, m,t,a,i,i,n,p,d,y,m,i,w,n,b,p,o,t,i,w,p,t ? these letters stood for. "When you gave me the answer 'It is not possible,' did you mean it would never be possible, or that it wasn't possible then?"

There wasn't the slightest likelihood of her being able to guess this complicated sentence; but he looked at her as though his life depended on whether she would.

She looked at him gravely; then she leaned her puckered forehead on her hand and began reading. Occasionally she looked up at him, her look asking him: "Is it what I think it is?"

"I understand it," she said, blushing.

"What's this word?" he said, pointing to the *n*, which stood for "never."

"That means 'never,' " she said, "but that's not so!"

He quickly rubbed out what he had written, gave her the chalk and got up. She wrote: *t,w,n,o,a,I,c,g,t.*

Dolly was quite consoled for the grief her conversation with Karenin had given her when she saw these two figures: Kitty with the piece of chalk in her hand, looking up at Levin with a timid happy smile, and his handsome figure leaning over the table, with his burning eyes fixed now on her and now on the table. Suddenly he was radiant: he had guessed it. What it meant was: "There was no other answer I could give then."

He looked at her questioningly, timidly.

"Only then?"

"Yes," her smile replied.

"And n–n–n–now?" he asked.

"Well, read this now. I'll tell you what I should like. Should like very much!" She wrote down these initial letters: *I,l,y,t, f,a,f,w,h.* That meant: "'I'd like you to forget and forgive what happened."

He seized the chalk in his taut, trembling fingers, broke it, and wrote down the initial letters of the following: "There's nothing for me to forget or forgive, I haven't stopped loving you."

She looked at him with a smile that did not falter.

"I understand," she said in a whisper.

He sat down and wrote out a long sentence. She understood it all and without asking him whether she had it right took the chalk and replied immediately.

For a long time he could not understand what she had written, and he kept looking into her eyes. He was numb with happiness. He could not fill in the words she meant at all, but in her lovely eyes, radiant with happiness, he understood everything he had to know. He wrote down three letters; but before he had even finished writing she had already read it under his hand; she had finished it herself, and written down the answer: "Yes."

"Playing 'secretary'?" said the old Prince, coming over to them. "Come along now. We really ought to be going if we're to be in time for the theater."

Levin got up and saw Kitty to the door.

Everything had been said in their conversation: what had been said was that she loved him and would tell her father and mother, and that he would call in the morning.

### XIV

WHEN Kitty went out and Levin was left alone, he felt so restless without her, and so impatient to get through the time quickly, as quickly as possible till the next day when he would see her once again and be united with her forever, that he was frightened to death of the fourteen hours he was going to have to pass without her. He had to be with and talk to someone, in order not to be left alone and to deceive the time. Oblonsky would have been the most agreeable one for him to talk to, but as he had said he was going off to an evening party, though actually it was to the ballet, Levin only had time enough to tell him that he was happy, that he was devoted to him, and would never, never forget what he had done for him. Oblonsky's look and smile showed Levin that he had understood this feeling rightly.

"What—it's not time to die?" said Oblonsky, pressing Levin's hand with emotion.

"N–n–no," said Levin.

When Dolly said good-by to him she also seemed to be congratulating him; she said: "I'm so happy you've seen Kitty again, old friendships ought to be treasured."

Levin disliked this remark of Dolly's. She was incapable of understanding how lofty and inaccessible to her all this was, and she ought not to have dared mention it. Levin said good-by to them, but in order not to be left alone he fastened on to his brother.

"Where are you off to?"

"I'm going to the Council meeting."

"Then I'll go with you. Can I?"

"Why not? Let's go," said Koznyshov with a smile. "What's happened to you today?"

"To me? Happiness!" said Levin, letting down the windows of the carriage they were driving in. "You don't mind? It's stifling in here. Yes, happiness! Why didn't you ever get married?"

Koznyshov smiled. "I'm delighted, she seems to be a wonderful gi—" he started saying.

"Don't say it, don't, don't!" Levin cried out, seizing the collar of his brother's fur coat with both hands and folding it over his face. "A wonderful girl" were such simple, commonplace words, so out of harmony with his feeling.

Koznyshov burst into a merry laugh, which happened with him rarely.

"Well, at least I can say I'm delighted."

"Tomorrow you can, tomorrow, and now not another word! Nothing, nothing, silence!" said Levin; folding the fur coat over his brother's face again he added: "I'm terribly fond of you! Now tell me, can I really go to the meeting?"

"Of course you can."

"What are you talking about tonight?" asked Levin, smiling without letup.

They arrived at the Council meeting. Levin listened to the secretary stammering through the minutes, which he obviously couldn't understand himself, but Levin saw by his face what a charming, kindhearted, and wonderful fellow he was. This was obvious by the way he got confused and embarrassed as he read the minutes. Then the speeches began. They were debating the grant of some sums of money and the laying of some pipes; Koznyshov got off some gibes at a couple of other members and said something at great length with a triumphant air; another member, after jotting something down on a slip of paper, got off to a timid start but went on to answer him very venomously and neatly. Then Sviyazhsky (he was there too) also made an eloquent, lofty speech. Levin listened to them and saw clearly that neither the sums of money allocated nor the pipes really existed, there was nothing of the kind; they were not in the least angry with one another, but were all kindhearted, splendid fellows, and that was why they were all getting on so nicely. They harmed no one and were all enjoying themselves. What Levin found remarkable was that they were all completely transparent to him today, and by tiny, previously unnoticed telltale signs he could recognize each one's soul and see clearly what kind hearts they all had, and especially how extraordinarily fond of him, Levin, they all were today. This was visible in the way they spoke to him, and the affectionate way even all the people he didn't know looked at him.

"Well, are you pleased?" Koznyshov asked him.

"Very! I never thought it was so interesting! It's wonderful, magnificent!"

Sviyazhsky came over to Levin and invited him to come home with him for some tea. Levin was completely incapable of understanding or recalling why he had ever been annoyed with Sviyazhsky, or what he had failed to find in him. He was an intelligent and wonderfully kindhearted fellow.

"Delighted," he said, and asked about his wife and his sister-in-law. And by a curious train of thought, since the idea of Sviyazhsky's sister-in-law was associated in his mind with marriage, it seemed to him that it would be impossible to find anyone better to tell about his own happiness than Sviyazhsky's wife and sister-in-law, and he was delighted to visit them.

Sviyazhsky asked him about his affairs in the country, as usual refusing to believe in the possibility of inventing anything not already invented in Europe; Levin didn't find this in the least disagreeable now. On the contrary he felt that Sviyazhsky was right, that this whole business was quite trivial, and he perceived the wonderful gentleness and delicacy with which Sviyazhsky avoided making a point of being in the right. Sviyazhsky's wife and sister-in-law were particularly charming. It seemed to Levin that they knew all about everything already and were in sympathy with him, and it was only tact that prevented their speaking of it. He stayed on at the house one hour, two hours, three hours, chatting away about a variety of subjects but thinking only of the one thing that filled his soul, and not noticing that they had grown terribly weary of him and that it was long past their bedtime. Sviyazhsky, yawning, saw him into the hall, wondering at his friend's strange mood. It was past one o'clock.

Levin returned to his hotel full of apprehension at the idea of how, alone now with his impatience, he was going to pass the ten hours that were still left. The attendant on night duty lighted his candles and was about to go away, but Levin stopped him. This servant, Yegor, whom Levin had never noticed before, turned out to be very intelligent, good, and above all kindhearted.

"Well, Yegor, it must be very hard, not sleeping?"

"What can be done! That's our job. Private service is easier, but we make more money here."

It turned out that Yegor had a family, three boys and a daughter, a seamstress, whom he wanted to marry off to a harnessmaker's assistant.

Levin took the occasion to convey to Yegor his own idea

that the main thing in marriage was love, and that you'd always be happy if you had love because happiness lay only in yourself.

Yegor listened to him attentively till he finished; he plainly understood Levin's idea fully, but by way of agreeing with it he made a remark Levin didn't expect, that when he had been in the service of good masters he had always been satisfied, and was completely satisfied now with his master, even though he was a Frenchman.

A wonderfully kindhearted fellow, thought Levin.

"And when you got married, Yegor, did you love your wife?"

"How could I help loving her?" Yegor replied.

And Levin saw that Yegor was also in a state of rapture, and bent on expressing all his most intimate thoughts.

"My life has also been wonderful. Since childhood I—" he began, his eyes shining, obviously infected by Levin's excitement, as people are infected by yawning.

But just then a bell rang; Yegor went out and Levin was left alone. He had eaten almost nothing at dinner, had refused tea and supper at the Sviyazhskys', but he couldn't think about eating. He had not slept the night before, but he couldn't even think of sleeping. His room was cool, but he felt stifled by the heat. He opened both the little panes in the window and sat down at a table in front of it. Beyond the snow-covered roofs he could see a cross hung with chains and above it the rising triangular constellation of the Charioteer with the bright yellow star Capella. He looked from the cross to the constellation and back, breathed in the fresh, moist air that blew evenly into the room, and as though he were in a dream followed the images and memories that rose up in his imagination. Toward four o'clock he overheard steps in the corridor and glanced out the door. It was a gambler he knew, by the name of Myaskin, on his way home from the club. He passed by gloomily, frowning and coughing. Poor wretch! thought Levin. And tears of love and pity for him came into his eyes. He wanted to speak to him, comfort him, but remembering he had nothing on but his shirt he changed his mind, and sat down in front of the window again, to bathe in the chilly air and look out at the strange shape of the cross, silent but full of meaning for him, and the bright yellow star ascending. At six o'clock the floor polishers began making a noise, bells began ringing

somewhere in the servants' section, and Levin began to feel
chilly. He closed the window, washed, dressed, and went
outside.

## XV

THE streets were still empty. Levin walked over to the
Shcherbatskys' house, where the front doors were locked and
everyone was asleep. He walked back, went up to his room
again and ordered some coffee. It wasn't brought to him by
Yegor, but by the day waiter. Levin wanted to start up a
conversation with him, but the waiter was rung for and went
out. Levin tried to drink some coffee and put a roll in his
mouth, but his mouth was completely at a loss what to do
with it. He spit out the roll, put on his overcoat and went
out to walk about again. It was after nine when he came to
the Shcherbatskys' front steps for the second time. The household had only just gotten up, and the cook was on his way
out to shop. He had to get through at least another two
hours.

That entire night and morning Levin had been living completely unconsciously; he felt utterly abstracted from the
conditions of material life. He had not eaten for a whole
day, had not slept for two nights, he had spent several hours
half-undressed in the frost, and not only did he feel completely fresh and healthy as he never had before, but he
felt quite independent of his body; he moved without any
muscular exertion, and felt he could do anything. He was
sure he could fly upward, or knock down the corner of a
house if he had to. He spent the rest of the time walking
about the streets, constantly looking at his watch and
gazing about him.

And never again did he see what he saw then. He was
moved in particular by two children going to school, some
silvery gray pigeons that flew down from the rooftop to the
pavement, and some little loaves of bread, sprinkled with
flour, that some invisible hand had set out in front of a
bakery. These loaves, pigeons, and two little boys seemed
unearthly. It all happened at the same time: a little boy ran
over to a pigeon, glancing over at Levin with a smile; the
pigeon flapped its wings and fluttered, gleaming in the sunshine among the snowdust quivering in the air, while the
smell of freshly baked bread was wafted out of a little win-

dow as the loaves were put out. All this together was so extraordinarily wonderful that Levin burst out laughing and crying for joy.

After making a big circle by way of Gazetny and Kislovka Streets, he went back to his hotel again; he put his watch in front of him and sat down to wait for noon. The people in the next room were saying something about machines and swindling, and coughing their morning coughs. They didn't realize that the watch hand was already approaching twelve. The hand reached twelve. Levin went out onto the front steps. It was evident that the cabmen knew all about it. They surrounded him with happy faces, bickering and offering him their services. Trying not to offend the other cabmen and promising to drive with them too, Levin took one of them and told him to drive to the Shcherbatskys'. The cabman looked charming in his white shirtband, which stuck out from under his coat and clung tightly to his full, red, powerful neck. This cabman's sleigh was high and comfortable; Levin had never driven in one like it before; the horse was a good one and did its best to run, but seemed rooted to the spot. The cabman knew the Shcherbatskys' house and, rounding his elbows and shouting "Whoa!" with particular deference to his passenger, he drew up at the entrance. The Shcherbatskys' hall porter surely knew all about it. This was obvious by the smile in his eyes, and by the way he said:

"Well, Mr. Constantine, it's a long time since you've been here!"

Not only did he know everything, but he was obviously delighted, and making an effort to conceal his joy. Looking into his kind old eyes Levin felt something else that was new, even in his own happiness.

"Are they up?"

"Just go in! And you can leave that here," he said with a smile, as Levin turned back for his cap. That meant something.

"Whom shall I announce you to, sir?" asked a footman.

The footman, even though he was young and one of the new kind of footmen—a dandy—was a very good and kindhearted fellow; he understood everything, too.

"The Princess—the Prince—the young Princess . . ." Levin said.

The first person he saw was Mlle. Linon. She was passing through the hall, her ringlets and face radiant. He had just started talking to her, when suddenly the rustle of a dress was heard behind the door, and Mlle. Linon vanished from Levin's sight; a joyous dread at his imminent happiness seized him. Mlle. Linon hastened off, leaving him, and went over to the other door. She had only just gone out when there was a sound of rapid, very rapid light steps along the parquet floor, and his happiness, his life, his very self— the best of himself, that which he had been seeking and longing for so long—quickly, very quickly, came close to him. She was not walking, but was being borne toward him by some invisible force.

He saw only her clear, candid eyes, frightened by the same joy of love that filled his own heart. Those eyes shone out nearer and nearer, blinding him with their radiant love. She stopped at his very side, close enough to touch him. Her arms rose, and sank down on to his shoulders.

She had done everything she could: she had run up to him and yielded herself entirely, shyly and joyously. He embraced her and pressed his lips to her mouth, which was seeking his kisses.

She had not slept all night either, and had been waiting for him all that morning. Her father and mother had given their unqualified consent and were happy in her happiness. She had been waiting for him. She wanted to be the first to tell him of his happiness and her own. She had prepared herself to meet him alone, and was overjoyed at the thought of it; she was shy, and bashful, and did not know herself what she was going to do. She had heard his step and his voice, and had been waiting behind the door for Mlle. Linon to go out. Mlle. Linon went out. Without thinking or asking herself how to do it or what would come of it she had gone over to him and done what she had done.

"Let's go and see Mama!" she said, taking him by the hand. For a long time he was speechless, not so much because he was afraid of destroying the loftiness of his feelings by saying something as because each time he tried to say something he felt that instead of words tears of joy would burst forth. He took her hand and kissed it.

"It's not true, is it?" he said finally, in a husky voice. "I can't believe you love me, darling!"

She smiled at his "darling," and at the timidity with which he looked at her.

"Yes . . ." she said slowly and meaningfully. "I'm so happy!"

Clinging to his hand she went into the drawing room. When the Princess saw them she started breathing rapidly; she immediately burst into tears, then all at once into laughter, and with an energetic stride Levin hadn't expected she ran up to them, put her arms around Levin's head and wetted his cheeks with her tears.

"Then it's all finished! I'm so glad. Love her—I'm so glad . . . Kitty!"

"Well, you settled all that quick enough!" said the old Prince, trying to look indifferent, though Levin noticed that his eyes were moist as he turned to him.

"For a long time, forever, this is just what I've wanted!" he said taking Levin by the hand and drawing him closer. "Even at that time, when this little flibbertigibbet took it into her head to—"

"Papa!" Kitty cried out, and shut his mouth with her hands.

"All right, then I won't!" he said. "I'm very, very hap— hap— Really, how stupid of me!"

He embraced Kitty, kissed her face and her hand, then her face again, and made the sign of the cross over her.

Levin was seized by a new feeling of affection for the old Prince, who had been a stranger to him before, when he saw how long and tenderly Kitty kissed his fleshy hand.

XVI

THE Princess sat smiling silently in the armchair; the Prince sat down beside her. Kitty stood close to her father's chair, still holding on to his hand. No one said anything.

The Princess was the first to put everything into words; she translated all their thoughts and feelings into practical terms. At first this seemed strange and even painful to all of them.

"Now, when is it to be? There is the betrothal, and announcements to be sent out. And when is the wedding to be? What do you think, Alexander?"

"There he is," said the old Prince, nodding at Levin. "He's the chief personage here."

"When?" said Levin, blushing. "If you ask me we ought to have the betrothal today, in my opinion, and the wedding tomorrow."

"Now, now, my dear boy, enough silliness!"

"Well, in a week then."

"He seems quite mad."

"No, but why not?"

"Really!" said the mother, with a happy smile at his haste. "And the trousseau?"

Is there really going to be a trousseau and all that? thought Levin in horror. But what if there is a trousseau, and a betrothal and the whole business—is that going to spoil my happiness? Nothing can spoil that! He glanced at Kitty and noticed that she was not in the least, not the slightest bit annoyed at the idea of a trousseau. So it must be necessary, he thought.

"Well, I don't really know, I was just saying what I wanted," he said apologetically.

"Then we'll be the ones to decide. We can have the betrothal now and make the announcements. That will be all right."

The Princess went over to her husband, kissed him and was about to leave, but he held her back, embraced her with a smile and kissed her tenderly, like a young man in love, several times. The old couple had obviously become confused for a moment and were not very clear about whether it was they who were in love again or just their daughter. When the Prince and Princess had gone out Levin went over to his betrothed and took her hand. He had recovered his self-control and could speak, and there was a great deal he needed to tell her. But what he said was not at all what was needed.

"I was so sure it would be this way! I never had any hope, but at heart I was always sure of it," he said. "I believe it was foreordained."

"And I?" she said. "Even at that time—" She stopped, then started again, looking at him resolutely with her candid eyes. "Even at that time, when I thrust my own happiness away from me. You were the only one I ever loved, but I was infatuated. I must ask you—can you forget it?"

"It may have been for the best. It is I you must forgive a great many things. I must tell you—"

This was one of the things he had decided to tell her. He had made up his mind to tell her two things straight off—that he was not so pure as she, and secondly that he was not a believer. It was agonizing, but he considered it his duty to tell her both one and the other.

"No, not now—later!" he said.

"Very well then, later, but you absolutely must tell me.

I'm not afraid of anything. I must know everything. It's all settled now—"

He finished it up for her.

"What's settled is that you're going to take me just as I am, you won't refuse me? Yes?"

"Yes, yes!"

Their conversation was interrupted by Mlle. Linon, who came in smiling affectedly though tenderly to congratulate her favorite pupil. She had not gone before the servants came in with their congratulations. Afterward relatives began arriving, and there began the blissful tumult Levin did not emerge from until the day after the wedding. He constantly felt ill at ease and bored, but the tension of happiness kept on increasing. He constantly felt that a great deal he didn't know was being demanded of him, and he did everything he was told to, and it all gave him joy. He had thought his courtship was going to be quite unlike any other, that the usual conditions of courtship would spoil his own special happiness; but it ended up by his behaving just like everyone else, and because of this his happiness simply increased and became more and more peculiar to himself, unlike what anyone else's was or would be.

"Now we'll eat some sweets," said Mlle. Linon, and Levin went off to buy some sweets.

"Well, I'm delighted," said Sviyazhsky, "I advise you to get your flowers from Fomin's."

"Are they necessary?" said Levin, and was off to Fomin's.

His brother told him he'd have to borrow some money, since there were going to be a great many expenses, presents . . .

"Are the presents necessary?" And he bounded off to Fulda the jeweler.

And at the sweetshop, at Fomin's, and at Fulda's he saw that he was expected, that they were pleased to see him, and were just as enraptured by his happiness as everyone else he had anything to do with during these days. What was extraordinary was that not only did everyone show affection for him, but all those people who had used to be antipathetic, cold and indifferent, yielded to him in everything in their delight with him, handled his feelings with tenderness and tact, and shared his own conviction that he was the happiest man on earth because his betrothed was the pinnacle of perfection. Kitty had the same feeling. When Countess Nordston took the liberty of hinting that she had wished for something better, Kitty grew so heated and proved so convincingly that there could be nothing on earth that was better than Levin that Countess Nordston was obliged to admit it; from then on she never met Levin in Kitty's presence without putting on a rapturous smile.

The confession he had promised Kitty was the one painful event of that period. He consulted the old Prince, and with his permission gave Kitty the diary in which what had been tormenting him was written down. He had actually started this diary with his future bride in mind. He was tormented by two things: his not being a virgin and his lack of faith. His confession of agnosticism passed without comment. She was devout, and had never doubted the truths of religion, but his external lack of faith did not affect her at all. Through her love she knew his whole soul through and through, and in his soul she saw what she desired, and it didn't matter to her at all that this spiritual condition was called agnosticism. But his other confession made her weep bitterly.

Levin had not handed her his diary without an inner struggle. He knew that there could not and must not be any secrets between him and her, and this was why he had decided that it was his duty; but he had not taken into account the effect it might have; he had not put himself in her place. It was not until the evening he came to their house before going to the theater, and went into her room, and there saw her tear-stained, sweet, pitiful face, wretched with the misery he had brought about, that he understood the abyss that divided his shameful past from her own dovelike purity, and was horrified at what he had done.

"Take these horrible books, take them away!" she said, pushing away the notebooks lying on the table in front of her. "Why did you give them to me? No—it was best after all," she added, moved to pity by his despairing face. "But it's horrible, horrible!"

He bowed his head in silence; he was incapable of speech.

"Won't you forgive me?" he whispered.

"Yes, I've forgiven you, but it's horrible!"

But his happiness was so great that this confession did not destroy it, but merely gave it a new shading. She forgave him, but from then on he considered himself still more unworthy of her, bowed still lower before her morally, and set a still higher value on his undeserved happiness.

## XVII

INVOLUNTARILY turning over in his mind the impression of the conversations during and after the dinner, Karenin returned to his solitary room. What Dolly had said about forgiveness had merely irritated him. The application or non-application of the Christian rule to his own case was too difficult a question to be discussed lightly, and it was a question that Karenin had long since decided in the negative. Of everything that had been said it was the remark of the stupid good-natured Turovtsyn that had sunk deepest into his mind: *"He acted like a man! Challenged him and killed him!"* Everyone evidently sympathized with this, even though out of politeness they had not said so.

But it's all over with, there's no point thinking about it, Karenin said to himself. Thinking only of his forthcoming trip and inspection tour, he went to his room and asked the porter who had accompanied him where his valet was. The porter said the valet had just gone out. Karenin ordered some tea, sat down at the table, took up a timetable and began planning his itinerary.

"Two telegrams," said his valet, as he came into the room. "Excuse me, Your Excellency, I just stepped out."

Karenin took the telegrams and opened them. The first reported that Stremov had been appointed to the post Karenin had wanted. Karenin flung it aside; turning red he got up and began pacing up and down the room. "Whom the gods would destroy they first make mad," he said, meaning by "whom" the ones who had had a hand in this appointment. It was not that he was annoyed at having lost the post himself, at having been conspicuously passed over; but he found it incomprehensible, astounding, that they failed to understand that that chatterbox Stremov was less suited for it than anyone else. How could they fail to see that by giving him this post they were ruining themselves and their own prestige!

Something else along the same lines, he said to himself bitterly as he opened the second telegram. It was from Anna. Her signature, written in a blue pencil, was the first thing to leap to his eyes. *"Dying, beg, implore you come. With your forgiveness will die more tranquilly,"* he read. He smiled contemptuously and flung the telegram aside. In the first moment it seemed to him that there could not be the slightest doubt of its being nothing but falsehood and guile.

There's no falsehood she would stop at, he thought. She was supposed to be having a child, perhaps that's the illness. But what can their purpose be? To legitimize the child, compromise me, and prevent the divorce. But what's that about "dying"?

He reread the telegram; suddenly the straightforward sense of what it contained struck him. What if it were true? he said to himself. Suppose it were true that at a moment of suffering, with death imminent, she was sincerely repentant, and I took it for a swindle and refused to go to her? That would not only be cruel, and I would be condemned for it by everyone, but it would be stupid from my own point of view.

"Peter, keep the carriage. I'm going to Petersburg," he said to his valet.

He made up his mind to go to Petersburg and see his wife. If her illness were a fraud he would say nothing and go away again. If she were really ill and dying and wanted to see him before her death he would forgive her, if he found her still among the living, and if he arrived too late he would perform his final duty to her.

For the whole of his journey he gave no further thought to what he had to do.

Feeling weary and filthy from a night in the train, Karenin made his way along the deserted Nevsky in the morning Petersburg mist, looking straight ahead of him without thinking of what lay ahead. He was incapable of thinking about it because in imagining what would happen he could not drive away the thought that her death would instantly resolve all the difficulty of his position. The bakers, the closed shops, the night cabmen, the pavement sweepers flashed by his eyes; he surveyed them all as he tried to stifle the thought of what was awaiting him and what he dared not wish for but wished for nevertheless. He drove up to the front steps. A cabman and a carriage with a sleeping coachman were standing out in front. As he entered the hallway Karenin seemed to drag forth as it were his resolution from a remote corner of his mind and come to grips with it. This is how it ran: If it's a fraud—then calm contempt and departure. If it's the truth—the proprieties are to be observed.

The hall porter opened the door even before Karenin rang.

Petrov, otherwise known as Kapitonych, looked very peculiar in an old coat without a tie, and in slippers.

"How is Madame?"

"Safely delivered yesterday."

Karenin halted and turned white. Now he understood clearly how intensely he had longed for her death.

"How is she?"

Korney, in his morning apron, came running down the staircase.

"Very bad," he replied. "There was a doctors' consultation yesterday; now the doctor's here."

"Take my things," said Karenin, and feeling somewhat relieved at the news that there was nevertheless some hope of her death he went into the anteroom.

A military greatcoat was hanging on the stand. Karenin noticed it and asked: "Who's here?"

"The doctor, the midwife, and Count Vronsky."

Karenin went on into the inner apartments.

There was no one in the drawing room; at the sound of his footsteps the midwife came out in a cap with lilac ribbons on it. She went over to Karenin and with the familiarity due to the nearness of death took him by the hand and led him into the bedroom.

"Thank God you've come! All she talks about is you, nothing but you," she said.

"Be quick and bring me some ice!" said the peremptory voice of the doctor from inside the bedroom.

Karenin entered her sitting room. At her desk, sitting sideways on a low chair and covering his face with his hands, Vronsky sat weeping. At the sound of the doctor's voice he took his hands from his face, jumped to his feet, and saw Karenin. At the sight of her husband he was so disconcerted that he sat down again, drawing his head down between his shoulders as though he wanted to disappear somewhere; then he made an attempt at self-control, got up and said:

"She's dying. The doctors say there's no hope. I'm entirely in your hands, but please, let me stay here . . . though I'm in your hands, I—"

At the sight of Vronsky's tears Karenin felt an access of that spiritual agitation produced in him by the sight of the sufferings of others; he turned his face away and without listening to Vronsky finish hurried to the door. Anna's voice could be heard from the bedroom, saying something or other. Her voice was gay and lively, with extremely distinct tones.

Karenin entered the bedroom and went over to the bed. She lay there facing him. Her cheeks were flushed and her eyes glittered; and her little white hands, sticking out of the cuffs of her dressing jacket, toyed with the corner of the blanket, twisting it about. She seemed to be not only healthy and fresh, but in the best possible mood. She spoke quickly, in a loud voice, with extraordinary precision and feeling.

"Because Alexis—I'm talking about my husband; what a strange, horrible fate, for them both to be called Alexis, isn't it?—Alexis would not have refused me. I could have forgotten and he would have forgiven me . . . But why is it he doesn't come? He's kind, he himself has no idea of how kind he is. Oh! My God, what anguish! Quickly, give me some water! Oh, that would be bad for her, for my little girl! Very well then, give her to a nurse. All right then, I agree, that may even be better. He's coming, it'll hurt him to see her. Take her away!"

"He's come, Madame! Here he is!" said the midwife, trying to direct Anna's attention to Karenin.

"Oh, such nonsense!" Anna went on, not seeing her husband. "But hand her over to me, the little girl, hand her over! He still hasn't come. You say he won't forgive me because you don't know him. No one knows him. I'm the only one, and it became hard for me too. You ought to realize that Seryozha has the same eyes he has, that's why I can't look at them. Has Seryozha been given his dinner? But of course everyone's going to forget. He wouldn't have forgotten. Seryozha must be moved into the corner room, and Mariette must be asked to sleep with him."

Suddenly she shrank together; she fell silent and in fright, as though she were afraid of being hit and were defending herself, she raised her hand to her face. She had seen her husband.

"No, no!" she began again. "I'm not afraid of him, I'm afraid of dying. Alexis, come over here. I'm only hurrying because there's not much time left for me to live, the fever's going to begin soon, and I won't understand anything at all. Now I do understand, I understand everything, I see everything."

A look of suffering came over Karenin's drawn face; he took her hand and tried to say something, but he couldn't speak. His lower lip quivered, but he kept struggling against his own agitation and looked over at her only rarely. Each time he looked at her he saw her eyes, which were gazing at him with a tender ecstatic affection he had never seen in them before.

"Wait a moment, you have no idea . . . Wait a moment, wait!" She stopped as though gathering her thoughts. "Yes!" she began again. "Yes, yes, yes! This is what I wanted to say. Don't be surprised at me; I'm still just the same. But there's someone else in me, I'm afraid of her. She fell in love with that other one, and I wanted to begin hating you, and I couldn't forget the other one who was there before. She's not the same as I. Now I'm the real one, all of me. I'm dying now, I know I'm dying, just ask him. That's what I feel right now—look at them, my hands, my feet, my fingers—they weigh tons! Look at my fingers—gigantic! But all that'll soon be over with . . . There's only one thing I need —you must forgive me, forgive me utterly! I'm horrible— but my nanny once told me: that holy martyr—what was her name—she was even worse. I'll go to Rome, there's a wilderness there, I won't bother anyone, I'll just take Seryozha and the little girl . . . No—you cannot forgive! I know—it can't be forgiven! No, no, get out, you're too kindhearted!" She held his hand with one burning hand, while with the other she thrust him away.

Karenin's distraction kept growing more and more violent; it had now reached such a point that he had stopped fighting it. He suddenly felt that what he had thought of as spiritual agitation was, on the contrary, a blissful spiritual state that gave him all at once a new happiness he had never felt before. It never occurred to him that the Christian law he had wanted to follow throughout his life instructed him to forgive his enemies and love them; but the joyful feeling of love and forgiveness for his enemies filled his soul. He knelt down; placing his head on the bend of her arm, which burned like a fire through her sleeve, he sobbed like a child. She embraced his bald head, moved closer to him and raised her eyes with defiant pride.

"Here he is, I knew it! Now, good-by to everything, goodby! They've come again now. Why don't they leave? Oh, take these furs away from me!"

The doctor moved her arms away, and carefully set her against the pillow and covered her shoulders. She lay back submissively and looked before her radiantly.

"There's one thing I remember—all I wanted was your forgiveness, nothing else . . . But why doesn't *he* come in?"

she cried, turning to Vronsky on the other side of the door. "Come now, come! Give him your hand."

Vronsky came over to the edge of the bed; when he saw her he covered his face with his hands again.

"Uncover your face! Look at him! He's a saint," she said. "Uncover your face, uncover it!" she cried angrily. "Alexis! Uncover his face! I want to see him."

Karenin took Vronsky's hands and moved them away from his face, which was horrifying because of the suffering and shame it expressed.

"Give him your hand! Forgive him!"

Karenin gave him his hand, letting the tears pour down without restraint.

"Thank God, thank God!" she cried. "Now everything is ready. If only I could stretch my legs a little. There, there, that's wonderful! Those flowers, the way they're drawn, what bad taste, not in the least like violets," she said, indicating the wallpaper. "My God! My God! When will it all be over? Give me some morphine! Doctor! Some morphine! Oh, my God, my God!"

And she began writhing in the bed.

The doctor and his colleagues said it was puerperal fever, which had ninety-nine chances to one of ending by death. She was feverish, delirious, and unconscious the whole day. Toward midnight she lay there insensible, almost without a pulse.

The end was expected at any moment.

Vronsky had gone home, but in the morning he came to inquire, and Karenin, who met him in the hallway, said: "Stay here, she may ask for you."

Toward morning Anna's excitement, animation, and quickness of thought and speech began all over again, to end once again in a coma. The third day it was the same, and the doctors said there was some hope. That same day Karenin went into his study, where Vronsky was sitting, and after closing the door sat down opposite him.

"I'm unable to speak," Vronsky said, feeling that an explanation was approaching, "I'm unable to understand. Take pity on me! However painful it is for you believe me, it's still more horrible for me."

He was about to get up, but Karenin took him by the arm and said:

"I beg you to hear me out; you must. I ought to explain to

you my feelings, which have been my guide and will go on being my guide, so that you will not misunderstand me. You know I had decided on a divorce and had even begun proceedings. I shall not conceal from you my indecision when I decided to take action; I was in torment. I confess I was haunted by a desire to revenge myself on you and her. When I got the telegram I came here with the same feelings —I will say more: I wished her to die. But—" He fell silent, in two minds as to whether to disclose his feeling to him or not. "But I saw her and I forgave her. And the happiness of forgiveness has revealed to me my duty. I've forgiven her completely. I want to turn the other cheek, I want to give away my cloak because my coat has been taken; I only beseech God not to take away from me the joy of forgiveness!"

His eyes were filled with tears, and their luminous, serene look struck Vronsky.

"That's my position. You can trample me in the mud and make me the laughingstock of the world—I will not forsake her and will never say a word of reproach to you," he went on. "My duty is clearly defined: I should be with her and I will be. If she wishes to see you I'll let you know, but for the time being I think it would be better for you to leave."

He stood up; sobs prevented him from speaking. Vronsky also got up, stooping; without straightening up he looked into his face from under his eyebrows. He had no understanding for Karenin's emotion but he felt there was something lofty and even inaccessible to him in Karenin's outlook on life.

## XVIII

AFTER this conversation Vronsky went out onto the front steps of the Karenin house and stopped, recalling with difficulty where he was and where he had to go. He felt ashamed of himself, humiliated, guilt-laden, and deprived of any possibility of purging his humiliation. He felt he was knocked out of the rut in which until then he had been moving along so proudly and easily. All the habits and principles of his life, which had seemed so firm, had suddenly proved false and inapplicable. The deceived husband, who up to then had constituted a pitiful creature, an accidental and somewhat ludicrous obstacle to his happiness, had suddenly been recalled by Anna herself and elevated to an awe-inspiring height; on that height the husband had shown himself to be not vindictive, or false, or ludicrous, but kind, straightforward, and noble. Vronsky could not help but feel this. The roles had suddenly been reversed. Vronsky felt Karenin's loftiness and his own degradation, Karenin's integrity and his own wrongdoing. He felt that the husband had been generous even in his grief, while he had been mean and trivial in his deception. But this awareness of his own abasement with respect to the man whom he had wrongfully despised constituted only a small portion of Vronsky's misery. He felt unspeakably unhappy now because his passion for Anna, which had cooled off lately, as it seemed to him, had become more powerful than it had ever been before, now that he knew he was losing her forever. During her illness he had come to know her through and through, to see into her very soul, and it seemed to him that until that time he had never loved her. And just now, when he had come to know her, and loved her as he ought to have loved her, he was humiliated before her; he was losing her forever, leaving her nothing but a shameful memory of himself. But what was most dreadful of all was the ridiculous, shameful position he had been in when Karenin pulled his hands away from his shame-covered face. He stood there on the front steps of the Karenin house like a lost soul, with no idea of what to do.

"A sleigh, sir?" asked the hall porter.

"Yes, a sleigh."

On his return home after his three sleepless nights, Vronsky stretched out prone on the sofa without undressing, with his head on his folded arms. His head was heavy. Images, memories, and ideas of the strangest kind followed one another with extraordinary swiftness and clarity: the medicine he had poured out for the patient, overfilling the spoon, the midwife's white hands, Karenin's strange posture on the floor in front of the bed.

To sleep, to forget! he said to himself, with the calm assurance of a healthy man that if he is tired and wants to go to sleep he'll do so at once. And as a matter of fact at that very moment his thoughts grew all mixed up and he began tumbling into the abyss of oblivion. Waves in the sea of his unconscious life were already beginning to close above his head when suddenly—as though an electric shock had run through him—he started so violently that his whole body jerked up on the springs of the sofa; leaning on his hands, he jumped to his knees in terror. His eyes were wide open, as though he had never been asleep at all. The heaviness in his head, and the limpness of his limbs, which he had been aware of a moment before, suddenly vanished.

"You can trample me in the mud"—he heard Karenin's words and saw him in front of him, and saw Anna's burning face and glittering eyes looking with tenderness and love not at him, but at Karenin; he saw the stupid, ridiculous figure he cut, as it seemed to him, when Karenin removed his hands from in front of his face. Once again he stretched out his legs and flung himself on the sofa in his former position, and closed his eyes.

Sleep, sleep! he repeated to himself. But with his eyes closed he saw still more clearly Anna's face as it had been that memorable evening before the races.

"It's all finished now, and it'll never happen again, and she wants to wipe it out of her mind. While I can't live without it. How can we be reconciled, how can we be reconciled?" he said aloud, and unconsciously began repeating these words. This repetition of words held back the appearance of other images and memories which he felt thronging through his head. But it did not repress his imagination for long. Once again his best moments with her and at the same time his recent degradation began appearing to him one after the other. "Take your hands away!" said Anna's voice: he took his hands away and felt the stupid, shame-filled expression on his face.

He still lay trying to fall asleep though he felt there was not the slightest hope of this; he kept repeating in a whisper random words associated with some thought or other, trying to stop in this way the appearance of new images. He listened to himself—and heard words repeated in a strange mad whisper: "Couldn't appreciate it, Couldn't make use of it, Couldn't appreciate it, Couldn't make use of it."

What is this? Or am I going mad? he said to himself. Perhaps . . . Why else do people go crazy, shoot themselves? he answered his own question; opening his eyes he was astonished to see beside his head a cushion embroidered for him by Varya, his brother's wife. He fingered a tassel of the cushion and tried to recall Varya and the last time he had seen her. But it was painful to think of anything extraneous. No —I must sleep! He pulled the cushion over and pressed his head against it, but he had to make an effort to keep his eyes shut. He jumped to his feet, then sat down. It's all over with for me, he said to himself; I'll have to think of what to do.

What is there left? His thoughts made a swift tour of his life outside of his love for Anna.

Ambition? Serpukhovskoy? Society? The Court? He couldn't dwell on any of these. It had all had some sense before, but now nothing was left of it at all. He got up from the sofa, took off his coat, loosened his belt, and baring his hairy chest to breathe more freely, paced about the room. So this is why people go crazy, he repeated, this is why they shoot themselves . . . in order not to be ashamed of themselves, he added slowly.

He went over to the door and closed it; then with a fixed stare and tightly clenched teeth he went to a table, took out a revolver, examined it, turned it over to a loaded chamber, and pondered. For a moment or two he stood motionless with the revolver in his hand, his head bowed, with an expression of great mental concentration, thinking. Of course! he said to himself, as though a logical, prolonged, and lucid train of thought had led him to an incontestable conclusion. In reality, though, this "of course" which he found so convincing was merely the result of a repetition of exactly the same round of fancies and memories he had already gone over dozens of times during the past hour. They were the same memories of happiness now lost forever, the same thought of the senselessness of everything life had in store for him, the same awareness of his own humiliation. And the sequence of these fancies and feelings was the same.

Of course, he repeated, as for the third time his thoughts were directed along this same enchanted circle of memories and ideas; placing the revolver to the left side of his chest and violently contracting his whole hand, as though suddenly squeezing it into a fist, he pressed the trigger. He didn't hear the sound of the shot, but a powerful blow on the chest knocked him off his feet. He tried to support himself on the end of the table; he dropped the revolver, staggered, and sat down on the floor, looking round him in astonishment. He could not recognize his room as he looked up from below at the curved legs of the table, the wastepaper basket and the tiger-skin rug. The rapid creaking footsteps of his servant, walking through the drawing room, forced him back to his senses. He made a mental effort and realized he was on the floor; when he saw the blood on the tiger skin and on his own hand he realized he had tried to shoot himself.

"How stupid! I missed," he muttered, feeling with his hand for the revolver. It was lying beside him, but he felt about for it farther off. As he went on looking he stretched himself over to the other side, and unable to keep his balance he fell over, dripping blood.

The elegant servant with the whiskers, who frequently complained to friends of the weakness of his nerves, was so frightened when he saw his master lying on the floor, that he left him there bleeding and ran off for help. An hour later Varya, Vronsky's sister-in-law, arrived and with the help of three doctors, whom she had sent for in all directions and who had all arrived simultaneously, she put the wounded Vronsky to bed and stayed to nurse him.

### XIX

KARENIN'S mistake, in failing to consider, during his preparation for the interview with his wife, the eventuality that her repentance would be genuine and that he would forgive her, but that then she wouldn't die—this mistake confronted him with its full force two months after he came back from Moscow. But his mistake had not come about only because he hadn't taken this eventuality into account, but also because he had not known his own heart before he saw his dying wife again. At the bedside of his sick wife he had surrendered for the first time in his life to the feeling of tender compassion that the sufferings of others evoked in him, and that he had been ashamed of before as a harmful weakness; pity for her, and remorse at having wished for her death, and above all the very joy of forgiveness had seen to it that he suddenly felt not only relief from his own sufferings, but also a spiritual peace he had never experienced before. He suddenly felt that the very same thing that had been the source of his sufferings had become a source of spiritual joy for him, and that what had seemed to him insoluble when he had been full of condemnation, reproach, and hatred, had become simple and clear when he yielded to forgiveness and love.

He forgave his wife and pitied her for her suffering and her repentance. He forgave Vronsky and pitied him, especially after rumors came to his ears about his desperate act. He also pitied his son more than he had before; now he reproached himself for having paid too little attention to him. But for the newly born little girl he experienced a sort of special feeling not only of pity but also of tenderness. At first it had been a feeling of compassion alone that had made him take care of the newborn feeble little girl, who was not his daughter and had been neglected during her mother's illness, and would certainly have died if he hadn't taken care of her. He himself did not notice how fond of her he had grown. Several times every day as he would go into the nursery and sit there a long time, so that the wet nurse and the nanny, who had been timid with him at first, got used to him. Sometimes he would look on in silence for half an hour at the saffron-red, downy, wrinkled little face of the sleeping infant, and contemplate the movements of her frowning forehead and the plump little hands with the curled-up fingers, rubbing the little eyes and nose with the backs of the fists. It was at such moments especially Karenin felt completely serene and at peace with himself, and saw nothing in his position that was unusual, nothing that needed to be changed.

But the more time passed the more clearly he saw that however natural the situation now was for him, he would not be allowed to remain in it. He felt that aside from the beneficent spiritual power that governed his soul there was another force, brutal and just as powerful or more so, that dominated his life, and that this force would not give him the humble calm he longed for. He felt that everyone was looking at him with questioning astonishment, without understanding him, and expecting something or other from him. He especially felt the instability and unnaturalness of his relations with Anna.

When the softening that had been brought about in her by the imminence of death had passed by, Karenin began to notice that Anna was afraid of him, found his presence oppressive, and was unable to look straight into his eyes. It was as though she wished to tell him something but could not make up her mind to it, and as though feeling that their relations could not continue she also expected something from him.

At the end of February, Anna's newborn daughter, also called Anna, happened to fall ill. Karenin had been in the nursery that morning, and, after ordering the doctor to be sent for, had gone off to the Ministry. He finished his business there and came back toward four o'clock. Going into the hall he saw a handsome footman in braided livery and a bearskin cape, holding a white fur cloak.

"Who is here?" Karenin asked.

"Princess Tverskoy," the footman replied, with what seemed to Karenin like a grin.

Throughout this painful time Karenin had been noticing that his society acquaintances, especially women, showed a particular interest in him and his wife. In all these acquaintances he noticed a glee about something that was concealed with difficulty, the same glee he had seen in the eyes of the lawyer and just now again in the eyes of the footman. Everyone seemed elated, as though they were giving away someone in marriage. When people met him they asked about Anna's health with this scarcely concealed glee.

The presence of Princess Tverskoy, both because of the memories associated with her and because he didn't like her in general, was unpleasant for Karenin, and he went straight to the children's rooms. In the front nursery Seryozha, stretched out on the table with his legs on a chair, was drawing something and chattering gaily. The Englishwoman who had replaced the Frenchwoman during Anna's illness was sitting beside the little boy doing some crochet work; she got up hurriedly, curtsied and nudged Seryozha.

Karenin stroked his son's head, answered the governess's question about Anna's health, and asked what the doctor had said about the baby.

"The doctor says it's nothing dangerous; he ordered some baths, sir."

"But she's still uncomfortable," said Karenin, listening to the child crying in the next room.

"I don't think the wet nurse is suitable, sir," said the Englishwoman firmly.

"Why d'you think that?" he asked, stopping short.

"It's the same thing that happened at Countess Paul's, sir. The baby was being treated, then it turned out to be hungry, nothing more: the wet nurse had no milk, sir."

Karenin stood there a moment or two reflecting, then went into the other room. The little girl, her head thrown back, was wriggling in the wet nurse's arms; she refused to take either the plump breast held out to her or to stop crying, in spite of the hushes of both the wet nurse and the nanny who was bending over her.

"Still no better?" said Karenin.

"She's very restless," the nanny whispered.

"Miss Edwards says that perhaps the wet nurse has no milk," he said.

"I think so myself, sir."

"Then why didn't you say so?"

"But whom could I have told? Madame is still ill," said the nanny in a disgruntled voice.

The nanny was an old family servant, and these simple words of hers seemed to Karenin an allusion to his situation.

The baby was screaming still louder, hiccupping and choking. The nanny made a gesture and went over to it, took it from the wet nurse and began walking up and down, rocking the baby in her arms.

"We'll have to ask the doctor to examine the wet nurse," said Karenin.

The healthy-looking, smartly dressed wet nurse, frightened that she might be dismissed, muttered something under her breath and covering up her big breast smiled contemptuously at the idea of her not having enough milk. In this smile too Karenin saw a sneer at his own situation.

"Unfortunate child!" said the nanny, hushing the baby and continuing to walk up and down with it.

Karenin sat down on a chair and with a look full of melancholy suffering watched the nanny walking up and down.

When the baby, finally subsiding, was lowered into the deep crib and the nanny had adjusted the pillow and left, Karenin got up and walking with difficulty on tiptoe went over to it. For a moment he looked at the infant with the same melancholy expression, then a smile, wrinkling his forehead and moving his hair, suddenly passed over his face, and he left the room just as quietly.

In the dining room he rang and ordered the servant who came in to send for the doctor again. He was annoyed with his wife for not concerning herself with this delightful infant, and in his state of annoyance with her had no desire to go in to see her, nor did he wish to see Princess Betsy; but since Anna might have been surprised by his not coming in as usual he made an effort and went into the bedroom. As he walked across the soft carpet to the door he involuntarily overheard a conversation he had no wish to hear.

"If he had not been going away I should have understood your refusal and his too. But your husband ought to be above that," Betsy was saying.

"It's not because of my husband that I don't want to, it's because of myself. Don't talk about it!" Anna replied in an excited voice.

"Yes, but you can't help but want to say good-by to a man who tried to shoot himself on your account—"

"That's just why I don't want to."

Karenin stopped, with a look of guilt and alarm, and was about to go back again unnoticed; but, reflecting that this would be undignified, he turned round again, coughed and went toward the bedroom door. The voices fell silent and he went in.

Anna, in a gray dressing gown, her black hair cropped short but already growing out again in a dense brush over her round head, was sitting on a couch. The animation suddenly vanished from her face, as it always did whenever she saw her husband; she lowered her head and glanced uneasily at Betsy. Betsy, dressed in the very latest fashion, her hat soaring somewhere over her head like a shade over a lamp, in a dove-colored dress with very pronounced stripes slanting one way on the bodice and the other way on the skirt, was sitting side by side with Anna, holding her flat tall figure upright; leaning her head to one side she nodded at Karenin and greeted him with an ironical smile.

"Ah!" she said, as though surprised. "I'm delighted you're at home. You never show yourself, and I haven't seen you since Anna's illness. I've heard all about it—all about your devotion. Yes, you're a wonderful husband!" she said with a portentous and affable expression, as though she were conferring an order of high-mindedness on him for his behavior toward his wife.

Karenin bowed coldly and kissing his wife's hand asked about her health.

"I think I'm better," she said, avoiding his eye.

"But your face has a feverish look about it," he said stressing the word "feverish."

"We've been chattering too much," said Betsy. "I feel it's selfishness on my part, and I'm leaving."

She got up, but Anna, suddenly blushing, quickly seized her by the hand.

"No, stay awhile, please! I must tell you something . . . No, I mean you," she said, turning to Karenin, her neck and forehead all crimson. "I don't wish to and I can't have any secrets from you," she said.

Karenin cracked his knuckles and bowed his head.

"Betsy was saying that Count Vronsky wanted to call on us in order to say good-by before leaving for Tashkent." She did not look at her husband and was obviously in a hurry to get everything said no matter how hard it was for her. "I said I couldn't receive him."

"What you said, my dear, was that it would depend on Karenin," Betsy corrected her.

"Oh no, I can't receive him, and it would be quite pointless to——" She stopped short and glanced at her husband questioningly (he wasn't looking at her). "In a word, I don't want to . . ."

Karenin drew nearer and was about to take her hand. Her first impulse was to jerk it back from his own moist hand, with its great, swollen veins, which was reaching for it; but making a visible effort to control herself she pressed his hand.

"I'm very grateful to you for your confidence in me, but——" he said, feeling with embarrassment and irritation that what he could make up his mind about so easily and clearly alone he could not discuss in the presence of Princess Betsy Tverskoy, who for him was the personification of the coarse power that was bound to dominate his life in the eyes of the world and that prevented him from yielding to his own feeling of love and forgiveness. He stopped, and looked over at Betsy.

"Well, good-by then, my sweet," said Betsy, getting up. She kissed Anna and went out. Karenin followed her.

"Alexis! I know you have a genuinely magnanimous nature," Betsy said, stopping in the small drawing room and pressing his hand once again with special warmth. "I'm an outsider, but I'm so fond of her and I respect you so much that I'm taking the liberty of giving you some advice. Receive him. Alexis Vronsky is the soul of honor, and he's leaving for Tashkent."

"Thank you, Princess, for your sympathy and advice. But the question of whom my wife will or will not receive is one to be decided by herself."

As he said this, raising his eyebrows in a dignified way by force of habit, he realized instantly that no matter what he said there could be no dignity in his position. And he saw this by the suppressed, malicious and ironical smile with which Betsy glanced at him after he had got off his remark.

## XX

KARENIN took leave of Betsy in the hall and went back to his wife. She was lying down, but when she heard his footsteps approaching she hastened to sit up in her former position, looking at him in fright. He saw she had been crying.

"I'm grateful to you for your confidence in me," he said gently, repeating in Russian the phrase he had said in French when Betsy had been present, and sat down beside her. Whenever he spoke to her in Russian, and used an intimate form of address, Anna felt uncontrollably irritated. "And I'm very grateful for your decision. I also think that since he's going away there's not the slightest need for Count Vronsky to come here. However—"

"But I've said so already, so why repeat it?" Anna interrupted him suddenly with an irritation she could not repress. No, she thought, not the slightest need for a man to come to say good-by to the woman he loves, for whom he wanted to die and has destroyed himself, and who cannot live without him. Not the slightest need!

She pressed her lips together and looked down at his hands with their swollen veins, which he was slowly rubbing together.

"Let us never mention it again," she added more calmly.

"I left the decision of this question to you, and I'm very glad that—" Karenin began.

"My wishes coincide with your own," she quickly finished his sentence, irritated by his speaking so slowly when she knew in advance everything he was going to say.

"Yes," he nodded. "And it is entirely out of place for Princess Tverskoy to meddle in the most difficult family matters. She of all people—"

"I don't believe anything they say about her," Anna said quickly. "I know she's sincerely attached to me."

Karenin sighed and was silent. She was agitatedly toying with the tassels of her dressing gown, looking at him with the painful feeling of physical revulsion toward him she reproached herself for but was incapable of overcoming. Just now all she longed for was to be rid of his loathsome presence.

"Well, I've just sent for the doctor," he said.

"I'm all right, why do I need a doctor?"

"No, it's the baby, she keeps on crying. They say the wet nurse hasn't got enough milk."

"Then why didn't you allow me to nurse her myself when I begged you to? Anyway"—Karenin understood what "anyway" meant—"she's an infant and they're going to kill her." She rang and ordered the baby brought in. "I asked to nurse it, I wasn't allowed, and now I'm being reproached for it."

"I'm not reproaching you for—"

"Yes, you are! Oh my God, why didn't I die!" She burst into sobs. "Forgive me, I'm upset, I'm being unfair," she said, controlling herself. "But go away now . . ."

No, things can't go on this way, Karenin resolutely said to himself as he left his wife.

The impossibility of his position in the eyes of the world, his wife's hatred for him, and in general the power of the crude mysterious force that was directing his life in opposition to his own inner mood, insisting on the execution of its own will and on a change in his relations with his wife, had never before confronted him so unmistakably as today. He saw clearly that his wife and all the world were demanding something from him, but just what it was he could not understand. He felt that because of this there was a feeling of malice rising up in his own soul that was destroying his serenity, and depriving his action of any value. He thought it would be best for Anna to break off all relations with Vronsky, but if everyone felt this was impossible he was even prepared to permit these relations to be renewed, as long as the children were not disgraced, he was not deprived of them, and his own position was not altered. However bad this would be, it would nevertheless be better than a rupture in which she would be left in a hopeless and shameful position while he himself was deprived of everything he loved. But he felt helpless; he knew in advance that everyone was against him and that he would not be allowed to do what now seemed to him so natural and good; he would be forced to do what was wrong but seemed to them proper.

XXI

BETSY was just leaving the drawing room when Oblonsky, who had just come from Eliseyev's, where some fresh oysters had arrived, came in and met her. "Ah! Princess! What a delightful encounter!" he began. "And I had gone to your place!"

"It's going to be a brief encounter, I'm just leaving," said Betsy, smiling and putting on her glove.

"Just a moment before putting on your glove, Princess, allow me to kiss your hand. There's nothing I'm so grateful for in the revival of old-fashioned manners as hand-kissing." He kissed Betsy's hand. "Then when shall we see each other?"

"You don't deserve it," said Betsy smiling.

"Oh I do, I do, I've become a most serious man! Not only do I arrange my own family affairs, but those of others as well," he said weightily.

"Oh I'm very glad!" replied Betsy, who realized at once that he was speaking of Anna. They went back into the drawing room and stood in a corner. "He's killing her," Betsy said in a portentous whisper. "It's impossible, just impossible . . ."

"I'm very glad you think so," said Oblonsky, shaking his head with a grave look of compassionate suffering. "That's why I've come to Petersburg."

"The whole town's talking about it," she said. "The situation is impossible. She keeps pining away, pining away! He doesn't understand that she's one of those women who cannot trifle with their feelings. There are only two alternatives —either he must act energetically and take her away, or he must give her a divorce. But all this is suffocating her."

"Yes, yes . . . exactly . . ." said Oblonsky with a sigh. "That's just why I came. That is, not exactly for that . . . I've been made a Chamberlain, and of course I had to come and say my thank-yous. But the main thing is that this has to be cleared up."

"Well, may God help you!" said Betsy.

After seeing Betsy to the hall, kissing her hand once again above the glove, where the pulse beats, and on top of that telling her some nonsense that was so indecent she couldn't make up her mind whether to get angry or burst out laughing, Oblonsky went to see his sister. He found her in tears.

Though he happened to be bubbling over with high spirits Oblonsky instantly slipped into a compassionate, lyrically romantic tone that suited her mood. He asked her about her health and how she had spent the morning.

"Very, very badly. Both the morning, and the day, and every single day past and future," she said.

"It seems to me you're succumbing to melancholy. You have to give yourself a shake—look life straight in the eye. I know it's hard, but—"

"I had heard that women love men even for their faults," Anna suddenly began, "but I hate him for his virtuousness! I cannot live with him! You must understand, the sight of him has a physical effect on me, I'm beside myself. I cannot, I simply cannot live with him! What can I do? I was unhappy, I thought it was impossible to be any unhappier, but

I could never have imagined to myself the horrible state I'm in now. Would you believe that I, knowing he's a kindhearted man, a fine man—I'm not worth his little finger—I hate him nevertheless! I hate him for his generosity. And there's nothing left for me but—"

She had been about to say "death," but Oblonsky did not let her finish.

"You're ill and upset," he said. "Believe me, you're exaggerating terribly. There's nothing so awful about it all."

And Oblonsky smiled. In his place no one dealing with such desperation would have allowed himself to smile (it would have seemed callous) but in his smile there was so much kindness, an almost feminine tenderness, that it was not offensive, but soothing and reassuring. His soft reassuring words and smiles had a soothing, tranquilizing effect like almond oil. And Anna soon felt this.

"No, Stiva," she said, "I'm finished, finished! Worse than finished—I'm not yet finished, I can't say that everything is over with; on the contrary I feel it's not over with. I'm like a taut string that is bound to break. But it's not yet ended—and it's going to have a dreadful end."

"Never mind, the string can be loosened little by little. There is no situation there's no way out of."

"I've been thinking and thinking. There's only one way—"

Again he saw by her frightened look that to her mind the one way out was death, and he didn't let her finish.

"Not a bit of it," he said. "Now listen. You can't see your own position as I can. Let me give you my honest opinion." Again he gave his cautious, almond-oil smile. "I'll begin from the beginning: you married a man twenty years older than yourself. You married without love, and without knowing love. Let's grant that was a mistake."

"A horrible mistake!" said Anna.

"But I repeat—it's an accomplished fact. Then you had, let's say, the misfortune of falling in love with someone who wasn't your husband. That's a misfortune, but it's also an accomplished fact. And your husband has accepted that and forgiven you." He paused after each phrase, waiting for her to protest, but she said nothing in reply. "That's how it is. Now the question is: Can you go on living with your husband any longer? Is that what you want? Is that what he wants?"

"I don't know, I just don't know."

"But you said yourself you couldn't stand him."

"No, I didn't say that. I take that back. I don't know anything and I don't understand anything."

"Yes, but after all—"

"You can't understand—I feel I'm flying headfirst over some precipice but mustn't try to save myself. And I cannot."

"Never mind—we'll spread something out and catch you. I understand you, I understand your not being able to take it on yourself to say what you want, what you feel."

"I want nothing, nothing—only for it all to be over with."

"But he sees that and knows it. D'you think it's any the less painful for him than for you? You're tormenting yourself, he's tormenting himself—how can it all end? And when a divorce would solve everything." With some effort Oblonsky got out his main idea, and looked at her significantly.

She said nothing in reply, and shook her cropped head. But by the expression of her face, which suddenly lit up with all its former beauty, he saw that the only reason she hadn't wanted that was because it had seemed to her to be an unattainable happiness.

"I'm dreadfully sorry for both of you! How happy I'd be if I could settle it all!" said Oblonsky, smiling more boldly now. "Don't say anything, not a word! If only God helps me speak as I feel! I'm going to him now."

Anna looked at him with her dreamy, shining eyes and said nothing.

## XXII

WEARING the same somewhat solemn expression with which he took his chairman's seat at his Council meetings, Oblonsky went into Karenin's study. Karenin, his arms crossed behind his back, was pacing around the room thinking of the same thing Oblonsky had just been talking about with Anna.

"Am I disturbing you?" said Oblonsky, who suddenly had an unfamiliar feeling of embarrassment at the sight of his brother-in-law. To hide it he got out a cigarette case he had just bought, with a new kind of clasp, and sniffing the leather took out a cigarette.

"No. D'you want anything?" Karenin answered reluctantly.

"Yes, I wanted to—I had to—yes, I had to talk to you," said Oblonsky, surprised at his unfamiliar feeling of shyness.

This feeling was so strange and unexpected that Oblonsky did not believe it was the voice of conscience telling him that what he intended to do was wrong. He controlled himself with an effort and conquered the shyness that had come over him.

"I hope you believe in my love for my sister and in my sincere affection and respect for yourself," he said blushing.

Karenin stood still and said nothing, but his face impressed Oblonsky with its look of submissive self-sacrifice.

"I had intended, I wanted to talk about my sister and about the position both of you are in," said Oblonsky, still struggling against his unaccustomed timidity.

Karenin smiled sadly, looked at his brother-in-law and without replying went over to the table, took a letter he had begun and handed it to Oblonsky.

"I think about the same thing without pause. This is what I started writing, thinking that I could express it better in a letter, since my presence irritates her," he said as he handed the letter over.

Oblonsky took the letter, looked in astonished perplexity at the dim eyes staring at him unwaveringly, and began reading.

> "I see that my presence is disagreeable to you. However painful it has been for me to become persuaded of this, I now see that it is so and that it cannot be otherwise. I do not blame you, and God is my witness that when I saw you during your illness I had resolved, from the bottom of my heart, to forget everything that had happened between us and start a new life. I do not regret what I did, and I never shall, but the only thing I had wished for was your own good, the good of your soul, and now I see I have not achieved this. Tell me yourself what it is that will give you genuine happiness and peace of mind. I yield entirely to your wishes and to your sense of justice."

Oblonsky handed back the letter, and went on looking at his brother-in-law with the same perplexity, at a loss for words. The silence was so uncomfortable for them both that Oblonsky's lips began twitching nervously as he kept his eyes fixed silently on Karenin's face.

"That is what I had wanted to say to her," said Karenin, turning away.

"Yes, yes . . ." said Oblonsky, choked with tears and speechless. "Yes, yes . . . I understand you," he finally managed to get out.

"I should like to know what it is she wishes," said Karenin.

"I'm afraid she herself doesn't know her own position. She is no judge of it," said Oblonsky, pulling himself together. "She's crushed, actually crushed by your generosity. If she reads this letter she'll be incapable of saying anything at all, she'll merely hang her head still lower."

"Yes, but what's to be done then, in such a situation? How can we clear it up—how can we find out what she wants?"

"If you'll allow me to express my own opinion, I think it's up to you to point out directly the steps you consider necessary to bring this situation to an end."

"Accordingly, you think it must be brought to an end?" Karenin interrupted him. "But how?" he added, making an uncharacteristic gesture with his hands before his eyes, "I see no way out."

"There's a way out of every situation," said Oblonsky, getting up and growing more animated. "There was a time when you wanted to break off . . . If you're convinced now that you cannot make each other happy . . ."

"Happiness can be understood in a variety of ways. But let's suppose that I agree to everything, I want nothing. Then what is the way out of our position?"

"If you want to know my opinion," Oblonsky began, with the same soothing smile of almond-oil tenderness with which he had spoken to Anna. His kindly smile was so convincing that in spite of himself Karenin, feeling his own weakness and yielding to it, was ready to believe whatever Oblonsky said. "She'll never say so herself. But there's only one thing possible, only one thing she can want," Oblonsky went on. "That is—a termination of all relations and everything bound up with them. To my mind what is essential in your position is a clarification of your new relationship. And that relationship can only be established on the basis of freedom on both sides."

"Divorce!" Karenin interrupted with revulsion.

"Yes, divorce, I think. Yes, a divorce," Oblonsky repeated, reddening. "That is the most reasonable way out, from all points of view, for a married couple in the relationship with each other that you are in. What can be done if husband and

wife have found that a life together is impossible? It can
happen to anyone." Karenin gave a deep sigh and closed his
eyes. "There is only one thing at issue—does either party
wish to enter on another marriage? If not it's all very simple,"
said Oblonsky, progressively getting rid of his embarrassment.

Karenin, his face drawn with emotion, muttered something under his breath without replying. What seemed to
Oblonsky so simple had been thought over by Karenin thousands of times. And it all seemed to him not only very simple,
but utterly impossible. Divorce, the details of which he was
already familiar with, now seemed to him impossible because his sense of his own dignity and his regard for religion
would not allow him to take on himself a false charge of
adultery; still less could he allow his wife, whom he loved
and had forgiven, to be detected in the act and disgraced.
Divorce seemed impossible for still other, even more important reasons.

What would happen to their son if they were divorced? It
would be impossible to leave him with his mother. His
mother, divorced, would have her own illegitimate family,
in which a stepson's position and his education would in all
probability be a bad one. Could he keep him himself? He
knew that this would be revenge on his part, and he had no
desire for that.

But aside from all this divorce seemed impossible to Karenin primarily because the very fact of his consenting to a
divorce would be what would ruin Anna. What Dolly had
said to him in Moscow had sunk deep into his heart, that in
deciding on a divorce he was thinking of himself, and not
realizing that it would ruin Anna irrevocably. Now that
he connected this remark with his own forgiveness, and
with his attachment to the children, he understood it in his
own way. In his own mind, agreeing to a divorce and giving
Anna her freedom meant taking away from himself the last
tie he had to the life of the children, whom he loved, and
from her the last support on the path of virtue; it meant
casting her to perdition. If she became a divorced wife he
knew she would unite with Vronsky, a liaison that would be
illegal and sinful, since according to the law of the Church a
wife could not remarry as long as her husband was alive.

She'll live with him, and in a year or two either he'll
abandon her or else form a new liaison, Karenin thought. And

I, by agreeing to an illegal divorce, should be the cause of her destruction.

He had turned all this over in his mind hundreds of times and was convinced that divorce was not only not very simple, as his brother-in-law said, but was completely impossible. He didn't believe a single word Oblonsky said; he had thousands of refutations for every single word of his, but he listened to him, feeling that what Oblonsky was saying reflected the coarse and mighty power that dominated his life and that he was obliged to submit to.

"It's simply a question of the terms on which you'd agree to have a divorce. She wants nothing, she would not dare ask for anything, she's leaving it all up to your own generosity."

Oh God, oh my God! How have I deserved this? Karenin thought, and recalling the details of a divorce suit in which the husband assumed all the blame, he hid his face in his hands with the same gesture as Vronsky's.

"You're upset, I quite understand, but if you take into consideration—"

And whosoever shall smite thee on thy right cheek, turn to him the other also . . . and if any man shall take away thy coat, let him have thy cloak also, thought Karenin.

"Yes, yes!" he cried in a shrill voice. "I'll assume the disgrace, I'll even give up my son, but—but, wouldn't it be better to leave the whole thing alone? Though do whatever you want to . . ."

And turning away from his brother-in-law so that the latter couldn't see him, Karenin sat down on a chair beside the window. His heart was filled with bitterness, and with shame, but together with this bitterness and shame he was moved by exultation over the loftiness of his own humility.

Oblonsky was touched; for a moment he was silent.

"Believe me," he said, "she will appreciate your magnanimity. Though manifestly it has been God's will," he added; as he said this he felt it had been stupid, and could scarcely restrain a smile at his own stupidity.

Karenin tried to say something in reply, but tears prevented him.

"It's a misfortune that is an act of destiny, it must be acknowledged. I acknowledge this misfortune as an accomplished fact and shall do my best to help both her and you," said Oblonsky.

Oblonsky felt moved as he left his brother-in-law's room, but that didn't prevent his being satisfied at having successfully settled things, since he was sure Karenin would not go back on what he had said. His satisfaction was added to by a notion that came to him, of a question he would ask his wife and friends once the affair was over and done with: "What's the difference between me and a chemist?" "A chemist makes a solution, which doesn't make anyone the happier, while I concocted a solution that made three people happier." Or perhaps: "What's the resemblance between me and a chemist? When . . ." But I'll improve on it, he said to himself with a smile.

## XXIII

VRONSKY'S wound had been a dangerous one, even though it had missed the heart. For several days he had lain between life and death. When he was able to speak for the first time no one was in the room but his brother's wife Varya.

"Varya!" he said, looking at her sternly. "I shot myself by accident. Please never speak about it; you must say that to everyone. Else it would really be too stupid!"

Without answering him Varya leaned over him and looked into his face with a joyful smile. His eyes were bright, and not feverish, but they had a severe expression.

"Well, thank God!" she said. "Are you in pain?"

"A little here," he said, indicating his chest.

"Then let me change the bandage."

His broad jaws clenched, he looked at her silently as she changed his bandage. When she had finished he said: "I'm not delirious; please see to it that there is no talk about my having shot myself on purpose."

"But no one's saying that. I only hope there'll be no more accidental shots," she said with a questioning smile.

"Doubtless there won't be, but it would have been better if—" and he smiled glumly.

In spite of these words of his, and his smile, which frightened Varya so much, when the inflammation had passed and he began to improve, he felt himself completely liberated from one part of his grief. By this act of his he had as it were purged the shame and humiliation he had felt before. Now he could think of Karenin calmly. He acknowledged all his magnanimity without feeling humiliated by it.

Aside from this he lapsed into his old rut again. He found he could look people in the eyes again without a feeling of shame, and could live in accordance with his old habits. The only thing he could not wrench out of his heart, though he kept struggling against the feeling, was a regret bordering on despair at having lost Anna forever. At heart he was firmly resolved that, having expiated his guilt toward her husband, he was bound to renounce her and never in future stand between her, with her remorse, and her husband; but he could not pluck out of his heart his regret at the loss of her love; he could not wipe out of his memory the moments of happiness he had known with her, which at that time he had set such little value on and which now pursued him with all their charm.

Serpukhovskoy had thought up a post for him in Tashkent, and Vronsky accepted the proposal without the slightest hesitation. But the closer the time for his departure approached the more painful seemed to him the sacrifice he was making to what he considered his duty.

His wound had healed and he was able to start making preparations for his trip to Tashkent.

If I could just see her once more, then bury myself—die, he thought, and while making his farewell visits he expressed this idea to Betsy, who went to see Anna on this mission and brought him back a refusal.

So much the better, Vronsky thought when he received the news. It was a weakness that would have destroyed all the strength I have left.

The next morning Betsy herself came to see him and told him she had heard, through Oblonsky, the definite news that Karenin was giving Anna a divorce and consequently Vronsky could see her.

Without even bothering about seeing Betsy to the door, having forgotten all his decisions, without asking when he could see Anna or where Karenin was, Vronsky immediately left for the Karenin house. He ran up the staircase, seeing nothing and nobody; at a rapid pace, barely keeping himself from running, he entered the room. And without thinking of or noticing whether anyone was in the room or not, he embraced her and began covering her face, hands, and neck with kisses.

Anna had prepared herself for this meeting; she had thought about what she was going to say to him, but she couldn't get any of it out: his passion overwhelmed her. She tried to calm him, and calm herself, but it was already too late. His emotion took hold of her. Her lips quivered so that for a long time she was incapable of saying anything.

"Yes, you've taken possession of me—I am yours," she managed to say at last, pressing his hand to her bosom.

"It had to be!" he said. "As long as we live, this is how it must be! I know that now."

"It is true," she said, growing paler and paler and putting her arms around his head. "But nevertheless there's something horrifying in it now, after everything that's happened."

"It will pass, it will all pass, we're going to be so happy! If our love could grow any stronger it would grow stronger because there is something horrifying in it," he said, raising his head and showing his strong teeth in a smile.

And she could not help but answer with a smile—not what he said, but the look in his enamored eyes. She took his hand and stroked her cold cheeks and cropped hair with it.

"I don't recognize you with such short hair. You've gotten so much prettier! A little boy! But how pale you are!"

"Yes, I'm very weak," she said with a smile. And her lips began quivering again.

"We'll go to Italy, you'll get well there," he said.

"Is it really possible that we'll be like man and wife, together, in one family—you and I?" she said, looking closely into his eyes.

"All that surprises me is that it could ever have been any other way."

"Stiva says *he's* agreed to everything, but I cannot accept *his* generosity," she said, dreamily gazing past Vronsky's face. "I don't want a divorce, nothing matters now. Only I don't know what he's going to decide about Seryozha."

He was quite incapable of understanding how at this moment of reunion she could remember and think about her son, about a divorce. Could any of that matter?

"Don't talk and don't think about it," he said, turning her hand over in his and trying to attract her attention; but she still kept her eyes away from him.

"Oh, why didn't I die, that would have been best!" she said, and tears streamed silently down her cheeks; but to avoid hurting him she tried to smile.

According to Vronsky's previous views it would have been shameful and impossible to refuse the flattering, dangerous post in Tashkent. But now, without a moment's hesitation, he refused it, and noticing that his superiors disapproved of his action he resigned at once.

A month later Karenin was left alone in the house with his son, while Anna and Vronsky went abroad; they had not received a divorce, having firmly refused it.

# PART FIVE

## I

PRINCESS Shcherbatsky thought it was out of the question to have the wedding before Lent, which was five weeks away, since half the trousseau could not be got ready in time; but she could not help agreeing with Levin that putting it off till after Lent would make it definitely too late, since Prince Shcherbatsky's old aunt was very ill and might soon die, in which case the mourning would delay the wedding still further. This was why, after deciding to divide Kitty's trousseau into two parts, a big trousseau and a small one, the Princess agreed to arrange for the wedding before Lent. She decided to prepare the whole small trousseau now, and send on the big part later; she got very angry with Levin for his being completely unable to give her a serious answer as to whether he agreed with this or not. This plan was all the more convenient since the young couple were leaving immediately afterward for the country, where the major part of the trousseau would not be needed.

Levin continued in the same state of lunacy in which it seemed to him that he and his own happiness constituted the principal and unique goal of all existence, and that thinking or bothering about anything was quite pointless for him, since everything was being and would be done for him by others. He did not even have any plans or aims for his future life; he left the settlement of this to others, certain that everything would turn out splendidly. His brother Koznyshov, Oblonsky, and the Princess told him what he had to do. He did nothing but agree completely to everything they proposed. His brother borrowed some money for him; the Princess advised him to leave Moscow for the country after the wedding; Oblonsky advised him to go abroad. He agreed to everything. Do whatever you like, if it makes you feel any better, he thought; I'm happy, and my happiness won't be any the greater or any the less whatever you do.

When he told Kitty of Oblonsky's advice on going abroad, he was very surprised that she didn't agree, but had some definite requirements of her own concerning their future life together. She knew that Levin had work in the country he liked. He saw that she not only did not understand this work, but did not even want to, but this did not prevent her from considering it very important. Because of this she knew their house was going to be in the country, and did she not want to go abroad, where she was not going to live, but to where their house was going to be. This intention, clearly expressed, astounded Levin. But since it was all exactly the same to him, he immediately asked Oblonsky to go to the country, as though it were his bounden duty to, and arrange everything there, as he knew how to, and with the good taste he had so much of.

"By the way," Oblonsky said one day to Levin after coming back from the country, where he had arranged everything for the arrival of the young couple, "have you got a certificate to show you've been to confession?"

"No—why?"

"You can't get married without it."

"Oh-h-h-h," Levin cried. "I think it must be nine years since I've been to communion. I never even thought of it."

"Very clever!" said Oblonsky laughing. "And you call *me* a nihilist! But that won't do at all, you know. You'll have to go to communion."

"But when? There are only four days left."

Oblonsky arranged that too. And Levin began fasting. For Levin, as an unbeliever who respected the beliefs of others, being present at and taking part in any church ceremonies was very tiresome. Now, in the softened mood he was in, sensitive to everything, pretense was not only tiresome to him but seemed quite impossible. Now, at the moment of his glory, just as he was bursting into flower, he was supposed to lie or blaspheme! He felt incapable of doing either one or the other. But however insistently he asked Oblonsky whether it wasn't possible to get a certificate without fasting, Oblonsky told him it was out of the question.

"Besides, what does it amount to—two days? And the priest is a terribly nice, bright old man. He'll pull the tooth for you so that you won't even feel it."

Standing in church during his first service Levin made an attempt to revive his youthful recollections of the powerful religious feeling he had experienced from the age of sixteen to seventeen. But he immediately convinced himself that this was quite impossible for him. Then he tried to look on it all as an empty formality like paying calls; but he felt that he couldn't do that either.

Like most of his contemporaries, Levin had the most indefinite views about religion. He could not believe, while at the same time he was not completely convinced it was all false. This was why, being incapable of believing in the significance of what he was doing, or of looking on it indifferently as an empty formality, throughout this whole period of fasting he had a feeling of awkwardness and shame, since an inner voice told him it was false and wrong to do something he didn't understand.

During the service he would sometimes listen to the prayers, trying to attribute some meaning to them that was not out of harmony with his own views, and sometimes, feeling he couldn't understand them and so ought to condemn them, he tried not to listen to them, but busied himself with his own thoughts, observations, and recollections, which during this idle standing about in church teemed in his mind with extraordinary vividness.

He stood through mass, vespers, and evensong, and the next day, after getting up earlier than usual and not having his tea, he got to the church at eight o'clock for morning prayers and confession.

There was no one in the church but a beggar soldier, and the clergy.

The young deacon, the two halves of his long back sharply outlined beneath his thin undercassock, met him, and going over at once to a small table beside the wall began reading the prayers. As the reading proceeded, and especially at the frequent and rapid repetition of the same words, "Lord have mercy upon us," which sounded like "Lordvmercpons," Levin felt that his mind was closed and sealed up, and that now was not the time to move it or shake it up, else confusion would result; so as he stood behind the deacon he went on thinking his own thoughts, without listening or trying to enter into what was being read. Her hand is amazingly expressive, he thought, recalling how they had been sitting at a corner table the day before. They had nothing to say to each other, as it almost always was with them at this time, and putting her hand on the table she opened and closed it, laughing herself as she watched it move. He remembered how he had kissed this hand, and then examined the converging lines on the rosy palm. Another "Lordvmercpons,"

Levin thought, crossing himself, bowing, and watching the supple movements of the bowing deacon's back.

Then she took my own hand and began examining the lines on it: "You have a wonderful hand," she said.

Levin looked at his own hand and at the deacon's short hand. Yes, now it'll soon be over; no, I think he's starting all over again, he thought, listening to the prayers. No, it's ending, there he is prostrating himself, that's always just before the end.

Unobtrusively accepting a three-ruble note in his hand under its velvet cuff, the deacon said he would put down Levin's name, and went into the chancel, his new boots clattering briskly over the flagstones of the empty church. A minute later he glanced out and beckoned to Levin. The thoughts that up to now had been sealed in Levin's head began stirring, but he hastily drove them back again. It'll all be settled somehow, he thought, and went toward the pulpit. He went up the little steps and when he turned to the right saw the priest, a little old man with a sparse graying beard and tired kindly eyes, who was standing beside the lectern turning over the pages of a missal. With a slight bow toward Levin he immediately began reciting the prayers in his stereotyped manner. When he finished he bowed down to the ground and turned to face Levin.

"Christ is present here, invisible, to receive your confession," he said, indicating the crucifix. "Do you believe in all the teachings of the Holy Apostolic Church?" the priest went on, turning his eyes away from Levin's face and folding his hands beneath his stole.

"I have doubted everything, and I still do," Levin replied in a voice he himself found unpleasant, and fell silent.

The priest waited a few seconds to see whether he was going to say something else, then closed his eyes and said quickly, in a provincial accent:

"Doubts are natural to human weakness, but we must pray, that we may be strengthened by divine compassion. What in particular are your sins?" he added without the slightest interval, as though trying not to lose any time.

"My principal sin is doubt. I doubt everything, and am in doubt most of the time."

"Doubt is natural to human weakness," the priest said, repeating the same words. "But what do you doubt most of all?"

"I doubt everything. Sometimes I doubt even the existence

of God," said Levin involuntarily, and was horrified at the indecency of what he had said. But Levin's words seemed to make no impression on the priest.

"But what doubts can there be of the existence of God?" he said hurriedly with a scarcely perceptible smile.

Levin was silent.

"How can you doubt the Creator, when you gaze upon His creation?" the priest continued in the rapid, customary jargon. "Who adorned the celestial firmament with stars? Who has decked out the earth in all its beauty? How could it all have happened without a Creator?" he said, looking at Levin inquiringly.

Levin felt it would be improper to enter into a philosophical debate with a priest, so the answer he gave referred only to the direct question.

"I don't know," he said.

"You don't know? Then how can you doubt that God created everything?" said the priest in cheerful perplexity.

"I don't understand anything," said Levin, blushing; he felt that his words were stupid and in such a situation could not be anything but stupid.

"Pray to God and entreat Him! Even the Holy Fathers had doubts, and entreated God to fortify their faith. The Devil has great power; we must not yield to him. Pray to God, entreat Him! Pray to God," he repeated hurriedly.

The priest was silent for a while, as though pondering.

"As I have heard you are about to enter into matrimony with the daughter of my parishioner and spiritual son, Prince Shcherbatsky?" he added with a smile. "A wonderful girl!"

"Yes," Levin replied, blushing for the priest. Why does he have to ask me about that at confession? he thought.

And as though in answer to this thought of his the priest said to him:

"You are about to enter into matrimony, and it may be that God will reward you with children, is it not so? Then what sort of education will you be able to give your little ones if you cannot conquer in yourself the temptations of the Devil, which are luring you into unbelief?" he said in gentle rebuke. "If you love your own offspring then, as a kind father, you will wish not only riches, luxury, and honors for your child, you will wish for its salvation, its spiritual illumination by the light of truth. Is that not so? Then what answer will you give your child when he asks you: 'Papa! Who created everything that pleases me in this world—the earth, the water, sun, flowers, grass?' Will you really say to him 'I don't know?' You cannot but know, when the Lord God in His great mercy has revealed it to you. Or when your child asks you: 'What awaits me in the afterlife?' What will you tell him when you know nothing? How will you answer him? Will you leave him to the temptations of the world and of the Devil? That is bad!" he said, and stopped, putting his head on one side and looking at Levin with his gentle, kindly eyes.

Levin said nothing, now not because he did not want to enter into an argument with a priest, but because no one had ever put such questions to him, and before his little ones began asking him questions like that there was still some time to think over how he would reply.

"You are entering upon a time of life," the priest went on, "when it is necessary to choose a path and keep to it. Pray to God that in His goodness He may help you and have mercy upon you," he concluded. "May the Lord our God Jesus Christ, in the goodness and bounty of His love for mankind, pardon this His child . . ." And having pronounced the absolution the priest blessed him and let him go.

When he went home that day Levin had the happy feeling that his uncomfortable position had come to an end, and come to an end in such a way that he had not had to tell any lies. Aside from this a vague recollection remained with him that what this kindly, charming little old man had said was not at all so silly as it had seemed to him at first, and that there was something there that had to be cleared up.

Not now, of course, Levin thought, some other time. Levin felt now more than before that there was something unclear and impure in his soul, and that in his attitude toward religion he was in just the same position that he saw so clearly and disliked in others, and that he reproached his friend Sviyazhsky for.

That evening, which he spent with his fiancée and Dolly, Levin was particularly cheerful, and when he explained to Oblonsky the state of excitement he was in he said he was as cheerful as a dog that was being taught to jump through a hoop, and, that once it's finally realized and accomplished what is being required of it, barks, and wagging its tail, jumps for joy onto the tables and window sills.

II

THE day of the wedding Levin, according to custom (the Princess and Dolly both insisted sternly on carrying out all customs) did not see his bride, and dined in his rooms at the hotel together with three bachelors who happened to drop in: Koznyshov, Katavasov, a friend from the university, now a professor of natural sciences, whom Levin had run into on the street and dragged home with him, and Chirikov, his best man, a Moscow magistrate and a bear-hunting comrade of Levin's. The dinner was very gay. Koznyshov was in the best of spirits, and found Katavasov's originality very entertaining. Katavasov, feeling that this originality was appreciated and understood, paraded it. Chirikov gaily and good-naturedly backed up every kind of conversation.

"There now," said Katavasov, drawling out of professorial habit, "what a talented young fellow our friend Constantine used to be! I'm speaking of one no longer among those present, since he's already gone. In those days he used to love science, when he left the university, and he had human interests; now one half of his abilities is aimed at deceiving himself, and the other half—at justifying the deception."

"A more determined enemy of marriage than yourself has never yet come to my notice," said Koznyshov.

"No, I'm no enemy of it. I'm a partisan of the divison of labor. People who can't produce anything else ought to produce people, while the rest—work for their enlightenment and happiness. That's the way I see things. There are hosts of people aspiring to mix the two trades, but I'm not one of them."

"How happy I'll be when I find out you've fallen in love!" said Levin. "Do invite me to the wedding!"

"I'm in love already."

"Yes—with a cuttlefish! You know," said Levin, turning to his brother, "Katavasov is writing a book on nutrition and—"

"At least don't get it all mixed up! It doesn't matter at all what it's about, the point is I really do love cuttlefish."

"But that wouldn't prevent your loving a wife."

"The cuttlefish wouldn't, the wife would."

"Why?"

"Oh, you'll soon see. Now you like farming, hunting—well then, wait and see!"

"Arkhip came today to tell me there are vast numbers of elk in Prudno and two bears," said Chirikov.

"Well, you won't need me to get them."

"There you are!" said Koznyshov. "You might as well say good-by to bear-hunting from now on, your wife will never allow it!"

Levin smiled. The idea that his wife would not allow it was so pleasant for him that he was ready to renounce the pleasure of ever setting eyes on a bear again.

"Though it's a pity after all that those two bears are going to be taken without you. D'you remember that last time in Khapilovo? It was a wonderful hunt!" said Chirikov.

Levin did not wish to disillusion him about the possibility of there being anything good anywhere without her, so he said nothing.

"There's some point to this custom of bidding farewell to bachelor life," said Koznyshov. "No matter how happy you may be you can't help regretting the loss of your freedom."

"Now admit, don't you feel like the bridegroom in Gogol's play, who wanted to jump out the window?"

"Of course he does, but he'll never admit it!" said Katavasov, and roared with laughter.

"Well, the window's still open . . . Let's leave for Tver right away! One is a she-bear, we can go into her lair. Really—let's leave by the five-o'clock train! And here they can do as they please," Chirikov said with a smile.

"Well," said Levin with a smile, "I'm ready to swear I can't detect any feeling of regret in my soul for my lost liberty!"

"But there's such chaos in your soul now you couldn't find anything there at all," said Katavasov. "Wait a bit till you've settled down, then you'll find it all right!"

"No, I should have felt some regret, even if only to some slight extent, that aside from my feelings"—he didn't want to say "love" in Katavasov's presence—"and my happiness, it's a pity nevertheless to be losing my freedom . . . But on the contrary, it's just this loss of freedom that makes me glad."

"A bad business! A hopeless specimen!" said Katavasov. "Well then, let's drink to his recovery, or let's just wish that at least a hundredth part of his dreams comes true. Even that would be happiness such as has never yet been seen on earth!"

Soon after dinner Levin's guests all left to change for the wedding.

Left alone with the remarks of these bachelors on his mind,

Levin asked himself once again: Did he have that feeling in his soul of regret for his lost freedom that they had been speaking of? He smiled at the question. Freedom? What for? Happiness lies simply in loving her, and in wishing and thinking her wishes and her thoughts, that is, no freedom at all—that's what happiness is!

But do I know her thoughts, her wishes, her feelings? a voice suddenly whispered to him. The smile vanished from his face, and he pondered. Suddenly a strange feeling came over him. Fear and doubt assailed him—doubt of everything.

What if she doesn't love me? What if she's marrying me just for the sake of getting married? What if she doesn't know herself what she's doing? he asked himself. She may come to her senses and realize only after getting married that she doesn't love me and never could have.

Strange and most evil thoughts about her began coming into his mind. He became jealous of Vronsky as he had the year before, as though the evening he had seen her with Vronsky had been only yesterday. He suspected that she had not told him everything.

Levin jumped up abruptly. No—this is impossible! he said to himself desperately. I'll go to her and ask her, I'll tell her for the last time—we're still free—wouldn't it be better if we stopped now? Anything is better than continual misery, shame, infidelity!

His heart full of despair and of bitterness toward everyone, toward himself and her, he left the hotel and went to see her.

He found Kitty in one of the back rooms. She was sitting on a trunk and making arrangements about something with one of the maids, sorting out a heap of differently colored dresses that were laid out over the backs of chairs and on the floor.

"Oh!" she cried out, all radiant with joy, when she saw him. "How did you—what—well, this is unexpected! I'm just sorting out my old dresses, to give them away . . ."

"Aha—very nice indeed!" he said, staring glumly at the maid.

"You may go now, Dunyasha, I'll call you later," said Kitty. "What's the matter with you?" she asked, the moment the maid had gone out. She had noticed his strange expression, excited and morose, and was seized with fear.

"Kitty—I'm in agony! I cannot bear it alone," he said in a despairing voice, standing in front of her and gazing into her eyes imploringly. He had already seen by her loving, candid face that nothing he had intended saying could lead to anything, yet he had to hear her own disavowal. "I came to tell you that it's still not too late. Everything can still be canceled and put right."

"What? I don't understand a thing! What's the matter with you?"

"What I've said a thousand times already and can't help thinking—I'm not worthy of you! You simply can't have agreed to marry me. You must think it over. You've made a mistake. Think it over seriously. You can't really love me . . . If you . . . You had better say so," he said, not looking at her. "I'll be unhappy. Let people say whatever they like, anything is better than the misfortune of—Anyhow it would be better now while there's still time . . ."

"I don't understand," she said, thoroughly frightened. "You mean you want to break it off? That there's no need to—?"

"Yes, if you don't love me."

"You're out of your mind!" she cried, flushing with irritation. But he looked so pitiful that she curbed her annoyance, and throwing the dresses off the armchair, she sat down closer to him. "What are you thinking about? Tell me everything."

"I don't think you can be in love with me. What could you love me for?"

"Oh God—what can I do?" she said and burst into tears.

"Oh, what have I done!" he cried, kneeling down in front of her and kissing her hands.

When the Princess entered the room five minutes later she found them quite reconciled. Kitty had not only assured him that she loved him, but in response to his question had even given him the reasons why. She told him she loved him because she understood him completely, because she knew that he had a loving heart and that everything he loved was good. And this seemed completely clear to him. When the Princess came in they were sitting side by side on the trunk sorting out the dresses and arguing because Kitty wanted to give Dunyasha the brown dress she had worn when Levin had proposed, while he insisted that that dress could not be given away to anyone, and that Dunyasha should be given a blue one instead.

"Why don't you see it? She's a brunette, it won't suit her . . . I've thought it all over."

When the Princess heard why he had come she lost her

temper, half-jokingly and half in earnest, and sent him home
to change and not to bother Kitty while her hair was being
done, since the hairdresser was going to be there any moment.

"As it is she hasn't eaten anything all these days and has
turned quite plain, then you come here and upset her even
more with all your nonsense!" she said to him. "Off with
you now, my dear, off with you!"

Levin, feeling guilty and shamefaced but reassured, went
back to his hotel. His brother, Dolly, and Oblonsky, all in
full evening dress, were already waiting for him in order to
bless him with the icon. There was no time to lose. Dolly
still had to go back home to fetch her son, who, his hair
oiled and curled, was supposed to drive in the bride's carriage holding an icon. Then a carriage had to be sent to
fetch the best man, and another one, which was to take
Koznyshov, had to be sent back. Altogether there were a
great many problems, all of them extremely complicated. One
thing was certain: they had to hurry, since it was already
half-past six.

The blessing with the icon did not come off. Oblonsky
struck a comic-solemn attitude beside Dolly, took the icon,
and ordering Levin to bow to the ground he blessed him
with a good-natured ironical smile and kissed him three times;
Dolly did the same thing, then hurried off at once and again
got all mixed up with the carriage schedules.

"Well, this is what we'll do then: you go fetch him in our
carriage; then, if Sergius will be so kind as to go on ahead
and send the carriage back?"

"Of course, I should be delighted."

"And we'll follow along immediately with him. Have your
things been sent off?" asked Oblonsky.

"Yes," Levin replied, and ordered Kuzma to lay out his
clothes.

## III

A throng of people, mostly women, had assembled around
the church, which was all lighted up for the wedding. Those
who had come too late to get into the middle pressed round
the windows, jostling one another, arguing, and trying to peek
in between the bars.

More than twenty carriages had already been lined up
along the street by the mounted police. A police officer, disre-

garding the frost, was standing at the entrance, resplendent in his uniform. More carriages kept driving constantly up; women with flowers in their hair, holding up their trains, and men doffing their military caps or black hats kept going into the church. In the church itself the two chandeliers were already lighted, as well as all the candles in front of the icons. The golden glitter against the crimson background of the altar screen, the gilt decorations of the icons, the silver of the chandeliers and candlesticks, the flagstones, on the floor, the little carpets, the banners above the choir, the steps of the pulpit, the age-blackened books, the cassocks, the surplices—everything was flooded with light. At the right side of the warm church, in the throng of swallowtail coats, white ties, uniforms, brocades, velvets and satins, hair, flowers, naked shoulders and arms and high gloves, a restrained and lively buzzing was going on that echoed oddly from the high dome above. Each time the creaking of the doors opening was heard the chattering of the crowd died down, as everyone looked round expecting to see the bride and bridegroom come in. But the door had already opened more than ten times and each time it turned out to be either a late guest who joined the circle of those invited on the right, or a spectator who had tricked the police officer or melted his heart and joined the crowd of strangers at the left. Both relatives and outsiders had already passed through every stage of expectation.

At first it was thought that the bride and bridegroom were arriving at any moment; no one thought the delay meant anything. Then people began looking at the door more and more often, wondering whether something might have happened. Then the delay actually began to make people ill at ease; relatives and guests tried to look as though they were not thinking about the bride and groom but were taken up by their own conversations.

The archdeacon, as though drawing attention to the value of his time, coughed impatiently, making the windowpanes vibrate. From the choir the bored singers could be heard trying out their voices or blowing their noses. The priest continually kept sending the chanter or the deacon to find out whether the bridegroom had arrived, and he himself, in his purple surplice with the embroidered girdle, kept going out to the side doors more and more often to look out for the bridegroom. Finally one of the ladies, looking at her watch, said: "Really this is too odd!" and all the guests grew restless and began expressing their astonishment and dissatisfaction in loud voices. The best man went to find out what had happened.

Throughout this time Kitty, long since ready, in her white dress, long veil, and crown of orange blossoms, was standing with her sister Princess Lvov and the old lady who was to accompany her, in the ballroom of the Shcherbatskys' looking out of the window; for more than half an hour she had been vainly expecting some news from her bridesman about the bridegroom's arrival at the church.

As for Levin, he had been pacing back and forth in his room, in his trousers but without waistcoat or coat, constantly sticking his head out the door and looking up the corridor. But he didn't see whom he was expecting, and coming back in and gesticulating in despair he said to Oblonsky, who was smoking serenely:

"Was anyone ever in this frightfully idiotic position!?" he said.

"Yes, it's silly," agreed Oblonsky, with a soothing smile. "But calm down, they'll be here right away."

"How can I help it?" said Levin in suppressed fury. "And these idiotic open waistcoats—it's impossible!" he said, looking at his crumpled shirt front. "And what if the things have already gone to the railroad station!" he cried out despairingly.

"Then you can put on mine."

"That's what I should have a long time ago."

"It's no good being ridiculous. Just wait—it'll all *turn out all right*."

What had happened was that when Levin had asked his old servant Kuzma to get his things ready, Kuzma had brought his coat, waistcoat, and everything else that was needed.

"What about the shirt?" Levin cried.

"You're wearing it," replied Kuzma with a tranquil smile. He had not thought of leaving out a clean shirt; when he had been told to pack everything and send it to the Shcherbatskys', from where the young couple were leaving that same evening, he had done just that, and packed everything but the dress suit. The shirt, which Levin had been wearing since morning, was crumpled; with the low-cut waistcoats in fashion it was out of the question. It was too far to get one from the Shcherbatskys', so a servant was sent to buy one; he came back—it was Sunday and everything was shut.

He was sent to Oblonsky's and brought back a shirt—it was impossibly wide and short. They finally sent to the Shcherbatskys', for the things to be unpacked. The bridegroom was expected at the church, and like a caged wild beast he was pacing up and down in his room looking out into the corridor and recalling with horror and despair what he had said to Kitty and what she might be thinking now.

Finally Kuzma, the culprit, gasping for breath, came flying into the room with the shirt.

"Just made it! They were hoisting the trunk into the cart already," said Kuzma.

Three minutes later, without looking at his watch, so as not to rub any more salt in the wound, Levin was running down the corridor at top speed.

"That won't help any," said Oblonsky with a smile, following him at a leisurely pace, "*it'll turn out all right,* I tell you."

## IV

HERE they are!" "There he is!" "Which one?" "Is it the younger one?" "And look at her, heavens, more dead than alive!" came the remarks from the crowd as Levin, having met Kitty at the entrance, entered the church together with her.

Oblonsky told Dolly why they had been late, and the guests smilingly whispered to one another. Levin noticed nothing and no one; he did not take his eyes off his bride.

Everyone said Kitty had grown much plainer during the past few days, and in her bridal dress was far less pretty than usual; but Levin didn't think so. He looked at her hair dressed high beneath the long white veil and the white flowers, at the high collar that in a particularly maidenly way covered her long neck at the sides and showed it off in front, and the strikingly slender waist, and it seemed to him that she was more beautiful than ever before—not because these flowers, that veil, that dress ordered from Paris added anything to her beauty, but because in spite of the intricate ornateness of her attire the look on her sweet face, her eyes, her lips was still her same characteristic look of innocent candor.

"I started thinking you wanted to run away," she said, smiling at him.

"It's so silly, the thing that happened, it's embarrassing to mention it," he said blushing; then he had to turn round to Koznyshov, who was approaching.

"A fine story that, about your shirt!" said Koznyshov, shaking his head and smiling.

"Yes, yes," Levin replied, unable to understand what was being said to him.

"Well, Constantine, you'll have to make a decision now," said Oblonsky with a look of mock alarm, "it's a very important question. You happen to be in a position now to appreciate its full importance. I've been asked whether to have used candles lighted or new ones. There's a difference of ten rubles," he added, a smile hovering round his lips. "I've made a decision, but I'm afraid you won't give your consent."

Levin realized it was a joke, but he couldn't smile.

"Then which is it? Used or new? That's the question."

"Yes, yes—new ones!"

"Well, I'm delighted. The question's settled!" Oblonsky said with a smile. "But really how silly people are in this situation," he said to Chirikov as Levin, casting a distraught look at him, moved off toward Kitty.

"Mind now, Kitty, you must step on the mat first," said Countess Nordston, coming over. "A fine one you are!" she said to Levin.

"Well, aren't you frightened?" said Kitty's old Aunt Mary.

"Are you chilly? You look pale. Wait a moment, lean over!" said Kitty's sister, Princess Lvov; raising her lovely, full arms with a smile she adjusted the flowers on Kitty's head.

Dolly came over and was about to say something, but she couldn't get it out; she started crying, then laughing unnaturally.

Kitty was looking at everyone with the same faraway eyes as Levin. The only response she could make to everything that was said to her was a smile of happiness, which came to her very naturally now.

Meanwhile the clergy had put on their vestments, and the priest and deacon went out to the lectern that stood near the church entrance. The priest turned to Levin and said something which Levin could not make out.

"Take the bride's hand and lead her," said Levin's best man.

For some time Levin was unable to grasp what was wanted of him. It took a long time to set him right, and they were about to give him up altogether—he kept taking her by the wrong hand or not taking her with the right one—when he finally realized he had to take her with his right hand by her right hand, without changing his position. When he finally took her by the hand properly, the priest walked a few steps in front of them and stopped beside the lectern. The crowd of relatives and acquaintances, voices buzzing and ladies' trains rustling, moved up after them. Someone leaned over and straightened out the bride's train. The church became so still that the drops of wax could be heard falling.

The old priest, in his sacerdotal headgear, and his locks of gray hair, gleaming like silver, combed back on two sides behind his ears, drew his wrinkled little hands out from under his heavy silver chasuble with the gold cross on the back, and began turning something over on the lectern.

Oblonsky stepped over to him cautiously, whispered something, signaled to Levin and stepped back again.

The priest lighted two wax candles decorated with flowers, and holding them at a slant in his left hand, so that the wax slowly dripped down, turned to face the young couple. The priest was the same one who had listened to Levin's confession. He gave a weary, mournful glance at the bride and bridegroom, sighed, and taking his right hand out from under his chasuble, blessed the bridegroom with it, then the bride, though there was a shade of watchful tenderness in the way he placed his folded fingers on Kitty's bowed head. Then he handed them the candles, took the censer and slowly moved away from them.

Can it really be true? thought Levin, and glanced round at his bride. He could see her profile slightly from above and he knew, by the scarcely perceptible movement of her lips and eyelashes, that she was aware of his look. She did not glance round, but her high frilled collar moved, rising to her pink little ear. He saw that a sigh had been halted in her breast; her little hand in the long glove, holding the candle, began trembling.

All the bother about the shirt, the delay, the conversation with acquaintances and relatives, their irritation, his ludicrous position—everything suddenly vanished; he felt joyous and fearful.

The handsome, sturdy, archdeacon in silver cloth alb, his curled hair parted in two, briskly strode forward, lifting his stole with a practiced movement of two fingers, and stopped in front of the priest.

"Ble-e-ess us, O Lo-o-rd!" slowly came the solemn sounds, one after the other, vibrating in the air.

"Blessed be the Lord our God, now and hereafter, forever and ever," responded the old priest meekly, in a singsong voice, continuing to turn something over on the lectern. And, harmoniously filling the whole church from the windows to the vaulted roof, a full chord sung by the unseen choir broadly swelled up, increased in volume, paused for a moment, and softly died away again.

The usual prayers were given for peace and salvation from above, for the synod, for the Sovereign; prayers were also given for the servants of God who were being betrothed that day, Constantine and Catherine.

"Let us pray to the Lord, that He may send them perfect love, peace, and help," the whole church seemed to breathe with the archdeacon's voice.

Levin listened to the words, and was struck by them. How did they realize that help was the thing I needed, just help? he thought, recalling all his recent fears and doubts. What do I know? What could I accomplish in this terrible business without help, he thought; help is just what I need now.

When the deacon had finished the prayer for the Imperial family, the priest, holding a book, turned to the bride and bridegroom:

"God eternal, who joineth together them that were separate," he read out in a gentle, singsong voice, "who hath ordained for them a union in love indissoluble; Thou who hast blessed Isaac and Rebecca and hast kept Thy promise to their heirs: bless these Thy servants Constantine and Catherine, and lead them along the path of righteousness. Most merciful God, lover of man, we praise Thee. Glory be to the Father, and to the Son, and to the Holy Ghost, now and hereafter and forever and ever." "A-a-a-men," from the unseen choir, floated out into the air once again.

"Who joineth together them that were separate, ordaining a union in love"—what profound words, and how they fit in with what I'm feeling at this moment! Levin thought. Does she feel the same thing as I?

And glancing round he met her eyes. By their expression he concluded that she understood them just as he did. But that was not so: she scarcely understood the words of the service at all; she was not even listening to them. She was unable to hear and understand them, so powerful was the one feeling that filled her soul and kept growing stronger and stronger. This feeling was one of joy at the complete consummation of what had been going on in her soul for more than a month and a half, and in the course of these past six weeks had been gladdening and tormenting her. That day in the ballroom of the house on Arbat Street, when she had gone over to him silently, in her brown dress, and promised herself to him—on that day and at that moment a complete break had been accomplished with the whole of her previous life, and a completely different, novel, utterly unknown life began, though in fact the old life still went on. These six weeks had been the most blissful and the most agonizing period for her. Her whole life, all her desires and hopes were concentrated in this one man, who was still incomprehensible to her, and whom she was bound to by a feeling that was even more incomprehensible than the man himself, and that alternately attracted and repelled her. And all this while she had gone on living in the conditions of her former life. While living her old life she was horrified at herself, and at her total and invincible indifference to her entire past: to objects, habits, people who had loved her and still did, to her mother, who was wounded by this indifference, to her darling, tender father whom she had used to love more than anything in the world. Sometimes she was horrified at this indifference, sometimes happy about what had brought her to it. She was unable to think of or desire anything outside of a life with this man; but this new life had not yet come into being; she could not even visualize it clearly. There was nothing but anticipation—fear and joy at the new and unknown. And now any moment the anticipation, and the unfamiliarity, and the remorse at the renunciation of her former life —all this was coming to an end, and the new life was about to begin. This new life, because of its unfamiliarity, could not help being terrifying, but terrifying or not, it had already been accomplished within her soul six weeks before; what had been accomplished in her soul a long time before was merely being sanctified now.

Going back again to the lectern the priest, with some difficulty, picked up Kitty's little ring; asking Levin for his hand he put it on the tip of his finger. "The servant of God, Constantine, is betrothed to the servant of God, Catherine." And putting a big ring on Kitty's pink, slender finger, pathetic in its puniness, the priest said the same thing.

Several times the betrothed couple tried to guess what they were supposed to do; each time they blundered, and the priest corrected them in a whisper. Finally, when everything necessary had been done, he made the sign of the cross over them with the rings, and again gave Kitty the big ring and Levin the small one; again they blundered and passed the rings from one hand to another twice without getting it right.

Dolly, Chirikov, and Oblonsky came forward to set them right. This resulted in some confusion, whispers, and smiles, but the expression of solemn emotion on the faces of the betrothed couple did not change; on the contrary, as they fumbled about with their hands they looked even more earnest and solemn than before, and the smile on Oblonsky's lips as he whispered that now each one was to put on his own ring involuntarily faded away. He felt that any kind of smile would wound them.

"Thou hast from the beginning created them male and female," the priest read out after the rings had been exchanged. "Through Thee the woman is united to the man, to be his helpmate and to procreate the human race. Therefore, O Lord our God, who hast bequeathed the truth to thy heritage, and gavest Thy promises to Thy servants our fathers, from generation to generation of Thy chosen people; look down upon Thy servant Constantine and upon Thy servant Catherine; strengthen their union with faith, with concord, with truth, and with love . . ."

More and more Levin kept feeling that all his ideas about marriage, and his dreams of how he was going to arrange his life, that all of that was mere childishness, that this was something he had never understood before and now understood even less, even though it was happening to him; in his breast a tremor swelled higher and higher, and intractable tears came to his eyes.

v

ALL Moscow was at the church—relatives and friends. During the marriage ceremony, in the brilliant illumination, conversation, decorously quiet, never flagged in the crowd of elegantly dressed women, girls, and men in evening dress and in uniforms. It was chiefly the men who started it, while the women were absorbed in the contemplation of all the details of this service that they always find so fascinating.

In the circle nearest the bride were her two sisters, Dolly and the older, the calm and beautiful Princess Lvov, who had come from abroad.

"Why is Marie in lilac? At a wedding it's like black!" said Madame Korsunsky.

"With her complexion it's the only salvation . . ." replied Princess Drubetskoy. "I'm astonished they're having the wedding in the evening, like tradespeople . . ."

"It's prettier. I was married in the evening too," replied Madame Korsunsky, sighing as she recalled how charming she had looked then, how preposterously in love with her husband she had been, and how everything was now quite different.

"They say anyone who's a best man more than ten times will never marry; I wanted to be one for the tenth time to insure myself, but the place was already taken," Count Sinyavin was saying to the pretty Princess Charsky, who had designs on him.

Her only answer was a smile. She was looking at Kitty, wondering how and when she was going to stand together with Count Sinyavin in Kitty's situation and how she would remind him then of the joke he had just made.

Young Shcherbatsky was telling an old Lady in Waiting that he intended to put the crown on Kitty's chignon to bring her luck.

"There was no need for a chignon," answered the Lady in Waiting, who had long since decided that if the old widower she was angling for ever married her their wedding was going to be the simplest possible. "I don't like all this opulence."

Koznyshov was chatting with Dolly, jocularly assuring her that the custom of going away after the wedding was spreading because the newly married couples always felt somewhat ashamed of themselves.

"Your brother has a right to be proud of himself. She's wonderfully sweet. I wonder—could you be jealous?"

"I'm past all that," he replied, and his face unexpectedly took on a grave, sad expression.

Oblonsky was telling his sister-in-law the pun he had made up about "solutions."

"I must straighten out her wreath," she said, without listening to him.

"What a pity she's grown so plain," said Countess Nordston to Princess Lvov. "But he's not worth her little finger anyhow. Don't you think so?"

"No, I like him. And not because he's my future brother-in-law," replied Princess Lvov. "How well he's behaving! And it's so difficult to behave well in this situation—not to look ridiculous. But he's not ridiculous, and he's not stiff—he's obviously moved."

"I suppose you expected this?"

"More or less; she's always been fond of him."

"Well, let's look and see who steps onto the mat first. I gave Kitty some advice about it."

"That doesn't matter," replied Princess Lvov, "we're all docile wives, that's our nature."

"Well, with Vasili I stepped onto the mat first. And you, Dolly?"

Dolly, who was standing beside them, heard them but made no reply. She was deeply moved. Her eyes were moist; she could not have said a word without bursting into tears. She was rejoicing over Kitty and Levin; going back in thought to her own wedding, she kept glancing at the radiant Oblonsky, forgetting all the present and recalling only her own first innocent love. She remembered not herself alone, but all the women she knew, intimates and acquaintances; she remembered them at this most solemn moment of their lives, as they stood beneath the nuptial crown, just like Kitty now, with love, hope, and terror in their hearts, renouncing the past and entering upon the mysterious future. Among all these brides who came to her mind she recalled her own darling Anna, the details of whose impending divorce she had recently heard. She too, just as pure, had once stood there in a veil, crowned with orange blossoms. And now? "Dreadfully odd," she murmured.

The two sisters, women friends, and relatives were not the only ones intent on all the details of the service; women onlookers who were complete strangers breathless with excitement and afraid to miss a single motion, followed the expressions on the face of the bridegroom or the bride; irritably they disregarded and most often did not hear what was said by the men, who in their indifference kept making jocular or irrelevant remarks.

"Why is she drenched in tears? Or is she doing it against her will?"

"Against her will, with a fine fellow like that? Isn't he a Prince, or something, eh?"

"And is that the sister, in the white satin? . . . Now just listen to the deacon roaring 'Obey your husband'!"

"Is that the Chudovsky choir?"

"No, the Synod's."

"I asked the footman, he said he was going to take her

straight off to his ancestral estate. He's terribly rich, they say. That's why they've given her to him, too."

"No, they're a handsome couple."

"There you are now, Mary, and you were arguing that crinolines were being worn fuller at the back! Just take a look at the one over there in the puce dress, an ambassador's wife, they say; see how it's draped? This way, then back again."

"What a darling the bride is, like a lamb ready for the slaughter! Say what you like, you feel sorry for another girl."

This was what was being said by the crowd of women who had managed to slip inside the church.

## VI

WHEN the first part of the marriage service was over, a verger spread out a piece of pink silk cloth in front of the lectern in the middle of the church, the choir began singing a psalm in some intricate and complicated melody in which the bass and tenor kept repeating each other, and the priest, turning round, motioned the couple to the spread out piece of pink cloth. However often they had both heard the saying that the one who was the first to step onto the mat would be the head of the household, neither Levin nor Kitty could remember it when they took these few steps. Nor did they hear the loud remarks and arguments about whether he had stepped onto it first, as some said, or they had both stepped onto it together, according to others.

After the customary questions about their desire to enter into matrimony, and whether they had promised themselves to others, and their answers, which sounded peculiar even to themselves, the second part of the service began. Kitty listened to the words of the prayer, hoping to understand what they meant, but she couldn't. A feeling of triumph and radiant joy went on filling her soul more and more as the ceremony progressed and made it impossible for her to pay attention.

A prayer was said: "That they may live in chastity for the good of the fruits of their womb, and find joy in the sight of their sons and daughters." It was mentioned that God had created woman from Adam's rib, and that "because of this shall a man leave his father and his mother and cleave unto his wife, and the twain shall be one flesh," and that "This is a great mystery." God was entreated to make them fruitful and bless them as He had Isaac, and Rebecca, Joseph, Moses, and Zipporah, and that they should see their children's children.

That was all beautiful, thought Kitty as she listened to these words, nor could it be any different. A smile of joy that automatically infected everyone looking at her shone on her radiant face.

"Put it on completely!" came the words of advice when the priest had put the crowns on them and Shcherbatsky, his hand trembling in its three-buttoned glove, held a crown high above her head.

"Put it on!" she whispered, smiling.

Levin glanced round at her and was struck by the radiant joy on her face; her feeling infected him involuntarily. He felt bright and joyous as she did.

They took joy in listening to the reading of the Epistle and the roll of the protodeacon's voice in the last verse, awaited with such impatience by the spectators. With light hearts they drank the warm red wine and water from the shallow cup, and they grew even more cheerful when the priest, throwing back his vestments, took their hands in his and to the gusts of the bass leading in *Rejoice, O Isaiah!* led them round the lectern. Shcherbatsky and Chirikov, who had been holding up the crowns and getting in the way of the bride's train, were also smiling, for some reason delighted; they would sometimes lag behind and sometimes jostle the young couple whenever the priest came to a halt. The tingle of joy glowing in Kitty's heart seemed to have infected everyone in the church. It seemed to Levin that both the priest and the deacon, like himself, had a desire to smile.

After taking the crowns from their heads the priest recited the final prayer and congratulated the young couple. Levin looked at Kitty; he had never seen her before as she looked then. She was enchanting with the light of her new happiness radiating from her face. Levin felt like saying something to her, but he didn't know whether it was all over yet. The priest brought him out of the difficulty; with a smile on his kindly mouth he said softly: "Kiss your wife, and you, kiss your husband," and took the candlesticks out of their hands.

Levin cautiously kissed her smiling lips, gave her his arm, and with a new sensation of peculiar closeness went out of the church. He did not, could not believe it was true. It was only when their astonished, shy glances met each other that he believed it, because he felt they were already one.

That same night, after supper, the newlyweds left for the country.

<br>

## VII

FOR some three months now Vronsky and Anna had been traveling around Europe. They had visited Venice, Rome, and Naples; now they had arrived in a small Italian town where they intended to settle down for a while.

The headwaiter, a handsome fellow with a part in his thick, greased hair that began at the nape of his neck, in a swallowtail coat and a wide white cambric shirt front, with a bunch of charms dangling on his round stomach, was frowning contemptuously, his hands in his pockets, and answering some passer-by in a severe tone. Overhearing footsteps going up the staircase on the other side of the entrance, the headwaiter turned round and when he saw the Russian Count who was occupying the best rooms in the hotel, he respectfully took his hands out of his pockets and bowing explained that the courier had been there and that the matter of renting the *palazzo* was settled. The manager was ready to sign the contract.

"Ah, I'm delighted," said Vronsky. "Is Madame in or not?"

"Madame went out for a walk, but has just come back," said the headwaiter.

Vronsky took off the soft, broad-brimmed hat and with a handkerchief wiped his damp forehead and his hair, which he had allowed to grow halfway down his ears and combed straight back to hide his bald spot. Looking absently at the passer-by who was still standing there and looking at him, he was about to go on.

"This gentleman is a Russian and has been asking about you," said the headwaiter.

With a feeling of vexation at never being able to escape from people you know, mixed with a desire to find some distraction from the monotony of his life, Vronsky glanced round once again at the man, who had moved a distance off and then stopped; their eyes lit up simultaneously.

"Golenishchev!"

"Vronsky!"

It was in fact Golenishchev, a friend of Vronsky's from the Corps of Pages. In the Corps Golenishchev had been one of the liberals, had left the Corps a civilian and had never served. The two friends had completely lost sight of each other after leaving the Corps and had met only once afterward.

At this encounter Vronsky gathered that Golenishchev had chosen some loftily intellectual liberal activity, and so had an inclination to despise Vronsky's profession and activities. On meeting him, accordingly, Vronsky had given him that chilly, haughty rebuff he was capable of, the sense of which was this: You may or may not like my style of life, it's a matter of total indifference to me: you must respect me if you wish to know me. As for Golenishchev he had been contemptuously indifferent to Vronsky's tone, so that one would have thought that this meeting would have alienated them still further. But when they recognized each other now they brightened up and exclaimed with delight. Vronsky would never have expected to be so overjoyed at seeing Golenishchev, but doubtless he didn't realize himself how bored he was. He had forgotten the disagreeable impression made by their last encounter; with a happy open expression he held his hand out to his old schoolfellow. The same joyful expression replaced the previous anxious look on Golenishchev's face.

"Delighted to see you!" said Vronsky, showing his strong white teeth in a friendly smile.

"I heard 'Vronsky,' but I didn't know which one. Delighted, simply delighted!"

"Come, let's go in. Well, what are you up to?"

"This is the second year I've been living here. I'm working."

"Oh!" said Vronsky with interest. "Well, come in!"

And as usual among Russians, instead of saying what he wanted to hide from the servants in Russian, he began speaking in French.

"D'you know Madame Karenin? We're traveling together. I'm going to see her now," he said in French, looking watchfully into Golenishchev's face.

"Oh? I didn't know," replied Golenishchev indifferently, though actually he did. "Have you been here long?" he added.

"I? This is the fourth day," answered Vronsky, once again looking watchfully into his friend's face.

Yes, he's a decent chap and takes it the right way, Vronsky said to himself, understanding what Golenishchev's expression meant, and his changing the subject. I can introduce him to Anna, he's taking it the right way . . .

During the three months Vronsky had spent with Anna abroad, whenever he met any new people he always asked himself how the new acquaintance would look upon his relationship with Anna, and in the men, for the most part, he would encounter *the right way* of looking at it. But if he or those who took it *the right way* were to be asked just what this meant, both he and they would have been greatly puzzled.

Essentially those who took it *the right way* in Vronsky's opinion didn't take it any way at all, but merely behaved as well-brought-up people do in general with respect to all the complicated and insoluble questions that encompass life on all sides—they behaved politely, avoiding any hints and disagreeable questions. They pretended that they completely understood the importance and meaning of the position, acknowledged and even approved of it, but considered it out of place and superfluous to explain it all.

Vronsky had guessed at once that Golenishchev was one of these, and so was doubly glad to see him. In fact, when Golenishchev was introduced to Anna he did behave with her as well as Vronsky could have desired. It was plainly no effort at all for him to avoid any topics that might have led to any awkwardnesses.

Golenishchev had not known Anna before; he was struck by her beauty and still more by the simplicity with which she accepted her situation. She blushed when Vronsky brought Golenishchev in, and this childish blush, which covered her beautiful, open face, pleased him very much. But what he liked particularly was that as though on purpose, in order to avoid any misunderstandings in the presence of a stranger, she called Vronsky simply Alexis and said they were about to move into a house they had just rented, locally referred to as a *palazzo*. Golenishchev liked this straightforward, simple attitude toward her own situation. Watching Anna's gay, brisk and good-natured manner, and knowing both Karenin and Vronsky, Golenishchev felt he understood her perfectly. It seemed to him that he understood just what she herself did not at all: just how, after making her husband unhappy, deserting him and her son, and losing her good name, she could still feel brisk, gay, and happy.

"It's in the guidebook," said Golenishchev, about the

*palazzo* being rented by Vronsky. "There's a magnificent Tintoretto there, his last period."

"D'you know what? The weather's wonderful, let's go out there and take another look at it," said Vronsky to Anna.

"Wonderful, I'll put on a hat right away. You say it's hot?" she said, stopping in the doorway and looking inquiringly at Vronsky. And again her face was suffused by a bright flush.

By her look Vronsky understood that she didn't know what terms he wanted to be on with Golenishchev, and that she was afraid of not behaving as he might want her to.

He gave her a tender, lingering look. "No, not very," he said.

It seemed to her that she had understood everything, mainly that he was pleased with her; she smiled at him and went out with her rapid steps.

The two friends looked at each other; both faces took on an embarrassed expression, as though Golenishchev, who plainly admired Anna, wanted to say something about her but couldn't think what, while Vronsky felt both eager for him to and apprehensive.

"So there you are," Vronsky began, in order to launch some kind of conversation. "So you've settled down here, eh? Then you're still doing the same thing?" he went on; he recalled being told that Golenishchev was writing something.

"Yes, I'm writing the second part of *Two Principles*," said Golenishchev, flushing with pleasure at the question. "To be precise, that is, I haven't begun writing yet, but I'm preparing the materials, assembling them. It's going to be far more comprehensive, it'll take in almost every question. In Russia we refuse to realize that we are the heirs of Byzantium . . ." He began a long, passionate discourse.

At first Vronsky felt embarrassed at not knowing even the first part of *Two Principles*, which the author was speaking to him about as though it were familiar. But afterward, as Golenishchev began expounding his ideas and Vronsky was able to follow him, he listened to him with some interest even without knowing anything about the *Two Principles*, since Golenishchev was an excellent talker. But Vronsky was surprised and annoyed by the excited irascibility with which Golenishchev talked about the subject that occupied him. The more he talked the more his eyes flashed, the more hastily he rebutted imaginary opponents, and the more agitated and offended grew the expression on his face. Remembering Golenishchev as a thin, lively, good-natured, and

generous boy who was always at the head of the class,
Vronsky was quite unable to grasp the reasons for this
irritability, and he disapproved of it. What he disliked
especially was that Golenishchev, who came from a good
family, was placing himself on the same level as some scrib-
blers or other who had annoyed him and whom he was losing
his temper at. Was it worth that? Vronsky disliked it; nevertheless he felt that Golenishchev was unhappy and felt sorry
for him. Unhappiness, almost insanity, was apparent in Golenishchev's mobile, rather handsome face as he went on
hotly and precipitately expressing his ideas, without even
noticing Anna's re-entering the room.

When Anna, in a hat and mantle, came back and stood
beside him toying with her sunshade with a rapid movement
of her beautiful hand, Vronsky wrenched himself away with a
feeling of relief from Golenishchev's eyes, which were fixed
on him plaintively, and with renewed love glanced at his
charming companion, full of life and gaiety. Golenishchev
recovered himself with difficulty; at first he was dejected
and morose, but Anna, who was tenderly disposed to everyone (as she was at this time) soon revived him with her simple, gay manner. After trying various topics of conversation
she led him on to art, which he spoke about very well,
and listened to him attentively. They went on foot to the
house they had taken and looked over it.

"There's one thing I'm very pleased about," Anna said to
Golenishchev, after they had returned. "Alexis will have an
excellent studio. You must have that little room without
fail Alexis," she said to Vronsky in Russian, having already
understood that in their isolation Golenishchev was going to
become an intimate and that there was no need to pretend in
front of him.

"Do you really paint?" said Golenishchev, turning quickly
to Vronsky.

"Yes, I used to a long time ago; now I've started in again
a little," said Vronsky with a blush.

"He's extremely talented," said Anna with a happy smile.
"Of course I'm no judge, but people who are able to judge
say so too."

## VIII

IN this first period of her liberation and rapid recovery, Anna felt unforgivably happy and full of the joy of life. The recollection of her husband's misery did not poison her own happiness. On the one hand the memory of this was too dreadful to think about; on the other her husband's misery had been the cause of too much happiness for her to feel remorse. The recollection of everything that had happened to her after her illness: her reconciliation with her husband, the rupture, the news of Vronsky's wound, his reappearance, the preparations for the divorce, her departure from her husband's house, her farewell to her son—it all seemed to her a delirious dream, from which she had woken up abroad alone with Vronsky. The recollection of the evil done to her husband aroused in her a feeling similar to revulsion, such as a drowning man might feel who had shaken off another who was hanging on to him. The other one was drowned; of course that was bad, but it was the only possible salvation and it's better not to think about all these dreadful details.

One comforting reflection about her behavior had come to her at that time at the very first moment of the rupture, and now, when she recalled what had taken place it was this one reflection that came to her mind. My making him unhappy was inevitable, she thought, but I don't want to profit by this unhappiness; I'm suffering too and shall go on suffering: I've deprived myself of what I treasured most—my good name and my son. What I did was wrong and because of that I don't wish for happiness, I don't want a divorce and I shall go on suffering from shame and from the loss of my son.

But however sincerely Anna wanted to suffer, she did not suffer. There was no shame of any kind. With the tact they both had so much of, by avoiding Russian ladies abroad they never put themselves in a false position, and they kept meeting people who pretended to understand their mutual relations fully, far better than they themselves did. Even the separation from her son, whom she loved so much, did not torment her at first either. The little girl, *his* child, was so darling and Anna had grown so attached to her ever since she was all that was left to her, that she seldom thought about her son.

The need to live, heightened by her recovery, was so powerful and the circumstances of their life were so novel and agreeable that Anna felt unforgivably happy. The more she came to know Vronsky the more she loved him. She loved him for his own sake and for the sake of his love for her. It was a continuous joy for her to have complete possession of him. His closeness was always pleasant for her. She found every trait in his character, which she was coming to know more and more, inexpressibly charming. His looks, changed by his civilian dress, were as attractive to her as to a girl in love. In everything he said, thought, and did she saw something peculiarly noble and lofty. Her raptures over him sometimes frightened even herself: she looked for and was unable to find anything in him that was not beautiful. She did not dare to disclose to him her consciousness of her own worthlessness compared with him. It seemed to her that if he found that out he would soon fall out of love with her; and there was nothing she was so afraid of now, though she had no grounds for it, as losing his love. But she could not help being grateful to him for his behavior toward her, and showing how she appreciated it. In her view of it he, who had such a decided vocation for statesmanship, in which he ought to have played an eminent role, had sacrificed his ambition for her sake, without ever showing the slightest regret. He was even more lovingly deferential to her than before; the thought that she must never be made aware of the awkwardness of her situation did not leave him for a moment. In relationship to her he, who was such a virile man, not only never contradicted her but had no will of his own, and seemed to be preoccupied by nothing but how to anticipate her wishes. And she could not help but appreciate this, even though this strained attentiveness of his, this atmosphere of solicitude with which he enveloped her, sometimes weighed on her.

Vronsky meanwhile, in spite of the complete realization of what he had desired for so long, was not entirely happy. He soon came to feel that the fulfillment of his desires had given him only one grain of the mountain of joy he had been expecting. This fulfillment showed him the eternal mistake people make when they imagine that happiness is the fulfillment of their wishes. At first, when he had united himself with her and put on civilian clothing, he had felt the full charm of freedom in general, which he had never known before, as well as of the freedom of love, and he was satisfied. But not for long. He soon came to feel that a desire for desires was rising in his soul—boredom. In spite of himself he began snatching at every passing caprice, mistaking it for a desire and a goal. Sixteen hours of the day had to be occupied somehow, since they were living abroad in complete liberty and outside that circle of social circumstance that took up the time in Petersburg. The mere thought of the pleasures of bachelor life that had occupied Vronsky on former trips abroad was out of the question, since his one attempt of this kind, a late supper with some acquaintances, had put Anna in a state of unexpected and disproportionate depression. It was also impossible to have any relations with local or Russian society, in view of the indefiniteness of their situation. Sight-seeing, aside from the fact that everything had been seen already, could not have for him—an intelligent Russian—the inexplicable importance attached to it by the English.

And just as a hungry animal seizes every object it comes across in the hope of finding some food in it, so Vronsky quite unconsciously snatched at politics, or new books, or paintings.

Since in youth he had had some talent for sketching, and since, at a loss for what to spend his money on, he had begun collecting engravings, he now settled on painting, began to devote himself to it and invested in it his unused store of desires in quest of satisfaction.

He had a gift for understanding art and for imitating with accuracy and taste, and he thought he had just what an artist needed; after hesitating for a while between different kinds of art—religious, historical, genre, or realistic—he set to work painting. He was at home in all styles and could be inspired by one or another equally, but he was quite incapable of imagining that it might be possible not to know anything at all about the various kinds of art, and be inspired directly by what was in your own soul without bothering about whether what he painted belonged to some particular school. Since he didn't know this and did not draw his inspiration from life directly, but indirectly from the life that was already embodied in art, he found himself inspired very quickly and easily, and just as quickly and easily got to the point where what he painted was very much like the kind of art he wanted to imitate.

He liked the graceful and showy French school more than

any other, and it was in this style that he began painting a portrait of Anna in Italian costume; it seemed a great success to him and to everyone who saw it.

## IX

THE neglected old *palazzo* with its high stucco ceilings and frescoes on the walls, its mosaic floors, heavy yellow damask curtains in high windows, with vases standing on console tables and mantelshelves, its carved doors and gloomy halls hung with pictures—this *palazzo*, after they moved into it, by its very appearance maintained Vronsky in his agreeable delusion that he was not so much a Russian landowner and unemployed equerry as an enlightened amateur and patron of the arts, and a modest artist in his own right, who had renounced the world, his connections, and his ambition for the woman he loved.

The role selected by Vronsky, with their moving into the *palazzo*, was a complete success; after meeting a number of interesting people through Golenishchev, Vronsky at first felt at peace. Under the guidance of an Italian professor of painting he painted some studies from nature, and took up the study of Italian life in the Middle Ages. Medieval Italian life had lately become so fascinating to him that he even began wearing his hat and flinging his cloak over his shoulder in the medieval manner, which suited him very well.

"Living here we never know anything," he said one morning to Golenishchev, who had come to see him. "Did you see Mikhailov's picture?" he said, handing him a Russian paper that had just been delivered that morning and indicating an article on the Russian painter, who was living in the same town and had just finished a picture that rumors had been circulating about for a long time, and that had been bought in advance. The article contained some reproaches directed at the government and the Academy for not having done anything to encourage or help out this remarkable artist.

"Yes, I did," replied Golenishchev. "Of course he's not devoid of talent, but he's in a completely false tendency. It's all that same Ivanov-Strauss-Renan attitude toward Christ and religious painting."

"What's the picture about?" asked Anna.

"Christ before Pilate. Christ is portrayed as a Jew, with all the realism of the new school."

And led on by the question about the subject of the picture to one of his favorite themes, Golenishchev began a disquisition:

"I don't understand how they can make such crude mistakes. Christ is already depicted in a definite way in the painting of the old masters. Consequently, if they want to portray not a God but a revolutionary or a sage let them choose some historical character like Socrates, Benjamin Franklin, Charlotte Corday—but not Christ! They take just the person it's impossible to use in art and then—"

"Is it true that this Mikhailov is so poor?" asked Vronsky, thinking that as a Russian Maecenas he had to help an artist regardless of whether his painting was good or bad.

"Hardly. He's a wonderful portrait painter. Have you seen his portrait of Princess Vasilchikov? But it seems he doesn't want to paint any more portraits, so he may actually be poor now. What I say is—"

"Would it be impossible to ask him to do a portrait of Anna?" said Vronsky.

"Why of me?" said Anna. "Now that you've done one I don't want any other. It would be better if he did one of Annie." (She had given that name to her baby daughter.) "Here she is now," she added, looking through the window at the beautiful Italian wet nurse who was taking the infant out into the garden, and then furtively looking round immediately at Vronsky. This beautiful nurse, whose head Vronsky had been painting for his picture, was the only secret sorrow in Anna's life. Vronsky while painting her had much admired her beauty and her "medievalism"; Anna dared not admit to herself that she was afraid of being jealous of this nurse, so she was particularly indulgent with her and spoiled both her and her infant daughter.

Vronsky also looked through the window and into Anna's eyes; then, turning round at once to Golenishchev, he said: "D'you know this Mikhailov?"

"I've met him. But he's a crank and quite uneducated. You know—one of those modern savages one runs across so often nowadays, one of those freethinkers, you know, who've been brought up all at once on notions of disbelief, negation, and materialism. Before," said Golenishchev, not noticing, or not wishing to, that both Anna and Vronsky wanted to say something, "a freethinker used to be a man who had been educated on ideas of religion, law, morality, and had arrived at free thought by virtue of his own struggle and toil; but now a new type of born freethinker has been appearing, who've never even heard that there have been laws of morality and religion, and that there are authorities, but who simply grow up with negative ideas about everything, that is, savages. That's the way he is. I think he's the son of a head footman in Moscow, and never had any education at all. When he entered the Academy and made a reputation for himself, he wanted to get some education, since he's not stupid, and turned to what seemed to him a source of instruction—the magazines. In the old days, you understand, a man who wanted to educate himself, let's say some Frenchman, would have begun studying all the classics: theologians, dramatists, historians, philosophers—you can imagine the intellectual labor he would have been faced by! But in Russia today he tumbled straight into the literature of negation, very quickly acquired the entire essence of negative thought, and there he was—all ready! Nor is that all: twenty years before he would have found signs in this literature too of a struggle against the authorities, against the age-old points of view, and this struggle would have shown him that there had been something else in existence; but now he falls straight into the sort of literature that doesn't even deign to contest these age-old views, but says straight out: there is nothing—it's all evolution, selection, the struggle for existence, and that's all. In my article I—"

"D'you know what?" said Anna, who after cautiously exchanging looks with Vronsky for some time, realized that Vronsky had no interest in the painter's education, but was simply concerned with the idea of helping him and of commissioning a portrait by him. "D'you know what?" she said, firmly interrupting Golenishchev, who was growing more and more heated. "Let's go to see him!"

Golenishchev recovered himself and gladly agreed. But since the artist lived in a remote quarter of the town they decided to hire a carriage.

An hour later Anna, sitting by Golenishchev's side, with Vronsky facing them, drove up to a pretty new house in this remote quarter. When they were told by the house porter's wife, who came out to meet them, that Mikhailov allowed visitors into his studio, but was just then in his own apartment a few steps away, they sent her to him with their cards, asking for permission to see his pictures.

## X

MIKHAILOV, the artist, was at work as usual when Count Vronsky's and Golenishchev's cards were brought to him. In the mornings he worked on the big picture in his studio. On returning home he had been angry with his wife for her not having been able to get round the landlady, who was asking for money.

"I've told you dozens of times—never make any explanations! As it is you're a fool, and when you start explaining something in Italian you turn into a triple fool!" he said to her at the end of a lengthy quarrel.

"Then it's up to you not to fall behind! It's not my fault, if I had any money—"

"Oh leave me in peace, for God's sake!" cried Mikhailov with tears in his voice; he stopped up his ears with his hands and went out into his own workroom, behind a partition, and locked the door behind him. Idiot! he said to himself; he sat down at the table and opening up a portfolio he immediately set to work with especial vigor at an unfinished drawing.

He never worked with greater vigor and success than when things were going badly for him, and especially when he had quarreled with his wife. Oh, if only I could escape somewhere! he thought, as he went on working. He was sketching the figure of a man in a fit of rage. He had done the sketch before, but was dissatisfied with it. No, the other one was better, he thought; where is it?

He went back to his wife; scowling, and without looking at her, he asked his eldest little girl where the paper was he had given them. The paper with the drawing he had cast aside was found, but it was dirty now and spotted with candle wax. He took it anyhow, put it on his table, and standing some distance away from it and screwing up his eyes, he began studying it. Suddenly he smiled and joyfully flung up his arms.

"That's it, that's it!" he cried, and taking a pencil he rapidly started drawing. A grease spot had given the man a new pose.

He copied this new pose, and suddenly he recalled the energetic face and prominent chin of a shopkeeper he had bought cigars from, and he gave his sketch just that face and chin.

He laughed aloud with joy. The figure had suddenly stopped being dead and contrived; it had come alive, and nothing further could be done to it. This figure was alive; it was clear and authoritatively defined. The sketch might be corrected to fit the demands of the pose, the legs might be, and even had to be placed farther apart, the position of the left hand completely altered, and the hair thrown back. But in making these corrections he did not change anything in the pose itself, but simply threw out what had been obscuring it. It was as though he were taking off the coverings because of which it had not all been quite visible; each new stroke simply disclosed more and more of the whole figure in all its energy and power, just as it had appeared to him because of the grease spot. He was carefully finishing the drawing when the visiting cards were brought to him.

"Coming right away!"

He went out to his wife. "Come now, Sasha, don't be angry!" he said to her, with a shy, tender smile. "It was your fault, and it was mine too, I'll fix everything." And making his peace with his wife he put on an olive-green overcoat with a velvet collar, and a hat, and went over to his studio. The successful drawing had already been forgotten. Now he felt happy and excited about the visit to his studio of these important Russians who had come to visit him in a carriage.

At the bottom of his heart there was only one opinion he had about the painting that was now standing on the easel —this was that no one else had ever painted a picture like it. He didn't think his painting was better than all of Raphael, but he knew that what he had wanted to express in this picture, and had expressed, had never been expressed by anyone before. He was absolutely sure of this, and had known it for a long time, from the moment he had begun painting it; but the opinions of others, whoever they were, had enormous importance for him nevertheless, and agitated him to the depths of his being. Any remark, however trivial, that showed that his critics saw even only a small part of what he himself saw in this picture, agitated him profoundly. He always attributed greater depth of judgment to his critics than he had himself, and always expected from them something he hadn't seen in his own painting. And it seemed to him that he often found this in the opinions of spectators.

With his swift stride he walked over to the entrance of his studio, and in spite of his agitation he was struck by the soft lighting on the figure of Anna, who was standing in the shad-

ow of the entrance listening to Golenishchev vehemently
telling her something, and at the same time obviously wanting
to look round at the painter as he approached. He himself was
unaware, as he walked over to them, of how he seized
on this impression and absorbed it, just as he had done with
the chin of the shopkeeper who sold him cigars, and hid it
away somewhere ready to be taken out when needed. The
visitors, who had been disillusioned in advance by what Golenishchev had told them of the painter, were disillusioned
still further by his appearance. Of medium height, stocky,
with a fidgety walk, Mikhailov, in his brown hat, olive-green
coat, and tight trousers, when wide ones had been in fashion
for a long time, made a disagreeable impression, especially
because of his commonplace broad face, which had a look of
shyness mingled with a desire to keep up his dignity.

"Do come in, please," he said, trying to put on an air of indifference; going into the hall he took a key from his pocket
and opened the door.

## XI

As he went into the studio the painter looked round at
his visitors once again, and mentally noted once again the expression on Vronsky's face, especially his jaw. In spite of the
unflagging activity of his artistic sensibility, which kept gathering material, in spite of his constantly increasing feeling of
agitation as the moment approached for his work to be crit-
icized, he rapidly and subtly formed an idea about these
three people on the basis of imperceptible signs. The other
fellow—Golenishchev—was a local Russian: Mikhailov did
not recall his name, where he had met him, or what he had
talked to him about. All he remembered was his face, just as
he recalled all the faces he had ever seen, but he also recalled
that it was one of those faces that in his mind had been
filed away in the enormous category of pseudoimportant,
meagerly expressive faces. The shock of hair and the very
open forehead lent some superficial significance to the face,
which had nothing but a petty, childish, restless expression
concentrated on the narrow bridge of the nose. To Mikhailov's
mind, Vronsky and Anna must be wealthy Russian aristocrats, who had no conception whatever of art, like all rich
Russians, but put on airs as art lovers and connoisseurs.
They've probably seen all the old things, and now they're

making a tour of the moderns, that German charlatan and that fool of an English pre-Raphaelite; they've only come to me so they can say they've seen everything, he thought. He was very familiar with the way dilettantes (the more intelligent they were the worse) examined the studios of contemporary painters with the sole aim of having the right to say that art had declined and that the more you looked at the moderns the more you saw how inimitable the old masters were. He expected all this; he saw it all in their faces, he saw it in the careless indifference with which they chatted with each other, looked at the lay figures and the busts, and casually strolled about waiting for him to uncover the picture. Nevertheless, as he turned over his studies, pulled up the blinds and took the sheet off the canvas, he felt intensely excited, especially since in spite of his having the idea that all rich Russian aristocrats must be beasts and nincompoops, he liked both Vronsky and, especially, Anna.

"There now, if you please," he said stepping to one side with his fidgety walk, and pointing to the picture. "This is *Pilate's Admonition, Matthew*, Chapter XXVII," he said, feeling his lips beginning to quiver with excitement. He stepped back, behind them.

During the few moments the visitors silently contemplated the painting, Mikhailov also looked at it, and looked at it with an indifferent, disengaged eye. In these few seconds he believed in advance that a lofty, extremely fair-minded judgment would be handed down by them, by just these visitors whom he had so despised a moment before. He forgot everything he had thought about his painting beforehand, during the three years it took him to paint it; he forgot all its merits, which had seemed to him incontestable—he saw the painting with their own indifferent, fresh, uninvolved eye, and saw no good in it at all. In the foreground he saw Pilate's irritated and Christ's serene face; behind them he saw the figures of Pilate's servants and of John, watching what was going on. Each one of these faces, that with so much searching, so many errors and corrections had grown up with its own special character, each face that had given him so much torment and joy, and all these faces, that had been shifted round so much so that it could all be seen as a whole, all the shades of color and tone that had been achieved at the cost of so much toil—all of it together, as he looked at it now with their eyes, seemed to him mere banality repeated a thousand times. The face that was dearest of all to him, that of Christ, the focus of the painting, that had put him into such raptures when he discovered it, was all lost for him as he looked at the picture with their eyes. What he saw was a well-painted (and for that matter not even that—now he clearly saw a multitude of shortcomings) repetition of those countless Christs by Titian, Raphael, Rubens, with the same soldiers and the same Pilate. It was all banal, impoverished, stale, and even badly painted—discordant and feeble. They would be quite right when they got off their hypocritically polite remarks in the artist's presence, only to pity and make fun of him when they were by themselves.

This silence, though it lasted no more than a moment, became too oppressive for him. To interrupt it and show that he was not agitated, he made an effort and turned to Golenishchev.

"I think I once had the pleasure of meeting you," he said to him, restlessly glancing back and forth between Anna and Vronsky, in order not to miss a single detail of their expressions.

"But of course! We met at Rossi's, you remember the evening that Italian girl recited, the new Rachel," Golenishchev began easily, taking his eyes off the picture without the slightest regret and turning to the painter. But on seeing that Mikhailov was expecting an opinion of the painting, he said: "Your painting has made a great deal of progress since the last time I saw it. And what makes an extraordinary impression on me now, like the last time, is the figure of Pilate. One understands him so well—a kindhearted, splendid fellow, but a bureaucrat to the bottom of his soul, who does not know what he's doing. But it seems to me that—"

The whole of Mikhailov's mobile face suddenly lit up: his eyes sparkled. He started to say something, but could not get it out because of his excitement, and pretended to be coughing. However low an opinion he had of Golenishchev's judgment of art, however trivial, though accurate, his remark about the fidelity of the expression on the face of Pilate the bureaucrat, however offensive it might have seemed to him that this triviality was the first remark made while nothing was said about the most important things, Mikhailov was enraptured by it. He had had the same thought about Pilate's expression as Golenishchev. That this opinion was no more than one of a million others that as Mikhailov knew very well would all have been true, did not detract from the significance he ascribed to what Golenishchev had said. He conceived a liking for Golenishchev because of this remark of his, and from a mood of depression he suddenly passed over to enthusiasm. His painting instantly came alive before him with all the inexpressible complexity of any living thing. Mikhailov tried once again to say that that was just as he had understood Pilate; but his lips refused to stop trembling; he could not get out a word. Vronsky and Anna also said something in the soft tone usually spoken in at picture expositions, partly not to hurt the artist's feelings and partly in order not to say something silly, which is so easy to do in discussing art. It seemed to Mikhailov that the picture had made an impression on them too. He went over to them.

"What a remarkable expression Christ has!" said Anna. She liked this expression best of all she saw; she felt it was the center of the painting, so that praising it would be particularly pleasing to the artist. "You can see he's sorry for Pilate."

This again was one of the million accurate observations that might have been made about the painting and about the figure of Christ. She said he was sorry for Pilate. Christ's face ought to have expressed pity too, since there was an expression of love in it, of other-worldly serenity, a readiness for death, and an awareness of the futility of words. It was a matter of course for Pilate to have the expression of a bureaucrat and for Christ to look pitying, since one was the incarnation of carnal and the other of spiritual life. All this and a great many other things flashed through Mikhailov's mind, and once again his face beamed with rapture.

"Yes, and how well that figure is done, how much atmosphere there is! You feel you could walk around it," said Golenishchev, evidently showing by this remark that he disapproved of the content and idea of the figure.

"Yes—amazing mastery!" said Vronsky. "How clearly those figures in the background stand out! Now there's technique!" he said, turning to Golenishchev, alluding to the argument they had had about Vronsky's despairing of acquiring technique.

"Yes, yes, amazing!" Golenischev and Anna chimed in. In spite of his state of excitement this remark about technique grated painfully on Mikhailov, and throwing an angry look at Vronsky he suddenly scowled. He had often heard the word technique and was absolutely unable to understand what was meant by it. He knew that what was meant by this word was a mechanical ability to paint and draw quite independently of the subject matter. He had often observed, as he did now in this compliment, that technique was contrasted with inner value, as though it were possible to paint something well that was bad. He knew a great deal of attention and caution was needed, in taking the wrappings off an idea, in order to take off all the wrappings without damaging the work of art itself; but as far as painting as an art was concerned there was no such thing as technique. If the things he saw could have been revealed to a small child or to his cook, they would also have been able to peel off the outer shell of what they saw, while the most experienced and skillful technical painter, by mere mechanical ability, could never paint anything if the boundaries of the subject matter had not been revealed to him beforehand. In addition he saw that if there was going to be any talk about technique then that was not what he could be praised for. In everything he painted or had painted he saw blinding defects that were due to the carelessness with which he had taken off the wrappings, and that he could now no longer correct without damaging the entire work. And in nearly all the figures and faces he still saw traces of inadequately removed wrappings that spoiled the picture.

"There is one thing that might be said, if you will allow me to make the remark—" Golenishchev began.

"Please do, I should be delighted," said Mikhailov with an insincere smile.

"It is this—what you have is a man-God, not a God-man. Though I know that's what you wanted to do."

"I couldn't paint a Christ I didn't have in my own soul," said Mikhailov morosely.

"Yes, but in that case, if you'll permit me to express my opinion . . . Your picture is so good it can't be hurt by anything I say, and besides it's only my own personal view— yours is different, the conception itself is different. Let's take Ivanov, for instance. To my mind, if Christ is reduced to the level of an historical personage it would have been better for Ivanov to have chosen some other historical theme —one that was fresh and untouched."

"But what if this is the greatest theme art can be confronted by?"

"If you looked for another theme you'd find it. But the point is that art cannot endure discussions and arguments. And in Ivanov's picture there is one question that emerges, for the believer and for the unbeliever—is this a God or not a God? And that destroys the unity of effect."

"But why? It seems to me that for educated people," said Mikhailov, "there really can't be any debate."

Golenishchev didn't agree with this; clinging to his first contention that art had to have a unity of effect, he refuted Mikhailov.

Mikhailov was upset, but didn't know what to say in defense of his own idea.

### XII

FOR some time Anna and Vronsky had been exchanging glances, regretting their friend's clever talkativeness; finally Vronsky, without waiting for their host, went on to another picture, a small one.

"But how charming! How charming! Marvelous! Charming!" he and Anna both cried with one voice.

What do they like so much? thought Mikhailov. He had already forgotten all about this picture, which he had painted three years before. He had forgotten all the sufferings and the ecstasies he had gone through because of this picture, when it had been the only thing that had obsessed him day and night without letup for several months—forgotten, as he always forgot his pictures once they were finished. He didn't even like looking at it; he had only put it out because he was expecting some Englishman who wanted to buy it.

"Oh that—that's only a study I did a long time ago."

"Oh, very fine!" said Golenishchev, who also, with obvious sincerity, yielded to the charm of the picture.

Two boys, in the shade of a willow, were angling. One of them, the older, had just cast his rod and was carefully drawing the float out from behind a bush, completely absorbed by what he was doing; the younger was lying on the grass, leaning on his elbows with his fair tousled head in his hands and looking into the water with dreamy blue eyes. What was he thinking about?

Their enthusiasm over this picture stirred up Mikhailov's previous excitement, but he feared and disliked this idle feeling about the past, and so, though their praise made him very happy, he tried to draw his visitors' attention to a third picture.

But Vronsky asked whether the picture was for sale. In

Mikhailov's excitement over his visitors any talk about money was extremely unpleasant.

"It's been put out to be sold," he said scowling darkly.

When the visitors had left Mikhailov sat down in front of the painting of Christ and Pilate and in his mind went over everything that had been said, or if not said, had been implied by these visitors. The strange thing was that what had had such weight for him when they had been there and he had looked at everything from their point of view suddenly lost all its significance for him. He began to look at his painting with his own full artistic perception, and reached that state of confidence in the perfection, and consequently the importance of his painting that was essential to him for the all-excluding concentration that was the only way he could work.

Now the foreshortening of Christ's foot, though, was wrong. He picked up his palette and set to work. As he corrected the foot he kept glancing at the figure of John in the background, which his visitors had not noticed but which he knew to be the height of perfection. When he finished the foot he was about to start in on this figure, but he felt too agitated. He couldn't work both when he was indifferent and when he was too excited, and saw everything too clearly. There was only one stage in this transition from indifference to inspiration when work was possible, and today he was too excited. He was about to cover the picture, but, holding the sheet in his hand and smiling blissfully, he paused to take a long look at the figure of John. Regretfully tearing himself away at last, he lowered the sheet and went home, tired but happy.

On their way home Vronsky, Anna, and Golenishchev were particularly animated and cheerful. They talked about Mikhailov and his pictures. The word "talent," by which they meant an inborn, almost physical ability, independent of mind or heart, and which they used to refer to everything experienced by an artist, cropped up in their conversation with particular frequency, since it was indispensable for them in order to be able to refer to things they had no conception of but wanted to talk about. They said it was impossible to deny that he had talent, but that his talent was incapable of developing because of his deficient education—the common misfortune of our Russian artists. But the picture of the boys angling had impressed itself on their memories, and they came back to it again and again.

"What charm it had! How well he managed it, and how simply! He doesn't understand himself how good it is. Yes, we mustn't miss this chance of buying it," said Vronsky.

XIII

Mikhailov sold Vronsky the picture and agreed to do Anna's portrait; on the appointed day he arrived and began working.

After the fifth sitting the portrait struck everyone, especially Vronsky, not only by its likeness but by its peculiar beauty. It was strange how Mikhailov had been able to discover that peculiar beauty of hers. One must have known and loved her as I did in order to find just that sweetest spiritual expression of hers, thought Vronsky, though it was only because of this portrait that he himself had learned to know this "sweetest spiritual expression of hers." But this expression was so true it seemed to him and others that they had known it for a long time.

"I struggled for so long and never got anything done," he said about the portrait he had been painting himself, "and he just took a look and painted it! There's technique for you."

"That will come," said Golenishchev comfortingly; he thought Vronsky had not only talent but above all an education that gave him a lofty outlook on art. Golenishchev's conviction that Vronsky had talent was strengthened still further by his need for Vronsky's sympathy and praise for his own articles and ideas; he felt that praise and support ought to be reciprocal.

In a strange house, and especially in Vronsky's *palazzo*, Mikhailov was completely different from the way he was in his own studio. He was deferential in a hostile way, as though afraid of any intimacy with people he had no respect for. He addressed Vronsky as "Your Excellency," and in spite of Anna's and Vronsky's invitations would never stay to dinner; he never came except for sittings. Anna was friendlier to him than to others and was grateful for her portrait. Vronsky was more than polite to him, and was obviously interested in his opinion of his own picture. Golenishchev didn't miss a chance of passing on to Mikhailov the right ideas about art. But Mikhailov remained uniformly cool to them all. Anna could see by his expression that he liked looking at her; but he avoided any conversation with her. Whenever Vronsky started talking about his painting he fell into a stubborn silence; he was just as stubbornly silent when he was shown Vronsky's own picture, and obviously found Golenishchev's discourses tedious and never responded to them.

Altogether Mikhailov's reserved and disagreeable, seemingly hostile manner, did not please them at all when they had come to know him better. They were glad when the sittings were over; they had a beautiful portrait in their hands, and he had stopped coming.

Golenishchev was the first to express the idea they all had in their minds, that is, that Mikhailov was simply envious of Vronsky.

"Perhaps not envy exactly, because there's no doubt he has *talent*, but it irritates him that someone connected with the Court, who's rich, and is a Count into the bargain—after all they hate all that—with no particular effort does the same, if not better, than he, who's devoted his whole life to it. The main thing is cultivation, which is what he lacks."

Vronsky defended Mikhailov, but at the bottom of his heart he believed it, since to his mind anyone from that other, lower world was bound to envy him.

Anna's portrait—the same thing painted from nature by both of them—ought to have shown Vronsky the difference between himself and Mikhailov, but he didn't see it. After Mikhailov had finished his painting, Vronsky simply decided that his own was now superfluous. But he went on with his medieval painting, which he, as well as Golenishchev, and Anna too, thought first rate, since it looked far more like celebrated paintings than Mikhailov's.

Mikhailov meanwhile, though Anna's portrait had absorbed him a great deal, was even happier than they when the sittings were over and he no longer had to listen to Golenishchev's disquisitions on art and could forget about Vronsky's painting. He realized that Vronsky couldn't be forbidden to divert himself by painting; he realized that Vronsky, like all dilettantes, had a perfect right to paint whatever he pleased, but Mikhailov found it irritating. A man cannot be prevented from making himself a large wax doll and kissing it. But if the man with the doll were to come and sit in front of someone in love and begin caressing his doll like the lover caressing his beloved, the lover would find it distasteful. Mikhailov had this same feeling of distaste when he saw Vronsky's painting; he found it absurd, irritating, pathetic, and offensive.

Vronsky's interest in painting and the Middle Ages didn't

last long. He had enough artistic taste to be unable to finish his picture. It came to a stop. He had a confused feeling that its shortcomings, which at first were not very noticeable, would be striking if he were to go on. The same thing happened with him as with Golenishchev, who felt that he had nothing to say, and who kept constantly deceiving himself by saying his ideas had not yet ripened, that he was developing them and preparing material. But Golenishchev was embittered by this and tormented, while Vronsky was incapable of deceiving and tormenting himself, and above all could not become embittered. With his characteristic decisiveness, without giving any explanations or apologies, he left off painting.

But without this occupation his life and Anna's—who was surprised by his disenchantment—seemed to him so boring in this Italian town, the *palazzo* suddenly became so unmistakably old and dirty, the spots on the curtains, the cracks in the floor, the stuccoes cracking off the cornices, looked so disagreeably familiar, and Golenishchev, who never varied, became so boring, just as an Italian professor and a German traveler did, that a change in their lives had to be made. They decided to go back to Russia, to the countryside. In Petersburg, Vronsky intended to separate his property from his brother's, while Anna could see her son. They intended to spend the summer on Vronsky's large family estate.

## XIV

LEVIN had been married three months. He was happy, but not at all in the same way as he had expected. At every step he found himself disillusioned in his former dreams while also discovering new, unexpected enchantments. Levin was happy, but on entering into family life he saw at every step that it was not at all what he had imagined. At every step he felt as a man might feel who, after admiring the smooth, cheerful motion of a boat on the water, actually gets into the boat himself. He saw that apart from having to sit steadily in the boat without rocking, he also had to keep in mind, without forgetting for a moment where he was going, that there was water beneath his feet, that he had to row, that his unaccustomed hands hurt, and that it was easy only when you looked at it, but that doing it, though it made you very happy, was very hard.

When he had been a bachelor, seeing the married life of

others, their petty cares, quarrels, jealousy, he had merely smiled to himself contemptuously. Not only was he convinced that in his own married life in the future there could be nothing of the sort, but it seemed to him that even all the outward forms were bound to be totally unlike the life of others. And suddenly, instead of that, his life with his wife not only did not shape itself in any special way, but on the contrary, it was all made up of the same petty trifles that he had despised so much before, but that now took on against his will an extraordinary and incontestable importance. And he saw that the arrangement of all these trifles was not at all so easy as it had seemed to him before. In spite of Levin's thinking that he had the most precise conceptions of family life, like all men he involuntarily imagined family life to be nothing but the enjoyment of love-making, which nothing ought to be allowed to hinder, and which petty cares ought not to distract you from. As he understood it, what he ought to do was his own work, then rest from it in the happiness of love. What she ought to do was be loved, and that was all. But like all men he forgot that she had to work too. And he was astounded at how she, his poetical, enchanting Kitty, not only in the first few weeks, but in the very first days of their married life was able to think, remember, and fuss about tablecloths, furniture, mattresses for the guest rooms, a tray, the cook, the dinner, and so forth. Even during their engagement he had been struck by the definiteness with which she had refused to go abroad and decided to come to the country, as though she knew something that had to be done and could think about something else beside their love. This had wounded him then, and now too her petty cares and worries wounded him often. But he saw this was necessary for her; and since he loved her, though he didn't understand what it was all for and laughed at all these cares, he could not help admiring her. He laughed at the way she arranged the furniture brought from Moscow, redid his room and her own, hung the curtains, prepared rooms for future visitors, for Dolly, arranged a room for her new maid, gave orders about dinner to the old cook, got into a collision with Miss Agatha and took the storekeeping away from her. He saw the old cook smile at her admiringly and listen to her inexperienced, impossible orders; he saw Miss Agatha shake her head thoughtfully and tenderly at the new arrangements of the young mistress in the storeroom, saw that Kitty was particularly charming when she came to him half-laughing, half-crying to say that her maid Masha was used to considering her a young miss and because of that no one would obey her. This seemed charming to him, but strange; he thought things would have been better without all that.

He was unaware of the feeling of change she was going through after her life at home, when she had sometimes felt like having cabbage with *kvas*, or sweets, and was not allowed to have either, while now she could order whatever she wanted, buy heaps of sweets, spend as much money as she wanted to and order as many puddings as she liked.

Now she looked forward with joy to Dolly's arrival with the children, especially since she would be ordering each child's favorite pudding, while Dolly would appreciate all the new arrangements she had made. She herself had no idea of how it was or why, but managing the house attracted her irresistibly. Instinctively sensing the approach of spring and knowing there would also be wet weather, she built her nest as best she could, hastening to build it while simultaneously learning how to.

This preoccupation of Kitty's with trifles, so contrary to Levin's early ideal of lofty happiness, was one disenchantment; yet this sweet preoccupation, the sense of which he could not understand but could not help liking, was one of his new enchantments.

Another disenchantment, and enchantment, was their quarreling. Levin had never been able to imagine that between him and his wife there could be anything but a tender, respectful, and loving relationship; and suddenly, even at the very beginning, they had a quarrel—she said he didn't love her and loved only himself, burst into tears and wrung her hands.

This first quarrel of theirs came about because Levin had ridden over to a new farm and got back half an hour late; he had tried to take a short cut and lost his way. He was riding home thinking only of her, of her love, of his own happiness and the nearer he approached the warmer grew his tenderness for her. He ran into the room with the same feeling, even more powerful, as when he had gone to the Shcherbatskys' to propose. Suddenly he was met by a morose expression he had never seen on her face before. He tried to kiss her; she thrust him away.

"What's the matter?"

"*You* look cheerful—" she began, trying to say something calm and venomous.

But the moment she opened her mouth reproachful words of senseless jealousy, everything that had tormented her during the half-hour she had spent sitting motionlessly at the window, burst out of her. It was only now for the first time that he clearly understood what he had been unable to when he had led her out of the church after the wedding. He understood that she was not only close to him but that now he no longer knew where she ended and he began. He realized this because of the agonizing feeling of cleavage he now underwent. At first he felt offended, but that same second he felt that he could not be offended by her, since she was himself. During this first moment he had a feeling such as a man might have when after suddenly receiving a powerful blow from behind, he turns around angrily with a desire for revenge to find his attacker, and discovers that he has unwittingly struck himself, that there is no one to get angry with and that he must endure the pain and soothe it.

He never felt this afterward with such force, but when it first happened he could not recover for a long time. A natural feeling would have required him to defend himself and demonstrate to her that she was at fault; but demonstrating her fault to her meant irritating her still more and widening the breach which was the cause of all the trouble. One feeling, based on habit, impelled him to shift the blame from himself to her; another feeling, more powerful, impelled him to smooth the breach over quickly, as quickly as possible, without giving it a chance to get wider. It was painful to remain under such an unfair accusation, but it was even worse to give her pain by defending himself. Like a man half-asleep and wracked with pain he wanted to tear out and cast away the aching part, and on recovering himself he felt that the aching part was—himself. All he could do was try to relieve the ache and endure it, which is what he did.

They made it up. Realizing she had been in the wrong, though without admitting it, she became more tender toward him, and they experienced a new and redoubled happiness in their love. But this did not prevent these collisions from repeating themselves, for that matter extremely often and for the most unexpected and trivial reasons. These collisions came about often both because they still did not realize that they were important to each other, and because throughout this whole first period they were both often in a bad mood. When one was in a good and the other in a bad mood, peace was not broken; but if they both happened to be in bad tempers, these collisions would come about for reasons that were so incomprehensibly trivial that later they were quite unable to recall what they had been quarreling about. When they were both in good tempers, to be sure, their life was doubly happy, but nevertheless this first period was painful for them.

Throughout this first period there was a peculiar feeling of intense strain, as though the chain that bound them together were being tugged first from one side then the other. Altogether this honeymoon—the month after the wedding which Levin had expected so much from, according to tradition—was not only no honeymoon, but remained in the memories of them both as the most painful and humiliating period of their lives. They both did their best in later life to erase from their memories all the ugly, shameful incidents of this unhealthy period, when both of them had rarely been in a normal frame of mind, had rarely been themselves.

It was not until the third month of their marriage, after they came back from Moscow, where they had gone for a month, that their life began to run more smoothly.

## xv

THEY had only just come back from Moscow and were delighted with their solitude. He was sitting in his study writing at his desk. She was doing embroidery, in the dark lilac dress that she had worn during the first days of marriage and had put on again that day, and that was particularly memorable and precious to him, as she sat on the sofa, the same old-fashioned leather-covered sofa that had stood forever in this study of Levin's father and grandfather. All the while, as he sat and wrote, he was happily conscious of her presence. His preoccupations, both with farming and with his book, which was to lay the foundations of a new agriculture, had not been abandoned; but just as these activities and ideas had seemed to him petty and trivial in comparison with the gloom that enveloped his whole life, so they seemed unimportant and trivial now in comparison with the bright and radiant happiness of the life that lay before him. He went on with what he had been doing, but now he felt that the focal point of his attention had shifted to something else, and that because of this he saw his work completely differently and much more clearly. Beforehand this work of his had been a way of escaping his life; beforehand he had felt that without this work his life would be too gloomy, while now these activities were essential if his life was not to be too monotonously bright. When he set to work on his book again, and read over what he had written, he was delighted to find that the work was worth doing. It was a novel and useful project. Many of his former ideas seemed to him superfluous and extreme, but as he revived the whole thing once more in his mind many of the gaps became clear.

He was now writing a new chapter on the reasons why Russian agriculture was unprofitable. He argued that the poverty of Russia had not come about only because of the unfair distribution of landed property and a fallacious policy, but had lately been contributed to by the abnormal transplanting to Russia of a foreign civilization, especially the means of communication, the railroads. This entailed urban centralization and a growth of luxury, the consequent development of factories at the expense of agriculture, and factory industry, credit, and its accompaniment—stock market speculation. It seemed to him that when a country's wealth developed normally all these phenomena would make their appearance only after a substantial amount of labor had been applied to agriculture, when it had been established along the right lines, or at any rate along definite lines; that a country's wealth ought to grow evenly, more especially in such a way that other branches of the national wealth should not outstrip agriculture; that a certain state of agriculture also ought to have corresponding means of communication, and that in view of the wrong use of land in Russia the railroads, which had been called into existence not by economic but by political necessity, were premature, and that instead of promoting agriculture as they had been expected to, they had outstripped agriculture, and by stimulating the growth of industry and credit had halted it, and that because of all this, just as the one-sided and premature development of one organ in an animal would hinder its development as a whole, so the system of credit, the means of communication, and the forced growth of industry, which were certainly indispensable in Europe, where the time was ripe for them, had simply harmed the growth of Russia's national wealth by thrusting aside the chief current question, the organization of agriculture.

Meanwhile, as he busied himself with what he was writing, Kitty was thinking about the unnatural attention he had paid young Prince Charsky, who had been flirting with her very tactlessly the day before they had left Moscow. So he's jealous! she thought; heavens, how sweet and silly he is! He, jealous of me! If he only knew that the lot of them don't mean any more to me than Peter the cook, she thought, looking at the nape of his red neck with a feeling of proprietorship that was strange to herself. It's a pity to tear him away from his work (though he'll have time enough!) but I must look at his face; will he feel me looking at him? I want him to turn around—now, turn round! and she opened her eyes wider in an attempt to heighten the effect of her look.

"Yes, they take away all the sap and give a false sheen," he muttered, pausing; then, feeling her looking at him and smiling, he turned round.

"Well?" he asked, smiling and getting up.

He turned round! she thought. "Nothing—I just wanted you to turn round," she said, looking at him and trying to guess whether he was annoyed at being interrupted or not.

"Isn't it wonderful, just the two of us together! That is, for me," he said, going over to her with a beaming smile of happiness.

"It's wonderful for me too! I'm never going away anywhere, especially not Moscow."

"And what were you thinking about?"

"I? I was thinking that— No, no! Go ahead and write, don't get distracted," she said, puckering up her lips. "Besides, I have to cut out these little holes here, d'you see?"

She took up her scissors and started cutting.

"No, tell me—what was it?" he said, sitting down beside her and watching the circular motion of the tiny scissors.

"What was I thinking about? I was thinking about Moscow . . . about the nape of your neck . . ."

"But why should I be just the one to have so much happiness? It's unnatural. It's too good," he said, kissing her hand.

"To me it's just the opposite—the better it is the more natural it is too."

"And your hair comes to a point behind," he said, carefully turning her head round.

"A point?"

"D'you see—right here . . ."

"No, no, we have important work to do!"

But there was no longer any going on with this important work; they jumped apart guiltily when Kuzma came in to announce that tea was served.

"Have they come from town?" Levin asked Kuzma.

"They've just come, they're unpacking."

"Come along as quick as you can then," she said to him, as she left the study. "Or else I'll read the letters without you. Then we can have a duet!"

When he was left alone, after putting away his notebooks in the new portfolio she had bought for him, he began washing his hands in the new washstand with the elegant new accessories that had also appeared through her doing. Levin smiled at his own thoughts and shook his head at them disapprovingly; a feeling something like remorse tormented him. There was something contemptible, effete, Capuan, as he called it, in the way he was living now.

It's no good living this way, he thought. It'll soon be three months now and I've done practically nothing. I started doing some serious work today for almost the first time, and what did it amount to? The moment I started I stopped. Even my usual activities—I've almost abandoned those too. The farm—I hardly ever take a look at it. Sometimes I'm sorry to leave her alone, I can see she's bored. And I used to think before marriage that life could be lived just anyhow, it didn't count, while real life only began after getting married. And now it'll soon be three months of it and I've never spent my time so idly and uselessly. No—it's impossible, I'll have to start on something! Of course it's not her fault; there's nothing to reproach her with. I ought to have been more decisive myself, made a point of my masculine independence. As it is I'm likely to get used to these bad habits myself and teach them to her as well . . . Of course it's not her fault, he said to himself.

But it's difficult for a discontented man not to reproach someone else, whoever is closest to him, for his own discontent. A vague notion came into Levin's head: it was not that she herself was to blame for anything (she could not be that), what was to blame, though, was her upbringing, which had been too superficial and frivolous (that fool Charsky! I know she wanted to stop him, but she didn't know how). Yes, aside from her interest in the house (which she had), aside from her interest in her clothes, and in embroidery, she has no serious interests at all. She's not interested in my own business, in the farming, or the peasants, or in music, which she knows a good deal about, or in reading. She does nothing and is completely satisfied!

At heart Levin condemned this; he still did not realize that she was preparing for that period of activity that was bound to arrive for her, when she would be simultaneously her husband's wife and mistress of a house, and bear, nurse, and bring up their children. It did not occur to him that she knew this instinctively and as she prepared herself for this fearful task she did not reproach herself for the carefree moments of happy love that she was enjoying now as she merrily built her future nest.

XVI

WHEN Levin went upstairs Kitty was sitting beside the new silver samovar with the new tea service in front of her and, having made old Miss Agatha sit at a little table with a cup of tea she had poured for her, was reading a letter from Dolly, with whom she was in regular and frequent correspondence.

"You see, your lady has ordered me to sit with her," said Miss Agatha, with a friendly smile at Kitty.

In these words of Miss Agatha's Levin read the dénouement of the drama that had been going on lately between her and Kitty. He saw that in spite of all the grief the new mistress had inflicted on Miss Agatha by taking away from her the reins of management, Kitty had conquered her nevertheless and forced her to love her.

"There, I've gone and opened your letter," said Kitty, handing him an illiterate sheet. "It's from that woman, I think, your brother's—" she said. "I didn't read it. And this is from home, and from Dolly. Just imagine—Dolly took Grisha and Tanya to a children's ball at the Sarmatskys'! Tanya went as a marquise."

But Levin wasn't listening to her; blushing, he took the letter, which was from Masha, his brother Nicholas's former mistress, and began reading it. This was her second letter. In the first she had written that his brother had sent her away for no reason, and went on to add, with touching naïveté, that though she was living in poverty once again she did not want anything and was not asking for anything, but was simply tormented by the thought that without her Nicholas would succumb because of weak health, and she was asking his brother to look after him. Now she was writing him this second letter. She had found Nicholas and joined him again in Moscow, and was going together with him to a town in the provinces where he had gotten a position in government service. Then he had had a quarrel with his department head and had gone back to Moscow, but had fallen so ill on the way that it was hardly likely he would ever get up again. She wrote, "He keeps on speaking of you, and there's no more money left either."

"Read this, Dolly says something about you," Kitty began with a smile, but she suddenly stopped when she noticed the changed expression on Levin's face.

"What is it? What's the matter?"

"She says my brother Nicholas is dying. I'm going to him."

Kitty's expression changed instantly. Thoughts about Tanya as a marquise, about Dolly—they all vanished.

"When are you leaving?" she said.

"Tomorrow."

"I'll go along, can I?" she said.

"Kitty! What does that mean?" he said reproachfully.

"What d'you mean—what?" she said, hurt at his apparent unwillingness, and irritation with her suggestion. "Why shouldn't I go along? I won't get in your way. I'll—"

"I'm going because my brother's dying," said Levin. "Why should you—"

"Why? For the same reason as you."

And at a time that's so important for me all she can think of is that she'll be bored by herself, Levin thought. This subterfuge in something so important made him angry.

"It's out of the question," he said sternly.

Miss Agatha, seeing a quarrel in the offing, quietly put her cup down and went out. Kitty did not even notice her. The tone in which her husband had said these last words irritated her particularly because it was obvious that he didn't believe what she had said.

"And I tell you that if you go I'm absolutely going along too," she said hastily and angrily. "Why is it out of the question? Why d'you say it's out of the question?"

"Because it means going God knows where, and by what roads, what inns! You'd be a burden on me," said Levin, trying to keep cool.

"Not in the least. I don't need anything. I can go anywhere you can—"

"Well then, if only because that woman's there, and you can't associate with her."

"I don't know anything about who's there or what and I don't care. All I know is that my husband's brother is dying and my husband's going to him, and I'm going along with him so that—"

"Kitty! Don't be angry! But you must remember, this is such an important matter that it hurts me to think you're mixing it up with a feeling of weakness, your dislike of being by yourself. Well, if it's boring to be by yourself you can go to Moscow."

"There—you *always* think I have bad, vile thoughts," she began, with tears of resentment and anger. "I'm all right, I'm not weak or anything—I just feel it's my duty to be with my husband in his grief, but you just want to hurt me on purpose, you refuse to understand on purpose—"

"No—this is horrible! It's being a sort of slave!" Levin cried out, getting up; he was incapable of restraining his fury any further. But at this same moment he felt that he was striking himself.

"Then why did you get married? You might have been free. Then why, since you regret it all?" she began; then she jumped up and ran into the drawing room.

When he came in after her she was sobbing.

He began speaking, trying to find words that might not so much dissuade her as simply pacify her. But she wouldn't listen to him and didn't agree with anything he said. He stooped over and took her hand, which resisted. He kissed her hand, kissed her hair, then kissed her hand again—she kept silent. But when he took her face in both his hands and said, "Kitty!" she suddenly recovered, cried a little more, and then they made it up.

It was decided they would leave the next day together. Levin told Kitty he believed she was going only in order to be of some use and agreed there was nothing improper about Masha's presence at his brother's; but at the bottom of his heart he went off dissatisfied with her and with himself. He was dissatisfied with her because she had been unable to take it on herself to let him go when it was necessary for him to (how strange it was for him to think that he, who such a short while before hadn't dared believe in the joy of her being able to love him, felt unhappy now because she loved him too much!) and dissatisfied with himself for not having kept firm. He was even more persuaded at the bottom of his heart that she ought to have nothing to do with the woman who was with his brother, and he kept thinking with horror of all the encounters that might take place. The mere thought that his wife, his Kitty, was going to be in the same room with a streetwalker made him shudder with horror and revulsion.

## XVII

THE hotel in the provincial town where Nicholas Levin was lying ill was one of those provincial hotels that are set up in accordance with the latest models of perfection, with the finest intentions of cleanliness, comfort, and even elegance, but which because of the people who use them change with extraordinary swiftness into filthy public houses with pretensions to modern improvements, and because of this very pretentiousness turn into something even worse than old-fashioned inns that are merely filthy. This hotel had already passed over into this state; the soldier in a dirty uniform smoking a cigarette at the entrance, who was passing himself off as a hall porter, the dismal and unpleasant ornamental iron staircase, the free-and-easy waiter in a filthy frockcoat, the common room with a dusty bouquet of wax flowers decorating the table, and the filth, dust, and sloppiness everywhere, together with a sort of modern, up-to-date, self-satisfied railway bustle about the hotel—everything made the most painful impression on the Levins after their fresh home life, especially because the false impression made by the hotel was completely out of harmony with what was awaiting them.

As usual, after they were asked how much they wanted to pay for rooms it turned out that there was not a single good room to be had: one good room was occupied by a railroad inspector, another by a lawyer from Moscow, and a third by Princess Astafyev from the country. All that was left was one dirty room; though an adjoining one was promised them by evening. Annoyed with Kitty because what he had expected had happened, which was just that at the moment of arrival, at a time when his heart was overwhelmed with emotion at the thought of his brother's condition, he had to be concerned about her instead of instantly running to his brother's side, Levin led her to the room.

"Go along now, go!" she said, looking at him with a shy, guilty expression.

He went out without a word, and in front of the door
ran across Masha, who had found out about his arrival but
didn't dare come inside. She was just as she had been when
he had seen her in Moscow; the same woolen dress with no
cuffs or collar and the same good-naturedly dull pock-marked
face, which had grown somewhat broader.

"Well? How is he?"

"He's very bad. He can't get up. He keeps expecting you.
He . . . You . . . Are you with your wife?"

At first Levin didn't understand what she was embarrassed
about, but she explained it at once.

"I'll go out, down to the kitchen," she got out. "He'll be
happy. He's heard; he knows and remembers her from
abroad."

Levin realized she meant Kitty; he didn't know what to
say in reply.

"Come along then, come along!" he said.

But the moment he started moving, the door of his room
opened and Kitty looked out. Levin blushed both for shame
and because of his annoyance with Kitty for having put both
herself and him in this painful position; but Masha blushed
even more. She shrank together into herself and blushed to
the point of tears; seizing the ends of her kerchief, she twisted
them with her red fingers, not knowing what to say or do.

In the first instant Levin saw an expression of avid curiosity
in Kitty's eyes as she looked at this woman, so dreadful and
incomprehensible to her, but this lasted only an instant.

"Well, how is he? How is he?" she said, turning first to her
husband then to Masha.

"But we can't go on chattering in the corridor!" said
Levin, looking around angrily at a man, evidently on business
of his own, who was walking jauntily along the corridor.

"Come in then," said Kitty, turning to Masha, who had
recovered herself, but when she saw Levin's frightened face
she said, "or go along, go on, and send for me," and went
back into her room. Levin went to his brother.

He had not in the least expected what he saw and felt at
his brother's side. He had expected to find the same state of
self-delusion that he had heard was so frequent among
consumptives, and that had made such a powerful impression
on him during his brother's visit in the autumn. He had
expected to find the physical signs of approaching death more
clear-cut, a greater weakness and a greater emaciation, but
still almost the same condition. He had expected that he him-

self would have the same feeling of grief at the loss of a beloved brother and of horror at death, as he had had at that time, simply to a greater degree. He had prepared himself for this; but what he found was quite different.

In a filthy little room, its painted panels splattered with spittle and stifling with the stench of impurities, with a thin partition behind which the sound of voices could be heard, lay a body covered with a blanket, on a bed pushed away from the wall. One arm of this body was lying on top of the blanket; an enormous hand, like a rake, was fastened in some mysterious way to a long thin spindle of an arm that was smooth from the beginning to the middle. The head was lying sideways on the pillow. Levin could see the sparse, damp hairs on the temples and the drawn, transparent-looking forehead.

It's not possible that this dreadful body is my brother Nicholas, thought Levin. But he came closer, saw the face, and there could be no further doubt. In spite of the frightful changes in the face all Levin had to do was look into the living eyes raised toward the newcomer, notice the slight movement of the mouth beneath the clammy mustache, for him to grasp the dreadful truth—this dead body was his living brother.

The glittering eyes looked at him with stern reproach as he came in. This look instantly re-established a living relationship between living people. Levin instantly felt the reproach in this look that was fixed on him, and remorse for his own happiness.

When Levin took him by the hand Nicholas smiled. It was a feeble smile, scarcely perceptible, but the stern expression of the eyes did not change in spite of it.

"You didn't expect to find me this way," Nicholas got out with difficulty.

"Yes . . . No . . ." said Levin, stumbling over his words. "How is it you didn't let me know before, I mean when I was getting married? I asked all over."

It was necessary to say something, in order not to be silent, but he didn't know what to say, especially since Nicholas said nothing in reply and simply kept looking without lowering his eyes, manifestly trying to penetrate to the meaning of each word. Levin told him his wife had come with him. Nicholas expressed satisfaction, but said he was afraid to frighten her with his condition. A silence followed. Suddenly Nicholas stirred and began saying something. By his expression Levin expected something particularly important and significant, but Nicholas started speaking about his health. He found fault with the doctor; he regretted not having any famous Moscow specialist, and Levin realized he still kept hoping.

Levin took advantage of the first moment of silence to get up; he wanted to rid himself if only for a moment of his agonizing feeling, and said he was going out to fetch his wife.

"All right then, and I'll have them clean up here. It's dirty, I suppose it smells. Masha! Tidy things up here!" the sick man said with difficulty. "And as soon as you've tidied up you can get out," he added, glancing at his brother questioningly.

Levin said nothing. Once he got out into the corridor he stopped. He had said he was going to fetch his wife, but now that he had weighed his own feeling he decided that on the contrary he would do his best to dissuade her from coming to see the sick man. Why should she go through the same torment as I? he thought.

"Well? How is he?" Kitty asked him, with a frightened look.

"Oh, it's frightful, frightful! Why did you have to come?" said Levin.

Kitty was silent for a few seconds, looking at him timidly and pathetically; then she went over to him and took hold of his elbow with both hands.

"Kostya! Take me to him, it'll be easier if we bear it together. Take me there, please, just take me there, then go out," she began. "You must understand that it's much more painful for me to see you without seeing him. If I'm there perhaps I can be of some use to you and to him. Let me, please!" she implored him as though her life's happiness depended on it.

Levin had to agree; having recovered and having by now completely forgotten all about Masha, he went back to his brother again together with Kitty.

Stepping softly and glancing over at her husband repeatedly, showing him her courageous and compassionate face, she went into the sick man's room, and turning around without haste she noiselessly closed the door. She went over to the bedside swiftly and silently, and going round so that he didn't have to turn his head she immediately took hold of his enormous skeleton of a hand in her own fresh young one, pressed it, and with that gentle animation, compassionate and unoffending, that only women have, she began speaking to him.

"I remember you from Soden, though we never met," she said. "You never imagined I was going to be your sister."

"You wouldn't have recognized me, would you?" he said, with the smile that had lit up his face at her entrance.

"Oh yes I would. How good of you it was to let us know! Not a day passed by without Kostya's mentioning you and being anxious."

But the sick man's animation did not last long.

She hadn't finished speaking before the stern reproachful look of envy the dying feel for the living settled on his face once again.

"I'm afraid you're not entirely comfortable here," she said, turning away from his insistent gaze and looking round the room. "We'll have to ask for another room," she said to Levin, "besides we have to be closer."

## XVIII

LEVIN could not look at his brother calmly; he couldn't be natural or tranquil in his presence. When he came into the sick man's room his eyes and his attention clouded over unconsciously; and he couldn't see or distinguish between the details of his brother's condition. He smelled the frightful stench, saw the filth and disorder, his agonizing posture, heard his groans, and felt it was impossible to help. It never even entered his mind to think of analyzing all the details of the sick man's condition, to think of how this body of his was lying there, under the blanket, how those emaciated legs, loins, and spine were doubled up, or whether it was possible somehow to arrange them better, to do something that would make it at least less difficult, if no easier. A cold shiver ran along his spine at the mere thought of all these details. He was unshakably convinced there was nothing that could be done either to prolong his life or to ease his sufferings. But this awareness that he regarded help of any kind as out of the question was felt by the sick man and irritated him. This made things still more painful for Levin. It was painful for him to be in the sick man's room, and still worse not to be. Under various pretexts he kept going out and coming in again, incapable of staying by himself.

But Kitty's thoughts, feelings, and actions were quite different. When she saw the sick man she pitied him, and in her womanly soul this pity did not produce anything like the feeling of horror and loathing it did in Levin, but a need to act, to learn all about the details of his condition and to help him. Since she didn't have the slightest doubt that it was her duty to help him, she also had no doubt of its being possible; so she instantly set to work. The same details the mere thought of which filled her husband with horror at once arrested her attention. She sent for the doctor, sent to the drugstore, bade the maid who had come with her, as well as Masha, to sweep, dust, and scrub, started washing and rinsing some things herself, and spread something under the blanket. On her orders things were brought in and taken out of the sickroom. She herself went back and forth several times to their own room, without being noticed by any of the people she came across, and brought back with her sheets, pillowcases, towels, and shirts.

The waiter, who was busy serving a meal to some engineers in the common room, answered her call several times with an angry look on his face; he could not help carrying out her orders, she gave them with such endearing insistence that there was no getting away from her. Though Levin didn't approve of any of this, he didn't believe it would do the sick man any good, and what he was afraid of most of all was that Nicholas might get angry. But the sick man, though apparently indifferent to it all, didn't get angry, but was simply ashamed, altogether as though he were interested in what she was doing for him. When he came back from the doctor's, where Kitty had sent him, Levin opened the door and saw the sick man just at the moment when his nightshirt was being changed, on Kitty's orders. The long white skeleton back with the enormous prominent shoulder blades, and ribs and vertebrae sticking out, was bare, and Masha and the waiter together had gotten one of the sleeves of the shirt tangled up and couldn't get the long dangling arm into it. Kitty, hastily shutting the door behind Levin, didn't look in that direction, but the sick man moaned and she quickly went over to him.

"Quickly now!" she said.

"Now don't come over here," said the sick man angrily. "I myself can—"

"What did you say?" Masha broke in.

But Kitty had overheard him and realized he felt embarrassed and uncomfortable at being undressed in front of her.

"I won't look, I won't look!" she said, helping his arm in.

"Masha, you go round the other side and put it right," she added.

"Please go to my room," she said to Levin, "there's a little bottle in my handbag, you know, in the little side pocket, please bring it. Everything here will be set straight meanwhile."

When he came back with the bottle Levin found the sick man arranged in bed and everything round him quite different. The foul smell had been replaced by that of aromatic vinegar, which Kitty, pouting her lips and puffing out her rosy cheeks, was blowing through a little glass tube. The dust had vanished and there was a mat beside the bed. Medicine bottles and a pitcher of water were standing neatly on the table, as well as a pile of needed linen, and Kitty's embroidery. On another table beside the sick man's bed there was something to drink, a candle, and some powders. The invalid himself, combed and washed, was lying on clean sheets, his pillows piled high up, in a clean nightshirt with a white collar round his unnaturally thin neck, staring fixedly at Kitty with a new expression of hope.

The doctor Levin had gone for, and whom he had found at a club, was not the one who had been treating Nicholas, and whom Nicholas had been displeased with. This new doctor took out a stethoscope and sounded the sick man; he shook his head, prescribed some medicine, and left minutely detailed instructions first for taking the medicine, then for the diet that was to be observed. He ordered raw or very lightly boiled eggs and seltzer water with warm milk at a certain temperature. After the doctor had left, Nicholas said something to his brother, but Levin only caught the last words—"Your Katya . . ." though by the look he gave her Levin understood he was praising her. He asked "Katya" to come nearer.

"I feel much better already," he said. "With you I should have been all well a long time ago now. How good it feels!" He took her hand and drew it to his lips, but as though afraid she might find it distasteful he changed his mind, let it drop and merely stroked it. Kitty took this hand in both her own and pressed it.

"Now turn me over on my left side and go to sleep," he murmured.

No one could catch what he said; Kitty was the only one who understood. She understood because she kept thinking incessantly of what he needed.

"On the other side," she said to Levin, "he always sleeps on that side. Turn him over, it's disagreeable to call for the servants. I can't do it. But can you?" she said, turning to Masha.

"I'm afraid," Masha replied.

Dreadful as it was for Levin to put his arms around this dreadful body, and to seize hold of those parts under the blanket that he didn't want to think about, he yielded to his wife's influence and putting on the look of determination she was familiar with he thrust his arms under the blanket and got ahold; but in spite of his strength he was struck by the strange heaviness of the emaciated limbs. While he was turning him, feeling his enormous thin arm embracing his neck, Kitty quickly and noiselessly turned the pillow over and beat it; she arranged the sick man's head and the sparse hair that was sticking to his temples again.

The sick man held his brother's hand in his own. Levin felt that he wanted to do something with his hand and was pulling at it. He surrendered it, with a sinking heart. Yes— Nicholas pulled it to his mouth and kissed it. Levin started shaking with sobs; unable to say a word he went out of the room.

### XIX

THOU hast hid these things from the wise and prudent, and hast revealed them unto babes." This is what Levin thought about his wife as he talked to her that evening.

Levin was not thinking of this Gospel text because he thought himself wise and prudent. He did not think himself wise, but he could not help knowing that he was more intelligent than his wife and than Miss Agatha, and could not help knowing that when he thought of death he thought about it with all his might. He also knew that the minds of many great men, whose thoughts on this he had read, after all their reflection did not know one-hundredth of what his wife and Miss Agatha knew about it. However different these two women were, Miss Agatha and Katya, as his brother Nicholas called her and as Levin now found it particularly agreeable to call her too, they were completely alike in this. Both knew beyond any question what life was and what death was, and though they wouldn't have been able to answer and wouldn't even have understood the questions that came to

Levin's mind, neither one had any doubt of the meaning of this phenomenon and had exactly the same view of it, a view that was not only theirs alone but that they shared with millions of people. The proof that they were quite sure of what death was lay in the assurance with which, without a second's hesitation, they knew what had to be done with people who were dying, and they had no fear of them. But Levin and the others, though they could talk a great deal about death, plainly didn't know they were afraid of death and hadn't the least idea what had to be done when someone was dying. If Levin had been alone now with his brother he would have looked at him with horror, and with even greater horror have waited about; he would have been unable to do anything beyond that.

That was the least of it: he didn't know what to say, how to look, how to walk. Talking about irrelevant things seemed to him offensive, out of the question; talking about death, about something gloomy, was also impossible. Keeping quiet —also impossible.

If I look he'll think I'm watching him, I'm afraid to; if I don't look he'll think I'm thinking about something else. If I walk around on tiptoe it'll annoy him; if I put my whole foot down I'll feel guilty.

But Kitty obviously was not thinking about herself, nor did she have the time to; she was thinking about him because she knew something, and so everything came out right. She talked about herself too, and about her wedding, and she smiled, and felt sorry for him, and caressed him, and talked about cases of recovery, and everything came out right; consequently she must have known. The proof that her activity and Miss Agatha's was not an instinctive, animal, irrational one was that aside from the physical care, the relief of suffering, both Miss Agatha and Kitty did something else for the dying person that was more important than physical care, something of a kind that had nothing in common with physical conditions. In speaking about an old man who was dying Miss Agatha had said: "Well, God be thanked! he was given communion and extreme unction, may God grant everyone a death like that!" Just in the same way Kitty, in addition to all her worries about linen, bedsores, and things to drink, had managed to persuade the sick man the very first day of the necessity of taking communion and extreme unction.

When Levin left the sick man to go back to their two rooms for the night, he sat there, his head bowed, not knowing what

to do. Not only couldn't he think of supper, of getting ready
for bed, or of considering what they were to do, he wasn't
even able to talk to his wife: he felt ashamed to. Kitty, on the
contrary, was more active and even livelier than usual. She
ordered supper, did the unpacking herself, helped make the
beds, and didn't forget to sprinkle them with insect powder.
There was an excitement and alertness about her which men
show before a battle or a struggle, in the dangerous and decisive moments of life, those moments when a man shows his
worth once and for all, and shows that his whole past has
not been in vain but has been a preparation for such moments.

She was very efficient in everything, and before midnight
everything had been sorted out, clean and neat, in such a
way that their rooms began to look like home, like her own
room: the beds were made, brushes, combs, and mirrors laid
out, and the table napkins spread.

It seemed to Levin unforgivable to eat, sleep, and talk even
now; he felt that every movement he made was indecent.
But she sorted out the brushes in such a way that nothing
she did was offensive.

But they could not eat anything, and for a long time they
couldn't fall asleep; for that matter it was a long time before they went to bed.

"I'm very glad I persuaded him to receive extreme unction
tomorrow," she said, sitting in her dressing jacket before her
folding mirror and combing her soft, fragrant hair with a fine
comb. "I've never been present, but I know, Mama's told me,
that there are prayers for recovery in it."

"Do you really think he can recover?" said Levin, looking
at the narrow parting at the back of her round little head,
which disappeared each time she drew the comb forward.

"I asked the doctor: he said he can't live more than three
days. But can they really be so sure? Anyhow, I'm very glad
I persuaded him to," she said, glancing over at Levin from
under her hair. "Anything can happen," she added with the
peculiar, somewhat sly look her face always had on it whenever she spoke about religion.

After their conversation about religion, while they were
still engaged, neither he nor she had ever begun talking
about it again, but she continued to go through the rites of
going to church and praying with the serene and unvarying
assurance that that was what had to be done. In spite of his
protestations to the contrary she was firmly convinced that he
was as good a Christian as she or better, and that everything

he said about it was no more than one of his absurd masculine quirks, like what he said about her embroidery, such
as that rightminded people stopped up holes while she made
a point of opening them up and so on.

"Yes, you see that woman Masha couldn't arrange any of
that," said Levin. "And—I must confess, I'm very, very happy
you came. You're so pure that—" He took her hand and
didn't kiss it (kissing her hand with death so close seemed to
him indecent), but simply squeezed it with a guilty look, as
he gazed into her brightening eyes.

"It would have been so painful for you by yourself," she
said, and lifting up her arms, which hid her cheeks, pink
with pleasure, she twisted back her braids and pinned them
up. "No," she went on, "she didn't know how to. Luckily I
learned a great deal in Soden."

"Don't tell me there were such sick people there?"

"Worse."

"What's dreadful for me is that I can't help seeing him as
he was when he was young . . . You wouldn't believe how
charming he was, but at that time I never understood him."

"I do believe it, I do. I'm so sure we *would have been*
friends—he and I," she said, and was frightened by her own
words; she looked around at her husband and tears came
into her eyes.

"Yes, *would have been*," he said sadly. "He's really just the
kind of man about whom people say, they're not for this
world."

"But we're going to have a lot to do, we have to go to
bed," said Kitty, glancing at her tiny watch.

## XX

THE next day the sick man was given communion and extreme unction. During the ceremony he prayed fervently. His
great eyes, fixed on an icon set up on a card table covered
with a colored cloth, expressed such passionate entreaty and
hope that Levin found them unendurable to look at. Levin
knew that this passionate entreaty and hope would only
make his parting from life, which he loved so much, still
more painful. Levin knew his brother and the way he thought;
he knew that his lack of faith had not come about because it
was easier for him to live without faith, but because the
modern scientific explanations of the phenomena of the uni-

verse had step by step squeezed out his beliefs, and so he knew that his present reversion to faith was not a legitimate one, based on reasoning, but was simply a temporary, selfish one due to a mad hope of recovery. Levin also knew that Kitty had strengthened this hope still further by stories she had heard of extraordinary recoveries. Levin knew all this, and it was painful, agonizing for him to see this imploring look, full of hope, and that emaciated wrist lifting itself with difficulty to make the sign of the cross and touching the drawn forehead, the protruding shoulders, and the hollow, rattling chest that could by now no longer hold the life the sick man was begging for. During the sacrament Levin prayed too, and did what he, an unbeliever, had done a thousand times before. He said, addressing God: "If You exist make this man well—after all that's happened often before—and You will save both him and me."

After receiving extreme unction the sick man suddenly felt much better. For a whole hour he didn't cough once; he smiled, kissed Kitty's hand, thanking her with tears in his eyes, and said that he felt well, he didn't hurt anywhere, and felt strong and hungry. He even raised himself when soup was brought to him, and asked for a cutlet as well. However hopeless he was, however obvious it was by a look at him that he could never get well, for that hour Levin and Kitty were both in the same state of excitement, happy yet fearful of being mistaken.

"Is he better?" "Yes, much." "Amazing!" "Not amazing at all!" "Nevertheless he's better," they said in whispers, smiling at each other.

This illusion did not last long. The sick man fell asleep calmly, but half an hour later a fit of coughing woke him up. And suddenly all hope vanished both in those around him and in himself. The reality of his sufferings destroyed it beyond any question and without leaving even a trace of the preceding hope either in Levin and Kitty, or in the sick man himself.

Without even referring to what he had believed half an hour before, as though he felt ashamed of recalling it, he asked to be given some iodine for inhaling, from a small bottle covered with perforated paper. Levin handed him the bottle, and the same look of passionate hopefulness he had received extreme unction with was now directed at his brother, demanding his confirmation of what the doctor had said about the miracles produced by the inhaling of iodine.

"Katya, isn't she here?" he said hoarsely, looking around him after Levin had reluctantly repeated what the doctor had said. "No? Then I can tell you . . . I put on that comedy just for her. She's such a darling, but you and I can't deceive ourselves. This is what I believe in," he said, and clutching the bottle in his bony hand he began inhaling from it.

After seven that evening Levin and Kitty were drinking tea in their rooms when Masha rushed in breathless. She was white, and her lips were quivering.

"He's dying!" she whispered. "I'm afraid he'll die any minute."

They both ran to him. He had lifted himself and was sitting on the bed, leaning on an elbow, his long back doubled up and his head hanging low.

"What do you feel?" Levin asked in a whisper, after a moment's silence.

"I feel I'm on my way," Nicholas murmured, squeezing the words out with difficulty, but with extraordinary distinctness. He did not try to raise his head, but simply looked up, his eyes not reaching his brother's face. Then he said: "Katya, go away!"

Levin jumped up and in a peremptory whisper made her go out.

"I'm on my way," he said again.

"Why do you think so?" said Levin, in order to say something.

"Because I'm on my way," he repeated, as though he had taken a liking for the phrase. "It's the end."

Masha went over to him. "You'd feel better if you lay down," she said.

"I shall soon be lying quietly," he muttered. "Dead—" he said ironically, angrily. "Well, stretch me out if you feel like it."

Levin lay his brother on his back, sat down beside him and holding his breath watched his face. The dying man was lying down, with his eyes closed, but now and then the muscles on his forehead would twitch like those of a woman plunged in concentrated thought. Involuntarily Levin thought together with him of what was taking place inside him now, but in spite of all his mental efforts to follow him he saw by the look on his calm, stern face, and by the play of the muscles above one eyebrow that something was being clarified for the dying man, and what was being clarified was just what remained as dark as before for Levin.

"Yes . . . yes . . . That's so," the dying man muttered slowly, pausing between words. "Wait a moment . . ." He fell silent again. "That's so!" he suddenly drawled out in a reassuring tone, as though everything had been solved for him. "O Lord!" he muttered and sighed heavily.

Masha felt his feet. "They're growing cold," she whispered.

For a long time, for a very long time, as it seemed to Levin, the sick man lay motionless. But he was still alive and would sigh now and then. Levin was already exhausted by the mental strain. He felt that in spite of all his intellectual effort he could not grasp just what it was that was "so." He felt that he had long since fallen behind the dying man. He was no longer able to think about the actual question of death, but in spite of himself thoughts kept coming into his mind about what he was going to have to do now, any minute: close his brother's eyes, dress him, order the coffin. Strangely enough, he felt completely cool; he felt neither grief, nor a sense of loss, and least of all pity for his brother. If he had any feeling for his brother now it was, rather, envy for the knowledge of the dying man now had and Levin could not have.

For a long time he went on sitting there over him, waiting for the end. But the end did not come. The door opened, and Kitty appeared. Levin got up to stop her. But just as he was getting up he heard the dying man move.

"Don't go away," said Nicholas, and stretched out his hand. Levin gave him his own and angrily gestured to his wife to go out.

Holding the dying man's hand in his own he sat there for half an hour, then an hour, and another hour. Now he was no longer thinking about death at all. He was thinking about what Kitty was doing, who lived in the next room, whether the doctor had a house of his own. He felt like eating and sleeping. He freed his hand cautiously and felt his brother's feet. The feet were cold, but the sick man was breathing. Once again Levin started to go out on tiptoe, but the sick man stirred again and said:

"Don't go . . ."

Dawn came up; the sick man's condition remained the same. Levin softly withdrew his hand, without looking at the dying man; he went to his own room and fell asleep. When he woke up, instead of hearing the news of his brother's death which he had been expecting he learned that the sick man had reverted to his previous condition. Once again he had begun sitting up, coughing; he had begun eating again, speaking again, and had again stopped talking about death; again he had begun expressing his hopes for recovery and had turned more irritable and morose than before. No one, neither Levin nor Kitty, could soothe him. He got angry at everyone, said disagreeable things to everyone, reproached everyone for his own sufferings and insisted that some celebrated Moscow specialist be brought to him. He answered every question put to him about how he felt in the same way, with a look of spiteful reproach: "I'm in terrible suffering—it's unbearable!"

The sick man was suffering more and more, especially because of his bedsores, which by now could no longer heal; he kept growing more and more angry at everyone round him, reproaching them for everything and especially for their not fetching a doctor from Moscow. Kitty tried to help and soothe him in every possible way, but it was all in vain and Levin saw that she herself was worn out both physically and spiritually, though she wouldn't acknowledge it. The feeling of death that had been evoked in them all by his farewell to life the night he had called his brother was destroyed. Everyone knew that he was going to die inevitably and soon, that he was half-dead already. Everyone longed for only one thing that he might die as quickly as possible; all of them hid this and gave him bottles of medicine, went off to fetch medicines and doctors, and deceived him, themselves, and one another. It was all a lie, a vile, offensive, and blasphemous lie. And this lie was felt with particular anguish by Levin, both because of his nature and because he loved the dying man more than anyone else.

Levin, who had long since been preoccupied by the idea of reconciling his brothers if only on the threshold of death, had written Koznyshov and when he got a letter in reply he read it to the sick man. Koznyshov wrote that he couldn't come himself, but in moving terms he asked his brother's forgiveness.

The sick man said nothing.

"What should I write him?" asked Levin. "I hope you're not angry with him?"

"No, not in the least!" Nicholas answered, irritated by the question. "Write him to send me a doctor."

Another three days of agony went by; the sick man was still in the same condition. Everyone who saw him now longed for his death: the waiters at the hotel, the proprietor, all the people staying there, the doctor, Masha, Levin, and Kitty. It was only the sick man alone who did not express this feeling, but on the contrary, got angry because a doctor hadn't been brought in, and went on taking medicine and talking about living. It was only at rare moments, when the opium made him forget his constant sufferings for a moment, that he sometimes, when half-asleep, said what he felt in his soul more intensely than any of the others: "Oh, if only it were over with!" or, "When will it end!"

His sufferings, which kept steadily increasing, did their work and prepared him for death. There was not a single position in which he didn't suffer; there was not a moment when he could forget himself; there was not a place on his body or a limb that didn't hurt and torture him. Even recollections, impressions, and thoughts about this body of his aroused the same revulsion in him by now as his body itself. The sight of other people, what they said, their own memories—everything was torture for him. Those around him felt this and unconsciously would not allow themselves to move freely in his presence, or speak, or express their own desires. His whole life fused into one single feeling of agony and a desire to be released from it.

It was plain that a change was taking place within him that was bound to make him look upon death as a fulfillment of his desires, as a joy. Each individual wish that had been brought about before by suffering or by privation, such as hunger, fatigue, or thirst, had been satisfied by some bodily function that gave him pleasure; now the privation and suffering could not be alleviated while any attempt to do so brought about a renewal of suffering. Consequently all his desires merged into one—a desire to be released from all his sufferings and from their source, his body. But he had no words to express this desire for liberation, and so he said nothing about it, but out of habit went on demanding the satisfaction of wishes which by now could no longer be fulfilled. "Turn me over on the other side," he would say, then immediately afterward ask to be turned back again. "Give me some bouillon. Take the bouillon away. Say something—what are you all so silent for?" And no sooner would they begin talking than he would close his eyes and express fatigue, indifference, and loathing.

The tenth day after their arrival Kitty fell ill. She had

a headache, vomited, and could not get out of bed all morning.

The doctor explained that her illness was due to fatigue and excitement; he prescribed spiritual calm.

After dinner, however, Kitty got up and went to Nicholas as usual, taking along her embroidery. He looked at her sternly when she came in, and smiled contemptuously when she said she had been ill. That day he kept blowing his nose incessantly and moaning pathetically.

"How do you feel?" she asked him.

"Worse," he answered, with an effort. "It hurts!"

"Where does it hurt?"

"Everywhere!"

"It's going to end today, you'll see," said Masha, but even though she whispered the sick man, whose senses were very acute, as Levin had noticed, was bound to hear her. Levin hushed her and glanced round at the invalid. Nicholas had heard her, but what Masha said made no impression on him at all; he still had the same tense, reproachful look.

"Why d'you think so?" Levin asked her after she followed him into the corridor.

"He's begun picking at himself."

"What d'you mean—picking?"

"Like this,'"she said, pulling at the folds of her woolen dress. As a matter of fact Levin had noticed that his brother had kept catching at himself that whole day as though he were trying to snatch something off.

Masha's prediction came true. Toward night the sick man was no longer able to lift his arms, and simply kept staring in front of him without changing the attentive, concentrated expression in his eyes. Even when his brother or Kitty leaned over him so that he could see them he kept staring the same way. Kitty sent for the priest to read the death service.

While the priest was reading the death service the dying man showed no signs of life; his eyes were shut. Levin, Kitty, and Masha were standing beside the bed. Before the prayer had been read through by the priest the dying man stretched out, sighed, and opened his eyes. The priest finished reading the prayer, touched the cold forehead with his cross, which he then wrapped up in his stole, and after standing in silence for another two minutes touched the enormous bloodless hand, which was turning cold.

"He is gone," said the priest and was about to move away; but suddenly the sticky mustache of the dying man stirred, and clearly in the stillness there came his voice, sharp and distinct, from the depths of his chest:

"Not quite. Soon. . . ."

And a moment later his face lit up, a smile appeared beneath the mustache, and the two women standing there carefully set to work laying out the body.

In Levin's soul the sight of his brother and the imminence of death renewed the feeling of horror at the enigma of death, as well as its nearness and inevitability, that had laid hold of him that autumn evening when Nicholas had come to visit him. This feeling was more powerful now than before; he felt himself even less capable than before of understanding the meaning of death and its inevitability seemed to him still more horrible. But now this feeling did not lead him into despair, thanks to the closeness of his wife: in spite of death he felt the necessity of living and loving. He felt that love had saved him from despair, and that this love of his had grown still more powerful and purer under the threat of despair.

This one mystery of death, that remained an enigma, had not had time to be consummated before his eyes before a second one, just as enigmatic, had emerged, summoning him to love and life.

The doctor confirmed his surmise about Kitty. Her illness had been pregnancy.

## XXI

FROM the moment Karenin, after talking to Betsy and Oblonsky, realized that what was required of him was simply that he leave his wife in peace, and not trouble her with his presence, and that his wife wanted this herself, he felt so lost that he couldn't make any decisions, had no idea what he wanted himself, and yielding to those who were coping with his affairs with such gusto he agreed to everything. It was only after Anna had already left his house, when the English governess sent to ask him whether she ought to dine together with him or separately, that he clearly grasped his situation for the first time and was horrified by it.

What was hardest of all was that he was quite incapable of identifying and reconciling the present state of affairs with the past. He was not troubled by the past when he had been living happily together with his wife; he had already painfully made the transition from that past to his learning of his wife's infidelity. That situation had been painful to him but comprehensible. If at that time his wife had told him of her infidelity and left him he would have been wounded and unhappy, but he would not have been in the incomprehensible, hopeless position he felt he was in now. What he could not reconcile with his present situation was his more recent forgiveness, his emotion, his love for his sick wife and for the stranger's child; that is, with the fact that, as though in reward for all of that, he now found himself alone, disgraced, and a laughingstock, of no use to anyone and despised by all.

The first two days after his wife left, Karenin received petitioners, his private secretary, drove to the Committee and had dinner in the dining room as usual. During these two days, without trying to explain to himself why he was doing all this, he exerted himself with all his might just to look calm, and even indifferent. When he answered questions about what disposition was to be made of Madame Karenin's rooms and belongings, he made the greatest effort to look like a man for whom what had happened had not been unforeseen and had nothing in the least extraordinary about it. He attained his object; no one could have detected any sign of despair in him. But on the third day, when Korney handed him a bill from a fashion house that Anna had forgotten to pay, and announced the presence of a clerk from the shop in person, Karenin had the clerk brought in.

"Forgive me, Your Excellency, for taking the liberty of troubling you. But if you wish us to address ourselves to Her Excellency, would you be so good as to let us have her address?"

Karenin sank into thought, as it seemed to the clerk, then suddenly turned round and sat down at the table. Dropping his head on his hands he sat in this position for a long time; he tried to speak several times and stopped again.

Understanding his master's feelings Korney asked the clerk to come some other time. When he was left alone again Karenin realized that he was incapable of sustaining his role of firmness and serenity any longer. He ordered the carriage waiting for him to be sent away, asked that no one be received, and did not appear for dinner.

He felt he could not bear the general pressure of con-

tempt and callousness he clearly saw on the face of the clerk,
of Korney, and of everyone without exception whom he
ran into during these two days. He felt he could not divert
people's hatred from himself, since this hatred was not due
to his being bad (in which case he might have tried to be
better) but to his being shamefully and repellently unhappy.
He knew that it was just because of this, just because his
heart was lacerated, that they would be merciless toward
him. He felt people would destroy him, as dogs will kill
a mangled dog whining with pain. He knew that the only
escape from people was to hide his wounds from them; he
had tried to do this unconsciously for two days, but now
he no longer felt capable of continuing the unequal struggle.

His despair was intensified still further by his knowing
that he was completely isolated in his grief. Not only did
he not have a single person in Petersburg to whom he could
have told everything he was going through and who would
have pitied him not as a superior functionary, not as a
member of society, but simply as a suffering human being,
he had no one like that anywhere.

Karenin had grown up an orphan. There had been two
brothers; they did not remember their father, and their
mother had died when Karenin was ten years old. They
had small means; their uncle, a Karenin who had been an
important functionary and at one time a favorite of the
late Tsar, had brought them up.

After finishing his school and university studies with
honors, Karenin had immediately set out on a prominent
career in government service with the help of his uncle;
from then on he had devoted himself exclusively to official
ambition. He had never formed any friendships with anyone,
either at school or the university, or later on in the service.
His brother had been closest to his heart, but he served in
the Ministry of Foreign Affairs and had always lived abroad,
where he died soon after Karenin's marriage.

While he was Governor of a Province, Anna's aunt, a
rich provincial, brought her niece together with him, a young
Governor though no longer a young man, and put him in such
a position that he was bound either to declare himself or
else leave the city. For a long time Karenin hesitated.
There were just as many arguments at the time for the
step as against it, and a decisive occasion was lacking that
would have forced him to change his principle—*when in
doubt do nothing*. But through an acquaintance Anna's aunt

suggested to him that he had already compromised the girl
and was in honor bound to propose. He proposed, and gave
his fiancée and his wife all the emotion he was capable of.

The attachment he felt for Anna took away any need he
might still have had for warm relations with other people.
And now, among all his acquaintances, there was no one
close to him. He had a great many so-called connections,
but no friendships. Karenin knew a great many people of
the sort he could invite to dinner, or ask to take part in
some matter of interest to him or use their influence on
behalf of some petitioner, and whom he could carry on
a frank discussion with of the activities of other people and
of the government; but his relations to these people were
restricted to one sphere, sharply defined by custom and
habit, that it was impossible to get out of. There was one
friend from the university whom he had become more intimate with afterward and whom he could have discussed his
personal grief with, but this friend now had a post as
educational supervisor in a remote part of the country. Of
the people who lived in Petersburg the closest and most ac-
cessible were his private secretary and his doctor.

Michael Slyudin, his private secretary, was a simple,
intelligent, kindhearted and moral man who Karenin felt
liked him personally; but their five years of official activity
together had set up a barrier in the way of any intimate
conversations.

Once Karenin, after signing the last of some documents
he had before him, was silent for a long time, glancing over
at Slyudin; he made a number of attempts to start speaking
but was unable to. He had a phrase all ready: "You've heard
about my difficulty, haven't you?" But he ended up by
saying the usual thing: "Then you'll get this ready for me,"
and on that let him go.

Another such person was the doctor, who also liked him.
But for a long time now it had been tacitly agreed that they
were both overwhelmed by work, with no time to spare.

As for his women friends, including the principal one
among them, Countess Lydia Ivanovna, Karenin did not even
think of them. All women, simply as women, terrified and
repelled him.

### XXII

KARENIN had forgotten Countess Lydia, but she had not forgotten him. At just this most painful moment of lonely despair, she came to see him, going into his study unannounced. She found him in the same position he had been sitting in, his head propped up on both hands.

"I've broken in," she said, coming in with quick steps and breathing heavily because of her excitement and her rapid movement. "I've heard all about it! My dear friend!" she went on, pressing his hand hard in both her own and gazing with her beautiful dreamy eyes into his.

Karenin rose to his feet with a frown; freeing his hand he drew up a chair for her.

"Won't you sit down, Countess? I'm not receiving because I'm not well," he said, his lips quivering.

"My dear friend!" Countess Lydia repeated, not taking her eyes off him; suddenly the inner corners of her eyebrows rose, forming a triangle on her forehead; her plain yellow face turned still plainer, but Karenin felt that she was sorry for him and ready to weep. He was moved; he seized her plump hand and kissed it.

"My dear friend!" she said in a voice broken by emotion. "You must not give way to sorrow. Your sorrow is great, but you must find consolation."

"I'm crushed, broken, I'm no longer a man!" said Karenin, releasing her hand but continuing to gaze into her tearful eyes. "My position is dreadful; I cannot find a point of support anywhere, not even in myself."

"You will find support, you must seek it, not in me, though I beg you to believe in my friendship," she said with a sigh. "Your support will be love, the love that He has bequeathed to us. His yoke is easy," she said with that ecstatic look Karenin knew so well. "He will support you and help you."

Though these words displayed her emotion over her own exalted sentiments, and something of that novel, ecstatic mystical mood that had lately been spreading in Petersburg and that Karenin thought excessive, he found it agreeable to listen to it now.

"I'm weak. I'm crushed. I foresaw nothing and now I don't understand anything."

"My dear friend," Countess Lydia repeated once more.

"It's not the loss of what's gone now, it's not that," Karenin went on. "I don't regret that, but I cannot help feeling humiliated before others because of my present position. It's wrong, but I can't help it, I can't help it!"

"It was not you who performed that lofty act of forgiveness that has filled me and everyone else with rapture, but He who dwells within your heart," said Countess Lydia, ecstatically raising her eyes, "and therefore you cannot be ashamed of your behavior."

Karenin frowned and bending his hands backward began cracking his knuckles.

"One must know all the details," he said in a high voice. "There are limits to a man's strength, Countess, and I've come to the limit of mine. All day long I've had to make domestic decisions resulting"—he emphasized the word *resulting*—"from my new solitary situation. The servants, the governess, the bills . . . These petty flames have devoured me, I can stand it no longer. At dinner . . . yesterday I very nearly left the table. I could not bear the way my son was looking at me. He didn't ask me the meaning of it all, but he wanted to, and I could not endure his expression. He was afraid to look at me . . . But that's not all . . ."

Karenin was about to mention the bill that had been brought to him, but his voice shook and he stopped. He could not think about this bill, on blue paper, for a hat and ribbons, without feeling sorry for himself.

"I understand, my dear," said Countess Lydia. "I understand everything. You will not find help and consolation in me, though I've come nevertheless only in order to help you if I can. If only I could take all these petty humiliating cares off your shoulders . . . I understand how much a woman's word, a woman's supervision is needed. Will you entrust me with that?"

Karenin pressed her hand in silent gratitude.

"We'll take care of Seryozha together. I'm not very efficient in practical matters, but I'll set to work, I'll be your housekeeper. Do not thank me. I'm not doing it of myself—"

"I cannot help thanking you!"

"But my dear, you must not give way to that feeling you were speaking of—being ashamed of what is the Christian's greatest glory—'He who humbles himself shall be exalted.' And you cannot thank me; it is He who must be thanked, and He who must be asked for help. It is in Him alone that we shall find peace, solace, salvation, and love," she said, and raising her eyes to Heaven she began praying, as Karenin realized from her silence.

Karenin listened to her now, and expressions that had seemed to him if not disagreeable at any rate superfluous now seemed natural and comforting. Karenin did not like this new spirit of ecstasy; he was a believer who was interested in religion primarily in the political sense, while the new doctrine, which allowed a number of novel interpretations just because it opened the door to argument and analysis, repelled him on principle. Beforehand he had had a chilly and even hostile attitude toward this new doctrine; he had never argued with Countess Lydia, who was carried away by it, but had taken pains to avoid her challenges by keeping silent. But for the first time he listened to what she said now with pleasure and with no inner protest.

"I'm very, very grateful to you both for your deeds and for your words," he said after she had finished praying.

Once again Countess Lydia pressed both her friend's hands.

"Now I shall get down to work," she said after a pause, smiling and wiping away the traces of tears from her face. "I'll go to Seryozha. I'll only appeal to you in emergencies." She got up and went out.

The Countess Lydia went to Seryozha's part of the house and there, bathing the cheeks of the frightened little boy in her tears, she told him his father was a saint and his mother dead.

Countess Lydia kept her promise. She really did assume all the cares of arranging and running Karenin's house. But she had not exaggerated in saying she was not efficient in practical matters. All the orders she gave had to be changed, since they were unfeasible, and they were changed by Karenin's valet, Korney, who was now imperceptibly running the whole house and would quietly and tactfully inform his master, while he was dressing, of whatever he ought to know. Nevertheless Countess Lydia's help was extremely effective: she gave Karenin moral support by making him conscious of her love and respect for him, and especially by almost converting him to Christianity, as it consoled her to think; that is, she converted him from an apathetic and indolent believer into a firm and ardent partisan of the new interpretation of Christian doctrine that had been spreading lately in Petersburg, and that it was easy for Karenin to be persuaded by. Karenin, like Countess Lydia and the others who shared their views, was completely devoid of any depth of imagination, of that spiritual faculty thanks to which the ideas summoned up by imagination become so real that they insist on being brought into harmony with other ideas and with actual fact. He saw nothing impossible or incongruous in the idea that death, which existed for unbelievers, did not exist for him, and that since he was in possession of the most complete faith, the extent of which he himself was the sole judge, there was no longer any sin in his soul, and he was already experiencing total salvation here on earth.

To be sure, Karenin vaguely felt the shallowness and falseness of this notion of his faith; he knew that when he had directly yielded to that feeling of forgiveness, without thinking at all about its being the action of a higher power, he had experienced greater happiness than when, as now, he kept constantly thinking that Christ was living in his soul, and that when he was signing documents he was fulfilling His will. But for Karenin it was so necessary to think in this way; it was so necessary for him in his humiliation to have a lofty, though contrived point of vantage from which, despised by all, he would be able to despise others, that he clung to his pseudosalvation as though it were salvation.

## XXIII

WHEN Countess Lydia had been a very young, ecstatic girl she had been married off to a rich and jovial aristocrat, very good-natured and extremely dissolute. By the second month of their marriage her husband had left her; his response to her ecstatic assurances of tenderness was mere irony and even hostility, which people who both knew the Count's kind heart and were unaware of any shortcomings in the ecstatic Lydia were quite unable to explain. Ever since then, though not divorced, they had lived apart; whenever the husband met his wife he always treated her with an unvarying venomous mockery, the cause of which remained incomprehensible.

Countess Lydia had long since stopped being in love with her husband, but from then on she had never stopped being in love with some one. She would be in love with several people at once, both men and women; she would be in love with practically anyone who was in any way particularly distinguished. She was in love with all the new Princes and

Princesses who married into the Imperial family, she was in love with a Metropolitan, a vicar, and a priest. She had been in love with a journalist, three Slavophiles, and with Komisarov; with one of the Ministers, a doctor, an English missionary, and now with Karenin. None of these loves of hers, which waxed and waned, interfered with her maintaining the most widespread and complicated relations around the Court and in society. But ever since Karenin's misfortune, when she took him under her special protection, ever since she began busying herself in Karenin's house and toiling for his welfare, she felt that none of her other loves was genuine and that now she was genuinely in love with Karenin alone. The feeling she now had for him seemed to her to be more powerful than all her previous feelings. When she analyzed it and compared it with her previous feelings, she saw clearly that while she would never have been in love with Komisarov if he hadn't saved the Sovereign's life, and would not have been in love with Ristich-Kudzhitsky if it hadn't been for the Slavonic question, she loved Karenin for himself alone, for his lofty misunderstood soul, for his high-pitched voice, whose drawling inflections she found charming, for his weary gaze, for his character, and for his soft white hands with their swollen veins. She was not only delighted whenever she met him, but she studied his face for signs of the impression she made on him. She wanted to please him not only by what she said, but by her whole person. For his sake she spent more time now on her dress than ever before. She would catch herself daydreaming about what might be if she hadn't been married and he were free. She blushed with excitement when he entered a room; she could not repress a smile of rapture when he said something nice to her.

For several days now Countess Lydia was in a state of the most violent excitement. She had learned that Anna and Vronsky were in Petersburg. Karenin had to be saved from a meeting with her, had to be saved even from the agonizing knowledge that this dreadful woman was in the same city as he and that he might run into her at any moment.

Through her acquaintances Countess Lydia kept herself informed of the intentions of these "disgusting people," as she called them, and exerted herself during these days to guide all the movements of her friend so that he would not encounter them. A young adjutant, a friend of Vronsky's, from whom she received reports and who hoped to obtain a concession through her influence, told her they had finished their business and were leaving the following day. Countess Lydia had just begun calming down when she was brought a note the very next morning: she recognized the handwriting with horror. It was Anna's. The envelope was of paper that was as thick as parchment; there was a gigantic monogram on the narrow yellow sheet, and it had a wonderful scent.

"Who brought it?"

"A commissionaire from the hotel."

For a long time Countess Lydia could not sit down to read the letter. Her agitation brought on an attack of the asthma she was subject to. When she had calmed down she read the following letter, which was in French:

> *Countess,*
> *The Christian feelings that fill your heart give me, I feel, the unpardonable boldness to write to you. I am unhappy at being parted from my son. I implore you for permission to see him once before my departure. Forgive me for recalling myself to you. I am turning to you and not to Alexis only because I do not wish to make that generous heart suffer by being reminded of me. Knowing your friendship with him I am sure you will understand me. Could you send Seryozha to me, or let me come to the house at a certain appointed hour, or let me know when and where I may see him away from the house? Knowing the magnanimity of the person this depends on, I do not expect a refusal. You cannot imagine my yearning to see him, and so cannot imagine the gratitude your help will awaken in me.*

> ANNA

Everything in this letter irritated Countess Lydia, both the content, the allusion to magnanimity, and especially what seemed to her its free-and-easy tone.

"Say there's no answer," she said, and instantly opened her blotting pad and wrote Karenin that she was hoping to see him after twelve at the birthday reception in the Palace.

"*I must speak to you about an important and melancholy subject. We shall make an appointment there. It would be best of all at my house, where I shall give orders to have your tea prepared. It is urgent. He gives us a cross, but He gives us strength to bear it, too,*" she added, to prepare him, if only a little bit.

Countess Lydia usually wrote Karenin two or three letters a day. She liked this method of communicating with him; it had an elegance and secrecy about it that was not achieved when they saw each other personally.

## XXIV

THE reception was ending. People going out ran into acquaintances and chatted about the latest news of the day, the newly awarded honors, and the important official changes.

"How would it be to make Countess Mary Minister of War, and Princess Vatkovsky Chief of Staff?" said a gray-haired old man in a gold-embroidered uniform to a tall and beautiful Lady in Waiting who had asked him about the promotions.

"And myself an aide-de-camp," replied the Lady in Waiting, smiling.

"You have a post assigned to you already—in the Ecclesiastical Department. Your assistant—Karenin."

"How d'you do, Prince!" said the old man, shaking hands with someone who had come up.

"What were you saying about Karenin?" said the Prince.

"He and Putyatov got the Order of Alexander Nevsky."

"I thought he had it already."

"No: look at him," said the old man, with his gold-trimmed hat indicating Karenin, in a Court uniform with a new red ribbon across his shoulder, who had stopped in the doorway with one of the influential members of the State Council. "Happy and gay as a brass kopeck," he added, stopping to shake hands with a handsome, athletically built Chamberlain.

"No, he's aged," said the Chamberlain.

"With worry. He keeps writing projects nowadays. He's not going to let that unlucky fellow go now until he's explained everything point by point."

"What d'you mean—aged! He's having one love affair after another! I think Countess Lydia is jealous of his wife now."

"Come now, you're not going to say anything bad about Countess Lydia, please!"

"But is it bad for her to be in love with Karenin?"

"Is it true his wife is here?"

"Not here in the Palace, but in Petersburg. I met them yesterday, her and Vronsky, walking arm in arm in Great Morskoy Street."

"He's a man who hasn't—" the Chamberlain began, then

paused to make way with a bow for a member of the Imperial family who was passing by.

They chattered on about Karenin in this way without a stop, criticizing and deriding him while he, barring the way to the member of the State Council whom he had buttonholed and not pausing for a moment, in order not to let him slip away, kept on expounding to him point by point some finance project of his.

Almost at exactly the same time his wife left him one of the most painful things that can happen to a functionary happened to Karenin—his movement upward in the government service came to a halt. This halt was a fact, and everyone saw it clearly, but Karenin himself was still unaware of it. Whether it was his collision with Stremov, or the misfortune with his wife, or simply that Karenin had arrived at his predestined limit, that year it became obvious to everyone that his official career was finished. He still occupied an important position, he was a member of many commissions and committees, but he was a man who was played out, from whom nothing further was expected. Whatever he said, whatever he proposed, he was listened to as though what he was proposing were long since familiar to everyone and were just what no one wanted.

But Karenin did not feel this; on the contrary, since he was now some distance away from any direct participation in governmental activity, he saw more clearly than before the defects and blunders of the activities of others, and considered it his duty to point out means to correct them. Soon after his separation from his wife he began writing his first memorandum on the new judicial procedure, the first of an innumerable series of unwanted notes he was destined to write on every branch of the administration.

Not only did Karenin fail to notice his hopeless position in the official world, and not only was he not upset about it, but he was more complacent than ever about what he was doing. "He who is married cares about the things of this world, how he may please his wife . . . he who is unmarried cares for the things of the Lord, how he may please the Lord," says St. Paul, and Karenin, who was now guided by the Gospel in everything, often recalled this text. It seemed to him that ever since he had been left without a wife he had been serving the Lord more than ever by means of these very projects.

The obvious impatience of the member of the State Council,

who wanted to get away from him, did not disconcert Karenin: he stopped giving his exposition only when the Council member, taking advantage of a royal personage passing by, slipped away.

When he was left alone Karenin bowed his head, collecting his thoughts, then glanced round absent-mindedly and turned to the door, where he hoped to meet Countess Lydia.

How strong and healthy they all are physically, Karenin thought, glancing at the powerfully built Chamberlain, with his well-brushed fragrant whiskers, and at the red neck of a Prince in a tight-fitting uniform, whom he had to pass by. Truly is it said that everything in the world is evil, he thought, with another sidelong look at the Chamberlain's calves.

Unhurriedly moving his feet Karenin, with his usual look of dignified fatigue, bowed to these gentlemen who had been talking about him, and glanced toward the door, on the look-out for Countess Lydia.

"Ah! Karenin!" said the old man, his eyes twinkling maliciously as Karenin drew level with him and inclined his head coldly. "I still haven't congratulated you," he said, indicating his newly awarded ribbon.

"Thank you," Karenin replied. "What a *beautiful* day it is," he added, laying special stress on the word "beautiful" as was his habit.

He knew they were laughing at him, but he expected nothing from them but hostility anyhow, and he had already grown accustomed to that.

When he caught sight of Countess Lydia as she entered, with her yellow shoulders squeezed up out of her corset, and her beautiful dreamy eyes summoning him, Karenin smiled, showing his impeccable white teeth, and went over to her.

Dressing had given Countess Lydia a great deal of trouble, as it always did lately. Her purpose in dressing was now the exact opposite of what it had been thirty years before. At that time she wanted to adorn herself somehow, the more the better. Now, on the contrary, she was bound to be made up in such disharmony with her years and looks that her only concern was that the contrast between her make-up and her appearance should not be too dreadful. As far as Karenin was concerned she had achieved this; to him she seemed attractive. For him she was the sole oasis not only of benevolence, but of love in the desert of hostility and scorn he was surrounded by.

Passing the file of mocking glances, he was drawn toward her infatuated look as naturally as a plant toward the sun.

"I congratulate you," she said, her eyes indicating the ribbon.

Repressing a smile of pleasure he closed his eyes and shrugged his shoulders, as though beyond being cheered up by such a thing. Countess Lydia was well aware that this was one of his chief joys, though he would never admit it.

"How is our angel?" said Countess Lydia, referring to Seryozha.

"I cannot say I'm entirely satisfied with him," said Karenin, raising his eyebrows and opening his eyes. "Sitnikov is also dissatisfied." (Sitnikov was Seryozha's secular tutor.) "As I've told you he has a sort of coldness toward the basic questions that ought to touch the heart of every man and of every child." Karenin began expounding his ideas on the only question outside the service that interested him, the education of his son.

When with Countess Lydia's help Karenin had returned once more to life and activity he felt it his duty to busy himself with the education of the son who had been left on his hands. Since he had never before had anything to do with questions of education, Karenin devoted some time to a theoretical study of the subject. After reading a number of books on anthropology, pedagogy, and didactics, he drew up a plan of education for his own use. Then he engaged the best teacher in Petersburg to supervise it and set to work. Now he was constantly preoccupied by it.

"Yes, but what a heart! I see his father's heart in him, and with a heart like that no child can be bad," said Countess Lydia enthusiastically.

"Yes, that may be . . . As far as I'm concerned I'm doing my duty. I can do no more."

There was a pause; then Countess Lydia said: "Will you come to see me? We must discuss something that will be distressing for you. I should give anything to free you of certain memories, but there are others who don't think that way. I've received a letter from *her*—*she's* here, in Petersburg."

At the mention of his wife Karenin started; then there instantly settled on his face the deathlike immobility that expressed his utter helplessness in this matter.

"I was expecting that," he said.

Countess Lydia looked at him ecstatically; her eyes filled with tears of rapture over the majesty of his soul.

## XXV

WHEN Karenin entered Countess Lydia's small, cozy sitting room, full of old china and hung with portraits, the hostess was not yet there. She was changing.

A round table covered with a cloth had a Chinese tea service and silver spirit lamp and teakettle standing on it. Karenin absently glanced round at the countless portraits of people he knew that decorated the sitting room, and sitting down at the table opened a New Testament that was lying on it. The rustle of the Countess's silk dress interrupted him.

"Well, now we can sit down quietly," said Countess Lydia, with an agitated smile as she hurriedly squeezed in between the table and the sofa, "and have a chat over our tea."

After a few preparatory remarks Countess Lydia, sighing heavily and blushing, put Anna's letter into Karenin's hands.

After reading it he was silent for some time.

"I don't think I have the right to refuse her," he said diffidently, raising his eyes.

"My dear friend! You see evil in no one!"

"On the contrary, I see that evil is everywhere. But is that right?"

His face expressed an irresoluteness and a desire for advice, support, and guidance in a matter beyond his understanding.

"No," Countess Lydia interrupted him. "There's a limit to everything. I can understand immorality," she said, not quite sincerely, since she had never been able to understand what it was that led women into immorality, "but I cannot understand cruelty—and to whom? To you! How can she stay in the same city as you? Really, it's 'live and learn.' And I am learning to understand your own loftiness and her baseness."

"But who will throw the stone?" said Karenin, obviously pleased with his own role. "I've forgiven everything and so I cannot deprive her of what is demanded by her love— her love for her son . . ."

"But is that love, my dear? Is it sincere? Let's grant

that you've forgiven her, you forgive her still . . . but do we have the right to affect the soul of this angel? He thinks of her as dead. He prays for her and begs God to forgive her her sins . . . And it's better that way. But what would he think now?"

"I hadn't thought of that," said Karenin, evidently agreeing.

Countess Lydia covered her face with her hands and was silent. She was praying.

"If you ask me for my advice," she said, having finished her prayer and uncovered her face, "I advise you not to do it. D'you think I don't see how you suffer, how all this has opened up your wounds? But let's suppose you have no thought of yourself, as usual. What can it lead to? To renewed sufferings of your own, and to torment for the child. If anything human had been left in her she herself ought not to want that. No, without any hesitation, I advise you against it, and if you will allow me to I'll write to her."

Karenin agreed, and Countess Lydia wrote the following letter in French:

*Madame,*

*If your son is reminded of you it may lead to questions on his part it would be impossible to answer without implanting in the child's soul a feeling of condemnation for what ought to be sacred to him. Therefore I beg you to understand, in the spirit of Christian love, your husband's refusal. I pray to the Almighty to be compassionate toward you.*

COUNTESS LYDIA

This letter achieved the secret purpose that Countess Lydia had concealed from herself. It wounded Anna to the depths of her soul.

Karenin for his part, on returning home that day from Countess Lydia's, could not devote himself to his customary activites and find the spiritual peace he had felt before, that of a believer who has found salvation.

The recollection of his wife, who was so guilt-laden toward him and with respect to whom he had been so saintly, as Countess Lydia had rightly said to him, ought not to have upset him; but he was not at ease; he could not understand the book he was reading, could not drive away the painful memories of his relations with her, of the mistakes that as it seemed to him now he had made with regard to her. The memory of how on their return from the races he had accepted her confession of infidelity (and in particular his having demanded merely external propriety from her, without having challenged Vronsky to a duel) tormented him like remorse. He was equally tormented by the recollection of the letter he had written her: in particular his forgiveness, unwanted by anyone, and his concern for the stranger's child seared his heart with shame and remorse.

And now he felt just this same feeling of shame and remorse as he turned over in his mind his entire past with her and recalled the clumsy way he had proposed to her, after lengthy vacillations.

But how am I to blame? he said to himself. And this question always evoked in him another question: Did other people feel differently? Did they love differently? Marry differently? These Vronskys, these Oblonskys? . . . All these Chamberlains with thick calves? And a whole series came to his mind of these juicy, powerful men with no doubts, who had always and everywhere involuntarily attracted his attentive curiosity. He drove these thoughts away; he tried to persuade himself that he was not living for the temporary life of here and now, but for eternity, and that his soul was full of peace and love. But the fact that in this temporary, trivial life he had made a number of trivial mistakes, as it seemed to him, tormented him as though the eternal salvation he believed in did not even exist. But this temptation did not last long; in Karenin's soul there was very soon re-established that serenity and loftiness thanks to which he was able to forget what he did not wish to remember.

## XXVI

WELL, Kapitonych?" said Seryozha, coming back pink and merry from a walk the day before his birthday and handing his overcoat to the tall old hall porter who was smiling down from his height at the little fellow. "Has that bandaged official been here today? Did Papa see him?"

"Yes, he did. The minute the secretary left I announced him," said the hall porter, with a gay wink. "Let me take it off for you."

"Seryozha!" said his tutor, stopping in the doorway leading to the inner rooms. "Take it off yourself."

But Seryozha, though he heard his tutor's feeble voice, paid no attention to him. He stood there holding the porter by the shoulder strap and looking into his face.

"Well, and did Papa do what he wanted?"

The hall porter nodded.

The bandaged official, who had already come to the house seven times to petition Karenin for something, interested both Seryozha and the hall porter. Seryozha had once met him in the hall and heard him pathetically begging the porter to announce him, saying he and his children would die otherwise.

From then on Seryozha, after meeting the official in the hall a second time, had taken an interest in him.

"Well, was he very happy?" he asked.

"How could he help being! He was practically jumping for joy when he left."

"Has anything come for me?" asked Seryozha, after a pause.

"Well, sir," said the porter in a whisper, shaking his head, "there's something from the Countess."

Seryozha immediately understood that what the hall porter was talking about was a birthday present from Countess Lydia.

"You don't say! Where is it?"

"Korney's taken it in to Papa. It must be something fine!"

"How big is it? Would it be this big?"

"Smaller, but a fine thing!"

"A book?"

"No—just something. Go on now, get along, your tutor's calling you," said the hall porter, hearing the approaching sound of the tutor's footsteps and carefully disengaging the little hand in the half-pulled-off glove that was holding him by the shoulder strap, and nodded toward the tutor.

"In just a second, Mr. Vasili!" replied Seryozha with the gay and affectionate smile that always conquered the painstaking tutor.

Seryozha was in too gay a mood, he found everything too delightful for him to be able not to share with his friend the hall porter another family joy he had found out about from Countess Lydia's niece on his walk in the public gardens. This joy seemed to him to be especially important since it coincided with the joy about the official and his own joy over the present that had been brought him. It seemed to Seryozha that today was one of those days on which everyone ought to be happy and gay.

"Did you know Papa's been given the Alexander Nevsky?"

"How could I help knowing! People have been calling already to congratulate him."

"Well, is he glad?"

"How can you help being glad at an honor from the Tsar! It shows he deserves it," said the hall porter sternly and solemnly.

Seryozha grew thoughtful as he gazed into the hall porter's face, which he had studied down to the smallest details, especially his chin, suspended between gray whiskers, which no one had seen but Seryozha, who never saw him except from below.

"Well, and has your daughter been here lately?"

The hall porter's daughter was a ballet dancer.

"When does she get time to come on weekdays? They also have to study. And you have your studies, too, sir, so get along now."

When he entered the schoolroom Seryozha, instead of sitting down to his studies, began telling his tutor his notion that what had been brought to him must be a machine. "What do you think?" he asked.

But all the tutor thought was that Seryozha had to learn his grammar lesson for the teacher Mr. Michael who was coming at two o'clock.

"Now just tell me, Mr. Vasili," he suddenly asked, when he was already sitting at his desk holding a book: "What's higher than the Alexander Nevsky? Did you know Papa's got the Alexander Nevsky?"

The tutor answered that the Vladimir was higher than the Alexander Nevsky.

"And higher than that?"

"The highest of all is the St. Andrew."

"And higher than that?"

"I don't know."

"What—you don't know either?" Seryozha, leaning on his elbows, sank into meditation.

His reflections were extremely complex and variegated. He imagined his father suddenly receiving both the Vladimir and the St. Andrew, and how because of that he would be much kinder today at lessontime, and how he himself when he grew up would receive all the decorations including whatever they thought up that was higher than the St. Andrew. The moment they thought it up he would get it. And even if one still higher was invented he would receive that immediately as well.

The time passed in reflections like these, and when his teacher came to the lesson on the Attributes of Time, Place and Modality he wasn't ready—and the teacher was not only displeased, but saddened. This sadness of his teacher's touched Seryozha. He didn't feel to blame for not having learned his lesson, since no matter how much he tried he definitely couldn't do it. As long as the teacher was explaining something to him he believed him and seemed to understand, but the moment he was left alone he was completely incapable of recalling or understanding how such a short and simple word like "suddenly" could be an Attribute of Modality. But nevertheless he was sorry for having hurt his teacher, and he had a desire to comfort him.

He chose a moment when the teacher was looking silently at the book.

"Mr. Michael, when is your birthday?" he asked abruptly.

"It would be better if you thought about your own work, birthdays don't mean a thing to rational people. It's just a day like another when it's necessary to do one's work."

Seryozha looked attentively at his teacher, at his thin little beard and at his glasses that had slipped down below a ridge he had on his nose, and became so engrossed in his thoughts that he no longer even heard what his teacher was explaining to him. He realized Mr. Michael didn't believe what he was saying; he felt this by the tone in which the teacher said it. But why have they all made an agreement to keep saying the same thing in exactly the same way, the most boring and useless things? Why does he thrust me away from him, why doesn't he love me? he asked himself sadly, and couldn't think of an answer.

## XXVII

AFTER his teacher left he was to have a lesson with his father. While waiting he sat at the desk, playing with a pocket knife, and began thinking. Among Seryozha's favorite occupations was watching out for his mother while he was walking. In general he didn't believe in death, and especially not in her death, even though Countess Lydia had told him that and his father had confirmed it; consequently, even after he had been told she was dead he kept looking for her while walking. Every shapely graceful woman with dark hair was his mother. At the sight of any woman like that a feeling of such tenderness rose up in his heart that he stopped breathing and tears came into his eyes. At any moment he expected her to come over to him and raise her veil. Her whole face would be visible, she would smile, embrace him, he would smell her aroma, feel the tenderness of her hands and weep happily, the way he had once lain at her feet one evening and she had tickled him, while he squealed with laughter and bit her white ring-covered hand. Then, when he accidentally learned from his nanny that his mother hadn't died, and his father and Countess Lydia had explained to him that she had died for his sake, because she was bad (which he didn't believe at all, since he loved her) he went on looking for her just as before and expecting her. There had been one woman today in the public gardens, in a purple veil, whom he had followed with his heart sinking, expecting it to be she, as she came toward him on the little path. This woman hadn't come up close; she had vanished somewhere. Today Seryozha felt a flood of tenderness for her more strongly than ever before, and now, sitting lost in thought waiting for his father, he cut into the whole edge of the table with his little knife, looking in front of him with shining eyes and thinking of her.

The tutor roused him. "Your Papa's coming!"

Seryozha jumped up, went over to his father, kissed his hand and looked at him attentively, on the lookout for signs of his joy at having been awarded the Alexander Nevsky.

"Did you have a nice walk?" said Karenin, sitting down in his own armchair, drawing up the Old Testament and opening it. In spite of Karenin's having told Seryozha more than once that every Christian ought to have a thorough knowledge of Biblical history, he himself often had to consult the Bible, and Seryozha had noticed this.

"Yes, Papa, it was all great fun," said Seryozha, sitting down on the chair sideways and rocking it, which was forbidden. "I met Nadenka." (This was Countess Lydia's niece, who was being educated at her house.) "She told me you've been given a new star. Are you glad, Papa?"

"First of all, don't rock the chair, please," said Karenin. "Secondly, what is precious is not the reward, but the work. And I should like you to understand that. For if you are going to exert yourself, and study in order to get a reward, then the work will seem hard to you, but if when you work you love your work"—Karenin said this remembering how he had sustained himself by an awareness of duty during the boring work he had done that morning, which had consisted of his signing one hundred and eighteen papers—"you will find a reward for yourself in just that."

Seryozha's eyes, which had been shining with tenderness and joy, grew dull and were cast down under his father's gaze. This was the same old familiar tone that his father had always used with him, and that Seryozha had already learned to adapt himself to. His father always spoke to him—so Seryozha felt—as though he were addressing some imaginary boy, one of those to be found in books, but quite unlike Seryozha. And with his father Seryozha always made an attempt to pretend to be that same boy out of a book.

"You understand that, I hope?" said his father.

"Yes, Papa," Seryozha replied, pretending to be the imaginary boy.

The lesson consisted of learning several verses of the Gospels by heart and repeating the beginning of the Old Testament. Seryozha had a fair knowledge of the Gospel verses, but while he was reciting them he became so absorbed in looking at the bone in his father's forehead, which turned very sharply above the temple, that he got mixed up, and tacked the end of one verse on to the beginning of another, because they had the same word. It was obvious to Karenin that Seryozha didn't understand what he was saying, and this annoyed him.

He frowned and began an explanation that Seryozha had already heard a great many times and could never remember because he understood it too clearly, along the same lines as "suddenly" being an Attribute of Modality. Seryozha looked at his father with frightened eyes and could think of only one thing: would his father force him or not to repeat what he had just said, as he sometimes did? This thought frightened Seryozha so much that he stopped understanding anything at all. But his father didn't make him repeat anything, and went on to the Old Testament lesson. Seryozha gave a good account of the events themselves, but when he had to answer questions about what some of the events stood for, he didn't know anything, even though he had already been punished before for not knowing this lesson. But the place where he couldn't think of anything to say at all, and floundered about, cutting the table and rocking the chair, was where he had to say something about the antediluvian patriarchs. He didn't know a single one of them except Enoch, who had been taken up to Heaven alive. He had been able to recall some names before, but now he had completely forgotten them, chiefly because Enoch was his favorite in the whole of the Old Testament; there was a whole long train of thought in his mind, associated with the taking of Enoch to Heaven alive, that he surrendered himself to now, his eyes fixed on his father's watch chain and a half-fastened button on his waistcoat.

Seryozha, who was spoken to about death so often, didn't believe in it at all. He didn't believe that people he loved could die, and especially not that he himself would. He found this completely impossible and incomprehensible. But he was told everyone died: he would even ask people whom he trusted and they confirmed it; his nanny also said so, though reluctantly. But Enoch hadn't died, therefore not everyone did. Then why shouldn't everyone be able to deserve the same in the sight of the Lord and be taken up into Heaven alive? Seryozha thought. Bad people, that is, the ones Seryozha didn't love, they might die, but the good ones could all be just like Enoch.

"Well then, who were the patriarchs?"

"Enoch, Enos . . ."

"But you've already said that. That's bad, Seryozha, very bad indeed. If you don't make an effort to learn what's the most important thing for a Christian," said his father, getting up, "then what can interest you? I'm displeased with you, and Mr. Peter"—this was his educational supervisor—"is also displeased with you . . . I shall be obliged to punish you."

His father and his educational supervisor were both displeased with Seryozha, and in fact he was a very poor student. But it would have been impossible to say he had no ability. On the contrary, he was far more able than the boys whom his supervisor set him as examples. From his father's point of view he didn't want to learn what he was taught. But essentially he couldn't, and he couldn't because there were more imperative demands on his soul than those made on him by his father and supervisor. These demands contradicted each other; he was in direct conflict with his instructors.

He was nine years old, a child; but he knew his own soul and it was precious to him, he guarded it as the eyelid guards the eye, and he would allow no one into his soul without the key of love. His instructors complained that he didn't want to learn anything, while his soul was overflowing with a thirst for knowledge. And he learned from Kapitonych, from his nanny, from Nadenka, from Mr. Vasili, but not from his instructors. The water that his father and supervisor expected would turn their own mill wheels had long since leaked out and was working away somewhere else.

Seryozha was punished by his father, who didn't allow him to go to see Countess Lydia's niece Nadenka; but this punishment turned out luckily for Seryozha. Mr. Vasili was in a good mood and showed him how to make windmills. He spent the whole evening at work, dreaming of how a windmill could be made you could ride on: either by hanging on to one of the sails or by tying yourself on, then turning round. Seryozha didn't think about his mother all evening, but after getting into bed he suddenly remembered her and prayed in his own words for his mother to stop hiding and come to him tomorrow, for his birthday.

"Mr. Vasili, d'you know what I said an extra prayer for?"

"To learn better?"

"No!"

"Toys?"

"No! You'll never guess. It's something wonderful, but it's a secret! When it comes true I'll tell you. Have you guessed it?"

"No, I haven't. You'll have to tell me," said the tutor smiling, which he seldom did. "Well lie down, I'll put out the candle."

"Without the candle I can see what I've been praying for much better. There, I almost told you the secret!" said Seryozha, with a merry laugh.

When the candle had been taken away Seryozha heard and felt his mother. She was standing over him and caressing him with a loving look. But then the windmills appeared, then a knife, and everything turned topsy-turvy and he fell asleep.

## XXVIII

ON their arrival in Petersburg, Vronsky and Anna stopped at one of the best hotels, Vronsky separately, on the first floor, Anna with the baby and nurse upstairs in a large four-room suite.

Vronsky went to see his brother the day he arrived. There he met his mother, who had come from Moscow on business.

His mother and sister-in-law met him as usual; they asked him about his trip abroad and chatted about mutual acquaintances, but didn't say a single word about his liaison with Anna. But his brother, who came to see him the next morning, asked him about her himself, and Vronsky told him straight out that he looked on his liaison with Anna as a marriage; that he hoped to arrange for a divorce and then marry her, and until then considered her just as much his wife as any other wife, and he asked him to say as much to their mother and his own wife.

"If the world disapproves I don't care," said Vronsky, "but if my family wish to treat me as a member of the family they must treat my wife the same way."

His older brother, who had always respected the opinions of his junior, did not have a very clear idea about whether he was right or not until the world had decided the question; but for his own part he himself had nothing against it and went to see Anna together with Vronsky.

In his brother's presence, as in everyone else's, Vronsky addressed Anna with a certain formality, as a close acquaintance, but it was understood that his brother knew of their relationship and they spoke of Anna's going to Vronsky's estate.

In spite of all his worldly sophistication Vronsky was strangely deluded as a result of the new position he found himself in. He might have been expected to realize that for him and Anna society was closed: but now a number of foggy notions sprang up in his mind that it had only been this way in olden times, while with all the rapid progress nowadays (without noticing it he had become a partisan of every sort of progress), the views of society had changed and the question of whether they would be received by society was not yet settled. Of course, he thought, Court society won't receive her, but intimates must and ought to have a proper understanding of it all.

It's possible to sit for several hours with your legs doubled up in the same position if you know nothing is preventing you from changing it; but if a man knows he has to sit that way, with his legs doubled up, he will get cramps, and his legs will begin to jerk and strain in the direction he would like to stretch them. This was just how Vronsky felt about society. Though at the bottom of his heart he knew that society was closed to them, he kept on testing it to see whether society hadn't changed by now and might not receive them. But he noticed very quickly that though society was open to him personally, it was closed to Anna. Like the game of cat-and-mouse the arms that were raised for him to enter were instantly lowered in front of Anna.

One of the first ladies in Petersburg society whom Vronsky saw was his cousin Betsy.

"At last!" she greeted him joyfully. "And Anna? I'm so glad! Where are you stopping? I can imagine how hideous you must find our Petersburg after your charming trip; I can imagine your honeymoon in Rome! What's happening with the divorce? Is that all settled?"

Vronsky noticed a drop in Betsy's enthusiasm when she learned there had been no divorce as yet.

"There will be stones thrown at me, I know," she said, "but I'm going to see Anna; yes, I'm going without fail! You're not staying here long, are you?"

In fact she did go to see Anna the same day; but her tone was no longer the same at all. It was plain that she was proud of her boldness; she wanted Anna to appreciate her fidelity. She didn't stay more than ten minutes, chatting about the latest society news, and on leaving she said:

"You haven't told me when the divorce is going to take place. Of course I don't mind stepping out of line, but a lot of sticklers are going to give you the cold shoulder until you get married. And nowadays it's so simple; it's the done thing. So you're leaving this Friday? It's a pity we'll not be seeing each other any more."

Betsy's tone should have told Vronsky what he had to expect from society; but he made one more attempt in his own family. He had no hopes of his mother. He knew that his mother, who had been so enthusiastic over Anna when they had first met each other, was now implacably set against her because she had brought about the ruin of his career. But he set great hopes on Varya, his brother's wife. It seemed to him that she would not be the one to throw a stone, but would see Anna and receive her with simplicity and assurance.

The day after his arrival Vronsky went to see her; finding her alone he told her straight out what he wanted.

"You know how fond I am of you, Alexis," she said after listening to him; "I'm ready to do anything for you, but I've kept silent because I know I cannot be of any use to you and to Madame Karenin." She said "Madame Karenin" with particular emphasis. "Please don't think I condemn her. Never: in her place I might very well have done the same. I'm not going into any details, nor can I," she said, looking timidly into his morose face, "but things must be called by their proper names. You want me to call on her, receive her, and thus rehabilitate her in society; but you must understand that I *cannot* do that. I have growing daughters, and I must live in society for the sake of my husband. If I call on Madame Karenin she will realize I cannot invite her to my house, or if I do I must do it in such a way that she won't run into those who may take a different view, and that will hurt her. I cannot raise her up—"

"But I don't consider that she's fallen any lower than hundreds of women whom you do receive!" Vronsky stopped her, still more morosely; he got up in silence, realizing that his sister-in-law's decision was inflexible.

"Alexis—don't be angry with me! Please understand that it's not my fault," Varya began, looking at him with a timid smile.

"I'm not angry with you," he said, just as morosely, "but I'm doubly pained. I'm pained also by the fact that this breaks up our friendship. Or if it doesn't break it up it weakens it. You understand that for me too there can be no other way."

And on that he left her.

Vronsky realized that any further efforts would be fruitless, and that they would have to spend their few days in Petersburg as though they were in a strange city, avoiding any contact with their former world in order not to be exposed to the humiliating unpleasantnesses he found so painful. One of the chief annoyances of the situation in Petersburg was that Karenin and his name seemed to be everywhere. It was impossible to start talking about anything without the conversation turning to Karenin; it was impossible to go anywhere without running into him At any rate so it seemed to Vronsky, as a man with a sore finger thinks that he is constantly knocking it up against everything as though on purpose.

Their stay in Petersburg seemed to Vronsky even more oppressive because throughout this whole period he kept seeing in Anna some sort of novel mood that baffled him. Sometimes she would seem to be in love with him, sometimes she would be chilly, irritable, and impenetrable. She was being tormented by something, and hiding something from him; she seemed unaware of the humiliations that were poisoning his life and for her, with her acute perception, ought to have been even more painful.

## XXIX

ONE of the reasons for their trip to Russia, for Anna, was to see her son again. From the day she left Italy the thought of this reunion had been a source of constant excitement to her, and the nearer she came to Petersburg the more the joyfulness and importance of this reunion kept growing in her imagination. She didn't even ask herself the question of how it was to be arranged. It seemed to her a simple, natural thing to see her son when she was living in the same city; but on her arrival in Petersburg she suddenly got a clear picture of her present position in society, and realized that arranging for the meeting would be difficult.

She had already been in Petersburg for two days. The thought of her son never left her for a moment, but she still hadn't seen him. She felt she had no right to go straight to the house, where she might meet Karenin. They might not let her in, and humiliate her. It was painful for her even to think of writing to her husband and establishing contact with him; she could only feel at ease when he was out of her thoughts. Seeing her son while he was taking a walk, after she had found out where and when he went out, wouldn't be enough for her: she had been preparing herself for this meeting for so long, there was so much she had to say to him, she longed so much to embrace him, to kiss him. Seryozha's old nanny could have helped and advised her, but she was no longer in Karenin's house. Two days went by in this way, while she vacillated and made inquiries about the nanny.

The third day, after she had learned of Karenin's intimate friendship with Countess Lydia, she decided to write her the letter that had cost her such an effort, in which she deliberately said that permission to see her son must depend on her husband's magnanimity. She knew that if the letter were shown to Karenin he would live up to the magnanimous role he was playing and not refuse her.

The commissionaire who delivered her letter brought back the cruelest and most unexpected answer—that there was no answer. She had never felt so humiliated as the moment when she called in the commissionaire and heard from him a detailed account of how he had waited and then been told: "There will be no answer." She felt wounded and humiliated, but she saw that from her own point of view Countess Lydia was right. Her grief was all the more bitter because she had to bear it alone. She could not and did not wish to share it with Vronsky. She realized that though it was he who had been the chief cause of her misfortune the question of her seeing her son again would seem to him completely trivial. She realized he would never be capable of understanding the full depth of her suffering; she realized that if he reacted in a chilly way to her mentioning it she would hate him. She was more afraid of this than of anything in the world, and so she hid from him everything to do with her son.

She spent the whole day at home, turning over in her mind ways and means of seeing her son again, and finally resolved to write to her husband. She had already composed a letter to him when Countess Lydia's letter was brought to her. The Countess's silence had made her feel humble and submissive, but this letter, and everything she read between the lines in it, made her so angry, its spitefulness seemed to her so outrageous in comparison with her rightful passionate love for her son, that she grew indignant against the others and stopped blaming herself.

Such coldness, such hypocrisy! she said to herself. They just want to wound me and torture the child—am I going to submit to that? Not for anything! She's worse than I, at least I'm not a liar!

She decided then and there that the very next day, Seryozha's birthday itself, she would go straight to her husband's house, bribe the servants, deceive them, but at all costs would see her son and destroy the monstrous deception in which they were enveloping the unfortunate child.

She went to a toyshop, bought a lot of toys, and thought out a plan of action. She would go there early in the morning, at eight o'clock, when Karenin would surely still be in bed. She would have some money ready in her hand which she would give to the hall porter and the footman so that they would let her in; without raising her veil she would say she had come from Seryozha's godfather with birthday greetings and that she had been instructed to put the toys near Seryozha's bed. The only thing she didn't prepare was what she would say to her son; no matter how much she thought about this she couldn't invent anything.

The next day, at eight in the morning, Anna got out of a hired carriage alone and rang the bell at the main entrance of her former house.

"Go and see what it is—it's some lady," said Kapitonych, who was still not dressed, in an overcoat and galoshes, looking through the window at the veiled woman standing in front of the door.

Kapitonych's assistant, a young fellow Anna didn't know, had no sooner opened the door when she had come in, taken a three-ruble note out of her muff and hastily slipped it into his hand.

"Seryozha . . . Master Sergius!" she said, and was about to move on. After examining the note the porter's assistant stopped her at the inner glass door.

"Whom do you want?" he asked.

She didn't hear this, and said nothing.

Noticing the stranger's confusion Kapitonych himself came out, admitted her inside, and asked what he could do for her.

"I've come from Prince Skorodumov, to see Master Sergius," she said.

"He's not up yet," said the hall porter, scrutinizing her intently.

Anna had not had the slightest expectation that the completely unchanged appearance of the hallway of the house she had lived in for nine years would have such a powerful effect on her. One after the other memories, joyful and painful, rose up in her mind; for a moment she had forgotten just why she was there.

"Would you like to wait?" said Kapitonych, helping her off with her cloak.

After taking off her coat Kapitonych looked at her face, recognized her and silently bowed.

"Please come in, Your Excellency," he said to her.

She wanted to say something, but her voice refused to produce any sounds: she gave the old man a guilty look full of entreaty and with rapid steps went up the staircase. Bending forward and tripping on the steps in his galoshes, Kapitonych ran after her, trying to overtake her.

"The tutor's there, he may not be dressed; let me announce you."

Anna continued up the familiar staircase, not understanding what the old man was saying.

"Here, please, to the left. You must excuse us, it's not clean. He's been put in the little sitting room now," said the hall porter, panting. "Allow me, just a moment, Your Excellency! I'll take a look," he said, and having overtaken her he opened a high door and vanished behind it. Anna stood there waiting. "He's just woken up," said the hall porter, coming out again.

Just as he said this Anna overheard the sound of a child yawning. By the sound of this yawn alone she recognized her son, and seemed to see him alive in front of her.

"Let me in now, let me in!" she cried and entered through the high door. A bed was standing to the right of the door, and a boy was sitting up in it, with nothing on but an unbuttoned nightshirt, bending his little body backward, stretching, and finishing his yawn. Just as his lips were closing they formed into a sleepily blissful smile, and still smiling he slowly and sweetly tumbled backward again.

"Seryozha!" she whispered, coming toward him noiselessly.

During the time they had been separated, and with the gush of love for him she had been feeling all this last time, she had imagined him as a four-year-old child, which was how she had loved him best. Now he was no longer even as she had left him; he had changed still more from the time he was four; he had grown more and gotten thinner. How could it be! How thin his face was! How short his hair! How long his arms were! How he had changed since the time she had left him! But it was he—the shape of his head, his lips, the soft neck, the broad little shoulders.

"Seryozha!" she repeated, just above the child's very ear.

He raised himself on his elbow again, moved his tousled head from side to side as though looking for something, and opened his eyes. For a few seconds he gazed quietly and questioningly at the motionless figure of his mother standing in front of him, then suddenly gave a ecstatic smile; closing his sleepy eyes again he tumbled once more, not backward, but forward toward her, into her arms.

"Seryozha! My darling little boy!" she murmured, catching her breath and putting both arms around his plump little body.

"Mama!" he muttered, wriggling about in her arms so as to touch them with different parts of his body.

Smiling sleepily, his eyes still closed, he moved his plump little hands from the back of the bed to clasp her by the shoulders, leaning against her and enveloping her in the sweet aroma of warmth and sleepiness that only children have, and began rubbing himself up against her neck and shoulders.

"I knew it!" he said, opening his eyes. "Today's my birthday. I knew you'd come! I'll get up right away."

And as he said this he began dozing off again.

Anna watched him avidly; she saw how he had grown and changed during her absence. She recognized and didn't recognize his naked legs, which were now so long, sticking out from under the quilt; she recognized his cheeks, thinner now, and those close-cropped locks of hair at the nape of his neck where she had kissed him so often. She kept touching all these things, speechless: tears were choking her.

"But what are you crying about, Mama?" he said, quite wide awake now. "Mama, why are you crying?" he cried in a tearful voice.

"I? I won't cry any more—I'm crying for joy. I haven't seen you for so long. I won't cry, no I won't," she said, swallowing her tears and turning away. "Well, now it's time for you to get dressed," she added after a moment's silence, when she had recovered; without letting go of his hand she sat down beside his bed on a chair where his clothes were lying ready.

"How do you get dressed without me? How—" She had wanted to start talking simply and gaily, but she could not and turned away again.

"I don't wash with cold water; Papa said not to. And have you seen Mr. Vasili? He's coming. And now you've sat down on my clothes!"

Seryozha burst out laughing. She looked at him and smiled.

"Mama! Darling Mama! Dearest!" he shouted, flinging himself at her again and embracing her. It was as though he clearly understood only now, after seeing her smile, what had happened. "You don't need that," he said, taking off her hat. And as though seeing her anew without her hat he flung himself at her again and kissed her.

"But what did you think about me? Did you think I was dead?"

"I never believed it!"

"You didn't believe it, darling?"

"I knew it, I knew it all along!" he cried, repeating his favorite phrase; seizing her hand which was caressing his hair he pressed the palm of it to his mouth and covered it with kisses.

## XXX

MEANWHILE the tutor, Mr. Vasili, who hadn't understood at first who this lady was, realized from the conversation that she was the mother who had deserted her husband; he hadn't known her because he had come to the house afterward. Now he was in doubt as to whether he should go in or not, or inform Karenin. He finally came to the conclusion that it was his duty to get Seryozha up at the appointed time, and so it was none of his business to bother about who was sitting there, the mother or anyone else, but he had to do his duty; he got dressed, went to the door and opened it.

But the caresses of the mother and son, the sounds of their voices, and what they were saying to each other—all this made him change his mind.

He shook his head, sighed and shut the door again. I'll wait another ten minutes, he said to himself, coughing and wiping away his tears.

Meanwhile there was intense excitement among the servants of the house. They all learned that Madame had arrived, that Kapitonych had let her in, that she was now in the nursery, and that all the while the master was going to the nursery at nine o'clock as usual; they all realized that an encounter between husband and wife was unthinkable and had to be forestalled. Korney, the valet, went down to the hall porter's room and asked who had let her in and how; when he learned Kapitonych had let her in and brought her upstairs he reprimanded the old man. The hall porter stubbornly kept silent, but when Korney told him he "ought to be fired for it" Kapitonych bounded at him and waving his hands about in front of Korney's face he started in:

"Yes, and I suppose you wouldn't have let her in! I've been in service here ten years and seen nothing but kindness; and you would have gone up to her now and said, 'All right now, please—out!' You're very clever at understanding everything, aren't you! You'd better watch out for yourself, cheating the master and stealing his fur coats!"

"Old fool!" Korney said contemptuously and turned to the nanny, who had just come in. "Judge for yourself," he said to her. "He let her in without telling anyone, and the master will be ready any minute and be going into the nursery."

"Oh dear, oh dear!" said the nanny. "You'd better keep him back somehow, the master, and I'll rush up and get her out somehow. A fine business!"

When the nanny went into the nursery Seryozha was telling his mother about how he and Nadenka had fallen down together rolling over and over, and done three somersaults. She listened to the sounds of his voice, watched his face and the play of expression on it, felt his arm, but didn't understand what he was saying. She had to leave now, she had to leave him—that was all she could think and feel. She heard the tutor's steps as he came up to the door and coughed, then the steps of the nanny coming in; but she sat there as though turned to stone, powerless to make a move, either to speak or to get up.

"Madame, my dearest!" the nanny began, going up to Anna and kissing her hands and shoulders. "Now there God has given some joy to our birthday boy! You haven't changed in the slightest!"

"Oh nanny, darling, I didn't know you were in the house," said Anna, coming to her senses for a moment.

"I don't live here, I live with my daughter. I just came to give him birthday greetings, darling Madame Anna!"

Suddenly the nanny burst into tears and began kissing her hand again.

Seryozha, his eyes and smile radiant, holding on to his mother with one hand and the nanny with the other, began stamping his plump little bare feet on the carpet. His beloved nanny's tenderness toward his mother filled him with rapture.

"Mama! She often comes to see me, and when she comes—" he began, but stopped as he noticed the nanny saying something to his mother in a whisper, and on his mother's face an expression of fear and something like shame, which was completely out of place there.

She went over to him. "My darling!" she said.

She could not say *good-by*, but the expression on her face said as much, and he understood. "Darling, darling Kutik!" she said, calling him by her name for him as a baby, "you won't forget me? You—" But she was unable to say anything further.

How many words she thought up later that she might

have said to him! But now she didn't know what to say; she was speechless. But Seryozha understood everything she wanted to tell him. He understood that she was unhappy and that she loved him. He even understood what the nanny had said to her in a whisper. He had caught the words "always before nine o'clock"; he understood that they referred to his father and that it was impossible for his father and mother to meet. He understood all this, but there was one thing he was unable to grasp: Why had there been an expression of fright and shame on her face? She could not have done anything wrong, but she was afraid of his father and ashamed of something. He wanted to ask a question that would clear up his doubt, but he didn't dare to: he saw she was suffering and he felt sorry for her. He pressed up against her in silence, and said in a whisper:

"Don't go yet, he's not coming for a while!"

His mother moved him away from her, to make sure he realized what he was saying, and by the frightened expression on his face she saw that he was not merely talking about his father, but seemed to be asking her in some way how he ought to feel about him.

"Seryozha, my darling," she said, "love him—he's better than I, and kinder, and I've done something to him that was wrong. When you're grown up you'll be able to judge."

"There's no one better than you!" he cried out in despair through his tears; clutching her by the shoulders he hugged her with all his might, his arms trembling with the effort.

"My darling little baby!" said Anna, and like a child began weeping just as weakly as he was himself.

Just then the door opened and the tutor came in. Steps were heard at the other door, and the nanny said, "He's coming!" in a frightened whisper and handed Anna her hat.

Seryozha sank down onto the bed and began sobbing, hiding his face in his hands. Anna took his hands away, kissed his damp face once again and with rapid steps went out the door. Karenin was coming toward her. When he saw her he stopped and bowed his head.

In spite of her having just said that he was better and kinder than she, the swift glance she cast at him, taking in his whole figure in the most minute detail, filled her with feelings of loathing and rage toward him, and of jealousy for her son. With a rapid movement she let down her veil and, quickening her steps, practically ran out of the room.

She had not had time even to unwrap the toys she had picked out in the shop with such love and sadness the day before, and she took them away with her.

### XXXI

INTENSELY as Anna had longed to see her son again, and as long as she had thought of it and prepared herself for it, she did not expect in the least that the reunion would affect her so powerfully. On returning to her lonely suite in the hotel she couldn't understand for a long time just why she was there. Yes, it's all finished, and I'm alone again, she said to herself; without taking off her hat she sat down in an armchair near the fireplace. Staring fixedly at a bronze clock standing on a table between the windows, she sank into thought.

The French maid, whom she had brought from abroad, came in to ask whether she wasn't dressing. She looked at her in astonishment and said: "Later." A waiter offered her coffee. "Later," she said.

The Italian nurse, having tidied up the baby girl, came in and held her out to Anna. The plump, well-fed little girl, as always when she saw her mother, turned over her little hands, that seemed to have threads tightly tied round them, with their palms down and her little mouth smiling a toothless smile began waving them like a fish moving its fins, making the starched folds of her embroidered frock rustle. It was impossible not to smile at the baby girl and kiss her; it was impossible not to hold out toward her a finger, which she caught, gurgling and wriggling with her whole body; it was impossible not to hold out your lip to her, which she drew into her little mouth by way of a kiss. And Anna did all this; she took her in her arms, dandled her, and kissed her fresh little cheek and bare elbows; but at the sight of this infant it was even clearer to her that the feeling she had for her was not love at all compared with what she felt for Seryozha. Everything about this little girl was charming, but for some reason nothing caught at the heart. The first child, even though its father had not been loved, had received all her unsatisfied powers of love; the little girl had been born in the most difficult circumstances, and had not received even a hundredth part of the care given the first. Aside from this, in the little girl everything was still in the future, while Seryozha was already almost a personality, and a beloved one; thoughts and feelings were already struggling within him; he understood her, he loved and judged her, she thought, recalling what he said and the way he looked. And now she was separated from him forever, not only physically but spiritually, and nothing could be done to set this right.

She handed the little girl to the nurse, dismissed her, and opened a locket with a portrait of Seryozha in it, at almost the same age as the little girl. She got up and removing her hat took from the little table an album containing pictures of her son at different ages. She wanted to compare the likenesses, and began taking them out of the album. She took them all out, leaving only one, the last and best. He was sitting astride a chair, frowning with his eyes and smiling with his mouth. This was his most characteristic and best expression. She pulled at a corner of the picture with her adroit little hands, whose slender white fingers had been moving with particular tension that day, but the picture kept slipping away and she couldn't get it out. The paper knife was not on the table, and she took out the picture next to it (one of Vronsky, taken in Rome, wearing his hair long and in a round hat) and used it to push out her son's picture. "Yes, there he is!" she said, with a glance at Vronsky's picture, and suddenly she recalled that he had been the cause of her present distress. She hadn't thought of him once that whole morning, but now, suddenly, when she looked at this virile, noble, charming face she knew so well, she felt an unexpected gush of love for him.

But where is he? How can he leave me alone with my suffering? she thought, with a sudden feeling of reproach, forgetting that it was she herself who hid everything that concerned her son from him. She sent to him asking him to come to see her at once; she waited for him with a sinking heart, planning the words in which she was going to tell him everything, and the expressions of his love with which he was going to comfort her. The servant came back with the reply that he had a visitor, but that he would come immediately, and had instructed him to inquire whether she could receive him together with Prince Yashvin, who had just arrived in Petersburg. He's not coming alone, she thought, and he hasn't seen me since dinner yesterday; he's coming with Yashvin, so that I won't be able to tell him everything. And suddenly a strange thought came to her mind: What if he had stopped loving her?–

And going over the events of the past few days it seemed to her that she saw a confirmation of this peculiar idea in everything: that he hadn't dined at home the evening before, that he had insisted on their having separate apartments in Petersburg, and that even now he was not coming to see her alone, as though he were avoiding a tête-à-tête with her.

But he ought to tell me! I must know! If I were to know then I'd know what to do, she said to herself, incapable of imagining the position she would be in if she were persuaded of his indifference. She thought he had stopped loving her, she felt on the verge of despair, and because of this she felt especially excited. She called for the maid and went into her dressing room. She took greater pains in dressing than she had done all these days, as though even if he had fallen out of love with her his love might be revived by her wearing the dress and the hairdo that was most becoming to her.

She heard the bell ring before she was ready.

When she went into the drawing room it was not his eyes, but Yashvin's that met her. Vronsky was looking at the pictures of her son, which she had forgotten on the table, and was in no hurry to look at her.

"We've met," she said, placing her little hand in the enormous hand of Yashvin, who looked acutely embarrassed, which was very peculiar in view of his gigantic height and coarse face. "We met last year, at the races. Let me have those," she said, with a swift movement taking away from Vronsky the pictures of her son he had been examining, her eyes flashing him a significant look. "Were the races good this year? I watched the races at the Corso in Rome instead. But you don't like life abroad, do you?" she said, with a friendly smile. "I know you and I know all your tastes, though we've seen so little of each other."

"I'm very sorry about that, my tastes are mostly very bad," said Yashvin, gnawing the left side of his mustache.

After chatting a while and noticing that Vronsky had glanced at his watch, Yashvin asked her whether she was going to stay on in Petersburg for some time, and unwinding his gigantic body picked up his cap.

"I don't think I am," she said, embarrassed, looking at Vronsky.

"Then we won't see each other again?" said Yashvin, getting up and turning to Vronsky. "Where are you dining?"

"Come and have dinner with me," said Anna firmly, as though annoyed with herself for her embarrassment, but blushing as she always did when she had to reveal her situation to some new person. "The dinner here isn't much good, but at any rate you'll be able to see each other. Of all his friends from the regiment there's no one Alexis likes so much as you."

"Delighted," said Yashvin with a smile that showed Vronsky he liked Anna very much.

Yashvin bowed and left. Vronsky stayed behind.

"Are you off too?" she said.

"I'm late as it is," he replied. "Go ahead! I'll catch up with you in a second!" he shouted after Yashvin.

She took him by the hand and looked at him fixedly, casting about in her mind for something to say that would keep him from going.

"Wait a moment, there's something I must tell you." Taking his hand she pressed it to her neck. "Yes—was it all right for me to ask him to dinner?"

"You did very well," he said with a calm smile, showing his closely set teeth and kissing her hand.

"Alexis—have you changed toward me?" she said, pressing his hand with both her own. "Alexis, I'm miserable here. When are we leaving?"

"Soon, very soon. You can't imagine how tiresome I find our life here too," he said, drawing back his hand.

"Well go then, go!" she said, wounded, and quickly walked off.

## XXXII

ANNA was still not home by the time Vronsky returned. Soon after he had left, he was told, some lady had come to see her and they had gone out together. Her going out without telling him where, her still not being there, her having gone somewhere that same morning without saying anything to him about it—all this, together with her peculiarly excited expression that morning and the recollection of the hostile manner with which she had almost snatched her son's pictures out of his hands in Yashvin's presence, forced Vronsky to reflect. He made up his mind that they had to clear things up between them, and he waited for her in the drawing room. But Anna did not return alone, but brought along her aunt, an old woman, Princess Barbara Oblonsky, who had also been there that morning and with whom Anna had gone off shopping. Anna seemed not to notice Vronsky's worried, inquiring expression, and merrily told him what she had bought that morning. He saw that something peculiar was going on inside her: there was a strained attentiveness in her glittering eyes when they rested on him for a moment, and in her speech and movements there was the nervous rapidity and gracefulness that had fascinated him when they were first becoming intimate but that now alarmed and frightened him.

Dinner was set for four. They were all assembled and about to go into the small dining room when Tushkevich arrived with a message for Anna from Princess Betsy. Princess Betsy was apologizing for not having come to say good-by; she was not well, but she asked Anna to come to see her between half-past six and nine o'clock. Vronsky glanced at Anna at this specific reference to time, which showed that steps had been taken for her not to meet anyone; but Anna did not seem to notice it.

"I'm terribly sorry, but just between half-past six and nine I can't make it," she said, smiling slightly.

"The Princess will be very sorry."

"So shall I."

"You're doubtless going to hear Patti?" said Tushkevich.

"Patti? You've given me an idea. I'd go if it were possible to get a box."

"I can get one," Tushkevich proposed.

"I should be very, very grateful to you," said Anna. "But wouldn't you like to dine with us?"

Vronsky shrugged his shoulders slightly. He had no idea of what Anna was up to. Why had she brought along this elderly Princess? Why had she asked Tushkevich to stay to dinner? Most surprising of all, why was she sending him off for a box? Surely it was out of the question, in her position, for her to go to a subscribers' performance of Patti's, when all her society friends would be there? He looked at her earnestly, but she responded with the same challenging look, either high-spirited or desperate, that baffled him. At dinner she was aggressively merry: it seemed as though she were flirting with both Tushkevich and Yashvin. When they got up from the dinner table and Tushkevich went off to get the box, while Yashvin went to have a smoke, Vronsky down with him to his own rooms. He sat there a little while, then ran upstairs again. Anna was already dressed in a light silk dress trimmed with velvet, which she had had made in Paris, very low-cut and with rich white lace on her head that framed her face and set off her dazzling beauty to particular advantage.

"Are you actually going to the opera?" he said, trying not to look at her.

"Why do you ask in such a frightened way?" she said, hurt once again by his not looking at her. "Why shouldn't I go?"

She seemed not to understand what he meant.

"Of course, there's no reason not to," he said frowning.

"That's just what I'm saying," she said, deliberately not understanding the irony of his tone and calmly pulling on her long perfumed glove.

"Anna—for God's sake! What's the matter with you?" he said, appealing to her in just the same way as her husband once had.

"I don't understand what you're asking me."

"You know it's impossible to go."

"Why not? I'm not going alone. Princess Barbara has gone to dress, she's going with me."

He shrugged his shoulders with a look of bewildered perplexity.

"But don't you realize—" he began.

"I don't want to realize!" she almost screamed. "I don't want to! Do I regret what I've done? No! No and no! And if it were all to be done over again, from the beginning, the same thing would happen. For us, for you and for me, there's only one thing that's important—whether we love each other. There are no other considerations. Why do we live here apart, without seeing each other? Why can't I go out? I love you, and I don't care about anything," she said, changing into Russian, looking at him with a peculiar glitter in her eyes which he couldn't understand, "as long as you haven't changed. Why don't you look at me?"

He looked at her. He saw the whole beauty of her face and evening dress, which was always so becoming to her. But now it was just this beauty and elegance of hers that irritated him.

"My feelings cannot change, you know that, but I'm asking you not to go—I beg of you," he said in French again, with a tender entreaty in his voice but with a cold look.

She did not hear what he said, but she saw the coldness

in his eyes and replied with irritation: "And I ask you to explain why I ought not to go out."

"Because it might cause you—" he began to stumble.

"I don't understand a thing. Yashvin is not compromising, and Princess Barbara is no worse than anyone else. And here she is!"

### XXXIII

For the first time Vronsky had a feeling of irritation, almost of anger with Anna because of her deliberate obtuseness about her position. This feeling was heightened because of his inability to express the cause of his annoyance. If he had told her frankly what he thought he would have said: "To appear at the opera in that dress, with the Princess, a woman whom everyone knows about, would mean not only acknowledging your position as a fallen woman, but also flinging a challenge in the face of society, that is, renouncing it forever."

He couldn't say this to her. But how can she fail to understand it? What's happening inside her? he said to himself. He felt that his respect for her diminished simultaneously as his awareness of her beauty increased.

Frowning, he returned to his rooms, and sitting down beside Yashvin, who had stretched his long legs out on a chair and was drinking brandy and seltzer, ordered the same for himself.

"You were talking about Lankovsky's Powerful. It's a fine horse, I advise you to buy him," said Yashvin, glancing at his friend's gloomy face. "He's got a drooping rump, but his legs and head—you couldn't ask for anything better."

"I think I'll take him," Vronsky replied.

He was interested in the conversation about horses, but he didn't forget about Anna for a moment; involuntarily he kept listening to the sounds of footsteps along the corridor and looking at the clock on the mantelpiece.

"Madame Karenin has asked me to inform you that she has gone to the opera," a servant came in to report.

Yashvin poured another glass of brandy into the sparkling water, drank it down, and got up, buttoning his coat.

"Well, let's go," he said, smiling slightly beneath his mustache and showing by this smile that he understood the reason for Vronsky's moroseness, but attached no importance to it.

"I'm not going," replied Vronsky glumly.

"But I have to, I promised. Well, *au revoir*. If you change your mind come to the orchestra, you can take Krasinsky's seat," Yashvin added as he went out.

"No, I've got something to do."

A wife's a nuisance, but when she's not your wife it's worse, Yashvin thought as he left the hotel.

After Vronsky was left alone he got up from his chair and began pacing about the room.

Now what's on today? It's the fourth subscription night . . . Yegor and his wife'll be there, and probably my mother. That means that all Petersburg will be there. By now she's come in, taken off her coat, and stepped forward into the light. Tushkevich, Yashvin, Princess Barbara . . . He visualized them all. And what about me? Either I was afraid, or I transferred her protection to Tushkevich, isn't that it? No matter how you look at it, it's stupid, very stupid . . . And why does she put me in this position? he said to himself, flinging a hand up.

It caught the little table the seltzer water and a decanter of brandy were standing on and almost knocked it over. He tried to catch it and overturned it; he angrily kicked it, then rang the bell.

"If you want to go on working for me," he said to his valet when he came in, "then keep your mind on your duties. There must be none of this sort of thing. You'll have to clear it away."

The valet, who felt quite blameless, was about to defend himself, but he glanced at his master and by the expression on his face he realized he had best keep quiet; hurriedly apologizing he knelt on the carpet and began collecting the bottles and glasses, whole and shattered.

"It's not up to you to do that! Send a waiter in to clear it up and get my dress suit ready!"

Vronsky entered the Opera House at half-past eight. The performance was in full swing. The little old man who was the box attendant took Vronsky's fur coat, and recognizing him called him "Your Excellency," and suggested that he not take a number but simply call for Theodore afterward. There was no one in the lighted corridor except for the box attendant and two footmen with coats over their arms, listening at the door. From behind a door that was ajar there came the sounds of a discreet staccato accompaniment of the orchestra and of one female voice that was enunciating a musical phrase with precision. The door opened, letting an attendant slip through, and the phrase, approaching its end, struck Vronsky's ear distinctly. But the door shut again immediately, and though Vronsky did not hear the end of the phrase or cadenza after it, he realized from the thunder of applause from behind the door that the cadenza was finished. As he entered the auditorium, brilliantly lighted by chandeliers and bronze gas brackets, the uproar was still going on. On the stage Adelina Patti, her diamonds and bare shoulders glittering, bowing low and smiling, with the help of the tenor who was holding her by the hand, was collecting the bouquets that came clumsily flying across the footlights. She went up to a man, his hair parted in the middle and gleaming with pomade, who was stretching his long arms out across the footlights to hand her something—and the entire audience in the orchestra and boxes stirred, leaned forward, shouted and clapped. From his raised stand the conductor helped to pass over the bouquets, and adjusted his white tie. Vronsky went to the middle of the floor, then stopped and began looking around. Today he paid less attention than ever to the familiar, customary setting: the stage, the hubbub, the whole familiar, uninteresting, motley herd of spectators in the packed Opera House.

There were the same ladies in the boxes, with the same kind of officers behind them; the same gaily dressed women—God knew who—the same uniforms and frock coats; the same filthy crowd in the gallery, and in this entire throng, in the boxes and front rows, there were some forty *real* men and women. It was these oases that Vronsky immediately turned his attention to and established contact with.

The act had just finished when he came in, so without going into his brother's box he went up to the first row and stopped in front of the footlights beside Serpukhovskoy, who was standing there with his knee bent tapping the wall of the orchestra with his heel; he had seen Vronsky in the distance and welcomed him over with a smile.

Vronsky had not yet seen Anna; he intentionally avoided looking her way. But he could tell where she was by the direction of people's eyes. He glanced round unobtrusively, though without looking for her; anticipating the worst his eyes looked for Karenin. But this time, luckily for him, Karenin wasn't in the auditorium.

"How little there is of the military man left in you!"

Serpukhovskoy said to him. "A diplomat, an artist—something like that."

"Yes, as soon as I came home I put on a dress suit," Vronsky replied with a smile, slowly taking out his opera glasses.

"Now there's something I envy you, I admit. When I get back from abroad and put on these—" he touched his epaulettes—"I regret my lost liberty."

Serpukhovskoy had long since shrugged his shoulders about Vronsky's military career, but he was as fond of him as before and was particularly affable to him now.

"It's a pity you missed the first act."

Vronsky, who was listening with one ear, shifted his opera glasses from the lower tier to the dress circle and scanned the boxes. Next to a woman wearing a turban and a bald old man who blinked angrily just as the moving opera glass came to him, Vronsky suddenly saw Anna's head, proud, startlingly beautiful, and smiling away in its lace frame. She was in the fifth box in the lower tier, some twenty paces from him. She was sitting in the front of the box, and had turned round slightly and was saying something to Yashvin. The poise of her head on her lovely broad shoulders, and the gleam of restrained excitement in her eyes and her whole face reminded him of just how she had been when he had seen her at the ball in Moscow. But now this beauty of hers affected him in a completely different way. There was nothing mysterious now in his feeling for her, and though her beauty attracted him more powerfully now than before, at the same time it hurt him. She was not looking his way, but Vronsky felt she had already seen him.

When Vronsky leveled his glasses that way again he noticed that Princess Barbara was singularly red, and was laughing unnaturally and constantly glancing over into the neighboring box, while Anna, who had folded her fan and was tapping it on the red velvet edge of the box, was gazing in some other direction, not seeing and obviously not wishing to see what was going on in the next box. Yashvin's face had the look it had whenever he was losing at cards. He was frowning and kept sucking the left tip of his mustache farther and farther into his mouth, looking askance at the same box, to the left.

The Kartasovs were in this box. Vronsky knew them and knew that Anna was acquainted with them. The wife, a small, thin woman, was standing up in the box with her back turned toward Anna and putting on an opera cloak, which her husband was holding for her. Her face was pale and angry; she was saying something excitedly. Kartasov, stout and bald-headed, kept glancing over at Anna and trying to calm his wife. When his wife went out, Kartasov dawdled behind for a long moment, trying to catch Anna's eye and obviously wanting to bow to her. But Anna was evidently disregarding him intentionally; she had turned round and was saying something to Yashvin, whose cropped head was bent toward her. Kartasov went out without bowing, and the box was left empty.

Vronsky didn't understand just what had happened between the Kartasovs and Anna, but he realized it was something that was humiliating for her. He realized this both because of what he saw and above all because of Anna's expression; he knew she was collecting her last reserves in order to sustain the role she had assumed. This role, of outward calm, was entirely successful. Anyone who didn't know her or her circle, who heard none of the expressions of compassion, indignation or astonishment uttered by the women at her having allowed herself to appear in society, and to appear so conspicuously in her lace headdress and in all her beauty, admired the serenity and beauty of this woman, without suspecting that she was undergoing the feelings of someone being pilloried.

Knowing that something had happened, but not knowing just what, Vronsky felt painfully agitated; he went over to his brother's box in the hope of finding out something. He purposely left the auditorium by the side opposite Anna's box, and as he went out he ran into the colonel of his old regiment talking to two acquaintances. Vronsky heard the Karenins being mentioned, and noticed how the colonel hastened to call him by name, with a significant glance at the others.

"Aha, Vronsky! And when are you coming to see us at the regiment? We can't let you go without having a supper. You're the oldest of the gang," said the colonel.

"I shan't have time, awfully sorry, some other time," said Vronsky and ran up the staircase to his brother's box.

The old Countess, Vronsky's mother, with her steel-gray curls, was in his brother's box. Varya and Princess Sorokin met him in the corridor outside.

After conducting Princess Sorokin back to Vronsky's mother, Varya held out her hand to her brother-in-law and immediately began talking to him about what he was interested in. He had seldom seen her so excited.

"I think it's mean and horrid! Madame Kartasov had no right to do it! Madame Karenin—" she began.

"But what is it? I have no idea."

"What, you haven't heard?"

"You understand that I'd be the last one to hear."

"Is there a creature more poisonous than that Kartasov woman?"

"But what's she done?"

"My husband told me . . . She insulted Madame Karenin. Her husband began talking to her from their box, and this Kartasov woman made a scene. They say she said something offensive in a loud voice and then went out."

"Count, your *maman* is calling you," said Princess Sorokin, looking out from the door of the box.

"I've been expecting you the whole time," his mother said to him with an ironical smile. "You've been completely invisible."

Her son saw that she could not repress a smile of glee.

"How are you, *maman*? I was coming to see you," he said coldly.

"How is it you're not going off to pay court to Madame Karenin?" she added, when Princess Sorokin had stepped aside. "She's making a sensation. They're forgetting all about Patti because of her."

"*Maman*, I've asked you not to speak about that to me," he replied frowning.

"I'm simply saying what everyone else is."

Vronsky said nothing, and after making a few remarks to Princess Sorokin he went out. He met his brother in the doorway.

"Ah, Alexis!" said his brother. "What a disgusting business! A fool, that woman, that's all. I was just going to see her, let's go together."

Vronsky didn't listen to him. He went downstairs with rapid strides: he felt he had to do something, but he didn't know what. His anger with her for having put both herself and him in such a false position, together with his compassion for her suffering, disturbed him deeply. He went down to the orchestra seats and walked straight over to Anna's box. Stremov was standing in front of it talking to her.

"There are no more tenors left. The mold's been broken."

Vronsky bowed to her and stopped to say hello to Stremov.

"You got here late, I suppose, and you've missed the finest aria," Anna said to Vronsky, with what seemed to him a mocking look.

"I'm a poor judge," he said, looking at her sternly.

"Like Prince Yashvin," she said with a smile, "who thinks Patti sings too loud."

"Thank you," she said, taking in her small hand with its long glove a program Vronsky had picked up for her; suddenly her beautiful face quivered for a second. She got up and went to the back of the box.

Noticing that her box remained empty when the next act began, Vronsky left the Opera House, to cries of *Hush!* from the audience, which had quieted down to listen to a *cavatina,* and went home.

Anna was back already. When Vronsky came in she was alone, still dressed as she had been for the opera. She was sitting in the first armchair beside the wall, staring in front of her. She glanced at him and immediately resumed her former posture.

"Anna—" he said.

"You're to blame for everything—you!" she cried, with tears of despair and fury in her voice, as she got up.

"I asked you, I begged you not to go, I knew it would be unpleasant for you . . ."

"Unpleasant!" she exclaimed. "It was horrible! I'll never forget it as long as I live. She said it was a disgrace to sit next to me."

"A silly woman's remark," he said, "but why take the risk, why provoke—"

"I hate your calmness! You should never have driven me to it. If you'd loved me—"

"Anna! What's it got to do with my love for you—"

"Yes, if you'd loved me as I love you, if you were going through the agony I'm—" she said, with a frightened glance at him.

He felt sorry for her and angry nevertheless. He assured her of his love, because he saw that it was the only thing that could soothe her now; he did not reproach her in words, but at the bottom of his heart he did reproach her.

She drank in these assurances of his love, which seemed to him so vulgar he was ashamed to pronounce them, and gradually calmed down. The next day, wholly reconciled, they left for the country.

# PART SIX

## I

DOLLY was spending the summer with her children in Pokrovsk, at her sister Kitty's. The house on her own estate was completely in ruins, and Levin and Kitty had persuaded her to spend the summer with them. Oblonsky was entirely in favor of this. He said he was very sorry that his duties prevented him from spending the summer in the country with his family, which would have been the ultimate in happiness for him, and he stayed behind in Moscow, coming out to the country now and then for a day or two. Aside from the Oblonskys, with all their children and a governess, the Levins also had as a guest the old Princess, who thought it her duty to watch over an inexperienced daughter who was *in a certain condition*. Also, Varenka, Kitty's friend from abroad, had kept her promise to come to see Kitty after she got married, and was staying there too. These were all relatives and friends of Levin's wife. And though he was fond of them all he regretted a little the Levin world and order of his own that had been swallowed up by this influx of the "Shcherbatsky element," as he called them to himself. Of his own relatives only one, Koznyshov, stayed with him that summer, but he too was a Koznyshov type of man and not a Levin, so that the Levin atmosphere was completely annihilated.

In the Levin house, which had been empty for so long, there were so many people now that nearly all the rooms were occupied; almost every day the old Princess, when sitting down to table, was obliged to count everyone, and send the thirteenth grandchild off to another little separate table. And Kitty, who was taking great pains running the household, had a lot of trouble getting all the chickens, turkeys, and ducks that were so badly needed to satisfy the summer appetites of the guests and children.

The whole family had sat down to dinner. Dolly's children, with the governess and Varenka, were making plans about where to go mushroom hunting. Koznyshov, whose intellect and erudition enjoyed a respect on the part of all the visitors that went almost as far as veneration, astonished everyone by joining in the conversation about mushrooms.

"You must take me along too! I'm very fond of mushroom hunting," he said, looking at Varenka. "I consider it an excellent occupation."

"Why, of course, we should be delighted," Varenka replied, with a blush. Kitty and Dolly exchanged significant looks. The suggestion of the learned and intellectual Koznyshov that he go mushroom hunting with Varenka reinforced some thoughts of Kitty's that had greatly occupied her mind lately. She hastened to start talking to her mother so that her look would not be noticed. After dinner Koznyshov sat down by a window in the drawing room with his cup of coffee, continuing a conversation he had begun with Levin and glancing over at the door that the children who were preparing to set out on the mushroom hunt would come through. Levin sat down on the window sill beside him.

Kitty was standing beside her husband, obviously waiting for the conversation, of no interest to her, to end so that she could tell him something.

"You've changed a great deal since you got married, and for the better," said Koznyshov to Levin, smiling at Kitty and plainly not very interested in the conversation either. "But you've remained faithful to your passion for defending the most paradoxical views."

"Katya, it's not good for you to stand," Levin said with a meaningful look, drawing up a chair for her.

"Ah yes, well, there's no time now," Koznyshov added as the children came running in.

Ahead of all of them, galloping in sideways in her tightly pulled-up stockings, waving a basket and Koznyshov's hat, Tanya came running in directly at him.

Boldly rushing up to Koznyshov, her beautiful eyes shining like her father's, she handed Koznyshov his hat, pretending to be about to put it on him, but softening her boldness by a shy, affectionate smile.

"Varenka's waiting," she said, carefully putting the hat on his head, seeing by Koznyshov's smile that it was all right.

Varenka was standing in the doorway, having changed into a yellow print dress with a white kerchief round her head.

"Coming, coming," Kozynyshov said to her, finishing

his coffee and putting his handkerchief and cigar case in different pockets.

"Oh what a darling my Varenka is, isn't she!" Kitty said to Levin as soon as Koznyshov had got up. She said this so that Koznyshov could hear it, which she evidently wanted him to. "And how beautiful—noble and beautiful! Varenka!" she called out to her. "Will you be in the wood by the mill? We'll drive over and join you."

"You really do keep forgetting your condition, Kitty," said the old Princess, hurrying in. "You mustn't shout that way."

Hearing Kitty's voice and her mother's reprimand, Varenka came over to Kitty with swift, light strides. The swiftness of her movements, the color that flushed her animated face, all showed that something unusual was taking place within her. Kitty knew what this unusual thing was and watched her attentively. She had only called Varenka now in order to give her a mental blessing for the important event that in Kitty's mind was due to happen in the woods that day after dinner.

"Varenka, I'll be very happy if a certain thing happens," she whispered, giving her a kiss.

"And are you coming along with us?" said Varenka to Levin, embarrassed and pretending that she hadn't heard what had been said to her.

"I'm coming, but only as far as the threshing floor; I'll have to stay there."

"But what d'you want to go there for?" said Kitty.

"I have to take a look at the new wagons and count them," said Levin. "And where are you going to be?"

"On the balcony."

II

ALL the women had gathered together on the balcony. They generally liked to sit there after dinner anyhow, but today there was some work to do as well. Aside from the sewing of little shirts and the knitting of swaddling bands, which they were all busy with, some jam was being made there according to a method that was novel to Miss Agatha, without adding any water. Kitty had introduced this new method, which had been used at her mother's. Miss Agatha, who had used to be in charge of this work, and who thought that nothing done in the Levin household could be wrong, had put some water in the strawberries and the wild strawberries, maintaining that it couldn't be done any other way; she had been detected, and now the raspberry jam was being made in everyone's presence; Miss Agatha had to be persuaded that jam too would turn out well without water.

Miss Agatha, with a flushed face and wounded expression, her hair ruffled and her thin arms bared to the elbows, was moving the perserving pan over the brazier with a rotating movement, morosely watching the raspberries and longing with all her heart for them to harden and not get cooked through. The Princess, who felt that Miss Agatha's wrath must be directed at her as the chief adviser in the boiling of jam, made an effort to look as though she were busy with something else and had no interest in raspberries; she talked about other things but from the corner of her eye kept glancing over at the brazier.

"I always buy my maids' clothes ready-made myself, at the sales," said the Princess, continuing a conversation. "Shouldn't the scum be taken off now, my dear?" she added, turning to Miss Agatha. "It's quite unnecessary for you to do that yourself, besides it's hot," she said, stopping Kitty.

"I'll do it," said Dolly, and getting up she began carefully moving the spoon over the bubbling sugar; now and then, to remove what stuck to it she would tap it against a plate that was already covered by the varicolored, yellowish-pink scum, with its blood-red streaks of syrup. How they'll lick it up with their tea! she said to herself, thinking of her children and recalling how when she was a child herself she used to be astonished at grown-ups' not eating the best part—the scum.

"Stiva says it's much better to give them money," Dolly said, continuing an absorbing conversation about the best presents to give servants, "but—"

"Money—how can you give them money!" Kitty and the Princess both began with one voice. "They *appreciate* presents so!"

"Well, for instance, last year I bought our Matrona not poplin, but something like it," said the Princess.

"Yes, I remember she wore it on your nameday."

"The pattern was absolutely charming: so simple and refined. I should have had some made up for myself, if she hadn't had it. It was something like Varenka's; so pretty and cheap."

"Well, I think it's ready now," said Dolly, letting the syrup drop off the spoon.

"When it begins to set it's ready. Boil it a little more, Miss Agatha."

"These flies!" said Miss Agatha angrily. "It's going to come out just the same," she added.

"Oh how sweet he is, don't frighten him!" said Kitty unexpectedly, looking at a sparrow that had settled on the railing; it had turned over a raspberry stalk and had begun pecking away at it.

"Yes, but you ought to stay farther away from the brazier," said her mother.

"About Varenka now," said Kitty in French, which they had been talking all along so that Miss Agatha couldn't understand them. "You know, *maman*, for some reason I expect things to be settled today; you know what I mean. How wonderful that would be!"

"Really, what a wonderful matchmaker!" said Dolly. "How carefully, how adroitly she brings them together!"

"No, tell me, *maman*, what d'you think?"

"But what am I to think? He"—*he* meant Koznyshov —"could have made the best match in Russia always; now of course he's not so young any more, but I know that even now a great many would be glad to marry him anyhow. She's got a very good heart, but he could—"

"No, Mama, you must understand why it would be impossible to think up anything better for either one of them. First of all—she's a darling!" said Kitty, crooking one finger.

"He likes her very much, that's sure," Dolly chimed in.

"Then he's got such standing in society that he hasn't the slightest need for either money or social position in his wife. He needs only one thing—a good, charming wife, who'll be quiet."

"Yes, she certainly wouldn't be upsetting," Dolly chimed in again.

"Thirdly, she'd have to love him. And she does! So, it would be just wonderful! I'm expecting them to come popping out of the woods now, with everything settled! I'll be able to tell at once by their eyes. I'd be so happy! What d'you think, Dolly?"

"But don't get excited now, there's no need at all for you to get excited," said her mother.

"But I'm not excited, Mama. I think he's going to propose today."

"Oh, that's so peculiar, when and how a man proposes. There's some sort of barrier, then suddenly it's burst through," said Dolly with a dreamy smile, recalling her own past with Oblonsky.

"Mama, how did Papa propose to you?" Kitty suddenly asked.

"There was nothing extraordinary about it, it was all very simple," replied the Princess, though her face was all radiant at the memory.

"No, but how? You really *loved* him even before you were allowed to speak to each other?"

Kitty felt a special charm in being able to talk to her mother now as an equal about these most important questions of a woman's life.

"Of course, I loved him: he used to come and stay with us in the country."

"But how was it decided? Mama—how?"

"I suppose you think you and Kostya invented something new? It's always exactly the same thing: it was settled by looks, smiles . . ."

"How well you put it, Mama! That's it exactly—looks and smiles," Dolly agreed.

"But just what words did he use?"

"What did Kostya say to you?"

"He wrote it with a piece of chalk. It was wonderful . . . How long ago it seems to me now!" she said.

And the three women fell to musing on the same thing. Kitty was the first to break the silence. She had recalled the whole winter that preceded her marriage, and her infatuation with Vronsky.

"There's one thing—that old love affair of Varenka's," she said, reminded of this by a natural association of ideas. "I wanted to say something to Koznyshov about it somehow, to prepare him. Men are terribly jealous, all of them," she added, "of our pasts."

"Not all of them," said Dolly. "You're judging by your own husband. To this day the thought of Vronsky tortures him, doesn't it? Isn't that so?"

"Yes, it is," replied Kitty, her eyes smiling dreamily.

"But what I don't know," said the old Princess, defending her maternal watchfulness over her daughter, "is just what there is in your past that could upset him? That Vronsky paid court to you? That happens to every young girl."

"Well, we weren't speaking about that," said Kitty blushing.

"No, excuse me," her mother went on, "and then you yourself didn't want to let me talk it over with Vronsky. D'you remember?"

"Oh, Mama!" said Kitty, with a pained look.

"Nowadays there's no holding you girls back . . . For that matter your relations with him couldn't have gone any further than they ought to have; I should have called him to account myself. But it's not good for you to get excited, my dear. Please remember that and keep calm."

"I'm quite calm, *maman*."

"How lucky it turned out for Kitty then that Anna came along," said Dolly, "and how unlucky for her. It's a complete turnabout," she added, struck by her own thought. "At that time Anna was so happy, while Kitty considered herself unhappy. Now it's just the reverse! I often think of her."

"There's someone to think about! A vile, disgusting woman, without a heart," said the mother, who couldn't forget that it was Levin whom Kitty had married and not Vronsky.

"What's the point in talking about that?" Kitty exclaimed irritably. "I never think about it and I don't want to . . . I don't want to think about it," she repeated, listening to the familiar footsteps of her husband coming up the staircase to the balcony.

"About what?" asked Levin, coming out on the balcony. "What don't you want to think about?"

But no one answered him, and he didn't repeat the question.

"I'm sorry I've broken into your feminine domain," he said, glancing round at them all with irritation, having realized that they had been talking about something they wouldn't have discussed in his presence.

For a second he felt that he shared Miss Agatha's displeasure at having to boil jam without water, and at the alien Shcherbatsky influence in general. But he smiled and went over to Kitty.

"Well, how are you?" he asked her, giving her the same look everyone did now.

"All right, very well," Kitty said with a smile. "And how are you getting on?"

"The wagons hold three times as much as the old carts. Should we go fetch the children? I've ordered the gig harnessed."

"What—d'you want to take Kitty in the gig?" said her mother reproachfully.

"But we'll go at a walk, Princess."

Levin never called the Princess *maman*, as sons-in-law do, and this annoyed her. But in spite of Levin's great fondness and respect for the Princess he could not call her that without violating his feelings for his own dead mother.

"Come along with us, *maman*," said Kitty.

"I don't want to look on at such follies."

"Well, then I'll go on foot. Walking is good for me." Kitty got up, went over to her husband and took him by the hand.

"It's good for you, but everything in moderation," said the Princess.

"Well, Miss Agatha, is the jam ready?" Levin said to Miss Agatha with a smile, wishing to cheer her up. "Is the new way any good?"

"I suppose so . . . We would think it overcooked."

"It's better that way, Miss Agatha, it won't ferment; besides our ice is all melted now and we have no place to keep it cool," said Kitty, who had immediately realized Levin's purpose and spoke to the old woman in the same spirit. "Anyhow, your pickling is so good Mama says she's never eaten the like of it anywhere," she added, smiling and straightening out the old woman's kerchief.

Miss Agatha gave Kitty an angry look.

"There's no need to comfort me, ma'am. The moment I look at you and him together I feel cheerful," she said; the coarse way she had of saying *him* touched Kitty.

"Come along with us mushroom hunting, you can show us the right places."

Miss Agatha smiled and shook her head, as much as to say: I should be delighted to get angry with you but it's impossible.

"Please follow my advice," said the old Princess. "Cover the jam with a sheet of paper soaked in rum; it'll never get moldy then even without ice."

## III

KITTY was particularly glad of an occasion to be alone with Levin because she had noticed the shadow of vexation that crossed his face, which always gave such a vivid reflection of everything, when he had come onto the balcony and asked what they had been talking about, without getting any answer.

When they walked ahead of the others and passed out of sight of the house onto the hard, dusty road, strewn with rye ears and grain, she leaned more heavily on his arm and pressed it to her. He had already forgotten his momentary irritation, and when he was alone with her, now that the thought of her pregnancy never left him for a moment, he had a joyous feeling, still novel, of completely unsensual pleasure in the nearness of a beloved woman. There was nothing to talk about, but he felt like hearing the sound of her voice, which like her looks had changed now with pregnancy. Her voice and looks had a softness and earnestness such as people have who are constantly concentrated on a favorite task.

"You're sure you won't be tired now? Lean on me more," he said.

"No, I'm so happy at the chance to be alone with you! I admit that no matter how I enjoy their presence I miss our winter evenings together."

"That was good then, but now it's even better. Both are better," he said, squeezing her hand.

"You know what we were talking about when you came in?"

"Jam?"

"Yes, about jam too; but then about how men propose."

"Ah!" said Levin, who was listening to the sound of her voice more than to what she was saying, and kept thinking about the path which was now passing by the woods, and about avoiding the places where she might make a false step.

"And about Sergius and Varenka. Have you noticed? I want it very much," she went on. "What d'you think about it?" She looked into his face.

"I don't know what to think," replied Levin with a smile. "Sergius is very strange to me about such things. You know I once told you—"

"Yes, that he was in love with that girl who died . . ."

"That was when I was a child; I know it by hearsay. I remember him at that time. He was wonderfully sweet. But ever since then I've been watching him with women: he's amiable, he likes some of them, but you feel that for him they're simply human beings, not women."

"Yes, but now with Varenka . . . There seems to be something there . . ."

"Perhaps there is. But you have to know him . . . He's

peculiar and wonderful. He lives a purely spiritual life; his soul is too pure and lofty."

"What! Would that lower him?"

"No, but he's so used to living a purely spiritual life that he can't reconcile himself to reality, and Varenka, after all, is a reality."

Levin had already grown accustomed now to speaking his mind boldly, without taking the trouble to put things precisely; he knew his wife at such loving moments as these would grasp what he meant from a mere hint. She understood him now.

"Yes, but she doesn't have the same sort of reality as I do; I realize he would never have fallen in love with me. She's all spirit . . ."

"Well, no, he's very fond of you as it is, it's always such a pleasure when my people like you—"

"Yes, he's very nice to me, but—"

"But not the way it was with poor Nicholas . . . You and he grew very attached to each other," said Levin, finishing the sentence. "Why shouldn't we speak about it?" he added. "Sometimes I reproach myself: it'll end by our forgetting him. Oh what a terrible, wonderful fellow he was! . . . Yes . . . Well, what were we talking about?" said Levin, after a moment's silence.

"You think he can't fall in love," said Kitty, translating his thoughts into her own language.

"Not so much that he can't fall in love," said Levin with a smile, "but he lacks that weakness that is necessary . . . I've always envied him; even now, when I'm so happy, I envy him anyhow."

"You envy him for not being able to fall in love?"

"I envy him for being better than I," said Levin, smiling. "He doesn't live for himself. His whole life is subordinated to duty. That's why he can be at peace and contented."

"And you?" said Kitty, with an ironical, loving smile.

She would have been quite unable to express the train of thought that had made her smile; but the final link in it was that in singing his brother's praises and abasing himself before him her husband was not being sincere. Kitty realized that this insincerity of his arose out of his love for his brother, out of a feeling of guilt at being too happy, and especially out of a desire to improve that never left him. She loved this in him, and so she smiled.

"And you? What are you discontented about?" she asked with the same smile.

Her lack of belief in his discontent with himself made him happy; unconsciously he drew her on to express her reasons for it.

"I'm happy, but dissatisfied with myself," he said.

"But how can you be dissatisfied if you're happy?"

"How can I explain to you? . . . At heart I wish for nothing more than that you shouldn't stumble. No, really, you mustn't jump so!" he interrupted himself with a reproach to her for making too rapid a movement in stepping over a branch that was lying across the path. "But when I examine myself and compare myself with others, especially with my brother, then I feel how bad I am."

"But why?" Kitty went on, still smiling in the same way. "Don't you do things for others too? What about your small holdings, your farming, your book?"

"No, I feel, and I feel it especially now—it's your fault," he said, squeezing her hand, "that that's not the thing. I do it just so, casually. If I could love everything I do as I love you . . . but as it is I've been doing it lately as though I were finishing a lesson assigned me."

"Then what d'you say about Papa?" asked Kitty. "Is he bad too because he's never done anything for society?"

"He? No. But you have to have the same simplicity, clarity, and kindness as your father—have I got that? I don't do anything and I torment myself. It's you who've done it all. When you weren't there, and when *that* still wasn't there," he said with a glance at her stomach which she understood, "I put all my energies into my work; now I can't, and I'm ashamed; I do it just as though it were a lesson assigned me, I pretend . . ."

"Well, would you like to change places now with Sergius?" said Kitty. "Would you like to do things for the common good and become attached to this assigned lesson, and only that?"

"Of course not," said Levin. "Though I'm so happy I no longer understand anything. So you think he's going to propose today?" he added, after a pause.

"I do and I don't. It's just that I want him to so awfully! But wait a minute . . ." She leaned over and plucked a daisy on the side of the road. "Well, start counting: he'll propose, he won't," she said, handing him the flower.

"He'll propose, he won't," Levin said, pulling off the narrow, white petals.

"No, no!" cried Kitty, who had been excitedly watching his fingers; she caught hold of his hand and stopped it. "You tore off two at a time!"

"Well this little one doesn't count," said Levin, picking off a short half-grown petal. "And there's the gig catching up with us."

"Aren't you tired, Kitty?" the Princess called out.

"Not in the least!"

"You'd better get in, if the horses are quiet; we'll go at a walk."

But it wasn't worth getting in the gig; they were close by already, and they all went on foot.

## IV

VARENKA, with the white kerchief round her black hair, surrounded by the children whom she was good-naturedly and gaily taking care of, and obviously excited by the prospect of a proposal from a man she liked, looked extremely attractive. Koznyshov walked by her side in constant admiration of her. Looking at her he recalled all the charming things he had heard her say, everything good he had heard about her, and became more and more aware that the feeling he had for her was something special he had not experienced for a very long time, and then only once, in his early youth. The feeling of happiness at her nearness, which kept growing stronger and stronger, reached a point when, as he dropped into her basket an enormous wood mushroom he had found, with a thin stem and turned-up top, he looked into her eyes and, noticing the flush of happy, apprehensive excitement that spread over her face, he was embarrassed himself, and silently gave her the sort of smile that said too much.

If this is so, he said to himself, then I must think it over and make up my mind, and not surrender to a momentary impulse like a boy.

"I'll go along now and collect my own mushrooms independently, or else my contribution won't be noticed," he said, and moved off from the edge of the wood, where they had been walking about in the short silky grass between the scattered old birch trees, into the middle of the wood, where there were some gray-stemmed aspens and dark hazel shrubs growing among the white birch. Going along some forty paces Koznyshov, knowing he could no longer be seen, stopped behind a spindle bush in full flower, with reddish pink catkins. All round him there was total silence. Only the hum of flies, like that of a swarm of bees, sounded continuously high up in the birch trees he was standing under, and now and then the voices of the children reached him. Suddenly there came the sound, not far from the edge of the wood, of Varenka's contralto, calling Grisha, and a happy smile came over Koznyshov's face. Becoming aware of this smile, he shook his head disapprovingly at his own state of mind, got out a cigar and lighted it. For some time he was unable to strike the match on the bole of a birch tree. The delicate scales of the white bark clung to the phosphorus, and the light would go out. Finally one of the matches caught, and the aromatic smoke of the cigar, like a broad swaying sheet with clear-cut outlines, moved forward and upward over the bush beneath the overhanging birch boughs. Following this column of smoke with his eyes, Koznyshov walked on slowly, pondering his condition.

Why not? he was thinking. If it were a sudden impulse or a passion, if all I felt were this attraction, this mutual attraction (I'm entitled to call it mutual), but felt that it went counter to the entire tenor of my life, if I felt that in surrendering to this attraction I should be betraying my calling and my duty . . . but it's not that. The only thing I can say against it is that when I lost Marie I told myself that I would remain faithful to her memory. That's the only thing I can say against this feeling of mine . . . That is important, Koznyshov said to himself, feeling at the same time that this consideration could have no importance for him personally, though it might spoil his poetic role in the eyes of others. Aside from that, no matter how hard I looked I could never find any other objection to this feeling of mine. If I were to make a choice based on reason alone I couldn't find anything better.

However many women and girls he called to mind whom he had known, he could not remember a single girl who combined to such a degree all those qualities, actually all of them, that he, reasoning cold-bloodedly, would like to see in his wife. She had all the freshness and charm of youth, but was not a child, and if she loved him she loved him consciously, as a woman ought to: that was one thing. Secondly: not only was she far from being worldly, but she obviously loathed worldliness, while at the same time she was familiar with society and had all the manners of a woman of good society, without which no life's companion would have been conceivable for Koznyshov. Thirdly: she was religious, not naïvely religious and kindhearted like a child, such as, for instance, Kitty; her life was founded on her religious convictions. Even in small details Koznyshov found in her everything he required of a wife: she was poor and alone, so that she wouldn't bring along a crowd of relations and their influence into her husband's house, as he saw Kitty doing, but would be indebted to her husband for everything, which was also what he had always wanted for his future family life. And this girl, who united all these qualities in herself, loved him. He was modest, but he could not help seeing this. And he loved her. The only negative consideration was his age. But he came of a long-lived breed, he didn't have a single gray hair, no one thought he was forty, and he recalled Varenka saying that it was only in Russia that people of fifty considered themselves old, while in France a man fifty years old considered himself to be in the prime of life, and a man of forty was a youngster. But what was the point of counting up years when he felt himself to be young at heart, just as he had been twenty years before? Wasn't the feeling he had now one of youth, as he came out to the edge of the wood again from the other side and saw, in the bright light of the sun's slanting rays, Varenka's graceful figure in a yellow dress with her basket, walking lightly past the trunk of an old birch tree, and when this impression, of the sight of Varenka, fused together with the view whose beauty struck him so, the field of oats turning yellow bathed by the slanting rays, and the old forest far beyond, flecked with yellow fading away into the bluish distance? His heart leaped for joy. He was seized by a melting feeling. He felt it was decided now. Varenka, who had just stooped over to pick up a mushroom, straightened up with a supple motion and looked round. Throwing his cigar away, Koznyshov resolutely strode toward her.

## V

Miss Varenka, when I was still very young I formed an ideal for myself of the woman I would fall in love with and *whom I would be happy to call my wife. I have lived a long life, and now for the first time I have encountered in you that which I have been seeking. I love you and I offer you my hand.*

This is what Koznyshov was saying to himself when he was already only ten steps away from Varenka. Kneeling and defending a mushroom against Misha with outstretched arms, she was calling little Masha.

"Here! Here! Children, there's lots!" she was saying in her sweet deep voice.

She did not get up or change her position when she saw Koznyshov approaching, but everything told him that she felt his closeness and that it made her happy.

"Well, did you find any?" she asked, from beneath her white kerchief, turning her handsome face toward him, with a gentle smile.

"Not a single one," said Koznyshov. "And you?"

Busy with the children surrounding her, she made no reply.

"There's another, near the branch," she said, pointing to a small mushroom, its rubbery pinkish cap cut across by a dry blade of grass it had sprung up underneath. She got up when Masha picked up the mushroom, breaking it into two white halves. "This reminds me of my childhood," she added, walking away from the children together with Koznyshov.

They walked a few steps in silence. Varenka saw that he wanted to say something; she could guess what it was, and felt her heart sink with joy and fear. They walked far enough away so that no one could have heard them any longer, but still he did not begin. It would have been better for Varenka to keep silent. It would have been easier to say what they wanted to say after a silence than after some talk about mushrooms; but in spite of herself, as though by accident, Varenka said:

"So you didn't find any? Though in the middle of the woods there are always fewer."

Koznyshov sighed and said nothing. He was annoyed at her having begun speaking about mushrooms. He wanted to make her turn back to what she had first said, in speaking about her childhood, but as though in spite of himself, after a moment's silence, he answered her last remark.

"I've heard that the edible white ones are mostly found

at the edge, though I can't tell the difference between the edible ones and the others."

Another few minutes passed; they had walked still farther away from the children and were altogether alone. Varenka's heart was beating so hard she could hear it; she felt herself turning red, then white, then red again.

Being the wife of a man like Koznyshov, after the situation she had been in with Madame Stahl, seemed to her the pinnacle of happiness. Aside from this she was very nearly convinced she was in love with him; and it was about to be settled any moment. She was afraid; she was afraid he would speak, and afraid he wouldn't.

He had to declare himself now or never; Koznyshov felt this too. Everything—the way she looked, her flushing, her downcast eyes—indicated a state of painful expectation. Koznyshov saw this and felt sorry for her. He even felt that saying nothing now would offend her. Mentally he rapidly went over all his arguments in favor of his decision. He also repeated to himself the words in which he had intended to propose; but instead of these words, because of some unexpected thought that came to his mind, he suddenly asked:

"What difference is there between the edible white mushrooms and the birch-tree kind?"

Varenka's lips quivered with emotion as she replied: "There's hardly any difference in the caps, it's just in the stems."

And the moment she said this, both he and she realized that it was all over, that what ought to have been said would not be said, and their excitement, which just before had reached its highest point, began to die down.

"The birch-tree mushroom's stem reminds one of a swarthy man's two-day-old beard," Koznyshov said, by now quite calm.

"Yes, that's true," Varenka replied with a smile, and involuntarily the direction they were strolling shifted. They began to get closer to the children. Varenka felt both hurt and ashamed, but at the same time she also had a feeling of relief.

On his return home, as he went over all his arguments again, Koznyshov decided his judgment had been at fault. He could not betray the memory of Marie.

"Gently, children, gently!" Levin shouted at the children,

actually angrily, stepping in front of his wife to protect her as the crowd of children, shrieking with delight, came hurtling toward them.

Behind the children Koznyshov and Varenka also came out of the woods. There was no need for Kitty to ask Varenka: by the serene and somewhat shamefaced expression on the faces of both of them she realized that her plans had not materialized.

"Well?" Levin asked her when they were on their way home again.

"It didn't take," said Kitty, with a smile and way of talking that recalled her father, which Levin with pleasure had often noticed in her.

"What d'you mean—it didn't take?"

"Like this," she said, taking Levin's hand, raising it to her mouth and touching it lightly to her lips. "The way you kiss the bishop's hand."

"But who didn't take what?" he said laughing.

"Neither one. And this is how it should have been . . ."

"Here are some peasants coming . . ."

"Oh, they didn't see!"

## VI

WHILE the children were having their tea the grown-ups were sitting on the balcony chatting as though nothing had happened, though all of them, especially Koznyshov and Varenka, knew very well that something had happened that even though it was negative was extremely important. They both had the same feeling, such as a pupil might have who had failed his examination and been left in the same class, or even permanently expelled. Everyone present spoke in an animated way about irrelevant things. Levin and Kitty felt especially happy and full of love for each other that evening, and their happiness in their own love entailed an unpleasant reflection on anyone who had wished for it and failed to obtain it: this made them feel ashamed.

"Mark my words, Alexander isn't coming," said the old Princess.

They were expecting Oblonsky by the evening train, and the old Prince had written he might be coming with him.

"And I know why," the Princess continued, "he says newly-weds have to be left by themselves at first."

"Yes but Papa's deserted us as it is. We haven't even seen him," said Kitty. "Besides, what sort of newlyweds are we? We're an old married couple by now."

"Well, but if he doesn't come then I'll be saying good-by to you too, children," said the Princess with a mournful sigh.

"Really, Mama, how can you!" Both her daughters fell on her at once.

"But how d'you suppose he can be feeling? Why now, after all—"

And suddenly, quite unexpectedly, the old Princess's voice began quavering. Her daughters fell silent and glanced at each other. *Maman* is always finding something to feel gloomy about, they said by these glances. They didn't realize that no matter how much the Princess enjoyed being with her daughters, no matter how needed she felt, she had been painfully depressed both for herself and for her husband ever since they had given away their last beloved daughter in marriage, and the family nest had been left empty.

"What is it, Miss Agatha?" Kitty suddenly asked Miss Agatha, who had stopped in front of her with a mysterious, portentous air.

"What about supper?"

"But that's perfectly all right," said Dolly, "you go and give the orders and I'll go off with Grisha for his lesson. Otherwise he won't have done a thing all day."

"Now there's a lesson for me! No, Dolly, I'll go," said Levin, jumping up.

Grisha, who had already entered a high school, had some homework to do over the summer. Dolly, who had learned Latin together with him while still in Moscow, had made it a rule on coming to stay with the Levins to go over with him the most difficult lessons—arithmetic and Latin —even if only once a day. Levin had offered to relieve her, but Dolly, who had once heard Levin give a lesson and noticed that he wasn't doing it in accordance with the method used by the teacher in Moscow, told him firmly, though she was embarrassed and tried not to hurt his feelings, that it had to be done according to the book, the way the teacher did, and that it would be better if once again she gave the lesson herself. Levin was annoyed both with Oblonsky for his carelessness in letting Dolly instead of himself take charge of the boy's education, which she had no understanding of at all, and with the teacher, for the children's being taught so badly; but he promised his sister-in-law to give the lessons in the way she wanted. And he went on taking charge of Grisha's lessons not in his own way, but according to the book, and so he did it unwillingly, often forgetting about lessontime. That was what had happened today.

"No, Dolly, I'll go, you just sit still," he said. "We'll do it all properly, by the little book. Only, when Stiva comes and we go shooting, then we'll miss the lessons."

And he went to see Grisha.

Varenka said the same thing to Kitty. Even in the Levins' well-run house Varenka was able to make herself useful.

"I'll order the supper, and you sit still," she said, and got up to go with Miss Agatha.

"Yes, yes, I'm sure they couldn't find any chickens. In that case our own will do . . ." said Kitty.

"Miss Agatha and I will attend to it," said Varenka, and they both vanished.

"What a sweet girl!" said the Princess.

"Not just sweet, *maman*, she's so charming there's no one like her."

"So you're expecting Stiva tonight?" said Koznyshov, obviously averse to continuing the conversation about Varenka. "It would be hard to find two brothers-in-law more unlike each other," he said with his subtle smile. "One is always on the move, only at home in society, like a fish in water; the other, our Kostya, is full of life, quick, sensitive to everything, but the moment he appears in society he either shuts up altogether or starts flopping around wildly like a fish on dry land."

"Yes, he's extremely thoughtless," said the Princess, turning to Koznyshov. "I was just going to ask you to tell him that it's impossible for her"—indicating Kitty—"to stay here. She simply must come to Moscow. He says we should get the doctor to come out here—"

"*Maman*, he's going to do everything that's necessary; he's agreed to everything," said Kitty, irritated at her mother for appealing to Koznyshov.

In the midst of their conversation they heard the snorting of horses and the sound of wheels scraping on the gravel in the driveway.

Dolly hadn't had time to get up to meet her husband before Levin had jumped out of the window of the room where Grisha had been doing his lesson, and had lifted Grisha out too.

"It's Stiva!" shouted Levin from below the balcony. "Don't worry Dolly, we've finished!" he added, and sprinted off like a boy toward the carriage.

"*Is, ea, id, ejus, ejus,*" shouted Grisha, hopping along down the driveway.

"And there's someone else, it must be Papa!" Levin called out, stopping at a bend in the driveway. "Kitty, don't come down by the steep steps, go round!"

But Levin was mistaken; the other person sitting in the carriage was not the old Prince. When Levin got close to the carriage he saw a handsome, stout young man wearing a Scottish bonnet, with long ribbons streaming behind. This was Vasenka Veslovsky, a second cousin of the Shcherbatskys'—a brilliant Moscow-Petersburg playboy, "a splendid young fellow and a passionate sportsman," as Oblonsky said when he introduced him.

Not in the least disconcerted by the disappointment he was responsible for in taking the place of the old Prince, Veslovsky gaily said hello to Levin, reminding him that they had known each other before, and lifted Grisha up into the carriage over the pointer Oblonsky had brought along.

Levin did not get into the carriage, but followed behind. He was somewhat irritated because the old Prince, whom the more he knew the more he had grown to like, had not come, and because of the appearance of this Veslovsky, a totally superfluous stranger. The latter seemed to him all the more superfluous and alien because as Levin approached the front steps where the whole animated crowd of children and grown-ups had assembled he saw Veslovsky kissing Kitty's hand with a particularly tender, gallant air.

"Your wife and I are cousins, and old friends too," Veslovsky said, once again giving Levin's hand a specially hard squeeze.

"Well now, is there any game?" said Oblonsky, who had scarcely had time to greet everyone, as he turned to Levin. "He and I have the most ferocious intentions . . . Here, Tanya, that's for you! . . . Please get it out of the carriage, in the back," he kept saying to everyone round him. "How much fresher you look, Dolly dear," he said to his wife, kissing her hand once again, holding it in one hand while he patted the back of it with the other.

Levin, who had been in the most cheerful mood a moment before, was now looking morosely at everyone, displeased by everything.

Whom was he kissing yesterday with those lips? he was thinking as he looked at Oblonsky caressing his wife. He looked at Dolly, and she displeased him too.

After all, she doesn't even believe in his love. Then why is she so happy? Disgusting! Levin thought.

He looked at the Princess, whom he had thought so charming a moment before; he disliked the way she welcomed this Veslovsky with his ribbons, as though she were in her own house.

Even Koznyshov, who had also come out onto the front steps, seemed disagreeable to him because of the hypocritical friendliness with which he met Oblonsky, when Levin knew his brother disliked Oblonsky and had no respect for him.

Varenka, too, seemed repellent to him because of her holier-than-thou air as she was introduced to this fellow, when the only thing she was thinking about was getting married.

And most repellent of all was Kitty, because of the way she surrendered to the atmosphere of gaiety with which this fellow, as though he were at a festival for himself and for everyone else, looked on his arrival in the country; what was particularly disagreeable was the special smile with which she responded to his smiles.

Chatting noisily they all went back into the house; but the moment they were all sitting down Levin turned round and went out again.

Kitty saw that something was wrong with her husband. She tried to snatch a moment to talk to him alone, but he hurried away from her saying there was something he had to do in the office. It had been a long time since his farming affairs seemed to him so important as they did that evening. For them it never stops being a holiday, he thought, yet these are no holiday matters here; they won't wait, and life without them is impossible.

## VII

LEVIN did not go back until they sent to call him to supper. Kitty and Miss Agatha were standing on the stairs conferring about the wines.

"But what are you making all this fuss about? Serve the usual things!"

"No, Stiva won't drink it; Kostya, wait a moment, what's the matter with you?" Kitty began, hurrying after him, but he mercilessly walked off with great strides into the dining room and immediately entered into the general conversation there which was being kept going by Veslovsky and Oblonsky.

"Well, are we going shooting tomorrow?" said Oblonsky.

"Please, do let's!" said Veslovsky, moving sideways onto another chair and doubling a stout leg up under him.

"I'd be delighted; let us. And have you had any shooting this year?" Levin said to Veslovsky, staring intently at his leg, but with the feigned affability that Kitty knew so well and that suited him so badly. "I don't know whether we'll come across any snipe, though there are a lot of woodcock. But we'll have to leave early. Won't you be too tired? Aren't you tired, Stiva?"

"Tired? Me? I've never been tired yet! Let's not go to bed at all! Let's go out for a walk!"

"Yes, really! Let's not go to bed! Splendid!" Veslovsky chimed in.

"Oh, we're quite sure you can go without sleep and stop others from getting theirs," said Dolly to her husband with that scarcely perceptible smile with which she nearly always addressed him now. "But in my opinion it's time already. I'm going; I shan't have any supper."

"No, no, stay here, Dolly dear," said Oblonsky, going over to her side of the long supper table. "I still have so much to tell you!"

"Probably nothing at all!"

"But d'you know Veslovsky's been to see Anna? And he's going to see them again. After all they're not more than fifty miles from us. And I'm certainly going over too. Veslovsky, come over here!"

Veslovsky came over to the ladies, and sat down beside Kitty.

"Oh, do tell me, please! You've been to see her? How is she?" Dolly said to him.

Levin stayed at the other end of the table, and while talking constantly with the Princess and Varenka he saw that a lively and mysterious conversation was going on between Oblonsky, Dolly, Kitty, and Veslovsky. Not only was there a mysterious conversation going on, but he saw Kitty's look of deep feeling as she gazed fixedly at Veslovsky's handsome face telling them something in a vivacious way.

"It's extremely nice at their place," Veslovsky was saying about Vronsky and Anna. "Of course it's not up to me to judge, but in their house you feel you're in a family."

"What are they planning to do?"

"I think they want to go to Moscow for the winter."

"How nice it would be for us all to go over and see them together! When are you going?" Oblonsky asked Veslovsky.

"I'm spending July with them."

"And will you go too?" said Oblonsky, turning to his wife.

"I've wanted to for a long time and certainly will," said Dolly. "I'm sorry for her, and I know her—she's lovely. I'll go over alone when you're away, then I won't inconvenience anyone. It would be even better without you."

"And very nice too," said Oblonsky. "What about you, Kitty?"

"Me? Why should I go?" said Kitty, crimsoning. She glanced round at her husband.

"Are you acquainted with Madame Karenin?" Veslovsky asked her. "She's a very attractive woman."

"Yes," Kitty replied, blushing still more deeply, then getting up and going over to her husband.

"So you'll be off shooting tomorrow?" she said.

His jealousy during these few moments, especially after the flush spread over her face while she had been talking with Veslovsky, had already gone far. By now, as he listened to her words, he already had his own interpretation of them. Strange as it was for him to recall this later, it now seemed clear to him that the only reason she was asking him whether he was going shooting the next day was her interest in finding out whether he was going to give this satisfaction to Veslovsky, whom she had already fallen in love with, according to his way of thinking.

"Yes, I'm going," he said to her, in an unnatural voice he himself found unpleasant.

"No, it would be better if you stayed home tomorrow, or else Dolly won't see her husband; you could go the day after tomorrow," Kitty said.

Now the sense of Kitty's words was translated by Levin in this way: Don't separate me from *him*. I couldn't care at all whether you go, but let me enjoy the society of this delightful young man.

"Oh, if you feel like it we can stay home tomorrow," Levin replied with particular affability.

Meanwhile Veslovsky, not having the slightest suspicion of the suffering being caused by his presence, got up from the table after Kitty and followed her with an affectionate smiling look.

Levin saw this look. He turned white; for a moment he couldn't draw his breath. How dare he take the liberty of looking at my wife that way! he thought, boiling.

"Tomorrow then? Do please let's go!" said Veslovsky, sitting down on a chair and doubling his leg up under him again as usual.

Levin's jealousy had now gone still further. He already saw himself as a deceived husband, who was needed by his wife and her lover only in order to provide them with the comforts of life and with pleasures . . . But in spite of this he amiably and hospitably questioned Veslovsky about his shooting, his gun, his boots, and agreed to go shooting the next day.

Luckily for Levin the old Princess put a stop to his suffering by getting up herself and advising Kitty to go to bed. But even here Levin did not escape without another torment. In saying good night to his hostess, Veslovsky once again wanted to kiss her hand, but Kitty, blushing, and with a naïve rudeness for which her mother reprimanded her later, said as she withdrew her hand:

"That's not the custom of the house."

In Levin's eyes she was to blame for laying herself open to such behavior, and still more to blame for having shown so clumsily that it displeased her.

"But what's the point of going to sleep, eh?" said Oblonsky, who after drinking a few glasses of wine at supper had lapsed into his most charming and lyrical mood. "Look, Kitty!" he said, indicating the moon rising behind the lime trees. "How lovely it is! Veslovsky—now's the time for a serenade! You know he has a magnificent voice, we kept on singing all the way here. He's brought along some lovely songs, two new ones. He and Mlle. Varenka will have to do a duet."

After they had all separated for the night, Oblonsky kept on walking about the drive with Veslovsky; their voices could be heard practicing a new song.

Levin, frowning, sat listening to them in an armchair in his wife's bedroom, keeping a stubborn silence as Kitty asked him what the matter with him was; but when finally she herself, with a timid smile, asked, "Could you be annoyed by something to do with Veslovsky?" it all burst out and he gave vent to everything. He felt humiliated himself by what he was saying, which irritated him still more.

He was standing in front of her, his eyes beneath their scowling brows blazing terrifyingly and his powerful arms pressed against his chest as though he were trying with all his might to restrain himself. His face would have looked harsh, and even cruel, if at the same time it had not had an expression of suffering that moved her. His jaw trembled, and his voice kept breaking.

"You must understand that I'm not jealous: that's a vile word! I cannot be jealous, or believe that—I don't know how to say what I'm feeling, but it's dreadful . . . I'm not jealous, but I feel humiliated, degraded by the idea that someone can dare imagine, can dare look at you with such eyes . . ."

"But with what eyes?" said Kitty, trying as conscientiously as possible to recall all the words and gestures of the evening, with all their nuances.

At the bottom of her heart she thought that there had been something just at that moment when Veslovsky had followed her to the other end of the table, but she dared not acknowledge this even to herself, much less make up her mind to tell him this and thus intensify his suffering.

"But what can there be that's attractive about me as I am now?"

"Ah!" he cried, clutching his head. "You'd better not say anything! So—if you were attractive, then—"

"But no, Kostya—wait a second, listen!" she said, looking at him with a look of suffering compassion. "What can you be thinking of, when men simply don't exist for me! No one! Not one! What is it, d'you want me to see no one at all?"

At first his jealousy had offended her; it vexed her that the slightest relaxation, even the most innocent, was forbidden her; but now she would willingly have sacrificed not only trifles like that but anything at all for the sake of his tranquillity, to free him from the anguish he was undergoing.

"You must understand the horror, the ludicrousness of my position," he went on in a despairing whisper. "He's in my house, he actually hasn't done anything improper except for his free and easy manners and the way he doubles up his legs. He considers that in the best possible form, so I have to be affable to him."

"But Kostya, you're exaggerating," said Kitty, at the bottom of her heart overjoyed at the force of his love for her that was now expressing itself in his jealousy.

"The worst of it all is that you—you're just as you always are, and now when you're such a shrine for me, and we're so happy, so particularly happy, and suddenly this good-for-nothing—no, he's not a good-for-nothing, why should I abuse him? I have nothing to do with him. But why should your happiness, mine—"

"D'you know, I understand how it all happened—" Kitty began.

"How? How?"

"I saw the way you looked when we were talking at supper."

"Well, yes—yes!" he said in a frightened voice.

She told him what they had been talking about. And as she told him she grew breathless with excitement. Levin was silent, then he peered into her pale, frightened face and suddenly clapped his hands to his head.

"Katya—I've been torturing you! My darling, forgive me! It was madness! Katya—it's all my fault, completely! How could I torment myself so about such nonsense?"

"Oh no—I'm sorry for you."

"For me? Me? What am I? A lunatic! But why should I torture you? It's a terrible thought that every stranger can destroy our happiness!"

"Of course, that's just what offends me—"

"Then I'll do the opposite and keep him on here all summer long on purpose, and lavish amiability on him!" said Levin, kissing her hands. "You'll see. Tomorrow—oh that's right, tomorrow we're going out."

## VIII

THE next day, before the women of the house had gotten up, the vehicles for the shooting party—a cart and a small gig—were standing at the entrance, and Laska, who had realized since early that morning that there would be a shoot, after yelping and bounding about to her heart's content, was sitting in the cart beside the coachman, who with excitement and disapproval over the delay was looking at the door the hunters were still to come through. Veslovsky was the first to come out, in big new boots that came halfway up his thick thighs, in a green blouse girdled round by a new cartridge belt smelling of leather, and his Scottish bonnet with the ribbons, and with a brand-new hammerless English gun without a sling. Laska bounded over to him, greeted him by frisking about, and asked him in her own way whether the others were coming out soon, but on receiving no answer from him she went back to her observation post and subsided again, turning her head to the side and pricking up one ear. Finally the door creaked open and Krak, Oblonsky's spotted tan pointer, came hurtling out, spinning and twisting about in the air, followed by Oblonsky himself, with a gun in his hand and a cigar in his mouth.

"Quiet, Krak, quiet!" he called out affectionately to the dog, which was flinging its paws up against his stomach and chest and entangling them in his game bag. Oblonsky was wearing rawhide shoes, with rough leggings, torn trousers and a short coat. There was the wreck of some kind of hat on his head, but his gun, a new model, was a jewel, and his game bag and cartridge belt, though very much worn, were of the best quality.

Veslovsky hadn't realized beforehand that this was what a sportsman's real stylishness consisted of—being dressed in rags but having the best shooting equipment. He understood this now, seeing Oblonsky in his rags, his aristocratic figure radiating elegance and well-fed gaiety, and decided that the next time he went shooting he would without fail get himself up that way too.

"Well, and what about our host?"

"He has a young wife," said Oblonsky with a smile.

"Yes, and what a charming one!"

"He was all dressed; doubtless he's run up to see her again."

Oblonsky had guessed right. Levin had run back to his wife to ask her once again whether she had forgiven him for his foolishness of the night before, and also to beg her to be more careful, "for the love of Jesus." The main thing was for her to keep farther away from the children, who might collide with her at any moment. Then he has to have her repeat her assurance that she wasn't angry with him for going off for two days, and to ask her in addition to be sure to send him a note the following morning by a man on horseback, even if it were only a couple of words, just so he knew she was all right.

It was painful as usual for Kitty to be separated from her husband for two days; but when she saw his animated figure, which looked particularly big and strong in his shooting boots and white blouse, radiating some kind of sportsman's exhilaration she found incomprehensible, she forgot her own pain because of his joy and said good-by to him cheerfully.

"Sorry, gentlemen!" he said, running out onto the front steps. "Have they put the lunch in? Why is the chestnut on the right? Well, it doesn't matter. Quiet there, Laska! Go and lie down!

"Turn them in with the heifers," he said turning to the herdsman who had been waiting for him at the steps with a question about some bullocks. "Awfully sorry, here comes another rascal."

Levin jumped off the cart, in which he had been about to sit down, to meet the carpenter, who was coming over to the steps with a footrule in his hand.

"You didn't come to the office last night, and here you are holding me up now. Well, what is it?"

"You must have another turning made, sir. It's just a matter of adding three more steps, that'll make it just fit. It'll be much more convenient."

"You should have listened to me," answered Levin, annoyed. "I told you to set up the string boards first, and then fit the treads in. You won't be able to fix it now. Do what I tell you—make a new staircase."

The point was that in the new wing that was under construction the carpenter had spoiled the staircase, having built it without calculating the elevation, so that when it was put in position the steps came out at a slant. What the carpenter wanted to do now was keep the same staircase and add three steps to it.

"It will be much better that way."

"But where will it come out, with those three extra steps?"

"Excuse me, sir," said the carpenter with a condescending smile. "It will come out to exactly the right spot. You see, it will just come up from the bottom," he said with a persuasive gesture, "it'll just go up and up until it gets there."

"Yes, but the three steps will add to its length as well. Where will it come out at?"

"That's what I mean, it will go up from the bottom and reach to the top," the carpenter said stubbornly and persuasively.

"It will reach up to the wall, right under the ceiling."

"Oh no, excuse me, after all, it'll be coming up from below —it'll go up and up, and just fit."

Levin pulled out his ramrod and began making a drawing of the staircase in the dust.

"Just as you please," said the carpenter, his eyes suddenly lighting up; evidently he had finally got the point. "It does seem as though another one will have to be made."

"Well then, go ahead and do as you're told!" Levin shouted as he got into the cart. "Let's be off now! Hold the dogs, Philip!"

Now that he had left behind him all his family and business worries, Levin had such a violent feeling of joy in living and of anticipation that he had no desire to talk. In addition he also had that feeling of concentrated excitement every sportsman experiences as he approaches the field of action. If there was anything on his mind now it was only the question of whether they would find anything in the Kolpensky marsh, how Laska would turn out compared with Krak, and how successful his own shooting would be that day. *If only I don't disgrace myself in front of this stranger! If only Oblonsky doesn't beat me!* also passed through his mind.

Oblonsky was in the grip of the same feeling, and also untalkative. Only Veslovsky kept merrily chattering without letup. Listening to him now Levin felt ashamed at recalling how unfair he had been toward him the day before. Veslovsky really was a splendid chap, simple, good-natured, and extremely cheerful. If Levin had come across him in his bachelor days they would have become friends. What Levin found a little disagreeable was his idle attitude toward life and a sort of looseness about his elegance. It was as though he laid claim to a lofty and unquestionable importance because he had long nails, a Scottish bonnet, and everything else that went with all that; but he might be forgiven this because of his good nature and his breeding. Levin liked him because he was well brought up, had an excellent accent in both French and English, and was a man of his own class.

Veslovsky had the greatest admiration for the Don Steppe horse attached on the left. He went into raptures over it.

"How wonderful it must be to gallop across the steppe on a horse like that, eh? Isn't that so?" he said.

He seemed to imagine something wild and poetical, which would lead to nothing, in this galloping about on a Don Steppe horse; but his naïveté especially in conjunction with his good looks, his sweet smile and his graceful movements was very attractive. Whether it was because his character was congenial to Levin, or because he was trying to atone for his sin of the day before by finding everything about him admirable, Levin liked his company.

When they had gone about two miles Veslovsky suddenly missed his cigars and his wallet; he didn't know whether he had lost them or left them on the table. There were three hundred and seventy rubles in the wallet, so the matter could not simply be disregarded.

"D'you know, Levin, I'll just gallop back on this Don side horse, eh?" he said, already preparing to get out.

"No, but why?" replied Levin, who had calculated that Veslovsky weighed at least two hundred pounds. "I'll send the coachman."

The coachman rode back on the side horse, and Levin drove the other two himself.

## IX

NOW, what's our schedule? Tell us all about it," said Oblonsky.

"Well, we're going as far as Gvozdevo now. There's a good snipe marsh on this side, and on the other side there are some marshes for woodcock, and some snipe as well. Now it's hot, but we'll get there toward evening—it's about fifteen miles—and shoot then; we'll sleep over, and by tomorrow morning we'll be in the big marshes."

"There's nothing on the way?"

"There is, but we'd be delayed, besides it's hot. There are two wonderful little spots, but we probably wouldn't find anything."

Levin himself felt like stopping at these little spots, but they were near the house, he could always shoot there, and they were small; there wasn't enough room for three there. This was why he stretched a point by saying they probably wouldn't find anything. When they came to a small marsh Levin wanted to drive past, but Oblonsky, with the practiced eye of a sportsman, immediately noticed the marshy place, which was visible from the road.

"Why not there?" he said, pointing to the marsh.

"Levin, please! It looks delightful!" Veslovsky begged, and Levin couldn't help giving in.

Before they had time to stop, the dogs had already hurtled toward the marsh, racing each other.

"Krak! Laska!"

The dogs turned round.

"There's not enough room for three. I'll wait here," said Levin, hoping they wouldn't find anything but the pewits there which the dogs had raised and which, swaying as they flew, were crying plaintively over the marsh.

"No! Come along, Levin, let's go together!" Veslovsky called out.

"Really, there's no room. Laska, back! Laska! You don't need two dogs, do you?"

Levin stayed at the gig and enviously watched the sportsmen. They went over the whole marsh, but there was nothing in it but some waterfowl and pewits, one of which was shot by Veslovsky.

"Now you see why I didn't miss this marsh," said Levin. "It was just a loss of time."

"It was great fun anyhow. Did you see it?" said Veslovsky, awkwardly climbing into the cart holding the gun and the pewit in his hands. "How well I got this one! Didn't I? Well, will we soon be coming to the real place?"

All at once the horses plunged forward: Levin knocked his head against the barrel of someone's gun and a shot rang out. The shot had actually rung out before, but that was how it seemed to Levin. What had happened was that Veslovsky in uncocking his gun had pulled one trigger while uncocking the other barrel. The charge flew into the ground without hurting anyone. Oblonsky shook his head and laughed reproachfully at Veslovsky. But Levin didn't have the heart to reprimand him: first of all, any reproach would have seemed to have been provoked by the danger he just escaped and by the bump that had sprung up on his forehead; secondly, Veslovsky was so naïvely upset at first and then broke out laughing so good-naturedly and infectiously at their general alarm that he couldn't help laughing himself.

When they reached the second marsh, which was quite large and sure to take a lot of time, Levin again tried to persuade them not to get out. But again Veslovsky talked him into it, and again, since the marsh was a narrow one, Levin, as a hospitable host, stayed behind with the vehicles.

Krak went off at once to the hummocks. Veslovsky was the first to follow the dog, and before Oblonsky had time to approach a snipe flew up. Veslovsky missed it, and it flew over to an unmown meadow. This snipe was left to Veslovsky. Krak found it again and pointed; Veslovsky killed it and went back to the vehicles.

"Now you go ahead, I'll stay with the horses," he said.

Hunter's envy had begun working in Levin. He handed the reins over to Veslovsky and went into the swamp.

Laska, who for some time had been whining pathetically, complaining about the injustice of it all, rushed straight forward to a reliable, hummock-covered spot Levin was acquainted with, where Krak had not yet been.

"Why don't you stop her?" Oblonsky shouted.

"She won't frighten them," replied Levin, delighted with the dog and hurrying after her.

Laska became more and more intent in her search the closer she got to the familiar hummocks. She was only distracted for a moment by a small marsh bird. She described one circle in front of the hummocks, started another and suddenly quivered and stopped dead.

"Come on, Stiva! Come ahead!" called Levin, who felt his heart beginning to beat more violently; all at once, as though some bar had been removed from his strained sense of hearing and losing all sense of distance, he began being struck by all sorts of sounds, which came to him all jumbled up but distinct. He heard Oblonsky's footsteps, which he took for the distant pounding of horses' hoofs; he heard the brittle sound of a patch of hummock he stepped on, tearing it off by the roots, and took this for the sound of snipe on the wing. Not far behind him he also heard a sound of splashing he couldn't make out.

He picked his way over to the dog.

"Get it!"

It was not a snipe but a woodcock that rocketed up in front of the dog. Levin raised his gun, but just as he was taking aim the same splashing sound grew louder and came closer, and was joined with Veslovsky's voice shouting out something in a strange loud voice. Levin saw he was aiming behind the woodcock but he fired anyhow.

After making sure he had missed, Levin looked round and saw that the horses and the cart were no longer on the road but in the swamp.

Veslovsky, in his desire to watch the shooting, had driven into the marsh and mired the horses fast.

The devil take him! Levin muttered to himself, going over to the bogged-down cart. "Why did you come in here?" he said to Veslovsky drily, and calling the coachman over he set to work freeing the horses.

Levin was annoyed at having had his shot disturbed, at the

horses' being bogged down, and most of all at the fact that neither Oblonsky or Veslovsky helped him and the coachman unharness the horses and get them out of the bog, since neither one nor the other had the slightest notion about harnesses. Saying nothing in reply to Veslovsky's assurances that it was really quite dry there, Levin worked silently together with the coachman to disengage the horses. But after getting warmed up by the work and seeing that Veslovsky was tugging away at the mudguard with such zeal that he actually broke it off, Levin reproached himself for being too chilly toward Veslovsky, under the influence of the feeling he had had the day before; he made an effort to smooth over his dryness by becoming specially amiable. When everything was in order and the vehicles had been brought back onto the road, Levin ordered lunch to be served.

"Good appetite and good conscience! This chicken's going to drop down to the bottom of my boots," Veslovsky, who had brightened up again, remarked, repeating the French saying as he finished a second chicken. "Well, now our misfortunes are over; from now on everything will be all right. Only I must sit on the box for my sins. Isn't that so? Eh? No, no, I'm Automedon, just watch the way I drive you!" he said, holding on to the reins when Levin asked him to let the coachman drive. "No, I must atone for my sins, and it's wonderful here on the box." And he drove off.

Levin was a little afraid he would strain the horses, especially the chestnut on the left, which he couldn't hold in; but in spite of himself he yielded to Veslovsky's gaiety, listened to the songs he sang the whole way, sitting on the coach box, or the stories he told, or the way he showed how the English drove a four-in-hand; after lunch, by the time they got to the Gvozdevo marsh, they were all in the best of spirits.

X

VESLOVSKY drove so fast that they got to the marsh too early, while it was still hot.

When they had gotten to the real marsh, the chief goal of the party, Levin involuntarily began thinking of how to get rid of Veslovsky and go about unhindered. Oblonsky evidently wished for the same; on his face Levin saw the expression of concern a real sportsman always has before the beginning of a shoot, also a little of the good-natured sly-ness peculiar to him.

"Now, how shall we go about it? It's a first-rate marsh, and there are some hawks too, I see," said Oblonsky, indi-cating two large birds wheeling about above the sedges. "If there are hawks here there's sure to be game."

"Well, gentlemen," said Levin, pulling up his boots with a somewhat morose expression and examining his percussion caps, "d'you see that sedge?" He pointed to a dark-green little island in an enormous, half-mown wet meadow stretch-ing along the right bank of the river. "That's where the marsh begins, right out there, you see? Where it's greener? From there it goes along off to the right, where those horses are; there are the hummocks, where there are snipe. It goes round that sedge down to that alder grove, as far as the mill, where you can see that little bay there. That's the best place. I once shot seventeen woodcock there. We'll sep-arate, going different ways together with the two dogs, and meet up over there by the mill."

"All right then, who goes to the right, and who to the left?" asked Oblonsky. "There's more space on the right, you two go off together, while I go to the left," he said, as though indifferent.

"Wonderful! We'll get more shooting in. Come on then, let's go!" Veslovsky chimed in.

Levin couldn't help agreeing, and they separated.

They had only just gone into the marsh when both dogs began searching together and started off toward a rusty-looking spot. Levin knew the way Laska searched—cautious and dubious; he also knew the spot, and expected to see a flight of woodcock.

"Veslovsky, come here! Walk beside me!" he whispered with bated breath to his companion, splashing in the water behind him; ever since Veslovsky's accidental shot at the Kolpensky marsh the direction of his gun preoccupied Levin against his will.

"No, I don't want to get in your way, just don't think about me."

But in spite of himself Levin did think about him; he re-called Kitty's parting remark: "Mind you, don't shoot each other!" The dogs were approaching closer and closer, pass-ing each other, each one following its own scent; the expecta-tion of finding woodcock was so strong that the smacking sound of his heel as he pulled it out of the rusty mud sounded to Levin like the cry of a woodcock, and he seized the butt of his gun and squeezed it.

"Bang! Bang!" he heard just above his ear. It was Veslovsky firing at a flight of ducks that were circling above the marsh, far out of range, and just then were flying toward the sportsmen. Before Levin could look round a woodcock cried out, then another, and a third, and about eight more rose one after the other.

Oblonsky got one just as it was about to go off on its zigzags, and the woodcock plummeted into the bog like a lump. Oblonsky unhurriedly aimed at another, which was flying low toward the sedges, and this woodcock also came down together with the sound of the shot; it could be seen jumping up among the cut sedges, fluttering with one white-edged uninjured wing.

Levin was not so lucky: he fired too close to the first woodcock and missed; he followed it with his gun when it was already on the rise, but just then another rose from under his feet and distracted him, and he missed again.

While they were reloading another woodcock rose, and Veslovsky, who had finished reloading, fired another two charges of small shot over the water. Oblonsky picked up his two birds and looked at Levin with sparkling eyes.

"Well, now we'll separate," he said; limping with his left leg and holding his gun ready, he whistled to his dog and went off to one side. Levin and Veslovsky went to the other.

What always happened to Levin was that when the first few shots were unsuccessful he got excited and annoyed, and shot badly for the rest of the day. It was the same that day. There turned out to be a great many woodcock. They kept rocketing up in front of the dogs and from beneath the very feet of the sportsmen; Levin could have recovered himself, but the more shots he took the more he disgraced himself in front of Veslovsky, who was firing merrily away in and out of range, not killing a thing but not in the least put out by it. Levin hurried, had no restraint, got more and more heated, and got to the point where even as he fired he had no hope of hitting anything. Laska seemed to understand this, too. She began to search more lazily, and she glanced round at the sportsmen as though perplexed or reproachful. One shot followed another. The sportsmen were surrounded by powder smoke, but in the large roomy net of the game bag there were only three light little birds; for that matter one of them had been shot by Veslovsky and another by them both.

Meanwhile from the other side of the marsh they could hear Oblonsky's shots, which were not frequent but which counted, as it seemed to Levin, and were almost always followed by the cry of "Krak, Krak, fetch it!"

This agitated Levin even more. The woodcock kept circling incessantly over the sedges. Their cries near the ground and calls in the air were constantly heard on all sides; the birds that had risen before and had been flying around settled again in front of the sportsmen. There were not two hawks wheeling and screaming above the marsh now, but dozens.

Levin and Veslovsky had gone through more than half the marsh; they came to that part where the peasants' meadowland was divided into long strips that ended up in the sedges; it was marked by strips that were trodden down or cut. Half the strips were already mown.

Though there was not much hope of finding as many birds in the unmown strips as in those that were mown, Levin, having promised Oblonsky to meet him there, walked farther on with his companion along the mown and unmown strips.

"Hey there—sportsmen!" one of some peasants sitting by an unhitched cart called out to them. "Come on over and have something with us! Vodka!"

Levin looked round.

"Come on over, it's all right!" a cheerful, bearded peasant with a red face cried out, showing his white teeth and holding up a greenish vodka bottle that glittered in the sunshine.

"What are they saying?" asked Veslovsky.

"They're inviting us over for some vodka. They've probably been dividing up the meadows. I ought to go over and have a drink," said Levin, with a certain guile, since he hoped Veslovsky would be tempted by the vodka and go off to join them himself.

"But why are they inviting us?"

"Oh, they're just having some fun. Really, why don't you go on over? It'll amuse you."

"Come along then! It looks interesting!"

"Go ahead, you'll find the way to the mill yourself!" Levin called out, and glancing round saw with satisfaction that Veslovsky, stooping over and stumbling along on his weary legs, holding his gun in an outstretched arm, was making his way out of the marsh toward the peasants.

"You come too!" shouted a peasant to Levin. "Come, have a bite of pie!"

Levin had a great longing for a drink of vodka and a piece

of bread. He was weak; he felt he could hardly drag his stumbling legs out of the bog and for a moment he was in doubt. But just then the dog pointed, and on the instant all his weariness vanished and he followed the dog through the bog with a light step. A woodcock flew up from under his feet; he fired and killed it—the dog kept on pointing. "Fetch it!" Another one rose from under the dog. Levin fired again. But it was an unlucky day: he missed and when he went to look for the one he had killed he couldn't find that one either. He tramped all through the sedge, but Laska didn't believe he had killed anything and when he sent her to search she pretended she was going but didn't do any actual searching.

Even without Veslovsky, whom Levin had blamed all his failures on, matters didn't right themselves. There were still a great many woodcock, but Levin missed one after the other.

The slanting rays of the sun were still hot; his clothes, soaked through with sweat, clung to his body; his left boot, full of water, was heavy and made a squelching sound; sweat was running down his powder-flecked face in drops; there was a bitter taste in his mouth, a smell of powder and rust in his nose, and the perpetual cry of the woodcock in his ears; the barrels of his gun were so hot they couldn't be touched; his heart was thumping with short, rapid beats; his hands were trembling with excitement, and his weary legs kept stumbling and staggering over the hummocks and through the bog; but he kept on going ahead and shooting. Finally, after one more terrible miss he flung his gun and cap on the ground.

No, I must pull myself together! he said to himself. He picked up his gun and cap, called Laska to heel, and got out of the marsh. Coming out onto the dry ground, he sat down on a hummock, took off his boot and poured the water out of it, then went back to the marsh, drank some rusty water, put some of it on the overheated barrels and splashed his face and hands in it. Feeling refreshed he moved back to the spot where a woodcock had settled, firmly resolved not to get flustered.

He was trying to stay calm, but the same thing happened. His finger squeezed the trigger before he had the bird in the sights. Things were getting worse and worse.

He only had five birds in his game bag when he left the swamp by the alder grove where he was supposed to meet Oblonsky.

He saw Oblonsky's dog before he saw him. Completely black with the stinking slime of the marsh, Krak bounded out from beneath the upturned root of an alder with the air of a conqueror and sniffed noses with Laska. In the shade of an alder Oblonsky's stately figure also came into view behind Krak. He came toward Levin red and sweating, his shirt unbuttoned and limping as before.

"Well? You've both been doing a lot of firing!" he said with a cheerful smile.

"And what about you?" asked Levin. But there was no need to ask, he had already seen the bulging game bag.

"Not bad!" He had fourteen birds.

"A terrific swamp! I suppose Veslovsky got in your way. It's awkward having one dog for two," said Oblonsky, softening his triumph.

## XI

WHEN Levin and Oblonsky got to the peasant's hut Levin always used to put up at, Veslovsky was already there. He was sitting in the middle of the hut, holding on with both hands to a bench from which a soldier, the brother of the peasant's wife, was pulling off his slime-covered boots, and laughing his infectiously merry laugh.

"I've just got here. They've been charming! Just imagine, they fed me and gave me something to drink. What bread, it's marvelous! Delicious! And the vodka—I've never tasted any better! And they absolutely refused to take any money. They kept saying 'No offense' or something."

"But why should they take money? They were entertaining you, don't you see. You don't suppose they keep vodka for sale?" said the soldier, who had finally tugged off one soaked boot together with a blackened stocking.

In spite of the filth of the hut, muddied up by the sportsmen's boots and the dirty dogs that were licking themselves, the smell of marsh and powder it was filled with, and the absence of knives and forks, the sportsmen drank tea and ate supper with a relish only hunters know. Washed and clean they went to a hay barn that had been swept out, where the coachmen had made up beds for them.

Though it was already dusk none of them wanted to go to sleep.

After wavering between reminiscences and tales of shooting, of dogs, and of former shooting parties, the conversation settled on a topic that interested them all. Taking as his cue some of Veslovsky's enthusiastic remarks, repeated several times, about the charm of camping out, the smell of the hay, the charm of a broken cart (it seemed broken to him because its front wheels had been taken off), the good nature of the peasants who had given him some vodka to drink, and about the dogs, each one lying at the feet of its master, Oblonsky told a story about the charm of a shooting party at Malthus's, which he had been on the summer before. Malthus was a well-known railway magnate. Oblonsky was speaking of the marshes this Malthus had leased in Tver Province, how they were preserved, and of the carriages that would drive the sportsmen over and the marquee that had been set up beside the marsh for lunch.

"I can't understand you," said Levin, rising on his pile of hay, "how is it you don't find these people repulsive? I can understand how pleasant a lunch with Laffitte may be, but isn't this very luxury repellent to you? All these people, like the drink monopolists we used to have, get hold of their money in ways that deserve everyone's contempt; they ignore this contempt and then buy it off with the money they've dishonestly come by."

"Absolutely true!" Veslovsky chimed in. "Absolutely! Oblonsky, of course, does it all out of good nature, but then others say, 'Well, if Oblonsky himself goes there . . .'"

"Not in the least," Oblonsky said, and Levin could tell he was smiling, "I simply don't think he's any more dishonest than any other rich merchant or nobleman. Both one and the other have come by their money in the same way, by work and brains."

"Yes, but what kind of work? D'you call that work—getting a concession and reselling it?"

"Of course it's work. It's work in the sense that if it weren't for him or others like him there wouldn't even be any railroads."

"But it's not work like the work of a peasant or scientist."

"All right, but it's work in the sense that it's an activity that produces results—railroads. But then you think railroads are useless!"

"No—that's a different question; I'm ready to admit they're useful. But any acquisition that doesn't correspond to the amount of work put into it is dishonest."

"But who's going to determine the degree of correspondence?"

"Something acquired in a dishonest way, by guile," said Levin, who felt he was going to be unable to make a clear distinction between honesty and dishonesty, "such as the profits made by banks is an evil, like this acquisition of vast fortunes without work, the way it used to be with the drink monopolies, simply in a changed form. The king is dead, long live the king! No sooner were the drink monopolies wiped out than the railroads appeared, and the banks: just other ways of making money without work."

"Yes, that may all be true and ingenious—Lie down, Krak!" Oblonsky exclaimed to the dog, which was scratching itself and turning round in the hay. Oblonsky was obviously sure of being in the right and so was calm and unhurried. "But you haven't drawn any distinction between honest and dishonest work. Is it dishonest for me to get a bigger salary than my chief clerk, though he knows the work better than I do?"

"I don't know."

"Well, then I'll tell you: your receiving a profit of, let's say, five thousand rubles for your work on the farm, while our peasant host, no matter how hard he works, can never get more than fifty, is just as dishonest as my getting more than my chief clerk and as Malthus getting more than a railway mechanic. On the contrary, I notice an attitude of perfectly groundless hostility on the part of society toward these men, and it seems to me it's due to envy—"

"No, that's unfair," said Veslovsky, "there's no question of envy, it's just that there's something sordid in the whole business."

"No, excuse me!" Levin went on. "You say it's unfair for me to get five thousand and the peasant fifty: that's true. It is unfair, and I feel it is, but—"

"It is indeed. How is it we eat, drink, go shooting, and never do anything, while he's constantly at work, constantly?" said Veslovsky, who had obviously had a clear thought about this for the first time in his life and so was completely sincere.

"Yes, you feel it's unfair, but you're not going to give him your estate," said Oblonsky, as though pricking Levin intentionally.

A sort of covertly hostile relationship had lately sprung up between the two brothers-in-law: ever since they had married two sisters a rivalry seemed to have arisen between them as to who would arrange his life better; now this hostility was expressed in the conversation, which was taking on a personal nuance.

"I'm not giving it away because no one is asking me to, and if I wanted to I couldn't," replied Levin, "nor is there anyone to give it to."

"Give it to this peasant, he won't refuse."

"Yes, but how can I give it to him? Should I go with him and have the title deed transferred?"

"I don't know, but if that's your conviction you have no right to—"

"It's not my conviction at all. On the contrary, I feel I haven't got the right to give it away, that I have my obligations both to the land and to my family."

"I beg your pardon—if you consider this inequality unfair why don't you act on it?"

"I am acting on it—negatively in the sense that I intend to try not to increase the difference in status that exists between me and them."

"Forgive me—that's a paradox."

"Yes, that's a sophistical explanation," Veslovsky chimed in. "Ah! Our host!" he said to the peasant, who had opened the creaking barn doors and come into the barn. "What, still not asleep?"

"Sleep—what an idea! I thought you gentlemen were sleeping, then I heard you chatting. I have to get a hook here. She won't bite?" he added, cautiously stepping with bare feet.

"And where are you going to sleep?"

"We're pasturing the horses tonight."

"Oh, what a night!" said Veslovsky, looking at the corner of the hut and the unhitched carts, which could be seen in the dim light of the afterglow, framed in the open doorway. "Just listen! Those are women's voices singing, not at all badly either. Who's that singing?"

"Why, the maid servants close by," replied the peasant.

"Let's go for a walk! We're not going to sleep anyhow. Oblonsky, let's go!"

"If you could only go without getting up," said Oblonsky, stretching. "It's wonderful, just lying down!"

"Then I'll go alone," said Veslovsky, getting up briskly and putting his boots on. *"Au revoir,* gentlemen! If there's some fun I'll call you. You've treated me to game, and I won't forget you!"

"Isn't he a splendid chap?" said Oblonsky, after Veslovsky

had gone out and the peasant had shut the doors behind him.

"Yes, splendid," replied Levin, who was still thinking about the subject of the conversation they had just had. It seemed to him that he had expressed his thoughts and feelings as clearly as he could, yet both of them, who were honest and not stupid, had said with one voice that he was comforting himself with sophistries. He was upset.

"So that's it, my boy. You have to do one of two things: either admit that the present order of society is equitable, and then defend your rights, or else admit that you're exploiting some inequitable advantages, as I do, and exploit them with satisfaction."

"No, if these advantages are inequitable you couldn't exploit them with satisfaction, at any rate I couldn't. For me the main thing is not to feel guilty."

"But actually now, what if we did go after all?" said Oblonsky, evidently tired of the mental strain. "We're not going to sleep, are we? Really, let's go!"

Levin made no reply. The remark he had made in the conversation about acting fairly only in a negative sense was on his mind. Surely it's not possible to be just only in a negative sense? he was wondering.

"What a strong smell fresh hay has!" said Oblonsky, sitting up. "Nothing can make me sleep now. Veslovsky has started something out there. D'you hear the laughter, and his voice? Shouldn't we go over? Come on, let's!"

"No, I'm not going," replied Levin.

"Don't tell me that's on principle too!" said Oblonsky with a smile, as he looked about for his cap in the dark.

"Not on principle, but why should I go?"

"D'you know, you're going to get yourself in trouble," said Oblonsky, finding his cap and getting up.

"Why?"

"D'you suppose I didn't see the footing you've put yourself on with your wife? I heard you discussing, as a question of primary importance, whether or not you could go off for two days' shooting. For an idyll that's all very well and good, but it's not going to last a whole lifetime. A man must be independent, he has his own masculine interests. A man must be a man," said Oblonsky, opening the doors.

"What does that mean? Going off courting maids?" asked Levin.

"And why not, if it's fun? It doesn't lead to anything. It's not going to hurt my wife, and it's fun for me. The main thing is to safeguard the sanctity of the home; there can't be anything like that at home. But just don't tie your hands."

"Perhaps," said Levin drily, and turned on his side. "We have to leave early in the morning; I'm not going to wake anyone, and I'm starting at daybreak."

"Gentlemen, come at once!" came the voice of Veslovsky, who had come back. "Charming! I've found her! Charming— a perfect Gretchen, and we're friends already. Really, extremely pretty," he said in a tone of approval as though she had been made pretty just for him, and he was pleased with whoever had prepared her for him.

Levin pretended to be asleep; Oblonsky, who had put on his slippers and lighted a cigar, left the barn and their voices quickly died away.

For a long time Levin couldn't sleep. First he heard his horses munching hay, then his host together with his oldest son getting ready to set out, then riding off to pasture the horses for the night; then he heard the soldier settling down to sleep on the other side of the barn together with his nephew, their host's small son; he heard the boy telling his uncle, in a high little voice, his impression of the dogs, which the boy thought terrifying and gigantic; then he heard the boy asking what these dogs were going to catch, and the soldier telling him in a hoarse sleepy voice that the sportsmen were going to the marsh the next day and were going to shoot off their guns; then, to stop the boy's questions, the soldier said: "Go to sleep now, Vaska, go to sleep, or watch out!" Then the soldier soon started snoring, and everything died down; all that could be heard was the neighing of the horses and the cries of the woodcock.

Surely it can't only be negative? Levin repeated to himself. But what if it is? It's not my fault. And he began thinking about the following day.

Tomorrow I'll start out early in the morning; I'll make a point of not getting excited. There are masses of woodcock, and snipe too. And when I get back there'll be a note from Kitty. Yes, Stiva may be right at that: I'm not man enough with her, I've grown effeminate. But what's to be done about it? Another negative attitude!

Through his sleep he heard the laughter and the merry talk of Veslovsky and Oblonsky. For a moment he opened his eyes: the moon had risen, and they were standing there chatting away in the open doorway, brightly lit up by the moon.

Oblonsky was saying something about the freshness of a girl, comparing her with a fresh kernel just taken from its shell, and Veslovsky, laughing his infectious laugh, was repeating some remark that had probably been made to him by the peasant: "You'd better try to get hold of a wife of your own!" Through his sleep Levin muttered: "Gentlemen, tomorrow at dawn!" and fell asleep.

XII

LEVIN awoke in the early dawn and tried to wake his companions. Veslovsky, who was lying on his stomach with one stockinged leg outstretched, was sleeping so soundly it was impossible to get any reply out of him. Oblonsky, half-asleep, refused to start so early. Even Laska, who was sleeping curled up into a ring on a corner of the stack of hay, got up reluctantly, lazily stretching out one hind leg at a time and adjusting it. Levin put on his boots, picked up his gun and, cautiously opening the creaking door of the barn, he went out into the street. The coachmen was sleeping beside the vehicles; the horses were drowsing. Only one of them was lazily eating oats, scattering them over the edge of the trough and snorting. It was still gray outside.

"Why have you got up so early, my dear sir?" said the peasant's old wife to him, who had just come out of the hut, addressing him like an old friend.

"Why, I'm going off shooting, Granny. Can I get to the marsh this way?"

"Straight along past the back of the huts, past our threshing floors, my dear sir, then through the hemp field—there's a path."

Stepping carefully with sunburned bare feet, the old woman showed Levin the way, and raised one of the bars for him at the threshing floor.

"Go straight ahead and you'll step right into the marsh. That's the way our boys took the horses out last night."

Laska bounded merrily along the path; Levin followed her with his rapid light stride, constantly glancing up at the sky. He didn't want the sun to rise before he got to the marsh. But the sun didn't dawdle. The moon, which had still been giving off some light when he had first come out, now merely gleamed like quicksilver; the morning star, which it was impossible to miss before, now had to be looked for; what had formerly been vague spots on the distant field could be clearly made out now. They were shocks of rye. In the tall fragrant hemp, already free of its pollen, the dew, which had been invisible until the sun had risen, wetted Levin's feet and blouse above his belt. The slightest sounds could be heard in the translucent stillness of the morning. A bee, whizzing like a bullet, flew past Levin's ear. He gave a close look and saw a second, then a third. They were all coming from behind the wattle fence of an apiary, and vanishing across the hemp field in the direction of the marsh. The path led directly to the marsh, which could be distinguished by the mists rising from it, denser in some spots, less so in others, so that the sedge and willow shrubs, like little islands, seemed to sway back and forth. At the edge of the marsh by the road the peasant boys and men who had been pasturing their horses at night were stretched out, having gone to sleep beneath their coats before daybreak. Not far off three hobbled horses were moving about. One of them was making a clatter with its chain. Laska was walking beside her master, begging him to let her run out ahead, and looking around. After passing the sleeping peasants and going as far as the first wet spot, Levin examined his percussion caps and let the dog go. One of the horses, a well-fed three-year-old chestnut, shied at the sight of Laska, raised its tail and snorted. The other horses were also frightened; splashing about in the water with their hobbled feet and making a slapping sound as they pulled their hoofs out of the thick clayey mud, they began floundering out of the marsh. Laska halted, looking scornfully at the horses and questioningly at Levin. Levin patted her and whistled as a sign that she could begin now.

Joyful and intent, Laska ran along the footpath that dipped beneath her feet.

On running into the marsh Laska immediately detected, among the familiar odors of roots, marsh grass, and rust, and the peculiar aroma of horse dung, the smell of birds that was scattered throughout the whole place, the same strong-smelling birds that excited her most of all. Here and there among the moss and swamp sage this smell was extremely powerful, but it was impossible to determine which side it grew stronger on or fainter. To find out the direction it was necessary to go farther off downwind. Hardly aware of her legs under her, Laska broke into a stiff gallop, so that she could come to a halt on any bound if she had to, and ran off to the right, away from the dawn breeze that blew from the east, and turned round into the wind. Inhaling the air with her nostrils distended, she immediately sensed that it was not only their traces, but *they* themselves that were there in front of her, and not only a single one of them, but a great many. Laska slackened her pace. They were there, but she could not yet make out just where. To find just the right place she had already started off on a circle when her master's voice suddenly distracted her. "Laska! Here!" he said, pointing to the other side. She stood still as though asking him whether it wouldn't be better to go on as she had started. But he repeated his order in an angry voice, pointing to a cluster of hummocks flooded with water, where there couldn't be anything at all. She obeyed him, pretending to search in order to give him the satisfaction; she went all over the cluster of hummocks and then returned to the first place, where she immediately scented them again. Now that he wasn't interfering with her, she knew what to do; without looking at what she was stepping into, and stumbling with annoyance over the tall hummocks and falling into the water only to right herself with her powerful supple legs, she began the circle which was bound to make everything clear to her.

She was struck more and more powerfully, more and more definitely, by *their* scent; suddenly it became perfectly clear to her that one of them was right there, behind that hummock, five steps in front of her; she halted and her whole body grew rigid. Her short legs made it impossible for her to see anything in front of her, but by the smell she could tell it was not more than five steps away. She stood there, more and more aware of its presence and enjoying the anticipation. Her rigid tail was outstretched, only its very tip twitching. Her mouth was slightly open and her ears pricked up. One of her ears had got folded back while she was running; she was breathing heavily, but cautiously, and she looked round her still more cautiously, more with her eyes than with her head, at her master. He, with his familiar face, and eyes that were always so terrifying, came stumbling over the hummocks, it seemed to her extraordinarily slowly. It appeared to her that he was walking slowly, though he was running.

When he noticed Laska's peculiar way of searching, as she hugged the ground with her whole body, as though she were dragging her hind legs in great strides, with her mouth slightly open, Levin realized she was pointing at snipe, and ran over to her with a prayer to God in his heart for success, especially with the first bird. He came up close

to her and from his height looked in front of him and saw
with his eyes what she had sensed with her nose. In a space
between two hummocks he caught sight of a snipe. It was
listening, its head turned. Then, fluttering its wings out a
little and folding them again, it vanished round a corner,
with a clumsy wiggle of its rump.

"Fetch it, fetch it!" shouted Levin, giving Laska a shove
from behind.

But I can't go, thought Laska: Where can I go to? From
here I can smell them, but if I move forward I won't
know where or what they are.

But there he was nudging her with his knee and muttering
to her in an excited whisper: "Fetch it, Laska darling,
fetch it!"

Well, if that's what he wants I'll do it, but I no longer
accept any responsibility for it now, she thought, and hurled
herself forward between the hummocks. She was no longer
on the scent, but simply used her eyes and ears without
understanding anything.

Some ten steps from its former spot a snipe, with the
guttural cry and the peculiar snipelike rounded beating of
the wings, rose and following the report of the gun fell
heavily on its white breast into the wet bog. Behind Levin
a second one took to the air without waiting for the dogs.
When Levin turned back it was already far off. But his
shot reached it; after flying another twenty feet the second
snipe rose sharply, and turning over and over like a ball
plummeted heavily onto a dry spot.

Now things are beginning to make sense! thought Levin,
tucking the warm fat snipe into his game bag. "Eh, Laska
darling, don't you think so?"

By the time Levin had reloaded and gone on again the
sun, though still not visible through the clouds, had already
risen. The moon, all its brightness gone, gleamed pale in
the sky like a small cloud; by now not a single star could
be seen. The marsh grass, silvery with dew before, now had
a golden gleam. The rusty patches were all amber. The bluish
grasses had turned a yellowish green. The marsh birds were
bustling about in the shrubs glittering with dew and casting
long shadows beside the brook. A hawk had woken up and
settled on a haycock, turning its head from side to side
and looking irritably at the marsh. Crows were flying about
the field and a barefooted little boy was already driving
the horses toward an old man who was sitting up under

his coat and scratching himself. The smoke from the shots was spreading white as milk over the green grass.

One of the boys ran over to Levin.

"There were ducks here yesterday!" he shouted, following Levin at a distance.

And in the sight of this little boy, who expressed full approval, it gave Levin a double pleasure to kill another three woodcock, one after the other.

XIII

THE hunter's proverb that if you don't miss your first beast or first bird you'll have a lucky day turned out to be correct.

Tired, hungry, and happy, Levin came back toward ten o'clock in the morning, after tramping some twenty miles, with nineteen fine head of game and one duck tied to his belt, since there was no longer any room for it in the game bag. His companions had woken up long before and had had time to get hungry and have their breakfast.

"Just a second, just a second, I know there are nineteen," said Levin, for the second time counting the snipe and woodcock, which no longer looked as impressive as they had when they were flying, but were twisted, dried up, and bloodstained, with their head flopping to one side.

The count was right, and Oblonsky's envy was pleasant to Levin. He was also delighted at having found on his return a messenger with a note from Kitty.

*"I'm quite well and happy. If you've been worried about me you can feel better now. I have a new bodyguard— Mary Vlasevna."* (This was the midwife, a new and important personage in Levin's family life.) *"She's come to look me over; she thinks I'm completely all right, and we've managed to keep her till you get back. Everyone is cheerful and well; please don't be in any hurry, and if the shooting's good stay on another day."*

These two joys, a good day's shooting and the note from his wife, were so great that two slightly disagreeable incidents that took place afterward passed off lightly for Levin. One was that the chestnut side horse, which had evidently been overworked the day before, was off its feed and looked listless. The coachman said it had been strained.

"Overdriven it was yesterday, Mr. Constantine," he said. "What an idea—driving like that for seven miles!"

The other unpleasantness, which spoiled his high spirits at first but which he laughed about a great deal later on, was that nothing was left of all the supplies Kitty had provided so abundantly it had seemed impossible to eat them up in a week. When he came back from the shooting tired and hungry, Levin had been dreaming so vividly about pies that as he approached his lodgings he could already smell and taste them, just as Laska had scented the game, and had ordered Philip to bring some at once. It turned out that not only were there no pies left, but there was no longer even any chicken.

"Now there's an appetite for you!" said Oblonsky, with a laugh, indicating Veslovsky. "I don't suffer from a bad appetite, but his is astounding—"

"Oh well, it can't be helped," said Levin, looking morosely at Veslovsky. "Bring me some beef then, Philip."

"The beef's all been eaten, I've given the bone to the dogs," replied Philip.

Levin was so annoyed he said angrily: "You really might have left me something!" He felt like crying.

"Well, clean the game then," he said to Philip in a trembling voice, trying not to look at Veslovsky, "and stuff them with nettles. And ask for some milk, for me at least."

As soon as he had drunk his fill of milk he felt ashamed of having shown a stranger his annoyance, and he began laughing over the irascibility due to his hunger.

In the evening they went out shooting again, and Veslovsky killed a few birds; they started back home at night.

The drive back was just as gay as the drive out. Sometimes Veslovsky sang, sometimes he recalled his adventures with the peasants who had treated him to vodka and said "No offense!" his night's adventures and games and the maid, and the peasant who asked him whether he was married and on finding out he wasn't said to him: "Don't hanker after other men's wives, you'd better try to get hold of a wife of your own!" This remark seemed particularly funny to Veslovsky.

"Altogether I'm delighted with our outing. How about you, Levin?"

"I'm very pleased indeed," said Levin sincerely. He was

especially glad not only that he no longer felt any of the hostility he had had for Veslovsky at home, but that, on the contrary, he had the friendliest feelings for him.

XIV

NEXT morning at ten o'clock, after having already made the round of the estate, Levin knocked at the door of Veslovsky's room.

"Come in!" Veslovsky shouted. "Excuse me—I've only just finished washing," he said smiling, standing there in nothing but his underclothes.

"Don't mind me, please." Levin sat down by the window. "Did you sleep well?"

"Like the dead. And what sort of a day is it for shooting?"

"Would you like something to drink—tea or coffee?"

"Neither. I'll wait for lunch. I'm really quite ashamed of myself. I suppose the ladies are up already? Splendid time for a walk. You must show me your horses."

After walking about the garden, visiting the stables, and even doing some gymnastics together on the parallel bars, Levin and his guest returned and went into the drawing room.

"It was wonderful, shooting, and there were so many new impressions!" said Veslovsky, going over to Kitty, who was sitting beside the samovar. "What a pity that ladies are deprived of such pleasures!"

Well, what of it, said Levin to himself; he's bound to say something to the mistress of the house.

Once again he was struck by something in the smile, in the triumphant expression with which his guest had addressed Kitty . . .

The Princess, who was sitting on the other side of the table with the midwife and Oblonsky, called Levin over and started up a conversation with him about moving to Moscow for Kitty's confinement and getting the house ready. Just as at the time of the wedding Levin had thought all forms of preparation were disagreeable and offensive because of their triviality compared with the majesty of what was taking place, now the preparations for Kitty's confinement, the time of which was being counted off on their fingers seemed to him even more offensive. He constantly kept trying not to listen to these conversations about methods of swaddling the future infant; he tried to turn away from and not to see those mysterious, endless strips of knitting, those linen triangles Dolly attached such special importance to, and so on. The birth of a son (he was sure it would be a son), which they promised him, but which he couldn't believe in nevertheless—it seemed so extraordinary —appeared to him on the one hand such a gigantic and therefore unrealizable joy, and on the other hand such a mysterious event, that this assumed knowledge of what was going to happen, and thus the preparations for it as though it were something ordinary, brought about by mere human beings, appeared to him shocking and degrading.

But the Princess had no understanding for his feelings and explained his aversion to thinking and talking about this as frivolity and indifference; because of it she gave him no peace. She was now commissioning Oblonsky to look for a house, and had called Levin over.

"I have no idea at all, Princess. Do as you think best," he said.

"You must decide when you're going to move."

"Really, I have no idea. All I know is that children are born by the millions without Moscow and without any doctors . . . So why—"

"Well, if that's—"

"Oh no, it's whatever Kitty wants."

"It's impossible to talk to Kitty about this! D'you want me to give her a fright? Only this spring Nataly Golitsyn died because she had a bad doctor."

"Just tell me what to do and I'll do it," he replied morosely.

The Princess began to tell him, but he wasn't listening to her. Though he was upset by this talk with the Princess, what had made him morose was not the conversation but what he had seen by the samovar.

No, it's impossible, he thought, glancing over occasionally at Kitty, blushing and agitated, and at Veslovsky leaning toward her and saying something to her with his beautiful smile.

There was something impure in Veslovsky's posture, in the way he looked and smiled. Levin also saw something impure both in Kitty's posture and expression. Once again the light died out of his eyes. Once again, like that last time, without the slightest transition, he felt that he had been flung from his height of happiness, peace, and dignity into an abyss of despair, spite, and degradation. Once again everything and everyone became repulsive to him.

"Then do whatever you think best, Princess," he said, looking round again.

"Heavy the autocrat's crown!" said Oblonsky jocularly, evidently alluding not only to the conversation with the Princess but to the reason for Levin's agitation, which he had noticed. "How late you are today, Dolly!"

They all got up to greet Dolly. Veslovsky got up for a second, and with the rudeness toward ladies peculiar to modern young men he scarcely bowed before going on with his conversation and laughing at something.

"Masha's been exhausting me. She slept badly and has been terribly capricious all morning," said Dolly.

The conversation Veslovsky had started with Kitty was once again about Anna and about whether love could transcend social conventions. This conversation was unpleasant to Kitty; it upset her by its very content, by the tone in which it was carried on, and particularly by the effect she now knew it would have on her husband. But she was too simple and innocent to know how to cut it short, or even to conceal the superficial pleasure this young man's evident attentiveness gave her. She wanted to stop the conversation, but didn't know how. Whatever she did she knew it would be noticed by her husband, and would all be interpreted in a bad light. And as a matter of fact when she asked Dolly what was the matter with Masha, and Veslovsky gazed at Dolly indifferently as he waited for this discussion, which was boring for him, to come to an end, the question seemed artificial to Levin, a revolting piece of guile.

"Well, what about going mushroom hunting today?" said Dolly.

"Oh let's! I'll go too!" said Kitty, and blushed. Out of politeness she had wanted to ask Veslovsky whether he was coming but she didn't. "Kostya, where are you going?" she asked her husband guiltily as he walked by her with his resolute stride. This guilty look of hers confirmed all his suspicions.

"The mechanic came while I was away, I haven't seen him yet," he said without looking at her.

He went downstairs, but before he had time to leave his study he heard his wife's familiar footsteps following him with reckless haste.

"What's the matter with you?" he said to her drily. "We're busy."

"Excuse me," she said, turning to the German mechanic, "I have something to talk over with my husband."

The German was about to go out, but Levin said to him: "Don't bother."

"Isn't the train at three?" the German asked. "I mustn't be late."

Levin made no reply; he went out with his wife.

"Well, what is it you have to say to me?" he asked in French.

He didn't look her in the face; he didn't wish to see her, in her condition; she was standing there with her whole face twitching, with a pitiful crushed look.

"I—wanted to say that—it's impossible to live this way, it's agony!" she blurted out.

"The servants are there in the pantry," he said angrily. "Don't make a scene!"

"Well, come in here then!"

They were standing in a passage; Kitty wanted to go into a neighboring room, but the English governess was there giving Tanya a lesson.

"Then let's go into the garden."

In the garden they came upon a peasant, weeding a path. But no longer thinking about whether the peasant had seen her tear-stained and his excited face, without thinking that they looked as though they were fleeing some catastrophe, they walked on rapidly, feeling they had to speak their minds and make each other see the light, that they had to be alone together and so rid themselves of the torment they were both undergoing.

"It's impossible to live this way! It's agony! I suffer, and you suffer. For what?" she said, when they finally got to a secluded garden seat at a turn in the lime-tree walk.

"Just tell me one thing: Was there anything in his tone that was improper, impure, horrid, degrading?" he said, standing in front of her once again in that same pose, with his hands clenched against his chest, that he had taken up that night.

"There was," she said in a trembling voice. "But Kostya, surely you see I'm not to blame? All morning I meant to strike a tone that would . . . But all those people . . . Why did he come? How happy we were!" she said, choking with sobs that made her whole swollen body heave.

As they passed the gardener on their way back he saw to his astonishment that though nothing had been pursuing them, and there had been nothing to run away from, and that there could have been nothing specially joyful on that seat, their faces were radiant with reassurance.

XV

AFTER seeing Kitty upstairs, Levin went to Dolly's part of the house. That day she was also in great distress. She was walking up and down the room scolding a little girl who stood howling in a corner.

"And you're going to stand in the corner all day, and have your dinner by yourself, and won't see a single doll, and I'm not going to sew you a new dress," she said, trying to think up some way of punishing her.

"Oh, what a horrid little girl she is!" she said to Levin. "I can't think where she gets hold of all these·nasty tendencies!"

"But what did she do?" said Levin rather indifferently; he had wanted to consult Dolly about his own problems and was annoyed at having picked the wrong moment.

"She and Grisha went off among the raspberry bushes and there they—I can't even repeat what they did. One regrets Miss Elliot a thousand times. This one doesn't look after anything at all, she's a machine. Just imagine, the child . . ."

And Dolly told him Masha's crime.

"That proves nothing. It's not a nasty tendency, it's just mischievousness," said Levin to reassure her.

"But you—are you upset? Why did you come?" asked Dolly. "What's happening over there?"

By the way she asked this Levin could tell it would be easy for him to say what he had intended to.

"I haven't been there, I've been in the garden alone with Kitty. This is the second quarrel we've had since—since Stiva came."

Dolly looked at him with intelligent, understanding eyes.

"Now tell me, hand on heart, was there—not in Kitty's manner, but in that fellow's, anything that might be disagreeable, not disagreeable but horrible and offensive to a husband?"

"I mean—how can I put it?— Stand there, stand in the corner!" she said turning to Masha, who when she noticed a scarcely perceptible smile on her mother's face started turning round. "The opinion of society would be that he's behaving as all young men behave. He's paying court to a young and pretty woman, and a worldly husband simply ought to be flattered by it."

"Yes, yes," said Levin morosely. "But you noticed it, didn't you?"

"Not only me; Stiva noticed it too. He said to me right after tea: 'I think Veslovsky's making eyes at Kitty.' "

"Well that's fine; now I feel better. I'll just kick him out," said Levin.

"What! Have you gone out of your mind!" Dolly cried out in horror. "What d'you mean? Pull yourself together, Kostya," she said, laughing. "You can go off to Fanny now," she said to Masha. "No, if you like I'll tell Stiva and he'll take him away. We can say you're expecting some visitors. All in all this isn't the place for him."

"No, no; I'll do it myself."

"But will you have a fight?"

"Not at all! It'll be so much fun for me," said Levin cheerfully, his eyes actually sparkling. "Well, forgive her now, Dolly. She won't do it again," he said referring to the small culprit, who hadn't gone to Fanny but was standing hesitatingly in front of Dolly, looking up from under her brows and waiting to catch her mother's eye.

Her mother looked at her. The little girl burst into sobs and buried her face in her mother's lap, and Dolly placed her thin, tender hand on her head.

And what has he in common with us? Levin thought, and went to look for Veslovsky.

As he passed through the hall he ordered the carriage to be harnessed to go to the station.

"One of the springs got broken yesterday," replied the footman.

"Well the covered gig then, but quickly. Where is the guest?"

"He's gone to his room."

Levin found Veslovsky, who had unpacked his valise and spread out some new songs, trying on some leather gaiters to go riding.

Whether it was because there was something peculiar in Levin's expression or whether Veslovsky himself felt that his making eyes at Kitty was out of place in this family, he was somewhat disconcerted by Levin's entry, or as much as a man of the world can be.

"D'you use gaiters to ride?"

"Yes, it's much cleaner," said Veslovsky, putting his stout leg on a chair, fastening the bottom hook, and giving his cheerful good-natured smile.

There was no doubt that he was a splendid young fellow, and Levin felt sorry for him and ashamed of himself, as the host, when he detected the shyness in Veslovsky's expression.

On the table there was a piece of a stick they had broken that morning while doing gymnastics together, when they were trying to raise the warped parallel bars. Levin picked up this broken stick and began pulling off the splintered bits at the end; he didn't know how to begin.

"I wanted to—" He was about to fall silent, but suddenly, as he recalled Kitty and everything that had happened, he said, looking straight into his eyes: "I've ordered the horses to be harnessed for you."

"Eh? What d'you mean?" Veslovsky began in astonishment. "To go where?"

"For you to go to the railway station," said Levin morosely, twisting off splinters.

"Are you leaving, or has something happened?"

"It turns out that I'm expecting some visitors," said Levin, breaking off splinters from the end of the stick more and more rapidly with his powerful fingers. "And I'm not expecting any visitors, and nothing's happened, but I'm asking you to leave. You can explain my rudeness any way you please."

Veslovsky straightened up.

"I ask *you* to explain it to me . . ." he said with dignity, finally having got the point.

"I can't explain it to you," Levin began, softly and slowly, trying to conceal the trembling of his jaw. "And it's better for you not to ask."

As the splinters he had been plucking at were now all broken off, Levin grasped the thick ends of the stick in his fingers, snapped the stick in two, and carefully caught one of the ends as it fell.

The sight of these taut arms, the same muscles he had felt that morning when doing gymnastics, the glittering eyes, the soft voice, and the quivering jaw, probably convinced Veslovsky more than what Levin said. Shrugging his shoulders and smiling disdainfully, he bowed.

"Will it be possible for me to see Oblonsky?"

His shrugging his shoulders and smiling did not annoy Levin. What else is there for him to do? he thought.

"I'll send him to you at once."

"What nonsense!" said Oblonsky, after learning that his friend was being expelled from the house, when he found Levin strolling about in the garden waiting for Veslovsky to leave. "It's simply ridiculous! What's been biting you? It really is utterly ridiculous! What can you have been thinking, just because a young man—"

But the place where Levin had been bitten was evidently still sore, since once again he grew pale at Oblonsky's attempt to explain his motive and hastily stopped him:

"Please don't go into my reasons! There's nothing else I can do! I feel ashamed of myself vis-à-vis yourself and him. But I don't suppose it'll cause him any great distress to leave, and his presence here is disagreeable to my wife and myself."

"But it's insulting to him! And then really it *is* ridiculous!"

"And it's both insulting to me and painful! I'm not to blame for anything, and there's no reason for me to suffer!"

"Well, I really didn't expect this of you! One can be jealous, but to such a degree . . . Really, how ridiculous!"

Levin swiftly turned aside and left him; he went to the end of one of the walks, where he went on pacing back and forth by himself. He soon heard the rattle of the leather-topped gig, and through the trees saw Veslovsky, in his Scottish bonnet, sitting on some hay (unluckily it had no seats) jolting over the ruts as he was driven along the other drive.

Now what's that? thought Levin as a footman ran out of the house and stopped the gig. It was because of the mechanic, whom Levin had forgotten all about. The mechanic bowed and said something to Veslovsky; then he climbed into the gig and they drove off together.

Oblonsky and the Princess were indignant over Levin's behavior. He himself felt not only ridiculous to the highest degree, but completely at fault and disgraced, though when he recalled what he and his wife had suffered through and asked himself how he would act some other time, he told himself he would do exactly the same again.

In spite of all this, at the end of that day everyone, with the exception of the Princess, who would not forgive Levin's conduct, became extraordinarily lively and gay, just like children after being punished, or adults after a burdensome official reception, so that after the Princess had retired that evening they talked about Veslovsky's expulsion as though it were ancient history. And Dolly, who had her father's gift for comedy, made Varenka collapse with laughter as she told for the third and fourth times, each time with new humorous additions, how she had just been putting on some new ribbons in the guest's honor and was already going into the drawing room when she suddenly heard the rattle of the old gig. And who was it in the old gig? Veslovsky himself, in his Scottish bonnet, with his songs and his gaiters, was sitting in the hay.

"You might at least have had the carriage hitched up for him! . . . And then the next thing I heard was 'Stop!' So I thought, well they've relented. I looked and there they were putting in that big, fat German beside him and driving off . . . And there were my ribbons—all wasted!"

## XVI

DOLLY carried out her intention and went to see Anna. She was very sorry to hurt her sister and to do anything to displease Levin; she realized how right the Levins were in not wishing to have anything to do with Vronsky; but she considered it her duty to visit Anna and show her that her own feelings could not change regardless of any change in Anna's position.

In order not to depend on the Levins for this trip Dolly sent to the village to hire some horses; but when Levin heard this he came and reproached her.

"But why should you think your going is disagreeable to me? For that matter even if it were it would be all the more so if you didn't take my horses," he said. "You never told me definitely you were going. For you to hire horses in the village is disagreeable for me, in the first place, but the main thing is that they would agree to do it but wouldn't get you there. I have some horses, and if you don't want to make me feel uncomfortable you'll take them."

Dolly was bound to agree, and on the appointed day Levin got four horses ready for his sister-in-law as well as a relay, which he made up out of work and saddle horses, far from handsome, but which could get Dolly there in one day. At this time, just when the horses were needed both for the Princess, who was leaving, and for the midwife, this was inconvenient, but his duty as a host made it impossible for him to allow Dolly to hire horses while she was in his house; aside from this he knew that the twenty rubles it would have cost her for the trip were very important to her; he felt that Dolly's financial affairs, which were in a very bad way, were a concern of his own.

On Levin's advice Dolly left before daybreak. The road was good, the carriage comfortable, the horses trotted along briskly; on the box beside the coachman sat the office clerk instead of a footman, whom Levin had sent along for safety's sake. Dolly dozed off and did not wake up until they had already arrived at the inn where the horses had to be changed.

After drinking some tea at the same rich peasant's where Levin had stopped off on his way to Sviyazhsky's, and having had a chat with the peasant women about children and with the old man about Count Vronsky, whom he praised to the skies, Dolly went on again at ten o'clock. When she was at home she never had time to think because of her worries about the children. To make up for it on this four-hour drive, all the thoughts that had been repressed now suddenly crowded into her mind, and she thought through her whole life, from all angles, as she never had before. Even to herself her thoughts seemed strange. First she thought about the children; even though the Princess, and above all Kitty (whom she relied on more), had promised to look after them she was very uneasy about them nevertheless.

If only Masha doesn't get into mischief; or Grisha isn't kicked by a horse; and Lily's stomach—if only that doesn't get any more upset.

But then the questions of the present began to be replaced by those of the immediate future. She began thinking about the new house they would have to move into that winter in Moscow, the furniture that would have to be reupholstered in the drawing room, and the winter coat she would have to have made for her eldest girl. Then questions of a more remote future began coming to mind: How was she going to start the children off in life? There won't be any trouble with the girls, she thought, but what about the boys?

Now it's all very well, I can take care of Grisha, but after all that's only because I'm free now myself, I'm not having a baby. Of course Stiva can't be counted on, though with the help of some kindhearted people I'll be able to start them off; but if I have another baby . . .

And the thought came to her how wrong it was to say

that the curse that had been laid on women was the bringing forth of children in travail. Giving birth is nothing, but carrying them—that's what's agonizing, she thought, recalling her last pregnancy and the death of the infant. And she thought of the conversation she had had with a young woman at the wayside inn. She had asked her whether she had any children, and the woman, a pretty girl, had answered cheerfully:

"There was one little girl, but God set me free—I buried her in Lent."

"And were you very upset?" Dolly asked.

"What was there to be upset about? The old man has plenty of grandchildren as it is. It's just a nuisance. You can't work or anything. It just ties you down."

This reply seemed loathsome to Dolly, in spite of the good-natured sweetness of the young woman's looks; but now she recalled involuntarily these words of hers. This cynical remark had a grain of truth in it.

All in all, she thought, looking back over the whole of her life during these fifteen years of marriage, it's just been pregnancy, sickness, mental torpor, apathy, and—above all—disfigurement. Even Kitty, pretty young Kitty, even she's grown plainer, and when I'm pregnant I look like a monster, I know. The travail, the suffering, the monstrous suffering, and that final moment! . . . Then the nursing, the sleepless nights, those terrible pains!

Dolly shuddered at the mere recollection of the pain she had had to undergo from sore nipples with almost every baby.

Then there are the children's illnesses, that never-ending fear; then their education, their horrid tendencies (she remembered little Masha's misbehavior among the raspberry bushes), lessons, Latin—it's all so incomprehensible and so difficult. And above all—the death of those children.

And once again there arose in her mind the bitter memory that constantly tore at her maternal heart, the death of her last infant, a little boy who died of croup; she recalled his funeral, the general indifference toward the little pink coffin, and her own heart-rending, lonely pain at the sight of that pale little forehead with the curly locks at the temples, the open surprised little mouth—the last thing she saw the moment before the pink lid with the gold lace cross was closed over him.

And what for? What's the point of it all? Just that I, without ever having a moment's peace, always either pregnant or nursing a child, in a state of constant irritability and bad temper, tormented myself and tormenting others, repulsive to my husband—live out my life bringing up unfortunate, badly brought up and penniless children. Even now, if we weren't spending the summer with the Levins I don't know what we would have done. Of course Kostya and Kitty are so tactful we don't notice anything, but it can't go on that way. They're going to have children of their own, it'll be impossible for them to help us: they're cramped even as it is. And Papa—he's left himself hardly anything, how can he help us? So I can't even give the children a start myself, except with the help of others, by humiliating myself. Even if we assume the best—that none of the other children dies, and I manage somehow to bring them up: at best they'll just escape being good-for-nothings. That's the most I can hope for. And because of all this to go through so much suffering, so much toil . . . My whole life ruined!

She recalled again what the young peasant woman had said, and again it seemed disgusting to her; but she could not help agreeing that there was a kernel of plain truth in it.

"Is it much farther, Michael?" Dolly asked the office clerk, to distract herself from these frightening thoughts.

"After this village it's less than five miles, they say."

The carriage was going down through the village street toward a small bridge. A crowd of merry peasant women, with ready-twisted sheaf binders across their shoulders, was crossing the bridge, chattering loudly and merrily. They stopped on the bridge, inquisitively examining the carriage. All the faces turned toward Dolly seemed to her healthy and gay, teasing her with their joy in living. They're all full of life, all enjoying life, Dolly went on thinking as she passed the women, reached the top of the hill, and was once again going at a trot, the old carriage swaying comfortably on its soft springs, while I, as though I were just let out of prison, out of a world killing me with worries, have only now collected myself for a moment. Everyone is living—these women, and my sister Nataly, and Varenka, and Anna, whom I'm going to see now—everyone but me!

And they're all down on Anna! What for? Am I any better? At least I have a husband whom I love. Not the way I wanted to love him, but I love him, while Anna didn't love hers. So what is she guilty of? She wants to live. God has put that into our hearts. It may very well be that I would have done just the same. To this day I don't know whether I was right to listen to her that horrible time she came to see me in Moscow. At that time I ought to have left Stiva and begun life all over again. I might have loved and been loved the real way. And is it any better now? I have no respect for him. I need him, she went on, thinking about her husband, and I put up with him. Is that any better? At that time I might still have been able to attract someone, I still had my looks, Dolly went on thinking, and she felt like looking into the mirror; she had a small traveling mirror in her bag, and she wanted to get it out, but glancing at the backs of the coachman and the clerk swaying beside him she felt she would be embarrassed if one of them were to look round, and she didn't take the mirror out.

But even without looking at a mirror she thought that it was still not too late even now; she recalled Koznyshov, who had been particularly affable toward her; Stiva's friend, the kindhearted Turovtsyn, who nursed her children together with her when they had had scarlet fever and who was in love with her. And there was still another one, a very young man who, as her husband told her jocularly, thought she was the most beautiful of all the sisters. And the most passionate and impossible romances rose up in Dolly's imagination.

Anna was absolutely right to behave as she did, and I in any case am not going to reproach her at all. She is happy, she's making someone else happy; she's not crushed as I am, but is doubtless just the same as ever, fresh, clever, and outgoing, thought Dolly, and a roguish smile curved her lips, primarily because in thinking about Anna's love affair Dolly imagined, parallel with it, a similar love affair for herself with an imaginary, composite man who was in love with her. Just like Anna she confessed everything to her husband. And Oblonsky's dumfounded amazement at the news made her smile.

Daydreaming away like this Dolly reached the turning off the highroad which led to Vozdvizhensk.

## XVII

THE coachman pulled up the horses and looked round to the right, at a field of rye where some peasants were sitting beside a cart. The clerk was about to jump down, then changed his mind and shouted peremptorily to a peasant, beckoning him over. The breeze they had had while driving died down when they stopped; horseflies settled on the steaming horses, which angrily tried to shake them off. The metallic sound of a scythe being hammered beside the cart stopped, and one of the peasants got up and came over to the carriage.

"Hurry up, stick-in-the-mud!" the clerk shouted angrily at the peasant, who was slowly stepping with bare feet along the ruts of the dry, uneven road. "Be quick about it!"

The curly-headed old man, with a piece of bast tied round his hair, and his curved back dark with sweat, started walking faster, came up to the carriage and put his sunburned hand on the mudguard.

"Vozdvizhensk? The manor house? The Count's?" he repeated. "There, just go to that bend in the road, and take the turn to the left. Go straight down the drive and you can't miss it. Whom d'you want there? The Count himself?"

"And are they at home, my dear man?" Dolly said vaguely; she didn't know how to refer to Anna even to a peasant.

"They ought to be," said the peasant, shifting from one bare foot to the other and leaving a clear imprint of the ball of his foot with the five toes in the dust. "They ought to be home," he repeated, evidently wishing to chat. "They had some more visitors yesterday. Visitors—a terrible lot of them . . . What d'you want?" he turned round toward a boy who was shouting something at him from the cart. "There you are! A while back they passed by here on horseback, to take a look at the reaper. They must be back again by now. And who might you be?"

"We're from a long way off," said the coachman, climbing back onto the box. "So you say it's not far?"

"I tell you it's right over there. Where you drive out of the hollow," he said, rubbing his arm along the mudguard.

The healthy, thick-set young man came over too.

"Would there be some harvesting work to do?" he asked. "I don't know . . ."

"So then you turn to the left and you won't be able to miss it," said the peasant, who was obviously reluctant to let them go.

The coachman started up the horses but they had hardly gone round the bend when the peasants called out:

"Hey there—stop, my friend! Stop!" Two voices cried out. The coachman stopped.

"Here they are themselves! The whole crowd, they're coming now!" the peasant shouted, pointing to four people on horseback and two in a charabanc coming along the road.

It was Vronsky with his jockey, Veslovsky and Anna on horseback, and Princess Barbara and Sviyazhsky in the charabanc. They had been out riding and had gone to see some newly arrived reaping machines in operation.

When the carriage pulled up the horseback riders were moving forward at a walk. Anna was in front together with Veslovsky; she was riding quietly on a small, sturdy English cob with a cropped mane and short tail. Dolly was struck by the beauty of her head, with its black curls escaping from under her top hat, her full shoulders, slender waist in a black riding habit, and the whole of her calm, graceful bearing.

At first it seemed to her improper for Anna to be riding horseback. Dolly mentally associated the idea of a lady's horseback riding with the idea of youthful frivolity and coquetry, which to her mind was out of harmony with Anna's situation. But when she saw her close by she was instantly reconciled to her horseback riding. In spite of her elegance everything was so simple, calm, and dignified in Anna's posture, her clothes, and movements, that nothing could have been more natural.

Riding at Anna's side, on a heated gray cavalry horse, stretching his thick legs out in front and obviously delighted with himself, was Veslovsky, in his Scottish bonnet with its waving ribbons; Dolly could not repress a merry smile when she recognized him. Vronsky was riding behind them. He was mounted on a dark thoroughbred bay, plainly heated from galloping. He was using the reins to hold it in.

A short man dressed as a jockey was riding behind him. Sviyazhsky and Princess Barbara, in a new charabanc hitched to a powerful jet-black trotter, were overtaking the riders.

The moment Anna recognized Dolly in the little figure pressed back into a corner of the old carriage her face suddenly broke into a radiantly happy smile. She gave an exclamation, started in the saddle, and touched her horse into a gallop. When she reached the carriage she jumped off without any help and holding up her riding habit ran toward Dolly.

"Just what I thought, without daring to! Oh, what a pleasure! You can't imagine what a joy this is for me!" she cried, first pressing her face to Dolly's and kissing her, then holding her off and scrutinizing her with a smile.

"What a delicious surprise, Alexis!" she said, looking round at Vronsky, who had dismounted and was walking toward them.

Vronsky, taking off his gray top hat, went over to Dolly.

"You can't imagine how glad we are you came," he said, giving his words special emphasis and showing his strong white teeth.

Veslovsky, without dismounting, took off his hat and welcomed the visitor with a joyous wave of the ribbons above his head.

"This is Princess Barbara," said Anna in response to a questioning look from Dolly as the charabanc drove up.

"Ah!" said Dolly, with an involuntary expression of displeasure on her face.

Princess Barbara was an aunt of her husband's; Dolly had known her a long time and had no respect for her. She knew Princess Barbara had spent her whole life sponging on her rich relations, but for her to be living now in the house of Vronsky, a complete stranger, offended Dolly because of her relationship to Stiva. Anna noticed Dolly's expression and was disconcerted; she blushed, let her riding habit slip out of her hand and stumbled over it.

Dolly went over to the charabanc that had stopped and coldly said hello to Princess Barbara. She was acquainted with Sviyazhsky too. He asked her how his cranky friend with the young wife was getting along, and after taking in with a rapid glance the ill-matched horses and the patched mudguards of the carriage he suggested that the ladies drive in the charabanc.

"I'll go on in that vehicle," he said. "My horse is quiet, and the Princess drives splendidly."

"No, just stay as you are," said Anna, who had come over too. "We'll go on in the carriage." Taking Dolly by the arm she led her away.

Dolly was dazzled by this elegant charabanc—a kind of carriage she had never seen before—by the magnificent horses, by these brilliant elegant faces surrounding her. But she was struck most of all by the change that had taken place in her beloved Anna, whom she knew so well. Some other woman who was less attentive, who hadn't known Anna before and especially one who hadn't been thinking Dolly's thoughts on the way, would not have noticed anything special in Anna. But now Dolly was struck by that fleeting beauty that women have only when in love and

that she now found in Anna's face. Everything in her face—
the definiteness of the dimples on her cheeks and chin, the
smile that seemed to flutter round it, the brilliance of her
eyes, the graceful swiftness of her movements, the fullness of
her voice, even the irritably tender way she answered
Veslovsky when he asked her permission to mount her cob
so that he could teach it to lead with the right leg in the
gallop—it was all peculiarly attractive; and she seemed to
know it herself and be glad of it.

When Anna and Dolly had gotten into the carriage they
were both seized by a sudden embarrassment. Anna was
embarrassed by the keenly inquiring look Dolly turned on
her; Dolly by the fact that after what Sviyazhsky had said
about the "vehicle" she involuntarily felt ashamed of the
filthy old carriage in which Anna was sitting next to her.
The coachman Philip and the office clerk had the same feeling. In order to hide his embarrassment the clerk bustled
about helping the ladies in, but Philip the coachman turned
morose and prepared himself in advance not to be downed
by this external superiority. He smiled ironically when he
looked at the jet-black trotter, and was already deciding that
the trotter was good for nothing but a promenade and would
never do thirty miles at a stretch on a hot day.

The peasants had all gotten up next to the cart and were
watching the meeting between the two parties with inquisitive
merriment, making their own comments meanwhile.

"Glad too; haven't seen each other for a long time," said
the curly-headed old man with the bast tied round his head.

"There now, Uncle Gerasim, that raven stallion would be
a one for carting the sheaves!"

"Look there—is that a woman, in the breeches?" said one
of them, pointing to Veslovsky who had gotten up onto the
sidesaddle.

"No, it's a man. Did you see how spry he was jumping up!"

"Well, boys, aren't we going to get some sleep?"

"What d'you mean—sleep, today?" said the old man,
blinking up at the sun. "Look, it's too late. Scythes now, and
to work!"

## XVIII

ANNA looked at Dolly's thin, worn face, its wrinkles filled
with dust, and wished to say exactly what she was thinking,
which was just that Dolly had grown thinner and worse-look-

ing but, remembering that her own looks had improved and that Dolly's glance told her as much, she sighed and started talking about herself.

"You're looking at me," she said, "and wondering whether I can be happy in the position I'm in. Well, there it is—I'm ashamed to admit it, but I'm—I'm unforgivably happy. What happened to me was something magical, like a dream, when you feel terrified, full of horror, then suddenly you wake up and see there's nothing left of all your fears. I've woken up! I lived through agony, horror, and now for a long time already, especially since we've been here, I've been so happy!" she said, looking at Dolly with a shy, questioning smile.

"I'm so glad!" said Dolly with a smile, in spite of herself more coldly than she had intended. "I'm very glad for you! Why didn't you write me?"

"Why? Because I didn't dare to . . . You're forgetting my position."

"To me? You didn't dare to? If only you knew how I—I consider . . ."

Dolly had meant to talk about what she had been thinking of that morning, but for some reason it seemed to her out of place now.

"But we can talk about that later. What are all those buildings over there?" she asked, wishing to change the subject, and pointing to some red and green roofs that could be seen above a living green wall of acacias and lilacs. "It looks like quite a little town."

But Anna did not answer her.

"No, no! What is it you consider about my position? Just what do you think?" she asked.

"I think that—" Dolly began, but just then Veslovsky, who had got the cob to lead off with its right foot, galloped past them in his short jacket, bumping heavily up and down on the chamois of the sidesaddle.

"It's going all right!" he shouted.

Anna didn't even glance at him, but once again it seemed out of place to Dolly to discuss this broad subject in the carriage, so she cut short her sentence.

"I don't think anything," she said, "but I've always loved you, and if you love anyone you love them as they are, not as you want them to be."

Looking away from her friend's face and screwing up her eyes (this was a new habit of hers Dolly had never seen), Anna sank into thought; she wanted to grasp fully the significance of this remark. Then, having evidently understood it in her own way, she looked at Dolly:

"If you had any sins," she said, "they would all be forgiven you for your coming here and for what you just said."

Dolly saw that tears were coming into her eyes; she squeezed her hand in silence.

"But what are those buildings? There are so many of them!" she said, repeating her question after the moment's pause.

"Those are the servants' cottages, the stud farm, and the stables," Anna replied. "And that's where the park begins. It had been neglected, but Alexis had it all renovated. He's very fond of this estate, and he's got passionately interested in running it, a thing I never expected. But he has so many facets in his character! No matter what he sets his mind to he does it all wonderfully. Not only doesn't he get bored, he throws himself into everything with passion. I can see for myself that he's turned into a first-rate, prudent landlord, for that matter he's even stingy about farming. But only about farming. Where it's a question of tens of thousands he's quite heedless," she said with the sly, happy smile with which women often speak of the secret traits, known only to them, of the man they love. "There, d'you see that big building? That's the new hospital. I think it's going to cost more than a hundred thousand. That's his hobby just now. And d'you know how he started it? The peasants asked him to let them rent some meadows for less money, I think, and he refused, and I reproached him for being stingy. It wasn't just that alone, of course, but everything taken together that was what started him on the hospital to prove, you see, how far from stingy he is. It's a trifle, if you like, but I love him all the more for it. You'll see the house in a moment now. It's his grandfather's house, and on the outside it hasn't been altered at all."

"How lovely!" said Dolly, looking with unfeigned astonishment at the beautiful columned house rising out of the variegated greenery of the old trees in the garden.

"It is lovely, isn't it? And the view from the house upstairs is wonderful."

They drove into a graveled courtyard bright with flowers where two laborers were making a border of rough porous stones round a well-turned flower bed, and stopped beneath a roofed portico.

"Oh, they're here already!" said Anna, looking at the riding horses that were just being led away from the front steps. "That's a beauty, that horse, don't you think? That's the cob, my favorite . . . Bring it over here, and get me some sugar. Where is the Count?" she asked the two footmen in gala livery who had rushed out. "Ah, there he is!" she said, seeing Vronsky and Veslovsky coming out to meet her.

"Where have you put the Princess?" Vronsky said in French to Anna, and without waiting for an answer he greeted Dolly again, this time kissing her hand. "I suppose in the big room off the balcony?"

"Oh no—that's too far away! The corner room is better, we'll be able to see more of each other. Well, shall we go in?" said Anna, after giving the sugar the footman had brought her to her favorite horse.

"And you're forgetting your duty," she said to Veslovsky, who had also come out to the portico.

"Pardon me—my pockets are full of it," he replied with a smile, thrusting his fingers into his waistcoat pocket.

"But you've come too late," she said, using a handkerchief to wipe her hand, which the horse had wetted taking the sugar. She turned to Dolly:

"Are you staying long? What—only a day? That's impossible!"

"I promised . . . besides, the children . . ." said Dolly, who felt embarrassed both at having to take her bag out of the carriage and because she realized her face must be completely covered with dust.

"No, Dolly darling— Well, we'll see. Let's go in, come along!" And Anna showed Dolly to her room.

This was not the gala room Vronsky had suggested, but one that Anna apologized to Dolly for. This room too, which had to be apologized for, was full of luxury, which Dolly had never lived in and which reminded her of the best hotels abroad.

"Well, darling, I'm so happy!" said Anna, sitting down beside Dolly for a moment in her riding habit. "Now tell me all about yourselves. I've seen Stiva, for a second, but he couldn't tell me anything about the children. How is my darling Tanya? I suppose she's a big girl now?"

"Yes, very big," Dolly replied briefly; she herself was surprised at her giving such chilly answers about her children. "It's very comfortable, staying with the Levins," she added.

"If only I'd known you didn't despise me!" said Anna. "You could all have come to stay with us. After all Stiva's such a great old friend of Alexis's," she added, and suddenly she blushed.

"Yes, but we're so comfortable now——" replied Dolly, embarrassed.

"But I feel so happy I'm talking nonsense. The main thing, darling, is that I'm so glad to see you!" said Anna, kissing her again. "You still haven't told me your attitude or what you think about me, and I want to hear it all. But I'm glad you're going to see me just as I am. Above all I shouldn't want anyone to think I'm trying to prove anything. I don't want to prove anything at all—all I want to do is live, harming no one but myself. I have a right to that, don't I? But that's a big subject and we'll have a long talk about it later. I'm going to change now; I'll send you the maid."

XIX

LEFT to herself Dolly took in the room with a housewife's eye. Everything she had seen while approaching the house and going through it, as well as her own room now, all gave her the impression of abundance, opulence, and of the modern European luxury she had read about only in English novels but had never yet seen in Russia and in the country. Everything was new, from the new French wallpaper to the carpet that covered the whole floor. The bed had a spring with an overlay mattress, a special sort of bolster, and small pillows with silk slips. The marble washstand, the dressing table, the couch, the tables, the bronze clock on the mantelpiece, the curtains and the door hangings were all new and expensive.

The smart maid who came in to offer her services, whose clothes and hairdo were more fashionable than Dolly's, was just as new and expensive as the whole room. Dolly liked her politeness, tidiness, and willingness, but she felt ill at ease with her; she was ashamed of her patched dressing jacket, which she unluckily had packed by mistake. She was ashamed of the very patches and darns she was so proud of at home. At home it was obvious that six jackets took over eighteen yards of nainsook at sixty-five kopecks a yard, which came to more than fifteen rubles, beside the trimmings and the labor, and she had saved these fifteen rubles. But in front of the maid she felt not exactly ashamed, but ill at ease.

Dolly was very much relieved when Annushka, whom she had known a long time, came into the room. The smart maid had to go to her mistress, and Annushka stayed with Dolly.

It was obvious that Annushka was delighted at her having come, and she chattered away without a stop. Dolly noticed that she wanted to express her own opinion about her mistress's situation, especially about the Count's love and devotion, but Dolly would assiduously stop her the moment she began speaking about it.

"I grew up with Madame, she's dearer to me than anything. After all, it's not up to us to judge. And then the way he seems to love—"

"Then you'll please have this washed, if possible," Dolly interrupted her.

"Yes, ma'am. There are two women specially kept for washing small things here; the clothes are all done by machine. The Count looks after everything himself. Now what a husband he—"

Dolly was glad when Anna came into the room and by her arrival cut short Annushka's chatter.

Anna had changed into a very simple muslin dress. Dolly carefully studied this simple dress. She knew what such simplicity meant and how much money it had cost.

"An old friend," said Anna, nodding at Annushka.

Anna was now no longer embarrassed. She was quite composed and at ease. Dolly saw that she had now completely recovered from the impression that had been made on her by Dolly's arrival, and had assumed the superficial tone of indifference that seemed to shut tight the door into the apartment where all her feelings and intimate thoughts were kept.

"Well, and how is your little girl?" Dolly asked.

"Annie? She's well. Very much better. Would you like to see her? Come along, I'll show her to you. There's been such a lot of trouble with the nannies," she began. "We had an Italian wet nurse. Very pretty, but so stupid! We wanted to dismiss her, but the little girl's grown so accustomed to her we've kept her on."

"But what arrangements did you make for—" Dolly was about to ask about the name the little girl would bear; but when she noticed a sudden frown on Anna's face she changed the point of the question. "What did you arrange for? Have you weaned her yet?"

But Anna had understood. "That's not what you were

going to ask, is it? Weren't you going to ask about her name? It worries Alexis. She has no name. That is, her name is Karenin," said Anna, screwing up her eyes until only the lashes could be seen. Then her face suddenly lit up. "But we'll be able to talk about all that later on! Come, I'll show her to you. She's very sweet. She's crawling about already."

The luxury that had struck Dolly throughout the house struck her in the nursery even more. There were some little gocarts ordered from England, instruments for teaching infants how to walk, a specially built sofa something like a billiard table for her to crawl on, some swings, and special baths of a novel kind. Everything was English, solid, of good quality, and obviously very expensive. The room was large, very high and full of light.

When they entered the little girl was sitting in a tiny armchair at the table, wearing nothing but a little chemise, drinking her bouillon, which she was spilling all over her little chest. A Russian nursemaid was feeding the little girl, and evidently having her own meal together with her. Neither the wet nurse nor the nanny was there; they were in the next room, from which they could be heard talking in the peculiar French that was their only means of communication.

On hearing Anna's voice a tall smartly dressed Englishwoman, with a disagreeable, dissolute-looking face, came through the doorway with a quick shake of her fair curls and immediately began excusing herself, though Anna had not found fault with her. At everything Anna said the Englishwoman kept saying quickly "Yes, my lady!" several times.

The dark-browed, dark-haired rosy-faced little girl, with her sturdy, ruddy little body covered with skin like goose flesh pleased Dolly very much in spite of the severe look she gave the newcomer; Dolly even felt a little envious of her healthy looks. Dolly also very much liked the way she crawled. Not one of her own children had crawled like that. When the little girl was placed on the carpet with her little dress tucked up behind she looked wonderfully sweet. Looking up at the grown-ups with her shining black eyes, like some little wild animal, obviously delighted with being admired, she drew herself vigorously along on her little arms, holding her legs out sideways, quickly pulling her little seat forward, then advancing again on her little arms.

But Dolly very much disliked the general atmosphere of the nursery, especially the Englishwoman. The only explanation Dolly could make to herself of how Anna, with her knowledge of people, could have taken on such an unlikable, disreputable Englishwoman for her little girl was that no nice woman would have gone into such an irregular household. Aside from this Dolly realized at once, from a few remarks, that Anna, the wet nurse, the nanny, and the child were strangers to one another, and that a visit from the child's mother was something exceptional.

Anna had wanted to get the little girl some toy and she couldn't find it. And what was most astonishing of all was that in answering a question about how many teeth the little girl had Anna made a mistake; she knew nothing at all about the two latest teeth.

"It's hard for me sometimes to realize how superfluous I am around here," Anna said on leaving, lifting up her train to avoid the toys lying beside the door. "It wasn't that way with the first one."

"I thought it was the opposite," said Dolly timidly.

"Oh no! You know I've seen him, Seryozha, don't you?" said Anna, screwing up her eyes as though she were peering at something in the distance. "But we can talk about that later. You can't imagine it, I'm like someone starving who's suddenly had a full meal set before him and doesn't know what to start on first. The full meal is—you, and the talks I'm going to have with you that I couldn't have with anyone else; and I don't know what talk to start with. But I'm not letting you off with a thing! I have to talk my heart out. Yes, I'll have to give you a sketch of the people you'll meet here," she began.

"I'll start with the women. Princess Barbara. You know her, and I know what you and Stiva think about her. Stiva says the sole purpose of her life is to prove her superiority to Aunt Catherine. That's all true, but she has a kind heart and I'm very grateful to her. There was a moment in Petersburg when what I needed was a chaperon. That was when she turned up. But she really does have a kind heart. She's made my situation very much easier. I see you don't understand the full difficulty of my situation—there in Petersburg," she added. "Here I'm completely calm and happy—"

"But about that later: I must go on with my list. Then there's Sviyazhsky; he's a Marshal of the Nobility and a very nice fellow, but he's trying to get something from Alexis. With his fortune, you understand, now that we've settled in the country Alexis can exercise a great deal of influence. Then there's Tushkevich—you've seen him, he's one of

Betsy's. Now he's been retired and he's come to see us. As Alexis says he's one of those people who are very nice if you take them at face value, and then he's very *comme il faut*, as Princess Barbara puts it. Then there's Veslovsky—you know him. A very nice boy," she said, and a roguish smile curved her lips. "What was that wild story about him and Levin? Veslovsky told Alexis about it; we can't believe it. He's very sweet and naïve," she said, again with the same smile. "Men have to be distracted, and Alexis needs an audience, which is why I set such store by all these people. Things have to be lively and gay here, so that Alexis doesn't start wanting something new. Then you'll see the estate manager. He's a German, a very good man who knows his business. Alexis has a high opinion of him. Then there's the doctor, a young fellow, not exactly a complete Nihilist but, you know—eats with his knife . . . Though he's a first-rate doctor. Then there's the architect. . . . Quite a little court!"

## XX

WELL, Princess, here's Dolly for you now, you wanted to see her so much," said Anna, as she and Dolly came out onto the large stone terrace where Princess Barbara was sitting in the shade in front of an embroidery frame embroidering a chair cover for Vronsky. "She says she doesn't want anything before dinner, but could you order some lunch? I'll go find Alexis and bring them all here."

Princess Barbara received Dolly affectionately, and somewhat patronizingly; she immediately began explaining to her that she was living with Anna because she had always been more attached to her than her sister Catherine, the same aunt who had brought Anna up, and that now that Anna had been deserted by everyone she considered it her duty to help her in this most difficult period of transition.

"Her husband is going to give her a divorce, and then I'll withdraw into my solitude once more, but for the time being I can be useful and do my duty, however hard it may be for me, unlike some others.

"And how sweet it was of you to come, how right you were to do it! They're living just like the best of married couples; God will judge them, not us. And what about Biryuzovsky and Madame Avenyev? And Nikandrov himself? Or Vasiliev and Madame Mamonov? And Lisa Merkalov? Did any one say anything against them? And it all ended by everyone receiving them. Then it's such a pretty home, so *comme il faut*. Altogether in the English style. We meet for breakfast, then we separate. Everyone does just as he pleases until dinner-time. Dinner's at seven. Stiva did very well to send you here. He must stick to them. You know the Count can do anything at all through his mother and brother; they do so much good. Has he told you about his hospital? It's going to be magnificent! All straight from Paris."

Their conversation was interrupted by Anna, who had found the men in the billiard room and was bringing them back to the stone terrace. As there was still a great deal of time until dinner and the weather was lovely, various methods of spending the remaining two hours were proposed. There were a great many ways of passing time in Vozdvizhensk, all different from those in Pokrovsk.

"What about a game of lawn tennis," suggested Veslovsky, with his charming smile. "We can be partners again," he said to Anna.

"No, it's too hot; let's rather take a walk through the garden and go for a row, to show Princess Dolly the banks," suggested Vronsky.

"I'll agree to anything," said Sviyazhsky.

"I suppose Dolly would find a walk the most agreeable of all, wouldn't you? Then in the boat for a row later, perhaps," said Anna.

So this was decided. Veslovsky and Tushkevich went to the bathing house, where they promised to get the boat ready and wait for the others.

They started walking down the garden path in two couples, Anna and Sviyazhsky, and Dolly and Vronsky. Dolly was somewhat embarrassed and troubled by the completely novel milieu she was in. Theoretically, in the abstract, she not only defended Anna's conduct but even approved of it. As often with women of irreproachable virtue generally, who are tired of the monotony of a virtuous life, she not only condoned illicit love, from afar, but even envied it. Besides she loved Anna with all her heart. But in reality, when she saw her in the midst of these people who were strangers to her, with their unfamiliar fashionable tone, which was new to Dolly, she felt uncomfortable. It was particularly unpleasant for her to see Princess Barbara, who forgave them everything for the sake of the comforts she was taking advantage of.

Altogether—in the abstract—Dolly approved of Anna's action, but it was unpleasant for her actually to see the man on whose account the action had been taken. Aside from this she had never liked Vronsky. She thought him very proud, and she saw nothing he could have been proud of except his wealth. But involuntarily, here in his own house, he impressed her more than ever, and she could not feel at ease with him. In his presence she had the same sort of feeling she had had when the lady's maid saw her sleeping jacket. Just as with the maid she had felt not so much ashamed as uncomfortable because of the patches, so with him she constantly felt not so much ashamed as uncomfortable because of herself.

Dolly felt embarrassed, and cast about for a topic of conversation. Even though she thought that with all his pride any praise of his house or garden would be displeasing to him, nevertheless, since she couldn't find any other topic she told him she liked his house very much.

"Yes, it's a very fine building, and in the good, old-fashioned style," he said.

"I particularly liked the courtyard in front of the portico. Had it been that way before?"

"Oh no!" he said, and his face lit up with pleasure. "If you had only seen that courtyard in the spring!"

And then, at first with some reserve but getting more and more carried away, he began drawing her attention to the various details of the improvements in the house and garden. It was plain that having taken great pains to improve and beautify his estate Vronsky felt obliged to boast of them to a fresh person, and was profoundly pleased by Dolly's compliments.

"If you'd like to take a look at the hospital, and you're not too tired, it's not very far away. Shall we go?" he said, glancing at her face to make sure she really wasn't being bored.

"D'you want to come too, Anna?" he said, turning to her.

"We'll come along, shall we?" she said to Sviyazhsky. "But we can't leave poor Veslovsky and Tushkevich to cool their heels in the boat. We must let them know."

"Yes, that's a monument he's putting up here," said Anna, turning to Dolly with the same sly, knowing smile with which she had previously spoken about the hospital.

"Oh, it's a monumental enterprise!" said Sviyazhsky, but to avoid the appearance of making up to Vronsky he immediately added a slightly derogatory remark. "Though I'm surprised, Count," he said, "that with all you're doing for the people from the point of view of hygiene you're so indifferent to the schools."

"The schools have become so commonplace," Vronsky replied. "You understand that's not the reason, it's just that I've been carried away. This is the way to the hospital," he said, turning to Dolly and indicating a side path that led off the avenue.

The ladies opened their sunshades and went out into the side path. After a number of turnings they passed through a gate, and on a rise in front of her Dolly saw a large, handsome, fancifully designed building that was almost finished. The still unpainted iron roof shone dazzlingly in the bright sunshine. Beside the finished building there was another going up, surrounded by scaffolding, on which laborers in aprons were laying bricks, pouring mortar from wooden tubs and leveling it off with trowels.

"How quickly your laborers have been getting on!" said Sviyazhsky. "The last time I was here the roof hadn't been put on yet."

"It'll all be ready by autumn. It's nearly all finished inside," said Anna.

"And what's that new building?"

"That'll be the doctor's quarters and the dispensary," replied Vronsky; seeing the architect in his short jacket coming toward them, he apologized to the ladies and went toward him.

Skirting the pit the men were taking mortar from, he stopped and began talking heatedly about something with the architect.

"The pediment is still too low," he said to Anna when she asked him what it was all about.

"I said all along the foundations have to be raised," said Anna.

"Yes, Madame, it would be better, of course," said the architect, "but it's done already."

"Yes, I'm very much interested in it," Anna said in reply to Sviyazhsky, who expressed his surprise at her knowledge of architecture. "The new building ought to have harmonized with the hospital, but it was thought of afterward and started without any plan."

When his conversation with the architect was over, Vronsky joined the ladies and led them inside the hospital.

Although outside the cornices were still being finished and the lower floor was still being painted, the upper storey was almost finished. After going up the broad cast-iron staircase to a landing they went into the first large room. The walls were stuccoed to look like marble; the enormous plate-glass windows had already been installed; only the parquet floor was not yet finished, and the carpenters, who were planing a parquet square, took the tapes off that kept their hair out of the way and left their work to greet the gentry.

"This is the waiting room," said Vronsky. "There's going to be a desk here, a table, and a cupboard—nothing else."

"This way—we can pass along here. Don't go near the window," said Anna, feeling to see whether the paint had dried. "Alexis, the paint's dry already," she added.

From the waiting room they went out into the corridor. Here Vronsky showed them the new system of ventilation that had been installed. Then he showed them the marble baths, and the beds with an unusual kind of springs. Then he showed them one after the other the wards, the storeroom, the linen room, then the stoves, built according to a novel design, then some trollies for carting necessary things along the corridor, and a great many other things. Sviyazhsky, as a connoisseur of all the latest improvements, appreciated everything fully. Dolly was simply astonished at all these things she had never seen before; wishing to understand everything she kept asking about it all in detail, which gave Vronsky manifest pleasure.

"Yes, I think this is going to be the only hospital in Russia built on completely correct lines," said Sviyazhsky.

"And aren't you going to have a maternity ward?" asked Dolly. "In the country that's needed so much. I often—"

Despite his courtesy, Vronsky interrupted her.

"This is not a maternity home, but a hospital, intended for all but the contagious diseases," he said. "Now take a look at this . . ." He rolled up to Dolly a newly ordered wheel chair for convalescents. "Just look . . ." He got into the chair and began moving it. "Some one can't walk, he's still too weak, or has something wrong with his legs, but he needs fresh air, so he goes out, rides himself around in this . . ."

Dolly took an interest in everything; she liked everything very much, but most of all she liked Vronsky himself, with this natural naïve enthusiasm of his.

Yes, he's a very sweet, kind fellow, she kept thinking, not listening but looking at him, trying to penetrate his expression and mentally changing places with Anna. She liked him so much now in this mood of animation that she understood how Anna had been able to fall in love with him.

## XXI

No, I think the Princess is tired, and horses don't interest her," Vronsky said to Anna, who had suggested going to the stud farm, where Sviyazhsky wanted to look at a new stallion. "You go ahead and I'll accompany the Princess back to the house and have a talk with her. That is, if you don't mind?" he added, turning to Dolly.

"I don't understand a thing about horses, and I should be delighted," said Dolly, somewhat taken aback.

She saw by Vronsky's expression that he wanted something. She was not mistaken. The moment they had gone back through the gate into the garden, he glanced over in the direction Anna had taken; after making sure she couldn't either hear or see them he began:

"You've guessed that I wanted to have a talk with you, haven't you?" he said, looking at her with laughing eyes. "I'm right in thinking you're a friend of Anna's." He took off his hat and getting out a handkerchief he wiped his head, which was beginning to go bald.

Dolly said nothing; she simply looked at him in alarm. Left alone with him, she suddenly felt fearful: his laughing eyes and stern expression frightened her.

The most variegated notions of what he might be about to say flashed through her head: he's going to ask me to come and stay with them, together with the children, and I'll have to refuse him; or that I should get together a social circle for Anna in Moscow . . . Or maybe it's about Veslovsky and his relations with Anna? Or perhaps about Kitty—does he feel guilty about her? Nothing she foresaw was anything but disagreeable; but she couldn't guess what he actually wanted to talk about.

"You have such influence over Anna, she loves you so much," he said, "—you must help me."

Dolly looked with shy inquiry into his energetic face, which kept wholly or partly coming out into the sunlight between the shadows of the lime trees, then was darkened again by their shadow; she waited for him to go on speaking; but he walked beside her in silence, prodding the gravel with his cane.

"If you've come to see us, you, the only one among Anna's former friends—I don't count Princess Barbara—I realize you've done so not because you consider our situation normal, but because though fully realizing the painfulness of that situation you love her nevertheless and want to help her. Is that how I am to understand you?" he asked, looking round at her.

"Oh yes," replied Dolly, closing her sunshade. "But—"

"No," he interrupted, and involuntarily, forgetting that he was putting his companion in an awkward position, he stopped, so that she was obliged to stop too. "No one understands how painful Anna's situation is more strongly than I. And that's understandable, if you will do me the honor of considering me a man with a heart. I am the cause of that situation, and so I feel it."

"I understand," said Dolly, involuntarily admiring him for the sincere and resolute way he said this. "But just because you feel you're the cause I'm afraid you exaggerate it," she said. "I realize that her position in society is difficult."

"In society it is hell!" he said quickly, with a somber scowl. "It's impossible to imagine greater moral torment than she endured in the course of two weeks in Petersburg . . . I beg you to believe that!"

"Yes, but here, as long as neither Anna nor yourself feels a need for society—"

"Society!" he said with contempt. "What need could I have for society?"

"As long as that's so—which may be forever—you can be tranquil and happy. I can tell by the way Anna looks that she's happy, completely happy, she's had time to tell me already," said Dolly with a smile; and involuntarily, as she said this, she began doubting whether Anna really was happy.

But Vronsky, it seemed, had no doubt of it.

"Yes, yes!" he said. "I know she's revived again after all her sufferings; she's happy. She's happy in the present. But I?— I'm afraid of what lies ahead of us . . . I beg your pardon—would you like to move on?"

"It doesn't matter."

"Then let's sit down here."

Dolly sat down on a garden bench at a bend in the avenue. He stood in front of her.

"I see that she's happy," he repeated, and Dolly was struck

even more strongly by a doubt as to whether she was. "But can it go on this way? Whether we behaved well or badly is another question: but the die is cast," he said, shifting from Russian into French, "and we're bound together for life. We are bound to each other by what are for us the most sacred ties of love. We have a child; we may have others. But the law, and all the conditions of our situation are such that thousands of complications are arising that she, resting now after all her trials and sufferings, does not see and does not wish to see. That is understandable. But I cannot help seeing. In law my daughter is not my daughter—but Karenin's. I am against this deceit!" he said with a vigorous gesture of protest; he gave Dolly a gloomily inquiring look.

She said nothing, but only looked at him. He went on.

"And if a son is born tomorrow, *my* son, in law he'll be— Karenin's; he won't be heir either to my name, or to my property, and regardless of how happy we were as a family, or how many children we had, there would be no legal bond between me and them. They will all be Karenin's. You must understand the pain and horror of this situation! I've tried speaking to Anna about it; it irritates her. She does not understand it, and I cannot speak of everything to *her*. Now look at it from the other side. I'm happy in her love, but I must have interests. I've found such an interest, and I'm proud of it; I consider it more honorable than the interests of my former comrades at the Court and in the service. There's certainly no doubt that I wouldn't change my work for theirs. I'm working here, staying in one place; I'm happy and contented, and there's nothing else we require for happiness. I love what I'm doing here. It's not a makeshift, on the contrary . . ."

Dolly noticed that at this point in his explanation he began getting confused; she couldn't understand the reason for his digression very well, but she felt that once having begun speaking about intimate affairs, which he could not speak about with Anna, he was now pouring out everything, and that the question of his work in the country was in the same category of intimate thoughts as the question of his relations with Anna.

"Well, to go on then," he said, recovering himself. "The main thing is that in carrying on my work I must be sure that what I'm doing isn't going to die with me, that I'm going to have heirs—which is just what I haven't got. Imagine the position of a man who knows in advance that the children he has with the woman he loves will not be his but someone else's, someone who will hate them and refuse to recognize them. Isn't that horrible?"

He fell silent, evidently profoundly agitated.

"Of course, I understand that. But what can Anna do?" asked Dolly.

"Yes, that brings me to the point of what I've been saying," he said, calming himself with an effort. "Anna can do something, it depends on her . . . Even in order to petition the Tsar, to permit the adoption a divorce is necessary. And that depends on Anna. Her husband had agreed to a divorce —at that time your own husband had practically arranged it. And I know he wouldn't refuse now. It would only be a question of writing to him. At that time he replied definitely that if she expressed a desire for it he wouldn't refuse. Of course," he said glumly, "it's one of those pharisaical cruelties only heartless people like that are capable of. He knows how she's tormented by any recollection of him, and since he knows her he insists that she write to him. I know how agonizing it is for her. But the reasons for it are so important that all these fine emotional points must be disregarded. It's a question of the happiness and the life of Anna and of her children. I'm not speaking about myself, though it's hard for me—very hard," he said, looking as though he were threatening someone for making it so hard for him. "So, Princess, I am clinging to you shamelessly as my anchor of salvation. Help me persuade her to write him and request a divorce!"

"Yes, of course," said Dolly thoughtfully, vividly recalling her last conversation with Karenin. "Yes, of course," she repeated resolutely, thinking of Anna.

"Use your influence with her; make her write. I don't want to, I'm almost unable to speak to her about it."

"Very well, I'll talk to her. But how is it she herself doesn't think of it?" said Dolly, for some reason suddenly recalling Anna's odd new habit of screwing up her eyes. And it came to her mind that it was just when the intimate aspects of life were touched on that Anna screwed up her eyes. It's as though she were shutting her eyes to her own life, so as not to see it all, thought Dolly. "I'll speak to her without fail, both for my own sake and for hers," said Dolly in reply to his expression of gratitude.

They got up and returned to the house.

## XXII

Anna found Dolly back already; she looked intently into her eyes, as though inquiring about the conversation she had had with Vronsky, but she did not put the question in words.

"I think it's time for dinner already," she said. "We haven't seen anything at all of each other yet. What I'm counting on is this evening. I have to go and dress now. I suppose you do too. We all got rather stained in that unfinished building."

Dolly went to her room; she felt like laughing. She had nothing to change into, since she already had her best dress on, but in order to signalize in some way her preparations for dinner, she asked the maid to brush her dress, put on a new bow and fresh cuffs, and placed some lace in her hair.

"This was all I could do," she said with a smile to Anna, who came into her room in still a third, again strikingly simple dress.

"Yes, we're very formal here," she said, as though apologizing for her own stateliness. "Alexis is delighted you've come, he's seldom been so pleased. He's definitely fallen in love with you," she added. "But aren't you tired?"

Before dinner there was no time to talk about anything. When they went into the drawing room they found Princess Barbara and the men, in black frock coats, already there. The architect was wearing a swallow-tail. Vronsky introduced the doctor and the estate manager to Dolly; she had already met the architect at the hospital.

A stout butler, his round clean-shaven face and starched white necktie radiant, announced that dinner was served, and the ladies got up. Vronsky asked Sviyazhsky to give his arm to Anna; he himself went over to Dolly. Veslovsky offered his arm to Princess Barbara before Tushkevich, so that Tushkevich, the doctor, and the estate manager went in alone.

The dinner, the dining room, the dinner service, the servants, the wine, and the food not only harmonized with the general tone of up-to-date luxury in the house, but seemed to be even more luxurious and more modern than the rest. Dolly observed all this unfamiliar luxury, and as a housewife in charge of a household herself—though she didn't even hope to apply in her own house any of the things she had seen, since such luxury was far beyond her own standard of living, she could not help taking note of all the details, and asking herself who had done it all and how. Veslovsky, her own husband, and even Sviyazhsky and a great many other people she knew never thought of it at all, but readily believed what every well-bred host tries to make his guests feel, which is that everything that is so well arranged at his host's has not cost him, the host, any effort at all but has come about of itself. But Dolly knew that not even the children's breakfast porridge comes about of itself, so that such a complicated and magnificent establishment had to have someone's concentrated attention behind it. And by the way Vronsky looked, the way he surveyed the table and nodded to the butler, the way he offered Dolly a choice between cold soup and hot, she realized that everything was accomplished and maintained by the efforts of the host himself. It was clear that none of it depended on Anna any more than on Veslovsky. Anna, Sviyazhsky, the Princess, and Veslovsky were all guests equally, cheerfully taking advantage of what had been prepared for them.

Anna was the hostess only with respect to the conduct of the conversation. And this conversation (extremely difficult for the hostess of a small dinner party that included people like the estate manager and the architect, people from a totally different world who were doing their best not to be intimidated by the unfamiliar opulence and were incapable of taking a substantial part in the general conversation) was conducted by Anna with her usual tact, naturalness, and, as Dolly noticed, even with pleasure.

The conversation started off with Tushkevich's and Veslovsky's solitary rowing party; Tushkevich began talking about the last races at the Petersburg Yacht Club. But Anna, after waiting for a pause, instantly turned to the architect in order to draw him out of his silence.

"Sviyazhsky was struck at how quickly the building has been going up since the last time he was here," she said. "But I'm there every day and every day I'm astonished at how quickly it's getting on."

"It's a pleasure to work with His Excellency," said the architect with a smile. (He was a respectful, composed man conscious of his own dignity.) "It's not the same as dealing with the local authorities. Where they would scribble out whole reams of paper, I just report to the Count, we talk it over, and in three words it's settled."

"American methods," said Sviyazhsky with a smile.

"Yes, there they do their building in a rational way . . ."

The conversation went on to the governmental abuses in the United States, but Anna immediately switched it to a different theme in order to draw the estate manager out of his silence.

"Have you ever seen a reaping machine?" she said, turning to Dolly. "We had just been to look at them when we met you. I saw one for the first time myself."

"How do they work?" asked Dolly.

"Just like a scissors. With a board and a lot of little scissors. Like this—"

Anna picked up a knife and fork in her beautiful, white, ring-covered fingers and began demonstrating. It was obvious that she knew her explanation would be quite incomprehensible, but knowing also that her voice was pleasant and her hands beautiful, she went on explaining.

"More like little penknives," said Veslovsky playfully, without taking his eyes off her.

Anna gave a barely perceptible smile, but didn't answer him. "Isn't it true, Mr. Karl, that it's just like a scissors?" she said to the estate manager.

"*Oh, ja!*" replied the German. "It's a very simple thing," and he began explaining the construction of the machine.

"It's a pity it doesn't bind too. I saw one at the Vienna Exhibition; it bound the sheaves with twine," said Sviyazhsky. "That kind would pay better."

"It all depends; the price of the wire must be taken into account." And the German, drawn out of his silence, turned to Vronsky. "That can be calculated, Your Excellency." The German was on the point of putting his hand to his pocket where he kept a notebook with a pencil in which he made all his calculations, but remembering he was at dinner and noticing Vronsky's cold loo ., he checked himself. "It's too complicated, too much trouble—*zu viel Klopot,*" he concluded.

"If you want some ducats you have to have *klopots,*" said Veslovsky, making fun of the German. "I adore German," he said, turning to Anna with the same smile.

"Stop it!" she said to him, with mock sternness.

"And we had thought we were going to find you on the field, Doctor," she said to the doctor, a sickly looking man. "Were you there?"

"I was there, but I had evaporated," replied the doctor, with gloomy jocularity.

"Then you must have had some good exercise."

"Magnificent!"

"And how is the old woman? I hope it's not typhus?"

"Typhus or not, it's not helping her any."

"What a pity!" said Anna, and having given the household staff the politeness that was their due she turned back to her friends.

"All the same, you know, it would be rather difficult to construct a machine on the basis of your description, Madame," Sviyazhsky said to her jokingly.

"Really, why not?" said Anna with a smile that showed she knew there had been something charming in her explanation of the machine, and that Sviyazhsky had also been aware of it. This new trait, of youthful coquetry, made a disagreeable impression on Dolly.

"To make up for that, though, Madame's knowledge of architecture is remarkable," said Tushkevich.

"Oh yes, only last night I heard you talking about damp courses and plinths," said Veslovsky to Anna. "Did I say that right?"

"There's nothing remarkable about it at all, when you see and hear so much," said Anna. "Doubtless you don't even know what houses are made of?"

Dolly saw that Anna was displeased by the playful tone between herself and Veslovsky, but fell in with it in spite of herself.

Vronsky behaved quite unlike Levin about it. He obviously didn't attach the slightest importance to Veslovsky's chatter; on the contrary he kept encouraging all these jokes.

"Come along now, Veslovsky—what keeps the bricks together?"

"Cement, of course."

"Bravo! And what is cement?"

"Something like paste—no, putty," said Veslovsky, making them all burst out laughing.

The conversation between the diners, except for the doctor, architect, and estate manager, who were sunk in gloomy silence, went on without a pause, sometimes sliding along, sometimes fastening on something and touching one or the other of them to the quick. Once Dolly was stung; she got so angry she even blushed, and afterward wondered whether she hadn't gone too far and said something rude. Sviyazhsky had begun talking about Levin, telling of his peculiar notion about machines doing Russian agriculture nothing but harm.

"I don't have the pleasure of knowing Levin," said Vronsky with a smile, "but he's probably never seen any of the machines he condemns. Or if he's seen them and tried them they're just homemade Russian ones, not foreign. So what ideas can he have about them?"

"Turkish ones, in general," said Veslovsky with a smile, turning to Anna.

"I can't defend his opinions," said Dolly, flaring up, "but I can say that he's extremely educated, and if he were here he'd answer you himself, though I'm incapable of it."

"I'm very fond of him, and we're great friends," said Sviyazhsky with a good-natured smile, "but if you'll forgive me he's a little cracked; he claims, for instance, that neither the District Councils nor the magistrates are of any use; he doesn't want to take part in anything."

"That's our Russian apathy," said Vronsky, pouring some water from an iced decanter into a thin glass with a stem. "Not to realize the duties imposed on us by our rights, and consequently to deny those duties."

"I know of no one who's more scrupulous in the observance of his duties," said Dolly, irritated by Vronsky's superior tone.

"I, on the contrary," said Vronsky, who was evidently touched to the quick for some reason by this conversation, "I, on the contrary, such as I am, feel very grateful for the honor which thanks to Sviyazhsky here they have done me in electing me a Justice of the Peace. I consider that for me the duty of going to the meetings to deliberate on a case of a peasant and a horse is just as important as anything else I can do. And I should consider it an honor to be elected to the District Council. That's the only way I can repay the advantages I enjoy as a landowner. Unfortunately there's no understanding of the importance the large landowners ought to have in state affairs."

Dolly found it strange, listening to him, that he was so assured of being in the right, here at his own table. She recalled how Levin, who held completely contrary opinions, was just as positive in expressing them at his own table. But being fond of Levin she was on his side.

"Then we can depend on you, Count, for the next session?" said Sviyazhsky. "But you'll have to leave in good time, so as to be there on the eighth. If you would do me the honor of coming to stay with me—?"

"To some extent I agree with your brother-in-law," said

Anna, "though I don't go quite so far," she added with a smile. "I'm afraid we've been having too many of these public obligations lately. Just as before there were so many functionaries around that you had to have one no matter what you wanted to do, now there are nothing but public figures. Alexis has been here six months now, and I think he's already a member of five or six different public institutions: a Guardian of the Poor, a Justice of the Peace, a District Councilor, a juryman, and something or other to do with horses. At the rate things are going he'll be spending all his time this way. And I'm afraid that with as many of these activities as there are it will be no more than a formality. How many institutions are you a member of, Sviyazhsky?" she said, turning to him. "More than twenty, isn't it?"

Anna was speaking in a playful way, but a note of irritation could be heard in her voice. Dolly, who was attentively watching Anna and Vronsky, noticed it at once. She also noticed that in this conversation Vronsky's face had instantly assumed a serious and obstinate expression. Noticing this, and the fact that all at once Princess Barbara started hastily speaking about people they knew in Petersburg, in order to change the subject, and recalling the irrelevant things Vronsky had been saying in the garden about his activities, Dolly realized that this question of public activity was bound up with some intimate dispute between Anna and Vronsky.

The dinner, the wine, the service—they were all excellent, but they were all of a kind Dolly had seen at formal dinners and balls, which she had grown out of the habit of, with the same character of impersonality and tension; consequently, on an ordinary day and in a small circle all this made a disagreeable impression on her.

After dinner they sat on the terrace for a while, then began playing lawn tennis. After choosing partners the players took their positions on the carefully leveled and rolled croquet lawn, on both sides of a net stretched between two gilded posts. Dolly tried to play, but it took her a long time to understand the game, and by the time she did she was so tired she sat down beside Princess Barbara and simply watched the others playing. Tushkevich, her partner, also gave in, but the others went on playing for a long time. Both Sviyazhsky and Vronsky played very well, and seriously. They kept their eyes fixed on the ball as it came to them, ran over to it adroitly, neither too fast nor too slow, waited for the bounce, then striking it firmly and accurately with the racket hit it back over the net. Veslovsky played worse than the others. He got too excited, but to make up for it his gaiety inspired the others. His laughter and shouts never ceased. Like the other men too he took off his frock coat, with the ladies' permission, and his massive handsome figure in his white shirt sleeves, with his ruddy sweating face and impetuous movements made an unforgettable picture.

When Dolly went to bed that night she saw Veslovsky hurtling about on the croquet lawn the moment she closed her eyes.

But during the game itself Dolly had not enjoyed herself. She disliked the playful tone between Veslovsky and Anna that was continued during the game, as well as the general artificiality of grown-ups playing a children's game in the absence of children. But in order not to disturb the others and pass the time somehow she joined in the game once again, after she had taken a rest, and pretended to be enjoying herself. It had seemed to her that whole day that she was acting in a theater with actors who were better than she, and that her bad performance was spoiling the whole show.

She had come with the intention of staying two days, if things worked out all right. But that same evening, during the game, she made up her mind to leave the following day. Those painful maternal worries she had detested so much on the way, by now appeared to her in a different light, after a day spent without them, and were drawing her back.

After evening tea, and a row in the boat at night, when Dolly went back to her room by herself, took off her dress and sat down to put up her thin hair for the night, she felt an immense sense of relief.

Even the idea of Anna coming to see her in a moment was disagreeable to her. She wanted to be left alone with her own thoughts.

### XXIII

SHE was about to get into bed when Anna came into the room in a white dressing gown.

In the course of the day Anna had begun talking about intimate things several times, and each time had come to a stop after saying a few words. "Later," she had said, "we'll talk everything over later, when we're alone. There are so many things I have to tell you."

Now they were alone, and Anna didn't know what to talk about. She was sitting beside the window, looking at Dolly and reviewing in her mind the store of intimate topics that had seemed to her inexhaustible, and she couldn't find one. It seemed to her now that everything had been said already.

"Well, and how is Kitty?" she said, sighing heavily, with a guilty glance at Dolly. "Tell me the truth, Dolly—isn't she angry with me?"

"Angry? No," said Dolly with a smile.

"But she hates me—despises me?"

"Oh no! But you know, it's not a thing to be forgiven."

"Yes, yes,ᴬ said Anna, turning away from her and looking through the open window. "But I wasn't to blame. And who is to blame? What does it mean—blame? Could it have been any different? Now, what do you think? Would it have been possible for you not to be Stiva's wife?"

"Really, I have no idea. But now I want you to tell me—"

"Yes, yes, but we haven't finished talking about Kitty. Is she happy? He's a very fine fellow, they say."

"Very fine is the least you can say. I don't know anyone better!"

"Oh, how glad I am! I'm so glad! Very fine is the least you can say," she repeated.

Dolly smiled. "But now tell me about yourself. I have so much to talk to you about. I've been talking to—" Dolly didn't know what to call him. She felt uncomfortable calling him either the Count or Alexis.

"To Alexis," said Anna. "I know you have. But I wanted to ask you frankly what you think about me, about the way I'm living."

"How can I tell you all at once? Really, I have no idea."

"No, you must tell me all the same . . . You see the way I live. But you mustn't forget you're seeing us now in summer, when you've come and we're not alone; but we came here in early spring and lived here completely alone, and we're going to be living alone again. I wish for nothing better. But imagine my living here alone, without him, *alone*, and that's what's going to happen . . . Everything tells me it will happen often, his being away from the house half the time," she said, getting up and seating herself closer to Dolly.

"Of course," she said, interrupting Dolly, who was about to protest, "of course, I won't hold him back by force. I don't hold him as it is. One day there are races and his horses are running—off he goes. I'm delighted. But just think of me, imagine my position . . . But why talk about it!" she smiled. "So what was he talking about with you?"

"He was talking about something I want to talk about myself; it's easy for me to be his spokesman: it's about whether it isn't possible, isn't necessary to—" Dolly hesitated. "Correct your position, improve it . . . You know what I think . . . Nevertheless, if you can you ought to get married . . ."

"You mean a divorce?" said Anna. "You know the only woman who came to see me in Petersburg was Betsy Tverskoy? You know her, don't you? At bottom she's the most depraved woman in existence. She had an affair with Tushkevich and deceived her husband in the vilest way. And *she* told me she didn't want to know me as long as my position was irregular. You mustn't think I'm making any comparison, I know you, my darling. But I couldn't help remembering it . . . Well, so what did he tell you?" she repeated.

"He said he suffers on your account as well as on his own. You may say it's egotism, but what legitimate, what noble egotism! What he wants is first of all to legitimize his daughter and be your husband; to have a right to you."

"What woman who's a slave can be a slave to such a degree as I, in my position?" Anna interrupted somberly.

"But the main thing he wants is . . . he wants you not to suffer."

"That's out of the question! And then?"

"And then, the most legitimate thing—he wants the children you and he have to have a name."

"What children?" said Anna, not looking at Dolly and frowning.

"Annie and those that are coming."

"He can feel at ease about that. I'm not going to have any more children."

"But how can you say that?"

"I'm not going to have any more because I don't want to."

And in spite of all her agitation Anna smiled as she noticed the naïve look of curiosity, astonishment, and horror on Dolly's face.

"After my illness the doctor told me how . . ."

"It's not possible!" said Dolly, opening wide her eyes. For her this was one of those discoveries that leads to consequences and conclusions of such enormous magnitude that at first you feel simply it's impossible to take it all in, but that there's a great deal there that will have to be thought about again and again.

This discovery, which suddenly explained to her all those families she had never been able to understand, which only had one or two children apiece, evoked so many thoughts, ideas, and contradictory feelings within her that she was incapable of saying anything, and could only look at Anna in astonishment, her eyes wide open. It was just what she had been daydreaming about during the drive, but now that she learned it was possible she was horrified. She felt it was too simple a solution for too complicated a problem.

After a silence, all she could say was: "Isn't it immoral?"

"Why? Remember that I have two alternatives: either being pregnant, that is, ill, or being a friend and companion to my husband—he is my husband after all!" said Anna in a tone of deliberately superficial frivolity.

"Well, yes—yes," said Dolly, listening to the same arguments she had been making herself, without finding them so convincing as before.

"For you, and for others," said Anna, as though guessing her thoughts, "there may be some doubt about it; but for me . . . You must understand I'm not a wife; he loves me only as long as he loves me. Well then, how am I going to keep his love? By being like this?"

And she curved her white arms out in front of her stomach.

With extraordinary swiftness, as happens in moments of excitement, ideas and recollections crowded into Dolly's mind. I couldn't keep Stiva attracted, she thought; he left me for others, and the first one he deceived me with, pretty and gay though she always was, didn't keep him either; he threw her over and got another. Can Anna really attract Count Vronsky and hold him this way? If that's what he's going to be looking for he'll find women whose dresses and manners are even gayer and more attractive. No matter how white and lovely her bare arms may be, no matter how beautiful the whole of her full figure, and her flushed face framed in that black hair, he'll find someone better, just as that loathsome, pathetic, charming husband of my own looks for and finds them . . .

Dolly said nothing; she only sighed. Anna noticed this sigh, which expressed dissent, and went on. She had some other arguments in store that were so powerful they were sure to be unanswerable.

"You say that's bad? But you must consider," she went on, "you're forgetting my situation. How can I wish for children? I'm not talking about the pains, I'm not afraid of them. But think of what my children would be? Unfortunate creatures bearing a stranger's name! By reason of their very birth they would be bound to be ashamed of their mother, their father, their birth itself."

"But, after all, that's just why a divorce is necessary."

But Anna was not listening to her. She wanted to give a full account of the arguments she had so often convinced herself with.

"Why is reason given me if I don't use it to avoid bringing unhappy creatures into the world?"

She glanced at Dolly, but without waiting for an answer went on again: "I would always feel guilty toward these unhappy children," she said. "If they don't come into existence they won't be unhappy, at least, while if they're unhappy then I'll be the only one to blame."

These were the same arguments Dolly had put to herself; but as she listened to them now she couldn't understand them. How can you feel guilty about nonexistent creatures? she thought. Suddenly the thought came into her mind: could it have been better in any case for her favorite, Grisha, if he had never existed? And this seemed to her so strange, so preposterous that she gave her head a shake to dispel this confusion of mad thoughts swirling about in her mind.

"No, I don't know—it's all wrong," was all she said, with a look of disgust.

"Yes, but you mustn't forget what you are and what I am. . . . Besides," Anna added, in spite of the wealth of her own arguments and the poverty of Dolly's, as though she were aware nevertheless that it was all wrong, "you mustn't forget the main thing, which is that I'm not in the same situation now as yourself. For you the question is: D'you want to stop having children? For me it's whether I want to have them. That's the great difference. You understand that in my situation I cannot want any."

Dolly did not reply. She suddenly felt that she was already far away from Anna, that there were questions that they would never be in agreement on and that it was better not to speak about.

## XXIV

THEN it's all the more necessary to regularize your situation if possible," said Dolly.

"Yes—if possible," said Anna, in a voice that was completely different, low and sad.

"Surely a divorce is possible? I've been told your husband had agreed."

"Dolly! I don't feel like speaking about it."

"Let's not then," Dolly hastened to say as she noticed a look of suffering on Anna's face. "It's just that I see you take too gloomy a view of things."

"I? Not in the least. I'm very gay and contented. You've seen what a success I've been having—Veslovsky . . . ."

"Yes . . . to tell the truth I didn't much like this Veslovsky's manner," said Dolly, trying to change the subject.

"Of course not! It just tickles Alexis, that's all; he's only a boy and entirely in my hands; you understand I manage him just as I please. He's just the same to me as your Grisha . . . Dolly!" she said with a sudden change of tone. "You say I take a gloomy view of things. You just don't understand—it's too horrible, I try not to look at things at all!"

"But it seems to me you must. You must do everything possible."

"But what's possible? Nothing. You say I should marry Alexis and that I'm not considering that. I—not considering that!" she repeated; a flush spread over her face. She rose, and straightened up, sighed heavily and began walking up and down the room with her light steps, stopping now and then. "I don't consider it? There's not a day or an hour when I don't think about it and blame myself for what I think . . . Because these thoughts are enough to drive you out of your mind! Out of your mind," she repeated. "Whenever I think about it I can't fall asleep without some morphia. All right then. Let's discuss it calmly. I'm told—divorce. First of all he wouldn't give me one; he's now under the influence of Countess Lydia."

Sitting upright in her chair, Dolly, with a look of pained compassion on her face, kept turning her head as she followed Anna's movements.

"One must try," she said gently.

"Let's suppose I do. What does that mean?" said Anna, obviously expressing a thought she had considered a thousand times and knew by heart. "It means that I who hate him, while nevertheless acknowledging my guilt toward him—and I consider him magnanimous—should have to humiliate myself by writing to him. Let's suppose I make an effort and do it. Either I'll get back an insulting answer, or his consent. Very well, let's say I get his consent . . ." Anna had stopped in the farther end of the room just then, doing something to the window curtain. "I get his consent; well, what about my—my son? They're not going to give him to me, are they? He's going to grow up, despising me, in the house of his father whom I left. You must understand that I love only two beings, I think equally, but both of them more than myself—Seryozha and Alexis."

She came back to the middle of the room and stood in front of Dolly, pressing her bosom with her arms. Her figure in its white dressing gown looked particularly tall and broad. She bowed her head and looked up with moist shining eyes from beneath her eyebrows at Dolly, a small, slight, and pathetic figure in her darned dressing jacket and nightcap, trembling all over with emotion.

"I love these two beings alone, and one excludes the other. I can't unite them, and that's the only thing I want. And if I can't have that then nothing else matters. Nothing else at all. And it will end somehow, and that's why I cannot and do not wish to talk about it. So you mustn't reproach me, you mustn't condemn me for anything. With your purity you cannot understand all my suffering."

She came over and sat down beside Dolly; looking into her face with a guilty expression she took her by the hand.

"What d'you think? What d'you think about me? You can't despise me, I don't deserve contempt. I'm simply unhappy. If there's anyone who's unhappy it's I," she murmured, and turning away she burst into tears.

When Dolly was left alone she said her prayers and got into bed. She had been sorry for Anna with all her heart while she had been talking to her, but now she could not make herself think about her. Thoughts of home and children rose up in her imagination with a special, novel charm, a sort of fresh radiance. This world of hers seemed to her so precious and charming now that on no account did she wish to spend another day away from it; she made up her mind she would leave the following day without fail.

Anna, meanwhile, on her return to her boudoir took a

wineglass and poured into it several drops of a medicine principally made up of morphia; after drinking it down and sitting there motionless for a few moments she went into the bedroom in a reassured and cheerful mood.

When she entered the bedroom Vronsky looked at her intently. He was searching for some trace of the conversation which he knew she must have been having with Dolly after staying there so long. But he could find nothing in her expression of repressed excitement, hiding something, except the beauty that though he was used to it still captivated him, her consciousness of this, and her desire to move him by it. He did not want to ask her what they had been talking about, though he hoped she would tell him something of her own accord. But all she said was:

"I'm so glad you like Dolly. You do, don't you?"

"But I've known her a long time, after all. She's very kind-hearted, I think, but a little too matter-of-fact. All the same I was glad she came."

He took Anna's hand and looked into her eyes inquiringly.

Misunderstanding the look she smiled at him.

The next morning, in spite of her hosts' entreaties, Dolly prepared to leave. Levin's coachman, in his far from new coat and shabby hat, the horses unmatched and the carriage with patched-up mudguards, resolutely and morosely drove up to the covered, sand-strewn portico.

Dolly disliked saying good-by to Princess Barbara and to the men. After spending a day together both she and her hosts clearly felt that they were unsuited to each other and that it was better for them not to associate. Only Anna felt sad. She knew that with Dolly gone there would be no one to stir up in her soul those feelings that had shown themselves during their talk. It was painful for her to have these feelings stirred up; nevertheless she knew that these were the best part of her soul and that this part of her soul was quickly becoming smothered by the life she was leading.

Dolly had a pleasant feeling of relief when they reached the open country; she wanted to ask the servants how they had liked Vronsky's place, when suddenly Philip the coachman started talking himself:

"They're rich, right enough, but they didn't give our horses more than three bushels of oats. The horses had eaten the last grain before cockcrow. And what's three bushels? Just a

mouthful. At an inn nowadays oats don't cost more than
forty-five kopecks. Well, we don't do it that way—when anyone comes we give his horses as much as they'll eat."

"A stingy gentleman," agreed the office clerk.

"Well, and did you like their horses?" asked Dolly.

"The horses—no two ways about *them*. And their feed is
good too. But somehow it all seemed dull to me, Princess, I
don't know about you," he said, turning his handsome, kindly
face toward her.

"I felt just the same. Well, will we get back by evening?"

"We'll have to."

After getting home and finding everyone very well and
especially sweet, Dolly with immense animation told all
about her excursion, about how well she was received, about
the Vronskys' luxury and good taste, their diversions; she
wouldn't let anyone say a word against them.

"You have to know Anna and Vronsky—I got to know
him better now—to understand how sweet and touching they
are," she said in all sincerity, forgetting all about the vague
feeling of dissatisfaction and embarrassment she had had
while there.

### XXV

VRONSKY and Anna spent that whole summer and part
of the autumn in the country, living in the same way and
still doing nothing about getting a divorce. They had agreed
not to go away anywhere, but they both felt, the longer they
lived alone, especially in autumn when there were no guests,
that they would not be able to endure the life they were
leading and that a change would have to be made.

It would have seemed that their life was impossible to improve upon; there was an abundance of everything, good
health, a child, while they both had something to do. In the
absence of any guests Anna went on as usual caring for her
appearance and reading a great deal, both novels and whatever serious books were in fashion. She ordered all the
books that were praised in the foreign newspapers and magazines she received, and gave them the attention that was possible only in solitude. Besides this she studied in books and
technical magazines all the subjects Vronsky was busy with,
so that he often came straight to her with questions on agriculture and architecture, sometimes even on horse breeding

or sport. He was astounded at her erudition and memory, and though at first, when he was in doubt, he would ask for confirmation she would find what he was asking about in some book and show it to him.

The building of the hospital interested her too. Not only did she help but she would arrange and think up a great many things herself. Nevertheless her main preoccupation remained herself—herself insofar as she was precious to Vronsky, insofar as she could replace for him everything he had given up. Vronsky appreciated this desire not only to please but to serve him, which had become the sole purpose of her life; at the same time he was oppressed by the loving web in which she kept trying to entangle him. The more time passed the more often he saw himself entangled in this web and the more he wanted not so much to get out of it as to test it, to see whether it interfered with his liberty. If it had not been for this constantly increasing desire to be free, and not to have scenes every time he had to go to town for a meeting or the races, Vronsky would have been entirely satisfied with his life. The role he had selected for himself, the role of a rich landowner, one of those who ought to constitute the kernel of the Russian aristocracy, was not only perfectly in keeping with his tastes, but now that he had lived in this way for half a year the pleasure it gave him kept constantly increasing. His estate, which occupied and absorbed him more and more, was doing magnificently. In spite of the vast sums of money the hospital, the machinery, the cows ordered from Switzerland, and a great many other things cost him, he felt sure that he was not wasting his fortune but adding to it. Where it was a question of income— the sale of forest land, of corn, wool, the leasing of land— Vronsky was as hard as flint and knew how to hold out for his price. In his massive farming operations, both on this and on his other estates, he stuck to the simplest and safest methods, and was economical and calculating in the extreme about all details. In spite of all the wiliness and adroitness of his German manager, who kept trying to involve him in expenditures and presented all his estimates in such a way as to make it seem that at first a great deal was needed, but that after consideration the same thing could be done more cheaply and bring in an immediate profit, Vronsky did not succumb. He would listen to the manager, question him, and only give his consent when what was to be ordered or built was the latest thing, still unknown in Russia and likely to create a sensation. Aside from this he would only agree to a major expenditure when there was some money to spare, and when he made it would go into every detail and insist on getting the very best for his money. His whole way of running things thus made it clear that he was not squandering his fortune but increasing it.

In October the nobility elections were taking place in Kashin Province, where the estates of Vronsky, Sviyazhsky, Koznyshov, Oblonsky, and a small part of Levin's were located.

These elections attracted a great deal of public attention because of the number of people participating in them, and for many ᵉᵣ reasons. They were discussed a great deal and preparations were made for them. People who had never attended any elections were coming to these from Moscow and Petersburg, as well as from abroad.

Vronsky had promised Sviyazhsky long before to be present, and before the elections Sviyazhsky, who often visited Vozdvizhensk, called for him.

The day before a quarrel had almost broken out between Vronsky and Anna about his proposed trip. It was the dullest and most oppressive autumn weather in the country, so Vronsky, preparing himself for a struggle, told Anna of his departure with a chilly, stern expression, in a way he had never spoken to her before. To his surprise Anna took the news very calmly, and merely asked when he was coming back. He looked at her intently, at a loss to understand her calm. She smiled at the way he looked at her. He knew her capacity for withdrawing into herself, and knew she only did it when she was making up her mind about something without telling him of her plans. He was afraid of it; but he was so eager to avoid any scene that he pretended to, and with some sincerity did believe in what he wanted to—in her reasonableness.

"I hope you won't be too bored?"

"I hope not," said Anna. "I received a box of books from Gauthier's yesterday. No, I shan't be bored."

If that's the tone she wants to take so much the better, he thought; otherwise it would be the same thing all over again.

And so, without challenging her to a frank explanation, he went off to the elections. This was the first time since their liaison that they parted without having talked things out. On the one hand this made him uneasy; on the other he thought it the best way. At first there will be something vague, something unexpressed, as there is now, but then she'll get used to it. In any case I can give up everything else for her, but not my masculine independence, he thought.

XXVI

IN September, Levin moved to Moscow for Kitty's confinement. He had already been living a whole month in Moscow without having anything to do when Koznyshov, who had an estate in Kashin Province and was playing an important part in the forthcoming elections, prepared to go and attend them. He invited Levin, who had a vote in the Seleznyov District, to go with him. Aside from this, Levin had some business in Kashin that was extremely important for his sister, who lived abroad, in connection with a trusteeship and with getting some money due for a transfer of land.

Levin was still vacillating, but Kitty, who saw how bored he was in Moscow and had been advising him to go, ordered the necessary nobleman's uniform, which cost eighty rubles, without telling him. It was these eighty rubles paid for the uniform that were the principal reason for Levin's going, and he left for Kashin.

He had been in Kashin for five days now, going to the assembly every day and fussing about on his sister's business, which kept hanging fire. The Marshals of the Nobility were all busy with the elections, and even such a simple matter as his sister's money, which depended on the trusteeship, could not be arranged. As for the other business, the money for the land, that kept running into obstacles too. After a great deal of trouble getting the money unblocked it was ready to be paid out; but the notary, who was extremely obliging, could not hand over the warrant because the president's signature was needed, and the president, who had not appointed a deputy, was attending the meeting.

All this bother, walking back and forth from one place to another and talking to very good and kindhearted people who fully understand how tiresome the petitioner's position was but were unable to help him, all this fruitless tension gave Levin an agonizing feeling similar to the feeling of helplessness one gets in a dream when trying to use physical force. He felt this frequently in talking to his extremely goodnatured legal adviser. This legal adviser seemed to be doing everything possible and straining all his intellectual powers to get Levin out of his difficulty. "Why not try this?" he would say more than once. "Just go to so-and-so, or go to so-and-so!" and he would outline a whole plan for getting round the fatal source of all the trouble. But then he would add at once: "They'll put you off in any case, but have a try all the same!" And Levin would keep trying, walking and driving back and forth. Everyone was very kind and amiable, but it would turn out that what had been got round would turn up again elsewhere and block the way once again. What was particularly annoying was that Levin could not begin to understand whom he was contending with, and who profited by the delay in terminating his business. It seemed that no one, including his legal adviser, knew this. If Levin had understood why, just as he realized the only way to get a train ticket was to stand in line in front of a ticket window, then he wouldn't have been irritated or offended; but no one could explain to him just why all the obstacles he kept running into existed at all.

But since getting married Levin had changed a great deal. He had become patient, and if he failed to see why things were arranged in this way he told himself that without knowing everything he was in no position to judge, that in all probability it had to be that way, and he tried not to lose his temper.

Now, when he attended the elections and took part in them, he tried not to condemn everything either, or to argue, but as far as possible to understand the issues the honest, upright people he respected so much were treating with such gravity and enthusiasm. Ever since marrying, so many new and serious aspects of life had been disclosed to him that because of his own frivolous attitude he had considered trivial before that he anticipated and looked for some weighty significance in this question of the elections too.

Koznyshov explained to him the point and importance of the upheaval anticipated at the elections:

By law the Marshal of the Nobility for the Province had in his hands a great deal of important public business—trusteeships (such as Levin was now suffering from), the custody of vast sums of money belonging to the nobility, high schools for boys and girls, military academies, public education according to the new decree, and finally the District Council. This Marshal of the Nobility, Snetkov, was a nobleman of the old school; he had run through an enormous fortune, and while kindhearted and honorable in his way lacked the slightest conception of what was required by the modern era. He always took the side of the nobility in everything, directly resisted the spread of popular education and was giving the District Council, which ought to have such enormous importance, a class character. What had to be done was to put a fresh, up-to-date, businesslike, and completely modern man in his place, who would do things so as to extract from all the rights conferred upon the nobility (not as nobility but as an element in the District Council) all the advantages of self-government that could be extracted. In the rich Province of Kashin, which had always been a leader in everything, forces had now been assembled so that this enterprise, if handled as it ought to be, might serve as an example for other provinces, for all Russia. This was why the whole matter was of such great consequence. It was proposed to replace Snetkov as Marshal by Sviyazhsky, or still better by Nevedovsky, a former professor, a remarkably able fellow and a great friend of Koznyshov's.

The assembly was opened by the Governor of the Province, who in his speech to the nobles told them they should elect office holders not because of who they were but according to merit, and for the good of the fatherland, and that he hoped the honorable nobility of Kashin would perform their sacred duty, as indeed they had in former elections, and vindicate their sovereign's exalted trust in them.

After finishing his speech the Governor left the hall, and the noblemen, with noisy animation, some of them even with enthusiasm, followed him out and stood round him as he was putting on his fur coat and chatting in a friendly way with the Marshal of the Province. Levin, who wanted to get to the bottom of everything and miss nothing, also stood there in the crowd and heard the Governor say: "Please tell Madame that my wife is very sorry, but she has to go to the orphanage." Then all the noblemen gaily sorted out their fur coats and went off to the cathedral.

In the cathedral Levin, raising his hand together with the others and repeating the words of the priest, vowed by the most awful oaths to fulfill all the things the Governor had hoped for. Church services always affected Levin, and when they pronounced the words "I kiss the cross," and he glanced round the throng of young and old men, all repeating the same thing, he felt moved.

The second and third days were devoted to the points concerning the funds of the nobility and the girls' high schools;

as Kozynshov explained, these were quite unimportant, and Levin, taken up as he was by his own affairs, paid no attention to them. On the fourth day the audit of the Provincial funds came up, and here for the first time a collision took place between the new party and the old. The Commission that had been charged with the financial audit reported to the assembly that it was all in order. The Marshal of the Province got up and with tears in' his eyes thanked the nobility for their confidence. The nobles hailed him noisily and pressed his hand. But just then one of the nobles from Koznyshov's party said he had heard that the Commission had not carried out any audit, since it considered an audit offensive to the Marshal of the Province. One of the members of the Commission incautiously confirmed this. Then a small, youthful-looking but extremely venomous nobleman got up to say that in all probability it would be a pleasure for the Marshal of the Province to give a financial accounting, and that the superfluous tact of the members of the Commission was depriving him of this moral satisfaction. Then the members of the Commission waived their own report, and Koznyshov began to prove logically that they had to admit that they had either audited the finances or not; he developed this dilemma in detail. Some chatterbox from the opposing party spoke against Koznyshov. Then Sviyazhsky spoke, followed by the venomous gentleman once again. The debate went on for a long time and came to no conclusion. Levin was surprised that this was being argued about for so long, especially because when he asked Koznyshov whether he thought there had been any abuse of the funds Koznyshov replied: "Oh no! He's an honest chap. But we have to give a jolt to this old-fashioned patriarchal and family management of the nobility's affairs."

On the fifth day the elections of the District Marshals took place. For some of the districts the elections were rather tempestuous. In the Seleznyov District, Sviyazhsky was unanimously elected without a ballot, and that evening he gave a dinner party at his house.

## XXVII

THE Provincial elections were scheduled for the sixth day. All the halls, large and small, were full of noblemen in various uniforms. A great many had come for that day only.

Men who hadn't seen one another for a long time, some from the Crimea, some from Petersburg, some from abroad, would meet one another in the halls. At the Marshal's table, beneath a portrait of the Tsar, a debate was in full swing.

In both the large and small halls the noblemen had grouped themselves by party, and from their hostile and mistrustful looks, the silence that would follow the approach of strangers, and the fact that some of them would go off whispering together into the farther corridor, it was obvious that each side had secrets from the other. In their external appearance the noblemen were sharply divided into two kinds: the old and the young. The older ones were for the most part wearing either the old-fashioned buttoned-up noblemen's uniforms, with swords and hats, or the naval, infantry, or cavalry uniforms that each was individually entitled to. The uniforms of the older noblemen were cut in the old-fashioned way, pleated at the shoulders; they were plainly too small for them, short-waisted and narrow, as though their wearers had grown out of them. The young men wore long-waisted loose uniforms, broad in the shoulders, with white waistcoats, or uniforms with black collars embroidered with laurel leaves, the emblem of the Ministry of Justice. The young group also included the Court uniforms that ornamented the crowd here and there.

But the division into old and young did not coincide with the division between the parties. Levin saw that some of the young men belonged to the older party while some of the oldest noblemen there, on the other hand, were whispering together with Sviyazhsky and were obviously ardent adherents of the new party.

Levin stood beside a group of his own people in the small hall, which was a smoking and snack room, listening to what was being said and vainly exerting all his mental powers in order to understand it all. Koznyshov was the center: just now he was listening to Sviyazhsky and Khlyustov, a Marshal of another district who belonged to their party. Khlyustov was refusing to go together with his people to ask Snetkov to be a candidate for election, while Sviyazhsky was trying to persuade him to, with Koznyshov's approval. Levin could not make out what the point was of the opposition party asking the Marshal to be a candidate when they intended to defeat him.

Oblonsky, who had just had something to eat and drink, came over to them in his Chamberlain's uniform, wiping his mouth with a scented lawn handkerchief with a border.

"We're holding our ground, Koznyshov," he said, smoothing back his whiskers. And after listening to the conversation he backed Sviyazhsky's opinion.

"One district will be enough, and Sviyazhsky is obviously in the opposition already," he said; this was understood by everyone but Levin.

"Well, Kostya, I see you're getting a taste for it too," he added, turning to Levin and taking him by the arm. Levin would have been glad to get a taste for it, but he couldn't understand what it was all about; stepping aside from the group, he expressed his perplexity to Oblonsky, about why the Marshal of the Province was being asked to be a candidate.

"*O, sancta simplicitas!*" said Oblonsky, and tersely and clearly explained to Levin what the point was:

If all the districts together nominated the Provincial Marshal, which was what had happened in previous elections, he would be unanimously elected. They didn't want that. Now eight districts were willing to nominate him, so if two others refused then Snetkov might decline to be a candidate, and then the old party might put up someone else, in which case all calculations would be upset. But if Sviyazhsky's district were the only one not to join in the nomination then Snetkov would be a candidate. Some of them would even vote for him and deliberately let him make a good showing, so that their opponents would be misled, and when one of their own people was put up he would get some of the others' votes.

Levin understood, but not fully, and was about to ask a few more questions when suddenly everyone started talking, making a racket and moving toward the large hall.

"What's that?" "Who?" "An authorization? Whose?" "What?" "Turned down?" "No authorization." "Flerov's not being let in." "Suppose he is being prosecuted? In that way they can refuse to let anyone in!" "What a disgrace!" "The law!" Levin heard on all sides, and together with all the others, who were hurrying on afraid of missing something, he made his way toward the large hall; hemmed in by a crowd of noblemen he tried to get close to the high table, where the Provincial Marshal, Sviyazhsky, and some other leaders were having a heated argument.

## XXVIII

Levin was standing some way off. The stertorous breathing of one nobleman next to him, and the heavy creaking shoes of another, prevented him from hearing distinctly. All he could hear from far off was the soft voice of the Marshal, then the strident voice of the venomous young nobleman, then Sviyazhsky's voice. As far as he could make out they were arguing about some legal clause and the meaning of the words: "against whom legal proceedings are pending."

The crowd separated to make way for Koznyshov, who was moving toward the table. After waiting for the venomous nobleman to finish what he was saying, Koznyshov said it seemed to him that the best thing would be to consult the wording of the clause, and he asked the secretary to find the paragraph. The paragraph provided that in case of disagreement a vote should be taken.

Koznyshov read the paragraph aloud and began to explain its meaning, but just then a tall, stout, round-shouldered landowner with dyed mustaches, wearing a tight uniform with a collar that squeezed up the back of his neck, interrupted him. He went over to the table and striking it with his ring shouted in a loud voice:

"The vote! Put it to the vote! Enough chatter! Put it to the vote!"

A number of other voices suddenly started speaking, and the tall nobleman with the ring, getting more and more infuriated, kept shouting louder and louder. But it was impossible to make out what he was saying.

He was proposing the same thing as Koznyshov, though he obviously detested him and all his party, and this feeling of hatred infected his whole party and evoked a reaction of similar though more politely expressed virulence from the opposing party. Some nobleman began shouting, and for a moment everything got all mixed up, so that the Provincial Marshal was obliged to call for order.

"The vote! The vote! All noblemen will understand . . . We have shed our blood . . . The sovereign's trust . . . No auditing of the Marshal, he's not a salesman . . ." "But that's not the point!" "The vote, please!" "Abominable!" Spiteful, furious voices were shouting on all sides. The faces were still more vindictive and frenzied than the words: they showed implacable hatred. Levin was completely incapable of understanding what it was all about; he was astonished by the passion with which the question of whether or not Flerov's case should be voted on was discussed. As Koznyshov explained to him later he had forgotten the syllogism that the Provincial Marshal had to be ousted for the sake of the common welfare; that for the Marshal to be ousted a majority of ballots was necessary; that to get that majority Flerov had to be given the right to vote; that for Flerov to be acknowledged as eligible the proper interpretation of the juridical clause had to be given.

"And one vote may decide the whole business; one must be serious and consistent if one wishes to serve the cause of the public," Koznyshov had concluded.

But Levin had forgotten that, and it was painful for him to witness all these nice men he respected so much in a state of such disagreeable, malevolent excitement. To get rid of this painful feeling he left without waiting for the end of the debate and went into the snack room, where there was no one but some waiters around the buffet. When he saw the waiters busying themselves wiping the crockery and arranging plates and wineglasses, and saw their lively, serene faces, Levin had an unexpected feeling of relief, as though he had come out of a stuffy room into the fresh air. He began walking up and down, watching the waiters with pleasure. He particularly liked the way one waiter with gray whiskers, expressing disdain for the other younger ones who were making fun of him, was teaching them how to fold napkins. Levin was just about to enter into a conversation with this old waiter when the secretary of the court of trusteeship, an old man who specialized in knowing all the noblemen of the province by their full name, drew him away.

"If you please," he said, "your brother is looking for you. The vote is being taken."

Levin entered the hall, was given a white ball, and followed his brother Koznyshov to the table Sviyazhsky was standing next to with a portentous and ironical look, gathering his beard in his hand and sniffing it. Koznyshov put his hand into the ballot box, dropped his ball somewhere, and stood aside for Levin. Levin moved up, but he had completely forgotten what it was all about; he felt embarrassed and turned to Koznyshov with a question: "Where should I put it?" He asked this in a low voice, while people nearby were talking, so that he hoped his question would not be overheard. But the talk subsided just then and his improper question was overheard. Koznyshov frowned.

"It's a matter of individual conviction," he said sternly.

Several men smiled. Levin blushed, hastily thrust his hand under the cloth and dropped the ball to the right, since it was in his right hand. After dropping it he recalled that the left hand had to be put into the box too, and he did so hastily, but it was already too late, and feeling still more embarrassed he hurried away to the back part of the hall.

"One hund'ed and twenty-six fo'! Ninety-eight against!" rang out the voice of the secretary, who couldn't pronounce *r*'s. Then laughter was heard: a button and two nuts had been found in the ballot box. Flerov was declared eligible, and the new party had had a victory.

But the old party didn't consider itself defeated. Levin heard that Snetkov was being nominated and he saw a crowd of noblemen surrounding the Provincial Marshal, who was saying something. Levin moved up closer. In his answer to the noblemen Snetkov spoke of the confidence and the affection the nobility had for him, which he did not deserve, for all his merit consisted of his love for the nobility, to whom he had devoted twenty years of service. Several times he repeated these words: ". . . have served to the limits of my powers, faithfully and truly . . . I appreciate and thank you . . ." Then he stopped suddenly because of the tears that were choking him and left the hall. Whether these tears came from a feeling of injustice toward himself, from love for the nobility, or from the strained situation he was in, feeling himself surrounded by enemies, his agitation was infectious; the majority of the noblemen were touched, and Levin had a feeling of tenderness for him.

The Marshal collided with Levin in the doorway.

"I beg your pardon! Excuse me, please," he said, as though to a stranger, but when he recognized Levin he smiled shyly. It seemed to Levin that he wanted to say something but was too excited to. The look on his face and his whole figure as he hurried past, in his uniform with crosses and gold-trimmed white trousers, reminded Levin of a hunted animal aware of being in a bad way. This expression on the Marshal's face was particularly moving to Levin because only the day before he had been to his house in connection with his trusteeship business and had seen him in all his grandeur as a kindhearted family man. The large house with old-fashioned family furniture; the old footmen, far from smart, shabby, but deferential, evidently former serfs who had not changed masters; the stout good-natured wife in a lace cap and Turkish shawl, caressing her pretty little granddaughter (a daughter's daughter); their sturdy young son in the sixth form in high school, who had just come home from school and had greeted his father by kissing his large hand; his host's impressive kindly words and gestures—the day before all that had aroused in Levin an involuntary respect and sympathy; now this old man seemed to him touching and pitiful, and he wanted to say something pleasant to him.

"So you're going to be our Marshal again!" he said.

"Hardly!" said the Marshal, with a frightened look round. "I'm tired—feeling my age. There are others worthier than I and younger; let them serve." And he vanished through a side door.

The most solemn moment had arrived. The elections were due to begin immediately. The leaders of both parties were calculating on their fingers the white and black balls they could muster.

The debate on Flerov had given the new party not merely Flerov's single vote, but a gain in time as well, so that three noblemen could be brought up who were to have been deprived by the intrigues of the old party of a chance to take part in the elections. Two of these noblemen, who had a weakness for wine, had been made drunk by Snetkov's agents, while the third one's uniform had been removed.

On learning of this, the new party had had time during the Flerov debate to send a sleigh with a uniform for one of the noblemen and to bring back one of the drunken ones to the assembly.

"I've brought back one of them, doused him with water," whispered the landowner who had gone to fetch him, going up to Sviyazhsky. "It's all right, he'll do."

"Is he very drunk? Will he fall down?" said Sviyazhsky, shaking his head.

"No, he's fine. If only they don't get at him here . . . I've told the barman on no account to give him anything."

## XXIX

THE narrow hall that served as smoking and snack room was full of noblemen. The excitement kept growing; anxiety was visible on every face. The party leaders, who knew all the

details and the estimates of the vote, were most excited
of all. They were the directors of the forthcoming skirmish;
the others were like the rank-and-file before a battle—though
they had prepared themselves for the fight they were seeking distraction for the time being. Some of them were eating,
standing up or sitting down at the table; others were smoking
cigarettes and walking up and down the long room chatting
with friends they hadn't seen for a long time.

Levin did not feel like eating, and he didn't smoke; he
didn't want to join his own set, that is, Koznyshov, Oblonsky,
Sviyazhsky, and some others, because Vronsky, in an equerry's uniform, was standing there with them engaged in a lively
conversation. Levin had already caught sight of him at the
elections the day before and had taken pains to avoid meeting him. He went over to the window and sat down, watching the various groups and listening to what was being said
around him. He felt particularly sad because everyone he
saw was animated, preoccupied and busy, and he alone, together with a toothless mumbling ancient in a naval uniform
who had sat down beside him, had nothing to do and no
interest in what was going on.

"What a rascal he is! I told him not to! Really, he'd never
collect it in three years," a short round-shouldered landowner with greased hair hanging over the embroidered collar of his uniform, was saying vehemently, stamping heavily
with the heels of some new boots he had evidently put on
for the elections. Throwing an irritated look at Levin the
landowner suddenly turned away.

"Yes, it's a dirty business, there's no gainsaying that," said
a short landowner in a high-pitched voice.

These two were immediately followed by a whole crowd of
landowners surrounding a stout general who were hurrying
toward Levin. They were obviously looking for a place where
they could talk things over in seclusion.

"How can he dare say I gave orders for his breeches to be
stolen! I expect he sold them for drink. I snap my fingers
at him and his princely title! Just let him dare say a word—
it's scandalous!"

"My dear fellow, excuse me! They're taking the articles
of the law as their authority," someone in another group
was saying: "the wife must be registered as noble."

"The hell with the statutes! I'm speaking from the heart.
That's what the nobility is there for. You have to have confidence."

"Come, Excellency—some cognac."

Another group was following close on the heels of some nobleman who was shouting something in a loud voice: this was one of those who had been made drunk.

"I always advised her to lease her estate, she'll never make it pay," said a landowner with a gray mustache, in the uniform of Colonel of the old General Staff, in an agreeable voice. It was the same landowner Levin had met at Sviyazhsky's; he recognized him immediately. The landowner gave Levin a close look too, and they shook hands.

"Delighted to see you. Of course I remember you very well. Last year at Sviyazhsky's, the Marshal's."

"Well, how is your farming getting on?" Levin asked.

"Oh it's still the same—running at a loss," replied the landowner, stopping beside Levin, with a resigned smile but an expression of calm conviction that this was how it was bound to be. "And how d'you happen to land in our province?" he asked. "Have you come to take part in our *coup d'état*?" he said, pronouncing the French words firmly but badly. "All Russia is assembled here: Chamberlains and practically Ministers." He indicated to Oblonsky's imposing figure in white trousers with a Chamberlain's uniform, walking beside a general.

"I feel obliged to tell you that I have a very poor understanding of the meaning of these nobility elections," said Levin.

The landowner looked at him. "But what is there to understand? They have no meaning whatsoever. It's an obsolete institution that goes on moving from mere inertia. Just look at the uniforms—they tell you as much: this is an assembly of Justices of the Peace, permanent officials and so on, but not of nobles."

"Then why do you come?" asked Levin.

"Out of habit, for one thing. Then you have to keep up connections. It's some kind of a moral obligation. And then, to tell you the truth, I have an ax of my own to grind. My son-in-law wants to be nominated for a permanent membership; they don't have much money and I want him to get him in. But why do people like that come?" he said, indicating the venomous nobleman who had spoken at the high table.

"That's one of the new generation of noblemen."

"They may be new, but they're not noblemen. They just own land; we're squires. As noblemen they're digging their own graves."

"But don't you say it's an obsolete institution?"

"Obsolete is what it is; all the same it ought to be treated more respectfully. Just take Snetkov . . . Good or not we've taken a thousand years growing. You know, if you had to make a little garden in front of your house, and plan it, and a hundred-year-old tree were growing on the spot, even though it was gnarled and old you wouldn't cut down the old giant for the sake of some flower beds, you'd lay out the flower beds so as to take advantage of the tree. It can't be grown in a year," he said guardedly, and immediately changed the subject. "Well, and how is your own farming getting on?"

"Far from well. I get about five per cent."

"Yes, but you're not counting yourself. After all, you're worth something too, aren't you? Now look at me: until I took up farming I was getting three thousand a year in the service. Now I work harder than I did in the service, and get about five per cent just like you, and then only with luck. My own labor goes for nothing."

"Then why d'you do it? If it's an out-and-out loss?"

"One just does it. What would you have? It's a habit, and you know it's necessary! Let me tell you something else," the landowner went on, now that he was started, leaning his elbow on the window. "My son has no taste at all for farming. It's obvious he's going to be a scholar, so there'll be no one to carry on in my place. But you do it anyhow. Just now I've been planting an orchard."

"Yes, yes," said Levin, "that's absolutely right. I always feel there's no real calculation in my own farming, but you do it anyhow. You feel some sort of an obligation toward the land."

"Let me tell you something," the landowner went on. "I had a neighbor, a merchant, visiting me; we walked round the farm and the orchard together. He says: 'Everything in the place is going properly, but your garden's neglected,' though actually it's not. 'If I were you I'd cut down those limes, but make sure it's when the sap's rising. You must have a thousand limes here, and each one would produce a lot of bark, which fetches a good price nowadays. I'd cut them all down.' "

"And for the money he'd buy cattle, or buy up some piece of land for next to nothing and lease it to the peasants," said Levin, finishing the sentence for him; he had evidently come across such calculations more than once before. "And he'll make a fortune for himself, while as for you and me, we'll be lucky if we can hang on to what we have and leave it to our children."

"You're married, I hear?" asked the landowner.

"Yes," replied Levin, with proud satisfaction. "Yes, it's odd," he went on, "we go on living without making anything, as though we were appointed like the ancient vestals to watch over some fire or other."

The landowner chuckled under his white mustache.

"There are some of us the other way too; take our friend Sviyazhsky, or Count Vronsky, who's settled here now; they want to make agriculture an industry; so far, though, it's only led to a waste of capital."

"But why is it we don't act like the merchants? And cut down the limes for their bark?" said Levin, reverting to a thought that had struck him.

"There, as you said, it's a question of watching over the fire. The other isn't a nobleman's business. And our nobleman's business isn't accomplished here, at these elections, but elsewhere, on our own land. We have a class instinct of our own about what's done and what's not done. The peasants, too, I see it in them sometimes; the way a good peasant tries to grab as much land as he can. No matter how bad it is he'll go on plowing it. He gets no profit out of it either, it's a straight loss."

"Just like us," said Levin. "I was delighted to meet you again, delighted," he added, seeing Sviyazhsky approaching.

"Here we've seen each other for the first time since we met at your place," said the landowner; "we've been having a talk."

"Yes, and running down the new order too, what?" said Sviyazhsky with a smile.

"That too."

"Unburdening ourselves."

### XXX

SVIYAZHSKY took Levin by the arm and went back with him to his own group.

Now it was no longer possible to avoid Vronsky. He was standing there together with Oblonsky and Koznyshov and looking straight at Levin as he came over.

"Delighted. I think I've had the pleasure before, at Princess Shcherbatsky's," he said, holding out his hand to Levin.

"Yes, I remember our meeting very well," said Levin; flushing crimson he turned away immediately and began talking to his brother.

Smiling slightly, Vronsky went on talking to Sviyazhsky, evidently having no desire to enter into a conversation with Levin; but Levin, while talking to his brother, kept glancing over at Vronsky constantly, trying to think of something he might start talking to him about to smooth over his rudeness.

"What are we waiting for now?" asked Levin, glancing at Sviyazhsky and Vronsky.

"For Snetkov. He must either decline or accept," replied Sviyazhsky.

"Well, which is it? Has he accepted or not?"

"That's just it: neither one nor the other," said Vronsky.

"And if he declines, who'll be nominated?" asked Levin, glancing at Vronsky.

"Anyone who wants to," said Sviyazhsky.

"Will you?" asked Levin.

"Certainly not," said Sviyazhsky, getting embarrassed and casting a look of alarm at the venomous young nobleman, who was standing beside Koznyshov.

"Then who? Nevedovsky?" said Levin, feeling he had put his foot in it somehow.

But that was still worse. Nevedovsky and Sviyazhsky were the two candidates.

"It won't be me on any account," replied the venomous gentleman.

This was Nevedovsky himself. Sviyazhsky introduced him to Levin.

"Well, has it got into you too?" said Oblonsky, winking at Vronsky. "It's something like the races; you could place bets."

"Yes, it does get into you," said Vronsky. "Once you get involved you want to see things through. It's a contest!" he said, frowning and setting his powerful jaws.

"What an able fellow Sviyazhsky is! How clear he makes everything!"

"Oh yes," said Vronsky absently.

There was a silence during which Vronsky, since one must look at something, looked at Levin, at his legs, his uniform, then his face, and noticing his morose eyes fixed on him, said, in order to say something:

"And how is it that you, living in the country permanently,

aren't a Justice of the Peace? You're not wearing a Justice's uniform."

"Because in my opinion it's a preposterous institution," replied Levin morosely, after waiting the whole time for a chance to start talking to Vronsky in order to make up for his rudeness at their first encounter.

"I don't think so, quite the contrary," said Vronsky, with calm surprise.

"It's a game," Levin interrupted him. "We don't need any Justices of the Peace. I haven't had a single case in eight years, and the one I did have was settled wrongly. The Justice of the Peace is nearly thirty miles from my place. To settle a matter worth two rubles I should have to send a lawyer who costs fifteen."

And he told a story about a peasant who stole some flour from a miller, and when the miller mentioned it to him the peasant sued him for slander. All this was irrelevant and silly, and while Levin was speaking he felt as much himself.

"Oh, what a crank!" said Oblonsky with his smoothest smile. "But let's go in, I think the voting's begun . . ."

And they separated.

"I don't understand," said Koznyshov, who had noticed his brother's clumsy sally. "I don't understand how it's possible to be so utterly devoid of any political tact. That's what we Russians lack. The Provincial Marshal is our political opponent, and here you and he are thick as thieves and you want to nominate him. While Count Vronsky—he's no friend of mine, he's invited me to dinner and I'm not going; but he's one of our own people, so why turn him into an enemy? Then you ask Nevedovsky whether he's going to be a candidate. That sort of thing isn't done."

"Oh, I don't understand a thing! And it's all nonsense," Levin replied morosely.

"You say it's all nonsense, and the moment you have anything to do with it you make a mess of everything."

Levin was silent, and they went into the large hall together.

The Provincial Marshal, though he felt in the air that a plot had been formed against him, and though he had not been unanimously nominated, had made up his mind to be a candidate anyhow. The hall fell silent, and the secretary announced in a loud voice that Michael Stepanovich Snetkov, Captain of the Guards, would now be voted on for the post of Provincial Marshal.

The District Marshals carried the little plates with the ballot balls from their own tables to the high table, and the election started.

"Drop it on the right," Oblonsky whispered to Levin, when he and Koznyshov followed the Marshal to the table. But Levin had now forgotten the calculation which had been explained to him, and he was afraid Oblonsky had made a mistake in telling him "on the right." After all, it was Snekov who was the enemy. As he went up to the ballot box he was holding the ballot ball in his right hand, but when it occurred to him that he was mistaken he transferred the ball to his left hand right in front of the ballot box, and visibly dropped it on the left. An expert standing beside the box, who could tell by the mere motion of an elbow who dropped the ball where, frowned with irritation. There was nothing for him to exercise his perspicacity on this time.

Everything fell silent again; and the counting of the balls began. Then a solitary voice announced the number for and against.

The Marshal had been elected by a substantial majority. Everyone started making an uproar and rushing for the door. Snetkov came in and the noblemen crowded round him with their congratulations.

"Well, is it over now?" Levin asked Koznyshov.

"It's only just beginning," Sviyazhsky, with a smile, answered for Koznyshov. "The other candidate may get more votes."

Again, Levin had forgotten about this too. All he could remember now was that there had been some subtlety about this, but he was too bored to recall just what it was. He was seized by depression, and began longing to get out of this crowd.

Since no one was paying any attention to him and he seemed to be of no use to anyone, he quietly made his way into the small hall that served as snack room, and felt greatly relieved again when he saw the waiters. The old waiter offered him something to eat and Levin accepted. After eating a cutlet and beans and talking to the waiter about masters he had had, Levin, who didn't feel like going back into the hall where he felt so ill at ease, went up into the gallery.

The gallery was crowded with women in gala dresses, leaning over the railing and doing their best not to miss a word of what was being said below. Some elegant lawyers, spectacled high-school teachers, and officers were sitting and standing around them. Everyone was discussing the election, the Marshal's fatigue, and what an excellent debate it was; in one group Levin heard his brother being praised. One of the women said to a lawyer:

"I'm so glad I heard Koznyshov! It was worth going a little hungry for. He was wonderful! Everything was so clear, so audible. Now in your court no one talks that way. At best it might be Maidel, and even he's far less eloquent."

Levin found a seat free near the railing; he leaned over it and began watching and listening.

All the noblemen were sitting behind partitions that divided their districts from each other. A man in uniform was standing in the middle of the room and announcing in a loud, high-pitched voice:

"The vote will now be taken on Captain Eugene Ivanovich Apukhtin, candidate for the post of Provincial Marshal!"

A sepulchral silence followed; then a single feeble old man's voice was heard:

"Declines!"

"The vote will now be taken on Court Council for Peter Petrovich Bohl—" the voice began again.

"Declines!" shouted a squeaky youthful voice.

The same thing began again, and again the candidate "declined." This went on for about an hour. With his elbows on the railing Levin watched and listened. At first he was surprised and tried to understand what it all meant; then, after making sure he would never be able to understand it, he grew bored. Then, as he thought of all the agitation and vindictiveness he saw on everyone's face he felt sad; he decided to leave and started downstairs. As he was passing through the aisle behind the gallery he came across a dejected high-school student with bloodshot eyes pacing back and forth. On the staircase he met a couple: a woman hurrying up on high-heeled shoes and the Assistant Public Prosecutor.

"I said you wouldn't be late," said the Assistant Prosecutor as Levin stepped aside to let the woman pass.

Levin was already at the bottom of the staircase near the exit and getting the cloakroom stub for his fur coat out of his vest pocket when the secretary caught him: "Please come, sir—the vote is beginning."

The vote was being taken on the candidacy of Nevedovsky—who had declined so firmly.

Levin went up to the door of the hall; it was shut. The

secretary knocked, the door opened, and two landowners with flushed faces plunged out past Levin.

"I can't stand it!" said one red-faced landowner.

The landowner was followed by the Provincial Marshal, who thrust his face through the door. He had a horrifying expression, due to exhaustion and fear.

"I told you not to let anyone out!" he shouted to the doorkeeper.

"I was letting them in, Your Excellency!"

"Oh Lord!" said the Marshal with a heavy sigh; his head drooping and his legs in their white trousers dragging wearily, he went through the middle of the room to the high table.

A majority had shifted to Nevedovsky, which was what had been calculated on, and he was now Provincial Marshal. Many people were gay, many were pleased and happy, many were in raptures, many were discontented and unhappy. The former Provincial Marshal was in despair, which he could not hide. When Nevedovsky went out of the hall he was surrounded by a crowd that followed him enthusiastically, just as it had followed the Governor on the first day, when he had opened the elections, and just as it had followed Snetkov when he had been given his election.

## XXXI

THE newly elected Marshal and many of the triumphant new party dined that evening at Vronsky's.

Vronsky had come to the elections because he was bored in the country and wanted to proclaim to Anna his right to freedom, in order to repay Sviyazhsky with his support at the elections for all the trouble he had gone to on Vronsky's behalf at the District Council elections, and most of all in order to perform strictly all the duties of the position he had chosen for himself as nobleman and landowner. But he had not had the least expectation that this business of the elections would preoccupy him so, get him so inflamed, or that he could do so well at it. He was a complete newcomer in this circle of noblemen, but he had evidently had a success and was not mistaken in thinking that he had already acquired some influence among them. This influence was contributed to by: his wealth and title; his splendid house in town, which had been lent him by an old acquaintance of his, Shirkov, a financier who had established a thriving bank in Kashin; his excellent cook, whom he had brought along from his country place; his friendship with the Governor, who had been a comrade of Vronsky's, and for that matter one whom he had even protected; and most of all by his simple manners; he treated everyone alike, and this very soon made the majority of the noblemen change their minds about his supposed pride. He felt himself that, except for that crackpot married to Kitty Shcherbatsky, who in a frenzy of spite had made a great many pointlessly stupid remarks to him for no reason at all, each nobleman he met became a partisan of his. He saw clearly, and the others acknowledged it, that he had contributed a great deal to Nevedovsky's success. And now at his own table, as he celebrated Nevedovsky's election, he had a pleasant feeling of triumph. The elections themselves had absorbed him so much that he began to think that if he were married by the next triennial election he would be a candidate himself—something like his wanting to ride himself whenever a jockey had won him a prize.

But now it was the jockey's victory that was being celebrated. Vronsky was sitting at the head of the table with the young Governor, a general of the Imperial suite, on his right. For everyone else there he was the master of the Province, who solemnly opened the election, made a speech, and as Vronsky saw aroused both respect and servility in many of them; but for Vronsky he was Maslov Katka—his nickname in the Corps of Pages—who had once been embarrassed in his presence and whom he had tried to put at his ease. Nevedovsky, with his youthful, unyielding, and venomous face, was sitting on Vronsky's left. Vronsky's manner with him was simple and respectful.

Sviyazhsky bore his failure cheerfully. It was not even a failure for him, as he said himself, turning to Nevedovsky with a champagne glass in his hand—no better representative of the new tendency the nobility ought to follow could have been found. Therefore all honest men, as he said, were on the side of that day's victory and triumphed with it.

Oblonsky was also glad that he had had some fun and that everyone was satisfied. Over the magnificent dinner various episodes of the election were gone over. Sviyazhsky gave a comical imitation of the old Marshal's tearful speech and remarked, turning to Nevedovsky, that His Excellency would have to pick out a different and more complicated way of auditing the accounts than tears. Another jocular nobleman told how footmen in knee breeches and stockings had been ordered for the ball the old Marshal had been going to give, and now they would have to be sent back unless the new Marshal gave a ball with stockinged footmen.

During the dinner Nevedovsky was constantly referred to as "our Provincial Marshal," and "Your Excellency."

This was said with the same pleasure with which a young woman is addressed as "Madame" and by her husband's name. Nevedovsky pretended to be not only indifferent to this title but contemptuous of it, though it was obvious that he was happy and holding a tight rein on himself in order not to give expression to the delight that was out of harmony with the modern liberal milieu they were all part of.

During the dinner several telegrams were sent to people interested in the outcome of the elections. Oblonsky, who was feeling very gay, also sent Dolly a telegram as follows: NEVEDOVSKY ELECTED MAJORITY TWENTY. CONGRATULATIONS. SPREAD NEWS. He dictated it aloud, saying: "They have to be cheered up." But when Dolly received the telegram she only sighed for the waste of a ruble on it and realized it had been toward the end of a dinner. She knew Stiva had a weakness for sending telegrams at the end of a dinner.

Everything, together with the first-rate dinner and the wines—which had not been ordered from Russian merchants but bought bottled abroad—was very distinguished, simple, and gay. The group of twenty men had been selected by Sviyazhsky from among like-minded, liberal members of the new tendency who were at the same time witty and respectable. Toasts, also half-jocular, were drunk to the new Provincial Marshal, the Governor, to the Director of the Bank, and to "our amiable host."

Vronsky was satisfied. He had not at all expected such an agreeable atmosphere in the provinces.

At the end of the dinner things grew even gayer. The Governor asked Vronsky to come along to a concert in aid of "our Serbian brothers," which was being arranged by his wife, who wanted to meet him.

"There'll be a bar there, and you'll be able to see the local beauty. She actually is remarkable."

"Not in my line," replied Vronsky, who was fond of this English expression, but he smiled and promised to come.

Just before they left the table, when they had all started smoking, Vronsky's valet came over to him with a letter on a tray.

"From Vozdvizhensk, by special messenger," he said meaningfully.

"Remarkable resemblance he has to Public Prosecutor Sventitsky," one of the guests said in French, referring to the valet, as Vronsky, with a frown, read the letter.

It was from Anna. He knew what was in it even before reading it. Thinking the elections would be over in five days he had promised to be back on Friday. It was Saturday already and he knew the letter would be full of reproaches for his not having come back on time. The letter he had sent off the evening before had probably not yet arrived.

The letter contained what he had expected, but it was put in an unexpected way he found particularly disagreeable. *"Annie very ill, doctor says it may be inflammation. When I'm alone I lose my head. Princess Barbara is not a help but a hindrance. I expected you the day before yesterday, then yesterday, and I'm sending this to find out where you are and what you're doing. I wanted to come myself, but I changed my mind, knowing it would annoy you. Give me an answer of some kind so that I'll know what to do."*

Their child was ill, and she had wanted to come herself; their daughter was ill, and this hostile tone.

The innocent gaiety of the elections, and the dismal, oppressive love he was obliged to return to struck Vronsky by their contrast. But he had to leave, and he returned home by the first train that night.

## XXXII

BEFORE Vronsky left for the elections, Anna, having reflected that the scenes that repeatedly took place between them whenever he went away could only alienate him and not bind him to her more closely, made up her mind to exert every effort possible to endure their separation calmly. But the chilly, stern look he gave her when he came to tell her he was going away hurt her, and even before he left, her composure was destroyed.

Later on, as she meditated in solitude on that look, which expressed his right to freedom, she came to only one conclusion, as she always did: an awareness of her own degradation.

He has the right to leave wherever and whenever he wants to, she thought. Not only to go away, but to leave me. He has every right, and I have none at all. But since he knows that he oughtn't to do it . . . But what did he do? He looked at me with a chilly, severe expression. Of course it's indefinite, and intangible, but it was not there before, and that look means a great deal. That look proves that he has begun to grow cold.

And though she was sure that he had begun to grow cold there was still nothing she could do; it was impossible for her to change her relations with him. It was just as it had been before—it was by love alone, by her charms, that she could hold him. And just as before, it was only by busying herself during the day and taking morphia at night that she could stifle the terrifying thoughts of what would happen if he fell out of love with her. There was, to be sure, one other means left: not to hold him, for which she wanted nothing beyond his love, but to unite herself with him by putting herself in such a position that he could not abandon her. This means was divorce and marriage. And she began to desire that; she made up her mind to agree to it the very first time either he or Stiva brought it up.

With thoughts like these she spent five days without him—the five days he was supposed to be away.

Walks, talks with Princess Barbara, visits to the hospital, and most of all reading, reading one book after another, took up her time. But on the sixth day, when the coachman came back without him, she felt she was no longer capable of stifling thoughts about him or about what he was doing there. Just then her daughter fell ill. Anna set about nursing her, but that didn't distract her either, especially since the illness was not serious. No matter how hard she tried she could not grow to love this little girl, and she was incapable of simulating love. Toward the end of the day, when she was left alone, Anna felt such terror on his account that she almost decided to go to town, but after thinking it over she wrote the contradictory letter Vronsky had received and without reading it over sent it by special messenger. The following morning she received his letter and regretted her own. Horrified, she anticipated a repetition of the stern look he had thrown at her when he had left, especially when he learned that the little girl had not been dangerously ill. Nevertheless she was glad she had written him. By now Anna had acknowledged to herself that he was tired of her, that he was abandoning his liberty with regret to come back to her, and nevertheless she was glad he was coming. Let him be tired of her, as long as he was there with her, so that she could see him and know every move he made.

She was sitting in the drawing room, under a lamp, reading a new book by Taine, listening to the sounds of the wind in the courtyard and expecting the carriage to draw up at any moment. It seemed to her a number of times that she heard the sound of the wheels, but she was mistaken; at last she heard not only the sound of the wheels but the coachman's voice as well, and a dull clatter in the covered portico. Even Princess Barbara, who was playing patience, confirmed this, and Anna, flushing, got up, but instead of going downstairs, as she had already done twice before, she stopped. Suddenly she felt ashamed of her deception, but above all she was afraid of how he would receive her. Her feeling of injury had already passed; she was simply afraid he would express displeasure. She recalled that the little girl was perfectly well now for the second day. She even felt annoyed with her for having recovered just at the moment the letter had been sent. Then she recollected that he was there, himself, with his hands, his eyes. She heard his voice. And forgetting everything she joyfully ran to meet him.

"Well, how is Annie?" he asked diffidently, looking up at Anna as she ran down to him.

He was sitting on a chair, with a footman pulling off a warm boot.

"It's all right, she's better."

"And yourself?" he asked, giving himself a shake.

She took his hand in both her own, and drew it to her waist, without taking her eyes off him.

"Well, I'm delighted," he said, coldly surveying her, and the coiffure and dress he knew were for him.

He liked it all, but how often he had liked it already! And the stonily severe expression she was so afraid of settled on his face.

"Well, I'm delighted. And are you well?" he said, wiping his damp beard with a handkerchief and kissing her hand.

It doesn't matter, she thought, as long as he's here; when he's here he cannot, he won't dare not to love me.

The evening passed contentedly and cheerfully in the company of Princess Barbara, who complained to him that when he wasn't there Anna took morphia.

"What can I do? I couldn't sleep . . . I lay awake thinking. When he's here I don't take any. Almost never."

He told them about the elections, and by her questions

Anna was able to draw him out to talk about just what made him lively—his success. She told him everything that could interest him at home; she had nothing but the most cheerful news for him.

But late at night, when they were alone, Anna, seeing that she had completely recovered her hold over him, wanted to wipe out the painful impression of the look he had given her on account of her letter.

"Now admit it," she said, "wasn't it a nuisance to get a letter from me? And you didn't believe me?"

The moment she had said this she realized that however lovingly he was disposed toward her now he had not forgiven her for that.

"Yes," he said. "The letter was so strange. First Annie was ill, then you wanted to come yourself."

"That was all true."

"I have no doubt of it."

"Yes, you do. You're annoyed, I can see it."

"Not for a moment. I'm simply annoyed, it's true, by your apparently refusing to admit that there are some obligations that—"

"Obligations to go to a concert?"

"But let's not talk about it," he said.

"But why shouldn't we?" she said.

"All I mean is that there are some business things that can't be avoided. Now, for instance, I'm going to have to go to Moscow to see about the house . . . Anna, *why* are you so irritable? Surely you know that I can't live without you?"

"If that's so," said Anna, her voice suddenly changing, "then what you're tired of is this life . . . Yes, you'll drop in for a day, and go away again, the way men do . . ."

"Anna, that's cruel. I'm ready to give up my whole life to—"

But she wasn't listening to him.

"If you go to Moscow I'm coming along too. I'm not going to be left here alone. Either we ought to separate, or live together."

"You know that's my sole wish. But for that—"

"There has to be a divorce? I'll write him. I see I can't live this way . . . But I'm going with you to Moscow."

"You say that as though you were threatening me. But there's nothing I want so much as never being separated from you," said Vronsky with a smile.

But it was not merely a chilly look, it was the malevolent look of a harried and exasperated man that flashed in his eyes as he said these tender words.

She saw this look and rightly guessed its meaning.

If that's so, then it's disaster! was what this look said. It was a fleeting impression, but she was never to forget it.

Anna wrote her husband a letter asking him for a divorce, and at the end of November, having parted from Princess Barbara, who had to go to Petersburg, she and Vronsky moved to Moscow. Expecting a letter from Karenin any day, and the divorce after that, they now settled down as a married couple.

# PART SEVEN

## I

THE Levins had been in Moscow for more than two months. The due date of Kitty's confinement, ascertained by the most precise calculations of people who knew about such things, had long since passed by; she was still with child, and there was not the slightest indication that her time was nearer now than it had been two months before. The doctor, the midwife, Dolly, the mother, and especially Levin, none of them able to think without horror of what was approaching, were beginning to feel impatient and alarmed; Kitty was the only one who felt completely calm and happy.

She was now distinctly aware of the awakening within her of a new feeling of love for her future child, already partly existent for her, and she attuned herself to the feeling with pleasure. The child was now no longer altogether a part of her; it sometimes lived its own independent life too. Often this hurt her, but at the same time she wanted to laugh aloud because of this strange new joy.

Everyone she loved was with her, and everyone was so kind to her, so attentive, everything was presented her in nothing but its most pleasant aspect, that if she hadn't known and felt that it was all going to end soon she wouldn't have wished for a better or more agreeable life. The one thing that spoiled the delight of this life was that her husband was not as she loved him, and as he used to be in the country.

She had loved his calm, affectionate, and hospitable tone in the country. But in the city he seemed constantly restless and on his guard, as though afraid someone would offend him, and, worse still, her. In the country, evidently feeling he was in his own place, he would never hurry anywhere and never be idle. Here in the city he was constantly rushing, as though anxious not to miss anything, and there was nothing he had to do. She felt sorry for him. She knew he didn't seem pathetic to others; on the contrary, when Kitty watched him sometimes in company, as you sometimes watch someone you love, trying to see them as though they were strangers in order to define for yourself the impression they make on others, she saw, actually with jealous fear, that he was not only not pathetic, but was extremely attractive, with his breeding, his rather old-fashioned deferential politeness to women, his powerful figure, and what seemed to her his unusually expressive face. But she saw him not from without, but from within—she saw that in town he was not himself; that was the only way she could define his condition. Sometimes she would reproach him in her heart for being unable to live in the city; then she would realize that it actually was difficult for him to arrange a life for himself in town that he could be satisfied with.

And in fact what was there for him to do? He didn't like playing cards; he didn't go to a club. As for hanging around with gay blades like Oblonsky she already knew what that meant—it meant drinking and after drinking going off somewhere . . . She could not think without horror of where men in such circumstances would be off to. Go out in society? But she knew that for that you had to enjoy being intimate with young women; she could not wish for that. Sit at home with her, with her mother and sisters? But pleasant and gay as she found these endless, unvarying conversations about "Alines and Nadines," as the old Prince referred to these sisterly chats, she knew they were bound to bore him. Then what was there left for him to do? Go on writing his book? He had actually tried to do that, and at first would go to the library to take notes and look up references for his book, but as he told her the longer he went on doing nothing the less time he had left. Also, he complained to her that he was talking too much about his book here, so that all his ideas about it were getting jumbled and losing their interest for him.

One advantage of this life in town was that there were never any quarrels between them. Whether it was because the conditions of town life were different or because they had both become more careful and reasonable in this respect, in Moscow they never had any quarrels due to jealousy, which they had been so afraid of on moving into town.

An event even took place that was very important for them both in this respect, that is, Kitty's meeting with Vronsky.

Kitty's godmother, the old Princess Mary, who had always loved her very much, wanted to see her without fail. Kitty, who never went anywhere in her condition, went with her father to the venerable old lady's and there she met Vronsky.

The only thing Kitty could reproach herself for at this encounter was that for a moment, when she recognized in the civilian clothes those features that had once been so familiar to her, she caught her breath, the blood rushed to her heart, and she could feel a flush crimsoning her face. But it only lasted a few seconds. Before her father, who had started talking to Vronsky in a purposely loud voice, had finished what he was saying she was already quite prepared to look at and talk to him if necessary just as she talked to Princess Mary, and above all in such a way that everything, down to the last intonation and smile would have been approved of by her husband, whose unseen presence she seemed to feel above her at that moment.

She said a few words to him, and even smiled calmly at a joke of his about the elections, which he called "our parliament." (She had to smile to show she had understood the joke.) But she turned aside at once to Princess Mary, and didn't glance at him once until he got up to say good-by; then she looked at him, but it was plain that it was only because it is rude not to look at a man when he bows to you.

She was thankful to her father for saying nothing to her about this encounter with Vronsky, but by the special tenderness he showed her after this call, during their usual walk together, she could tell he was pleased with her. She too was pleased with herself. She had not at all expected she would have had the strength to stop up somewhere deep in her heart all the memories of her former feeling for Vronsky, and not only seem to be but actually to feel completely indifferent and serene.

Levin got far redder than she when she told him she had met Vronsky at Princess Mary's. It was very hard for her to tell him, but it was even harder to go on talking about the details of the encounter, since he didn't ask her any questions but simply kept looking at her with a frown.

"I'm very sorry you weren't there," she said, "I don't mean there in the room, if you had been I shouldn't have been so natural. I'm blushing much more now, much much more," she said, blushing to the point of tears, "but I'm sorry you couldn't peep through a crack."

Her candid eyes told Levin she was pleased with herself, and in spite of her blushing he was instantly reassured, and began asking her questions, which was just what she wanted. When he had learned everything, down to the detail that it was only the first second she hadn't been able to help

blushing, but that afterward she found it was all as simple
and easy as meeting someone for the first time, Levin was
completely cheered up and said he was very glad and now
would no longer behave as foolishly as he had at the elections, but would try to be as friendly as possible with Vronsky the next time he met him.

"It's painful to think there's a man around who's almost
an enemy, whom it makes me uncomfortable to meet," said
Levin. "I'm very, very glad."

## II

THEN please call on the Bohls," Kitty said to her husband,
when he came to see her at eleven in the morning, before
going out. "I know you're dining at the club; Papa's put
your name down. But what are you doing this morning?"

"Only going to see Katavasov," replied Levin.

"But why so early?"

"He's promised to introduce me to Metrov. I wanted to talk
to him about my work, he's a famous Petersburg scholar,"
said Levin.

"Oh yes, that was his article you were praising so, wasn't
it? Well, and then?" said Kitty.

"Then maybe to the courts, I have to see about my sister's
case."

"And the concert?"

"The concert—all by myself!"

"No, do go; they're giving those new pieces . . . It used to
interest you so much. I should certainly go."

"Well, in any case I'll come back to the house before dinner," he said, glancing at his watch.

"But put on your frock coat, so that you can call on
Countess Bohl on the way."

"But is that absolutely necessary?"

"Oh absolutely! He called on us. How much effort is it?
You drop in, sit down, chat about the weather for five minutes,
get up and go."

"Well, you won't believe it but I've gotten so unaccustomed
to all that I'm ashamed of myself. Really—a stranger
comes in, sits down, dawdles around without anything to do,
gets in their way and upsets himself, then goes away again!"

Kitty burst out laughing. "But didn't you pay calls when
you were a bachelor?" she said.

"I did, but I always felt ashamed of myself, and now I've gotten so unaccustomed to it that really I'd rather go without dinner for two days than pay this call now. It's so embarrassing! I always think they're going to be offended and say, 'But why did you come if you have no business here?' "

"No, they won't be offended. I'll vouch for that myself," said Kitty, looking laughingly into his face. She took him by the hand. "Well, good-by then . . . and please call on them!"

He kissed her hand and was about to go out, when she stopped him.

"Kostya, you know I only have fifty rubles left."

"Well, all right, I'll drop in at the bank and get some. How much?" he said with a dissatisfied look she was familiar with.

"No, wait a moment." She held him by the hand. "Let's talk it over; it upsets me. I don't think I buy anything we don't need, but the money just evaporates. There's something we're not doing right."

"Not at all," he said, coughing and looking at her from under his eyebrows.

She knew that cough of his. It was a sign of intense dissatisfaction, not with her but with himself. He really was displeased, not because a great deal of money was being spent, but because he was being reminded of something he knew was wrong somewhere and wanted to forget about.

"I've told Sokolov to sell the wheat and get some money for the mill in advance. In any case we'll have enough money."

"No, but I'm afraid that altogether a great deal of—"

"Not at all, not at all," he repeated. "Good-by then, darling."

"No really, sometimes I'm sorry I listened to Mama. How nice it would have been in the country! As it is I've been wearing you all out and we're wasting money . . ."

"Not at all, not at all. Not once since I've been married have I said things could be any better than the way they are."

"Is that true?" she said, looking into his eyes.

He had said this without thinking, simply to comfort her. But when he looked at her and saw those sweet candid eyes of hers fixed on him inquiringly, he repeated the same words, this time from the bottom of his heart. Definitely, I forget about her, he thought, and he recalled what was awaiting them so soon.

"Will it be soon? How do you feel?" he whispered, taking both her hands.

"I've so often thought so that now I no longer think or know anything."

"And you're not afraid?"

She smiled disdainfully. "Not a jot," she said.

"Well, if anything happens I'll be at Katavasov's."

"No, nothing's going to happen; don't think about it. I'll go for a stroll on the boulevard with Papa; we'll call on Dolly. I'll expect you before dinner. Oh yes! You know that Dolly's situation is getting to be completely impossible? She's head over heels in debt; she has no money at all. Mama and I were discussing it yesterday with Arseny." (This was how she referred to Prince Lvov, her sister's husband.) "We decided to turn you and him loose on Stiva. It's definitely impossible. We can't talk to Papa about it, but if you and Arseny . . ."

"But what can we do?" said Levin.

"Well anyhow, you're going to see Arseny, you can talk it over with him, he'll tell you what we decided."

"Well, with Arseny I'm ready to agree to everything beforehand. Then I'll go to see him. By the way, if I do go to the concert I'll go with Nataly. Well, good-by."

At the front steps Kuzma, the old servant Levin had had while still a bachelor, who was now managing the household in town, stopped him.

"Beauty has been reshod, but he still limps," he said. "What d'you want done with him?" (Beauty was one of the pair of carriage horses brought from the country.)

On first coming to Moscow, Levin had been occupied by the horses brought from the country. He had wanted to arrange this aspect of their lives as well and cheaply as possible; but it turned out that their own horses cost them more than hired ones would have, and then they hired horses anyhow.

"Send for the vet, maybe it's a bruise."

"And what will Madame do?" asked Kuzma.

Levin was no longer struck, as he had been when he first began living in Moscow, by the fact that to go from Vozdvizhensky Street to Sivtsev-Vrazhek you had to harness a pair of powerful horses to a heavy carriage, drive the carriage through the slush for three hundred yards, have it stand about for four hours, and pay five rubles for it all. By now all this seemed to him a matter of course.

"Hire a pair for our carriage," he said.

"Yes, sir."

And having found, thanks to the conditions of life in town, such a simple, easy solution to a difficulty that in the country would have required so much personal labor and attention Levin went out, hailed a sleigh, got into it and drove to Nikitsky Street. On the way he was no longer thinking about money, but reflected on his forthcoming introduction to the Petersburg scholar, who was a sociologist, and what he would say to him about his book.

It was only when he had first begun living in Moscow Levin was struck by the unproductive but inevitable expenses that were so strange to people living in the country, and that were required from him every step he took. By now he was used to them. The same thing had happened to him that is said to happen with drunkards: the first glass sticks in your throat, the second flies down like a hawk, but the third is like wee little birds. When Levin had changed his first hundred-ruble note to buy liveries for the footman and the hall porter, he had involuntarily calculated that these liveries—of no use to anyone but absolutely indispensable to judge by the Princess's and Kitty's astonishment at his suggestion that you could get along without them—that these liveries would cost as much as it would to hire two summer laborers, that is, around three hundred working days, from Easter to Advent, and each day one of hard work from early in the morning to late at night. This hundred-ruble note did stick in his throat. But the next one, which he changed to buy supplies for a family dinner that cost twenty-eight rubles, even though it evoked in Levin the thought that twenty-eight rubles meant about seventy-two bushels, mown, bound, threshed, winnowed, sifted and sacked, with sweat and groans, this second note went down more easily than the first anyhow. And by now the notes he changed no longer aroused such calculations, but flew away like wee little birds. As to whether the labor applied to the acquisition of the money corresponded to the pleasure it bought, that was a consideration that had long since vanished. His farmer's calculation that there was a certain price below which a certain amount of grain could not be sold was also forgotten. The rye, whose price he kept up for such a long time, was finally sold at fifty kopecks a measure cheaper than it had been the month before. Even the calculation that at that rate of expenditure it would be impossible to live for a whole year without getting into debt no longer had any meaning either. Only one thing was called for: to have money in the bank, without asking any questions about where it came from, just so that you always knew you would be able to buy some beef for the following day. And up to now he had always observed this rule: he always had money in the bank. But now the money in the bank had run out, and he had no clear idea where he could get hold of any. When Kitty reminded him of money it upset him for a moment, but he had no time to think about it. He drove along reflecting on Katavasov and his forthcoming meeting with Metrov.

III

ON this visit of his Levin had renewed his former intimacy with his university friend, Professor Katavasov, whom he hadn't seen since his marriage. He liked Katavasov because of the clarity and simplicity of his outlook on life. Levin thought that the clarity of Katavasov's outlook was due to the poverty of his character, whereas Katavasov thought the inconsistency of Levin's thinking was due to his inadequate intellectual discipline; but Katavasov's clarity was agreeable to Levin, and the abundance of Levin's undisciplined ideas was agreeable to Katavasov, and they liked meeting and arguing.

Levin had read Katavasov some parts of his book, and he had liked them. When he happened to meet Levin the day before at a public lecture Katavasov had told him that the celebrated Metrov, whose article Levin had liked so much, was in Moscow, and was extremely interested in what Katavasov had told him about Levin's work, and that Metrov would be at his house the following day at eleven o'clock and would be delighted to meet Levin.

"You're definitely improving, old man, it's a pleasure to see it," said Katavasov, as he came to meet Levin in his little drawing room. "When I heard the bell I thought to myself, 'It's not possible he's on time!' Well, what d'you think of the Montenegrins? Born fighters!"

"Why, what is it?" asked Levin.

Katavasov told him the latest news in a few words, and leading Levin to the study he introduced him to a short, stocky man with a very pleasant-looking face. This was Metrov. For a short time the conversation settled on politics and on the views of the highest Petersburg spheres about the latest incidents. Metrov passed on something he had heard about them from a reliable source as coming from the Tsar and one of the Ministers. But Katavasov, just as reliably, had heard something the Tsar was supposed to have said that was just the opposite. Levin made an effort to imagine a situation in which both remarks might have been made, and the subject was dropped.

"Now Levin here has written what amounts to a book on the natural condition of the laborer in relationship to the land," said Katavasov. "I'm not a specialist, but as a naturalist what I liked about it is that he doesn't take the human race as something independent of zoological laws: on the contrary, he sees it as dependent on its environment, and he looks for the laws of its evolution in this dependence."

"That's very interesting," said Metrov.

"What I actually began writing was a book on agriculture, but since I was dealing with the principal instrument of agriculture, the laborer," said Levin, blushing, "I involuntarily arrived at results that were completely unexpected."

Cautiously, as though feeling out the terrain, Levin began expounding his views. He knew that Metrov had written an article against the generally accepted doctrine in political economy, but he had no idea how much he could rely on his having any sympathy for his own novel views; he could not tell anything from the professor's calm, intelligent face.

"But where do you see the special traits of the Russian laborer?" said Metrov. "In his zoological traits, so to speak, or in his social circumstances?"

Levin saw that the question itself expressed an idea he didn't agree with, but he went on expounding his own thought, which was that the Russian laborer had a view of the land that was completely different from any other people's. To prove this proposition he hastened to add that in his opinion this view of the Russian people was due to an awareness of their mission of settling the vast, unpopulated spaces in the East.

"It's easy to be misled in drawing conclusions about a people's general mission," said Metrov, interrupting Levin. "The laborer's condition will always depend on his relationship to the land and to capital."

And without even allowing Levin to finish expressing his thought, Metrov began explaining to him the special point of his own doctrine.

Just what this special point consisted of Levin did not understand, since he made no effort to: he saw that Metrov, just like everyone else, in spite of the article in which he had refuted the doctrines of the economists, also looked at the position of the Russian laborer from the point of view of capital, wages, and rent. Though he was obliged to acknowledge that in the Eastern part of Russia, which was the greater, rent was still zero, and that for the nine-tenths of the eighty million people in Russia wages constituted no more than subsistence for themselves, and that capital still did not exist except in the form of the most primitive tools, he kept looking at every laborer only from this point of view, even though he disagreed with the economists about a great many things and had a new theory of his own about wages, which was what he was now expounding to Levin.

Levin listened reluctantly, and at first made objections. He wanted to interrupt Metrov in order to state his own idea, which he thought was bound to make any further exposition on the part of Metrov superfluous. Then, when he became convinced that they were both looking at the subject so differently that they would never be able to understand each other, he no longer protested but simply listened. Though he now no longer had the slightest interest in what Metrov was saying, it nevertheless gave him a certain pleasure to listen to him. His self-esteem was flattered that so learned a man was setting forth his views to Levin, so eagerly, so painstakingly, and with such confidence in Levin's knowledge of the subject, that he sometimes indicated a whole aspect of the matter by a mere hint. Levin assumed this was because of his own merit, not knowing that Metrov, after having exhausted the subject with all his own intimates spoke about it with particular relish to every new person he met; for that matter he talked to everyone with relish on this subject he was coping with, which was still unclear to himself.

"I'm afraid we'll be late," said Katavasov, glancing at his watch the moment Metrov had finished his disquisition.

"Yes, there's a meeting today of the Society of Amateurs in memory of Svintich's jubilee," said Katavasov in answer to Levin's inquiry. "Metrov and I were going. I promised to read something about his work in zoology. Come along, it'll be very interesting."

"Yes, it's high time," said Metrov. "Come along with us and from there, if you care to come home with me, I should very much like to hear your work."

"No, really, it's not finished at all. But I'd be delighted to go to the meeting."

"And have you heard?" Katavasov called out from the next

room, where he was putting on a frock coat, "I sent in a special report."

And they started talking about the "university question."

This was a controversy that had created a great stir that winter in Moscow. Three old professors on the council had not accepted the opinion of some younger ones, who had handed in a separate resolution. According to some this resolution was horrifying, according to others it was most simple and fair-minded, and the professors split up into two camps.

The side Katavasov was on saw nothing but vile treachery and deceit in the opposing side, who in their turn accused them of juvenile impudence and lack of respect for the authorities. Though Levin didn't belong to the university he had already heard and talked about this dispute several times during his stay in Moscow and had formed his own view of it. He took part in the conversation that continued in the street until the three of them got to the Old University.

The meeting had already begun. At the cloth-covered table, which Katavasov and Metrov sat down at, six men were sitting, one of whom was reading something aloud, with his head bent over a manuscript. Levin sat down on one of the empty chairs standing around the table and in a whisper asked a student sitting there what was being read. The student gave Levin a look of annoyance and said: "The biography."

Though Levin had no interest in the scientist's biography he could not help listening; he learned a few interesting new facts about the famous scientist's life.

When the reader had finished, the chairman thanked him and read aloud some verses sent to him for this jubilee by Ment the poet, and added a few words of thanks to the poet. Then Katavasov, in his loud, strident voice read off his paper on the scientific works of the man whose jubilee was being celebrated.

When Katavasov finished, Levin looked at his watch and saw it was past one already; he thought he would never have time before the concert to read his work to Metrov, and for that matter he now no longer even wanted to. During the reading he had also been thinking about the talk they had had. It was clear to him now that even if Metrov's ideas might have had some importance, so did his own; these ideas could only be clarified and lead to something if each of them went on working along his own lines, while nothing at all could come of bringing them together. Having made up his mind to decline Metrov's invitation, Levin went over to him at the end of the meeting. Metrov introduced him to the chairman, whom he was chatting with about the political news. Metrov was telling the chairman the same thing he had told Levin, while Levin made the same remarks he had already made that morning, but for the sake of variety also expressed a new opinion of his own, which had just come into his head. Then the university question came up again. Since Levin had heard it all before he hastened to tell Metrov he regretted being unable to take advantage of his invitation, shook hands, and drove off to Prince Lvov's.

IV

LVOV, who was married to Kitty's sister, had spent all his life in the capitals and abroad, where he had also been educated and had been in the diplomatic service.

He had left the diplomatic service the year before, not because of any unpleasantness (he never had any unpleasantness with anyone); he had had himself transferred to the Moscow Court Department in order to give his two boys the best education possible.

In spite of the most acute contrast between their habits and opinions, and the fact that Lvov was older than Levin, they became very intimate that winter and grew very fond of each other.

Lvov was at home, and Levin entered unannounced.

Lvov, wearing an indoor jacket with a belt, and in chamois slippers, was sitting in an easy chair, a pince-nez with blue tinted glasses on his nose, reading a book held on a reading stand before him, with one beautiful hand holding a half-smoked cigar away from his face.

His handsome, sensitive, and still youthful face, to which his curly, glossy silver hair lent a still more aristocratic look, broke into a radiant smile when he saw Levin.

"Wonderful! And I was just going to send you a note. Well, how is Kitty? Sit down over here, it's more comfortable . . ." He got up and moved a rocking chair forward. "Have you read the last circular in the *Journal de St. Pétersbourg*? I think it's first-rate," he said with a slight French accent.

Levin told him what he had heard from Katavasov about what was being said in Petersburg, and after they talked about politics he told him about meeting Metrov and going to the meeting. Lvov was very interested in all this.

"How I envy you your access to all that interesting world of scholarship!" he said. And having started talking he changed at once, as he usually did, into French, in which he felt more at ease. "It's true I have no time; both the service and the time taken up with the children prevent it; besides, I'm not ashamed to say my education is far too deficient."

"I don't think so," said Levin with a smile, feeling touched as he always did by Lvov's low opinion of himself, which was not in the least put on from any desire to appear or even to be modest, but was entirely sincere.

"Yes indeed, now I feel how little education I have. Even for the children's lessons I often have to refresh my memory, or even simply learn things. For it's not enough just to have teachers, you have to have a supervisor, just as you need an overseer on your farm as well as laborers. Look at what I'm reading now—" He showed Levin a copy of Buslaev's *Grammar* which lay on the reading stand. "Misha has to know this, and it's so difficult . . . Here now, explain this to me: he says that . . ."

Levin tried to explain that it was impossible to understand, but had to be memorized, but Lvov didn't agree.

"No, you're just laughing at it!"

"On the contrary, you can't imagine how much I learn about what lies ahead of me whenever I look at you, that is, the children's education."

"Oh, there's nothing to learn from me," said Lvov.

"All I know," said Levin, "is that I've never seen children that were better brought up than yours, and wouldn't want to have children that were any better."

Lvov visibly tried to avoid showing his delight, but his face lit up with a radiant smile.

"If only they turn out better than I! That's all I want. You have no idea of all the difficulties you have with children like mine," he began, "who've been neglected because of our living abroad."

"You'll soon make up for it; they're so gifted. The main thing is their moral training. That's what I learn about by watching your children."

"You say 'moral training.' You can't imagine how hard that is! The moment you thrust down one fault another crops up, and the struggle is on again. If we didn't have the support of religion—you remember we spoke about that—no father could bring up a child by his own strength alone, without its aid."

Their conversation about this, which always interested Levin, was interrupted by the entrance of Lvov's beautiful wife Nataly, who was already dressed to go out.

"Oh, I didn't know you were here," she said, obviously not only not sorry but happy about interrupting the conversation, which she was so familiar with and bored to death by. "Well, how is Kitty? I'm dining with you today. I'll tell you, Arseny," she said, turning to her husband, "you take the carriage . . ."

And husband and wife began discussing how they were going to spend the day. The husband had to go to see someone in the service, and the wife had to go to a concert and then to a public meeting of the South-Eastern Committee, so there was a great deal that had to be decided on and considered. As one of the family Levin had to take part in all this scheduling. It was decided that Levin would go with Nataly to the concert and to the public meeting, and from there the carriage would be sent to the office to fetch Arseny, who would then call for her and take her on to Kitty's, or if he hadn't finished his business he would send the carriage back and Levin would take Nataly.

"He spoils me, you know," Lvov said to his wife. "He assures me that our children are wonderful, when all the while I know there's so much that's wrong with them."

"Arseny goes to extremes, I always say," said his wife. "If you're going to look for perfection you'll never be satisfied. What Papa says is perfectly true: when we were being brought up they went to one extreme—the children were kept in the attic while the parents lived in the best rooms; now it's just the reverse—the parents are in the lumber room and the children are in the best rooms. Nowadays the parents are not supposed to live at all—everything's for the children."

"Why not, if that's pleasanter?" said Lvov, with his beautiful smile, touching her hand. "Anyone who didn't know you would think you're not a mother but a stepmother."

"No, extremes are no good in anything," said Nataly calmly, putting his paper knife in a particular place on the table.

"Ah! Come in here, you paragons!" said Lvov to two handsome boys as they came in, bowed to Levin, and went over to their father, obviously wishing to ask him something.

Levin wanted to talk to them, and listen to what they said to their father, but Nataly started talking to him, then Makhotin, a colleague of Lvov's, came into the room, in Court uniform, to go off to meet someone together with Lvov, and then an interminable discussion began about Herzegovina, Princess Korzinsky, the Duma, and Countess Apraxin's sudden death.

Levin had forgotten what he had been told to do; he recalled it only when he was already on his way out into the hall.

"Oh—Kitty asked me to talk to you about Oblonsky," he said, when Lvov was seeing him and Nataly out; he paused on the staircase landing.

"Yes, yes, *maman* wants us, the brothers-in-law, to pounce on him," Lvov said, blushing and smiling. "But why should I be the one?"

"Then I'll do the pouncing," said Nataly with a smile, standing there in her white fur-lined cloak waiting for them to stop talking. "Come along now!"

## V

TWO very interesting pieces were given at the matinee concert.

One was a fantasia, *King Lear on the Heath*; the other was a quartet dedicated to the memory of Bach. Both pieces were new, and in the new style, and Levin wanted to form an opinion of his own about them. After seeing his sister-in-law to her seat he took up his stand by a pillar and made up his mind to listen as attentively and conscientiously as possible. He tried not to be distracted or spoil his impression by watching the white-tied conductor's gesticulations, that always distract one's attention so from the music, or the ladies with their hats, who had tied their ribbons over their ears so carefully for the concert, or all those faces that were preoccupied either by nothing at all or by the most variegated interests, with the sole exception of the music. He tried to avoid encounters with connoisseurs of music and with chatterboxes; he stood there looking down in front of him, listening.

But the longer he listened to the *King Lear* fantasia the more incapable he felt of forming any definite opinion about it. It seemed to be on the verge of beginning over and over again, as though a musical expression of emotion were gathering its forces, but then it would immediately break up into fragments of musical themes expressing some other emotion, and sometimes simply into nothing but the composer's whims —unrelated but extraordinarily complicated sounds. But even the fragments of these musical themes, though some were good, were disagreeable, since they were completely unexpected and unprepared for. Merriment, sadness, despair, tenderness, and triumph all appeared without cause, like the emotions of a madman. And like a madman's these emotions passed away equally unexpectedly.

Throughout the performance Levin felt like a deaf man watching people dance. He was in total perplexity when the piece came to an end; he felt exhausted by the unrewarded strain on his attention. Loud applause was heard on all sides. Everyone got up and began walking about and talking. Wishing to clarify his own perplexity through the impressions of others, Levin started walking about looking for the experts, and was pleased to see one of the famous ones talking to Pestsov, whom he knew.

"Wonderful!" Pestsov was saying in his deep bass. "How d'you do, Levin. What was particularly shapely and sculptural, so to speak, and rich in color, was the passage where you feel the approach of Cordelia, where the woman, the eternal feminine, enters upon a struggle with fate. Don't you think so?"

"Well, just what has it to do with Cordelia?" asked Levin timidly; he had quite forgotten that the fantasia was supposed to represent King Lear on the heath.

"Cordelia comes in, right here!" said Pestsov, tapping his fingers on the glossy program he was holding and handing it to Levin.

It was only then that Levin recalled the title of the fantasia and hastened to read the Russian translation of Shakespeare's verses that were printed on the back of the program.

"It's impossible to follow it without that," said Pestsov, turning to Levin, since the man he had been talking to had gone away and he had no one else left.

During the intermission Levin and Pestsov got into an argument about the merits and shortcomings of Wagnerian music. Levin maintained that the mistake of Wagner and all his followers lay in trying to carry music into the domain of an alien art, the same mistake poetry made in describing the features of a face, which ought to be done by painting; as an example of this kind of error he mentioned a sculptor who had the notion of carving in marble the phantasms of poetic forms rising up round the figure of a poet on a pedestal. "These phantasms of the sculptor have so little to do with phantasms they even cling to the ladder," said Levin.

He liked this phrase, but he didn't know whether he had used the same phrase before, to Pestsov himself, in fact, and he got embarrassed as soon as he said it.

Pestsov, on the other hand, argued that all art was one, and that it could only achieve its loftiest manifestation in a fusion of all genres.

Levin was incapable of listening to the second part of the concert. Pestsov, who was standing beside him, kept talking to him practically the whole time, condemning the piece because of its superfluous, affected pretense of simplicity, and comparing it with the simplicity of the pre-Raphaelites in painting. While going out Levin met a great many other people he knew whom he started to talk to about politics, music, and mutual acquaintances. Among others he met Count Bohl; he had forgotten all about calling on him.

"Well, why not go along now?" said Nataly, when he told her this. "Maybe they won't receive you, then you'll be able to call for me at the meeting. You have plenty of time."

## VI

PERHAPS they're not receiving today?" said Levin as he entered the hall of the Bohl house.

"Yes, they are, sir. Please come in," said the hall porter, firmly removing his fur coat.

Oh what a nuisance! thought Levin, pulling off a glove with a sigh and smoothing his hat. What's the point of my going in? And what am I going to talk about with them?

As he entered the first drawing room he met Countess Bohl in the doorway; looking worried and severe, she was giving some orders to a servant. When she saw Levin she smiled and asked him into the adjoining room, the small drawing room, where voices could be heard. The Countess's two daughters and a Moscow colonel whom Levin knew were sitting there in easy chairs. Levin went up to them, greeted them, and sat down beside the sofa, holding his hat on his lap.

"How is your wife? Were you at the concert? We couldn't go. Mama had to attend the funeral."

"Yes, I heard . . . How sudden it was," said Levin.

The Countess came in, sat down on the sofa and also asked about his wife and about the concert.

Levin answered, repeating his remark about the suddenness of Countess Apraxin's death.

"But her health was always delicate."

"Were you at the opera last night?"

"Yes, I was."

"Lucca was very good."

"Yes, very good," he said, and since he didn't care at all what they might think of him he began repeating what he had heard hundreds of times about the singer's extraordinary talent. Countess Bohl pretended to be listening. Then, when he had said enough and fell silent, the colonel, who had been silent until then, began speaking. The colonel also talked about the opera, and about the illumination of the Opera House. Finally, after making a remark about the wild party being planned at Tyurin's, the colonel laughed, got up noisily, and left. Levin also got up, but he noticed by the look on the Countess's face that it wasn't time yet for him to leave; he had to stay another couple of minutes. He sat down.

But since he kept thinking how silly it all was he couldn't think of anything to talk about and said nothing.

"Are you going to the public meeting? They say it will be very interesting," the Countess began.

"No, but I promised my sister-in-law I would call for her," said Levin.

There was a pause; mother and daughter exchanged glances.

Well, I suppose it's time now, thought Levin and got up. The ladies shook his hand and asked him to give his wife their love.

The hall porter asked him, as he helped him on with his coat: "Where are you stopping, sir?" and immediately entered his address in a large, well-bound book.

Of course it doesn't matter to me, all the same it's embarrassing, it's so frightfully stupid, thought Levin, comforting himself with the reflection that everyone did it, and he drove off to the public meeting of the Committee, where he was to pick up his sister-in-law and go home with her.

There were a great many people at the public meeting of the Committee, and almost the whole of society. Levin came in time to hear a report, which everyone said was very interesting. After the report was read people began moving about; Levin met Sviyazhsky, who asked him to be sure and come that evening to a meeting of the Agricultural Society where an important lecture was to be given, Oblonsky who had only just come from the races, and a great many other people he knew; Levin again expressed and listened to various opinions about the meeting, the new fantasia, and some trial. But doubtless because of the mental exhaustion he was beginning to feel, he made a slip in speaking about the trial; he recalled it often afterward with irritation. In speaking about the punishment in store for some foreigner who was on trial in Russia, and about the injustice of punishing him by deportation, Levin repeated what he had heard said the day before by someone he knew.

"I think deporting him would be just the same as punishing a pike by throwing it into the water," Levin said; he only remembered later that this thought, which he was apparently passing off as his own, and which he had heard from his acquaintance, came from one of Krylov's fables, and that his acquaintance had picked it up from a newspaper article.

After taking his sister-in-law home with him, and finding Kitty cheerful and perfectly all right, Levin left for the club.

## VII

He arrived there at just the right moment. Members and visitors were driving up at the same time. Levin had not been to the club for a long time, not since he had lived in Moscow and moved about in society after leaving the university. Though he remembered the club and all its external details, he had completely forgotten the impression it used to make on him. But the moment he entered the semicircular courtyard and stepped out of the sleigh onto the front steps, where a hall porter in a shoulder band met him and opened the door for him with a bow; the moment he saw in the hall the galoshes and fur coats of the members who realized it was less trouble to take off their galoshes below than to wear them upstairs; the moment he heard the mysterious ring of the bell announcing him and saw, as he mounted the shallow, carpeted steps, the statue on the landing and a third aging hall porter in club livery whom he knew in the upper doorway, examining each guest as he opened the door for him with unhurried regularity, Levin felt himself enveloped by the old atmosphere of the club, an atmosphere of repose, comfort, and decorum.

"Your hat, sir," said the hall porter to Levin, who had forgotten the club rule about leaving hats in the hall. "We haven't seen you for a long time. The Prince entered your name yesterday. Prince Oblonsky hasn't arrived yet."

The hall porter not only knew Levin, he knew all his connections and relatives as well, and at once mentioned some of his friends.

Passing through the outer hall, divided up by screens, then a partitioned room on the right in which there was a fruit buffet, Levin overtook an old man walking slowly along and entered the noisy, crowded dining room.

He walked past the tables, nearly all taken already, surveying the guests. Here and there he saw all sorts of acquaintances, both old and young, intimates and ones he scarcely knew. There was not a single angry or worried face among them. It seemed as though they had all left their cares and worries behind in the hall together with their hats and were preparing to enjoy the material blessings of life at their leisure. Sviyazhsky was there, and Shcherbatsky, and Nevedovsky, and the old Prince, and Vronsky, and Koznyshov.

"Aha! Why are you so late?" said the old Prince to him with a smile, holding out his hand over his shoulder. "How's Kitty?" he added, smoothing out the table napkin which he had tucked in behind a button of his waistcoat.

"Oh, all right; the three of them are dining at home together."

"Ah—Alines-Nadines! Well, there's no room here. Go over to that table and get yourself a seat, quickly now!" said the Prince, and turning away he carefully took a plate of fish soup.

"Levin! Over here!" a good-natured voice called out to him a little way off: it was Turovtsyn. He was sitting with a young officer; there were two chairs tilted against the table. Levin happily went over to him. He had always liked this good-natured playboy Turovtsyn—he was associated with the memory of his proposal—but today, after all the strain of the intellectual conversations he had been through, Turovtsyn's good-natured face was especially pleasant.

"That's for you and Oblonsky. He'll be here any minute."

The officer, with gay, constantly laughing eyes, who held himself very erect, was Gagin, from Petersburg. Turovtsyn introduced him.

"Oblonsky's always late."

"Ah, there he is!"

"Did you just get here?" said Oblonsky, hurrying over. "How d'you do? Had some vodka? Come along then."

Levin got up and went over with him to a large table spread with various kinds of vodka and a great variety of appetizers. It would have seemed that out of the couple of dozen kinds of appetizer something could have been picked out to suit anyone's taste, but Oblonsky ordered something special, and one of the liveried footmen standing about brought it at once. They drank a glass of vodka each and went back to the table.

Gagin was brought a bottle of champagne immediately, while they were still at their soup, and he had the four glasses filled. Levin did not refuse the wine that was offered, and he ordered another bottle. He was hungry, and ate and drank with great pleasure, and with still greater pleasure took part in the gay, simple talk at the table. Gagin, lowering his voice, told a new Petersburg anecdote, and the anecdote, though indecent and silly, was so funny that Levin burst out laughing so loud people turned round to look at him.

"That's the same story as that other one, 'But that's just what I can't stand!' D'you know it?" said Oblonsky. "That's delicious! Another bottle!" he said to the waiter, and he began telling it.

"With Peter Ilyich Vinovsky's compliments," interrupted an old waiter, bringing over two delicate glasses of still sparkling champagne on a tray, and addressing Oblonsky and Levin. Oblonsky took a glass, and looking over at a bald man with a ginger mustache at the other end of their table, he smilingly nodded his head at him.

"Who's that?" asked Levin.

"You met him at my place once, don't you remember? A very nice chap."

Levin did the same as Oblonsky and took the glass.

Oblonsky's anecdote was very amusing, too. Levin told an anecdote of his own, which also went down. Then they started talking about horses, about the races that day, and how smartly Vronsky's Atlas had won the first prize. Levin scarcely noticed how the time passed.

"Ah—there they are!" exclaimed Oblonsky just as they were already finishing; he leaned back in his chair and stretched his hand out toward Vronsky, who was coming over to them together with a tall colonel of the Guards. Vronsky's face also radiated the general merry good-nature of the club. He gaily leaned his elbow on Oblonsky's shoulder, whispering something to him, and with the same gay smile stretched his hand out to Levin.

"Delighted to see you again," he said to him. "I was looking for you that time after the elections but I was told you'd left."

"Yes, I left that same day. I've just been hearing about your horse. Congratulations!" said Levin. "Very good going."

"But you keep race horses too, don't you?"

"No, that was my father; but I remember them, so I know a little about them."

"Where did you dine?" asked Oblonsky.

"We were at the second table, behind the pillars."

"He's been getting his congratulations," said the tall colonel. "It's his second Imperial prize; if only I had the luck at cards he has with horses! . . . but why waste the golden moments— I'm off to the 'inferno,'" said the colonel and walked away.

"That's Yashvin," Vronsky said in reply to Turovtsyn's question, and sat down in a vacant chair beside them. After drinking a glass of champagne they offered him he ordered a bottle. Whether it was the influence of the club atmosphere or the wine he had drunk, Levin started chatting away with Vronsky about the best breeds of cattle and was very pleased at not having the slightest feeling of hostility toward him. Among other things he even told him he had heard from his wife that she had run into him at Princess Mary's.

"Oh, Princess Mary—isn't she delightful!" said Oblonsky, and told an anecdote about her that made them all laugh. Vronsky in particular burst into such good-natured laughter that Levin felt completely reconciled to him.

"Well, have we finished?" said Oblonsky, getting up with a smile. "Then let's go!"

## VIII

On leaving the table Levin, feeling that his arms were swinging with unusual regularity and ease as he walked along, went off with Gagin through the high-ceilinged rooms toward the billiard room. As they crossed the big hall he met his father-in-law.

"Well, how d'you like our temple of idleness?" said the Prince, taking him by the arm. "Come along, let's walk about."

"Yes, that's just what I feel like, taking a walk and looking round. It's all very interesting."

"Yes, you must find it so, but my own interest is different

from yours. Just take a look at these little old men," he said, indicating a club member with bent back and hanging lower lip, who was coming toward them, scarcely able to shuffle along in his soft boots, "you'd imagine they were born *shlyupiks*."

"*Shlyupiks*? What's that?"

"You don't even know what the word means! That's a club expression. You know the game of egg-rolling? Well, when an egg's been rolled round a great deal it becomes a *shlyupik*. That's how it is with us: you keep coming and coming to the club and you wind up a *shlyupik*. Yes, go on, laugh, but we're already looking out for the time we'll be one of the *shlyupiks* ourselves. D'you know Prince Chechensky?" asked the Prince; Levin saw by his expression that he was preparing to tell some funny story.

"No, I don't."

"What, really not? I mean Prince Chechensky, he's famous. Well, never mind; anyhow, he was always playing billiards. Only three years ago he was still not a *shlyupik;* he was putting on a great show, calling everyone else a *shlyupik* himself. Well, one day he came in and our hall porter—d'you know him, Vasili? You know, that fat one, he's a great wit. Prince Chechensky asked him, 'Well, Vasili, who's here now? Any *shlyupiks* around?' And Vasili said, 'Why yes, sir, you're the third.' Yes, my boy, that's how it is!"

Chatting and exchanging greetings with acquaintances they ran into, Levin and the Prince passed through all the rooms: the big one, where the card tables were already set up and habitual partners were playing for small stakes; the sofa room, where people were playing chess, and Koznyshov sat chatting with someone; the billiard room, where a merry party including Gagin were drinking champagne by a sofa in a recess; they also glanced into the "inferno," where a great many betters were crowding round a table Yashvin had already taken his seat at. Trying not to make any noise, they also went into the dim reading room, where two people were sitting under the shaded lamps, a young man with an angry expression, turning over one newspaper after the other, and a bald-headed general, sunk in a book. They also went into the room the Prince called the "intellectual" room. Three men were having a heated discussion there about the latest political news.

"If you please, Prince, we're all ready," said one of his partners who had been looking for him, and the Prince went off. Levin sat down for a while and listened, but when he recalled all the conversations he'd heard that day he suddenly felt frightfully bored. He hastily got up and went off to look for Oblonsky and Turovtsyn; they were always cheerful to be with.

Turovtsyn, with a tankard of something to drink, was sitting on the high sofa in the billiard room; Oblonsky and Vronsky were standing by the door in the far corner of the room talking about something.

"It's not so much that she's bored, it's the vagueness, the indecisiveness of her situation . . ." Levin overheard, and was about to beat a hasty retreat when Oblonsky called him over.

"Levin!" Oblonsky called out, and Levin noticed that his eyes did not have tears in them, but were moist, as they always were when he had either been drinking or was moved. Just now it was both. "Levin, don't go," he said, clasping him tightly by the elbow, evidently determined not to let him go for anything.

"This is a real friend of mine, perhaps my best friend," he said to Vronsky. "And you've also become nearer and dearer to me. And I want you both to be close friends, and I know you will because you're both good fellows."

"Well, there's nothing for it then but to kiss and be friends," said Vronsky, joking good-naturedly as he held out his hand.

Levin swiftly held out his own and gave it a powerful squeeze.

"I'm very, very glad, " said Levin, pressing Vronsky's hand.

"Waiter—a bottle of champagne!" Oblonsky called out.

"I'm very glad, too," said Vronsky.

But in spite of Oblonsky's desire, and in spite of their own mutual desire, they had nothing to say to each other, and they both felt it.

"D'you know he doesn't know Anna?" Oblonsky said to Vronsky. "And I'm determined to take him to see her. Levin —let's go there!"

"Really?" said Vronsky. "She'll be delighted. I would go home right away, but I'm anxious about Yashvin; I'd like to stay here till he finishes."

"Oh, is he doing badly?"

"He keeps on losing; I'm the only one who can hold him back."

"Well, what about a game of pyramids? D'you want to

play, Levin? Wonderful!" said Oblonsky. "Set the balls for pyramids," he said, turning to the billiard marker.

"They've been ready a long time," replied the marker, who had already set out the balls in a triangle and was rolling the red one back and forth to kill time.

"Let's begin then."

After the game Vronsky and Levin sat down at Gagin's table; at Oblonsky's suggestion Levin began betting on aces. Vronsky sat beside the table, surrounded by acquaintances who kept constantly coming over to him, or else he would walk over to the "inferno" to keep an eye on Yashvin. Levin had an agreeable feeling of relief from his intellectual fatigue of the morning. He was glad the hostility between Vronsky and himself had ended, and the feeling of tranquillity, decorum, and well-being never left him.

When the game was over Oblonsky took Levin by the arm. "Well, let's go to see Anna. Right now, eh? She's at home. I promised her a long time ago to bring you along. Where were you thinking of going tonight?"

"Nowhere in particular. I promised Sviyazhsky to go to a meeting of the Agricultural Society, but I'll go with you if you like," said Levin.

"Splendid! Let's go then! See whether my carriage has come," said Oblonsky to a footman.

Levin went over to the table, paid the forty rubles he had lost betting on aces, paid his club bill to an old footman standing by the door who in some mysterious way knew what it amounted to, and swinging his arms in a peculiar way he walked through all the rooms to the exit.

IX

THE Oblonsky carriage!" shouted the hall porter in an irascible bass. The carriage drew up and they both got in. It was only for the first few moments, while they were leaving the courtyard of the club, that Levin retained his feeling of the calm, the well-being and the unassailable decorum of his club surroundings; but the moment the carriage had passed out into the street and he felt it jolting along the uneven road, heard the angry shout of a sleigh driver coming toward them, saw in the dim light the red signboards of a tavern and of a small shop, this feeling was shattered, and he began reflecting on his behavior and wondering whether he was doing a good thing in going to see Anna. What would Kitty say? But Oblonsky gave him no time for reflection; as though guessing his doubts he dissipated them.

"I'm so glad you're going to meet her," he said. "You know Dolly's wanted it for a long time. Lvov's called on her too and goes to see her. Even though she's my own sister," Oblonsky continued, "I must say she's a remarkable woman. You'll see. She's in a very difficult situation, especially just now."

"Why just now?"

"We're negotiating with her husband about a divorce. He's willing, but there are some difficulties concerning their son, and the whole thing, which ought to have been finished a long time ago, has been dragging on now for three months. The moment she gets the divorce she'll marry Vronsky. How stupid that old ceremony is—walking round and round singing *Rejoice, O Isaiah!* which no one believes in and which stands in the way of people's happiness!" Oblonsky interjected. "And then their situation will be definite, like yours or mine."

"But what's the difficulty?" asked Levin.

"Oh, it's a long and boring story! All that sort of thing is so vague in this country. But the point is this—for three months she's been waiting for this divorce here in Moscow, where everyone knows him and her; she doesn't see any of the women except for Dolly, because, you understand, she doesn't want anyone to call on her out of pity; even that fool Princess Barbara has left her, she thinks it's improper. Well, any other woman in a situation like that wouldn't be able to have found any inner resources. But you'll see how she's arranged her life, how calm and dignified she is. To the left, in that side street opposite the church!" Oblonsky shouted, leaning through the window of the carriage. "Phew, how hot it is!" he exclaimed, throwing his already unbuttoned overcoat still further open in spite of the twenty-seven-degree cold.

"But she has a daughter, doesn't she? She's probably busy with her?" said Levin.

"I suppose you imagine every woman is just a female, a brood hen," said Oblonsky. "If she's busy at all it could be only with children! No, she's bringing her up splendidly, but you don't hear anything about it. She's busy primarily with her writing. I can see an ironical smile on your face already, but it's no use. She's writing a children's book, she doesn't speak about it to anyone but she's read it to me and I showed the manuscript to Vorkuyev, you know, the publisher—I think he's a writer himself. He knows what he's talking about and he says it's a remarkable piece of work. But you may think she's a female author? Not in the least. Above all she's a woman with a heart—you'll see! She has a little English girl now, and a whole family she's interested in."

"Why, is she some kind of a philanthropist?"

"There you are—always looking for trouble! It's nothing to do with philanthropy, it's just her warm heart. They had—I mean Vronsky had an English trainer, an expert in his profession but a drunkard. He soaked himself in drink, got delirium tremens, and the family's deserted. She saw them, helped them out, got more and more involved, and now she's taking care of the entire family; but she doesn't do it patronizingly, just with money; she's coaching the boys in Russian for high school, and she's taken the girl into the house. But you'll see her in a minute . . ."

The carriage drove into the courtyard and Oblonsky gave a loud ring at the entrance, in front of which there was a sleigh standing.

Without asking the porter who opened the door whether they were in, Oblonsky went into the hall. Levin followed him, his doubts as to whether he was doing right or wrong constantly increasing.

Glancing in the mirror Levin noticed he was red in the face; but he was sure he wasn't drunk and he followed Oblonsky up the carpeted steps. Upstairs Oblonsky asked the footman, who bowed to him as a familiar of the house, who was with Madame, and was told it was Mr. Vorkuyev.

"Where are they?"

"In the study, sir."

Passing through a small dining room with dark-paneled walls, Oblonsky and Levin crossed a soft carpet into the study, dimly lighted by a single lamp with a large dark shade. Another lamp on the wall, with a reflector, lighted up a full-length portrait of a woman Levin found himself involuntarily staring at. It was the portrait of Anna that had been done in Italy by Mikhailov. While Oblonsky went behind a trellis screen, and the voice of a man who had been saying something fell silent, Levin gazed at the portrait, which in the bright illumination seemed to step out of the frame, and could not tear himself away. He even forgot where he was; without listening to what was being said he stared fixedly at the wonderful portrait. It was not a picture—it was a living, enchanting woman with black curly hair, bare shoulders and arms, and a dreamy half-smile on softly downy lips, who was looking tenderly and triumphantly at him with eyes that disturbed him. The only thing that showed she was not living was that she was more beautiful than a living woman can be.

"I'm very pleased," he suddenly heard a voice beside him obviously addressed to him, the voice of the same woman he had been admiring in the portrait. Anna had come out toward him from behind the trellis screen, and in the dim light of the study Levin saw the same woman of the portrait in a dark dress of varying shades of blue, not in the same posture, nor with the same expression, but on the same pinnacle of beauty as that on which the artist had caught her in the portrait. She was less dazzling in reality, but to make up for that there was something novel and attractive about the living woman that was not in the portrait.

x

SHE had risen to meet him, without concealing her pleasure at his being there. The serenity with which she held out her small, vigorous hand to him, introduced him to Vorkuyev, and indicated a pretty red-haired little girl sitting at her work, whom she called her ward, showed the manners of a woman of the world, always serene and natural, which Levin was at home with and liked.

"Very, very pleased," she repeated, and on her lips these simple words took on some special significance for Levin. "I've known you a long time, and have liked you both because of your friendship with Stiva and because of your wife . . . I knew her for a very short time, but she left on me the impression of a lovely flower—just that, a flower. And here she is, soon to become a mother!"

She spoke easily and without haste, shifting her glance now and then from Levin to her brother, and Levin felt he had made a good impression on her, and he immediately felt at ease with her, as simple and happy as though he had known her since childhood.

"That's just why we came to Alexis's study, to smoke," she said in answer to Oblonsky's question whether it was all right to smoke; then, glancing at Levin, instead of asking whether he smoked she moved over a tortoise-shell cigar case and took out a cigarette.

"How are you feeling today?" her brother asked.

"All right. Nerves as usual."

"It's wonderful, isn't it?" said Oblonsky, noticing that Levin kept looking at the portrait.

"I've never seen a better portrait."

"A wonderful likeness, too, isn't it?" said Vorkuyev.

Levin looked from the portrait to the original. A peculiar sheen lit up Anna's face as she felt his eyes on her. Levin blushed and to his embarrassment started to ask whether she had seen Dolly recently, but just then Anna started saying something herself:

"Vorkuyev and I were just talking about Vashchenkov's latest pictures. Have you seen them?"

"Why, yes, I have," Levin replied.

"But I beg your pardon, I interrupted you—you were saying?"

Levin asked whether she had seen Dolly lately.

"She was here yesterday; she's very angry with Grisha's high school. It seems the Latin teacher's been unfair to him."

"Yes, I've seen his pictures, I didn't like them very much," said Levin, returning to the topic she had touched on.

This time Levin did not speak at all in the routine way he had that morning. Every word they said to each other took on a special meaning. It was a pleasure to talk to her, and an even greater pleasure to listen to her.

Anna not only talked naturally and intelligently, but intelligently and offhandedly, attaching no value to her own ideas but great value to those of the person she talked to.

The conversation turned on the new tendency in art, and the new illustrations of the Bible by a French artist. Vorkuyev accused the artist of realism carried to the point of coarseness. Levin said the French had carried conventionality in art further than anyone else, which was why they saw some special merit in a reversion to realism. They saw poetry in the mere fact of not lying.

No clever thing ever said by Levin before gave him so much pleasure as this. Anna's face grew all radiant as she suddenly appreciated this notion. She broke into a laugh.

"I'm laughing the way one laughs at seeing a very good likeness," she said. "What you just said completely sums up French art today, both painting and for that matter literature —Zola, Daudet. But perhaps that's how it always is—conceptions are built up out of contrived, conventional figures, and then, after all the possible combinations have been made the contrived figures become tiresome and people begin devising more natural, realistic figures."

"Now that's it exactly!" said Vorkuyev.

"So you've been to the club?" she said, turning to her brother.

Yes, yes, now there's a woman! thought Levin; forgetting himself completely he gazed insistently into her lovely, mobile face, which was now abruptly transformed. Levin couldn't hear what she was saying as she leaned toward her brother, but he was struck by the change in her expression. Her face, which had been so beautiful before in its tranquillity, suddenly expressed anger, pride, and a strange curiosity. But it only lasted a moment. She screwed up her eyes as though she were recalling something.

"Well, but all that's of no interest to anyone," she said, and turned to the little English girl: "Please order tea in the drawing room."

The little girl got up and went out.

"Well, did she pass her examination?" Oblonsky asked.

"Splendidly! She's a very gifted child, with a sweet nature."

"It'll all end by your loving her more than your own."

"That's how a man talks. In love there's no such thing as greater or less. I love my daughter with one kind of love, her with another."

"I was just telling Madame," said Vorkuyev, "that if she devoted only a hundredth part of the energy she gives to this little English girl to the general cause of Russian children's education she would be performing a great and useful work."

"Yes, but say whatever you like, I can't do it. Count Vronsky used to urge me." (As she pronounced his name she looked at Levin in timid inquiry; involuntarily he answered her with a look of respectful reassurance.) "He urged me to take an interest in the village school. I went there several times. They're all very sweet but I couldn't get attached to the work. You talk about energy: energy is founded on love. And love can't just be picked up anywhere; it can't be forced. I've become fond of that little girl, I don't know why myself."

And she glanced at Levin again. Both her smile and her look told him she was speaking for him alone, had a high regard for his opinion and at the same time knew in advance that they would understand each other.

"I quite understand," replied Levin. "It's impossible to put

your heart into a school or into any institutions of that kind
in general; I think that's just why these philanthropic institutions always give such poor results."

After a pause she smiled. "Yes, yes," she agreed. "I could
never do it. My heart isn't big enough to get attached to an
entire orphanage full of horrible little girls. I've never been
able to manage it. There are so many women who've bet-
tered themselves socially that way. And now more than
ever, I can't do it." With a sudden frown (Levin understood
that she was frowning at herself for talking about herself)
she changed the subject. "I've heard you called a bad citizen,"
she said to Levin, "and I've defended you as best I could."

"But how were you able to defend me?"

"It depended on the kind of attack. But won't you come
and have some tea?" She rose and picked up a morocco-
bound book.

"Do let me have it, Madame," said Vorkuyev, indicating
the book. "It's well worth it."

"Oh no—it's so unfinished."

"I told him about it," Oblonsky said to his sister, nodding
at Levin.

"You shouldn't have. My writing is like those little carv-
ings and baskets Lisa Merkalov used to sell me, which were
made in prison. She used to be chairman of the prison section
in that Society," she said to Levin. "Those poor wretches
achieved miracles of patience."

And Levin saw still another trait in this woman he liked
so much. In addition to her mind, grace, and beauty, she
was also honest. She had no desire to hide from him the full
hardship of her situation. After she said this she sighed; her
face suddenly took on a look of sternness, as though turned
to stone. With such an expression she was even lovelier than
before; but it was a new expression—it was outside the domain of the expressions radiating and creating happiness,
which had been caught by the artist in the portrait. Levin
looked at the portrait once again, then back at her as she
took her brother's arm and passed through the high doorway
with him: he felt a tenderness and pity for her that surprised
himself.

She asked Levin and Vorkuyev to go on ahead into the
drawing room, while she stayed behind to talk something

over with her brother. The divorce? Vronsky? What he had
been doing in the club? Me? thought Levin. He was so excited about what she might be saying to Oblonsky that he
scarcely heard what Vorkuyev was telling him about the
merits of the children's book she had written.

Over tea the same agreeable conversation, full of meat,
was continued. Not only was there never a moment it was
necessary to hunt for a topic; on the contrary, there was a
feeling that one didn't have enough time to say what one
wanted to oneself, and one gladly held back to hear what the
other was saying. And everything that was said, not only by
her but by Vorkuyev and Oblonsky, everything took on a
special importance, as it seemed to Levin, thanks to her attentiveness and her comments.

While following the absorbing conversation Levin kept constantly admiring her—her beauty, her intelligence, her cultivation, and at the same time her simplicity and straight-
forwardness. As he listened and spoke he kept thinking about
her and her inner life, trying to guess her feelings. After having condemned her so severely before he now, by some
peculiar chain of thought, tried to vindicate her, while at the
same time pitying her and fearing that Vronsky did not understand her fully. Toward eleven o'clock, when Oblonsky
got up to go (Vorkuyev had already left) Levin felt he had
only just arrived. Regretfully he got up too.

"Good-by," she said, holding him by the hand and looking into his face with an expression that drew him to her,
"I'm very pleased the ice is broken."

She let go his hand and screwed up her eyes. "Tell your
wife that I'm as fond of her as before, and that if she cannot
forgive me my situation then I wish her never to forgive me.
To forgive she would have had to have gone through everything I've gone through, and may God spare her that."

"Without fail, yes, I'll tell her . . ." said Levin blushing.

## XI

WHAT a wonderful, sweet, pathetic woman, thought Levin
as he went out into the frosty air with Oblonsky.

"Well? I told you," said Oblonsky, seeing that Levin had
been completely conquered.

"Yes," replied Levin thoughtfully. "An extraordinary

woman! It's not only her mind; she has a wonderfully warm heart. I'm terribly sorry for her!"

"Everything will soon be settled now, God willing. Next time don't judge things beforehand," said Oblonsky, opening the carriage door. "Good-by, we're not going the same way."

Thinking of Anna incessantly, and of the simplest things they had said to each other, while recalling every detail of the expression on her face and entering more and more into her situation and feeling more and more sorry for her, Levin reached home.

At home Kuzma told him that Kitty was well, that her sisters had been gone just a little while; and he gave him two letters. Levin read them at once, there in the hall, in order not to be distracted later. One was from Sokolov, his foreman. Sokolov wrote that it was impossible to sell the wheat, people were offering only five-and-a-half rubles a measure, and there was no way of getting any more money. The other letter was from his sister: she was reproaching him because her business had not been settled yet.

Well, we'll sell it at five-and-a-half then, if they're not giving any more, thought Levin, with extraordinary facility deciding the first question, which had seemed so difficult to him before. Amazing, how your time is taken up here, he thought about the second letter. He felt guilty about his sister for still not having accomplished what she had asked him to do. I didn't go to the court again today, but really there was no time at all, he thought.

Having decided that he would do it without fail the following day, he went to see his wife. On his way he quickly reviewed in his mind the whole of the past day. All the day's events had been conversations, conversations he had listened to and taken part in. They had all been about subjects that if he had been alone in the country he would have paid no attention to, but here in town were very interesting. And the conversations had all been good; there were only two points he felt uncomfortable about. One was what he had said about the pike, the other was that there was something *not quite right* about the tender pity he felt for Anna.

Levin found his wife sad and depressed. The dinner of the three sisters would have gone off very well, but then they had waited and waited for him, had all grown bored, the other sisters had gone away and she had been left alone.

"And what did you do?" she asked, looking into his eyes,

which had a peculiarly suspicious glitter. But in order not to prevent his telling her everything she concealed her alertness and with an encouraging smile listened to his story of how he had spent the evening.

"Well, I was very glad to meet Vronsky. I felt very simple and easy with him. Now, you understand I'm going to try to avoid meeting him again, but at least that awkwardness is over with . . ." he said, and recalling that while "trying to avoid meeting him again" he had instantly gone to see Anna, he blushed. "There, we talk about the peasants drinking; I don't know who does more drinking, the peasants or ourselves. At least the peasants drink on holidays, but—"

But Kitty had no interest in a discussion of the peasants' drinking. She had noticed that he had blushed and wanted to know why.

"Well, and then where did you go?"

"Stiva absolutely begged me to go and see Anna."

And on saying this Levin blushed even more, and his doubts about whether he had been right or wrong in going to see Anna were settled once and for all. He knew now he shouldn't have done it.

At the mention of Anna's name Kitty's eyes opened wide in an odd way and flashed, but by making an effort to control herself she concealed her agitation and deceived him.

"Ah!" was all she said.

"I'm sure you won't be angry I went. Stiva asked me to and Dolly wanted it," Levin went on.

"Oh no," she said, but in her eyes he could see the effort she was making, which boded him no good.

"She's a very sweet, very, very pathetic, and good woman," he said, telling her about Anna, her interests, and the message she had sent.

"Yes, of course, she's very pathetic," said Kitty, when he had finished. "Whom were your letters from?"

He told her, and taken in by her calm manner he went off to undress.

When he came back he found Kitty still sitting in the same armchair. When he came over to her she looked up at him and burst into sobs.

"What is it? What's the matter?" he asked, knowing perfectly well what it was.

"You've fallen in love with that horrid woman, she's bewitched you! I could see it in your eyes. Yes, yes! How will it all end? You kept drinking at the club, drinking and drinking and gambling, then you went off—to see whom? No—let's go away. I'm leaving tomorrow."

It took Levin a long time to pacify her. Finally he managed it by admitting that his feeling of pity in conjunction with the wine had undone him, that he had yielded to Anna's guileful influence and would avoid her in future. One thing he confessed to most sincerely of all was that living in Moscow for so long, with nothing to do but talk, eat, and drink, he had been getting more and more confused. They kept talking until about three in the morning, and it was only at three o'clock that they had become sufficiently reconciled to be able to go to sleep.

XII

AFTER seeing her visitors out Anna did not sit down, but began pacing back and forth in the room. Unconsciously she had been doing everything in her power all evening to kindle in Levin a feeling of love for her (which she had been doing lately with respect to all young men), and she knew she had achieved this as far as it was possible to in a single evening with respect to a married man of honor. But though she liked him very much (in spite of the acute contrast from a man's point of view between Vronsky and Levin, as a woman she had seen in both of them a common quality, which was why Kitty too had fallen in love with both Vronsky and Levin) the moment he left the room she stopped thinking about him.

There was one thought and one thought only that in different forms pursued her implacably. If I have this effect on others, on that loving husband and family man, why is it that *he's* so cold toward me? Not coldness; he loves me, I'm sure of it. But there's something new now that divides us. Why has he stayed away a whole evening? He sent a message with Stiva that he couldn't leave Yashvin and had to keep an eye on his playing. Is Yashvin such a child? But let's assume it's true; he never tells lies. But there's something else behind this truth. He's glad of an opportunity to show me that he has other obligations. I know that and I don't object. But why keep proving it to me? He wants to prove to me that his love for me must not interfere with his freedom. But I don't need proofs, I need love. He ought to understand the full hardship of this life of mine here in Moscow.

Can it be called a life? I'm not living, I'm waiting for a solution that goes on and on being put off. Again there's no answer! And Stiva says he can't go to see Karenin. And I can't write him again. I can't do anything, can't begin anything, can't change anything; I just hold myself in and wait, thinking up amusements for myself—the English family, writing, reading, but it's all nothing but a fraud, it's just so much morphia. He ought to be sorry for me, she said to herself, feeling tears of self-pity welling up.

She heard Vronsky's peremptory ring and hastened to wipe away her tears; she not only wiped them away but sat down by the lamp and opened up a book, pretending to be calm. She had to show him that she was displeased at his not having returned when he had promised to, though merely displeased, and on no account to show him her distress and least of all her self-pity. She might pity herself, but he must not. She did not want any strife; though she reproached him for wanting to quarrel, it was she who willy-nilly took up a truculent attitude.

"Well, have you been bored?" he said, going over to her with cheerful animation. "What a frightful passion—gambling!"

"No, I haven't been bored, it's a long time since I learned not to be. Stiva and Levin were here."

"Yes, they wanted to come to see you. Well, how did you like Levin?" he said, sitting down beside her.

"Very much. They only left a little while ago. What did Yashvin do?"

"He was ahead, he had won seventeen thousand. I called him away, and he was very nearly on the point of leaving, but he went back again and now he's behind."

"Then what was the point of staying on there?" she asked, suddenly looking up at him. Her face looked cold and hostile. "You told Stiva you were staying on to bring Yashvin away, and now you've left him."

The same cold look—of readiness for a fight—came over his face.

"In the first place I didn't ask him to tell you anything; secondly, I never say anything untrue. And the main thing is that I wanted to stay on and I did," he said scowling. "Anna—why? Why d'you do this?" he said after a moment's pause, leaning toward her and opening his hand, hoping she would place her own in it.

She was glad of this appeal for tenderness. But some

strange force of evil did not allow her to yield to her own impulse, as though the rules of warfare would not allow her to submit.

"Of course you wanted to stay and you stayed. You do whatever you please. But why d'you say that to me? Why?" she said, getting more and more agitated. "Is anyone contesting your rights? But you want to be in the right, so be in the right."

His hand closed, he leaned back, and his face took on an even more stubborn expression than before.

"For you it's a question of obstinacy," she said, looking at him intently and suddenly finding a word to describe this expression of his that irritated her. "It's just obstinacy. For you it's a question of whether you'll conquer me, whereas for me—" Again she felt sorry for herself, and nearly burst into tears. "If you knew what it means to me! When I feel as I do now that your attitude toward me is hostile, actually hostile—if you knew what that means for me! If you knew how close I am to a catastrophe at such moments, how afraid I am, afraid of myself!" And she turned aside to hide her sobs.

"But what is this all about?" he said, horrified by her look of despair; he leaned toward her again, took up her hand and kissed it. "What have I done? Do I go looking for distractions away from home? Don't I avoid the company of women?"

"That's all I'd need!" she said.

"Then tell me what I have to do for you to feel at ease. I'm ready to do anything to make you happy," he said, touched by her despair. "Anna, what wouldn't I do to save you from distress of any kind, like this!" he said.

"Nothing, nothing!" she said. "I don't know myself whether it's my lonely life, or my nerves . . . Well, let's not speak about it. What about the races? You haven't told me . . ." she asked, trying to hide her triumph over the victory which was now hers after all.

He asked for supper and began telling her the details of the races; but by his tone and looks, which kept growing colder and colder, she saw that he didn't forgive her for her victory, that the feeling of obstinacy she had been struggling against was reasserting itself within him. He was colder to her than before, as though regretting his submission. And recalling the words that had assured her victory—"I'm close to a catastrophe and I'm afraid of myself"—she realized this was a dangerous weapon, which she wouldn't be able to use again. And she felt that together with the love that bound them together some evil spirit of strife had grown up between them that she could not cast out of his heart, and still less out of her own.

## XIII

THERE are no circumstances a man cannot grow accustomed to, especially if he sees everyone around him living the same way. Three months before, Levin would not have believed he could calmly fall asleep in the circumstances he was in now: living in aimless, senseless life, which for that matter was beyond his means, after a bout of drunkenness (there was no other word for what had happened at the club), and after establishing unsuitably friendly relations with a man his wife had once been in love with, after a still more unsuitable visit to a woman who could only be called a fallen woman, after being infatuated by such a woman and upsetting his wife—he would never have believed that he could calmly fall asleep. But under the influence of fatigue, a sleepless night, and the wine he had drunk he slept soundly and peacefully.

At five in the morning he was awakened by the creak of the door opening. He jumped up and looked around. Kitty was not in the bed beside him. But there was a light moving on the other side of the partition and he heard her walking about.

"What—what is it?" he muttered, half-asleep. "Kitty! What is it?"

"Nothing," she said, coming out from behind the partition with a candle in her hand. "I didn't feel very well," she said, with a peculiarly sweet and meaningful smile.

"What—has it begun? Has it begun?" he asked in a frightened voice. "We'll have to send for—" And he hastily began dressing.

"No, no," she said, smiling and holding him back with her hand. "I'm sure it's nothing. I only felt a little unwell. It's gone now."

And going over to the bed she put out the candle, stretched out and quieted down. Though he was suspicious of her stillness, as though she were holding her breath, and particularly of the expression of peculiar tenderness and excitement with which on coming out from behind the partition she had said "Nothing," he was so sleepy he dozed off at once. It was only later that he recalled the stillness of her breathing and understood everything that was taking place in her sweet, precious soul as she lay motionless beside him awaiting the greatest event in a woman's life. At seven o'clock he was awakened by the touch of her hand on his shoulder and a soft whisper. She seemed to be hesitating between regret at waking him up and a desire to speak to him.

"Kostya, don't be frightened. It's nothing. But I think . . . we'd better send for Miss Mary."

She had lighted the candle again, and was sitting on the bed holding the knitting she had been busy with lately.

"Please don't be afraid, it's nothing. I'm not the least bit afraid," she said, seeing his frightened face; she pressed his hand to her breast, then to her lips.

He leaped to his feet, unaware of himself and without taking his eyes off her, put on a dressing gown and stood still, staring at her. He had to go, but he couldn't tear himself away from the sight of her. He would have thought he loved her face and knew every expression it had, every look, but he had never seen her like this. Standing before her as she was now how vile and horrible he seemed to himself when he recalled the grief he had given her the evening before! Her flushed face, framed in the soft curls that had escaped from under her nightcap, was radiant with joy and resolution.

Little as there was of affectation and conventionality in Kitty's general character, Levin was nevertheless dazed by what he saw revealed before him now, when suddenly all the wrappings had been removed and the very kernel of her soul shone out through her eyes. And in this simplicity of hers, in this nakedness, she whom he loved was still more apparent than before. She looked at him smilingly; but suddenly her eyebrows twitched, she raised her head and quickly coming over to him she took hold of his hand and pressed all of herself against him, enveloping him in her hot breath. She was in pain; it was as though she were complaining to him of her suffering. And for a moment at first it seemed to him by force of habit that he was to blame. But there was a tenderness in her gaze that told him not only that she did not reproach him but that she loved him for just this suffering. If not I, then who is to blame for it? he thought involuntarily, seeking some culprit to punish for it; but there was no culprit. She suffered, she complained, and she triumphed in this suffering; she rejoiced in it and she loved it. He saw that something splendid was taking place in her soul, but what was it? He could not understand. It was too lofty for his comprehension.

"I've sent for Mama—you go as quickly as you can for Miss Mary . . . Kostya! No, nothing, it's gone."

She moved away from him and rang. "Well, go on now, Pasha's coming. I'm all right."

And to Levin's amazement he saw her take up again the knitting she had fetched during the night and start working on it again.

While Levin was going out through one door he heard the maid coming in through the other. He paused at the door, and listened to Kitty give detailed instructions to the maid, and with her help start moving the bed herself.

He got dressed, and while the horses were being harnessed, since there were still no hired sleighs about, he ran to the bedroom again, not on tiptoe but as it seemed to him on wings. Two maids were carefully moving something in the bedroom. Kitty was walking back and forth knitting, swiftly looping the thread over the needle, and giving orders.

"I'm going to the doctor's right now. They've already gone for Miss Mary, but I'll call there too. Is anything else needed? Oh yes, Dolly too, what?"

She looked at him, obviously not listening.

"Yes, yes. Go then, go," she murmured quickly, frowning and motioning him off with her hand.

He was already going through the drawing room when suddenly a pitiful moan, instantly silenced, reached him from the bedroom. He paused; for a moment he could not absorb it.

Yes, that's her, he said to himself, and clutching his head he ran downstairs.

"Lord have mercy! Pardon and help us!" he repeated the words that suddenly and unexpectedly somehow leaped to his lips. And unbeliever though he was he kept repeating these words and not only with his lips. Now, at this moment, he knew that not merely his doubts but even that incapacity to believe in accordance with his reason, which he had known to be within him, did not at all prevent him from turning to God. It all flew off his soul now like dust. Whom then could he have turned to, if not to Him in whose hands he felt himself, his soul, and his love to be?

The horse had not yet been hitched up, but feeling unusually tense physically, and all keyed up for what lay ahead, he didn't wait; in order not to lose a single moment he set out on foot, telling Kuzma to catch up with him.

At the corner he found a night cabman hurrying along. In the little sleigh sat Miss Mary in a velvet cloak with a shawl round her head. "Thank God, thank God!" he muttered, as he recognized with delight her small, fair face, which now had a specially grave and even severe expression. Telling the driver not to stop he ran back alongside her.

"Two hours ago, you say? No more?" she asked. "Go and fetch the doctor, only don't hurry him. And go get some laudanum at the pharmacy."

"So you think it may be all right? Lord have mercy and help us!" Levin said, as he saw his own horse coming out of the gateway. Leaping into the sleigh at Kuzma's side he ordered him to drive to the doctor's.

### XIV

THE doctor had not gotten up yet; his servant said he had gone to bed late and given orders not to be awakened, but that he "would be up soon." The servant was cleaning lamp glasses and seemed to be extremely preoccupied by what he was doing. This attention to his glasses and his indifference to what has taken place at the Levins' astounded Levin at first, but he instantly realized, on reflection, that no one knew or was obliged to know his feelings, and that this was all the more reason for behaving calmly, deliberately, and firmly in order to break through this wall of indifference and attain his goal. Don't hurry and don't omit anything, he said to himself, feeling a constantly swelling upsurge of physical strength and alertness for everything he was going to have to do.

When he found out that the doctor had not yet gotten up a number of different plans came to Levin's mind; he settled on the following: Kuzma would go off with a note to another doctor, while he himself would go to the pharmacy to get the laudanum, and if the doctor had not yet gotten up when he came back he would either bribe the servant or if need be force his way in and wake the doctor up himself at all costs.

At the pharmacy a skinny assistant was sealing up a packet of powders for a waiting coachman with the same indifference as the doctor's servant in cleaning his glasses, and refused to let Levin have any laudanum. Trying not to hurry and not to get excited, after mentioning the names of the doctor and the midwife and explaining what he needed the laudanum for, Levin tried to talk him into it. The attendant, in German, asked someone behind a partition whether he might release it, and on receiving permission took down a funnel and a small bottle, which he slowly filled from a larger one, stuck on a label, sealed it in spite of Levin's asking him not to, and was about to wrap it up as well. This was too much for Levin's endurance; he firmly snatched the little bottle out of his hands and rushed out the big glass doors. The doctor had still not gotten up, and the servant, who was now busy laying a carpet, refused to wake him. Levin unhurriedly got out a ten-ruble note and slowly pronouncing each word, though without wasting time, gave him the note and explained that the doctor (how grand and important this formerly insignificant little doctor now seemed to Levin!) had promised to come at any time, that he would surely not be angry, and consequently must be called at once.

The servant consented and went upstairs, asking Levin to go into the waiting room.

Behind the door Levin could hear the doctor, coughing, walking about, washing, and saying something. Some three minutes passed by; Levin thought it was more than an hour. He could wait no longer.

"Doctor!" he called through the open door in an imploring tone, "Doctor! Forgive me—but for Heaven's sake receive me as you are! It's over two hours."

"Immediately, immediately!" a voice replied, and to his astonishment Levin could detect a smile in it.

"Just for a second!"

"Immediately . . ."

Another couple of minutes went by while the doctor put on his boots, and another couple while he put on his clothes and brushed his hair.

"Doctor!" Levin was beginning again in a pitiful voice, but just then the doctor came out, dressed and with his hair brushed. Heartless people, thought Levin: brushing his hair while we're expiring!

"Good morning!" the doctor said to him, holding out his hand as though teasing him by his serenity. "There's no hurry! Well?"

Trying to be as circumstantial as possible, Levin began giving him every useless detail about his wife's condition, continually interrupting himself to beg the doctor to come along with him at once.

"Now don't be in such a hurry. After all you're new at this. I'm sure I shan't be needed, but I've promised and if you like I'll come. But there's no rush. Sit down, please; would you like some coffee?"

Levin stared at him: was he laughing at him? But the doctor hadn't the slightest intention of laughing at him.

"I know, I know," he said with a smile. "I'm a family man myself, but at moments like these we husbands are the most pathetic creatures. I have a patient whose husband always flees to the stable when this happens."

"But what d'you think, Doctor? D'you think it may be all right?"

"All the symptoms point to a successful outcome."

"Then you'll come at once?" said Levin, with an angry look at the servant, who had brought in the coffee.

"Within the hour."

"No, for the love of God!"

"Well, at least let me finish my coffee."

The doctor started on his coffee. They were both silent.

"Well, the Turks are getting a terrific beating. Did you read yesterday's telegram?" said the doctor, munching a roll.

"No, I can't stand it!" said Levin, jumping up. "Then you'll be there in a quarter of an hour?"

"Half an hour."

"Word of honor?"

Levin got home just as the Princess was arriving, and together they went to the door of the bedroom. The Princess had tears in her eyes, and her hands were trembling. When she saw Levin she embraced him and began to weep.

"Well how is everything, darling Miss Mary?" she said, clutching the hand of the midwife, who came toward them with a radiant but preoccupied look.

"It's going all right," she said. "Persuade her to lie down, it'll be easier."

From the moment he had awakened and realized what had happened, Levin had prepared himself to endure everything that lay ahead of him, without reflecting, without anticipating anything, repressing all thought and feeling, determined not to upset his wife but on the contrary to comfort and fortify her courage. Without allowing himself even to think about what was going to happen or how it would end, and judging by the inquiries he had made about how long such things usually lasted, Levin had been mentally prepared to endure and to keep a grip on his heart for some five hours, which it seemed to him he could do. But when he got back from the doctor's and again saw her in pain, he began repeating more and more often: "Lord have mercy, help us," sighing, and jerking his head up; he felt afraid of not being able to endure, of bursting into tears or running away, it was such agony for him. And only one hour had gone by.

But after this hour another two and three hours passed, then all five that he had set for himself at the most remote limit of endurance, and the situation was still the same; and he still kept on enduring, since there was nothing else to do but endure, every thinking moment that he had come to the ultimate limits of endurance and that at any moment his heart would burst with compassion.

But the minutes still kept passing by, hours and then hours more; his feelings of suffering and horror grew and kept growing tenser and tenser.

None of the usual circumstances of life without which nothing can be imagined existed for Levin any longer. He had lost all sense of time. Sometimes the minutes would seem to him hours—those minutes when she would call him to her side and he would hold her sweating hand, which sometimes pressed his with extraordinary strength and sometimes pushed him away—while sometimes the hours would seem to him like minutes. He was surprised when Miss Mary asked him to light a candle behind the screens and he learned that it was already five o'clock in the afternoon. If he had been told it was now only ten o'clock in the morning he would have been no more surprised. He didn't know where he was any more than he knew when anything took place. He saw her burning face, sometimes perplexed and suffering, sometimes reassuring him with a smile. He saw the Princess too, red-faced, overwrought, with her gray curls in disorder, biting her lips to swallow her tears; he saw Dolly, and the doctor smoking his thick cigarettes, and Miss Mary with her firm, resolute, and reassuring expression, and the old Prince pacing up and down the ballroom with a frown. But how they came and went or where they were he had no idea. Sometimes the Princess was in the bedroom with the doctor, sometimes in the study, where a table laid for a meal suddenly appeared; next it was not the Princess but Dolly.

Afterward Levin remembered that he had been sent some-where. Once he was sent to fetch a table and a sofa. He did this with zeal, thinking she needed it, only to learn later that he had been preparing his own bedstead. Then he was sent to the study to ask the doctor about something. The doctor answered and then began talking about the disorders in the Council. Then he was sent to the Princess's bedroom to fetch an icon with a silver-gilt mount, and together with the Princess's old lady's maid climbed up onto a cupboard to get the icon and broke the little lamp in front of it; the Princess's maid comforted him about his wife and about the icon lamp, and he took the icon and put it at the head of Kitty's bed, carefully pushing it in behind the pillows. But where, when, or why all this had happened he didn't know. He didn't even understand why the Princess took him by the hand and looking at him pitifully begged him to remain calm, or why Dolly tried to persuade him to eat something, to lead him out of the room, or even why the doctor gave him a grave look of commiseration and offered him some drops.

All he knew and felt was that what was happening was similar to what had happened the year before in the hotel of the provincial town, on his brother Nicholas's deathbed. But that had been grief—this was joy. But both that grief and this joy alike were outside all the usual circumstances of life; in this ordinary life they were like an opening through which something sublime could be seen. And now as then what was being accomplished came harshly, in agony, and just as incomprehensibly the soul soared aloft in the contemplation of this sublimity to a height it had never even understood before, where reason could no longer keep up with it.

"Lord forgive and help us," he repeated to himself in-cessantly, in spite of his lengthy and apparently total es-trangement, feeling that he was turning to God just as trust-fully and simply as he had in childhood and early youth.

Throughout this time he was in two different moods. One was when he was not in her presence: when he was with the doctor, who kept smoking one thick cigarette after another, extinguishing them against the rim of the overflowing ash-tray, or with Dolly and the Prince, where what was talked about was dinner, politics, and Mary so-and-so's illness, and for a moment Levin would suddenly forget all about what was happening, and feel as though he were waking up. The other mood was when he was with her, by her pillow, where his heart was ready to burst with pity yet never did, and where he prayed to God without pause. And each time, whenever he was taken out of a moment's forgetfulness by a scream that came to him from the bedroom, he fell into the same strange error that had seized hold of him in the very first moment; each time he heard a scream he leaped up and ran over to justify himself, recollecting only on the way that he was not to blame, and that he longed to protect and help her. But when he looked at her he saw again that there was no way he could help; he would lapse into horror and say, "Lord have mercy and help us!" And the more time went by the more powerful grew both these moods: the calmer he would be when he was not in her presence, completely forgetting her, and the more agonizing grew both her suffering itself and his feeling of helplessness. He would jump up, wishing to run away somewhere, but then run over to her.

Sometimes, when she had called him again and again, he blamed her. But when he saw her submissive, smiling face and heard her say "I've been wearing you out," he blamed God, but when he thought of God he immediately prayed for forgiveness and mercy.

## XV

He didn't know whether it was late or early. The candles were all burning low. Dolly had just been to the study and suggested that the doctor lie down. Levin was sitting down, listening to the doctor's stories of some quack hypnotic therapist, and staring at the ash on his cigarette. It was an interval of repose and oblivion. He had completely forgotten about what was now going on. He listened to the doctor's story and understood it. Suddenly a scream like nothing on earth was heard. This scream was so awful that Levin did not even jump up; breathless, he gave the doctor a look of frightened inquiry. The doctor leaned his head to one side, listening, then smiled approvingly. Everything was so extraordinary that by now nothing could surprise Levin. Probably that's the way it should be, he thought, and went on sitting. But whose scream had it been? He jumped, ran into the bedroom on tiptoe, past Miss Mary and the Princess, and halted at his place by the head of the bed. The screaming had

stopped, but now there was a change. What it was he could
not see or understand, and he had no desire to. But he could
see it by Miss Mary's expression: her face was stern and white.
and still just as resolute, though her jaw was trembling a
little and her eyes were fixed intently on Kitty. Kitty's burning, agonized sweating face, with a lock of hair sticking to
it, was turned toward him trying to catch his eye. Her hands
rose, seeking his. Clutching his cold hands with her own
sweating ones she began pressing them to her face.

"Don't go, don't go! I'm not afraid, I'm not afraid!" she
said quickly. "Mama! Take off my earrings, they're in my
way. Are you afraid? Soon now, Miss Mary, soon . . ."

She spoke rapidly, very rapidly, and tried to smile. But
suddenly her face was distorted and she thrust him away.

"No, this is horrible! I'm going to die, die! Go—go!" she
cried out, and once again he heard that same unearthly
scream.

Levin clutched his head and ran out of the room.

"It's all right! It's all right!" Dolly called out after him.

But no matter what they said he knew that now it was all
over. Leaning his head against the doorpost in the next room,
he stood there listening to someone shriek and moan in a
way he had never heard before, and he knew these sounds
were coming from what had once been Kitty. He no longer
had any desire for a child. Now he hated that child. He did
not even want her to live any more; all he wanted was an
end to this horrible suffering.

"Doctor! What is that? What is it? Oh, my God!" he said,
grasping the hand of the doctor, who had just come in.

"It's finished," said the doctor. And the doctor's face
was so grave as he said this that Levin understood "it's
finished" to mean "she's dying."

Beside himself he ran into the bedroom. The first thing
he saw was Miss Mary's face. It was even more frowning and
severe. Kitty's face was not there. In the place where it had
been before there was something strange, because of its look
of distortion and the sounds that came from it. He let his
head sink on to the wood of the bed; he felt his heart was
breaking. The horrible screaming did not stop, it grew still
more horrible, and then as though reaching the ultimate limit
of horror it suddenly subsided. Levin could not believe his
ears, but there would be no doubt of it: the screaming had
subsided; a soft stirring was heard, a rustling, hurried

breathing, and her voice, faltering, alive, tender and happy, said softly: "It's finished."

He lifted his head. Her arms nervelessly outstretched on the quilt, usually lovely and still, she lay there speechless, looking at him, trying to smile but unable to.

And suddenly, from that mysterious, horrible and unearthly world he had been living in for the last twenty-two hours, Levin felt instantaneously transported to the former, everyday world, but now radiant with a new light of such joy that he could not bear it. The taut strings snapped. Sobs and tears of joy he had not in the least anticipated rose up within him with such force that they shook his whole body and for a long time prevented him from speaking.

Falling on his knees by the bed, he held his wife's hand to his lips and kissed it; the hand responded with a feeble movement of the fingers. Meanwhile, there at the foot of the bed, in the skillful hands of Miss Mary there flickered, like the small flame of a night lamp, the life of a human being who had never existed before, and who now, just like others, with the same right and with the same importance for himself, would live and create others in his own image.

"Alive! Alive! And a boy too! Stop worrying!" Levin heard Miss Mary's voice as she slapped the baby's back with a trembling hand.

"Mama, is it true?" said Kitty's voice.

The Princess's only answer was a sob. And amidst the silence, as an irrefutable answer to the mother's question, a voice was now heard in the room that was completely different from all the other voices that had been speaking with such restraint. It was the bold, arrogant, self-centred screech of this new human being who had incomprehensibly appeared from somewhere else.

Before, if Levin had been told that Kitty had died, and that he had died with her, and that the children they had were angels, and that God was there, present before them —he would not have been at all astonished. But now, on his return to the world of reality, he had to make an immense effort of the mind to realize that she was alive and well, and that the creature yelling so desperately was his son. Kitty was alive; the suffering was over; he was unspeakably happy. He understood this, and it made him utterly happy.

But the child? Where did it come from? Why? Who was it? . . .

He was quite unable to grasp this, unable to accustom himself to the idea. It seemed to him something excessive, a superabundance, and it took him a long time to get used to it.

## XVI

TOWARD ten o'clock the old Prince, Koznyshov, and Oblonsky were sitting at Levin's. After talking about the young mother they had begun chatting about other things too. Levin was listening to them and, involuntarily remembering the day that had just passed, he also remembered himself as he had been until then. A hundred years seemed to have gone by since then. He felt as though he were on some unattainable heights from which he was taking pains to descend in order not to hurt the feelings of those he was talking to. As he talked he was thinking incessantly about his wife, the details of her present condition, and about his son, the idea of whose existence he was trying to accustom himself to. The whole female world, which after his marriage had taken on a new and unfamiliar significance for him, now loomed so large in his thoughts that his imagination could not encompass it. As he listened to a conversation about the dinner at the club the night before he thought: What's happening to her now? Has she fallen asleep? How is she? What is she thinking? Is our son Dmitri crying? And in the middle of the conversation, in the middle of a sentence, he jumped up and left the room.

"Let me know whether I can go in to see her," said the Prince.

"All right, directly," Levin replied, and without pausing he went to her room.

She was not sleeping, but talking quietly with her mother, making plans for the christening.

Tidied up, her hair brushed, in a smart cap trimmed with blue, her arms stretched out on the quilt, she was lying on her back; she met his look with a look that drew him toward her. Her eyes, bright as they were, grew still brighter the nearer he came. Her face still showed the same change from the earthly to the unearthly that is seen on the faces of the dead; but there it is farewell, here it was a welcome. Again an agitation such as he had felt during the moment of the birth gripped his heart. She took his hand and asked whether he had slept. He could make no answer and turned aside, aware of his own feebleness.

"And I've had a nap, Kostya," she said, "and now I feel so well."

She looked at him, but suddenly her face changed.

"Give him to me," she said, hearing the baby's whimper. "Give him to me, Miss Mary, and he can see him too."

"Well then, let Papa have a look," said Miss Mary, picking up something red, strange, and quivering, and bringing it over. "But wait a moment, first let's make him tidy;" and Miss Mary placed the squirming red object on the bed and began unwrapping it and then swaddling it again, raising it with one finger and turning it around, and powdering it with something.

Levin looked at this pathetic little thing and vainly searched his soul for any signs of paternal feeling. All he felt was loathing. But when it was undressed and he caught a glimpse of tiny, tiny little saffron-colored hands and feet, with little fingers and toes and even little thumbs and big toes distinguishable from the others, and when he saw Miss Mary bend these little hands that were sticking up as though they were soft springs and put them into linen garments, such pity for this creature came over him and such a fear of her hurting him that he was about to hold back her hand.

Miss Mary laughed. "Don't be afraid, don't be afraid!"

When the baby had been tidied up and transformed into a rigid little doll Miss Mary turned it over as though proud of her work and stepped aside, so that Levin might see his son in all his beauty.

Kitty watched sideways, also keeping her eyes fixed on the baby.

"Give him to me, give him to me!" she said and was even about to lift herself up.

"Really, Madame, you mustn't make such movements! Wait a moment I'll give him to you. Now we'll show Papa what a fine fellow we are!"

And Miss Mary held up to Levin this strange, squirming red creature hiding its head in the swaddling clothes, on one hand, only the fingers of the other propping it up by the nape of the neck. But there was also a nose, squinting eyes, and smacking lips.

"A beautiful baby!" said Miss Mary.

Levin sighed bitterly. This beautiful baby inspired him

with nothing but loathing and pity, feelings he hadn't at all expected.

He turned aside while Miss Mary held the child to the unaccustomed breast.

Suddenly a laugh made him raise his head. It was Kitty laughing. The infant had taken the breast.

"Well, enough now, enough!" said Miss Mary, but Kitty wouldn't release it. It fell asleep in her arms.

"Look at him now," said Kitty, turning the baby so that Levin could see it. The tiny little old man's face wrinkled even more, and the baby sneezed.

Smiling, scarcely able to hold back his tears of emotion, Levin kissed his wife and left the darkened room.

What he felt for this tiny creature was not at all what he had expected to. There was nothing merry or joyous in his feeling; on the contrary there was a new and painful fear—the consciousness of a new area of vulnerability. And this consciousness was so painful at first, the fear that this helpless creature might suffer was so strong, that it actually hid the strange feeling of unreasoning joy and even pride he felt when the baby sneezed.

## XVII

OBLONSKY'S affairs were in a bad way.

Two of the three payments of the money for the forest had been spent already, and by giving the merchant a discount of ten per cent he had gotten an advance of almost the whole of the last third. But the merchant would not give him any more of the money, especially since Dolly had asserted her rights to her own property for the first time that winter, and refused to endorse the contract with a receipt for the final third. All Oblonsky's salary went for household expenses and the settlement of small pressing bills. There was no money at all.

This was disagreeable, awkward, and in Oblonsky's opinion ought not to continue. To his mind the cause of it was that he was getting too small a salary. The post he held had certainly been a very good one five years before, but now it no longer was. Petrov, a bank director, was getting twelve thousand; Sventitsky, a company director, was getting seventeen thousand; Mitin, who had founded a bank, fifty thousand. It's obvious I've fallen asleep, I've been forgotten, thought Oblonsky. And he began keeping his eyes and ears open; toward the end of the winter he spied a very good post and began an attack on it, at first from Moscow, by way of aunts, uncles, and friends; then in the spring, when the matter had ripened, he came to Petersburg himself. It was one of those soft, lucrative posts, carrying salaries between one thousand to fifty thousand rubles a year, that were now much more numerous than they had been. It was the position of member of the Committee of the Joint Agency of the Mutual Credit Balance of the Southern Railways and Banking Houses. This post, like all such posts, required a vast knowledge and energy that would have been hard to find in any one man. And since there was no one combining all these qualities it was better at any rate for the post to be occupied by someone who was honest rather than dishonest. And Oblonsky was not only an honest man (without quotation marks) but he was an "honest" man with the special emphasis given the word in Moscow, when they speak of an "honest" politician, an "honest" writer, an "honest" newspaper, an "honest" institution, an "honest" tendency, and which means not only that the man or the institution is not dishonest, but also that they are capable on occasion of making some mischief for the government. Oblonsky moved in those circles in Moscow where the word was used; he was considered an "honest" man there and so had a better claim to the post than anyone else.

This post carried between seven thousand and ten thousand a year and Oblonsky could hold it without giving up his government office. It depended on two Ministers, a lady and two Jews, and though these people had already been prepared Oblonsky had to see them all in Petersburg. In addition he had promised his sister Anna to get a definitive answer out of Karenin about the divorce. So, having got fifty rubles from Dolly, he left for Petersburg.

As he sat in Karenin's study listening to a memorandum of his on the reasons for the parlous state of Russian finance, Oblonsky was only waiting for the moment he finished to start talking about his own business and about Anna.

"Yes, that's very true," he said when Karenin, after taking off the pince-nez he couldn't read without nowadays, looked inquiringly at his brother-in-law. "That's very true in detail, but all the same the principle of our age is—freedom."

"Yes, but I lay down another principle that embraces the principle of freedom," said Karenin, emphasizing the word "embraces" and putting his pince-nez on again in order to reread the section where this point was made.

And turning over the beautifully written manuscript, with huge margins, Karenin reread the convincing passage.

"I do not desire a system of protection for the benefit of private individuals, but for the common welfare—for upper and lower classes equally," he said, looking at Oblonsky over his pince-nez. "But *they* can't grasp that, all they're concerned with is their personal interests, they get carried away by phrases."

Oblonsky knew that when Karenin began to talk about what *they* were doing and thinking, the ones who refused to accept his memoranda and were the root of all the evil in Russia, he was already nearing the end; consequently Oblonsky gladly gave up his principle of freedom now and agreed entirely. Karenin fell silent, thoughtfully turning over the pages of his manuscript.

"Oh, by the way," said Oblonsky, "I wanted to ask you, in case you happen to run into Pomorsky, to drop him a hint that I should very much like to occupy the vacant post of member of the Committee of the Joint Agency of the Mutual Credit Balance of the Southern Railways."

The name of this post that was so close to Oblonsky's heart was already familiar to him, and he pronounced it fluently without a slip.

Karenin asked what the activity of this new Committee consisted of, and started thinking. He was considering whether there might be something in the activity of this Committee that ran counter to his own projects. But since the activity of this new institution was extremely complicated and his own projects covered an immense area he could not form an immediate opinion; taking off his pince-nez he said:

"Certainly I can speak to him, but actually just why d'you want it?"

"It carries a good salary, up to nine thousand, and my means—".

"Nine thousand . . ." repeated Karenin and frowned. The high salary reminded him that from this point of view Oblonsky's proposed activity was contrary to the main point of his own projects, which always leaned toward thrift.

"I consider, and I've written a memorandum to that effect, that the enormous salaries paid nowadays are a symptom of the fallacious economic policy of our Administration."

"Yes, but what would you like me to do?" said Oblonsky. "Let's take a bank director who gets ten thousand—he's worth it, isn't he? Or an engineer who's getting twenty thousand. It's vital work, after all."

"I take the view that a salary is a payment for a commodity, and it ought to be subject to the law of supply and demand. Hence, if a salary is fixed in a way that departs from this law, such as when I saw two engineers graduating from the same institute, both equally able and expert, and one receives forty thousand and the other has to be satisfied with two thousand, or when lawyers or hussars with no special knowledge are appointed bank directors with enormous salaries, I conclude that the salary is fixed not in accordance with the law of supply and demand, but simply through favoritism. This constitutes an abuse, important in itself and pernicious for the government service. I take the view—"

Oblonsky hastened to interrupt his brother-in-law.

"Yes, but you'll agree that a new and unquestionably important institution is being established—really vital work, after all! It's particularly desirable for it to be conducted honestly," said Oblonsky with special emphasis.

But the Moscow nuance of "honest" was incomprehensible to Karenin.

"Honesty is merely a negative quality," he said.

"All the same you'd oblige me greatly by dropping Pomorsky a hint," said Oblonsky. "Just like that, during a chat."

"But I have the impression it really depends more on Bolgarinov," said Karenin.

"As far as Bolgarinov is concerned he fully agrees," said Oblonsky, blushing.

Oblonsky blushed at the mention of Bolgarinov, a Jew, because he had been to see him that morning and the visit had left him with an unpleasant impression. Oblonsky was firmly convinced that the enterprise he wanted to get a position in was novel, alive, and honest, but that morning, when Bolgarinov, obviously intentionally, had made him wait two hours in his waiting room with some other petitioners, he suddenly began feeling uncomfortable.

Whether he was uncomfortable because he, a Prince Oblonsky, a descendant of Rurik, had been waiting around for two hours in a Jew's waiting room, or because for the first time in his life he was not following the example of his ancestors and serving the State but was embarking on a new career, he was in any case extremely uncomfortable. During these two hours of waiting at Bolgarinov's, Oblonsky, strolling jauntily back and forth in the waiting room, smoothing his whiskers, chatting with the other petitioners, and trying to contrive a pun about *"jewing his cud* at the Jew's," took great pains to conceal this feeling of his from others, and even from himself.

But he had felt uncomfortable the whole time and disgruntled, without knowing why himself: whether it was because the pun didn't come out right, or something else. And when Bolgarinov finally received him with exceptional politeness, obviously triumphing in his humiliation, and almost refused him, Oblonsky hastened to forget about it as quickly as possible. He was blushing now at the mere recollection.

## XVIII

I HAVE something else to discuss with you now, and you know what it is. It's about Anna," Oblonsky said, after a short pause, when he had shaken off his unpleasant memory.

The moment Oblonsky mentioned Anna's name Karenin's face changed completely: instead of its previous animation it now expressed only fatigue and lifelessness.

"Just what is it you want of me?" he said, turning round in his armchair and snapping his pince-nez shut.

"A decision, Alexis, some kind of decision. I am now addressing myself to you not as to"— Oblonsky meant to say, "not as to a wronged husband," but being afraid to spoil his case by that he changed it—"not as to a statesman"—which sounded incongruous—"but simply as a human being, a kind man and a Christian. You should pity her," he said.

"Just what do you mean?" said Karenin in a low voice.

"Yes, pity her. If you had seen her as I have—I've spent the whole winter with her—you would take pity on her. Her situation is horrible, actually horrible."

"It had seemed to me," replied Karenin in a more high-pitched, almost squeaky voice, "that she has everything she herself desired."

"Oh Alexis, for God's sake let's not have any recriminations! What's past is past, and you know what she wants and is waiting for—a divorce."

"But I thought she declined a divorce if I made it a condition that I be left the boy. That was how I answered her and

I thought the matter closed. And I still consider it closed!" cried Karenin.

"For God's sake don't excite yourself," said Oblonsky, touching his brother-in-law's knee. "It is not closed. If you'll allow me to recapitulate, this was how matters stood: when you separated you were greathearted, you were as magnanimous as a man can be; you gave her everything—freedom, and even a divorce. She appreciated that. Yes, you must believe that. She actually did appreciate it. To such a point that at first, feeling as she did that she was to blame for it all she did not take everything into consideration, nor could she have. She renounced everything. But experience and time have shown that her situation is agonizing and impossible."

"Her life cannot possibly interest me," interrupted Karenin, raising his eyebrows.

"Allow me not to believe that," Oblonsky retorted gently. "Her situation is both agonizing for her and of not the slightest benefit to anyone else. You will say she's deserved it. She knows that; she is not asking you for anything, she says plainly that she dare not. But I, all her family, all those of us who love her, we beg of you, we implore you—why should she be tortured so? Who benefits by it?"

"Excuse me—I think you're acting as though I were the defendant," said Karenin.

"But no, no, not at all, you must understand me," said Oblonsky, touching his arm again, as though sure this contact would mollify him. "All I'm saying is this: her situation is agonizing, and it can be relieved by you, and with no disadvantage to yourself. I'll arrange everything for you so that you won't even be aware of it. After all, you promised."

"The promise was given before. And I thought the question of the child was decisive. Besides, I had hoped she would have enough generosity—" Karenin, turning white, managed to say, his lips quivering.

"She leaves everything to your own generosity. She begs you—implores you for one thing, to get her out of the impossible situation she's in. She no longer asks for her son. Alexis, you have a kind heart. Put yourself in her position for a moment. For her, in her situation, the question of the divorce is a question of life and death. If you had not promised before she would have reconciled herself to her situation and lived in the country. But you promised; she wrote to you and moved to Moscow. And she's been living in Moscow now for six months, expecting your decision. Every time she meets anyone it's like twisting a knife in her heart. It's just like keeping a man condemned to death with a rope around his neck for months, promising him either death, or perhaps, a reprieve. Take pity on her, and I'll undertake to arrange everything so that . . . Your scruples . . ."

"I'm not speaking of that . . . of that . . ." Karenin interrupted him in a voice full of disgust. "But I may have promised something I had no right to promise."

"Then you're going back on your promise?"

"I've never gone back on a promise to do what was possible, but I want to have time to consider how far what I promised is possible."

"Alexis—no!" said Oblonsky, jumping up. "I won't believe that! She's as unhappy as only an unhappy woman can be, and you cannot refuse such a—"

"How far what I promised is possible. You profess to be a freethinker, but in such a grave matter I, as a believing Christian, cannot act contrary to Christian law."

"But in Christian communities, and in ours too, as far as I know, divorce is allowed," said Oblonsky. "Divorce is also allowed by our Church. And we see—"

"It is allowed, but not in that sense."

"Alexis, I don't recognize you," said Oblonsky after a pause. "Was it not you who forgave everything—and did we not appreciate it?—and, moved by just this Christian feeling, were ready to sacrifice everything? You yourself said, 'Give your coat when they would take your cloak' . . . and now—"

"I beg you—" Karenin suddenly stood up, pale and with his jaw trembling, and said in a shrill voice, "I beg you to stop . . . stop . . . this conversation!"

"Oh, no! Well, forgive me then, forgive me if I've wounded you," said Oblonsky with an embarrassed smile, holding out his hand. "I was simply delivering my message, like an envoy."

Karenin gave him his hand, and reflected for a moment.

"I must think it over and seek for guidance," he said. "I'll give you a final answer the day after tomorrow," he added, after thinking something over.

## XIX

OBLONSKY was about to leave when Korney entered and announced: "Master Sergius!"

"Who is Master Sergius?" Oblonsky was about to ask, but then he remembered immediately.

"Oh, Seryozha!" he said. " 'Master Sergius'—it sounded like the head of something or other." He remembered Anna had asked him to see the boy.

He remembered the timid, pathetic look on Anna's face as she said to him before parting: "In any case you'll see him. Find out exactly where he is, who's with him. And Stiva . . . if it's possible! Might it be possible?" Oblonsky realized this meant: Is it possible to arrange the divorce so that she got her son back? Now he saw that this could not even be thought of, but even so he was glad to see his nephew.

Karenin had reminded his brother-in-law that they never spoke to the boy about his mother, and asked him not to say a word about her.

"After he saw his mother that time, which we had not anticipated, he was very ill," Karenin said. "We even feared for his life. But sensible treatment and some sea bathing in the summer have restored his health, and now on the doctor's advice, I've sent him to school. The influence of his school fellows has really had a good effect on him, he's completely well and is a good student."

"Well, what a fine fellow you've turned into! And not even Seryozha any more, but Sergius!" said Oblonsky with a smile, looking at the handsome, broad-shouldered boy in a blue jacket and long trousers who walked with brisk assurance. The boy looked healthy and happy. He bowed to his uncle as to a stranger, but as he recognized him he blushed and quickly turned away from him as though offended and angry about something. He went over to his father and handed him his school report.

"Well, this looks all right," said Karenin. "You may go now."

"He's grown thinner and taller; he's stopped being a child and become a real boy. I like that," said Oblonsky. "D'you remember me?"

The boy glanced swiftly at his father.

"I remember you, Uncle," he replied, looking at him, then lowering his eyes again.

His uncle called him over and took him by the hand.

"Well, how are you? How are things?" he said, wanting to start a conversation and not knowing what to say.

Without answering, the boy blushed and cautiously withdrew his hand from his uncle's. The moment Oblonsky released his hand he gave his father an inquiring look and like a bird set free quickly left the room.

A year had passed since Seryozha had last seen his mother. Since then he had heard nothing more about her. During this year he had been sent to school where he had become acquainted with and fond of his school fellows. The dreams and thoughts about his mother that had made him ill after seeing her by now no longer occupied him. When they came he took pains to drive them away again, considering them shameful and fit only for girls, not for a real boy. He knew there had been a quarrel between his father and mother that had separated them; he knew it had been his fate to remain with his father, and he made an effort to accustom himself to the idea.

It was unpleasant for him to see his uncle, who resembled his mother, because it evoked in him just the memories he considered shameful. It was all the more unpleasant because from the few words he could overhear while waiting at the door of the study, and from the expressions of his uncle and his father he could guess that they had been speaking about his mother. And in order not to have to condemn his father, whom he was living with and dependent on, and above all not to yield to the emotions he considered so humiliating, Seryozha tried not to look at this uncle of his who had come to upset his peace of mind, and not to think about what he reminded him of.

But when Oblonsky, who followed him out of the room, saw him on the staircase and called him over to ask how he spent his time in school between classes Seryozha, away from his father's presence, started talking with him.

"We're playing railroad now," he said in reply to his question. "You see, this is how it works: two of us sit down on a bench—they're the passengers. Then one of us gets up on the bench and stands there; we all harness ourselves by our arms or belts, then we start off through all the rooms. The doors have been opened up first. Well, then it's not so easy to be the conductor!"

"He's the one standing up?" asked Oblonsky with a smile.

"Yes: you have to be plucky and quick, especially when they stop all of a sudden or someone falls down."

"Yes, that's no joke," said Oblonsky, looking sadly into his animated eyes so like his mother's, no longer a child's eyes, no longer altogether innocent. And even though he had made Karenin a promise not to speak of Anna he could not restrain himself.

"And d'you remember your mother?" he suddenly asked.

"No, I don't," Seryozha said quickly; blushing crimson he lowered his eyes. And that was all his uncle could get out of him.

Half an hour later the tutor found his pupil on the staircase; it took him a long time to make out whether he was in a bad temper or crying.

"What is it, I suppose you hurt yourself when you fell down?" said the tutor. "I told you it was a dangerous game. I'll have to tell the headmaster."

"If I had hurt myself no one would have noticed anything, that's quite certain."

"Then what is it?"

"Leave me alone! Whether I remember or whether I don't—whose business is it anyhow? Why should I remember? Leave me in peace!" he said, not to his tutor now but to the whole world.

XX

As usual Oblonsky did not waste his time while in Petersburg. Aside from his business there—his sister's divorce and his appointment—he found it necessary as usual to refresh himself, as he called it, after the stuffiness of Moscow.

Moscow, in spite of all its *cafés chantants* and its omnibuses, was just a stagnant swamp. Oblonsky always felt this. Living in Moscow, especially in the bosom of his family, always lowered his spirits. After living in Moscow for a long time without going away he got to the point where he would begin getting upset by his wife's ill temper and reproaches, the health and the education of his children, the petty details of his work: even the fact that he had debts upset him. But all he had to do was to go to Petersburg and stay there for a while, in the circle he moved in, where people lived, really *lived*, instead of vegetating as they did in Moscow, and all these thoughts vanished instantly, melting away like wax in front of a fire.

His wife? Only that day he had been talking to Prince Chechensky. Prince Chechensky had a wife and family; his grown sons were Pages at Court. He also had another illegitimate family, also with children. Though the first family was all right too Prince Chechensky felt happier with the second. He took his eldest son to see the second family and told Oblonsky he considered it useful and formative for his son. What would they have said about that in Moscow?

Children? In Petersburg children did not stop their fathers from living. In Petersburg children were brought up in schools; there was none of the preposterous notion now spreading in Moscow—take Prince Lvov, for instance—that all the luxury in life was supposed to be for the children, while all the parents got was toil and worry. There it was understood that a man had to live for himself, as a cultivated man should.

The service? There the service was not that grinding hopeless treadmill it was in Moscow; there it was interesting. An encounter with the right person, a service rendered, a neat remark, a talent for mimicry, and a man suddenly made a career for himself, like Bryantsov, whom Oblonsky had met the day before and who was now a top-flight functionary. Service of that kind was interesting.

But it was the Petersburg attitude toward money that had a particularly reassuring effect on Oblonsky. Bartnyansky, who at the rate he was living got through at least fifty thousand a year, had made a noteworthy remark to him about this the day before.

While chatting before dinner Oblonsky had said to him: "I think you know Mordvinsky very well; you can do me a favor, if you don't mind, just drop him a hint about me. There's a post I'd like to get hold of. Member of the Joint Agency—"

"Never mind, I'll never remember it anyhow . . . But why should you want to get into all this railway business with Yids? Why, it's horrible!"

Oblonsky didn't tell him it was vital work; Bartnyansky wouldn't have understood that.

"I'm broke; I've got nothing to live on."

"But you go on living?"

"Yes, on debts."

"Really? A lot?" said Bartnyansky commiseratingly.

"A great deal—about twenty thousand."

Bartnyansky burst out into merry laughter.

"You lucky fellow!" he said. "I owe a million and a half and I haven't got a thing; as you see it's still possible to go on living!"

And Oblonsky saw how true this was not only by hearsay

but in fact. Zhivakhov owed three hundred thousand rubles and didn't have a kopeck, yet he lived, and how he lived! Count Krivtsov had long since been given up altogether, but he went on keeping two mistresses. Petrovsky had run through five million and went on living just as he always did; he even directed the Finance Department, where he got a salary of twenty thousand.

But aside from all this Petersburg had a physically pleasant effect on Oblonsky. It made him younger. In Moscow he would sometimes notice his gray hairs, fall asleep after dinner, stretch himself, walk slowly upstairs breathing heavily, find young women boring, not do any dancing at balls. But in Petersburg he always felt he had shaken off ten years.

In Petersburg he had the same feeling sixty-year-old Prince Peter Oblonsky, who had just got back from abroad, had spoken of to him only the day before.

"We don't know how to live here," said Peter Oblonsky. "Would you believe it, I spent the summer in Baden, and d'you know, I actually felt like a very young man. I would see a young woman and all sorts of ideas. . . . I'd dine, drink a little, and feel full of vigor, high-spirited. I come back to Russia—I had to see my wife, in the country into the bargain—well, would you believe it, two weeks later I put on a dressing gown and stopped dressing for dinner. As for thinking about young women—what an idea! I'd turned into a complete dotard; the only thing left was the salvation of my soul. Then I went to Paris and there I was, perfectly all right again!"

Oblonsky felt exactly the same difference as Peter Oblonsky. In Moscow he let himself go to such an extent that if he went on living there for a long time he would actually have also wound up saving his soul; but in Petersburg he felt like a man again.

Princess Betsy and Oblonsky were on a very strange footing with each other that had lasted a long time. Oblonsky would always jocularly pay court to her and tell her, also jocularly, the most indecent things, knowing she liked hearing them better than anything. The day after his talk with Karenin, Oblonsky called on her and felt so young that he unexpectedly went so far in his jocular courtship and nonsense that he was at a loss to extricate himself, since not only did he not like her, he unfortunately found her repulsive. But this atmosphere had grown up between them because she liked him very much. Consequently he was simply delighted with the arrival of Princess Myagky, which put an end to their tête-à-tête.

"Aha, so you're here too!" she said when she saw him. "Well, how is your poor sister? Don't look at me like that," she added. "Ever since everyone has been attacking her—people who are a hundred thousand times worse than she—I've been of the opinion that she's acted magnificently. I can't forgive Vronsky for not having let me know when she was in Petersburg. I would have called on her and taken her with me everywhere. Please give her my love. Now tell me all about her."

"Yes, her situation is very painful, she—" Oblonsky began; in his simplicity he took Princess Myagky's remark, "Tell me all about her," at face value. But she interrupted him at once, as she always did, and began to talk herself.

"She's what everyone but myself does and conceals; but she disliked deceit, and she's acted magnificently. And she did even better in leaving that half-witted brother-in-law of yours. You must excuse me: everyone says he's clever, so clever, I'm the only one who says he's stupid. Now that he's thick as thieves with Countess Lydia and that Landau everyone says he's half-witted; I should be delighted to disagree with everyone again but this time I can't."

"But explain to me, please, what does it all mean?" said Oblonsky. "Yesterday I went to see him on my sister's business and I asked for a definite answer. He didn't give me one and said he would think it over, and this morning instead of an answer I received an invitation to go to Countess Lydia's this evening."

"Ah, that's it, that's it!" said Princess Myagky gleefully. "They're going to ask Landau, to see what he says."

"What d'you mean, ask Landau? Who's Landau?"

"What—you've never heard of Jules Landau, the celebrated Jules Landau, the clairvoyant? He's also a half-wit, but the fate of your sister depends on him. That's what comes of living in the provinces—you don't know a thing! You see this Landau was a salesman at a shop in Paris, and went to see a doctor. He fell asleep in the doctor's waiting room and while asleep began giving advice to all the invalids there, and remarkable advice too. Then Yury Meledinsky's wife—you know him, the invalid?—heard about this Landau and took him to see her husband, and now he's treating him. In my opinion he hasn't done him any good, since he's still as debilitated as ever, but they believe in him and take him around with them. They've brought him to Russia, and now everyone's chasing around after him; he's begun treating everyone. He cured Countess Bezzubov, and she's grown so attached to him that she's adopted him."

"What d'you mean, adopted him?"

"Just that, adopted him. He's no longer Landau, but Count Bezzubov. That's not the point, though: Lydia—of course I'm very fond of her, but her head isn't screwed on right —has gone and fallen for this Landau and neither she nor Karenin can make the slightest decision without him; consequently the fate of your sister is now in the hands of this Landau, alias Count Bezzubov."

XXI

AFTER a splendid dinner and a large quantity of cognac at Bartnyansky's, Oblonsky arrived at Countess Lydia's only a little late.

"Who else is with the Countess—a Frenchman?" Oblonsky asked the hall porter, glancing at Karenin's familiar overcoat and a peculiar, rather primitive overcoat with clasps.

"Mr. Karenin and Count Bezzubov, sir," the hall porter replied in a stern voice.

Princess Myagky guessed right, thought Oblonsky as he went up the stairs. Very strange! But it would be a good thing to get close to Lydia, she has enormous influence. A hint from her to Pomorsky and it's in the bag.

It was still quite light out of doors, but in Countess Lydia's small drawing room the blinds were down and the lamps were already burning.

The Countess and Karenin were sitting at a round table beneath a lamp, quietly talking. A short thin man, with hips like a woman's, knock-kneed, very pale and handsome, with beautiful shining eyes and long hair hanging over the collar of his frock coat, was standing at the other end of the room, looking at the portraits on the wall. After greeting his hostess and Karenin, Oblonsky glanced involuntarily at the stranger again.

"Monsieur Landau!" said the Countess softly, turning to him with a caution that struck Oblonsky. She introduced them to each other.

Landau looked round quickly, came over and with a smile placed his damp motionless hand in Oblonsky's outstretched one, and immediately moved back and resumed his inspection of the portraits. The Countess and Karenin exchanged significant looks.

"I'm delighted to see you, especially today," said Countess Lydia, indicating a seat beside Karenin.

"I introduced him to you as Landau," she said in a low voice, glancing at the Frenchman and then instantly at Karenin, "but actually he's Count Bezzubov, as you doubtless know. It's just that he dislikes the title."

"Yes, I've heard," Oblonsky replied. "They say he cured Countess Bezzubov completely."

"She called on me today, she's so pathetic!" said the Countess to Karenin. "The separation is dreadful for her. Such a blow!"

"Is he definitely leaving?" asked Karenin.

"Yes, he's going to Paris. Yesterday he heard a voice," said the Countess, looking at Oblonsky.

"Ah, a voice!" repeated Oblonsky, feeling it was necessary to be as cautious as possible in this company, where something peculiar was happening or supposed to be, to which he still lacked the key.

There was a moment's silence, after which Countess Lydia, as though coming to the main point, said to Oblonsky with a subtle smile:

"I've known you for a long time and I'm very pleased that I shall be knowing you more intimately. The friends of our friends are our friends. But in order to be a friend one must enter into a friend's state of mind, and I'm afraid you're not doing that with respect to Karenin. You understand what I'm speaking about," she said, lifting her beautiful dreamy eyes.

"To some extent, Countess, I realize that Karenin's situation—" said Oblonsky, who didn't have a very clear idea of what the point was and wanted to keep to generalities.

"The change is not in his external situation," said Countess Lydia sternly, as her infatuated eyes followed Karenin, who had stood up and gone over to Landau; "his heart has been transformed, he has been given a new heart, and I'm afraid you haven't fully realized the change that has taken place within him."

"Well, in a general way I can imagine what it is. We've always been friends, and now—" Oblonsky responded tenderly to the Countess's look, meanwhile considering which of the two Ministers she was closer to, so that he could make up his mind which one he should ask her to influence.

"The change that has taken place in him cannot weaken his feeling of love for his neighbor; on the contrary, it is bound to increase it. But I'm afraid you don't understand me. Won't you have some tea?" she said, indicating with her eyes a footman who was handing tea round on a tray.

"Not entirely, Countess. Of course, his misfortune——"

"Yes, a misfortune that has turned into the greatest good fortune by giving him a new heart, which it filled with Him," she said, turning her lovesick gaze on Oblonsky.

I think it'll be possible to ask her to mention me to both, he thought.

"Oh certainly, Countess," he said, "but I think such changes are so intimate that no one, not even one's closest friend, likes to speak of them."

"On the contrary! We must speak, and help each other."

"Undoubtedly, but there are such differences of conviction, and besides——" said Oblonsky with a gentle smile.

"There can be no differences in the cause of the holy Truth."

"Oh yes, of course, but——" Oblonsky, embarrassed, fell silent. He had realized it was a question of religion.

"I think he'll fall asleep in a moment," said Karenin in a portentous whisper as he came over to Countess Lydia.

Oblonsky looked round. Landau was sitting by the window, leaning against the arm and back of an easy chair, with his head hanging down. Noticing the looks directed at him he raised his head and gave a childishly naïve smile.

"Pay no attention to him," said Countess Lydia; with an agile movement she moved a chair up for Karenin. "I've noticed that——" she began, when a footman came into the room with a letter. Countess Lydia read it rapidly and, excusing herself, wrote an answer to it with extraordinary speed, handed it to the footman and came back to the table. "I've noticed," she went on, "that people from Moscow, especially men, are most indifferent to religion."

"Oh no, Countess, I think Muscovites have the reputation of being firmest in the faith," Oblonsky replied.

"Yes, though as far as I know you're one of the indifferent ones," said Karenin, turning to him with a tired smile.

"How can one be indifferent!" said Countess Lydia.

"In this respect it's not so much that I'm indifferent, as in a state of expectation," said Oblonsky with his most mollifying smile. "I don't think that for me the time for such questions has arrived yet."

Karenin and Countess Lydia exchanged glances.

"We can never know whether our time has come or not," said Karenin severely. "We should not think of whether we are ready or not ready: grace does not depend on human considerations—sometimes it does not descend on those who strive after it, and does descend on those who are unprepared for it, like Saul."

"No, not yet, I think," said Countess Lydia, who had been following the movements of the Frenchman.

Landau got up and came over to them. "Will you permit me to listen?" he asked.

"Oh yes! I didn't want to disturb you," said Countess Lydia, looking at him tenderly. "Sit down here beside us."

"All one has to do not to deprive oneself of light is not to shut one's eyes," Karenin continued.

"Oh, if you only knew the happiness it gives us to feel His presence constantly in our souls!" said Countess Lydia with a beatific smile.

"But sometimes one may feel incapable of ascending to such a height," said Oblonsky, feeling somewhat insincere in acknowledging that there were such religious heights, while at the same time reluctant to admit his freethinking in the presence of someone who by a mere word to Pomorsky might get him the post he wanted.

"You mean he might be prevented by sin?" said Countess Lydia. "But that is a false view. For believers there is no sin; sin has already been atoned for. Excuse me," she added, looking at the footman, who had come in with another note. She read it and answered it orally: "Say tomorrow, at the Grand Duchess's." Then she went on with the conversation: "For believers there is no sin."

"Yes, but faith without works is dead," said Oblonsky, who recalled this phrase from the catechism, defending his independence now only by a smile.

"There it is, from the Epistle of St. James," Karenin said to Countess Lydia, looking at her somewhat reproachfully, evidently in reference to something they had discussed more than once. "How much harm has been done by a fallacious interpretation of that passage! Nothing repels people from faith so much. 'I have no good works, so I cannot believe.' When there is no place where that is said, and what is said is just the reverse."

"To labor for God with works, save one's soul by fasting," said Countess Lydia with contemptuous disgust. "Those are barbarous opinions of our monks . . . When there is no place where that is said. It's far simpler and easier," she added, looking at Oblonsky with the same approving smile with which she encouraged young Ladies in Waiting who were confused by their novel Court surroundings.

"We are saved by Christ, who suffered for us. We are saved by faith," Karenin chimed in, looking his approval.

"Do you understand English?" asked Countess Lydia; when Oblonsky answered affirmatively she got up and began looking through a shelf of books. "I want to read *Safe and Happy, or Under the Wing*," she said, with an inquiring glance at Karenin. When she had found the book and taken her seat again she opened it. "It's very short. It describes the way faith is acquired and the happiness, beyond everything earthly, that then fills one's soul. The believer cannot be unhappy, since he is not alone. But you'll see—" She was about to begin reading when the footman came in again. "Madame Borozdin? Tell her tomorrow at two o'clock . . . Yes," she went on, keeping her finger in the book to mark the place; she sighed, her beautiful soulful eyes looking straight ahead of her. "This is how genuine faith acts. D'you know Mary Sanin? D'you know of her misfortune? She lost her only child. She was in despair. Well—what happened? She found this Friend and now she thanks God for the death of her child. There is the happiness given by faith!"

"Oh, yes, it's very—" Oblonsky began, pleased that they were going to read and let him recover himself a little. No, obviously it's better not to ask for anything today, he thought, if only I can get myself out of this without botching things up.

"You'll find this boring, since you don't know English," said Countess Lydia to Landau. "But it's quite short."

"Oh I'll understand," said Landau with the same smile, and shut his eyes.

Karenin and Countess Lydia exchanged significant looks again, and the reading started.

## XXII

OBLONSKY felt completely baffled by the strange talk he was listening to, which was new to him. Generally the complexities of Petersburg life had a stimulating effect on him, raising him out of the stagnation of Moscow; but he was fond of these complexities and understood them in familiar, intimate circles; but in this alien domain he was baffled, dazed, and could not grasp it all. Listening to Countess Lydia and feeling fixed on him the beautiful eyes, either naïve or knavish—he didn't know which himself—of Landau, Oblonsky began to be aware of a peculiar heaviness in his head.

The most variegated notions were getting all jumbled together in his head. Mary Sanin is glad her child is dead . . . all you have to do is believe, the monks don't know how to do this, but Countess Lydia does . . . Why is my head so heavy? From the cognac, or is it just that all this really is very odd? Anyhow, so far I don't think I've done anything improper. Still—asking her now is out of the question. They say they make you pray. What if they make *me* pray? That really would be too idiotic. And what nonsense she's reading . . . but she has a good accent. Landau—Bezzubov—why is he Bezzubov? Suddenly Oblonsky felt his lower jaw dropping irresistibly into a yawn. He smoothed his whiskers to hide it and shook himself. Then he felt that he had already dozed off, and was on the point of snoring. He recovered himself just as Countess Lydia said, "He's asleep."

Oblonsky came to with a frightened start and the guilty feeling of having been caught out. But he was reassured at once when he saw that the words "he's asleep" referred not to him but to Landau. The Frenchman had fallen asleep just as Oblonsky had. But while Oblonsky thought his falling asleep would have offended them (though he didn't think even that, everything seemed so odd by now) Landau's made them extraordinarily happy, especially Countess Lydia.

"My dear," Countess Lydia said, carefully holding the folds of her silk dress to prevent its rustling, and in her excitement calling Karenin not by his name but "my dear."

"Give him your hand—you see? Hush!" she said to the footman, who had come in again. "I'm not receiving."

The Frenchman was sleeping or pretending to; he had leaned his head against the back of the easy chair and his damp hand, lying on his knee, was making feeble motions as though it were catching something. Karenin got up; he went over to him, trying to be careful but catching against the table, and put his hand in the Frenchman's. Oblonsky also got up, opening his eyes wide to wake himself up in case he was sleeping, and kept looking from one to the other. It was all quite real. Oblonsky felt his head getting worse and worse.

"Let the person to arrive last, the one who wants something, let him go out! Let him go out!" the Frenchman said, without opening his eyes.

"You must excuse me—but you can see . . . come back around ten o'clock, or better still tomorrow."

"Let him go out!" the Frenchman repeated impatiently.

"He means me, doesn't he?"

And on receiving an affirmative reply Oblonsky, forgetting both the favor he had wanted to ask of Countess Lydia and his sister's business, anxious only to get out of there as quickly as possible, left on tiptoe; he ran out into the street as though leaving an infected house; to put himself in a good mood again he chatted and joked for a long time with the cabman.

At the French Theatre, where he arrived in time for the last act, and later at the Tatar Restaurant, over champagne, Oblonsky was able to restore himself in the atmosphere he felt at home in. But that whole evening he was far from being himself.

When he got back to Peter Oblonsky's house, where he was staying in Petersburg, Oblonsky found a note from Betsy. She wrote that she very much wanted to finish the conversation they had been having, and asked him to call the following day. He had scarcely had time to read it through and frown at it when he heard the heavy steps of men carrying some weight.

Oblonsky went out to take a look. It was the rejuvenated Peter Oblonsky. He was so drunk he could not get up the stairs, but when he saw Oblonsky he ordered the men to put him on his feet; clinging to Oblonsky he went with him to his room, began telling him how he had spent the evening, and fell asleep at once.

Oblonsky was in low spirits, something that rarely happened to him; for a long time he couldn't go to sleep. Everything that came to his mind was disgusting, but most disgusting of all, like something shameful, was his memory of the evening he had spent at Countess Lydia's.

The following day he got a definite refusal from Karenin with respect to the divorce, and he realized that the decision was due to what the Frenchman had said the night before during his real or feigned sleep.

## XXIII

FOR anything to be undertaken in a household what is essential is either total discord between husband and wife or loving harmony. When their relationships are vague, neither one thing nor the other, it is impossible to do anything at all.

A great many families stick for years in the same old ruts hated by both husband and wife, simply because there is neither out and out strife nor harmony.

Both for Vronsky and Anna life in Moscow, in the heat and dust, when the sun was no longer a spring but a summer sun, and the trees along the boulevards had long since been in leaf and the leaves were covered with dust, was unendurable; but they didn't move to Vozdvizhensk, which had been decided on long before, but went on living in Moscow, which had become repugnant to both of them, because lately there had been no harmony between them.

The irritation that divided them had no external cause, and every attempt to clear things up not only failed to eliminate it, but increased it. It was an inner irritation, which for her was due to the diminishing of his love, and for him to a regret that for her sake he had put himself in a distressing situation that she, instead of alleviating, was making even more distressing. Neither one ever mentioned the cause of their irritation but each thought the other in the wrong and attempted to prove it to the other at every opportunity.

For her he—all of him, with all his habits, thoughts, and desires, his whole spiritual and physical temperament—was just one thing: love for women, and this love, which she felt ought to be concentrated altogether on her alone, was diminishing. Consequently, to her mind, he must have transferred a part of this love to other women, or some other woman. She grew jealous: she was not jealous of any particular woman, but of the diminution of his love. Since she had no object for her jealousy she looked for one. At the slightest hint she would transfer her jealousy from one object to another. Sometimes she would be jealous of the low women it would be so easy for him to establish relations with, thanks to his bachelor connections; then she would be jealous of the society women he might meet; or she would be jealous of some imaginary girl he wanted to marry after breaking off with her. It was this last jealousy that tormented her most of all, particularly because he himself in an unguarded moment had imprudently told her that his mother had so little understanding of him that she had allowed herself to try to persuade him to marry young Princess Sorokin.

And since she was jealous Anna kept losing her temper with him; she seized on everything to justify her indignation. She blamed him for all the hardships of her situation. The painful state of anticipation she had to undergo in Moscow, suspended in midair; Karenin's dilatory indecisiveness; her own solitude—she attributed everything to him: if he loved her he would understand the full hardship of her situation and get her out of it. It was also he who was to blame for her living in Moscow and not in the country. He could not live buried in the country as she would have liked to. He had to have society, and so he had placed her in this horrible situation and refused to realize how distressing it was. Also, it was his fault that she was separated forever from her son.

Even the rare moments of tenderness that took place between them did not reassure her; in his tenderness she now saw a shade of matter-of-factness, of complacency, that had not been there before and that irritated her.

It was dusk already. She was alone, waiting for him to come back from some bachelor dinner; she was walking back and forth in his study (where there was less noise from the street), and turning over in her mind every detail of what they said to each other during a quarrel they had had the day before. As she kept tracing to their source the well-remembered offensive words of the quarrel, she finally worked her way back to the beginning of their conversation. For some time she couldn't believe that the quarrel had begun with such a harmless conversation, which was of no concern to either one of them. But it was actually so. It had all begun by his making fun of girls' high schools, which he considered unnecessary, while she had gone to their defense. He had a disrespectful attitude toward women's education generally, and said that Hannah, her little English protégée, had no need whatever to know anything about physics.

This irritated Anna. She regarded it as a contemptuous allusion to her own activities. She invented and uttered a phrase to pay him back for the pain he had caused her.

"I don't expect you to remember me or my feelings as a man who loved me would, but I did expect some simple tact," she said.

And as a matter of fact he had flushed with annoyance and said something disagreeable. She didn't remember her own reply, but then he had said something at that point with the evident intention of causing her pain, too:

"It's true that I have no interest in your infatuation with that little girl, since I see how unnatural it is."

This cruelty of his in destroying the world she had built for herself with such toil, in order to endure her burdensome life, and the unfairness with which he accused her of affectation and falseness, made her indignant.

"I'm very sorry that the only thing you find understandable and natural is whatever is coarse and material," she said, and left the room.

When he came to her in the evening they did not mention the quarrel, but they both felt it was only smoothed over, and not settled.

Today he had been away from home all day; she was so lonely and miserable feeling herself at odds with him that she wanted to forget everything, forgive him and be reconciled; she wanted to blame herself and vindicate him.

I'm to blame; I'm irritable and senselessly jealous. I'll make up with him, and we'll go to the country; I'll be more at peace there, she said to herself.

"Unnatural." She recalled what had hurt her most, which was not so much the word as his desire to hurt her.

I know what he meant to say: he meant to say that it's unnatural for me, not loving my own daughter, to love a strange child. What does he know about love for children? About my love for Seryozha, whom I sacrificed for his sake? But his longing to hurt me! No, he loves some other woman, it can't be anything else.

And when she saw that in her desire to comfort herself she had again completed the same circle she had gone around so many times before, and reverted to her previous state of irritation, she was horrified at herself. Is it really impossible? Am I really incapable of taking the blame on myself? she said to herself, and began again from the beginning. He's truthful, he's honorable, he loves me; and I love him, and I'll be getting the divorce any day now. What more do I want? I must have peace of mind, confidence; I'll take the blame on myself—yes, when he comes in now I'll say it was all my fault, though it wasn't, and we'll go away.

And in order to stop thinking any more and giving way to

her irritation she rang and ordered her trunks brought to be packed for the country.

Vronsky came back at ten o'clock.

## XXIV

WELL, did you have a good time?" she asked, coming toward him with a timid guilty look on her face.

"Just as usual," he replied, instantly realizing by one look that she was in one of her good moods. He was already used to these transitions, and was especially glad of it today, since he himself was in the best of spirits.

"But what do I see! Now that's nice!" he said, indicating the trunks in the hall.

"Yes, we must go away. I went out for a drive, and it was so lovely I suddenly longed to be in the country. There's nothing to keep you back, is there?"

"That's the only thing I want. I'll be back in a moment and we'll talk; I'm just going to change. Order tea."

And he went to his room.

There had been something offensive in his having said, "Now that's nice!", as one speaks to a child who has stopped being capricious, and what was even more offensive was the contrast between her guilty tone and his self-assurance; for a moment she felt a desire for battle rising within her, but making an effort to control herself she suppressed it and met him as cheerfully as before.

When he came back she told him—in a speech she had partly prepared—how she had spent her day and what her plans were for their leaving.

"D'you know, it was almost an inspiration that came over me," she said. "Why wait for the divorce here? Being in the country won't make any difference. I can't wait any longer. I don't want to hope; I don't want to hear anything more about the divorce. I've decided it's not going to have any further influence over my life. Do you agree?"

"Oh yes!" he said, looking uneasily at her excited face.

"What did you all do? Who was there?" she said, after a pause.

Vronsky named the guests. "The dinner was first-rate, and the boat races and everything were all quite nice, but in Moscow they can't do anything without being ridiculous. Some woman turned up, the Queen of Sweden's swimming teacher; she demonstrated her skill."

"What? She swam?" Anna asked with a frown.

"In some kind of red bathing costume; a hideous old woman. So when shall we leave?"

"What a silly notion! Did she swim in some special way?" Anna said, without replying.

"Not in the least. And as I say it was all frightfully silly. When were you thinking of leaving?"

Anna shook her head, as though trying to drive away some unpleasant thought.

"When shall we leave? The sooner the better. We should be able to by tomorrow. The day after."

"Yes . . . no, wait a moment. The day after tomorrow is Sunday, I have to see my mother," said Vronsky; he felt embarrassed because the moment he mentioned his mother he felt a piercing, suspicious look fixed on him. His embarrassment confirmed her suspicions. She flushed and moved away from him. It was no longer the Queen of Sweden's swimming teacher in her mind now, but young Princess Sorokin, who lived with Countess Vronsky in the country near Moscow.

"Can't you go tomorrow?" she said.

"Why no! The power of attorney and the money for the business I'm going there on won't be there by tomorrow," he replied.

"If that's so we won't leave at all."

"But why not?"

"I won't leave any later. Monday or never!"

"But why?" said Vronsky, as though surprised. "What's the sense of that?"

"It has no sense for you because you're not concerned about me. You don't want to understand what my life is. The only thing that's been occupying me here is Hannah. You say it's all pretense. After all, you said yesterday that I don't love my daughter but pretend to love this little English girl, and that it's unnatural—I'd like to know what life would be natural for me here!"

For a second she recovered herself and was horrified at her going back on her resolution. But even though she knew she was destroying herself she could not refrain; she could not help showing him how wrong he was; she could not give in to him.

"I never said that; I said I had no sympathy for this sudden affection."

"You boast of your uprightness—why don't you tell the truth?"

"I never boast and I always tell the truth," he said softly, holding back the anger that was rising up in him. "It's a pity you don't respect—"

"Respect was invented in order to hide the empty spot where love ought to be. And if you don't love me any more it would be better and more honest to say so."

"No—this is becoming unbearable!" cried Vronsky, getting up from his chair; stopping in front of her he said: "Why are you trying my patience?" he said, looking as though he could have said a great deal more, but were restraining himself. "It has its limits."

"What d'you mean by that?" she cried, looking with horror at the unmistakable look of hatred that filled his whole face, especially his cruel, menacing eyes.

"I mean—" he began, but stopped. "I must ask you what it is you want of me."

"What can I want? I can only want you not to leave me, as you are thinking of doing," she said, understanding everything he had left unsaid. "But I don't want that—that's secondary. What I want is love, and there is none. Therefore everything is finished!"

She started toward the door.

"Wait! W-a-i-t!" said Vronsky, not changing the morose set of his brows, but holding her back by the hand. "What is the matter? I said we had to put off leaving for three days, and on that you said to me I was lying, that I'm dishonorable."

"Yes, I repeat, that a man who reproaches me by saying he has sacrificed everything for my sake," she said, remembering the words used in a still earlier quarrel, "is worse than dishonorable—he is heartless!"

"No—there are limits to endurance!" he cried, and abruptly let go her hand.

He hates me, that's clear, she thought, and without looking round, in silence, her steps uncertain, she left the room.

He loves some other woman, that's even clearer, she said to herself, as she went into her own room. I want love, and there is none. Therefore everything is finished, she said, repeating her own words, and it must be finished.

But how? she asked herself, and sat down in the armchair before the mirror.

Thoughts about where she would go now—to her aunt, who had brought her up, or to Dolly; or simply abroad by herself; about what *he* was doing now in his study alone; whether this was a definitive quarrel or whether a reconciliation was still possible; about what all her former Petersburg acquaintances would say about her now; what view Karenin would take of it; and a great many other thoughts about what was going to happen now after this rupture came into her mind, but she did not give herself up to them whole-heartedly. She had some obscure thought in her mind; it was the only thing that interested her but she could not quite get hold of it. When she recalled Karenin again, she also recalled the time she had been ill after the birth of the child, and the feeling that at that time would not leave her: Why didn't I die? She recalled her words at the time, and the feeling she had had. Suddenly she realized what was in her heart. Yes—*that* was the thought that was the only thing that could solve everything.

Yes—die! she thought. Both Karenin's shame and his disgrace, and Seryozha's, and my own dreadful shame—everything will be saved by my death. Die—then he'll feel sorry, he'll love me, and suffer for me.

With a fixed smile of self-pity she sat down in the armchair, taking off and putting on the rings on her left hand, and vividly imagining to herself from all angles his feelings after her death.

The sound of approaching footsteps, his footsteps, distracted her. She busied herself pretending to put away her rings, without even turning toward him.

He came up to her; taking her by the hand he said softly: "Anna, let's leave the day after tomorrow, if you like. I agree to everything."

She said nothing.

"What is it?" he asked.

"You know yourself," she said, and then, unable to restrain herself any longer, she burst into tears.

"Abandon me—abandon me!" she murmured between her sobs. "I'll go away tomorrow. I'll do more. What am I? A depraved woman. A millstone round your neck. I don't want to torment you, I don't! I'll give you your freedom. You don't love me, you love someone else!"

Vronsky implored her to calm herself; he assured her that

there was no trace of justification for her jealousy, that he
had never stopped loving her and never would, that he loved
her more than he ever had.

"Anna, why is it you torture yourself and me?" he said,
kissing her hands. His face had a look of tenderness now,
and it seemed to her that her ear could detect the sound
of tears in his voice, she felt their moisture on her hand. And
instantly her despairing jealousy changed into a despairing
passionate tenderness; she embraced him, and covered his
head, his neck, and his hands with kisses.

## xxv

FEELING that there had been a complete reconciliation,
Anna began making active preparations the next morning
for their departure. Though it was not yet decided whether
they were leaving Monday or Tuesday, since they had both
yielded to each other the night before, Anna energetically did
everything necessary for the trip, since she now felt completely indifferent as to whether they left a day sooner or
later. She was in her room standing over an open trunk, sorting clothes, when he came in to see her, already dressed,
earlier than usual.

"I'm going to my mother at once, she may be able to send
me money through Yegorov; I'll be ready to go tomorrow," he
said.

Good as her mood was, the reference to his going out to
see his mother at her villa in the country stung her.

"No, I won't be ready in time myself," she said; at once she
thought, So it was possible to arrange things the way I
wanted. "No, do just as you had wished to. Go into the
dining room, I'll be right there; I'm just sorting out these
useless things," she said, handing something else to
Annushka, who was already carrying a heap of old clothes.

Vronsky was eating his beefsteak when she entered the
dining room.

"You wouldn't believe how repellent I find these rooms
now," she said, sitting down beside him for her coffee. "Nothing is worse than these furnished apartments. They have no
expression, really quite soulless. This clock, these curtains,
and especially the wallpaper—a nightmare! I think of Vozdvizhensk as the Promised Land. Have you sent the horses off
yet?"

"No, they'll follow us. Were you driving anywhere?"

"I wanted to go to the Wilsons', to take her a dress. Then it's definitely tomorrow?" she said in a cheerful voice; but suddenly her expression changed.

Vronsky's valet had come in to ask for a receipt for a telegram from Petersburg. There was nothing peculiar in Vronsky's getting a telegram, but he said the receipt was in his study, as though he wanted to hide something from her, and hastily turned to her.

"I'll have everything ready tomorrow without fail."

"Whom is the telegram from?" she asked, without listening to him.

"Stiva," he replied, reluctantly.

"Why didn't you show it to me? What secrets can there be between Stiva and me?"

Vronsky called the valet back and told him to bring the telegram.

"I didn't want to show it to you because Stiva has a passion for sending telegrams: What is there to wire about, when nothing has been settled?"

"About the divorce?"

"Yes, but he writes he hasn't been able to get any answer yet; he promises a decisive answer any day now. But here it is, read it."

Anna took the telegram with trembling hands and read just what Vronsky had told her, but then there was something added: "Not much hope, but I'll do everything possible and impossible."

"Last night I said I didn't care at all when I got the divorce or even if I got it," she said, flushing. "There was not the slightest need to hide it from me." That's just how he may be hiding and is hiding his correspondence with women from me, she thought.

"Oh, Yashvin wanted to come here this morning with Voytov," said Vronsky. "It seems he won from Pevtsov all he can pay, and even more—about sixty thousand."

"No," she said, irritated at his showing her so ostentatiously by this change of subject that she was irritated, "why do you imagine this news is so interesting to me that it actually has to be concealed? I said I didn't want to think about it; I'd like it to be of as little interest to you as to me."

"I'm interested because I like clarity," he said.

"Clarity doesn't depend on forms, but on love," she said, getting more and more irritated, not by what he was saying but by his tone of cool tranquillity. "Why do you want it?"

Love again, my God, he thought, frowning. "But you know why," he said; "for your sake and for the children we're going to have."

"We're not going to have any."

"That's a great pity," he said.

"You want it for the children, but you're not thinking of me," she said, completely ignoring or not hearing the words, "*for your sake* and for the children."

The question of children had long been a source of dispute between them, and of irritation to Anna. She explained his desire for children by a lack of appreciation for her beauty.

"Oh—what I said was 'for your sake.' Most of all for your sake," he repeated, his face twisting as though in pain. "Because I'm sure that most of your irritability comes from the indefiniteness of our situation."

Yes, there's he stopped pretending; you can see all his cold hatred for me, she thought, not listening to what he was saying but looking horror-struck at the cold, cruel judge who was provocatively glaring out of his eyes.

"That's not the cause," she said, "for that matter I don't understand how what you call my irritability could be caused by my being completely in your power. In what way is the situation indefinite? Quite the contrary."

"I'm extremely sorry you don't want to understand," he interrupted her, stubbornly intent on expressing his own thought. "The indefiniteness consists in your supposing that I'm free."

"As far as that's concerned you can set your mind completely at rest," she said, and turning away from him she began to drink coffee.

She raised her cup, sticking out her little finger, and put it to her lips. She took a few sips, and glanced at him; by the expression on his face she clearly realized that he was repelled by her hands, and by the gesture, and by the sound she made with her lips.

"It doesn't matter to me in the slightest what your mother thinks and whom she wants to marry you off to," she said, putting the cup down with a trembling hand.

"But that's not what we were talking about."

"No—it was just that very thing. Believe me, a woman who has no heart, whether she's old or not, or your mother or a stranger, is of no interest to me, and I have no desire to know her."

"Anna, I must ask you not to speak disrespectfully of my mother."

"A woman whose heart has not told her where the happiness and the honor of her son are to be found has no heart."

"I repeat my request: please do not speak disrespectfully of my mother, whom I respect," he said raising his voice and looking at her sternly.

She did not reply. Looking insistently at him, at his face, his hands, she remembered their reconciliation of the day before and his passionate caresses in full detail. The same caresses, she thought, that he has been lavishing, and is going to lavish, and wants to lavish on other women!

"You don't love your mother. It's all just words, words, words!" she said, looking at him with hatred.

"If that's so we have to—"

"We have to make up our minds, and I've made up mine," she said, and was about to go out, but just then Yashvin came in. Anna greeted him and stayed.

Just why, when there was a tempest in her soul and she felt she was standing at a turning point in her life that might have frightful consequences, why at that moment she had to keep up appearances in front of a stranger who in any case would find out everything sooner or later, she did not know: but immediately silencing the tempest within her she sat down and began talking to the visitor.

"Well, how are your affairs? Have you gotten the money?" she asked Yashvin.

"Oh all right; I don't think I'm going to get it all, and on Wednesday I have to leave. And when are you off?" said Yashvin, looking at Vronsky with eyes half-closed, evidently guessing there had been a quarrel.

"I think the day after tomorrow," said Vronsky.

"But you've been planning to leave for some time."

"Now, though, it's definite," said Anna, looking straight into Vronsky's eyes with an expression that told him he was not even to think of the possibility of any reconciliation.

"Aren't you sorry for that unlucky fellow Pevtsov?" she asked, continuing the conversation with Yashvin.

"I've never asked myself whether I'm sorry or not. After all, my whole fortune is right here," he indicated a side pocket, "and now I'm a rich man; but I'm going to the club tonight and I may come out a pauper. Anyone who sits down with me, after all, also wants to leave me without a shirt to my back, and I want to do it to him. So we struggle, and there's where the fun is!"

"Well, and what if you were married?" said Anna. "How would your wife feel about it?"

Yashvin laughed. "That's evidently why I never married and never meant to."

"And what about Helsingfors?" said Vronsky, entering into the conversation; he glanced at Anna, who had smiled.

Meeting his gaze Anna's face suddenly took on a chilly expression, as though she were saying to him, It's not forgotten; it's still just the same!

"Don't tell me you've been in love?" she said to Yashvin.

"Oh Lord! How many times! But you understand some people can sit down to play cards, but in such a way as always to get up again when the time for a rendezvous comes round. Now, I can devote myself to love, but in such a way that I don't come late for a game in the evening. And that's how I arrange things."

"No, I'm not talking about that, but about the real thing." She was about to say Helsingfors, but she didn't want to use a word that had been pronounced by Vronsky.

Voytov, who was buying a stallion from Vronsky, came in; Anna got up and left the room.

Before going out Vronsky came to her room. She was about to pretend to be looking for something on the table, but ashamed of the pretense she coldly looked him straight in the eye.

"What do you want?" she asked in French.

"Gambetta's pedigree; I've sold him," he replied, in a tone that said more clearly than words: I have no time for explanations, and they would lead nowhere.

As far as she's concerned I'm not to blame for anything, he thought; if she wants to punish herself so much the worse for her. But as he was going out he thought she said something, and his heart suddenly ached with pity.

"What is it, Anna?"

"Nothing," she answered, in the same cold, calm tone.

If it's nothing, then so much the worse, he thought, chilled again. He turned away and went out; as he left he caught a glimpse in the mirror of her pale face and quivering lips. He even wished to stop again and say something comforting to her, but his legs carried him out of the room before he could think of what to say. He was away all day; when he got back late at night the maid told him that Madame had a headache and had asked him not to go to her room.

## XXVI

NEVER before had a quarrel lasted a whole day. This was the first time, and it was not a quarrel—it was a manifest admission that the estrangement was complete. How was it possible for him to look at her as he had when he went into the room for the pedigree? To look at her, to see that her heart was torn with despair, and then to go out in silence with that calmly indifferent expression? Not only had he cooled off toward her, he hated her, because he loved some other woman—that was clear.

And recalling all the cruel things he had said, Anna kept inventing other things that he obviously wanted to say to her and might have, and grew more and more exasperated.

"I'm not holding you," he might have said; "you can go wherever you please. You probably did not want to be divorced from your husband so that you could go back to him. Go back then. If you need money I'll give it to you. How many rubles d'you need?"

In her imagination he said all the cruel things to her that a coarse man could say, and she didn't forgive him; it was as though he had actually said them.

And wasn't it only last night that he, a truthful, honorable man, after all, swore he loved me? Haven't I very often despaired before, and all for nothing? she told herself immediately afterward.

The whole of that day, except for a call on Mrs. Wilson, which took a couple of hours, Anna spent wondering whether it was all over or whether there was still some hope of reconciliation, whether she should leave immediately or see him once more. She waited for him all day, and when she went to her room in the evening after leaving a message with the maid that she had a headache, she said to herself: If he comes in spite of what the maid tells him it means he still loves me. If he doesn't it means it's all over; then I'll make up my mind what to do! . . .

At night she heard his carriage stop, his ring, his footsteps, and his voice talking to the maid: he believed what he was told, did not want to learn anything more about it, and went to his room. Therefore, it was all over.

And death, as the only means of reviving love for her in his heart, of punishing him, and of winning a victory in the struggle the evil spirit in her heart was carrying on against him, came to her mind clearly and vividly.

Now nothing mattered at all: whether to go to Vozdvizhensk or not, whether to get a divorce from her husband or not—it was all futile. The only thing she wanted was to punish him.

When she poured out her usual dose of morphia, and thought that all she had to do was drink the whole phial in order to die, it seemed to her so easy and simple that she started thinking once again with enjoyment of how he would torment himself, repent, and love the memory of her when it was already too late. She lay in bed with her eyes open, looking at the stucco cornice of the ceiling in the light of a single burned-down candle, and at the shadow of the screen that covered part of it, vividly imagining what he would feel when she was no longer there and was no more than a memory for him. "How could I say those cruel things to her?" he would say. "How could I leave the room without saying anything to her? But she's not there any longer. She's gone away from us forever. She is *there* . . ." Suddenly the shadow of the screen began moving; it spread over the whole cornice, the whole ceiling, and other shadows swooped to meet it from the other side; for a second they rushed together, then they spread out again with renewed swiftness, wavered, melted together, and all went dark. Death! she thought. And such horror seized her that for some time she couldn't understand where she was; it took her trembling hands a long time to find some matches and light another candle in place of the one that had burned down and gone out. No—anything, as long as I'm alive! Don't I love him? Doesn't he love me? What's happened has happened, it will all pass away, she thought, feeling tears of joy running down her cheeks at this return to life. And to save herself from her fears she hastily went to see him in his study.

He was sound asleep. She went over to him; holding the light, over his face she looked at him for a long time. Now, as he lay sleeping, she loved him so much that at the sight of him she could not hold back tears of tenderness; but she knew that if he woke up he would look at her with a cold look, sure of his own rectitude, and that before she told him she

loved him she would have to prove to him how much to
blame he was. She returned to her room without waking him
up, and toward morning, after a second dose of morphia, she
fell into a heavy, troubled sleep during which she never quite
lost consciousness.

In the morning a dreadful nightmare she had had a number of times even before her liaison with Vronsky came
to her again and woke her up. The little old man with the
matted beard was leaning over an iron bar doing something,
muttering senseless words in French, while she, as usual in
this nightmare (this was what made it so horrible) felt that
the little old man was paying no attention to her but was
doing something dreadful to her with the iron bar. She woke
up in a cold sweat.

When she got up the day before came back to her as
though in a fog.

We had a quarrel, like the ones we've had several times
before. I said I had a headache; he didn't come to see me.
We're leaving tomorrow; I'll have to see him and get ready
for the trip, she said to herself, and on hearing that he was in
his study she went to see him. As she crossed the drawing
room she heard a carriage stop at the front door, and looking through the window she saw a young girl in a lilac hat
leaning out of it giving an order to the footman who was
ringing the bell. After some talking in the hall someone went
upstairs, and she heard Vronsky's step outside the drawing
room. He was running swiftly downstairs. Anna went to the
window again. There he was without a hat, on the front
steps, going over to the carriage. The young girl in the lilac
hat handed him a package. Vronsky said something to her
with a smile. The carriage drove off; he quickly ran back
upstairs.

The fog that had enveloped everything in Anna's soul was
suddenly dissipated. The feelings she had had yesterday
pierced her aching heart with fresh pain. Now she could not
understand how she had been able to humiliate herself to the
point of spending a single day with him in his house. She
went into his study to announce her decision to him.

"That was Princess Sorokin and her daughter, who came
by to bring me the money and the documents from my
mother. I couldn't get them yesterday. How is your head—
is it better?" he said calmly, ignoring her gloomy, solemn
expression.

She stood silent in the middle of the room, gazing at him

intently. He glanced at her, frowned for a moment, then went on reading a letter. She turned away and slowly walked out of the room. He could still have called her back, but she had reached the door and he still kept silent; all that could be heard was the sound of the paper rustling as he turned a page.

"Oh, by the way," he said, when she was already in the doorway, "we're definitely leaving tomorrow, aren't we?"

"I'm not, you are," she said, turning round toward him.

"Anna—it's impossible to live like this—"

"I'm not, you are," she repeated.

"This is becoming unbearable!"

"You—you'll regret this," she said and went out.

Frightened by her look of despair as she said this he jumped up and was about to run after her, but he recollected himself, sat down again and frowned, clenching his teeth. This vague threat, which seemed to him indecent, irritated him. I've tried everything, he thought; there's only one thing left to do—pay no attention; and he began making ready to drive to town again and see his mother; he had to get her signature for the power of attorney.

She heard the sounds of his footsteps in his study and in the dining room. He stopped in the drawing room. But he did not return to her; he simply left instructions to let Voytov have the stallion in his absence. Then she heard the carriage drive up and the door open, and he went out. But then he came back again into the hall, and someone ran upstairs. It was his valet running to fetch some gloves he had forgotten. She went over to the window and saw him take the gloves without looking back, and touching the coachman's back with his hand tell him something. Then without looking up at the windows he took up his usual position in the carriage; he crossed his legs and as he put on a glove vanished round the corner.

## XXVII

HE'S gone! It's over! Anna said to herself, standing by the window; and as though in response all the impressions of darkness, when the candle had gone out and she had had that terrible dream, merged into one and filled her heart with icy horror.

No, it's impossible! she cried; and crossing the room she

vigorously rang the bell. She was so frightened of being left alone now that she didn't wait for the man to come but went to meet him.

"Find out where the Count has gone," she said.

He answered that the Count had gone to the stables.

"The Count told me to let you know that if you wished to go out the carriage would be back immediately."

"Very well. Wait a moment. I'll write a note at once. Send Michael to the stables with it, as quickly as possible."

She sat down and wrote: *"I've been to blame. Come back, we must talk it over. For God's sake come; I'm afraid."*

She sealed it and gave it to the servant.

She was afraid to be left alone now; following the servant out of the room she went to the nursery.

What's happened—there's something wrong, this isn't he! Where are his blue eyes, his sweet, shy smile? was her first thought when she caught sight of her plump, rosy little girl with her curly black hair instead of Seryozha, whom in the confusion of her mind she had expected to see in the nursery. The little girl was sitting at the table and banging on it loudly and persistently with a bottle stopper; she turned her black eyes, like two raisins, on her mother in a blank stare. Anna told the Englishwoman that she was quite well and was leaving for the country the next day, then sat down beside the little girl and began twirling the stopper round in front of her. But the child's loud, ringing laugh and the way she moved her eyebrows reminded Anna so vividly of Vronsky that choking back her sobs she hastily got up and went out. Can everything be finished? No, it's impossible, she thought; he'll come back. But how will he explain that smile, that animation of his after speaking with her? But even if he doesn't explain it I'll believe him anyhow. If I don't believe him there's only one thing left for me—and I don't want to . . . .

She looked at the clock. Twelve minutes had passed. By now he's received the note and is on his way back. It won't be long—another ten minutes. . . . But what if he doesn't come? No, that's impossible. He mustn't see I've been crying. I'll go and wash. Yes—and did I brush my hair or not? she asked herself. And she couldn't recall. She felt her head with her hand. Yes, it's brushed, but I absolutely can't remember when. She didn't even trust her hand, and went up to the mirror to see whether her hair was actually brushed or not. It was, and she was quite unable to recall when she had done it. Who's that? she thought, looking into the mirror at the feverish face with the peculiarly glittering eyes that looked out at her in fright. But that's me, she suddenly realized, and taking in her whole body she suddenly felt his kisses on her, and shuddering moved her shoulders. Then she raised her hand to her mouth and kissed it.

What is it?—I'm going out of my mind. . . . And she went to the bedroom where Annushka was tidying up.

"Annushka," she said, stopping in front of the maid and looking at her, without knowing herself what she was going to say to her.

"You were going to see Princess Oblonsky," said the maid, as though she understood her.

"Princess Oblonsky? Yes, I'm going."

Fifteen minutes there, fifteen back; he's left already, he'll be here right away, she thought; she took out her watch and looked at it. But how could he go away leaving me in such a state? How can he go on living, without having made up with me?

She went over to the window and began looking out into the street. He had had time to get back already, but her calculation might have been wrong; again she tried to remember just when he had left, and began counting the minutes.

Just as she was going out to compare her watch with the big clock, someone drove up. Looking through the window she saw his carriage, but no one came upstairs; she heard voices below. It was her messenger, who had returned in the carriage. She went down to him.

"I couldn't catch the Count. He took the Nizhny road, to the station."

"What d'you want? What is this?" she said to the merry-looking red-faced Michael, who handed her back her note.

Of course, he didn't receive it, she remembered.

"Take this same note to Countess Vronsky in the country —you know where it is? And bring back an answer at once," she said to the messenger.

And what am I going to do now myself? she thought. Yes, I'm going to Dolly's, that's right, or else I'll go out of my mind. And I can telegraph too. She wrote out a telegram: I SIMPLY MUST SPEAK TO YOU, COME AT ONCE.

After sending the telegram she went to dress. When she was already dressed and in a hat she looked again into Annushka's placid face, which had grown plumper. Manifest compassion could be seen in her small gray, kindly eyes.

"Annushka, my dear, what am I to do?" Anna muttered sobbing, as she sank helplessly into an armchair.

"What is there to be so upset about! After all, these things happen. Go out—you'll feel better," said the maid.

"Yes, I'll go," said Anna, recovering herself and standing up. "If a telegram arrives while I'm gone send it to Princess Oblonsky's . . . No, I'll come back myself."

Yes, I mustn't think, I must do something, go away, above all get out of this house, she said to herself, listening horror-struck to the terrible beating of her heart; she hurried out and got into the carriage.

"Where to, ma'am," asked Peter before getting up onto the box.

"To the Znamenka—the Oblonskys'."

## XXVIII

THE weather was bright. There had been a fine drizzle all morning, which had just cleared up now. The iron roofs, the flagstones of the pavement, the cobblestones, the wheels, leather, brass and metalwork of the carriages, all shone brightly in the May sunshine. It was three o'clock; the streets were at their busiest.

As Anna sat in a corner of the quiet carriage, gently rocking on its resilient springs to the fast trot of the pair of grays, turning over in her mind again the events of the last few days, amidst the incessant clatter of the wheels and the rapidly shifting impressions in the open air, she saw her situation quite differently from the way it had seemed to her at home. Now even the thought of death no longer appeared to be so terrifying or clear, and death itself no longer seemed inevitable. Now she reproached herself for the humiliation she had sunk to. I'm imploring him to forgive me; I've surrendered to him; I've admitted I was to blame. What for? Is it impossible for me to live without him? Without answering this without answering this she began reading the signboards. OFFICE AND WARE-HOUSE . . . DENTIST . . . Yes, I'll tell Dolly everything. She doesn't like Vronsky. It'll be humiliating, painful, but I'll tell her everything. She loves me, and I'll follow her advice. I won't surrender to him; I won't permit him to be my trainer. FILIPPOV, BAKERY . . . They say the dough is sent to Peters-burg, the Moscow water is so good. Oh, and the wells at

Mitishchen, and the pancakes . . . She recalled how a long, long time ago, when she was only seventeen, she had gone with her aunt to visit the Trinity Monastery. We still drove with horses; could that really have been I, with those red hands? How much of what seemed to me then to be lovely and inaccessible has become insignificant, and the things that existed then are now eternally beyond reach. Would I have believed then that I could descend to such humiliation? How proud and happy he'll be when he gets my note! But I'll show him . . . What a terrible smell that paint has. Why do they keep on building and painting? DRESSMAKER AND MILLINER . . . she read. A man bowed to her; it was Annushka's husband. "Our parasites"—she remembered the way Vronsky had said this. Ours? Why ours? What's dreadful is that it's impossible to tear the past out by the roots. It's impossible to tear it out, but we can hide the memory of it. And I will hide it. Then she remembered her past with Karenin, and how she had erased it from her memory. Dolly's going to think I'm leaving a second husband, so that it must be me who's in the wrong. As though I want to be in the right! I can't help it! she said to herself; she felt like weeping. But then she instantly began wondering what those two girls could have been smiling about. Probably love? They have no idea how sad it is, how base . . . The boulevard, the children. The three little boys running around playing horses. Seryozha! I'm going to lose everything, and not get him back. Yes, I'll lose everything unless he comes back. Perhaps he missed the train and is back already. Looking for more humiliation! she said to herself. No, I'll go to see Dolly and tell her straight out: "I'm unhappy, I deserve it, I'm to blame, but I'm unhappy anyhow, help me!" These horses, this carriage—how disgusting I seem to myself in his carriage: everything is his, but I won't see them any more . . .

Thinking of the words in which she was going to tell Dolly everything, and deliberately lacerating her own heart, Anna went up the stairs.

"Is there anyone here?" she asked in the hall.

"Madame Levin," answered the footman.

Kitty! The same Kitty whom Vronsky was in love with, thought Anna; the one he remembers so lovingly. He regrets he didn't marry her. And he remembers me with hatred and regrets he ever met me.

When she arrived the two sisters had been having a conference on baby feeding. Dolly went out alone to meet the visitor who was interrupting their talk.

"So you haven't left yet? I was going to see you myself," she said, "I had a letter from Stiva today."

"We also had a telegram from him," said Anna, looking round to see Kitty.

"He says he can't understand just what it is that Karenin wants but won't leave without an answer."

"I thought there was someone with you. May I read the letter?"

"Yes—Kitty," said Dolly, embarrassed. "She's stayed in the nursery; she's been very ill."

"So I heard. May I read the letter?"

"I'll bring it at once. But he hasn't refused; on the contrary, Stiva is hopeful," said Dolly, standing in the doorway.

"I have no hopes, but no regrets either," said Anna.

What, does Kitty think it degrading to meet me? thought Anna, when she was left alone. Perhaps she's right too. But it's not for her, whom Vronsky was in love with, it's not for her to be the one to show me that, even if it is the truth. I know that in my situation not a single respectable woman can receive me. I knew that from the first moment I sacrificed everything for him! Now this is my reward! Oh, how I hate him! And why did I come here? I feel even worse, even more miserable. In the next room she heard the voices of the two sisters talking. And what am I going to tell Dolly now? Give Kitty consolation, by showing her that I'm unhappy? Submit to her patronizing me? No, and even Dolly would never understand anything. And I have nothing to say to her; it would just be interesting to see Kitty and show her how I despise everyone and everything, how nothing matters to me now!

Dolly came in with the letter. Anna read it and silently handed it back.

"I knew all that," she said. "And it's not of the slightest interest to me."

"But why? On the contrary, I'm hopeful," said Dolly, looking at Anna curiously. She had never seen her in such a strange and irritable state. "And when are you leaving?" she asked.

Screwing up her eyes, Anna looked ahead of her without replying.

"Why is Kitty hiding from me?" she said, looking at the door and blushing.

"What nonsense! She's nursing her baby. It's not going very well and I was giving her some advice . . . She's very pleased; she'll be here in a moment," said Dolly awkwardly; she didn't know how to tell lies. "And here she is."

When she heard Anna had arrived Kitty didn't want to come out, but Dolly had persuaded her to. Rallying her forces Kitty came out blushing, went over to Anna and held out her hand.

"I'm very glad to see you," she said in a trembling voice.

Kitty was confused by the struggle going on in her between her hostility to this wicked woman and a desire to be indulgent; but the moment she saw Anna's beautiful, endearing face all hostility vanished at once.

"I shouldn't be surprised if you hadn't wanted to meet me. I've grown accustomed to everything. Have you been ill? Yes, you've changed," said Anna.

Kitty felt that Anna was looking at her with animosity. She explained this animosity by the awkward position Anna, who had used to patronize her, felt herself to be in now, and she was sorry for her.

They talked about her illness, about the baby, about Stiva, but it was obvious that none of this interested Anna.

"I came to say good-by to you," she said as she got up.

"When are you leaving?"

But again Anna didn't answer; she turned to Kitty.

"Yes, I'm very glad I've seen you," she said with a smile. "I've heard so much about you from all sides, even from your husband. He came to see me. I liked him very much," she added, with obvious spite. "Where is he?"

"He's gone to the country," said Kitty, blushing.

"Remember me to him—be sure you don't forget!"

"Oh, I won't forget," Kitty repeated after her naïvely, looking compassionately into her eyes.

"Then good-by, Dolly!" And kissing Dolly and shaking Kitty by the hand Anna hurried out.

"She's just the same, and just as attractive. She's so pretty!" said Kitty, when she and Dolly were alone. "But there's something pathetic about her—terribly pathetic!"

"No, there's something odd about her today," said Dolly. "When I was seeing her out I thought she felt like crying."

## XXIX

ANNA got into the carriage in an even worse mood than she had been in when she left home. Her previous tortures were now added to by a feeling that she had been insulted and rejected, which she had been clearly aware of when meeting Kitty.

"Where to, ma'am? Home?" asked Peter.

"Yes, home," she said, no longer even thinking of where she was going.

How they looked at me, as though I were something strange, incomprehensible, and curious. What can he be telling the other one with so much heat? she thought, looking at two passers-by. Is it possible to tell anyone else what you feel? I wanted to tell Dolly, and it's a good thing I didn't. How happy she would have been over my misfortune! She would have concealed it, but her main feeling would have been joy at my having been punished for the pleasures she's always envied me. Kitty—she would have been even happier. How I can see through her! She knows that I was more than ordinarily pleasant to her husband. And she's jealous of me, she hates me. She despises me too. In her eyes I'm an immoral woman. If I were an immoral woman I could have made her husband fall in love with me . . . if I'd wanted to. And I did too. Now there's someone very pleased with himself, she thought, looking at a stout, ruddy gentleman driving toward them; he had taken her for an acquaintance and raised his shiny hat above his shiny bald head, only to see he was mistaken. He thought he knew me. And he knows me just as little as anyone else on earth. I don't even know myself. I know my appetites, as the French say. Now those boys there want some of that dirty ice cream, they know that for a certainty, she thought, looking at two boys who had stopped an ice-cream vendor, who had lifted down a tub from his head and was wiping his sweating face with the end of the cloth. We all want something sweet, something delicious. If not candy then dirty ice cream. Kitty's the same: if not Vronsky, then Levin. And she envies me. And hates me. And we all hate each other. I hate Kitty, she hates me. That is the truth. TYUTKIN, COIFFEUR. Tyutkin's *my* hairdresser . . . I'll tell him that when he comes back, she thought, and smiled. Just then she remembered that she had no one she could tell funny things to. And there *is* nothing funny, nothing cheerful. Everything is nasty. They're ringing for vespers; look at that tradesman crossing himself so carefully! As though he were afraid of dropping something. What are all these churches for, all that ringing, all these lies? Only to hide the fact that we all hate one another, just like those cabmen cursing one another so furiously. Yashvin says: "He wants to leave me without a shirt to my back, and I want to do it to him." Now there's the truth!

These thoughts preoccupied her so much that she had already stopped thinking about her situation when she came to a stop in front of her house. It was only when she saw the hall porter coming out to meet her that she remembered sending the note and the telegram.

"Is there any answer?" she asked.

"I'll look at once," replied the hall porter; after glancing at his desk he took up and handed to her the thin square envelope of a telegram. I CAN'T GET BACK BEFORE TEN. VRONSKY, she read.

"And the messenger hasn't returned?"

"No, ma'am," answered the hall porter.

In that case I know what I have to do, she said to herself, and feeling a vague fury and desire for vengeance surging up within her she ran upstairs. I'll go to him myself. Before going away forever I'll tell him everything. I've never hated anyone as I do that man! she thought. When she saw his hat on the stand she shuddered with loathing. It didn't occur to her that his telegram was an answer to her telegram, that he hadn't yet received her note. She visualized him now calmly chatting with his mother and Princess Sorokin, and rejoicing over her suffering. Yes, I must go at once, she said to herself, still not knowing where to go to. She felt like escaping as quickly as possible from the feelings she had had in this dreadful house. The servants, the walls, the things in the house—everything aroused her revulsion and spite, and crushed her like a weight.

Yes, I must go to the railway station, if I don't find him then I'll go there and unmask him. Anna looked up the timetable printed in the newspaper. There was a train leaving at 8:02 that evening. Yes, I'll make it. She gave orders for the other horses to be harnessed and set about packing her handbag with the things she needed for a few days. She knew she would never go back there again. She vaguely settled on one of the plans that came into her mind: after what would happen there at the station or on the Countess's estate she would take the Nizhny line to the first town she came to.

Dinner was on the table; she went over and sniffed the bread and cheese; seeing that the smell of all food revolted her she ordered the carriage and went out. The house was already casting a shadow across the whole street, and it was a clear evening, still warm in the sunshine. Annushka, who was carrying her things out, and Peter, who put them into the carriage, and the coachman, who was evidently disgruntled—they were all repulsive to her; everything they said and did irritated her.

"I shan't be needing you, Peter."

"But what about your ticket?"

"As you like then, but I don't care," she said with annoyance.

Peter jumped on to the box; arms akimbo he told the coachman to drive to the station.

### XXX

THERE—it's that girl again! Again I understand it all, Anna said to herself, as soon as the carriage started and rattled swaying over the stones, and once again changing impressions succeeded each other.

Now what was that last thing I thought of that was so good? She made an effort to remember. *Tyutkin, coiffeur?* No, not that. Oh, it was what Yashvin was saying—a struggle for existence, and hatred—the one thing that unites people. No, it's no use your going there, she said, mentally addressing a group of people in a carriage with four horses, who were obviously driving to town for a good time. And that dog you're taking along isn't going to help you—you'll never escape from yourselves. Glancing in the direction Peter was looking she saw a workman, almost dead drunk, his head wobbling back and forth, being led away by a policeman. Now that one is more likely to, she thought. Count Vronsky and I also failed to find the satisfaction we expected so much from. And now for the first time Anna turned that bright light by which she saw everything on her relations with Vronsky, which she had always avoided thinking about before. What was he looking for in me? Not so much love as the gratification of his vanity. She remembered the way he spoke, that expression of his, like a docile setter, during the first period of their liaison.

And everything confirmed this now. Yes, what he felt was the triumph of successful vanity. Of course, love was there too, but the major part of it was pride in his success. He boasted of me . . . Now that's past. There's nothing to be proud of. Not only that, it's something to be ashamed of. He took from me everything he could, and now I'm of no use to him. He finds me burdensome, and is trying not to behave dishonorably toward me. He betrayed himself yesterday through what he said—he wants divorce and marriage in order to burn his boats. He loves me—but in what way? *The zest is gone,* she said to herself in English. That one over there wants to astonish everyone, very pleased with himself he is too, she thought, looking at a red-faced shop salesman riding a hired horse. No, as far as he's concerned my flavor has gone wrong. At the bottom of his heart, if I leave him, he'll be glad.

This was not a supposition—she saw it clearly in that piercing light that was now disclosing to her the meaning of life and of human relations.

My love keeps growing more and more passionate and egotistical, while his goes on dwindling away, and that's why we're separating, she went on thinking. And it can't be helped. There is nothing for me except what's in him, and I require him to give himself up to me, all of him, more and more completely. Up to the time of our liaison we were really together, but from then on we began irresistibly drifting in different directions. And that can't be changed. He tells me I'm senselessly jealous, but it's not true. I'm not jealous, though I am discontented. But—she opened her mouth; she had a sudden thought that excited her so much she changed her seat in the carriage. If I could be anything but a mistress passionately loving nothing but his caresses; but I cannot be and don't want to be anything else. And this desire of mine arouses his revulsion, which makes me vindictive; and there's no other way it can be. Don't I know he would never begin deceiving me, that he has no designs on that Sorokin girl, that he's not in love with Kitty, that he won't be unfaithful to me? I know all that, but it doesn't make it any easier for me. If, without loving me, he were kind and tender to me out of *duty,* but weren't what I want him to be —that would be a thousand times worse even than malice! That would be—hell! And that's what it is too. He hasn't been in love with me now for a long time. And hate begins where love leaves off . . . I don't know these streets at all . . .

those hills there, and houses, houses, houses . . . And in all those houses there are people, people . . . So many of them, countless, each one hating everyone else. Well, let me try to imagine what I want in order to be happy. Well? I get a divorce, Karenin lets me have Seryozha, and I marry Vronsky. When she recollected Karenin she instantly, with extraordinary vividness, imagined him alive in front of her, with his mild, dull, extinct eyes, the blue veins on his white hands, his intonations, his crackling knuckles; and as she recalled the feeling that there had been between them and that had also been called love she shuddered with revulsion. I'll get a divorce and be Vronsky's wife. Well—will Kitty stop looking at me as she did today? No. Will Seryozha stop asking or thinking about my two husbands? And what sort of new feeling can I think up for Vronsky and myself? Will it be possible for me to have, not even happiness, but just not torture? No, no, no!—she answered herself now without the slightest hesitation. It's impossible! It is life that is separating us, and I'm the cause of his unhappiness, and he of mine, and neither he nor I can be made over. Every effort has been made, but the screw doesn't hold. Yes, there's a beggarwoman with a baby; she thinks I feel sorry for her. Aren't we all cast into the world only in order for us to hate one another and so to torment ourselves and each other? . . . There are some high-school children walking along laughing . . . Seryozha? she recalled—I also thought I loved him, I grew tearful over my tenderness for him. But then I went on living without him, and I changed him for the other love and didn't regret the change as long as I was satisfied by that other love. And she remembered with revulsion what she called the "other love." And the clarity with which she now saw her own life and the life of other people made her happy. That's how it is with me, and with Peter, and with the coachman Theodore, and that tradesman there, and all the people living along the Volga that those advertisements invite you to go to, and everywhere and always, she thought as she drove up to the low building of the Nizhny station, where the porters came running out toward her.

"Should I get a ticket to Obiralovka?" said Peter.

She had completely forgotten where she was going and why; it was only by making a great effort that she could grasp the question.

"Yes," she said, giving him her purse, and putting her

small red handbag over her arm she stepped down from the
carriage.

Making her way through the crowd into the first-class
waiting room, she gradually recalled all the details of her
situation and the decisions she was wavering between. And
again hope and despair, flickering round all the old sore
spots, began lacerating the wounds in her tortured, violently
fluttering heart. As she sat on the star-shaped sofa waiting
for the train, looking with revulsion at people going in and
coming out (she found them all repellent) she was thinking
first of how she would reach the station and write him a
note, and what she would write him, then of how he was
now, not understanding her sufferings, complaining to his
mother of his own situation, and how she was going to enter
the room there and what she would tell him. Then she
thought of how her life might still be happy, and how agonizingly she loved and hated him, and of how violently her
heart was pounding.

<br>

XXXI

A BELL rang. Some young men, ugly, arrogant, and impetuous, yet at the same time watchful of the impression
they were making, passed by; Peter also came through the
waiting room in his livery and gaiters, with his dull animal
face, and came over to her to escort her to the train. The
noisy young men subsided as she passed them on the platform, and one of them whispered something about her to
another—of course something vile. She mounted the high
step of the carriage and sat down in the empty compartment on the soiled spring sofa, which had not been white
for a long time. Her handbag, after trembling on the springs,
fell over on its side. With a foolish smile Peter raised his
gold-braided cap at the window in a gesture of farewell;
the impudent conductor slammed the door shut and drew the
latch. An ugly woman with a bustle (Anna mentally undressed
the woman and was horrified by her monstrosity) and a
girl, laughing affectedly, ran past outside.

"Catherine's got everything, Auntie!" cried the little girl.

Even that little girl is already full of affectation and gri-
maces, thought Anna. In order not to see anyone she swiftly
got up and sat down at the opposite window of the empty
compartment. A grimy, hunched-over peasant in a cap, from

under which his tousled hair was sticking out, passed by this window, stooping over the carriage wheels. There's something familiar about that misshapen peasant, thought Anna. Then she recalled her dream, and shuddering with fear she went to the opposite door. The conductor opened it, letting in a husband and wife.

"Would you like to get out?"

Anna made no reply. The conductor and the couple who were going in did not notice the horror on her face beneath the veil. She turned back to her corner and sat down. The couple sat down on the opposite side, intently but stealthily scrutinizing her dress. Both husband and wife repelled Anna. The husband asked whether she would allow him to smoke, not in order to smoke but to start up a conversation with her. On receiving her consent he began speaking to his wife in French about things there was even less point in his talking about than there was in smoking. They talked a lot of insincere nonsense meant only for her ears. Anna clearly saw how sick of each other they were and how they hated each other. It was impossible not to hate such wretched monsters.

The second bell rang, followed by a moving of baggage, noise, shouting and laughter. It was so obvious to Anna that no one had anything to be happy about that this laughter irritated her so much it hurt; she felt like stopping up her ears in order not to hear it. Finally the third bell rang, a whistle was heard, then the screech of the locomotive; the coupling chains tugged, and the husband crossed himself. It would be interesting to ask him what he means by that, thought Anna, with a malevolent glance at him. She looked past the woman through the window at the people standing on the platform, seeing the train off, who looked as though they were sliding backward. Jolting regularly over the points, the carriage Anna was sitting in rolled past the platform, the stone wall, the signal, and some other carriages; the wheels began ringing slightly on the rails, more smoothly and evenly, the window lit up with the bright evening sunshine, and a breeze moved the blind. Anna forgot about her companions in the compartment, and breathing in the fresh air to the slight sway of the train she began thinking again:

Yes, where did I leave off? That I couldn't think up a situation in which life would not be torture, that we're all created in order to torture ourselves, that we all know it, and all think up ways of deceiving ourselves about it. But when you see the truth what is there to be done?

"Reason was given man to help him escape his anxiety," said the woman in French, evidently pleased by her phrase and twisting her tongue to get it out.

These words seemed like a response to what Anna was thinking.

To escape his anxiety, Anna repeated. And glancing at the red-cheeked husband and his thin wife, she realized that the sickly looking wife considered herself a misunderstood woman, that the husband was deceiving her and encouraging her in this opinion of herself. Directing her beam of light on them, Anna seemed to see their whole history and all the recesses of their soul. But there was nothing of any interest there and she went on with her thoughts.

Yes, I'm very anxious, and reason was given to escape that; consequently, I have to escape. Why not put out the light when there's nothing more to look at, when looking at all this is horrid? But how? Why did that conductor run past holding the handrail? What are they shouting about, those young men in the next carriage? What are they talking for, why are they laughing? It's all falsehood, all lies, all deceit, all evil!

When the train came into the station Anna went out with the crowd of other passengers, and moving away from them as though they were lepers she stopped on the platform, trying to remember why she had come there and what she had intended to do. Everything that had seemed possible to her before was now too hard to imagine, especially in the noisy crowd of these monstrous people who would not leave her in peace. Either the porters would come running up to her offering their services, or the young men, clattering their heels along the platform boards and talking in loud voices, would look her up and down, or the people she met would be walking on the wrong side. Then she remembered that she had wanted to go on farther if there was no reply, and she stopped one of the porters and asked him whether a coachman was there with a note from Count Vronsky.

"Count Vronsky? Someone from there was here just now, meeting Princess Sorokin and her daughter. What is the coachman like?"

As she was speaking to the porter the coachman, Michael, ruddy and cheerful, in a smart blue coat with a watch chain, manifestly proud of having carried out his assignment so well, came over and handed her a note. She opened it; her heart felt constricted even before she read it.

"*I'm very sorry your note didn't catch me. I'll be back at ten o'clock,*" Vronsky had written in a negligent hand.

Yes—I expected that! she said to herself, with a malicious smile.

"All right, you may go home," she said to Michael in a low voice. She spoke softly because her heart was beating so rapidly it hampered her breathing. No, I won't let you torture me, she thought, addressing the threat not to him, not to herself, but to what was forcing her to suffer, and she walked along the platform past the station building.

Two maids strolling along the platform, turned their heads to look at her, saying something about her dress. "It's real," they said about the lace she was wearing. The young men would not leave her in peace: once again they passed by, looking into her face and laughingly shouting out something in unnatural voices. The stationmaster asked her as he passed whether she was going on. A boy who was selling *kvas* could not take his eyes off her. Oh my God, where am I to go? she thought as she kept going farther and farther along the platform. At the end of it she came to a stop. Some women and children who were meeting a man in glasses, and noisily laughing and talking, fell silent and looked at her as she passed them. She started walking faster and moved away from them to the very edge of the platform. A freight train was approaching. The platform started shaking; it seemed to her that she was in the train again.

And suddenly, as she recalled the man who had been run over the day she first met Vronsky, she realized what she had to do. With a quick, light stride she descended the steps that went from the water tank to the rails and stopped next to the train that was passing right beside her. She looked at the bottom of the freight cars, at the bolts and chains and at the great iron wheels of the first car that was slowly rolling by, and tried to measure with her eye the middle point between the front and the back wheels, and the moment that point would be opposite her.

There! she said to herself, looking at the shadow of the freight car on the mixture of sand and coal the ties were sprinkled with. There—right in the middle! I'll punish him and escape from everyone and from myself . . .

She tried to fall under the middle of the first freight car as it drew level with her. But the red handbag, which she had

started taking off her arm, hindered her, and by then it was
too late: the middle of the car had passed her. She had to
wait for the next car. A feeling gripped her like the one she
had had on getting ready to go into the water when bathing;
she crossed herself. The familiar gesture of making the sign
of the cross evoked in her mind a whole series of memories
from childhood and girlhood, and suddenly the gloom that
hid everything from her broke and, for a second, life appeared to her with all its bright past joys. But she didn't
take her eyes off the wheels of the second car, which were
coming nearer. And just at that moment, when the middle
point between the wheels drew level with her, she flung
aside the red handbag and drawing her head down between
her shoulders she fell underneath the car on her hands, and
with a light movement, as though she were preparing to get
up again at once, she sank to her knees. And just at this
moment she was horror-struck by what she was doing. Where
am I? What am I doing? Why? She tried to get up, to throw
herself back, but something huge and implacable struck her
on the head and dragged her down. "Lord, forgive me for
everything!" she murmured, feeling the impossibility of
struggling. . . . A little peasant was working at the rails
muttering something to himself. And the candle by which
she had been reading that book that is filled with anxiety,
deceit, sorrow, and evil flared up with a brighter flame than
ever before, lighted up everything for her that had previously
been in darkness, flickered, dimmed, and went out forever.

# PART EIGHT

## I

Almost two months had gone by. It was already the middle of the hot summer, and Koznyshov was only now getting ready to leave Moscow.

In Koznyshov's life some events of consequence for him had been taking place. A year before his book had been finished; the fruit of six years of work, it was entitled *An Attempt at a Survey of the Foundations and Forms of Government in Europe and in Russia*. Some sections of the book and the introduction had appeared in periodicals, and other parts had been read by Koznyshov to members of his own circle, so that the ideas embodied in the work could no longer be a complete novelty for the public: nevertheless Koznyshov had been expecting his book to make a serious impression on society by its actual publication, and if not a revolution in scholarship at any rate a violent upheaval in the world of learning.

After careful revision the book had been published the year before and sent to the booksellers.

Without asking anyone about the book, and reluctantly, with feigned indifference, answering his friends' questions about how it was going, without even asking the booksellers how it was selling, Koznyshov watched keenly, with taut attentiveness, for the first impression his book made on society and on the literary world.

But a week went by, then a second and a third, and no impression at all was visible among the public; the specialists and scholars among his friends would sometimes, obviously out of politeness, begin talking about it, but the other people he knew, who had no interest in technical works, didn't mention it to him at all. And in society, which was taken up with something else, particularly at this time, there was total indifference. In periodicals, too, not a word was said about the book for a whole month.

Koznyshov calculated with precision the amount of time

817

necessary for the reviews to be written, but one month passed
by, then another, and the same silence continued.

It was only in the *Northern Beetle,* in a humorous article
about a singer, Drabanti, who had lost his voice, that a few
contemptuous references were made to Koznyshov's book,
pointing out that the book had long since been condemned by
everyone and given over to general derision.

At last, during the third month, a critical article appeared
in a serious magazine. Koznyshov even knew the writer; he
had met him once at Golubtsov's.

The writer was a very young and sickly journalist, very
bold as a writer, but with an extraordinarily meager education and very shy in personal relations.

In spite of his total contempt for him, Koznyshov began
reading his article with total respect. The article was dreadful.

It was obvious that the journalist had misunderstood the
entire book. But he had picked out excerpts so adroitly that
for anyone who hadn't read the book (which evidently meant
almost everyone) it was utterly clear that the whole book
was nothing but a collection of highfalutin words, not even
used appropriately (as was shown by question marks) and
that the author was a thoroughgoing ignoramus. All this was
done with so much wit that Koznyshov himself would not
have been reluctant to make use of the same wit himself; but
that was just what was so dreadful.

In spite of the thorough conscientiousness with which
Koznyshov tested the accuracy of the reviewer's arguments,
he did not dwell for a moment on any of the shortcomings
and errors that had been ridiculed—it was too obvious that
everything had been picked out on purpose—but immediately
began involuntarily recalling, in the most minute detail, the
time he had met and talked to the writer of the article.

Could I have offended him somehow? Koznyshov asked
himself.

And when he recalled that on meeting him he had corrected
the young man's use of a word that showed up his ignorance, Koznyshov found an explanation of what lay behind
the article.

This article was followed by a deathlike silence about the
book, both in writing and in conversation, and Koznyshov
saw that his work, which had taken him six years, and had
been worked on with such love and effort, had drifted by
without a trace.

Koznyshov's position was even more painful because now

that he had finished the book he no longer had any literary work to do; formerly that had taken up most of his time.

Koznyshov was able, educated, healthy, and active, and he did not know how to make use of all his energy. Discussions in drawing rooms, meetings, assemblies, committees —everywhere it was possible to talk—took up part of his time; but since he had been living in the city for such a long time he couldn't allow himself to become entirely absorbed in conversations as his inexperienced brother did when he came to Moscow; there was still a great deal of leisure and mental energy left over.

Luckily for him, during this period, which because of his book's failure was most painful for him, all the questions to do with the schismatics in Poland, "our American friends," the famine in Samara, exhibitions, and spiritualism, were replaced by the Slavic question, which previously had only been smoldering in society, and Koznyshov, who had been one of its promoters even before this, devoted himself to it wholeheartedly.

In the group of people Koznyshov belonged to nothing was spoken or written of at this time except the Slavic question and the Serbian war. Everything usually done by idle crowds to kill time now began to be done on behalf of the Slavs. Balls, concerts, dinners, speeches, ladies' dresses, beer, restaurants—everything bore witness to Russian sympathy for the Slavs.

Koznyshov did not agree in some details with a great deal of what was being said and written about all this. He saw that the Slav question had been turned into one of those fashionable diversions that in constant succession always serve society as a focus of interest; he also saw how many people took the question up for motives of self-interest and vanity. He admitted that the papers printed a good deal that was useless and exaggerated, with the sole object of attracting attention and shouting down their rivals. He saw that in the general upsurge of society those who leaped out in front and bellowed louder than the others were all those who were unsuccessful or felt injured: commanders in chief without armies, Ministers without portfolios, reporters without newspapers, Party leaders without followers. He saw how much of it was frivolous and ridiculous; but he also saw and admitted the unquestionable, constantly growing enthusiasm unifying all classes of society, which it was impossible not to sympathize with. The massacre of our co-religionists and Slavic brothers aroused compassion for the sufferers and indignation against their oppressors. And the heroism of the Serbs and Montenegrins who were battling in a great cause kindled a desire throughout the nation to help their brothers not only with words now but by deeds.

But there was, also, another fact that delighted Koznyshov: this was that public opinion was manifesting itself. Society had definitely expressed its wishes. As Koznyshov put it, the soul of the nation had achieved expression. And the more he busied himself with this question the more evident it became to him that it was a cause that ought to attain gigantic proportions, and become epoch-making.

He devoted himself wholeheartedly to the service of this great cause and forgot to think about his book.

His time was all taken up now, so that he couldn't get round to answering all the letters and demands addressed to him.

Having spent the whole spring and part of the summer working, he only got ready in July to go off to the country to his brother's.

He went both to rest for two weeks and, in that holy of holies, the very heart of the country, to enjoy the sight of that swelling up of the people's spirit which he and all city dwellers were completely convinced of. Katavasov, who for some time had been preparing to keep the promise he had made Levin to pay him a visit, went along.

## II

KOZNYSHOV and Katavasov hardly had time to get to the Kursk station, which was especially crowded that day, and get out of their carriage to look for the footman who had followed with their baggage, when some Volunteers drove up in four cabs. The Volunteers were met by some ladies with bouquets; accompanied by a crowd surging behind them they went into the station.

As one of the ladies who had met the Volunteers was leaving the waiting room she spoke to Koznyshov: "Have you come to see them off too?" she asked in French.

"No, Princess, I'm leaving myself. I'm going to my brother's for a rest. And d'you always come to see them off?" said Koznyshov, with a slight smile.

"But that's impossible!" replied the Princess. "Is it true that eight hundred have already been sent off from here? Malvinsky didn't believe me."

"More than that. If you count those who haven't left from Moscow directly it's more than a thousand," said Koznyshov.

"There you are, it's just as I said!" the lady said joyfully. "And it's true, isn't it, that about a million rubles have already been contributed?"

"More, Princess."

"And what a telegram there was today! The Turks have been beaten again!"

"Yes, I saw it," Koznyshov replied. They were speaking about the last telegram, confirming the fact that the Turks had been beaten three days before at all points and were fleeing, and that a decisive engagement was being expected the following day.

"Oh yes, by the way, there's a young man, a splendid fellow, who wants to go. I don't know why they've been making difficulties. I wanted to ask you—I know him—to write a note if you would. He's been sent to me by Countess Lydia."

After getting whatever details the Princess could give him about the young applicant, Koznyshov went into the first-class waiting room, wrote a note to the man it depended on, and gave it to the Princess.

"You know the famous Count Vronsky is on this train?" said the Princess with a triumphant and meaningful smile, as he gave her the note.

"I heard he was going, but I didn't know when. On this train?"

"I saw him. He's here; his mother is seeing him off. After all, it's the best thing he could have done."

"Oh yes, of course."

While they were speaking the crowd had been streaming past them toward the dining table. They also moved forward and heard a man with a loud voice making a speech to the Volunteers. "To serve the Faith, mankind, and our brothers," he was saying, raising his voice higher and higher. "Mother Moscow blesses you in the great cause! Hail!" he bellowed tearfully in conclusion.

Everyone yelled *Hail!* and a fresh crowd surged into the refreshment room, nearly knocking the Princess off her feet.

"Ah Princess! Well, what d'you think!" said Oblonsky, suddenly popping up with a radiant smile in the middle of the crowd. "He spoke magnificently, didn't he? Such warmth! Bravo! And Koznyshov! Now you ought to say something, just a few words, you know, to encourage them; you do that so well," he added with a tender, respectful and solicitous smile, gently pushing Koznyshov forward by the arm.

"No, I'm just leaving."

"Where to?"

"To my brother's in the country," replied Koznyshov.

"Then you'll be seeing my wife. I've written her, but you'll see her before; please tell her you've seen me and that it's *all right*. She'll understand. Though you might tell her, if you'll be so kind, that I've been appointed Member of the Committee of the Joint— Well, she'll understand! You know, the little miseries of human life," he said to the Princess, as though apologizing. "And Princess Myagky—not Lisa but Bibish—is really sending a thousand rifles and twelve nurses. Did I tell you?"

"Yes, I heard," Koznyshov answered reluctantly.

"But it's a pity you're leaving," said Oblonsky. "Tomorrow we're giving a dinner to two men who're off to the war—Bartnyansky from Petersburg and our own Veslovsky, Vasenka. They're both going. Veslovsky got married a little while ago. Now there's a fine fellow! Don't you think so, Princess?"

The Princess looked at Koznyshov without answering. But Oblonsky wasn't in the least disconcerted by the fact that Koznyshov and the Princess seemed anxious to get rid of him. He looked smilingly at the feather on the Princess's hat, or all round him as though trying to recall something. Catching sight of a lady walking about with a collection box, he called her over and put in a five-ruble note.

"I can't keep calm when I see those collection boxes, as long as I have any money on me," he said. "And what a telegram that was today! Gallant chaps, those Montenegrins!"

"You don't say!" he exclaimed, when the Princess told him that Vronsky was leaving on that train. For a second Oblonsky's face looked sad, but a moment later, when, bouncing slightly at every step and smoothing his whiskers, he entered the waiting room where Vronsky was, Oblonsky had already forgotten how desperately he had sobbed over his sister's corpse, and saw in Vronsky only a hero and an old friend.

"With all his faults one must do him justice," said the Princess to Koznyshov the moment Oblonsky had left them. "There's someone with a totally Russian, Slavic character! I'm only afraid it'll be unpleasant for Vronsky to see him. Say what you will, I find that man's fate touching. Have a talk with him on the trip," said the Princess.

"Yes, perhaps I shall, if I can."

"I never liked him, but this atones for a great deal. He's not only going himself, he's taking along an entire squadron at his own expense."

"Yes, so I heard."

The bell rang. Everyone crowded toward the door.

"There he is!" murmured the Princess, indicating Vronsky, in a long overcoat and black, broad-brimmed hat, who was walking by with his mother on his arm. Oblonsky was walking beside him, talking animatedly.

Vronsky was looking straight before him with a frown, as though paying no attention to what Oblonsky was saying.

Probably at a sign from Oblonsky he glanced round toward where the Princess and Koznyshov were standing, and silently lifted his hat. His face, which had aged and looked full of suffering, seemed turned to stone.

Going up to the train Vronsky, letting his mother pass before him, silently vanished into one of the compartments.

On the platform "God Save the Tsar" was struck up, followed by shouts of *Hurrah!* and *Hail!* One of the Volunteers, a tall, very young man with a sunken chest, was bowing in a particularly noticeable way, waving a felt hat and a bouquet over his head. From behind him two officers and an elderly man with a large beard in a greasy cap, thrust their heads out and also bowed.

### III

AFTER saying good-by to the Princess, Koznyshov made his way into the packed carriage together with Katavasov, who had joined him. The train started.

At the Tsaritsyn station it was met by a melodious choir of young people singing "Slavsya." Once again the Volunteers bowed and stuck their heads out, but Koznyshov paid no attention to them; he had had so much to do with Volunteers that by now he was familiar with their general type, and it had no interest for him. But Katavasov, whose scholarly pursuits had given him occasion to observe them, was very much interested and questioned Koznyshov about them. Koznyshov advised him to go into the second-class car-

riage and talk to them himself. At the next station Katavasov
followed his advice.

As soon as the train stopped he went into the second-class
to introduce himself. The Volunteers were sitting in a corner
of the carriage, talking loudly and obviously aware that the
attention of the passengers, as well as of Katavasov who had
just come in, was concentrated on them. The tall young
man with the sunken chest was talking louder than anyone
else. He was obviously drunk and was telling a story about
something that had happened at his school. Sitting opposite
him was an officer, no longer young, in the military jacket of
the Austrian Guards. He was listening to the storyteller with
a smile and trying to stop him. The third Volunteer, wearing
an artillery uniform, was sitting beside them on a valise.
The fourth was asleep.

Starting up a conversation with the young man, Katavasov
learned that he had been a rich Moscow merchant, who had
run through a large fortune before he was twenty-two.
Katavasov disliked him for being effeminate, spoiled, and
sickly; he was obviously convinced, especially in his drunken
state, that he was going to perform some heroic exploit, and
was bragging in the most offensive way.

The other, the retired officer, also made a disagreeable impression on Katavasov. He was plainly someone who had
tried his hand at everything. He had had a post on a railway, been an estate manager, had started factories himself;
he talked about everything quite needlessly and kept hap-
hazardly using technical words.

On the other hand, Katavasov liked the third one, the
artilleryman, very much. He was a modest, quiet fellow,
who obviously deferred to the erudition of the retired Guards
officer and to the heroic self-sacrifice of the merchant; he
said nothing about himself. When Katavasov asked what had
impelled him to go to Serbia he answered modestly:

"Well, everyone's going. We have to help the Serbs too.
You feel sorry for them."

"Yes, especially since there are so few of you artillerymen
there," said Katavasov.

"Well, I didn't really serve very long in the artillery; maybe
they'll assign me to the infantry, or the cavalry."

"Why the infantry, when they need artillerymen more than
anything else?" said Katavasov, imagining by the artilleryman's age that he must have reached a considerable rank.

"I didn't serve long in the artillery, I'm a retired cadet," he said, and began to explain why he had failed the examination.

All this together made an unpleasant impression on Katavasov, and when the Volunteers went out at the station to get a drink he wanted to verify this unfavorable impression by talking to someone. One of the passengers, a little old man in a military greatcoat, had been listening in all the while on Katavasov's conversation with the Volunteers. When they were left alone Katavasov started talking to him.

"What different situations they all come from, all these people going off there," said Katavasov vaguely, wishing to express his own opinion while at the same time drawing out the old man.

The old man had been a soldier and had taken part in two campaigns. He knew what a soldier was, and by the look and talk of these men, and by the swagger with which they applied themselves to the bottle while traveling, he considered them bad soldiers. Also, he lived in a provincial town and wanted to tell the story of some soldier from his town who had volunteered, a drunkard and thief, whom no one would give work to any longer. But knowing by experience that with the present public mood it was dangerous to express any opinion contrary to what was generally thought, and especially to condemn the Volunteers, he also just looked at Katavasov.

"Well, they need men there," he said, with laughing eyes. And they started talking about the latest war news; both of them concealed from each other their perplexity about whom the engagement was expected with the following day, when according to the latest reports the Turks had been beaten at all points. So they separated, neither one expressing any opinion.

When Katavasov went back to his own carriage he couldn't help coloring the truth: he told Koznyshov his observation of the Volunteers in a way that made it look as though they were splendid fellows.

At the station of a big town singing and shouts met the Volunteers once again; women and men appeared again with collection boxes, and provincial ladies brought the Volunteers bouquets and followed them into the buffet; but by now it was all much weaker and more toned down than it had been in Moscow.

## IV

DURING the stop in the Provincial capital Koznyshov did not go out to the buffet but started walking back and forth along the platform.

Passing by Vronsky's compartment for the first time he noticed that the blind was drawn. But when he passed by again he saw the old Countess by the window. She beckoned to him.

"There, I'm going too; I'm taking him as far as Kursk," she said.

"So I heard," said Koznyshov, stopping by her window, and glancing inside. "What a splendid thing for him to do!" he added, seeing that Vronsky was not in the compartment.

"Yes, but after that misfortune of his what else was there for him to do?"

"What a frightful thing it was!" said Koznyshov.

"Oh, what I've had to endure! But do come in . . . Oh, what I've had to endure!" she repeated, after Koznyshov had come in and sat down beside her on the sofa. "It was unimaginable! For six weeks he didn't speak to anyone; he didn't eat anything unless I begged him to. And it was impossible to leave him alone for a second. We took away everything he might have used to kill himself with; we lived on the ground floor, but you couldn't tell what he might do. Of course you know he had once tried to shoot himself on her account," she added; the old woman frowned at the recollection. "Yes, she ended just as such a woman ought to have ended. Even the death she chose was base and common."

"It's not for us to judge, Countess," said Koznyshov with a sigh. "But I can understand how painful it was for you."

"Oh, don't speak about it! I was living on my estate, and he was with me. A note was brought in; he wrote an answer and sent it off. We hadn't the least idea she was right there at the station herself. That evening I had just gone to my room when my Mary told me that a lady had thrown herself under a train. It was as though I'd been hit with something —I knew it was she! The first thing I said was—don't tell him! But they had already told him. His coachman had been there and seen the whole thing. When I ran to his room he was beside himself—it was dreadful to see him. He didn't say a word; he just raced to the station. I don't actually know what happened there, but he was brought back like a corpse. I should never have recognized him. The doctor said it was 'complete prostration.' Then he almost went raving mad.

"Oh, what's the use of talking!" said the Countess, with a gesture of her hand. "It was a frightful time! No, no matter what you say she was a bad woman. Such desperate passions! It's all just to prove something special. Well, now she's proved it; she's destroyed herself and two fine men—her husband and my unfortunate son."

"How is her husband?" asked Koznyshov.

"He's taken her daughter. At first Alexis agreed to everything. But now he's terribly tormented at having given his daughter away to a stranger, and he can't go back on his word. Karenin went to the funeral. But we tried to see to it that they didn't meet. For him, the husband, it's easier: she set him free. But my poor son had given himself up to her entirely. He abandoned everything—his career, me—and then she didn't even pity him but deliberately destroyed him altogether. No, say what you like, her death itself was the death of a base woman with no religion. May God forgive me, but I cannot help hating her memory when I look at the ruin of my son."

"But how is he now?"

"It's a godsend for us, this Serbian war. I'm an old woman, I don't understand a thing about it, but for him it's a godsend. Of course it's terrible for me as a mother; and then the main thing is that it's said not to be very well regarded in Petersburg. But what can be done! It was the only thing that could get him on his feet again. Yashvin, that friend of his, had lost everything he had at cards and was about to go to Serbia. He went to see him and persuaded him to come along. Now it's an occupation for him. Please have a talk with him, I want him to have some distraction. He's so sad. And on top of everything else unluckily his teeth have started aching. But he'll be delighted to see you. Please talk to him, he's walking about on the other side."

Koznyshov said he would be very glad to, and went over to the platform on the other side of the train.

## V

IN the slanting evening shadow of a pile of sacks heaped up on the platform Vronsky, in his long overcoat, his hat pulled down and his hands in his pockets, was walking up and down like a caged animal, turning sharply every twenty paces. As Koznyshov approached it seemed to him that Vronsky saw him but pretended not to. It didn't matter to Koznyshov; there was nothing personal in his relations with Vronsky.

At that moment Vronsky was an important factor in a great cause, in Koznyshov's eyes, and Koznyshov considered it his duty to commend and encourage him. He went over to him.

Vronsky stopped short, peered at Koznyshov, recognized him, and taking a few steps toward him pressed his hand very very hard.

"It's very possible you don't want to see me," said Koznyshov, "but is there no way I can be of any service to you?"

"There's no one I should dislike seeing any the less," said Vronsky. "Forgive me—there's nothing left in life for me to like."

"I understand; I wanted to offer my services," said Koznyshov, gazing into Vronsky's face, which was plainly marked by suffering. "Would a letter to Ristich, or Milan, be of any use to you?"

"Oh no!" said Vronsky, as though finding it difficult to understand. "If it's all the same to you let's walk up and down. It's so stuffy in the train. A letter? No, thank you; there's no need for any letters of introduction in order to meet death. Unless they're to the Turks. . . ." he said, smiling with his mouth alone. His eyes kept their expression of angry suffering.

"Yes, but you might find it easier to establish connections —which in any case are necessary—if the person is prepared. But as you like. I was very pleased to hear of your decision. There are so many attacks on the Volunteers as it is that a man like yourself will raise them in the eyes of the public."

"The only merit I have as a man is that life means nothing to me," said Vronsky, "and that I have enough physical energy to hack my way into a fight and slay or fall—I'm sure of that. I'm glad there's something for which I can lay down a life that is not only useless to me but loathsome. It'll be of some use to somebody." And he made an impatient movement of his jaw, because of the constant gnawing pain in his tooth, which even prevented him from speaking with the expression he wanted.

"It'll make a new man of you, I predict," said Koznyshov, who felt touched. "The liberation of one's brothers from oppression is a goal that is worth both dying and living for. May God give you outward success—and inner peace," he added, holding out his hand.

Vronsky grasped it warmly. "Yes, as a utensil I may be of some use—but as a man—I am—a wreck," he said, pausing between words.

And suddenly something completely different, not a pain but a general, agonizing inner discomfort made him forget his toothache for a moment. When he saw the tender and the rails, under the influence of his conversation with an acquaintance he had not met since his misfortune, *she* suddenly came to mind, that is, what had been left of her when he had run like a madman into the railway shed: the mangled body, still full of recent life, stretched out shamelessly on a table before the eyes of strangers; the head, unhurt, flung back with its heavy plaits and curls round the temples, and on the lovely face, with its red, half-open lips, a frozen expression, strange and pitiful around the lips and dreadful in the fixed open eyes, which seemed to be saying in words the dreadful thing—about his being sorry—that she had said to him during their quarrel.

And he tried to remember her as she had been when he met her the first time, also at a station, mysterious, charming, loving, seeking happiness and giving it, and not cruelly vindictive, as he recollected her at the last. He tried to recall their best moments; but those moments were poisoned forever. He could only remember her as triumphant in having carried out her threat of inflicting on him a futile but indelible remorse. He stopped feeling his toothache, and sobs contorted his face.

After walking past the sacks twice and regaining control over himself, he turned calmly to Koznyshov: "Have you seen any telegrams since the one yesterday? Yes, they've been beaten for the third time; but a decisive engagement is expcted tomorrow."

And after talking some more about the proclamation of Milan as King and about the enormous consequences this might have, they separated when the second bell rang to go to their own carriages.

## VI

SINCE he hadn't known when he was going to leave Moscow, Koznyshov had not telegraphed his brother asking to be met. Levin was not at home when Katavasov and Koznyshov, dusty as Arabs, arrived at the steps of the Pokrovsk house at noon in the little carriage they had hired at the station. Kitty, who was sitting on the balcony with her father and sister, recognized her brother-in-law and ran down to meet him.

"Really, not letting us know—aren't you ashamed of yourself!" she said, holding her hand out to Koznyshov and putting her forehead up for a kiss.

"We got here splendidly, and didn't upset you all," replied Koznyshov. "I'm so dusty I'm afraid to touch you. I've been so busy I didn't know when I could tear myself away. And you as usual," he said smiling, "are enjoying your peaceful happiness in your peaceful backwater beyond reach of the current. And here is our friend Katavasov, who's managed to come at last."

"But I'm not a Negro—I'll just have a wash, then I'll look human," said Katavasov with his habitual facetiousness, holding out his hand and smiling, his teeth particularly bright by contrast with his smudged face.

"Kostya will be delighted. He's gone to the farm; he should be back by now."

"Always busy with his farming! Just as we said—a backwater," said Katavasov. "And in town we're unaware of anything but the Serbian war. Well, what's my friend's attitude toward that? Surely not the same as everyone else's?"

"Well, nothing special, the same as everyone's," Kitty replied, with a somewhat embarrassed look at Koznyshov. "Well, I'll send for him. Papa's staying with us; he came back from abroad a little while back."

And after giving instructions to send for Levin, to show the dust-stained guests where to wash—one in Levin's study and the other in Dolly's big room—and to prepare their lunch, Kitty, taking advantage of the right to move quickly, which she had been deprived of during her pregnancy, ran up to the balcony.

"It's Koznyshov and Katavasov, the professor," she said.

"Oh what a nuisance this heat is!" said the Prince.

"No, Papa, he's very sweet, and Kostya's very fond of him," said Kitty with a smile, as though she were appealing to him; she had noticed a sarcastic expression on her father's face.

"But I wasn't saying anything."

"You go and entertain them, darling," said Kitty to her sister. "They saw Stiva at the station, he's all right. And I'll run in to see Mitya. Just my luck that I haven't fed him since breakfast. He's awakened by now and sure to be screaming." And feeling a gush of milk she hurried off to the nursery.

Actually it was not that she had guessed it (the bond between her and the child had not yet been broken) she knew with certainty by the gush of milk in her that he had not been fed enough.

She knew he would be screaming even before she reached the nursery. And in fact he was. She heard his voice and walked more rapidly. But the faster she walked the louder he screamed. His voice was fine and healthy; he was just hungry and impatient.

"Has he been screaming long, Nanny? Really long?" Kitty said hurriedly, seating herself on a chair and making preparations to nurse him. "But give him to me at once, quickly. Oh, Nanny, really, how tiresome you are—tie his cap on later!"

The baby was convulsed with hungry yells.

"But you can't do that, my dear," said Miss Agatha, who was almost always in the nursery. "He has to be properly tidied up. Goo! Goo!" she cooed to the baby, paying no attention to his mother.

The nanny brought the baby to its mother. Miss Agatha followed behind, her face melting with tenderness.

"He knows me, he knows me! It's God's truth, Madame, he recognized me!" cried Miss Agatha, outshouting the baby.

But Kitty wasn't listening to what she was saying. Her impatience kept increasing together with that of the baby's.

Because of their impatience it took a long time for things to go right. The baby caught hold of the wrong place and lost its temper.

At last, after a great deal of desperate choking screams, and of sucking away with no results, things settled down; both mother and child felt calmer at the same time, and they both subsided.

"But the poor little thing's all bathed in sweat too," said Kitty, feeling him with her hand. "But why d'you think he knows you?" she added, moving her eyes to watch the baby's roguish eyes, as it seemed to her, peeping out from under his cap, which had slipped forward, his little cheeks regularly sucking, and his little hand with the red palm which he was moving round in circles.

"It's not possible! If he knew anyone at all it would be me," said Kitty in response to Miss Agatha's claim, and she smiled.

She was smiling because, though she said he couldn't know anyone, she knew in her heart that not only did he know Miss Agatha, but that he knew and understood a great many other things that no one else knew, and that she, his mother, knew and had begun to understand herself only thanks to him. For Miss Agatha, for the nanny, for his grandfather, and even for his father, Mitya was a living creature that required only material care; but for his mother he had been a thinking being for a long time now, with whom she was already involved in a long series of spiritual relations.

"Well, you'll see for yourself when he wakes up, God willing. When I do this he just beams, the darling! He beams away like a sunny morning!" said Miss Agatha.

"All right, all right, we'll see later," whispered Kitty. "Now go away, he's falling asleep."

## VII

Miss Agatha went out on tiptoe; the nanny pulled down the blind, drove away a fly from under the muslin curtain of the cot, as well as a bumblebee buzzing against the windowpane, and sat down, waving a withered birch branch over the mother and child.

"Oh what heat, what heat! If only God would send down a little shower!" she said.

"Yes, yes, sh-sh-sh . . ." was all Kitty answered, rocking gently back and forth and tenderly pressing the plump little arm that looked as though it had a thread tied round the wrist; Mitya kept waving it feebly about, opening and closing his eyes. This little hand disturbed Kitty; she felt like kissing it, but she was afraid she might wake the baby. At last the little hand stopped moving, and the eyes closed. Only from time to time, as he went on sucking, the baby, raising his long, curved eyelashes, would look at his mother with moist eyes that in the half-light seemed black. The nanny had

stopped fanning them and had dozed off. Upstairs the
Prince's booming voice and Katavasov's guffawing could be
heard.

They've probably started up a conversation without me,
Kitty thought; all the same it's annoying that Kostya's not
here. He must have gone to see the beehives again. It's sad
he spends so much time there, but I'm pleased about it anyhow. It's a distraction for him; he's become more cheerful
now than he was in spring. He was so glum and worried
then, I felt so alarmed about him. He really is so funny!

She knew what it was that had been worrying her husband.
It was his lack of faith. If she had been asked whether she
thought he would find no salvation in the afterlife if he had
no faith, she would have had to agree that he wouldn't, but
his lack of faith did not make her unhappy; while admitting
that there could be no salvation for an unbeliever, and loving
her husband's soul more than anything in the world, she
thought about his lack of faith with a smile and told herself he was funny.

Why does he keep reading all that philosophy all year
round? she thought. If it's all written down in those books
he can understand it. If what they say is false what's the
good of reading them? He says himself he'd like to be a believer. Then why doesn't he believe? He thinks too much,
that must be it. And he thinks such a lot because of his solitude. He's always alone, alone. He can't talk to us about
everything. I think he'll like these visitors, especially Katavasov. He likes arguing with him, she thought, and all at
once she started thinking about where it would be most convenient to have Katavasov sleep—whether separately or together with Koznyshov. Then a thought suddenly occurred to
her that made her quiver with excitement and even upset
Mitya, who gave her a stern look. I don't think the laundry-
woman has brought back the laundry yet, and the spare
sheets are all being used. If I don't see to it Miss Agatha will
give Koznyshov some used sheets; the mere thought of this
made the blood rush to Kitty's face.

Yes, I'll have to see about it, she decided and returning to
what she had been thinking before she remembered that there
was something spiritual that still hadn't been thought
through; she began trying to recall what it was. Oh yes,
Kostya's an unbeliever, she thought again with a smile.

Well, an unbeliever! I'd rather have him stay that way
than be like Madame Stahl, or the way I wanted to be that

time when I was abroad. No—he would never put on any pretense about anything.

And a recent example of his goodness came vividly to her mind. Two weeks before Dolly had received a penitent letter from Oblonsky. He had implored her to save his honor and sell her estate, in order to settle his debts. Dolly was in despair; she was full of hatred for her husband, contempt, pity; she was determined to divorce him and refuse, but it ended by her agreeing to sell off a part of her estate. With an involuntary smile of tenderness Kitty then remembered her husband's embarrassment, his repeated clumsy efforts to approach the subject that was on his mind, and how he finally thought up the only way of helping Dolly without offending her; he suggested that Kitty give her sister part of her own estate, which had never occurred to her.

How can he be an unbeliever? With such a heart, with his fear of hurting anyone's feelings, even a child's! Everything is for everyone else, nothing is for himself. Sergius just assumes that it's Kostya's duty to act as his foreman. His sister too. Now Dolly and her children are wards of his. And all those peasants who turn up here every day to see him, as though he were obliged to serve them.

"Yes, you just be like your father, just like him," she murmured, handing Mitya to the nanny and touching her lips to his little cheek.

## VIII

FROM the moment Levin saw his beloved brother dying and for the first time looked at the problems of life and death in the light of what he called the new convictions that between the ages of twenty and thirty-four had imperceptibly taken the place of the beliefs of his childhood and youth, he was horrified not so much by death as by a life without the slightest knowledge of where it came from, what it was for, and why, and what it was. The organism, its dissolution, the indestructibility of matter, the law of the conservation of energy, evolution—these were the words that had replaced his former faith. These words and the concepts associated with them were very useful for intellectual purposes, but they made no contribution to life, and Levin suddenly felt he was in the position of a man who had exchanged a warm fur coat for a muslin blouse, and who the first time he finds himself in the frost is persuaded beyond question, not by arguments but by the whole of his being, that he's no better than naked and is inevitably bound to perish miserably.

From that moment on, even though he didn't realize it and went on living as before, Levin never ceased feeling this terror at his own ignorance.

Aside from this he had an obscure feeling that what he called his convictions was not only ignorance, but represented an order of ideas that made it impossible to acquire the knowledge he needed.

After he married, the new joys and obligations he became aware of stifled these thoughts completely at first; but lately, since his wife had given birth to their child, while he was living in Moscow with nothing to do, this problem, which demanded a solution, began occupying his mind more and more often, more and more insistently.

For him the problem was this: If I don't accept the answers given by Christianity to the questions of my life, what answers do I accept? And in the whole arsenal of his convictions he was quite incapable of finding not only answers of any kind, but even anything that resembled an answer.

He was in the position of someone looking for food in a toyshop or a gunshop.

Involuntarily and unconsciously, he now sought in every book, every conversation, every human being, some relationship to these problems and to their solution.

What astounded and upset him most of all was that most people of his milieu and his age, who like himself had also replaced their former beliefs with just the same modern convictions as he himself, saw no calamity in it and were all quite serene and contented. So in addition to the cardinal question Levin was tormented by still other questions: Were these people sincere? Weren't they pretending? Or did they somehow understand, in a different way and more clearly than he did, the answers science gave to the questions that preoccupied him? And he painstakingly studied both the opinions of these people and the books that gave expression to these answers.

One thing he had discovered since the time these questions began to occupy him was that he had made a mistake in thinking, on the basis of recollections of his youthful university milieu, that religion had already outlived its time and no longer existed. Everyone close to him who lived a good life was a believer. The old Prince, and Lvov, whom he was so fond of, and Koznyshov, and all the women; his wife believed as he had in early childhood, and ninety-nine hundredths of the Russian people, the whole of that people whose life inspired him with the deepest respect, were believers.

Another thing was that after reading a great many books he became convinced that those who shared the same views understood them no better than he did, and that without explaining anything they simply ignored those questions he felt he had to have an answer to in order to go on living, to solve totally different questions that could not interest him, such as, for instance, the evolution of organisms, the mechanical explanation of the soul, and so on.

Aside from this, during his wife's confinement something extraordinary had happened to him. He, an unbeliever, had begun praying, and at the moment of praying he had believed. But the moment would pass and he could not find a place in his life for the mood he had been in at the time.

He could not admit that he had known the truth at that time, and was mistaken now, because the moment he would begin to think about it calmly everything would fall to pieces; nor could he admit that he had been mistaken at the time, because he prized the spiritual condition he had been in then, and if he had admitted that it had been a result of weakness he would have been denigrating those moments. He was in a state of agonizing discord with himself, and strained all his spiritual powers to get out of it.

IX

THESE thoughts oppressed and tormented Levin with varying degrees of intensity, but they never left him. He kept reading and thinking, and the more he read and thought the farther away he felt from the goal he was pursuing.

During the last part of his stay in Moscow, and after he went back to the country, he convinced himself that he would find no answer among the materialists, and he read through once again Plato, and Spinoza, and Kant, and Schelling, and Hagel, and Schopenhauer, philosophers who gave a nonmaterialistic explanation of life.

These ideas seemed fruitful to him when he either began reading or devising refutations of other doctrines, especially those of the materialists; but as soon as he began reading or himself devised the answers to these questions the same thing would invariably happen. As long as he followed the given definitions of vague words like *spirit, will, freedom, substance,* and deliberately entered the verbal trap set by the philosophers or himself, he would seem to begin to understand something. But all he had to do was to forget this artificial train of thought, and taking real life as a starting point go back to what gave him satisfaction as long as he followed a given thread of argument—and suddenly all this artificial structure collapsed like a house of cards and it was clear that the structure had been made out of the same words rearranged, and in disregard of something that was more important in life than reason.

At one time, while reading Schopenhauer, he replaced his word *will* by *love,* and this new philosophy comforted him for a day or two, as long as he stayed close to it; but it also collapsed just like the others when he looked at it later from the standpoint of life, and turned out to be a muslin blouse with no warmth in it.

His brother Koznyshov advised him to read the theological works of Khomyakov. Levin read the second volume of Khomyakov's works, and in spite of the polemical, elegant, and witty tone that at first repelled him, he was struck by its teaching concerning the Church. He was struck at first by the idea that the attainment of divine truth was not given to the individual, but was given to a community of people united by love—the Church. He was gladdened by the thought that it was easier to believe in an existing Church that was living in the present, that embraced all the beliefs of mankind and had God at its head, and was therefore holy and infallible, and to accept from that the beliefs in God, in the Creation, in the Fall, in Redemption, than to begin with God, a remote, mysterious God, Creation and so on. But after reading a history of the Church, first by a Roman Catholic and then by a Greek Orthodox writer, and seeing that both Churches, infallible by their very essence, repudiated each other, he became disillusioned with Khomyakov's teaching about the Church too, and this edifice crumbled to dust just like other philosophical structures.

That whole spring he was not himself, and he lived through dreadful moments.

I cannot live without knowing what I am and why I'm here. And I cannot find that out; therefore I cannot live, Levin said to himself.

In time that is infinite, in matter that is infinite, in space than is infinite, an organic cell is formed; this cell maintains itself for a while, then bursts, and that cell is—myself.

This was an agonizing falsehood, but it was the sole, ultimate result of the millennial labors of human thought in this direction.

This was the ultimate belief underlying all systems of human thought, in almost all its branches. It was the prevalent conviction, and involuntarily Levin, without knowing when or how himself, had made just this his own, as being at any rate the clearest.

But it was not only a falsehood, it was a cruel mockery on the part of some evil power, a power that was repugnant, and that it was impossible to submit to.

You had to free yourself from this power. And every man had the means of escape in his hands. You had to put an end to this dependence on evil. And there was one means —death.

And Levin, a happy, healthy family man, was so close to suicide a number of times that he hid a rope, in order not to hang himself, and walked about without a gun for fear of shooting himself.

But he did not shoot himself, and did not hang himself; he went on living.

x

WHEN Levin thought about what he was and what he was living for he found no answer and fell into despair; but when he stopped asking himself about it he seemed to know both what he was and what he was living for, since he acted and lived firmly and definitely; in this last period, indeed, he lived far more firmly and definitely than he had before.

When he returned to the country in the beginning of June he also returned to his usual activities. His farming, his relations with the peasants and the neighbors, his household, the affairs of his sister and brother, which were in his hands, his relations with his wife and relatives, worries about the baby, his new hobby, beekeeping, which he had been carried away by that spring, took up all his time.

These things occupied him not because he justified them to himself by any general views, as he had used to do; on the contrary; how his being disappointed on the one hand in the failure of his previous undertakings for the general welfare, and his preoccupation on the other hand by his own thoughts and by the sheer mass of business that overwhelmed him from all sides, made him abandon any consideration of the common welfare. These things occupied him only because it seemed to him that he was bound to do what he was doing—that there was nothing else he could do.

Beforehand (this had begun with his childhood and kept growing until he was completely adult) when he had tried to do something for the good of everyone, for mankind, for Russia, for the whole village, he would notice that thinking about it was agreeable, but that the activity itself was always incoherent; there was an absence of complete conviction that the work was absolutely necessary, and the activity itself, which at first had seemed so great, kept dwindling away till it was reduced to nothing; whereas now that since his marriage he had begun confining himself more and more to living for himself he felt certain that his work was vital, even though he no longer felt any joy at the *thought* of his own activity; he saw that it was advancing much better than before, and that it kept growing more and more.

Now it seemed that against his will he kept cutting into the soil more and more deeply, like a plow, so that he could no longer extricate himself without turning over the sod.

The family unquestionably had to live in the way their fathers and grandfathers had been accustomed to, that is, on the same level of cultivation, and to bring their children up in the same way. This was just as necessary as dining when hungry; and for this it was just as necessary for the farming in Pokrovsk to produce an income as it was necessary to make preparations for dinner. Just as it was necessary beyond question to settle debts, so it was necessary to maintain his patrimony in such a condition that his son on inheriting it would be able to thank his father just as Levin had thanked his grandfather for everything he had built and planted. And for this it was necessary not to lease the land, but to farm it himself, to keep cattle, manure the fields, and plant woods.

It was impossible not to attend to the business of Koznyshov, of his sister, and of all the peasants who came to ask his advice and were used to doing so, just as it would be impossible to abandon a baby you were already holding in your arms. It was necessary to see to the comforts of his sister-in-law and her children, who had been invited, and of his wife and child; and it was impossible not to spend at least a small part of the day with them.

And all this, together with his shooting and his new bee-keeping hobby, filled Levin's whole life, which when he thought about it had no meaning for him.

But aside from the fact that Levin knew definitely what he had to do, he knew in just the same way how he had to do all this, and what order of importance his interests had.

He knew that laborers had to be hired as cheaply as possible, but that they couldn't be put into bondage for less than they were worth by advancing them money, even though this would have been very profitable. He could sell straw to the peasants during a shortage, even though he felt sorry for them; but an inn or a tavern, even though they produced income, had to be eliminated. The chopping down of trees had to be punished as severely as possible, but it was impossible to levy any fines for cattle allowed to stray on to his land, and even though it exasperated the watchmen and did away with the peasants' fear of him he couldn't help releasing the strayed cattle.

Peter, who was paying a moneylender ten per cent a month, had to be given a loan to tide him over; but it was impossible to let off or reduce the payments of peasants defaulting on their rent. The foreman could not be excused if the small meadow hadn't been mowed and the grass went to waste; but the two hundred acres planted with young trees couldn't be mowed at all. A laborer who went home during the working season because his father had died couldn't be forgiven, however sorry he might be for him; part of his pay had to be docked for those precious months of idleness; but it was impossible not to give old house servants of no use to him at all their monthly allowances.

Levin also knew that when he came home the first thing he had to do was to go and see his wife, who was unwell, whereas the peasants who had been waiting for him for three hours already could be allowed to wait some more; he also knew that in spite of all the pleasure it gave him to hive a swarm he had to deprive himself of this pleasure, let the old beekeeper hive the swarm without him, and go off to talk to any peasants who had found him at the hives.

He had no idea whether he was behaving well or badly, and not only would he not have argued about it now, he avoided talking or thinking about it.

Thinking about it led him into doubt, and prevented him from seeing what he should and what he should not do. Whereas when he stopped thinking but lived, he constantly felt in his soul the presence of an infallible judge who decided which of two possible actions was better and which worse; and the moment he behaved as he shouldn't have he felt it at once.

This was how he lived, without knowing or seeing any possibility of knowing what he was and what he was living in the world for; he both suffered from this ignorance to the point of fearing suicide while at the same time he went on resolutely cutting his own individual, definite path through life.

## XI

THE day Koznyshov arrived in Pokrovsk was one of Levin's most anguished days.

It was the most pressing time of the season, when an extraordinary self-sacrificing tension of labor was displayed among all the peasants, which is never displayed in any other circumstances of life and would be highly esteemed if the people who displayed this quality had any esteem for it themselves, if it were not repeated every year, and if the results of this tension were not so simple.

Mowing and reaping the rye or oats and carting them, mowing the meadows, replowing the fallow land, threshing the seed and sowing the winter rye—it all seems simple and ordinary; but in order to have time to do all this every peasant, young and old, must work without letup twice as much as usual during these three or four weeks, living on *kvas*, onions, and black bread, threshing and carting the sheaves by night and not sleeping more than two or three hours out of twenty-four. And all over Russia this is done every year.

Having lived the greater part of his life in the country and in close contact with the peasants, Levin always felt, during this busy time, that he too was infected by this general stimulation of the peasants.

Early in the morning he had ridden to where the first rye was being sown, then to where the oats were being carted and stacked; he returned home when his wife and sister-in-law were getting up, drank some coffee with them and went off on foot to the farm, where the new threshing machine was supposed to be started to thresh the seed corn.

That whole day, while talking to the foreman and to the peasants, and talking at home to his wife, to Dolly, to her chil-

dren, to his father-in-law, Levin kept thinking about the one
and only thing that was on his mind beside his farming. In
everything he did he kept seeking for its relationship to his
question: What am I? Where am I? And what am I here
for?

Standing in the cool shade of the newly thatched barn, with
its wattle walls of hazel, its fragrant leaves still unshed,
pressed against the freshly stripped aspens of the beams
underneath the thatch, Levin gazed through the open doorway through which the dry, bitter chaff dust rushed and
whirled, or at the hot, sunlit grass round the threshing floor
and the fresh straw that had just been brought out of the
shed, or at the white-breasted swallows with the motley heads
that flew chirping under the roof and stopped in the light of
the doorway fluttering their wings, or at the peasants bustling about in the dark and dusty barn, and kept thinking
strange thoughts:

Why is all this being done? he thought. Why am I standing here, making them work? Why do they go to all the
trouble of trying hard and showing me how energetic they
are? Why is that old woman Matrona, my friend, straining
herself (I doctored her when that beam fell on her during
the fire)? he thought, looking at a thin peasant woman who
was pushing the grain with a rake, her bare, sun-blackened
feet moving painfully across the hard, uneven barn floor.
She got well then, but today or tomorrow, or ten years from
now, she'll be in her grave, and nothing will be left of her,
nor of that chic girl in the red jacket who's beating the chaff
from the ears with such a delicate, nimble movement. And
she'll be buried too, and that piebald gelding as well—that
one very soon, he thought, looking at a horse breathing
heavily, its nostrils distended and its belly heaving as it
trod the slanting wheel turning round under it. That'll be
buried too, and so will Theodore, who's feeding the machine,
with his curly beard full of chaff and the shirt torn on his
white shoulder—he'll be buried too. Yet there he is loosening
the sheaves and giving some orders or other, shouting at the
women, and with a brisk movement straightening out the
strap on the flywheel. And what's more they're not going
to be the only ones to be buried—I am too, and nothing will
be left. What's it all for?

He thought this while looking at his watch at the same time
to calculate how much was being threshed an hour. He had to

know this to have something to go by in assigning the day's work.

It'll soon be an hour, and they've only begun on the third heap, Levin thought; he went up to Theodore and shouting above the din told him to put in less at a time.

"You're putting in too much, Theodore! Don't you see, it gets jammed and doesn't work right! Put it in evenly!"

Black with the dust clinging to his sweating face, Theodore shouted something in reply, but he still didn't do it as Levin wanted him to.

Going over to the drum Levin motioned Theodore aside and began feeding the machine himself.

After working until the peasants' mealtime, which was not far away, he left the barn together with Theodore and started talking to him, stopping beside the tidy stack of freshly reaped yellow rye laid out on the threshing floor for seed.

Theodore came from a distant village, the one where Levin used to rent out land on a co-operative basis. Just now it had been let to a retired house porter.

Levin got into conversation with Theodore about this land and asked him whether it would be taken next year by Plato, a rich, goodhearted peasant from the same village.

"The rent's high, Mr. Constantine, it wouldn't pay Plato," replied the peasant, plucking the ears of rye off his sweat-soaked shirt.

"Then how does Kirilov make it pay?"

"Oh, Mityukha!" (He contemptuously called the house porter Mityukha.) "He could make anything pay, Mr. Constantine! He's a squeezer. He gets what he wants. No pity for a Christian from *him*. But Uncle Fokanich!" (This was his name for the old man Plato.) "D'you think he'd skin anyone! Sometimes he gives credit, and he'll let a man off. Then he runs short himself. That's how he is."

"But why should he let anyone off?"

"Just so—people are different; one man lives just for his own needs—take Mityukha, he just stuffs his own belly, but Uncle Fokanich is an honest old man. He lives for his soul, he remembers God."

"How does he remember God? How does he live for his soul?" Levin almost shouted.

"Everyone knows that—he lives righteously, in a godly way. People are different, after all. Take yourself, you don't hurt anyone either . . ."

"Yes, yes—good-by!" said Levin, breathless with excitement; turning away he took his stick and hurried off toward home. At hearing what the peasant had said about Plato living for his soul, righteously, in a godly way, vague but important thoughts seemed to burst out from under lock and key somewhere in throngs, and all rushing forward toward a single goal swirled round in his head, dazzling him with their light.

XII

LEVIN walked along the highroad with great strides, attending not so much to his own thoughts (he was still unable to disentangle them) as to a spiritual condition he had never experienced before.

The peasant's words had affected his soul like an electric spark, suddenly transforming and fusing into one a whole swarm of disjointed, impotent individual thoughts that had never stopped interesting him. These thoughts had occupied his mind, though he hadn't known it, even while he had been talking about letting the land.

He felt something new in his soul, and palpated this new thing with pleasure, not yet knowing what it was.

To live not for one's needs, but for God. For what God? And what could you say that was more senseless than what he said? He said it was unnecessary to live for one's own needs; that is, it's not necessary to live for what we understand, for what we're drawn to, for what we want, but we must live for something incomprehensible, for God, which no one can understand or define. Well, and what of it? Didn't I understand those senseless words of Theodore's? And after I understood did I have any doubt of their truth? Did I find them stupid, obscure, inexact?

No, I understood them, just as he understands them; I understood them completely, and more clearly than I understand anything in life; I've never doubted it in my life, nor can I doubt it. And not I alone, but everyone, the whole world understands this alone completely, it's the only thing it has no doubt of and always agrees with.

Theodore says that Kirilov the house porter lives for his belly. That's understandable and rational. As rational creatures none of us can live in any other way than for our bellies. Then suddenly this same Theodore says living for your belly is bad, and that you have to live for the truth, for God, and

I understand him from a mere hint! And I and millions of people who lived ages ago and are living now, peasants, the poor in spirit, and wise men who've thought and written about this, and said the same thing in their unclear way—we all agree on this one thing: what we should live for, and what it is that's good. There's only one thing I, together with everyone, know with certainty, know clearly and beyond question, and this piece of knowledge cannot be explained by reason—it is beyond that; it has no causes and can have no consequences.

If goodness has a cause, it is no longer goodness; if it has a consequence it is also not goodness. Consequently, goodness is outside the chain of cause and effect.

It is just this that I know, and that we all know.

And I had been seeking miracles; I regretted not having seen a miracle that would have convinced me. And here is a miracle, the only possible one, everlasting, surrounding me on all sides—and I never noticed it!

What miracle can be greater than that?

Can I really have found the solution of everything? Can my suffering really be over now? thought Levin, striding along the dusty road, unaware of either the heat or his fatigue, and with a feeling of relief after long-drawn-out suffering. This feeling gave him so much joy it seemed to him improbable. He was panting with excitement; incapable of walking any farther he left the road for the woods, and sat down on the uncut grass in the shade of the aspens. He took his hat off his sweating head and lay down, leaning on his elbows in the juicy, feathery forest grass.

Yes, I must think it through and clear things up, he thought, staring intently at the untrodden grass before him, and watching the movements of a little green beetle that was climbing up a stalk of couch grass and being hindered by a leaf of goutwort. Let's start all over again, he said to himself, turning aside the leaf of goutwort so that it wouldn't be in the beetle's way, and bending down another blade of grass for the beetle to pass on to. What is making me so happy? What have I discovered?

Before I used to say that in my body, in the body of this grass and of this beetle (there, he didn't want that blade of grass, it's spread its wings and flown away) a certain transformation of matter was accomplished in accordance with physical, chemical, and physiological laws. And in all of us, including the aspens, the clouds, and the misty nebulae in space, evolution takes place. Evolution from what? Into what? Infinite evolution and struggle? As though there could be any direction or struggle in the infinite! And I was astonished that in spite of the greatest mental concentration along those lines the meaning of life was not revealed to me, the meaning of my impulses and my aspirations. Whereas the meaning of my impulses is so clear to me that I live by them constantly, and I was astonished and overjoyed when a peasant expressed it to me: to live for God, for the soul.

I've discovered nothing. I've simply learned what I knew already. I've understood the force that gave me life not in the past alone, but is giving me life at this very moment. I've liberated myself from deception; I've learned to know my Master.

He summarized to himself the whole course of his thinking during the preceding two years, the beginning of which had been a clear, obvious thought about death at the sight of his beloved brother hopelessly ill.

At that time, having understood clearly for the first time that for every human being and for himself nothing lay ahead but suffering, death, and eternal oblivion, he decided that it was impossible to live that way, that he either had to interpret his life in such a way that it did not seem to be an evil mockery on the part of some devil, or else shoot himself.

But he did neither one thing nor the other; he went on living, thinking, and feeling; he even married at just this time, had many joys, and was happy whenever he wasn't thinking about the meaning of his life.

What did that mean? It meant he was living well but thinking badly.

He was living (without being aware of it) in accordance with the spiritual truths he had drunk in with his mother's milk, but he was thinking not only without acknowledging these truths but taking pains to evade them.

Now it was clear to him that he could live only thanks to those beliefs in which he had been brought up.

What would I be, how would I have lived my life, if I had lacked those beliefs? If I hadn't known you had to live for God and not for your own needs? I should have robbed, lied, murdered. None of the things that constitute the chief joys of my life would have existed for me. And though he made the greatest effort of the imagination he could nevertheless not picture to himself the bestial creature he himself would have been if he hadn't known what he was living for.

I was looking for an answer to my question. But thinking could not give me any answer to my question—it is not commensurate with it. It was life itself that gave me the answer, through my knowledge of what is good and what is bad. And I didn't acquire this knowledge in any special way; it was given to me just as it is to everyone—*given* just because I couldn't have gotten it anywhere.

Where did I get it from? Was it through reason that I managed to see that you had to love your neighbor and not throttle him? I was told that as a child, and I was glad to believe it because what was told me was what I already had in my soul. But who discovered it? Not reason. Reason discovered the struggle for existence and the law requiring anyone who interfered with the satisfaction of my desires to be throttled. That is a deduction made by reason. But it was not reason that could have discovered love of one's fellows, because that is unreasonable.

## XIII

LEVIN recalled a recent scene with Dolly and her children. The children, who had been left alone, had begun cooking raspberries over candles and squirting jets of milk into their mouths. Their mother, who had caught them in the act, tried to impress on them in front of Levin how much work it had taken the grown-ups to make what they were destroying, that the work had been done on their behalf, and if they broke the cups they wouldn't have anything to drink tea out of, and if they spilled the milk they wouldn't have anything to eat and would die of hunger.

And Levin was struck by the stolid, weary skepticism with which the children listened to what their mother was telling them. They were only annoyed that their absorbing game had been stopped, and didn't believe a word of what she was saying. Nor could they have believed, since they were unable to imagine the full volume of everything they made use of, and so could not realize that what they were destroying was the same as what they lived on.

All that comes about by itself, they thought, and there's nothing the least bit interesting or important about it, because it's always been that way and always will be. It's always the same thing over and over again. There's no reason for us to think about it, it's all there ready for us; what we want is to think up something of our own, something novel. Now there we thought up the idea of putting raspberries into a cup and cooking them over a candle, and squirting the milk into each other's mouth. That's something novel, it's fun and not in the least worse than drinking out of cups.

Don't we do the same thing, didn't I do the same thing when I was using reason to look for the meaning of the forces of nature and the point of human existence? Levin went on thinking.

And don't all philosophical theories do the same thing when they embark on ways of thought strange and alien to man in order to lead him to a knowledge of what he's known for a long time, and knows with such certainty that he couldn't even go on living without it? Isn't it obvious and clear in the development of every philosopher's theory that he starts off by knowing just as unquestionably as the peasant, Theodore, and not in any way more clearly, the cardinal meaning of life, and simply wants to take a dubious intellectual path in order to return to what everyone knows?

Well then, what if the children were left alone to get hold of or manufacture cups for themselves, milk the cows, and so on? Would they start any mischief? They would just die of hunger. And suppose we were left with all our nonsense and ideas, with no conception of the one God, the Creator! With no conception of what goodness is, no explanation of moral evil!

Just try to build anything without these conceptions!

We destroy because we are spiritually sated. We're just children after all!

Where did I get the joyful knowledge I have in common with the peasant, which is the only thing that gives me any peace of mind? Where did I get it?

I who have been brought up in the conception of God, as a Christian, and have filled my whole life with those spiritual blessings given me by Christianity, overflowing with these blessings and living by them, I too am a destroyer just like the children, that is, I want to destroy what I live by. And the moment an important moment in life comes, just like the children when they're cold and hungry, I go to Him, and I feel even less than the children when they're scolded by their mother for their childish mischief that my own childish attempts at wanton madness should be reckoned against me.

Yes—what I know I don't know by reason, it has been given to me, disclosed to me, and I know it by my heart, and by my faith in the chief things taught by the Church.

The Church? The Church! Levin repeated to himself, turning over on the other side; leaning on his elbow he began gazing into the distance at a herd of cattle that were going down to the river along the farther side.

But can I believe in everything taught by the Church? he thought, testing himself by thinking up everything that might destroy his present peace of mind. He deliberately began recalling all the doctrines of the Church that had always seemed to him the most strange and used to put him off. The Creation? But how did I explain existence? By existence? By nothing? The Devil, sin? But how do I explain evil? Atonement?

But I know nothing, nothing, and there's nothing I can know except what is told to me as to everyone.

And now it seemed to him that there was not a single one of the beliefs of the Church that disturbed the chief thing—faith in God, in goodness, as the sole purpose of mankind.

Every doctrine of the Church could be led back to the belief in the service of the truth rather than of personal needs. And each one would not only not disturb that, but was necessary for the consummation of the principal miracle constantly being manifested on earth, which consists in enabling every individual, in common with millions of the most diverse human beings, sages and fools, children and graybeards—everyone, the peasant, Lvov, Kitty, paupers and kings—to understand beyond question one and the same thing, and to live that life of the spirit that is the only thing worth living for and the only thing we cherish.

Lying on his back now he gazed high up into the cloudless sky. Don't I know that to be infinite space, and not a rounded vault? But no matter how I screw up my eyes and strain my eyesight I cannot help seeing it as rounded and limited, and in spite of my knowledge of its being infinite space I'm undoubtedly right in seeing it as a firm blue vault; I'm more right than when I strain to see beyond it.

Levin had stopped thinking now and was merely listening in as it were to mystic voices that seemed to be carrying on a gay and earnest discussion of something.

Can this be faith? he thought, afraid to believe in his

happiness. "I thank Thee, my God!" he murmured, gulping down the sobs that were rising within him, and with both hands wiping away the tears that filled his eyes.

## XIV

LEVIN was looking straight before him at the herd of cattle; then he caught sight of his gig with Raven harnessed to it, and Ivan the coachman who had driven up to the cattle and was saying something to the herdsman; then, close by now, he heard the sound of wheels and the snorting of a well-fed horse; but he was so preoccupied by his own thoughts that he didn't even wonder why the coachman was driving toward him.

This occurred to him only when the coachman, after driving all the way over to him, called out:

"Madame sent me. Your brother's here, with some other gentleman."

Levin got into the gig and took the reins.

It took him a long time to come to his senses; it was as though he were waking up from a dream. He looked at the well-fed horse, flecked with lather between the haunches and on the neck where the harness chafed, looked at Ivan the coachman sitting beside him, and recalled that he was expecting his brother and that his wife was doubtless anxious because of his lengthy absence, and tried to guess who was the visitor who had arrived with his brother. His brother, his wife, and the unknown visitor appeared to him in a different light now. It seemed to him that from now on his relations with everyone were going to be different.

Now there won't be that alienation there's always been between my brother and myself; there won't be any disputes; I'll never have any quarrels with Kitty, I'll be agreeable and nice to the visitor, whoever he is, and with the servants, with Ivan—it's all going to be different.

Tightly reining in the willing horse, which was snorting with impatience and begging for its head, Levin kept looking round at Ivan beside him, who didn't know what to do with his idle hands and kept tucking in his shirt; he tried to think of a topic he could start talking to him about. He was about to say that it was a pity Ivan had pulled the girths so tight, but that would have sounded like a reproach, while what he felt like was a loving chat. But nothing else came to mind.

"Bear to the right, sir—there's a stump," said Ivan, pulling at Levin's rein.

"Please leave that alone, and don't try to teach me!" said Levin, irritated by the coachman's interference. Interference always infuriated him; and at once he sadly felt how mistaken he had been in imagining that a state of mind could instantly change him in his contact with reality.

While still a couple of hundred yards from the house Levin saw Grisha and Tanya running to meet him.

"Uncle Kostya! Mama's coming, and Grandpapa, and Uncle Sergius, and some one else," they cried, climbing into the gig.

"But who?"

"Oh, he's awfully dreadful! This is how he goes with his arms," said Tanya, standing up in the gig and mimicking Katavasov.

"But is he old or young?" asked Levin laughing; Tanya's performance reminded him of someone.

If only he's not someone disagreeable! thought Levin.

The moment he turned the bend in the road and saw the group approaching, Levin recognized Katavasov in a straw hat, walking along swinging his arms just as Tanya had demonstrated.

Katavasov was very fond of discussing philosophy; his notions about it were acquired from naturalists who had never studied it, and, toward the end of his stay in Moscow, Levin had had a great many arguments with him.

And it was one of these conversations, in which Katavasov evidently thought he had come out on top, that was the first thing Levin recalled on recognizing him.

No, I'm not going to argue with him on any account, or express my ideas lightly, he thought.

Getting out of the gig, and saying hello to his brother and Katavasov, Levin asked where Kitty was.

"She's taken Mitya to Kolok." (This was the wood near the house.) "She wants him to sleep there; it's so hot in the house," said Dolly.

Levin had always advised his wife against taking the baby to the forest; he thought it was dangerous, and the news annoyed him.

"She keeps carrying him around with her from one place

to another," said the old Prince with a smile. "I advised her to try putting him in the ice cellar."

"She wanted to go to the beehives. She thought you were there. That's where we're going," said Dolly.

"Well, and what are you doing?" said Koznyshov, falling behind the others to walk beside his brother.

"Nothing in particular. I'm looking after the estate as usual," answered Levin. "You're staying some time, aren't you? We expected you long ago."

"A couple of weeks. I have a great deal to do in Moscow."

At these words the brothers' eyes met, and Levin, in spite of his constant desire, which was particularly strong now, to be on friendly and above all on simple terms with his brother, felt uncomfortable looking at him. He lowered his own eyes, not knowing what to say.

Going over in his mind the topics of conversation that might please Koznyshov and keep him from talking about the Serbian war and the Slavic Question, which he had hinted at by his remark about his Moscow activities, Levin started talking about Koznsyshov's book.

"Well, have there been any reviews of your book?" he asked.

Koznyshov smiled at the calculated question.

"No one bothers about it, least of all myself," he said. "Look there, Dolly, it's going to rain," he added, pointing with his umbrella at some white clouds that had come up over the aspen tops.

And these words were enough to re-establish the not exactly hostile, but chilly relationship between the two brothers that Levin was so eager to avoid.

Levin went over to Katavasov. "How nice it was of you to think of coming," he said to him.

"I've been intending to for a long time. Now we'll have some talks and we'll see! Have you read Spencer?"

"I haven't finished him," said Levin. "But I don't need him now."

"How is that? That's interesting. Why not?"

"That is, I've become absolutely convinced that I shan't find the answers to the questions that interest me now in him or in anyone like him. Now—"

But the calm, cheerful expression on Katavasov's face suddenly struck him, and he felt so concerned about his new mood, which he was obviously spoiling by this conversation, that recalling his resolution he stopped.

"But we can talk about that later," he added. "If we're going to the apiary it's this way, by that little path," he said turning to them all.

Going along the narrow path until they got to an unmowed glade covered on one side by a dense growth of bright pansies, with a great many tall, dark-green tufts of sneezewort between them, Levin settled his guests in the deep cool shade of the young aspens, on a bench and some tree stumps specially arranged for visitors to the apiary who might be afraid of the bees, and he himself went to the hut to fetch some bread, cucumbers, and fresh honey for both children and grown-ups.

Trying to make as few rapid movements as possible and listening to the bees that were flying past him more and more often, he went along the path to the hut. At the very entrance one bee got itself tangled up in his beard and began buzzing, but he carefully let it loose. Going into the shady passageway he took his veil down from a peg on the wall, put it on, and with his hands thrust deep in his pockets went out into the fenced-in apiary, where in the middle of a cleared space, in straight rows, each one tied with bast to stakes, all the old familiar hives were standing, each one with its own history, while along the wattle fence were the hives for the new swarms of that year. In front of the entrances to the hives, flickering before his eyes, were the fluttering bees and drones, circling and swirling over the same spot, and among them, always taking the same course, there flew the workers on their way to the blossoming lime trees in the wood for a load, or bringing one back to the hives.

There rang incessantly in his ears a variety of sounds, the swiftly flying busy worker bees, the buzzing idle drones, or the alarmed sentry bees, preparing to sting to protect their treasure against an enemy. On the other side of the fence an old man was planing a hoop, and didn't notice Levin, who stopped in the middle of the apiary without calling him.

He was glad of this chance to be alone, and to recover from reality, which had already deflated his mood so much.

He remembered that he had already managed to lose his temper with Ivan, to treat his brother with coldness, and to speak to Katavasov thoughtlessly.

Can it really have been nothing but a momentary mood, which will pass away without leaving any trace? he thought.

But just then as he reverted to his former mood, he joyfully felt that something novel and important had taken place within him. It was only for a moment that reality had cast a veil over the spiritual peace he had found; it was still intact.

Just as the bees, which were now buzzing round him, threatening and distracting him, deprived him of complete physical tranquillity and forced him to shrink away to avoid them, so the worries that had beset him from the moment he got into the gig deprived him of his peace of mind; but that only lasted as long as he was in their midst. Just as his bodily strength remained intact in spite of the bees so his newly realized spiritual strength also remained intact.

XV

KOSTYA, d'you know whom Sergius traveled with on his way here?" said Dolly, after distributing the cucumbers and honey among the children. "Vronsky! He's on his way to Serbia."

"And not alone either; he's taking along a squadron at his own expense!" said Katavasov.

"That's just like him," said Levin. "But are there really any Volunteers still leaving?" he added, glancing at Koznyshov.

Koznyshov made no reply: he was using the blunt edge of a knife to get out of the bowl a still living bee that had got itself caught in the running honey of a wedge of white honeycomb.

"I should think so! You ought to have seen what went on at the station yesterday!" said Katavasov, noisily munching a cucumber.

"But what be the meaning of it all? For the love of God, Sergius, explain to me where all these Volunteers are going? Whom are they going to fight?" asked the old Prince, evidently continuing a conversation that had started during Levin's absence.

"The Turks," replied Koznyshov, with a placid smile, having freed the bee, black with honey and helplessly waving its little legs as he pushed it from the knife onto a juicy aspen leaf.

"But who's declared war on the Turks? Ivan Ragozov and Countess Lydia, plus Madame Stahl?"

"No one has declared war, but people sympathize with the

sufferings of their kinsmen and want to help them," said Koznyshov.

"The Prince isn't speaking about help," said Levin, coming to the aid of his father-in-law, "but about war. The Prince is saying that private individuals cannot take part in a war without the permission of the government."

"Kostya, look—there's a bee! Really, we're going to get stung!" said Dolly, waving away a wasp.

"That's not a bee, it's a wasp," said Levin.

"Well, then, and what's *your* theory?" said Katavasov with a smile, evidently challenging Levin to an argument. "Why don't private individuals have the right?"

"This is my theory: on the one hand war is such a bestial, cruel, and frightful thing that not a single human being, not to mention Christians, can assume the responsibility for starting a war; that can only be done by a government, whose function that is, and which is drawn into war inevitably. On the other hand, in state affairs, especially in warfare, as a matter both of common sense and of law, citizens renounce their personal will."

Both Koznyshov and Katavasov were ready with their objections and started talking at the same time.

"But that's just the point, my dear boy; cases may arise where the government is not fulfilling the will of the citizenry, whereupon society declares its own will," said Katavasov.

But Koznyshov evidently disapproved of this retort. He frowned at Katavasov's point and said something different.

"It's a pity you put the question that way. There's no question of war being declared here, it's the simple expression of a humane, Christian feeling. Our brothers are being killed, our kinfolk and co-religionists. Let's even suppose they're not our brothers, not our co-religionists, that they're just children, women, old men; our feelings are outraged, and Russians are hastening to help stop these atrocities. Imagine that you're walking along the street and see some drunkards beating a woman or a child; I don't suppose you'd start asking whether war had been declared on the men or not, but you'd fling yourself on them and defend the victim."

"But I shouldn't kill them," said Levin.

"Yes, you would."

"I don't know. If I were to see it I would surrender to my immediate impulse; though I can't say beforehand. But there's no such immediate feeling with respect to the oppression of the Slavs, nor can there be."

"Maybe you don't have any, but others do," said Koznyshov with a frown of annoyance. "There are traditions still alive among the people, of Orthodox Christians suffering under the yoke of the 'infidel Mussulman.' The people have heard about the sufferings of their brethren and have spoken out."

"That may be," said Levin evasively. "But I don't see it; I'm one of the people myself, and I don't feel that."

"Nor do I," said the Prince. "I was living abroad, reading the newspapers, and I must confess that even before the Bulgarian atrocities I simply could not understand why all the Russians were suddenly falling in love with their Slavic brothers, while I feel no love for them at all. I was very upset; I thought that I was a monster, or that the Carlsbad waters were having that effect on me. But I calmed down when I got here and saw I wasn't the only one interested in nothing but Russia, and not in our Slavic brothers. Constantine, for instance."

"Personal opinions are irrelevant," said Koznyshov. "It's not a question of personal opinions when all Russia—the whole people—has expressed its will."

"But forgive me—I don't see it. The people know nothing at all about it," said the Prince.

"Oh no, Papa—they do! What about last Sunday in church?" said Dollý, who had been following the conversation. "Please get me a towel," she said to the old man, who was looking smilingly at the children. "It would be impossible for all—"

"But what happened in church on Sunday? The priest was ordered to read something and he read it. They didn't understand a thing, they just kept sighing as they do during every sermon," the Prince went on. "Then they were told there was going to be a collection in the church for some salutary cause, so they reached for a kopeck and handed it over. As for what it was all about they didn't know themselves."

"The people cannot help knowing; there is always an awareness of their destiny among the people, and at moments such as these it becomes clear to them," said Koznyshov categorically, glancing at the old beekeeper.

The handsome old man, with a black graying beard and thick silvery hair, was standing there motionless, with a bowl of honey in his hand, looking down from his height at the gentlefolk with an air of amiable tranquillity, evidently neither understanding anything nor wishing to.

"Yes, that is so," he said, wagging his head weightily on hearing Koznyshov's remarks.

"Now just ask him. He doesn't know anything and doesn't think," said Levin. "Well, Mikhailych, have you heard about the war?" he asked, turning to him. "What they read in church, eh? Well, what d'you think of it? Should we go and fight for the Christians?"

"Why should we think about it? Alexander Nikolayevich, the Emperor, has done our thinking for us, and he will go on thinking for us about everything. He can see better . . . Should I bring some more bread? Give the little boy some more?" he said to Dolly, nodding at Grisha, who was finishing his crust.

"There's no need for me to ask," said Koznyshov. "We've seen and still see hundreds and hundreds of people leaving everything they have in order to serve the cause of justice, who have come from every corner of Russia and are expressing, openly and clearly, their thoughts and their aims. They bring their pennies or go themselves, and they give their reason unequivocally. What does that mean?"

"To my mind what it means," said Levin, who was beginning to get excited, "is that in a nation of eighty million people there will always be found, not hundreds, as at present, but tens of thousands of men who have lost their social position, daredevils who will always be ready to go anywhere into Pugachov's band of robbers, to Khiva, to Serbia—"

"I tell you it's not hundreds, and they're not daredevils, but the best representatives of the nation!" said Koznyshov with annoyance, just as though he were defending the last remnant of his property. "And what about the donations? There at least the whole people is directly expressing its will."

"The word 'people' is so vague," said Levin. "District office clerks, teachers, and perhaps one out of a thousand peasants have any idea what it's all about. As for the rest of the eighty million, not only do they not express their own will, like Mikhailych, but they haven't the slightest conception of what there is to express it about. So what right have we to say it's the will of the people?"

## XVI

AN experienced debater, Koznyshov made no reply but
instantly turned the conversation into another region.

"Yes, if you want to learn what the spirit of the people is
by means of arithmetic it goes without saying that that's
extremely difficult. Balloting hasn't yet been introduced into
this country, and cannot be, since it does not represent the
will of the people; but there are other means. It is felt in the
air, it is felt in the heart; to say nothing of the underwater
currents that have begun stirring in the placid ocean of the
people and are clear to every unprejudiced person .But let
us simply look at society in the narrow sense. All the most
diverse parties in the world of the intelligentsia, which used
to be so hostile to each other, have all fused into one. All
bickerings are finished, all the public organs say one and the
same thing, everyone has felt an elemental power that has
snatched them up and is carrying them all in one direction."

"Yes, all the papers are saying the same thing, that's true,"
said the Prince. "In fact it's so much the same that they're
all just like frogs croaking before a storm. You can't even
hear anything because of it."

"Frogs or no frogs, I'm not a publisher of newspapers and
I have no wish to defend them; I'm only speaking about the
unanimity of opinion in the intellectual world," said Koznyshov, turning to his brother.

Levin was about to reply, but the old Prince interrupted
him.

"Well there's something else that can be said about that
unanimity," said the Prince. "There's my son-in-law Stiva,
you all know him. He's just got a post as Member of the
Committee of the Commission of something or other, I forget
what. Only there's nothing at all to do there—now Dolly, it's
no secret!—and it has a salary of eight thousand. Just try
asking him whether his work is of any use, and he'll prove
to you that it's indispensable. Now he's a truthful fellow, but
it's impossible not to believe in the usefulness of eight thousand rubles."

"Yes, he asked me to tell Dolly he'd gotten the post," said
Koznyshov, irritated; he thought the Prince's remarks beside
the point.

"That's just how it is with the unanimity of the newspapers.

I've had it explained to me—the moment there's a war they make twice as much money. How can they help thinking that the fate of the nation, the Slavs—and all the rest of it?"

"There are not many papers I like, but that's unfair," said Koznyshov.

"There's only one condition I would make," continued the Prince. "Alphonse Karr put it wonderfully well before the war with Prussia. 'D'you think a war is absolutely necessary? Splendid. Everyone who preaches war—off with him into a special front-line legion, and on to the assault, on to the attack, ahead of everyone else!'"

"The editors would be terrific," said Katavasov, roaring with laughter as he imagined in this picked legion the editors he knew.

"Really, they'd just run," said Dolly. "They'd only be in the way."

"And if they start running we'd put some grapeshot into their backsides or station some Cossacks there with whips," said the Prince.

"But that's a joke, and a bad one at that, if you'll forgive me, Prince," said Koznyshov.

"I don't see why it's a joke, it's—" Levin began, but Koznyshov interrupted him.

"Every member of society is called upon to do the task he is fitted for," he said. "Thinking people perform theirs by expressing public opinion. And this unanimity, this complete expression of public opinion is a merit of the press, and at the same time a heartening phenomenon. Twenty years ago we would have been silent—today we hear the voice of the Russian people, which is ready to rise as one man and ready to sacrifice itself for its oppressed brethren; that is a great step forward and a token of strength."

"But it's not just a question of sacrificing oneself, is it, but of killing Turks," said Levin diffidently. "The people sacrifice themselves and are ready to go on sacrificing themselves for the good of their souls, but not for the sake of murder," he added, involuntarily connecting the conversation with the ideas that were so much on his mind.

"How d'you mean—their souls? You understand that for a naturalist the expression presents a problem. What is the soul, after all?" said Katavasov, smiling.

"Oh—you know perfectly well!"

"No, I swear I haven't the slightest idea!" said Katavasov with a loud laugh.

" 'I come not to bring peace, but a sword,' as Christ said,"
Koznyshov remarked, quoting quite simply, as though it were
a matter of course, just the passage from the Gospels that
had always perplexed Levin more than any other.

"Yes, that is so," repeated the old man, who was standing
near them, in answer to a glance accidentally thrown his way.

"No, my boy, you're beaten, beaten—completely beaten!"
Katavasov shouted gaily.

Levin flushed with irritation, not at having been beaten,
but at having been unable to refrain from arguing.

No, he thought, I mustn't argue with them; they're invulner-
able in their armor, and I'm naked.

He saw it was impossible to convince his brother and Katavasov, and still less did he see any possibility of agreeing
with them himself. What they were advocating was just
that intellectual arrogance that had nearly undone him. He
could not agree that a few dozen people, including his
brother, had the right, on the strength of what they were
told by a few hundred grandiloquent Volunteers coming into
the capitals, to say that they and the newspapers together
were expressing the will and the opinion of the people, especially when that opinion was expressed by vengeance and
murder. He could not agree with this, because he neither
saw any expression of these ideas in the people in whose
midst he was living, nor could he find such ideas in himself
(and he could only think of himself as one of the individuals
who constituted the Russian people) but most of all because
he together with the people was ignorant of what the general
welfare consisted of, while being perfectly sure that the attainment of this general welfare was only possible through a
strict observance of the law of goodness that has been disclosed to everyone, and therefore could not wish for war or
advocate it for any kind of general aims whatever. He
agreed with Mikhailych, and with the people who expressed
their thought in the traditional invitation to the Varangians*:
"Come and rule over us. We gladly promise complete obedience. We will take on ourselves all the labor, all the
humiliations and all the sacrifices—but we will not be the
ones to decide and judge." But now, according to what
Koznyshov had said, the people were renouncing the right
they had purchased at so high a price.

---

* The Scandinavians who were invited by the early Slav tribes of
Russia to be their rulers. (Tr.)

Also, he wanted to say that if public opinion was an infallible judge then why wasn't a revolution, a Commune, just as legitimate as the movement on behalf of the Slavs? But none of these thoughts could settle anything. There was only one thing that was plain beyond question—at this moment the argument was irritating Koznyshov, and consequently it was wrong to argue; Levin fell silent and pointed out to his visitors that some clouds were gathering and that they had better go home because of the rain.

## XVII

THE Prince and Koznyshov got into the gig and drove off; the rest of the company, hastening their steps, started home on foot.

But a cloud, turning white and then black, moved up so quickly that they had to walk still more rapidly in order to get back to the house before it started raining. The outlying streamers of the cloud, low and black like soot-laden smoke, were racing across the sky with extraordinary swiftness. The company were still a couple of hundred paces from the house when a wind sprang up; a downpour was to be expected at any moment.

The children were running on ahead shrieking with fright and glee. Dolly, coping strenuously with the skirts that clung to her legs was no longer walking but running, her eyes glued to the children. The men, holding their hats, were walking ahead with great strides. They had already reached the front steps when a large drop broke against the edge of the iron gutter. Chattering merrily the children ran under the shelter of the roof followed by the grown-ups.

"And where is Madame?" Levin asked Miss Agatha, who met them in the hall carrying shawls and rugs.

"We thought she was with you," she said.

"And Mitya?"

"He must be in Kolok; nanny's with them."

Levin snatched up some rugs and rushed off to Kolok.

In this short space of time the center of the cloud had advanced so far over the sun that it had grown as dark as during an eclipse. The wind kept stubbornly pushing Levin back, as though insisting on its own rights, ripping the leaves and blossoms off the lime trees, stripping the white birch boughs down to a strange, grotesque nakedness, and bending everything in the same direction—acacias, flowers, burdocks, grass, and treetops. The peasant girls who had been working in the garden ran shrieking to the servants' quarters for shelter. A white sheet of pelting rain was already enveloping the whole of the distant wood and half the neighboring field, and swiftly advancing toward Kolok. The moisture of the rain as it broke up into tiny drops could be smelled in the air.

Lowering his head and fighting against the wind that was trying to snatch the wraps out of his grip Levin was approaching Kolok; he could already see something gleaming white behind an oak, when suddenly there was a burst of light, the whole earth seemed on fire, and the skies seemed to crack open just over his head. When he opened his dazzled eyes the first thing he saw with horror, through the dense curtain of rain that now separated him from Kolok, was the peculiarly altered position of the familiar green crown of the oak in the middle of the wood. Can it have been hit? he barely had time to think, when the top of the oak, falling faster and faster, vanished behind the other trees, and he heard the crash of a great tree falling on top of others.

The lightning flash, the roar of the thunder, and the instantaneous chill that ran through his body all merged for him into a single feeling of horror.

"Oh, my God, my God! If only it's not on them!" he muttered.

Though it instantly occurred to him how senseless it was for him to pray that they had not been killed by the oak that had already fallen, he repeated his prayer, knowing there was nothing he could do that was any better than this senseless prayer.

He ran over to the place they usually went, but didn't find them.

They were at the other end of the wood, under an old lime tree, and were calling him. Two figures in dark dresses (which had been light-colored before) were stooping over something. They were Kitty and the nanny. The rain was already letting up and it was beginning to grow lighter when Levin came running up to them. The lower part of the nanny's dress was dry, but Kitty's clothes were soaked through and clung to her. Though it was no longer raining they were still standing in the same posture they had been in when the storm broke. Both of them were stooping over a baby carriage with a green hood.

"Alive? Safe? Thank God!" he muttered, running up to

them splashing through the puddles, with one shoe half off and full of water.

Kitty's wet rosy face was turning to him, timidly smiling beneath her shapeless hat.

"Well, aren't you ashamed of yourself now? I can't understand how it's possible to be so careless!" he said, turning on her in anger.

"Really it wasn't my fault. We were just going home when he got all upset and we had to change him. We had just . . ." Kitty began excusing herself.

Mitya was safe and dry, and was still fast asleep.

"Well, thank God! I don't know what I'm saying!"

They collected the wet diapers; the nanny picked the baby up and carried him. Levin walked beside his wife, feeling guilty about his own irritation, and furtively squeezing her hand when the nanny wasn't looking.

## XVIII

THAT whole day, during the most diverse conversations in which he took part as it were with only the exterior side of his mind, Levin, in spite of his disappointment at not finding the change in himself that should have taken place, remained constantly and joyfully aware of the fullness of his heart.

It was too wet after the rain to go for a walk; apart from that the thunderclouds had not left the horizon and here and there kept passing along the borders of the sky, black and rumbling. The whole company spent the rest of the day at home.

No more arguments sprang up; on the contrary, after dinner everyone was in excellent spirits.

At first Katavasov amused the ladies with his original jokes, which on first meeting him everyone always liked so much, but afterward, prompted by Koznyshov, he told them of the very interesting observations he had made of the differences in the character and even physiognomy of male and female houseflies, and about their life. Koznyshov was also cheerful; over tea, urged by his brother, he expounded his views of the future of the Eastern Question. He did it so simply and well that everyone listened to him with interest.

Kitty was the only one who couldn't hear it all; she was called away to give Mitya his bath.

A few minutes after Kitty had gone out, Levin was also called to her in the nursery.

Leaving his tea, and also regretting the break in the interesting talk while at the same time anxious about why he was being called, since that happened only for something important, Levin went to the nursery.

In spite of his having been extremely interested in Koznyshov's partially heard plan for the emancipated world of the Slavs, forty million strong, to launch a new epoch in history together with Russia, which was a complete novelty to him, and in spite of his being agitated by both anxiety and curiosity about why he had been called, the moment he was by himself on leaving the drawing room he immediately recalled his thoughts of the morning. And all these considerations about the importance of the Slavic element in world history seemed to him so trivial in comparison with what was taking place in his own soul, that he instantly forgot all about them and lapsed into the mood he had been in that morning.

Now he no longer recalled, as he had done before, his whole train of thought (he had no need to now). He instantly returned to the feeling which had guided him and which had been bound up with those thoughts, and he found this feeling in his soul even more powerful and clear-cut than before. It was no longer as it had been with his previous contrived consolations, when he had had to recapitulate a whole sequence of ideas in order to arrive at the feeling. On the contrary: now his feeling of joy and solace was more vivid than before, while his thoughts could not keep up with the feeling.

He walked across the terrace and looked at the two stars that were coming up in the sky, already darkening, and suddenly he remembered: Yes, while I was looking at the sky and thinking that the vault I could see was not an illusion, there was something I didn't think through, something I was hiding from myself, he thought; but whatever it was it couldn't have been a refutation. All I have to do is think it through, and it will all be cleared up!

And just as he was entering the nursery he remembered what it was that he had been hiding from himself. It was this: If the chief proof of the existence of a Deity is His revelation of what is good, then why is that revelation restricted to the Christian Church alone? What is the relationship to it of the beliefs of the Buddhists and Moslems, who also teach and do good?

It seemed to him he had an answer to this question, but he had no time to express it to himself before he entered the nursery.

Kitty, sleeves rolled up, was standing beside the bath the baby was splashing about in; when she heard her husband's footsteps she turned her face toward him and beckoned him over with a smile. With one hand she was supporting the head of the plump baby, who was lying on his back and kicking out his little feet, with the other she was squeezing the sponge out over him, her muscles rhythmically tensing.

"Look—look!" she said, when Levin came over to her. "Miss Agatha's right—he does know us!"

The point was that on that day Mitya had obviously and incontestably begun recognizing the people near him.

The moment Levin went near the bathtub an experiment was tried on him which was a complete success. The cook, called in specially for this purpose, leaned over the child. Mitya frowned and shook his head in protest. Kitty leaned over him, and his face lit up with a smile, he started squeezing the sponge with his little hands and bubbled with his lips, producing such a peculiar, contented sound that not only Kitty and the nanny but Levin too went into unexpected raptures.

The nanny lifted the baby out of the water on one hand and doused him in fresh water; then he was wrapped up, dried off, and after a penetrating yell handed to his mother.

"Well, I'm glad you're beginning to like him," said Kitty to her husband, after she had settled herself placidly in her usual place with the child at her breast. "I'm very glad. I was beginning to get upset about it; you said you had no feeling for him."

"No, surely I didn't say I had no feeling? All I said was that I was disappointed."

"What—disappointed in him?"

"Not so much in him as in my own feelings; I had been expecting more. I had expected a new and pleasant feeling to blossom out inside me, like a surprise. Then suddenly, instead of that—revulsion, pity . . ."

She listened to him attentively, on the other side of the baby, as she put on her slender fingers the rings she had taken off in order to wash Mitya.

"And the main thing is that there was far more anxiety and

pity than pleasure. After that terror during the storm today I realized how much I love him."

Kitty smiled radiantly.

"Were you very frightened?" she said. "I was too, but I'm even more frightened now that it's over. I'm going to take a look at that oak. But how sweet Katavasov is! Altogether the whole day has been so pleasant. And you're so nice with Sergius when you feel like it . . . Well, go back to them now, it's always so hot and steamy here after his bath."

When Levin found himself alone after leaving the nursery, he immediately recalled again the thought that had had something unclear about it.

Instead of going to the drawing room, where he could hear voices, he stopped on the terrace and, leaning his elbows on the balustrade, gazed up at the sky.

It had turned quite dark already and to the south, where he was looking, the sky was clear. The clouds were in the opposite direction. Lightning was flashing there, and a distant rumble of thunder could be heard. Levin listened to the even dripping of the raindrops from the lime trees in the garden and looked at the familiar triangular constellation, with the Milky Way and its ramifications passing through the middle of it. At every flash of lightning not only would the Milky Way vanish but the bright stars as well, but the moment the lightning was gone they would reappear in the same spots, as though tossed there by some unerring hand.

Well, what is it that's puzzling me? Levin said to himself, feeling in advance that the resolution of his doubts, even though he still did not recognize it, was already present in his mind.

Yes, the one obvious and incontestable manifestation of the Deity are the laws of goodness, which have been disclosed to the world by revelation, and which I feel in myself, and in the acknowledgment of which I do not so much unite myself as I am willy-nilly united with other people in one community of believers, which is called the Church. Well, and what about the Jews, the Moslems, the Confucians, the Buddhists—what are they? he thought, putting to himself the question that seemed to him dangerous. Surely these hundreds of millions of people can't be deprived of that highest blessing without which life has no meaning? He started pondering, but corrected himself at once. But what is it I'm asking? he said to himself. I'm asking about the relationship to the Deity of all the diverse beliefs of all mankind; I'm asking about the general revelation of God to the whole universe with all its cloudy nebulae. Then what is it I'm doing? There has been revealed beyond question to me personally, to my own heart, a knowledge unattainable by reasoning, and I'm obstinately trying to express that knowledge by means of reason and language.

Don't I know the stars don't move? he asked himself, looking at a bright planet that had already shifted its position to the top branch of a birch tree. But in watching the movement of the stars I can't imagine to myself the rotation of the earth, so I'm right in saying that it is the stars that are moving.

And would the astronomers have been able to understand and calculate anything if they had taken into account all the diverse and complicated movements of the earth? All their marvellous conclusions about the distances, weight, movements, and disturbances of the celestial bodies are based only on the apparent movement of the stars around a stationary earth, on the same movement that I see before me now and that was the same for millions of people in the course of centuries, and has been and always will be the same, and can always be verified. And just as the conclusions of the astronomers would be idle and uncertain if they had not been founded on the observations of an apparent sky in relationship to a single meridian and a single horizon, so would my own conclusions be idle and uncertain too if they were not founded on that understanding of goodness that has been and always will be the same for everyone, and that has been revealed to me by Christianity and can always be verified in my soul. Thus I don't have the right or the possibility of deciding about these other faiths and their relationship to the Deity.

"Oh, haven't you gone in yet?" he suddenly heard Kitty's voice as she passed by that way to the drawing room. "Are you upset about anything?" she asked, looking intently into his face by the starlight.

But even so she wouldn't have been able to distinguish its expression if a flash of lightning that blotted out the stars had not lit it up. By the light of that flash she could see the whole of his face, and when she saw he was calm and happy she smiled at him.

She understands, he thought, she knows what I'm thinking about. Should I tell her or not? Yes—I'll tell her! But just as he was about to begin she also started talking.

"Oh, Kostya! Do me a favor, go to the corner room and see how they've arranged everything for Sergius," she said. "I can't very well go myself. See whether they've put in the new washstand."

"All right, I'll go at once," said Levin, straightening up and kissing her.

No, there's no need to tell her, he thought, after she had passed in before him. This is a secret that's necessary and important for no one but me, and can't be expressed in words.

This new feeling has not changed me, it has not made me happy, it has not given me any sudden illumination, as I dreamed it would, any more than my feeling for my son did. It has also been no surprise. But whether it's faith or not —I don't know what it is—through suffering this feeling too has imperceptibly entered into me rooted itself firmly in my soul.

I'll go on getting angry at Ivan the coachman, I'll go on arguing, go on expressing my ideas inappropriately, there will still be a wall between the inmost shrine of my soul and other people, including my wife; I'll go on blaming her because of my own fears, then repent; I'll go on not understanding with my reason why I pray, and go on praying— but from now on my life, my whole life, no matter what happens to me, every second of it, is not only not meaningless as it was before, but it has the incontestable meaning of the goodness I have the power to put into it!

# ON RETRANSLATING A RUSSIAN CLASSIC

## by Joel Carmichael

TOLSTOY, one of the few great writers with a public that genuinely reads him, (as distinct from a restricted coterie of specialists) has been immensely popular for so long that a new translation must inevitably run special hazards. The two celebrated translations that have carried his work throughout the English-speaking world have been cherished by so many readers that there is a natural tendency to resent any poaching on such familiar preserves.

The first thing I thought necessary, in embarking on this new translation of *Anna Karenina,* was a strong line on what may be called the Ivan Petrovich approach. This is the Russian habit, quite exotic for us, of addressing people by their given name and a patronymic: i.e., if the son's name is Ivan and the father's Peter the son may be referred to and addressed as Ivan son-of-Peter, or Ivan Petrovich.

This is of course not peculiar to Tolstoy; Russians actually do talk to each other that way, and this habit, perfectly natural and simple for them, has unaccountably been imported lock, stock and barrel into translations from the Russian, where, though trifling in itself, it injects a huge element of utterly superfluous, stilted inertia into both narrative and dialogue.

It seemed to me that the simplest way of getting round it was to disregard it altogether, and have the various characters address or refer to each other as they would if speaking English. Thus "Kitty" can consistently be called Kitty by the narrator, her family, and so on; but if a servant talks to her he will have to say Princess Shcherbatsky. Constantine Levin, the chief character of the book, can be referred to as Levin by the narrator and by masculine acquaintances, as Kostya by good friends or family, as Master Constantine by his servants. It will be seen from all this that the Russian habit is actually very useful, socially speaking, because it provides a simple form of address that can be used in nearly all circumstances, while in English and other languages specific nuances have to be devised to suit each particular relationship.

Thus, when Anna is being asked for a dance at the ball by the dancing director who scarcely knows her, it is perfectly all right for him to say "Anna Arkadyevna." But in translation this gives us a weighty problem: he cannot call her "Anna Arkadyevna" without opening the breach to a flood of the cumbersome chunks of alien cliché that act as such a deadweight on Russian novels and plays; he cannot call her just "Anna," still less Mrs. Karenin: the fact is he would say just "Madame," and that would be quite enough. If this has a lesson for us it is perhaps simply that in English there is often no need for people to address each other by name at all: the whole business of such formal address is old-fashioned as well as exotic.

But such details are of course the least of the problems of translation. They are, so to speak, a mere matter of mechanics: a more or less sensible rule is simply applied and that is that.

Far more serious is the fact that translations from the Russian, because of the difficulty of the language and its historic remoteness, have always tended to be a refuge for all sorts of decaying literary lumber. Archaic or quaint forms of speech, abuse of English idiom and rhythm, all the classic problems of translation confront the English reader who hopes to get at the individuality of the Russian writer. The success of Russian literature in the West must be credited to the originality and talent that were capable of bursting through these great obstacles.

The difficulty of translation varies enormously from medium to medium: almost impossible in poetry, it becomes both easier and less arbitrary as poetry is left behind.

The criterion of all this is summed up in the concept of style; it is doubtless to be expressed as a formula:

Insofar as the form of a written work can be dissociated from the content it expresses, to that extent the translator's contribution requires an original effort. In the case of a technical treatise, for instance, there is nothing special in the form at all: a word-for-word translation would be adequate at worse.

In the case of poetry, on the other hand, when it is precisely the form that tends to fuse indissolubly with the content—or in fact *is* the content—the translator is attempting to substitute his own effort for just that effort of the poet's that was the most special, the most original, and the most characteristic of the creative work to begin with. Even if the translator achieves a *tour de force*, the reader is in fact confronted by the artistic endeavor of the translator himself, and not of the poet. Even if the translator's effort is fused, if you like, with the poet's "idea" or theme, the overwhelming difficulty will have been the duplication of the original mold that embodied the theme and made it worth reading—and that was of course the *raison d'être* of the poem. This new mold will be the result of the translator's effort and not the poet's.

Creative prose falls between these extremes. The same problem is presented—to a lesser degree of course—by all those writers who make a point of style. In the case of a novelist like Henry James, for instance, or Proust, it would seem clear that the burden of their communication is in fact almost exhausted by their stylistic virtuousity. As in poetry the style is itself the essential, irreplaceable and characteristic element of the communication.

In the case of such a magnificently complex, involuted and personal style as James's, what vanishes in translation is clearly the man himself: James in a different style is a contradiction in terms. One can only admire the boldness of his translators, and perhaps even more the gullibility of the reading public in thinking, if they do, that what they are being served up is the authentic James—with only a certain amount "lost in translation."

But the literary milieu being what it is, it is a fact that people long to be on the inside with respect to the giants of world literature, and are thus reduced to dependence on authorized translations. Faulkner has a coterie of readers in France and Germany who discuss him ardently on the basis of "more or less satisfactory" translations; it may even be that an author will have more of a vogue via a translation than in his own language. This was what happened to Thomas Mann, whose spectacular international celebrity, as distinct from his entirely respectable but far from unique reputation in Germany, was doubtless due to his unprecedented success in the English-speaking world.

Tolstoy presents a far simpler problem, for a reason equally simple. He has no style at all. He seems to be stringing statements together so as to convey all the facts needed to make up an unadorned description of real situations. He lacks the slightest interest in using language for its own sake, in order to show off virtuosity. Perhaps his writing is best characterized as flat-footed.

So much has been said about Tolstoy's talents that there is no need to refer to them here except by way of illustrating the translator's task. In Tolstoy's case the performance of this essentially linguistic function illustrates his essential nature as an artist.

For of course Tolstoy has style—but it is the style not of a writer, but of a man.

It is, indeed, just this universal aspect of Tolstoy's style that is so impressive. His flat-footedness means his planting the flat of an immense foot on whatever he wants to say, then pressing it into the reader's mind with irresistible force. It is a question of acumen: what he has selected from among the myriads of available details can be depended on to convey exactly the impression he wishes to. At any rate that is the effect on the reader, whose attention is so absorbed by the content of Tolstoy's writing that its form—his "literary style"—seems to be a mere sheath, limpid and unobtrusive.

This apparent plainness of Tolstoy's has sometimes made his translators a little uneasy, I think; they must have felt it would be much nicer if Tolstoy had somehow managed to write more elaborately. English, with its far greater syntactical resources and more opulent vocabulary, can unquestionably do a great deal to help complicate and sophisticate Tolstoy's prose. A recurrent process of polishing, of smoothing out, of abridging an excess of detail, of fining down sentences thought too cumbrous, of discrete pruning, will indicate spots where translators have become editors.

Sometimes, of course, this process of tidying up does no damage to the essential elements of Tolstoy's writing; he too may nod. But the danger is that it may very well fall foul of his basic method of communication, which again is not so much a matter of style as of perspective. We must recall that Tolstoy was far from indifferent to his own view of stylistic nicety: he never heaped up details for the fun of it; he was neither careless nor verbose. In spite of his contempt for mere literariness he was so scrupulous about relevant detail that he would actually *telegraph* last-minute verbal corrections to the type-setter!

What Tolstoy achieves by his exploration of detail is a completely solid material framework that acts as a camera's eye through which our contact with whatever he is talking about is made intimate. His writing transposes us to a wholly real world; and his extraordinary ability to convey this effect of three-dimensionality is due to this selection of appropriate detail.

And when he uses his delicate, far-reaching probe for a methodical and seemingly dispassionate examination of emotions, his power is compelling. His method of what may be called molecular circumstantiality conquers us completely: we are swept by his art into the very presence of his creations, who not only live and breath about us, but display a marvellous transparency that the real people around us can never have.

For what places his style beyond literary artifice is his character as a man, a character marked by an altogether singular blend of luminous intelligence, nervous hypersensitivity, physical vitality, and exasperated passion. It is these qualities of his as a man that precisely fit his aim as an artist.

Hence, though it is difficult to be Tolstoy, it is much easier to be his translator. A translator who conscientiously articulates Tolstoy's thought as sparely and precisely as possible will not feel called upon to evolve any style independent of what Tolstoy is saying. He need merely perform his function with humility, and he can be sure of reaping the added dividend of a "literary" effect as well.

In short, whatever Tolstoy's art is, we are unconscious of it; I imagine that is what art should be. Tolstoy represents *par excellence*, in fact, the profound and well-known distinction between art and artfulness, summed up in a quotation from Goethe he was fond of: art is bad when "you see the intent and get put off." In Tolstoy one is unaware of the intent, and sees only the thing itself.

Tolstoy can pull his own weight: his translators merely need to clear the way.

# BIBLIOGRAPHICAL NOTE

AUTOBIOGRAPHY:

*Private Diary.* Edited by Aylmer Maude. Translated by Aylmer and Louise Maude. New York: Doubleday, 1927.

*Tolstoy: New Light on New Life and Genius.* Edited by Rene Fülöp-Miller. Translated by Paul England. New York: Dial, 1931.

*Tolstoy's Letters.* Selected, Edited and Translated by R. F. Christian. New York: Scribner. 1978.

*Tolstoy: A Collection of Critical Essays.* Edited by Ralph E. Matlaw. Englewood Cliffs, New Jersey: Prentice-Hall. A Spectrum Book (Twentieth Century Views), 1967.

*Last Diaries.* Edited and translated by Leon Stillman. New York: Putnam, 1960.

REMINISCENCES:

Gorki, M. *Reminiscences of Leo Nikolaevich Tolstoy.* Translated by S. S. Koteliansky and Leonard Woolf. New York: Viking, 1920. *Reminiscences of Tolstoy, Chekhov and Andreev.* Viking, 1959.

Kuzminskaya, T. A. B. *Tolstoy As I Knew Him.* Translated by Nora Sigerist and others. Introduction by Ernest J. Simmons. New York: Macmillan, 1948.

Maude, A. (ed.). *Family Views of Tolstoy.* Boston: Houghton, 1927.

Sukhotina, T. L. T. *Tolstoy Home.* Translated by Alec Brown. New York: Columbia, 1951.

Tolstoy, A. L. *Tolstoy: A Life of My Father.* Translated by Elizabeth Reynolds Hapgood. New York: Harper, 1953.

——*The Tragedy of Tolstoy.* Translated by Elena Varneck. New Haven: Yale, 1933.

Tolstoy, L. L. *Truth About My Father.* New York: Appleton, 1924.

Tolstoy, S. A. *The Autobiography of Countess Tolstoy.* Translated by S. S. Koteliansky and Leonard Woolf. New York: Viking, 1922.

——*Countess Tolstoy's Later Diary.* Translated by Alexander Werth. New York: Brewer, 1930.

——*Final Struggle.* Translated with an introduction by A. Maude. New York: Oxford, 1937.

Baudouin. C. *Tolstoy: the Teacher*. Translated by Fred Rothwell. New York: Dutton, 1924.

Bayley, John. *Tolstoy and the Novel*. New York: Viking, 1966.

Benson, Ruth Crego. *Women in Tolstoy: The Ideal and the Erotic*. Urbana: University of Illinois Press, 1973.

Berlin, Isaiah. *The Hedgehog and the Fox*. New York: Simon and Schuster, 1954.

Bodde, D. and G. S. *Tolstoy and China*. Princeton, 1950.

Christian, R. F. *Tolstoy: A Critical Introduction*. London: Cambridge University Press, 1969.

Crankshaw, Edward. *Tolstoy: The Making of a Novelist*. New York: Viking, 1974.

Fausset, H. I. *Tolstoy, the Inner Drama*. New York: Harcourt, 1928.

Hoffman, Modest and André Pierre. *By Deeds of Truth: the Life of Leo Tolstoy*. New York: Orion, 1958.

Knight, G. Wilson. *Shakespeare and Tolstoy*. London: Oxford, 1934.

Lavrin, J. *Tolstoy: an Approach*. New York: Macmillan, 1946.

Mann, T. *Three Essays*. Translated by H. T. Lowe-Porter. New York: Knopf, 1930.

Nazaroff, A. I. *Tolstoy, the Inconstant Genius*. New York: Stokes, 1929.

Noyes, G. R. *Tolstoy*. New York: Duffield, 1918.

Philipson, Morris. *The Count Who Wished He Were a Peasant*. New York: Pantheon, illustrated, 1967.

Polner, T. I. *Tolstoy and His Wife*. Translated by Nicholas Wreden. New York: Norton, 1945.

Rolland, Romain. *Tolstoy*. Translated by B. Miall. New York: Dutton, 1911.

Simmons, E. J. *Leo Tolstoy*. Boston: Little, Brown, 1947.

Simmons, Ernest J. *An Introduction to Tolstoy's Writings*. Chicago: University of Chicago Press, 1968.

Speirs, Logan. *Tolstoy and Chekhov*. Cambridge (England) University Press, 1971.

Steiner, George. *Tolstoy or Dostoevsky*. New York: Knopf, 1959.

Troyat, Henri. *Tolstoy*. Garden City, New York: Doubleday, 1967 (revised).

Wasiolek, Edward. *Tolstoy's Major Fiction*. Chicago: University of Chicago Press, 1978.

Zweig, S. *Adepts in Self-Portraiture*. New York: Viking, 1929.

Bantam Classics bring you the world's greatest literature—books that have stood the test of time—at specially low prices. These beautifully designed books will be proud additions to your bookshelf. You'll want all these time-tested classics for your own reading pleasure.

☐ 21137 **PERSUASION** Jane Austen
☐ 21051 **DAVID COPPERFIELD** Charles Dickens — $2.95
☐ 21148 **DRACULA** Bram Stoker — $2.50
☐ 21044 **FRANKENSTEIN** Mary Shelley — $1.95
☐ 21171 **ANNA KARENINA** Leo Tolstoy — $1.50
☐ 21035 **THE DEATH OF IVAN ILYICH** Leo Tolstoy — $2.95
☐ 21163 **THE BROTHERS KARAMAZOV** — $1.95
    Fyodor Dostoevsky — $2.95
☐ 21175 **CRIME AND PUNISHMENT**
    Fyodor Dostoevsky — $2.50
☐ 21136 **THE IDIOT** Fyodor Dostoevsky
☐ 21166 **CANDIDE** Voltaire — $3.50
☐ 21187 **THE COUNT OF MONTE CRISTO** — $2.25
    Alexandre Dumas — $3.50
☐ 21118 **CYRANO DE BERGERAC** Edmond Rostand
☐ 21048 **SILAS MARNER** George Eliot — $1.75
☐ 21089 **FATHERS AND SONS** Ivan Turgenev — $1.75
☐ 21032 **THE HUNCHBACK OF NOTRE DAME** — $1.95
    Victor Hugo — $1.95
☐ 21101 **MADAME BOVARY** Gustave Flaubert
☐ 21059 **THE TURN OF THE SCREW AND** — $2.50
    **OTHER SHORT FICTION** Henry James — $1.95

---

**Prices and availability subject to change without notice.**

Buy them at your local bookstore or use this handy coupon for ordering:

---

Bantam Books, Inc., Dept. CL, 414 East Golf Road, Des Plaines, Ill. 60016

Please send me the books I have checked above. I am enclosing $_____ (please add $1.25 to cover postage and handling). Send check or money order —no cash or C.O.D.'s please.

Mr/Mrs/Miss_____

Address_____

City_____ State/Zip_____

CL—1/85

Please allow four to six weeks for delivery. This offer expires 9/85.

Bantam Classics bring you the world's greatest literature—books that have stood the test of time—at specially low prices. These beautifully designed books will be proud additions to your bookshelf. You'll want all these time-tested classics for your own reading pleasure.

*Titles by Charles Dickens*

| | | | |
|---|---|---|---|
| ☐ | 21123 | **THE PICKWICK PAPERS** | $4.95 |
| ☐ | 21108 | **BLEAK HOUSE** | $3.95 |
| ☐ | 21086 | **NICHOLAS NICKLEBY** | $4.50 |
| ☐ | 21189 | **DAVID COPPERFIELD** | $3.50 |
| ☐ | 21113 | **GREAT EXPECTATIONS** | $2.50 |
| ☐ | 21106 | **A TALE OF TWO CITIES** | $1.95 |
| ☐ | 21016 | **HARD TIMES** | $1.95 |

*Titles by Thomas Hardy:*

| | | | |
|---|---|---|---|
| ☐ | 21191 | **JUDE THE OBSCURE** | $2.95 |
| ☐ | 21024 | **THE MAYOR OF CASTERBRIDGE** | $1.95 |
| ☐ | 21080 | **THE RETURN OF THE NATIVE** | $1.95 |
| ☐ | 21168 | **TESS OF THE D'URBERVILLES** | $2.95 |
| ☐ | 21131 | **FAR FROM THE MADDING CROWD** | $2.75 |

| | | | |
|---|---|---|---|
| ☐ | 21059 | **THE TURN OF THE SCREW AND OTHER SHORT FICTION** Henry James | $1.95 |
| ☐ | 21021 | **WUTHERING HEIGHTS** Emily Brontë | $1.75 |
| ☐ | 21149 | **LADY CHATTERLEY'S LOVER** D. H. Lawrence | $2.75 |
| ☐ | 21159 | **EMMA** Jane Austen | $1.95 |

Prices and availability subject to change without notice.

Buy them at your local bookstore or use this handy coupon for ordering:

Bantam Books, Inc., Dept. CL3, 414 East Golf Road, Des Plaines, Ill. 60016

Please send me the books I have checked above. I am enclosing $_____ (please add $1.25 to cover postage and handling). Send check or money order —no cash or C.O.D.'s please.

Mr/Mrs/Miss _____

Address_____

City_____State/Zip_____

CL3—5/85

Please allow four to six weeks for delivery. This offer expires 11/85.

These books have been bestsellers for generations of readers. Bantam Classics now bring you the world's greatest literature in specially low-priced editions. From the American epic Moby Dick to Dostoevsky's towering works, you'll want all these time-tested classics for your own.

| | | | |
|---|---|---|---|
| ☐ | 21138 | **THE HOUSE OF MIRTH** Edith Wharton | $2.25 |
| ☐ | 21133 | **THE DIVINE COMEDY: PURGATORIO** Dante (trans. by Allen Mandelbaum) | $3.50 |
| ☐ | 21041 | **THE AENEID** Virgil (trans. by Allen Mandelbaum) | $2.95 |
| ☐ | 21005 | **THE CALL OF THE WILD** and **WHITE FANG** Jack London | $1.75 |
| ☐ | 21166 | **CANDIDE** Voltaire | $2.25 |
| ☐ | 21082 | **THE CANTERBURY TALES** Geoffrey Chaucer | $2.95 |
| ☐ | 21130 | **THE COUNT OF MONTE CRISTO** Alexandre Dumas | $2.95 |
| ☐ | 21175 | **CRIME AND PUNISHMENT** Fyodor Dostoevsky | $2.50 |
| ☐ | 21134 | **THE SECRET AGENT** Joseph Conrad | $2.95 |
| ☐ | 21088 | **HEART OF DARKNESS & THE SECRET SHARER** Joseph Conrad | $1.75 |
| ☐ | 21007 | **MOBY DICK** Herman Melville | $1.95 |
| ☐ | 21021 | **WUTHERING HEIGHTS** Emily Bronte | $1.75 |
| ☐ | 21117 | **KIM** Rudyard Kipling | $2.25 |
| ☐ | 21115 | **LITTLE WOMEN** Louisa May Alcott | $2.95 |
| ☐ | 21190 | **CAPTAINS COURAGEOUS** Rudyard Kipling | $1.95 |
| ☐ | 21067 | **KIDNAPPED** Robert Louis Stevenson | $1.50 |
| ☐ | 21079 | **THE ADVENTURES OF HUCKLEBERRY FINN** Mark Twain | $1.75 |

**Prices and availability subject to change without notice.**

Buy them at your local bookstore or use this handy coupon for ordering:

---

Bantam Books, Inc., Dept. CL4, 414 East Golf Road, Des Plaines, Ill. 60016

Please send me the books I have checked above. I am enclosing $_____ (please add $1.25 to cover postage and handling). Send check or money order —no cash or C.O.D.'s please.

Mr/Mrs/Miss _____

Address_____

City_____ State/Zip_____

CL4—3/85

Please allow four to six weeks for delivery. This offer expires 9/85.

# SPECIAL
# MONEY SAVING
# OFFER

Now you can have an up-to-date listing of Bantam's hundreds of titles plus take advantage of our unique and exciting bonus book offer. A special offer which gives you the opportunity to purchase a Bantam book for only 50¢. Here's how!

By ordering any five books at the regular price per order, you can also choose any other single book listed (up to a $4.95 value) for just 50¢. Some restrictions do apply, but for further details why not send for Bantam's listing of titles today!

Just send us your name and address plus 50¢ to defray the postage and handling costs.